Frames Trilogy

JOHN BANVILLE was born in Wexford, Ireland, in 1945. His first book, *Long Lankin*, was published in 1970. His other books are *Nightspawn*, *Birchwood*, *Doctor Copernicus* (which won the James Tait Black Memorial Prize in 1976), *Kepler* (which was awarded the *Guardian* Fiction Prize in 1981), *The Newton Letter* (which was filmed for Channel 4), *Mefisto*, *The Book of Evidence* (shortlisted for the 1989 Booker Prize and winner of the 1989 Guinness Peat Aviation Award), *Ghosts*, *Athena*, *The Untouchable* and *Eclipse*. He has also received a literary award from the Lannan Foundation. He lives in Dublin, where he is at work on his next novel, *Shroud*.

JOHN BANVILLE

Frames Trilogy

THE BOOK OF EVIDENCE

GHOSTS

ATHENA

PICADOR

The Book of Evidence first published in Great Britain 1989 by Martin Secker & Warburg Ltd
First published by Picador 1998
Ghosts first published in Great Britain 1993 by Martin Secker & Warburg Ltd
First published by Picador 1998
Athena first published in Great Britain 1995 by Martin Secker & Warburg Ltd
First published by Picador 1998

This omnibus edition first published 2001 by Picador

This edition published 2001 by Picador
an imprint of Macmillan Publishers Ltd
25 Eccleston Place, London SW1W 9NF
Basingstoke and Oxford
Associated companies throughout the world
www.macmillan.com

ISBN 0 330 37348 X

Copyright © John Banville 1989, 1993, 1995, 2001

The right of John Banville to be identified as the
author of this work has been asserted by him in accordance
with the Copyright, Designs and Patents Act 1988.

1 3 5 7 9 8 6 4 2

A CIP catalogue record for this book is available from
the British Library.

Typeset by SetSystems Ltd, Saffron Walden, Essex
Printed and bound in Great Britain by
Mackays of Chatham plc, Chatham, Kent

Contents

MY LORD, when you ask me to tell the court in my own words, this is what I shall say. I am kept locked up here like some exotic animal, last survivor of a species they had thought extinct. They should let in people to view me, the girl-eater, svelte and dangerous, padding to and fro in my cage, my terrible green glance flickering past the bars, give them something to dream about, tucked up cosy in their beds of a night. After my capture they clawed at each other to get a look at me. They would have paid money for the privilege, I believe. They shouted abuse, and shook their fists at me, showing their teeth. It was unreal, somehow, frightening yet comic, the sight of them there, milling on the pavement like film extras, young men in cheap raincoats, and women with shopping bags, and one or two silent, grizzled characters who just stood, fixed on me hungrily, haggard with envy. Then a guard threw a blanket over my head and bundled me into a squad car. I laughed. There was something irresistibly funny in the way reality, banal as ever, was fulfilling my worst fantasies.

By the way, that blanket. Did they bring it specially, or do they always keep one handy in the boot? Such questions trouble me now, I brood on them. What an interesting figure I must have cut, glimpsed there, sitting up in the back like a sort of mummy, as the car sped through the wet, sunlit streets, bleating importantly.

Then this place. It was the noise that impressed me first of all. A terrible racket, yells and whistles, hoots of laughter, arguments, sobs. But there are moments of stillness, too, as if a great fear, or a great sadness, has fallen suddenly, striking us all speechless. The air stands motionless in the corridors, like stagnant water. It is laced with a faint stink of carbolic, which bespeaks the charnel-house. In the beginning I fancied it was me, I mean I thought this smell was mine, my contribution. Perhaps it is? The daylight too is strange, even outside, in the yard, as if something has happened to it, as if something has been done to it, before it is allowed to reach us. It has an acid, lemony cast, and comes in two intensities: either it is not enough to see by or it sears the sight. Of the various kinds of darkness I shall not speak.

My cell. My cell is. Why go on with this.

Remand prisoners are assigned the best cells. This is as it should be. After all, I might be found innocent. Oh, I mustn't laugh, it hurts too much, I get a terrible twinge, as if something were pressing on my heart – the burden of my guilt, I suppose. I have a table and what they call an easy chair. There is even a television set, though I rarely watch it, now that my case is *sub judice* and there is nothing about me on the news. The sanitation facilities leave something to be desired. Slopping out: how apt, these terms. I must see if I can get a catamite, or do I mean a neophyte? Some young fellow, nimble and willing, and not too fastidious. That shouldn't be difficult. I must see if I can get a dictionary, too.

Above all I object to the smell of semen everywhere. The place reeks of it.

I confess I had hopelessly romantic expectations of how things would be in here. Somehow I pictured myself a sort of celebrity, kept apart from the other prisoners in a special wing, where I would receive parties of grave, important people and hold forth to them about the great issues of the day, impressing the men and charming the ladies. What insight! they would cry. What breadth! We were told you were a beast, cold-blooded, cruel, but now that we have seen you, have heard you, why—! And there am I, striking an elegant pose, my ascetic profile lifted to the light in the barred window, fingering a scented handkerchief and faintly smirking, Jean-Jacques the cultured killer.

Not like that, not like that at all. But not like other clichés either. Where are the mess-hall riots, the mass break-outs, that kind of thing, so familiar from the silver screen? What of the scene in the exercise yard in which the stoolie is done to death with a shiv while a pair of blue-jawed heavyweights stage a diversionary fight? When are the gang-bangs going to start? The fact is, in here is like out there, only more so. We are obsessed with physical comfort. The place is always overheated, we might be in an incubator, yet there are endless complaints of draughts and sudden chills and frozen feet at night. Food is important too, we pick over our plates of mush, sniffing and sighing, as if we were a convention of gourmets. After a parcel delivery word goes round like wildfire. *Psst! She's sent him a battenberg! Homemade!* It's just like school, really, the mixture of misery and cosiness, the numbed longing, the noise, and everywhere, always, that particular smelly grey warm male fug.

It was different, I'm told, when the politicals were here. They used to goose-step up and down the corridors, barking at each other in bad Irish, causing much merriment among the ordinary criminals. But then they all went on hunger strike or something, and were moved away to a place of their own, and life returned to normal.

Why are we so compliant? Is it the stuff they are said to put in our tea to dull the libido? Or is it the drugs. Your honour, I know that no one, not even the prosecution, likes a squealer, but I think it is my duty to apprise the court of the brisk trade in proscribed substances which is carried on in this institution. There are screws, I mean warders, involved in it, I can supply their numbers if I am guaranteed protection. Anything can be had, uppers and downers, tranqs, horse, crack, you name it – not that you, of course, your worship, are likely to be familiar with these terms from the lower depths, I have only learned them myself since coming here. As you would imagine, it is mainly the young men who indulge. One recognises them, stumbling along the gangways like somnambulists, with that little, wistful, stunned smile of the truly zonked. There are some, however, who do not smile, who seem indeed as if they will never smile again. They are the lost ones, the goners. They stand gazing off, with a blank, preoccupied expression, the way that injured animals look away from us, mutely, as if we are mere phantoms to them, whose pain is taking place in a different world from ours.

But no, it's not just the drugs. Something essential has gone, the stuffing has been knocked out of us. We are not exactly men any more. Old lags, fellows who have committed some really impressive crimes, sashay about the place like dowagers, pale, soft, pigeon-chested, big in the beam. They squabble over library books, some of them even knit. The young too have their hobbies, they sidle up to me in the recreation room, their calf eyes fairly brimming, and shyly display their handiwork. If I have to admire one more ship in a bottle I shall scream. Still, they are so sad, so vulnerable, these muggers, these rapists, these baby-batterers. When I think of them I always picture, I'm not sure why, that strip of stubbly grass and one tree that I can glimpse from my window if I press my cheek against the bars and peer down diagonally past the wire and the wall.

*

Stand up, please, place your hand here, state your name clearly. Frederick Charles St John Vanderveld Montgomery. Do you swear to tell the truth, the whole truth and nothing but the truth? Don't make me laugh. I want straight away to call my first witness. My wife. Daphne. Yes, that was, is, her name. For some reason people have always found it faintly comic. I think it matches very well her damp, dark, myopic beauty. I see her, my lady of the laurels, reclining in a sun-dazed glade, a little vexed, looking away with a small frown, while some minor god in the shape of a faun, with a reed pipe, prances and capers, vainly playing his heart out for her. It was that abstracted, mildly dissatisfied air which first drew my attention to her. She was not nice, she was not good. She suited me. Perhaps I was already thinking of a time to come when I would need to be pardoned – by someone, anyone – and who better to do that than one of my own kind.

When I say she was not good I do not mean she was wicked,

or corrupt. The flaws in her were nothing compared with the jagged cracks that run athwart my soul. The most one could accuse her of was a sort of moral laziness. There were things she could not be bothered to do, no matter what imperatives propelled them to her jaded attention. She neglected our son, not because she was not fond of him, in her way, but simply because his needs did not really interest her. I would catch her, sitting on a chair, looking at him with a remote expression in her eyes, as if she were trying to remember who or what precisely he was, and how he had come to be there, rolling on the floor at her feet in one of his own many messes. Daphne! I would murmur, for Christ's sake! and as often as not she would look at me then in the same way, with the same blank, curiously absent gaze.

I notice that I seem unable to stop speaking of her in the past tense. It feels right, somehow. Yet she often visits me. The first time she came she asked what it was like in here. Oh, my dear! I said, the noise! – and the people! She just nodded a little and smiled wanly, and looked about her idly at the other visitors. We understand each other, you see.

In southern climes her indolence was transformed into a kind of voluptuous languor. There is a particular room I remember, with green shutters and a narrow bed and a Van Gogh chair, and a Mediterranean noon pulsing outside in the white streets. Ibiza? Ischia? Mykonos perhaps? Always an island, please note that, clerk, it may mean something. Daphne could get out of her clothes with magical swiftness, with just a sort of shrug, as if skirt, blouse, pants, everything, were all of a piece. She is a big woman, not fat, not heavy, even, but yet weighty, and beautifully balanced: always when I saw her naked I wanted to caress her, as I would want to caress a piece of sculpture, hefting the curves in the hollow of my hand, running a thumb down the long smooth lines, feeling the coolness, the velvet texture of the stone. Clerk, strike that last sentence, it will seem to mean too much.

Those burning noons, in that room and countless others like it – my God, I tremble to think of them now. I could not resist her careless nudity, the weight and density of that glimmering flesh. She would lie beside me, an abstracted *maya*, gazing past me at the shadowy ceiling, or at that chink of hot white light between the shutters, until at last I managed, I never understood exactly how, to press a secret nerve in her, and then she would turn to me heavily, quickly, with a groan, and cling to me as if she were falling, her mouth at my throat, her blind-man's fingertips on my back. She always kept her eyes open, their dim soft grey gaze straying helplessly, flinching under the tender damage I was inflicting on her. I cannot express how much it excited me, that pained, defenceless look, so unlike her at any other time. I used to try to have her wear her spectacles when we were in bed like this, so she would seem even more lost, more defenceless, but I never succeeded, no matter what sly means I might employ. And of course I could not ask. Afterwards it would be as though nothing at all had happened, she would get up and stroll to the bathroom, a hand in her hair, leaving me prostrate on the soaked sheet, convulsed, gasping, as if I had suffered a heart attack, which I suppose I had, in a way.

She never knew, I believe, how deeply she affected me. I was careful that she should not know it. Oh, don't mistake me, it was not that I was afraid I would give myself into her power, or anything like that. It was just that such knowledge would have been, well, inappropriate between us. There was a reticence, a tactfulness, which from the first we had silently agreed to preserve. We understood each other, yes, but that did not mean we knew each other, or wanted to. How would we have maintained that unselfconscious grace that was so important to us both, if we had not also maintained the essential secretness of our inner selves?

How good it was to get up then in the cool of afternoon and amble down to the harbour through the stark geometry of sun and shadow in the narrow streets. I liked to watch Daphne walking ahead of me, her strong shoulders and her hips moving in a muffled, complex rhythm under the light stuff of her dress. I liked to watch the island men, too, hunched over their pastis and their thimbles of turbid coffee, swivelling their lizard eyes as she went past. That's right, you bastards, yearn, yearn.

On the harbour there was always a bar, always the same one whatever the island, with a few tables and plastic chairs outside, and crooked sun-umbrellas advertising Stella or Pernod, and a swarthy, fat proprietor leaning in the doorway picking his teeth. It was always the same people, too: a few lean, tough types in bleached denim, hard-eyed women gone leathery from the sun, a fat old guy with a yachting cap and grizzled sideburns, and of course a queer or two, with bracelets and fancy sandals. They were our crowd, our set, our friends. We rarely knew their names, or they ours, we called each other pal, chum, captain, darling. We drank our brandies or our ouzos, whatever was the cheapest local poison, and talked loudly of other friends, characters every one, in other bars, on other islands, all the while eyeing each other narrowly, even as we smiled, watching for we knew not what, an opening, perhaps, a soft flank left momentarily unguarded into which we might sink our fangs. Ladies and gentlemen of the jury, you have seen us, we were part of the local colour on your package holiday, you passed us by with wistful glances, and we ignored you.

We presided among this rabble, Daphne and I, with a kind of grand detachment, like an exiled king and queen waiting daily for word of the counter-rebellion and the summons from the palace to return. People in general, I noticed it, were a little afraid of us, now and again I detected it in their eyes, a worried, placatory, doggie sort of look, or else a resentful glare, furtive and sullen. I have pondered this phenomenon, it strikes me as significant. What was it in us – or rather, what was it *about* us – that impressed them? Oh, we are large, well-made, I am handsome, Daphne is beautiful, but that cannot have been the whole of it. No, after much thought the conclusion I have come to is this, that they imagined they recognised in us a coherence and wholeness, an essential authenticity, which they lacked, and of which they felt they were not entirely worthy. We were – well, yes, we were heroes.

I thought all this ridiculous, of course. No, wait, I am under oath here, I must tell the truth. I enjoyed it. I enjoyed sitting at ease in the sun, with my resplendent, disreputable consort at my side, quietly receiving the tribute of our motley court. There was a special, faint little smile I had, calm, tolerant, with just the tiniest touch of contempt, I bestowed it in particular on the sillier ones, the poor fools who prattled, cavorting before us in cap and bells, doing their pathetic tricks and madly laughing. I looked in their eyes and saw myself ennobled there, and so could forget for a moment what I was, a paltry, shivering thing, just like them, full of longing and loathing, solitary, afraid, racked by doubts, and dying.

That was how I got into the hands of crooks: I allowed myself to be lulled into believing I was inviolable. I do not seek, my lord, to excuse my actions, only to explain them. That life, drifting from island to island, encouraged illusions. The sun, the salt air, leached the significance out of things, so that they lost their true weight. My instincts, the instincts of our tribe, those coiled springs tempered in the dark forests of the north, went slack down there, your honour, really, they did. How could anything be dangerous, be wicked, in such tender, blue, watercolour weather? And then, bad things are always things that take place elsewhere, and bad people are never the people that one knows. The American, for instance, seemed no worse than any of the others among that year's crowd. In fact, he seemed to me no worse than I was myself – I mean, than I imagined myself to be, for this, of course, was before I discovered what things I was capable of.

*

I refer to him as the American because I did not know, or cannot remember, his name, but I am not sure that he was American at all. He spoke with a twang that might have been learned from the pictures, and he had a way of looking about him with narrowed eyes while he talked which reminded me of some film star or other. I could not take him seriously. I did a splendid impression of him – I have always been a good mimic – which made people laugh out loud in surprise and recognition. At first I thought he was quite a young man, but Daphne smiled and asked had I looked at his hands. (She noticed such things.) He was lean and muscular, with a hatchet face and boyish, close-cropped hair. He went in for tight jeans and high-heeled boots and leather belts with huge buckles. There was a definite touch of the cowpoke about him. I shall call him, let me see, I shall call him – Randolph. It was Daphne he was after. I watched him sidle up, hands stuck in his tight pockets, and start to sniff around her, at once cocksure and edgy, like so many others before him, his longing, like theirs, evident in a certain strained whiteness between the eyes. Me he treated with watchful affability, addressing me as friend, and even – do I imagine it? – as *pardner*. I remember the first time he sat himself down at our table, twining his spidery legs around the chair and leaning forward on an elbow. I expected him to fetch out a tobacco pouch and roll himself a smoke with one hand. The waiter, Paco, or Pablo, a young man with hot eyes and aristocratic pretensions, made a mistake and brought us the wrong drinks, and Randolph seized the opportunity to savage him. The poor boy stood there, his shoulders bowed under the lashes of invective, and was what he had always been, a peasant's son. When he had stumbled away, Randolph looked at Daphne and grinned, showing a side row of long, fulvous teeth, and I thought of a hound sitting back proud as punch after delivering a dead rat at its mistress's feet. Goddamned spics, he said carelessly, and made a spitting noise out of the side of his mouth. I jumped up and seized the edge of the table and overturned it, pitching the drinks into his lap, and shouted at him to get up and reach for it, you sonofabitch! No, no, of course I didn't. Much as I might have liked to dump a table full of broken glass into his ludicrously overstuffed crotch, that was not the way I did things, not in those days. Besides, I had enjoyed as much as anyone seeing Pablo or Paco get his comeuppance, the twerp, with his soulful glances and his delicate hands and that horrible, pubic moustache.

Randolph liked to give the impression that he was a very dangerous character. He spoke of dark deeds perpetrated in a far-off country which he called Stateside. I encouraged these tales of

derring-do, secretly delighting in the aw-shucks, 'tweren't-nuthin'
way he told them. There was something wonderfully ridiculous
about it all, the braggart's sly glance and slyly modest inflexion,
his air of euphoric self-regard, the way he opened like a flower
under the warmth of my silently nodding, awed response. I have
always derived satisfaction from the little wickednesses of human
beings. To treat a fool and a liar as if I esteemed him the soul of
probity, to string him along in his poses and his fibs, that is a
peculiar pleasure. He claimed he was a painter, until I put a few
innocent questions to him on the subject, then he suddenly
became a writer instead. In fact, as he confided to me one night
in his cups, he made his money by dealing in dope among the
island's transient rich. I was shocked, of course, but I recognised
a valuable piece of information, and later, when—

But I am tired of this, let me get it out of the way. I asked
him to lend me some money. He refused. I reminded him of that
drunken night, and said I was sure the *guardia* would be interested
to hear what he had told me. He was shocked. He thought about
it. He didn't have the kind of dough I was asking for, he said, he
would have to get it for me somewhere, maybe from some people
that he knew. And he chewed his lip. I said that would be all
right, I didn't mind where it came from. I was amused, and rather
pleased with myself, playing at being a blackmailer. I had not
really expected him to take me seriously, but it seemed I had
underestimated his cravenness. He produced the cash, and for a
few weeks Daphne and I had a high old time, and everything was
grand except for Randolph dogging my steps wherever I went. He
was distressingly literal-minded in his interpretation of words such
as *lend* and *repay*. Hadn't I kept his grubby little secret, I said,
was that not a fair return? These people, he said, with an awful,
twitching attempt at a grin, these people didn't fool around. I
said I was glad to hear it, one wouldn't want to think one had
been dealing, even at second-hand, with the merely frivolous.
Then he threatened to give them my name. I laughed in his face
and walked away. I still could not take any of it seriously. A
few days later a small package wrapped in brown paper arrived,

addressed to me in a semi-literate hand. Daphne made the mistake of opening it. Inside was a tobacco tin – Balkan Sobranie, lending an oddly cosmopolitan touch – lined with cotton wool, in which nestled a curiously whorled, pale, gristly piece of meat crusted with dried blood. It took me a moment to identify it as a human ear. Whoever had cut it off had done a messy job, with something like a breadknife, to judge by the ragged serration. Painful. I suppose that was the intention. I remember thinking: How appropriate, an ear, in this land of the toreador! Quite droll, really.

I went in search of Randolph. He wore a large lint pad pressed to the left side of his head, held in place by a rakishly angled and none-too-clean bandage. He no longer made me think of the Wild West. Now, as if fate had decided to support his claim of being an artist, he bore a striking resemblance to poor, mad Vincent in that self-portrait made after he had disfigured himself for love. When he saw me I thought he was going to weep, he looked so sorry for himself, and so indignant. You deal with them yourself now, he said, you owe them, not me, I've paid, and he touched a hand grimly to his bandaged head. Then he called me a vile name and skulked off down an alleyway. Despite the noonday sun a shiver passed across my back, like a grey wind swarming over water. I tarried there for a moment, on that white corner, musing. An old man on a burro saluted me. Nearby a tinny churchbell was clanging rapidly. Why, I asked myself, why am I living like this?

*

That is a question which no doubt the court also would like answered. With my background, my education, my – yes – my culture, how could I live such a life, associate with such people, get myself into such scrapes? The answer is – I don't know the answer. Or I do, and it is too large, too tangled, for me to attempt here. I used to believe, like everyone else, that I was determining the course of my own life, according to my own decisions, but gradually, as I accumulated more and more past to look back on, I realised that I had done the things I did because I could do no other. Please, do not imagine, my lord, I hasten to say it, do not imagine that you detect here the insinuation of an apologia, or even of a defence. I wish to claim full responsibility for my actions – after all, they are the only things I can call my own – and I declare in advance that I shall accept without demur the verdict of the court. I am merely asking, with all respect, whether it is feasible to hold on to the principle of moral culpability once the notion of free will has been abandoned. It is, I grant you, a tricky one, the sort of thing we love to discuss in here of an evening, over our cocoa and our fags, when time hangs heavy.

As I've said, I did not always think of my life as a prison in which all actions are determined according to a random pattern thrown down by an unknown and insensate authority. Indeed, when I was young I saw myself as a masterbuilder who would one day assemble a marvellous edifice around myself, a kind of grand pavilion, airy and light, which would contain me utterly and yet wherein I would be free. Look, they would say, distinguishing this eminence from afar, look how sound it is, how solid: it's him all right, yes, no doubt about it, the man himself. Meantime, however, unhoused, I felt at once exposed and invisible. How shall I describe it, this sense of myself as something without weight, without moorings, a floating phantom? Other people seemed to have a density, a thereness, which I lacked. Among them, these big, carefree creatures, I was like a child among adults. I watched them, wide-eyed, wondering at their calm assurance in the face of a baffling and preposterous world. Don't mistake me, I was no wilting lily, I laughed and whooped and boasted with the best of them – only inside, in that grim, shadowed gallery I call my heart, I stood uneasily, with a hand to my mouth, silent, envious, uncertain. They understood matters, or accepted them, at least. They knew what they thought about things, they had opinions. They took the broad view, as if they did not realise that everything is infinitely divisible. They talked of cause and effect, as if they believed it possible to isolate an event and hold it up to scrutiny in a pure, timeless space, outside the mad swirl of things. They would speak of whole peoples as if they were speaking of a single individual, while to speak even of an individual with any show of certainty seemed to me foolhardy. Oh, they knew no bounds.

And as if people in the outside world were not enough, I had inside me too an exemplar of my own, a kind of invigilator, from whom I must hide my lack of conviction. For instance, if I was reading something, an argument in some book or other, and agreeing with it enthusiastically, and then I discovered at the end that I had misunderstood entirely what the writer was saying, had in fact got the whole thing arse-ways, I would be compelled at once to execute a somersault, quick as a flash, and tell myself, I mean my other self, that stern interior sergeant, that what was being said was true, that I had never really thought otherwise, and, even if I had, that it showed an open mind that I should be able to switch back and forth between opinions without even noticing it. Then I would mop my brow, clear my throat, straighten my shoulders and pass on delicately, in stifled dismay. But why the past tense? Has anything changed? Only that the watcher from inside has stepped forth and taken over, while the puzzled outsider cowers within.

Does the court realise, I wonder, what this confession is costing me?

I took up the study of science in order to find certainty. No, that's not it. Better say, I took up science in order to make the lack of certainty more manageable. Here was a way, I thought, of erecting a solid structure on the very sands that were everywhere, always, shifting under me. And I was good at it, I had a flair. It helped, to be without convictions as to the nature of reality, truth, ethics, all those big things – indeed, I discovered in science a vision of an unpredictable, seething world that was eerily familiar to me, to whom matter had always seemed a swirl of chance collisions. Statistics, probability theory, that was my field. Esoteric stuff, I won't go into it here. I had a certain cold gift that was not negligible, even by the awesome standards of the discipline. My student papers were models of clarity and concision. My professors loved me, dowdy old boys reeking of cigarette smoke and bad teeth, who recognised in me that rare, merciless streak the lack of which had condemned them to a life of drudgery at the lectern. And then the Americans spotted me.

How I loved America, the life there on that pastel, sun-drenched western coast, it spoiled me forever. I see it still in dreams, all there, inviolate, the ochre hills, the bay, the great delicate red bridge wreathed in fog. I felt as if I had ascended to some high, fabled plateau, a kind of Arcady. Such wealth, such ease, such innocence. From all the memories I have of the place I select one at random. A spring day, the university cafeteria. It is lunchtime. Outside, on the plaza, by the fountain, the marvellous girls disport themselves in the sun. We have listened that morning to a lecture by a visiting wizard, one of the grandmasters of the arcanum, who sits with us now at our table, drinking coffee from a paper cup and cracking pistachio nuts in his teeth. He is a lean, gangling person with a wild mop of frizzed hair going grey. His glance is humorous, with a spark of malice, it darts restlessly here and there as if searching for something that will make him laugh. The fact is, friends, he is saying, the whole damn thing is chance, pure chance. And he flashes suddenly a shark's grin, and winks at me, a fellow outsider. The faculty staff sitting around the table nod and say nothing, big, tanned, serious men in short-sleeved shirts and shoes with broad soles. One scratches his jaw, another consults idly a chunky wristwatch. A boy wearing shorts and no shirt passes by outside, playing a flute. The girls rise slowly, two by two, and slowly walk away, over the grass, arms folded, their books pressed to their chests like breastplates. My God, can I have been there, really? It seems to me now, in this place, more dream than memory, the music, the mild maenads, and us at our table, faint, still figures, the wise ones, presiding behind leaf-reflecting glass.

They were captivated by me over there, my accent, my bow-ties, my slightly sinister, old-world charm. I was twenty-four, among them I felt middle-aged. They threw themselves at me with solemn fervour, as if engaging in a form of self-improvement. One of their little foreign wars was in full swing just then, everyone was a protester, it seemed, except me – I would have no truck with their marches, their sit-downs, the ear-splitting echolalia that passed with them for argument – but even my politics, or lack of them, were no deterrent, and flower children of all shapes and colours fell into my bed, their petals trembling. I remember few of them with any precision, when I think of them I see a sort of hybrid, with this one's hands, and that one's eyes, and yet another's sobs. From those days, those nights, only a faint, bittersweet savour remains, and a trace, the barest afterglow, of that state of floating ease, of, how shall I say, of balanic, ataraxic bliss – yes, yes, I have got hold of a dictionary – in which they left me, my muscles aching from their strenuous ministrations, my flesh bathed in the balm of their sweat.

It was in America that I met Daphne. At a party in some professor's house one afternoon I was standing on the porch with a treble gin in my hand when I heard below me on the lawn the voice of home: soft yet clear, like the sound of water falling on glass, and with that touch of lethargy which is the unmistakable note of our set. I looked, and there she was, in a flowered dress and unfashionable shoes, her hair done up in the golliwog style of the day, frowning past the shoulder of a man in a loud jacket who was replying with airy gestures to something she had asked, while she nodded seriously, not listening to a word he said. I had just that glimpse of her and then I turned away, I don't quite know why. I was in one of my bad moods, and halfway drunk. I see that moment as an emblem of our life together. I would spend the next fifteen years turning away from her, in one way or another, until that morning when I stood at the rail of the island steamer, snuffling the slimed air of the harbour and waving half-heartedly to her and the child, the two of them tiny below me on the dockside. That day it was she who turned away from me, with what seems to me now a slow and infinitely sad finality.

*

I felt as much foolishness as fear. I felt ridiculous. It was unreal, the fix I had got myself into: one of those mad dreams that some ineffectual fat little man might turn into a third-rate film. I would dismiss it for long periods, as one dismisses a dream, no matter how awful, but presently it would come slithering back, the hideous, tentacled thing, and there would well up in me a hot flush of terror and shame – shame, that is, for my own stupidity, my wanton lack of prescience, that had landed me in such a deal of soup.

Since I had seemed, with Randolph, to have stumbled into a supporting feature, I had expected it would be played by a comic cast of ruffians, scarified fellows with low foreheads and little thin moustaches who would stand about me in a circle with their hands in their pockets, smiling horribly and chewing toothpicks. Instead I was summoned to an audience with a silver-haired hidalgo in a white suit, who greeted me with a firm, lingering handshake and told me his name was Aguirre. His manner was courteous and faintly sad. He fitted ill with his surroundings. I had climbed a narrow stairs to a dirty, low room above a bar. There was a table covered with oilcloth, and a couple of cane chairs. On the floor under the table a filthy infant was sitting, sucking a wooden spoon. An outsize television set squatted in a corner, on the blank, baleful screen of which I saw myself reflected, immensely tall and thin, and curved like a bow. There was a smell of fried food. Señor Aguirre, with a little moue of distaste, examined the seat of one of the chairs and sat down. He poured out wine for us, and tipped his glass in a friendly toast. He was a businessman, he said, a simple businessman, not a great professor – and smiled at me and gently bowed – but all the same he knew there were certain rules, certain moral imperatives. One of these in particular he was thinking of: perhaps I could guess which one? Mutely I shook my head. I felt like a mouse being toyed with by a sleek bored old cat. His sadness deepened. Loans, he said softly, loans must be repaid. That was the law on which commerce was founded. He hoped I would understand his position. There was a silence. A kind of horrified amazement had taken hold of me: this was the real world, the world of fear and pain and retribution, a serious place, not that sunny playground

in which I had frittered away fistfuls of someone else's money. I
would have to go home, I said at last, in a voice that did not
seem to be mine, there were people who would help me, friends,
family, I could borrow from them. He considered. Would I go
alone? he wondered. For a second I did not see what he was
getting at. Then I looked away from him and said slowly yes, yes,
my wife and son would probably stay here. And as I said it I
seemed to hear a horrible cackling, a jungle hoot of derision, just
behind my shoulder. He smiled, and poured out carefully another
inch of wine. The child, who had been playing with my shoelaces,
began to howl. I was agitated, I had not meant to kick the
creature. Señor Aguirre frowned, and shouted something over his
shoulder. A door behind him opened and an enormously fat,
angry-looking young woman put in her head and grunted at him.
She wore a black, sleeveless dress with a crooked hem, and a
glossy black wig as high as a beehive, with false eyelashes to
match. She waddled forward, and with an effort bent and picked
up the infant and smacked it hard across the face. It started in
surprise, and, swallowing a mighty sob, fixed its round eyes
solemnly on me. The woman glared at me too, and took the
wooden spoon and threw it on the table in front of me with a
clatter. Then, planting the child firmly on one tremendous hip,
she stumped out of the room and slammed the door behind her.
Señor Aguirre gave a slight, apologetic shrug. He smiled again,
twinkling. What was my opinion of the island women? I hesitated.
Come come, he said gaily, surely I had an opinion on such an
important matter. I said they were lovely, quite lovely, quite the
loveliest of their species I had ever encountered. He nodded
happily, it was what he had expected me to say. No, he said, no,
too dark, too dark all over, even in those places never exposed to
the sun. And he leaned forward with his crinkled, silvery smile
and tapped a finger lightly on my wrist. Northern women, now,
ah, those pale northern women. Such white skin! So delicate! So
fragile! Your wife, for instance, he said. There was another,
breathless silence. I could hear faintly the brazen strains of music
from a radio in the bar downstairs. Bullfight music. My chair

made a crackling noise under me, like a muttered warning. Señor Aguirre joined his El Greco hands and looked at me over the spire of his fingertips. Your whife, he said, breathing on the word, your beautiful whife, you will come back quickly to her? It was not really a question. What could I say to him, what could I do? These are not really questions either.

I told Daphne as little as possible. She seemed to understand. She made no difficulties. That has always been the great thing about Daphne: she makes no difficulties.

*

It was a long trip home. The steamer landed in Valencia harbour at dusk. I hate Spain, a brutish, boring country. The city smelled of sex and chlorine. I took the night train, jammed in a third-class compartment with half a dozen reeking peasants in cheap suits. I could not sleep. I was hot, my head ached. I could feel the engine labouring up the long slope to the plateau, the wheels drumming their one phrase over and over. A washed-blue dawn was breaking in Madrid. I stopped outside the station and watched a flock of birds wheeling and tumbling at an immense height, and, the strangest thing, a gust of euphoria, or something like euphoria, swept through me, making me tremble, and bringing tears to my eyes. It was from lack of sleep, I suppose, and the effect of the high, thin air. Why, I wonder, do I remember so clearly standing there, the colour of the sky, those birds, that shiver of fevered optimism? I was at a turning point, you will tell me, just there the future forked for me, and I took the wrong path without noticing – that's what you'll tell me, isn't it, you, who must have meaning in everything, who lust after meaning, your palms sticky and your faces on fire! But calm, Frederick, calm. Forgive me this outburst, your honour. It is just that I do not believe such moments mean anything – or any other moments, for that matter. They have significance, apparently. They may even have value of some sort. But they do not mean anything.

There now, I have declared my faith.

Where was I? In Madrid. On my way out of Madrid. I took another train, travelling north. We stopped at every station on the way, I thought I would never get out of that terrible country. Once we halted for an hour in the middle of nowhere. I sat in the ticking silence and stared dully through the window. Beyond the littered tracks of the upline there was an enormous, high, yellow field, and in the distance a range of blue mountains that at first I took for clouds. The sun shone. A tired crow flapped past. Someone coughed. I thought how odd it was to be there, I mean just there and not somewhere else. Not that being somewhere else would have seemed any less odd. I mean – oh, I don't know what I mean. The air in the compartment was thick. The seats gave off their dusty, sat-upon smell. A small, swarthy, low-browed man opposite me caught my eye and did not look away. At that instant it came to me that I was on my way to do something very bad, something really appalling, something for which there would be no forgiveness. It was not a premonition, that is too tentative a word. I knew. I cannot explain how, but I knew. I was shocked at myself, my breathing quickened, my face pounded as if from embarrassment, but as well as shock there was a sort of antic glee, it surged in my throat and made me choke. That peasant was still watching me. He sat canted forward a little, hands resting calmly on his knees, his brow lowered, at once intent and remote. They stare like that, these people, they have so little sense of themselves they seem to imagine their actions will not register on others. They might be looking in from a different world.

I knew very well, of course, that I was running away.

I HAD EXPECTED to arrive in rain, and at Holyhead, indeed, a fine, warm drizzle was falling, but when we got out on the channel the sun broke through again. It was evening. The sea was calm, an oiled, taut meniscus, mauve-tinted and curiously high and curved. From the forward lounge where I sat the prow seemed to rise and rise, as if the whole ship were straining to take to the air. The sky before us was a smear of crimson on the palest of pale blue and silvery green. I held my face up to the calm sea-light, entranced, expectant, grinning like a loon. I confess I was not entirely sober, I had already broken into my allowance of duty-free booze, and the skin at my temples and around my eyes was tightening alarmingly. It was not just the drink, though, that was making me happy, but the tenderness of things, the simple goodness of the world. This sunset, for instance, how lavishly it was laid on, the clouds, the light on the sea, that heartbreaking, blue-green distance, laid on, all of it, as if to console some lost, suffering wayfarer. I have never really got used to being on this earth. Sometimes I think our presence here is due to a cosmic blunder, that we were meant for another planet altogether, with other arrangements, and other laws, and other, grimmer skies. I try to imagine it, our true place, off on the far side of the galaxy, whirling and whirling. And the ones who were meant for here, are they out there, baffled and homesick, like us? No, they would have become extinct long ago. How could they survive, these gentle earthlings, in a world that was made to contain *us*?

*

The voices, that was what startled me first of all. I thought they must be putting on this accent, it sounded so like a caricature.

Two raw-faced dockers with fags in their mouths, a customs man in a cap: my fellow countrymen. I walked through a vast, corrugated-iron shed and out into the tired gold of the summer evening. A bus went past, and a workman on a bike. The clocktower, its addled clock still showing the wrong time. It was all so affecting, I was surprised. I liked it here when I was a child, the pier, the promenade, that green bandstand. There was always a sweet sense of melancholy, of mild regret, as if some quaint, gay music, the last of the season, had just faded on the air. My father never referred to the place as anything but Kingstown: he had no time for the native jabber. He used to bring me here on Sunday afternoons, sometimes on weekdays too in the school holidays. It was a long drive from Coolgrange. He would park on the road above the pier and give me a shilling and slope off, leaving me to what he called my own devices. I see myself, the frog prince, enthroned on the high back seat of the Morris Oxford, consuming a cornet of ice cream, licking the diminishing knob of goo round and round with scientific application, and staring back at the passing promenaders, who blanched at the sight of my baleful eye and flickering, creamy tongue. The breeze from the sea was a soft, salt wall of air in the open window of the car, with a hint of smoke in it from the mailboat berthed below me. The flags on the roof of the yacht club shuddered and snapped, and a thicket of masts in the harbour swayed and tinkled like an oriental orchestra.

My mother never accompanied us on these jaunts. They were, I know now, just an excuse for my father to visit a poppet he kept there. I do not recall him behaving furtively, or not any more so than usual. He was a slight, neatly-made man, with pale eyebrows and pale eyes, and a small, fair moustache that was faintly indecent, like a bit of body fur, soft and downy, that had found its way inadvertently on to his face from some other, secret part of his person. It made his mouth startlingly vivid, a hungry, violent, red-coloured thing, grinding and snarling. He was always more or less angry, seething with resentment and indignation. Behind the bluster, though, he was a coward, I think. He felt sorry for himself. He was convinced the world had used him badly. In recompense he pampered himself, gave himself treats. He wore handmade shoes and Charvet ties, drank good claret, smoked cigarettes specially imported in airtight tins from a shop in the Burlington Arcade. I still have, or had, his malacca walking-cane. He was enormously proud of it. He liked to demonstrate to me how it was made, from four or was it eight pieces of rattan prepared and fitted together by a master craftsman. I could hardly keep a straight face, he was so laughably earnest. He made the mistake of imagining that his possessions were a measure of his own worth, and strutted and crowed, parading his things like a schoolboy with a champion catapult. Indeed, there was something of the eternal boy about him, something tentative and pubertal. When I think of us together I see him as impossibly young and me already grown-up, weary, embittered. I suspect he was a little afraid of me. By the age of twelve or thirteen I was as big as he, or as heavy, anyway, for although I have his fawn colouring, in shape I took after my mother, and already at that age was inclined towards flab. (Yes, m'lud, you see before you a middling man inside whom there is a fattie trying not to come out. For he was let slip once, was Bunter, just once, and look what happened.)

I hope I do not give the impression that I disliked my father. We did not converse much, but we were perfectly companionable, in the way of fathers and sons. If he did fear me a little, I too was wise enough to be wary of *him*, a relation easily mistaken, even by us at times, for mutual esteem. We had a great distaste for the world generally, there was that much in common between us. I notice I have inherited his laugh, that soft, nasal snicker which was his only comment on the large events of his time. Schisms, wars, catastrophes, what did he care for such matters? – the world, the only worthwhile world, had ended with the last viceroy's departure from these shores, after that it was all just a wrangle among peasants. He really did try to believe in this fantasy of a great good place that had been taken away from us and our kind – our kind being Castle Catholics, as he liked to say, yes, sir, Castle Catholics, and proud of it! But I think there was less pride than chagrin. I think he was secretly ashamed not to be a Protestant: he would have had so much less explaining, so much less justifying, to do. He portrayed himself as a tragic figure, a gentleman of the old school displaced in time. I picture him on those Sunday afternoons with his mistress, an ample young lady, I surmise, with hair unwisely curled and a generous décolletage, before whom he kneels, poised trembling on one knee, gazing rapt into her face, his moustache twitching, his moist red mouth open in supplication. Oh but I must not mock him like this. Really, really, I did not think unkindly of him – apart, that is, from wanting deep down to kill him, so that I might marry my mother, a novel and compelling notion which my counsel urges on me frequently, with a meaning look in his eye.

But I digress.

The charm I had felt in Kingstown, I mean Dun Laoghaire, did not endure into the city. My seat at the front on the top deck of the bus – my old seat, my favourite! – showed me scenes I hardly recognised. In the ten years since I had last been here something had happened, something had befallen the place. Whole streets were gone, the houses torn out and replaced by frightening blocks of steel and black glass. An old square where Daphne and I lived for a while had been razed and made into a vast, cindered car-park. I saw a church for sale – a church, for sale! Oh, something dreadful had happened. The very air itself seemed damaged. Despite the late hour a faint glow of daylight lingered, dense, dust-laden, like the haze after an explosion, or a great conflagration. People in the streets had the shocked look of survivors, they seemed not to walk but reel. I got down from the bus and picked my way among them with lowered gaze, afraid I might see horrors. Barefoot urchins ran along beside me, whining for pennies. There were drunks everywhere, staggering and swearing, lost in joyless befuddlement. An amazing couple reared up out of a pulsating cellar, a minatory, pockmarked young man with a crest of orange hair, and a stark-faced girl in gladiator boots and ragged, soot-black clothes. They were draped about with ropes and chains and what looked like cartridge belts, and sported gold studs in their nostrils. I had never seen such creatures, I thought they must be members of some fantastic sect. I fled before them, and dived into Wally's pub. Dived is the word.

I had expected it to be changed, like everything else. I was fond of Wally's. I used to drink there when I was a student, and later on, too, when I worked for the government. There was a touch of sleaze to the place which I found congenial. I know much has been made of the fact that it was frequented by homosexuals, but I trust the court will dismiss the implications which have been tacitly drawn from this, especially in the gutter press. I am not queer. I have nothing against those who are, except that I despise them, of course, and find disgusting the thought of the things they get up to, whatever those things may be. But their presence lent a blowsy gaiety to the atmosphere in Wally's and a slight edge of threat. I liked that shiver of embarrassment and gleeful dread that ran like a bead of mercury up my spine when a bevy of them suddenly exploded in parrot shrieks of laughter, or when they got drunk and started howling abuse and breaking things. Tonight, when I hurried in to shelter from the stricken city, the first thing I saw was a half dozen of them at a table by the door with their heads together, whispering and giggling and pawing each other happily. Wally himself was behind the bar. He had grown fatter, which I would not have thought possible, but apart from that he had not changed in ten years. I greeted him warmly. I suspect he remembered me, though of course he would not acknowledge it: Wally prided himself on the sourness of his manner. I ordered a large, a gargantuan gin and tonic, and he sighed grudgingly and heaved himself off the high stool on which he had been propped. He moved very slowly, as if through water, billowing in his fat, like a jellyfish. I was feeling better already. I told him about the church I had seen for sale. He shrugged, he was not surprised, such things were commonplace nowadays. As he was setting my drink before me the huddled circle of queers by the door flew apart suddenly in a loud splash of laughter, and he frowned at them, pursing his little mouth so that it almost disappeared in the folds of his fat chin.

He affected contempt for his clientele, though it was said he kept a bevy of boys himself, over whom he ruled with great severity, jealous and terrible as a Beardsleyan queen.

I drank my drink. There is something about gin, the tang in it of the deep wildwood, perhaps, that always makes me think of twilight and mists and dead maidens. Tonight it tinkled in my mouth like secret laughter. I looked about me. No, Wally's was not changed, not changed at all. This was my place: the murmurous gloom, the mirrors, the bottles ranged behind the bar, each one with its bead of ruby light. Yes, yes, the witch's kitchen, with a horrid fat queen, and a tittering band of fairy-folk. Why, there was even an ogre – Gilles the Terrible, *c'est moi*. I was happy. I enjoy the inappropriate, the disreputable, I admit it. In low dives such as this the burden of birth and education falls from me and I feel, I feel – I don't know what I feel. I don't know. The tense is wrong anyway. I turned to Wally and held out my glass, and watched in a kind of numbed euphoria as he measured out another philtre for me in a little silver chalice. That flash of blue when he added the ice, what am I thinking of? Blue eyes. Yes, of course.

I did say dead maidens, didn't I. Dear me.

So I sat in Wally's pub and drank, and talked to Wally of this and that – his side of the conversation confined to shrugs and dull grunts and the odd malevolent snigger – and gradually the buzz that travel always sets going in my head was stilled. I felt as if, instead of journeying by ship and rail, I had been dropped somehow through the air to land up in this spot at last, feeling groggy and happy, and pleasantly, almost voluptuously vulnerable. Those ten years I had passed in restless wandering were as nothing, a dream voyage, insubstantial. How distant all that seemed, those islands in a blue sea, those burning noons, and Randolph and Señor Aguirre, even my wife and child, how distant. Thus it was that when Charlie French came in I greeted him as if I had seen him only yesterday.

I know Charlie insists that he did not meet me in Wally's pub, that he never went near the place, but all I am prepared to admit is the possibility that it was not on that particular night that I saw him there. I remember the moment with perfect clarity, the queers whispering, and Wally polishing a glass with a practised and inimitably contemptuous wrist-action, and I sitting at the bar with a bumper of gin in my fist and my old pigskin suitcase at my feet, and Charlie pausing there in his chalkstripes and his scuffed shoes, a forgetful Eumaeus, smiling uneasily and eyeing me with vague surmise. All the same, it is possible that my memory has conflated two separate occasions. It is possible. What more can I say? I hope, Charles, this concession will soothe, even if only a little, your sense of injury.

People think me heartless, but I am not. I have much sympathy for Charlie French. I caused him great distress, no doubt of that. I humiliated him before the world. What pain that must have been, for a man such as Charlie. He behaved very well about it. He behaved beautifully, in fact. On that last, appalling, and appallingly comic occasion, when I was being led out in handcuffs, he looked at me not accusingly, but with a sort of sadness. He almost smiled. And I was grateful. He is a source of guilt and annoyance to me now, but he was my friend, and—

He was my friend. Such a simple phrase, and yet how affecting. I don't think I have ever used it before. When I wrote it down I had to pause, startled. Something welled up in my throat, as if I might be about to, yes, to weep. What is happening to me? Is this what they mean by rehabilitation? Perhaps I shall leave here a reformed character, after all.

Poor Charlie did not recognise me at first, and was distinctly uneasy, I could see, at being addressed in this place, in this familiar fashion, by a person who seemed to him a stranger. I was enjoying myself, it was like being in disguise. I offered to buy him a drink, but he declined, with elaborate politeness. He had aged. He was in his early sixties, but he looked older. He was stooped, and had a little egg-shaped paunch, and his ashen cheeks were inlaid with a filigree of broken veins. Yet he gave an impression of, what shall I call it, of equilibrium, which seemed new to him. It was as if he were at last filling out exactly his allotted space. When I knew him he had been a small-time dealer in pictures and antiques. Now he had presence, it was almost an air of imperium, all the more marked amid the gaudy trappings of Wally's bar. It's true, there was still that familiar expression in his eye, at once mischievous and sheepish, but I had to look hard to find it. He began to edge away from me, still queasily smiling, but then he in turn must have caught something familiar in my eye, and he knew me at last. Relieved, he gave a breathy laugh and glanced around the bar. That I did remember, that glance, as if he had just discovered his flies were open and was looking to see if anyone had noticed. Freddie! he said. Well well! He lit a cigarette with a not altogether steady hand, and released a great whoosh of smoke towards the ceiling. I was trying to recall when it was I had first met him. He used to come down to Coolgrange when my father was alive and hang about the house looking furtive and apologetic. They had been young together, he and my parents, in their cups they would reminisce about hunt balls before the war, and dashing up to Dublin for the Show, and all the rest of it. I listened to this stuff with boundless contempt, curling an adolescent's villous lip. They sounded like actors flogging away at some tired old drawing-room comedy, projecting wildly, my mother especially, with her scarlet fingernails and metallic perm and that cracked, gin-and-smoke voice of hers. But to be fair to Charles, I do not think he really subscribed to this fantasy of the dear dead days. He could not ignore the tiny trill of hysteria that made my mother's goitrous throat vibrate, nor the way my father looked at her sometimes, poised on the edge of his chair, tense as a whippet, pop-eyed and pale, with an expression of incredulous loathing. When they got going like this, the two of them, they forgot everything else, their son, their friend, everything, locked together in a kind of macabre trance. This meant that Charlie and I were often thrown into each other's company. He treated me tentatively, as if I were something that might blow up in his face at any moment. I was very fierce in those days, brimming with impatience and scorn. We must have been a peculiar pair, yet we got on, at some deep level. Perhaps I seemed to him the son he would never have, perhaps he seemed to me the father I had never had. (This is another idea put forward by my counsel. I don't know how you think of them, Maolseachlainn.) What was I saying? Charlie. He took me to the races one day, when I was a boy. He was all kitted out for the occasion, in tweeds and brown brogues and a little trilby hat tipped at a raffish angle over one eye. He even had a pair of binoculars, though he did not seem to be able to get them properly in focus. He looked the part, except for a certain stifled something in his manner that made it seem all the time as if he were about to break down in helpless giggles at himself and his pretensions. I was fifteen or sixteen. In the drinks marquee he turned to me blandly and asked what I would have, Irish or Scotch – and brought me home in the evening loudly and truculently drunk. My father was furious, my mother laughed. Charlie maintained an unruffled silence, pretending nothing was amiss, and slipped me a fiver as I was stumbling off to bed.

Ah Charles, I am sorry, truly I am.

Now, as if he too were remembering that other time, he insisted on buying a drink, and pursed his lips disapprovingly when I asked for gin. He was a whiskey man, himself. It was part of his disguise, like the striped suit and the worn-down, handmade shoes, and that wonderful, winged helmet of hair, now silvered all over, which, so my mother liked to say, had destined him for greatness. He had always managed to avoid his destiny, however. I asked him what he was doing these days. Oh, he said, I'm running a gallery. And he glanced about him with an abstracted, wondering smile, as if he were himself surprised at such a notion. I nodded. So that was what had bucked him up, what had given him that self-sufficient air. I saw him in some dusty room, a forgotten backwater, with a few murky pictures on the wall, and a frosty spinster for a secretary who bickered with him over tea money and gave him a tie wrapped in tissue-paper every Christmas. Poor Charlie, forced to take himself seriously at last, with a business to take care of, and painters after him for their money. Here, I said, let me, and peeled a note from my rapidly dwindling wad and slapped it on the bar.

To be candid, however, I was thinking of asking him for a loan. What prevented me was – well, there will be laughter in court, I know, but the fact is I felt it would be in bad taste. It is not that I am squeamish about these matters, in my time I have touched sadder cases than Charlie for a float, but there was something in the present circumstances that held me back. We might indeed have been a father and son – not *my* father, of course, and certainly not *this* son – meeting by chance in a brothel. Constrained, sad, obscurely ashamed, we blustered and bluffed, knocking our glasses together and toasting the good old days. But it was no use, in a little while we faltered, and fell gloomily silent. Then suddenly Charlie looked at me, with what was almost a flash of pain, and in a low, impassioned voice said, Freddie, what have you done to yourself? At once abashed, he leaned away from me in a panic, desperately grinning, and puffed a covering cloud of smoke. First I was furious, and then depressed. Really, I was not in the mood for this kind of thing. I glanced at the clock behind the bar and, purposely misunderstanding him, said yes, it was true, it had been a long day, I was overdoing it, and I finished my drink and shook his hand and took up my bag and left.

*

There it was again, in another form, the same question: why, Freddie, why are you living like this? I brooded on it next morning on the way to Coolgrange. The day looked as I felt, grey and flat and heavy. The bus plunged laboriously down the narrow country roads, pitching and wallowing, with a dull zip and roar that seemed the sound of my own blood beating in my brain. The myriad possibilities of the past lay behind me, a strew of wreckage. Was there, in all that, one particular shard – a decision reached, a road taken, a signpost followed – that would show me just how I had come to my present state? No, of course not. My journey, like everyone else's, even yours, your honour, had not been a thing of signposts and decisive marching, but drift only, a kind of slow subsidence, my shoulders bowing down under the gradual accumulation of all the things I had not done. Yet I can see that to someone like Charlie, watching from the ground, I must have seemed a creature of fable scaling the far peaks, rising higher and ever higher, leaping at last from the pinnacle into marvellous, fiery flight, my head wreathed in flames. But I am not Euphorion. I am not even his father.

The question is wrong, that's the trouble. It assumes that actions are determined by volition, deliberate thought, a careful weighing-up of facts, all that puppet-show twitching which passes for consciousness. I was living like that because I was living like that, there is no other answer. When I look back, no matter how hard I try I can see no clear break between one phase and another. It is a seamless flow – although flow is too strong a word. More a sort of busy stasis, a sort of running on the spot. Even that was too fast for me, however, I was always a little way behind, trotting in the rear of my own life. In Dublin I was still the boy growing up at Coolgrange, in America I was the callow young man of Dublin days, on the islands I became a kind of American. And nothing was enough. Everything was coming, was on the way, was about to be. Stuck in the past, I was always peering beyond the present towards a limitless future. Now, I suppose, the future may be said to have arrived.

None of this means anything. Anything of significance, that is. I am just amusing myself, musing, losing myself in a welter of words. For words in here are a form of luxury, of sensuousness, they are all we have been allowed to keep of the rich, wasteful world from which we are shut away.

O God, O Christ, release me from this place.

O Someone.

I must stop, I am getting one of my headaches. They come with increasing frequency. Don't worry, your lordship, no need to summon the tipstaff or the sergeant-at-arms or whatever he's called – they are just headaches. I shall not suddenly go berserk, clutching my temples and bawling for my – but speak of the devil, here she is, Ma Jarrett herself. Come, step into the witness box, mother.

IT WAS EARLY AFTERNOON when I reached Coolgrange. I got down at the cross and watched the bus lumber away, its fat back-end looking somehow derisive. The noise of the engine faded, and the throbbing silence of summer settled again on the fields. The sky was still overcast, but the sun was asserting itself somewhere, and the light that had been dull and flat was now a tender, pearl-grey glow. I stood and looked about me. What a surprise the familiar always is. It was all there, the broken gate, the drive, the long meadow, the oak wood – home! – all perfectly in place, waiting for me, a little smaller than I remembered, like a scale-model of itself. I laughed. It was not really a laugh, more an exclamation of startlement and recognition. Before such scenes as this – trees, the shimmering fields, that mild soft light – I always feel like a traveller on the point of departure. Even arriving I seemed to be turning away, with a lingering glance at the lost land. I set off up the drive with my raincoat over my shoulder and my battered bag in my hand, a walking cliché, though it's true I was a bit long in the tooth, and a bit on the beefy side, for the part of the prodigal son. A dog slid out of the hedge at me with a guttural snarl, teeth bared to the gums. I halted. I do not like dogs. This was a black-and-white thing with shifty eyes, it moved back and forth in a half-circle in front of me, still growling, keeping its belly close to the ground. I held the suitcase against my knees for a shield, and spoke sharply, as to an unruly child, but my voice came out a broken falsetto, and for a moment there was a sense of general merriment, as if there were faces hidden among the leaves, laughing. Then a whistle sounded, and the brute whined and turned guiltily toward the house. My mother was standing on the front steps. She laughed. Suddenly the sun

came out, with a kind of soundless report. Good God, she said, it
is you, I thought I was seeing things.

*

I hesitate. It is not that I am lost for words, but the opposite.
There is so much to be said I do not know where to begin. I feel
myself staggering backwards slowly, clutching in my outstretched
arms a huge, unwieldy and yet weightless burden. She is so much,
and, at the same time, nothing. I must go carefully, this is perilous
ground. Of course, I know that whatever I say will be smirked at
knowingly by the amateur psychologists packing the court. When
it comes to the subject of mothers, simplicity is not permitted.
All the same, I shall try to be honest and clear. Her name is
Dorothy, though everyone has always called her Dolly, I do not
know why, for there is nothing doll-like about her. She is a large,
vigorous woman with the broad face and heavy hair of a tinker's
wife. In describing her thus I do not mean to be disrespectful.
She is impressive, in her way, at once majestic and slovenly. I
recall her from my childhood as a constant but remote presence,
statuesque, blank-eyed, impossibly handsome in an Ancient
Roman sort of way, like a marble figure at the far side of a lawn.
Later on, though, she grew to be top-heavy, with a big backside
and slim legs, a contrast which, when I was an adolescent and
morbidly interested in such things, led me to speculate on the
complicated architecture that must be necessary to bridge the gap
under her skirt between those shapely knees and that thick waist.
Hello, mother, I said, and looked away from her, casting about
me crossly for something neutral on which to concentrate. I was
annoyed already. She has that effect on me, I have only to stand
before her and instantly the irritation and resentment begin to
seethe in my breast. I was surprised. I had thought that after ten
years there would be at least a moment of grace between our
meeting and the first attack of filial heartburn, but not a bit of it,
here I was, jaw clenched, glaring venomously at a tuft of weed
sprouting from a crack in the stone steps where she stood. She
was not much changed. Her bosom, which cries out to be called

ample, had descended to just above her midriff. Also she had grown a little moustache. She wore baggy corduroy trousers and a cardigan with sagging pockets. She came down the steps to me and laughed again. You have put on weight, Freddie, she said, you've got fat. Then she reached out and – this is true, I swear it – and took hold of a piece of my stomach and rolled it playfully between a finger and thumb. This woman, this woman – what can I say? I was thirty-eight, a man of parts, with a wife and a son and an impressive Mediterranean tan, I carried myself with gravitas and a certain faint air of menace, and she, what did she do? – she pinched my belly and laughed her phlegmy laugh. Is it any wonder I have ended up in jail? Is it? The dog, seeing that I was to be accepted, sidled up to me and tried to lick my hand, which gave me an opportunity to deliver it a good hard kick in the ribs. That made me feel better, but not much, and not for long.

Is there anything as powerfully, as piercingly evocative, as the smell of the house in which one's childhood was spent? I try to avoid generalisations, as no doubt the court has noticed, but surely this is a universal, this involuntary spasm of recognition which comes with the first whiff of that humble, drab, brownish smell, which is hardly a smell at all, more an emanation, a sort of sigh exhaled by the thousands of known but unacknowledged tiny things that collectively constitute what is called home. I stepped into the hall and for an instant it was as if I had stepped soundlessly through the membrane of time itself. I faltered, tottering inwardly. Hatstand with broken umbrella, that floor tile, still loose. Get out, Patch, damn you! my mother said behind me, and the dog yelped. The taste of apples unaccountably flooded my mouth. I felt vaguely as if something momentous had happened, as if in the blink of an eye everything around me had been whipped away and replaced instantly with an exact replica, perfect in every detail, down to the last dust-mote. I walked on, into this substitute world, tactfully keeping a blank expression, and seemed to hear a disembodied held breath being let go in relief that the difficult trick had worked yet again.

We went into the kitchen. It looked like the lair of some large, scavenging creature. Lord, mother, I said, are you *living* in here? Items of clothing, an old woman's nameless rags, were stuffed between the dishes on the dresser. The toes of three or four pairs of shoes peeped out from under a cupboard, an unnerving sight, as if the wearers might be huddled together in there, stubby arms clasped around each other's hunched shoulders, listening. Pieces of furniture had migrated here from all over the house, the narrow little bureau from my father's study, the walnut cocktail cabinet from the drawing-room, the velvet-covered recliner with balding armrests in which my Great-Aunt Alice, a tiny, terrible woman, had died without a murmur one Sunday afternoon in summer. The huge old wireless that used to lord it over the lounge stood now at a drunken tilt on the draining-board, crooning softly to itself, its single green eye pulsing. The place was far from clean. A ledger was open on the table, and bills and things were strewn amid the smeared plates and the unwashed teacups. She had been doing the accounts. Briefly I considered bringing up the main matter straight away – money, that is – but thought better of it. As if she had an inkling of what was in my mind she glanced from me to the papers and back again with amusement. I turned away from her, to the window. Out on the lawn a stocky girl in jodhpurs was leading a string of Connemara ponies in a circle. I recalled dimly my mother telling me, in one of her infrequent and barely literate letters, about some hare-brained venture involving these animals. She came and stood beside me. We watched in silence the ponies plodding round and round. Ugly brutes, aren't they, she said cheerfully. The simmering annoyance I had felt since arriving was added to now by a sense of general futility. I have always been prone to accidie. It is a state, or, I might even say, a force, the significance of which in human affairs historians and suchlike seem not to appreciate. I think I would do anything to avoid it – anything. My mother was talking about her customers, mostly Japs and Germans, it seemed – They're taking over the bloody country, Freddie, I'm telling you. They bought the ponies as pets for their spoilt offspring, at what she happily admitted were outrageous prices. Cracked, the lot of them, she said. We laughed, and then fell vacantly silent again. The sun was on the lawn, and a vast white cloud was slowly unfurling above the sweltering beeches. I was thinking how strange it was to stand here glooming out at the day like this, bored and irritable, my hands in my pockets, while all the time, deep inside me somewhere, hardly acknowledged, grief dripped and dripped, a kind of silvery ichor, pure, and strangely precious. Home, yes, home is always a surprise.

She insisted that I come and look the place over, as she put it. After all, my boy, she said, someday all this will be yours. And she did her throaty cackle. I did not remember her being so easily amused in the past. There was something almost unruly in her laughter, a sort of abandon. I was a little put out by it, I thought it was not seemly. She lit up a cigarette and set off around the house, with the cigarette box and matches clutched in her left claw, and me trailing grimly in her smoking wake. The house was rotting, in places so badly, and so rapidly, that even she was startled. She talked and talked. I nodded dully, gazing at damp walls and sagging floors and mouldering window-frames. In my old room the bed was broken, and there was something growing in the middle of the mattress. The view from the window – trees, a bit of sloping field, the red roof of a barn – was exact and familiar as an hallucination. Here was the cupboard I had built, and at once I had a vision of myself, a small boy with a fierce frown, blunt saw in hand, hacking at a sheet of plywood, and my grieving heart wobbled, as if it were not myself I was remembering, but something like a son, dear and vulnerable, lost to me forever in the depths of my own past. When I turned around my mother was not there. I found her on the stairs, looking a little odd around the eyes. She set off again. I must see the grounds, she cried, the stables, the oak wood. She was determined I would see everything, everything.

Out of doors my spirits rose somewhat. How soft the air of summer here. I had been too long under harsh southern skies. And the trees, the great trees! those patient, quietly suffering creatures, standing stock-still as if in embarrassment, their tragic gazes somehow turned away from us. Patch the dog – I can see I am going to be stuck with this brute – Patch the dog appeared, rolling its mad eyes and squirming. It followed silently behind us across the lawn. The stable-girl, watching sidelong as we approached, seemed on the point of taking to her heels in fright. Her name was Joan, or Jean, something like that. Big bum, big chest – obviously mother had felt an affinity. When I spoke to her the poor girl turned crimson, and wincingly extended a calloused little paw as if she were afraid I might be going to keep it. I gave her one of my special, slow smiles, and saw myself through her eyes, a tall, tanned hunk in a linen suit, leaning over her on a summer lawn and murmuring dark words. Tinker! she yelped, get off! The lead pony, a stunted beast with a truculent eye, was edging sideways in that dully determined way that they have, nudging heavily against me. I put my hand on its flank to push it away, and was startled by the solidity, the actuality of the animal, the coarse dry coat, the dense unyielding flesh beneath, the blood warmth. Shocked, I took my hand away quickly and stepped back. Suddenly I had a vivid, queasy sense of myself, not the tanned pin-up now, but something else, something pallid and slack and soft. I was aware of my toenails, my anus, my damp, constricted crotch. And I was ashamed. I can't explain it. That is, I could, but won't. Then the dog began to bark, rushing at the pony's hoofs, and the pony snorted, peeling back its muzzle and snapping its alarming teeth. My mother kicked the dog, and the girl hauled the pony's head sideways. The dog howled, the line of ponies plunged and whinnied. What a racket! Everything, always, turns to farce. I remembered my hangover. I needed a drink.

*

Gin first, then some sort of awful sherry, then successive jorums of my late father's fine Bordeaux, the last, alas, of the bin. I was already half-soused when I went down to the cellar to fetch the claret. I sat on a crate amid the must and gloom, breathing gin fumes out of flared nostrils. A streaming lance of sunlight, seething with dust, pierced the low, cobwebbed window above my head. Things thronged around me in the shadows – a battered rocking-horse, an old high bicycle, a bundle of antique tennis racquets – their outlines blurred, greyish, fading, as if this place were a way-station where the past paused on its way down into oblivion. I laughed. Old bastard, I said aloud, and the silence rang like a rapped glass. He was always down here in those last months before he died. He had become a potterer, he who all his life had been driven by fierce, obsessive energies. My mother would send me down to look for him, in case something might have happened to him, as she delicately put it. I would find him poking about in corners, fiddling with things, or just standing, canted at an odd angle, staring at nothing. When I spoke he would give a great start and turn on me angrily, huffing, as if he had been caught at something shameful. But these spurts of animation did not last long, after a moment he would drift off again into vagueness. It was as if he were not dying of an illness, but of a sort of general distraction: as if one day in the midst of his vehement doings something had caught his attention, had beckoned to him out of the darkness, and, struck, he had turned aside and walked towards it, with a sleepwalker's pained, puzzled concentration. I was, what, twenty-two, twenty-three. The long process of his dying wearied and exasperated me in equal measure. Of course I pitied him, too, but I think pity is always, for me, only the permissible version of an urge to give weak things a good hard shake. He began to shrink. Suddenly his shirt collars were too big for that wobbly tortoise-neck with its two slack harp-strings. Everything was too big for him, his clothes had more substance than he did, he seemed to rattle about inside them. His eyes were huge and haunted, already clouding. It was summer then, too. Light was not his medium any more, he preferred it down here, in the mossy half-dark, among the deepening shades.

I hauled myself to my feet and gathered an armful of dusty bottles and staggered with them up the damp stone steps.

Yet he died upstairs, in the big front bedroom, the airiest room in the house. It was so hot all that week. They opened wide the window, and he made them move his bed forward until the foot of it was right out on the balcony. He lay with the covers thrown back, his meagre chest bared, giving himself up to the sun, the vast sky, dying into the blue and gold glare of summer. His hands. The rapid beat of his breathing. His—

Enough. I was speaking of my mother.

I had set the bottles on the table, and was clawing the dust and cobwebs off them, when she informed me that she did not drink now. This was a surprise – in the old days she could knock it back with the best of them. I stared at her, and she shrugged and looked away. Doctor's orders, she said. I examined her with renewed attention. There was something wrong with her left eye, and her mouth drooped a little on that side. I recalled the odd way she had clutched the cigarette box and matches in her left hand when she was conducting me around the house. She shrugged again. A slight stroke, she said, last year. I thought what an odd term that is: a slight stroke. As if a benevolent but clumsy power had dealt her a fond, playful blow and accidentally damaged her. She glanced at me sidelong now with a tentative, almost girlish, melancholy little smile. She might have been confessing to something, some peccadillo, trivial but embarrassing. Sorry to hear it, old thing, I said, and urged her to go on, take a drop of wine, the doctors be damned. She seemed not to hear me. And then a really surprising thing happened. The girl, Joan or Jean – I'll compromise, and call her Jane – got up suddenly from her place, with a gulp of distress, and put her arm awkwardly around my mother's head, clutching her in a sort of wrestling hold, and laying a hand along her brow. I expected my mother to give her a good push and tell her to get off, but no, she sat there, suffering calmly the girl's embrace and looking at me still with that small smile. I stared back at her in startlement, holding the wine bottle suspended above my glass. It was the strangest thing. The girl's great hip was beside my mother's shoulder, and I thought irresistibly of the pony pressing against me on the lawn with that stubborn, brute regard. There was a silence. Then the girl, I mean Jane, caught my eye, and blenched, and withdrew her arm and sat down again hurriedly. Here is a question: if man is a sick animal, an insane animal, as I have reason to believe, then how account for these small, unbidden gestures of kindness and of care? Does it occur to you, my lord, that people of our kind – if I may be permitted to scramble up and join you on the bench for a moment – that we have missed out on something, I mean something in general, a universal principle, which is so simple, so obvious, that no one has ever thought to tell us about it? They all know what it is, my learned friend, this knowledge is the badge of their fellowship. And they are everywhere, the vast, sad, initiated crowd. They look up at us from the well of the court and say nothing, only smile a little, with that mixture of compassion and sympathetic irony, as my mother was smiling at me now. She reached across and patted the girl's hand and told her not to mind me. I stared. What had I done? The child sat with eyes fixed on her plate, groping blindly for her knife and fork. Her cheeks were aflame, I could almost hear them hum. Had a look from me done all that? I sighed, poor ogre, and ate a potato. It was raw and waxen at the heart. More drink.

You're not getting into one of your moods, are you, Freddie? my mother said.

Have I mentioned my bad moods, I wonder. Very black, very black. As if the world had grown suddenly dim, as if something had dirtied the air. Even when I was a child my depressions frightened people. In them again, is he? they would say, and they would chuckle, but uneasily, and edge away from me. In school I was a terror – but no, no, I'll spare you the schooldays. I noticed my mother was no longer much impressed by my gloom. Her smile, with that slight droop at the side, was turning positively sardonic. I said I had seen Charlie French in town. Oh, Charlie, she said, and shook her head and laughed. I nodded. Poor Charlie, he is the kind of person about whom people say, Oh, like that, and laugh. Another, listless silence. Why on earth had I come back here. I picked up the bottle, and was surprised to find it empty. I opened another, clamping it between my knees and swaying and grunting as I yanked at the cork. Ah! and out it came with a jolly pop. Outside on the lawn the last of the day's sunlight thickened briefly, then faded. My mother was asking after Daphne and the child. At the thought of them something like a great sob, lugubrious, faintly comical, ballooned under my breastbone. Jane – no, I can't call her that, it doesn't fit – Joan cleared the table, and my mother produced, of all things, a decanter of port and pushed it across the table to me. You won't want us to withdraw, will you? she said, with that grin. You can think of me as a man, anyway, I'm ancient enough. I began earnestly to tell her about my financial troubles, but got into a muddle and had to stop. Besides, I suspected she was not really listening. She sat with her face half-turned to the nickel light of evening from the window, rheum-eyed and old, showing the broad brow and high cheekbones of her Dutch forebears, King Billy's henchmen. You should have a ruff, Ma, I said, and a lace cap. I laughed loudly, then frowned. My face was going numb. Jean carefully offered me a cup of coffee. No, thank you, my dear, I said gravely, in my grandee's voice, indicating my port-glass, which, I noticed, was unaccountably empty. I refilled it, admiring the steadiness of the hand that held the decanter. Time passed. Birds were calling through the blue-grey dusk. I sat bemused, bolt-upright, in happy misery, listening to them. Then with a snort and a heave I roused myself and looked about me, smacking my lips and blinking. My mother and the girl were gone.

He died at evening. The room was still heavy with the long day's heat. I sat on a chair beside his bed in the open window and held his hand. His hand. The waxen feel of. How bright the air above the trees, bright and blue, like the limitless skies of childhood. I put my arm around him, laid a hand on his forehead. He said to me: don't mind her. He said to me—

Stop this, stop it. I was not there. I have not been present at anyone's death. He died alone, slipped away while no one was looking, leaving us to our own devices. By the time I arrived from the city they had trussed him up, ready for the coffin. He lay on the bed with his hands folded on his breast and his eyes shut tight, like a child being good. His hair was brushed in a neat lick across his forehead. His ears, I remember, were very white. Extraordinary: all that anger and resentment, that furious, unfocused energy: gone.

I took what remained of the port and staggered away upstairs. My knees quaked, I felt as if I were lugging a body on my back. The light-switches seemed to have been moved, in the half-darkness I kept banging into things, swearing and laughing. Then I found my way by mistake into Joanne's room. (Joanne: that's it!) She must have been awake, listening to me barging about, I hardly got the door open before she switched on her lamp. I stood teetering on the threshold, goggling at her. She lay in a vast, sagging bed with the sheet pulled to her chin, and for some reason I was convinced that she was still wearing her jodhpurs and her baggy pullover, and even her riding boots. She said nothing, only smiled at me in fright, and for a wild moment I considered climbing in beside her, shoes and all, so that now she might cradle *my* poor whirling head in her plump young accommodating arm. I had not really noticed before her extraordinary flame-red hair, the sight of it spread out on the pillow in the lamplight almost made me cry. Then the moment was gone, and with a grave nod I withdrew silently, like an old sad grey fading ghost, and marched at a careful, dignified pace across the landing to the room where a bed had been made up for me. There I discovered that somewhere along the way I had mislaid the port.

I sat on the side of the bed, arms dangling between my knees, and was suddenly exhausted. My head fizzed, my eyes burned, but yet I could not make myself lie down to sleep. I might have been a child come home after a day of wild excursions. I had travelled far. Slowly, with underwater movements, I untied my shoelaces. One shoe dropped, and then—

I WOKE WITH A DREADFUL START, my ears ringing, as if there had been an explosion in my head. A dream: something about meat. It was light, but whether it was dawn or still dusk I was not sure. Grey. Nor did I know where I was. Even when I realised it was Coolgrange I did not recognise the room at first. Very high and long, with lofty windows that came down to the floor. Shabby, too, in a peculiar, offended way, as if it were conscious of once having been an important place. I got up carefully from the bed and went and looked down at the lawn. The grass was grey, and there were pigeon-coloured shadows under the trees. My brain thudded. It must be dawn: in the oak wood, under an iron sky, a solitary bird was testing out the lightening air with a single repeated flute-note. I pressed my forehead against the windowpane, and shivered at the clammy, cold touch of the glass. I had been travelling for the best part of a week, with scant food and too much alcohol, and now it was all catching up with me. I felt sick, sodden, reamed. My eyelids were scalding, my spit tasted of ash. It seemed to me the garden was watching me, in its stealthy, tight-lipped way, or that it was at least somehow aware of me, framed here in the window, wringing my hands, a stricken starer-out — how many other such there must have been, down the years! — with the room's weightless dark pressing at my back. I had slept in my clothes.

The dream. (The court will need to hear about my dreams.) It came back to me suddenly. Nothing very much happened in it. My dreams are not the riotous tumble of events that others claim to enjoy, but states of feeling, rather, moods, particular humours, gusts of emotion, accompanied often by extreme physical effects: I weep, or thrash my limbs, grind my teeth, laugh, cry

46

out. On this occasion it had been a dry retching, the ache in my throat when I woke was what brought it back to me. I had dreamed I was gnawing the ripped-out sternum of some creature, possibly human. It seemed to have been parboiled, for the meat on it was soft and white. Barely warm now, it crumbled in my mouth like suet, making me gag. Believe me, your lordship, I do not enjoy relating these things any more than the court enjoys hearing them. And there is worse to come, as you know. Anyway, there I was, mumbling these frightful gobs of flesh, my stomach heaving even as I slept. That is all there was, really, except for an underlying sensation of enforced yet horribly pleasurable transgression. Wait a moment. I want to get this right, it is important, I'm not sure why. Some nameless authority was making me do this terrible thing, was standing over me implacably with folded arms as I sucked and slobbered, yet despite this – or perhaps, even, because of it – despite the horror, too, and the nausea – deep inside me something exulted.

By the way, leafing through my dictionary I am struck by the poverty of the language when it comes to naming or describing badness. Evil, wickedness, mischief, these words imply an agency, the conscious or at least active doing of wrong. They do not signify the bad in its inert, neutral, self-sustaining state. Then there are the adjectives: dreadful, heinous, execrable, vile, and so on. They are not so much descriptive as judgmental. They carry a weight of censure mingled with fear. Is this not a queer state of affairs? It makes me wonder. I ask myself if perhaps the thing itself – *badness* – does not exist at all, if these strangely vague and imprecise words are only a kind of ruse, a kind of elaborate cover for the fact that nothing is there. Or perhaps the words are an attempt to make it be there? Or, again, perhaps there *is* something, but the words invented it. Such considerations make me feel dizzy, as if a hole had opened briefly in the world. What was I talking about? My dreams, yes. There was the recurring one, the one in which – but no, no, leave that to another time.

I am standing by the window, in my parents' bedroom. Yes, I had realised that it was, used to be, theirs. The grey of dawn was giving way to a pale wash of sunlight. My lips were tacky from last night's port. The room, the house, the garden and the fields, all was strange to me, I did not recognise it today – strange, and yet known, too, like a place in – yes – in a dream. I stood there in my wrinkled suit, with my aching head and soiled mouth, wide-eyed but not quite awake, staring fixedly into that patch of sunlit garden with an amnesiac's numbed amazement. But then, am I not always like that, more or less? When I think about it, I seem to have lived most of my life that way, stalled between sleep and waking, unable to distinguish between dream and the daylight world. In my mind there are places, moments, events, which are so still, so isolated, that I am not sure they can be real, but which if I had recalled them that morning would have struck me with more vividness and force than the real things surrounding me. For instance, there is the hallway of a farmhouse where I went once as a child to buy apples. I see the polished stone floor, cardinal red. I can smell the polish. There is a gnarled geranium in a pot, and a big pendulum clock with the minute-hand missing. I can hear the farmer's wife speaking in the dim depths of the house, asking something of someone. I can sense the fields all around, the light above the fields, the vast, slow, late-summer day. I am there. In such remembered moments I am there as I never was at Coolgrange, as I seem never to have been, or to be, anywhere, at any time, as I, or some essential part of me, was not there even on that day I am remembering, the day I went to buy apples from the farmer's wife, at that farm in the midst of the fields. Never wholly anywhere, never with anyone, either, that was me, always. Even as a child I seemed to myself a traveller who had been delayed in the middle of an urgent journey. Life was an unconscionable wait, walking up and down the platform, watching for the train. People got in the way and blocked my view, I had to crane to see past them. Yes, that was me, all right.

I picked my way down through the silent house to the kitchen. In the morning light the room had a scrubbed, eager aspect. I moved about warily, unwilling to disturb the atmosphere of hushed expectancy, feeling like an uninitiate at some grand, rapt ceremony of light and weather. The dog lay on a dirty old rug beside the stove, its muzzle between its paws, watching me, a crescent of white showing in each eye. I made a pot of tea, and was sitting at the table, waiting for it to draw, when Joanne came in. She was wearing a mouse-grey dressing-gown belted tightly about her midriff. Her hair was tied up at the back in a thick, appropriately equine plume. It really was remarkable in colour, a vernal russet blaze. Immediately, and not for the first time, I found myself picturing how she must be flossed elsewhere, and then was ashamed, as if I had misused the poor child. Seeing me, she halted, of course, ready to bolt. I lifted the teapot in a friendly gesture, and invited her to join me. She shut the door and edged around me with a panic-stricken smile, keeping the table between us, and took down a cup and saucer from the dresser. She had red heels and very white, thick calves. I thought she must be about seventeen. Through the fog of my hangover it occurred to me that she would be bound to know something about the state of my mother's finances – whether, for instance, those ponies were making money. I gave her what was intended to be a boyish, encouraging smile, though I suspect it came out a broken leer, and told her to sit down, that we must have a chat. The tea, however, was not for her, but for my mother – for Dolly, she said. Well! I thought, Dolly, no less! She made off at once, with the saucer grasped in both hands and her agitated smile fixed on the trembling liquid in the cup.

When she was gone I poked about morosely for a while, looking for the papers that had been on the table yesterday, the bills and ledgers and chequebook stubs, but found nothing. A drawer of the little bureau from my father's study was locked. I considered forcing it open, but restrained myself: in my hungover mood I might have smashed the whole thing to bits.

I wandered off through the house, carrying my teacup with me. In the drawing-room the carpet had been taken up, and a pane of glass in one of the windows was broken, and there was glass on the floor. I noticed I had no shoes on. I opened the garden door and stepped outside in my socks. There was a smell of sun-warmed grass and a faint tang of dung in the rinsed, silky air. The black shadow of the house lay across the lawn like a fallen stage-flat. I ventured a step or two on the yielding turf, the dew seeping up between my toes. I felt like an old man, going along shakily with my cup and saucer rattling and my trouser-cuffs wet and crumpled around my ankles. The rosebeds under the window had not been tended for years, and a tangle of briars rioted at the sills. The faded roses hung in clusters, heavy as cloth. Their particular wan shade of pink, and the chiaroscuro of the scene in general, put me in mind of something. I halted, frowning. The pictures – of course. I went back into the drawing-room. Yes, the walls were empty, with here and there a square patch where the wallpaper was not as faded as elsewhere. Surely she hadn't—? I put my cup down carefully on the mantelpiece, taking slow, deep breaths. The bitch! I said aloud, I bet she has! My feet had left wet, webbed prints behind me on the floorboards.

I went through room after room, scanning the walls. Then I tackled the upstairs. But I knew there would be nothing. I stood on the first-floor landing, cursing under my breath. There were voices nearby. I flung open a bedroom door. My mother and Joanne were sitting up side by side in the girl's big bed. They looked at me in mild astonishment, and for a moment I faltered as something brushed past my consciousness, a wingbeat of incredulous speculation. My mother wore a knitted yellow bed-jacket with bobbles and tiny satin bows, which made her look like a monstrously overgrown Easter chick. Where, I said, with a calm that surprised me, where are the pictures, pray? There followed a bit of comic patter, with my mother saying *What? What?* and I shouting *The pictures! The pictures, damn it!* In the end we both had to shut up. The girl had been watching us, turning her eyes slowly from one to the other of us, like a spectator at a tennis match. Now she put a hand over her mouth and laughed. I stared at her, and she blushed. There was a brief silence. I will see you downstairs, mother, I said, in a voice so stiff with ice it fairly creaked.

As I was going away from the door I thought I heard them both sniggering.

My mother arrived in the kitchen barefoot. The sight of her bunions and her big yellow toenails annoyed me. She had wrapped herself in an impossible, shot-silk tea-gown. She had the florid look of one of Lautrec's ruined doxies. I tried not to show too much of the disgust I felt. She pottered about with a show of unconcern, ignoring me. Well? I said, but she only raised her eyebrows blandly and said, Well what? She was almost smirking. That did it. I shouted, I waved my fists, I stamped about stiff-legged, beside myself. Where were they, the pictures, I cried, what had she done with them? I *demanded* to know. They were mine, my inheritance, my future and my son's future. And so on. My anger, my sense of outrage, impressed me. I was moved. I might almost have shed tears, I felt so sorry for myself. She let me go on like this for a while, standing with a hand on her hip and her head thrown back, contemplating me with sardonic calm. Then, when I paused to take a breath, she started. Demand, did I? – I, who had gone off and abandoned my widowed mother, who had skipped off to America and married without even informing her, who had never once brought my child, her grandson, to see her – I, who for ten years had stravaiged the world like a tinker, never doing a hand's turn of work, living off my dead father's few pounds and bleeding the estate dry – what right, she shrilled, what right had I to demand anything here? She stopped, and waited, as if really expecting an answer. I fell back a pace. I had forgotten what she is like when she gets going. Then I gathered myself and launched at her again. She rose magnificently to meet me. It was just like the old days. Hammer and tongs, oh, hammer and tongs! So stirring was it that even the dog joined in, barking and whining and dancing up and down on its front paws, until my mother gave it a clout and roared at it to lie down. I called her a bitch and she called me a bastard. I said if I was a bastard what did that make her, and quick as a flash she said, If I'm a bitch what does that make *you*, you cur! Oh, it was grand, a grand match. We were like furious children – no, not children, but big, maddened, primitive creatures – mastodons, something like that – tearing and thrashing in a jungle clearing amidst a storm of whipping lianas and uprooted vegetation. The air throbbed between us, blood-dimmed and thick. There was a sense of things ranged around us, small creatures cowering in the undergrowth, watching us in a trance of terror and awe. At last, sated, we disengaged tusks and turned aside. I nursed my pounding head in my hands. She stood at the sink, holding on to one of the taps and looking out the window at the garden, her chest heaving. We could hear ourselves breathe. The upstairs lavatory flushed, a muted, tentative noise, as if the girl were tactfully reminding us of her presence in the house. My mother sighed. She had sold the pictures to Binkie Behrens. I nodded to myself. Behrens: of course. All of them? I said. She did not answer. Time passed. She sighed again. You got the money, she said, what there was of it – he left me only debts. Suddenly she laughed. I should have known better, she said, than to marry a mick. She looked at me over her shoulder and shrugged. Now it was my turn to sigh. Dear me, I said. Oh, dear me.

*

Coincidences come out strangely flattened in court testimony – I'm sure you have noticed this, your honour, over the years – rather like jokes that should be really funny but fail to raise a single laugh. Accounts of the most bizarre doings of the accused are listened to with perfect equanimity, yet the moment some trivial simultaneity of events is mentioned feet begin to shuffle in the gallery, and counsel clear their throats, and reporters take to gazing dreamily at the mouldings on the ceiling. These are not so much signs of incredulity, I think, as of embarrassment. It is as if someone, the hidden arranger of all this intricate, amazing affair, who up to now never put a foot wrong, has suddenly gone that bit too far, has tried to be just a little too clever, and we are all disappointed, and somewhat sad.

I am struck, for instance, by the frequent appearance which

paintings make in this case. It was through art that my parents knew Helmut Behrens – well, not art, exactly, but the collecting of it. My father fancied himself a collector, did I mention that? Of course, he cared nothing for the works themselves, only for their cash value. He used his reputation as a horseman and erstwhile gay blade to insinuate himself into the houses of doddering acquaintances, on whose walls thirty or forty years before he had spotted a landscape, or a still-life, or a kippered portrait of a cross-eyed ancestor, which by now might be worth a bob or two. He had an uncanny sense of timing, often getting in only a step ahead of the heirs. I imagine him, at the side of a four-poster, in candlelight, still breathless from the stairs, leaning down and pressing a fiver urgently into a palsied, papery hand. He accumulated a lot of trash, but there were a few pieces which I thought were not altogether bad, and probably worth something. Most of these he had wheedled out of a distrait old lady whom his own father had courted briefly when she was a girl. He was hugely proud of this piece of chicanery, imagining, I suppose, that it put him on a par with the great robber barons of the past whom he so much admired, the Guggenheims and Pierpont Morgans and, indeed, the Behrenses. Perhaps these were the very pictures that led to his meeting Helmut Behrens. Perhaps they tussled for them over the old lady's deathbed, narrowing their eyes at each other, mouths pursed in furious determination.

It was through painting also that I met Anna Behrens – or met her again, I should say. We knew each other a little when we were young. I seem to remember once at Whitewater being sent outside to play with her in the grounds. Play! That's a good one. Even in those days she had that air of detachment, of faint, remote amusement, which I have always found unnerving. Later on, in Dublin, she would appear now and then, and glide through our student roisterings, poised, silent, palely handsome. She was nicknamed the Ice Queen, of course. I lost sight of her, forgot about her, until one day in Berkeley – this is where the coincidences begin – I spotted her in a gallery on Shattuck Avenue. I had not known she was in America, yet there was no sense of surprise. This is one of the things about Anna, she belongs exactly wherever she happens to be. I stood in the street for a moment watching her – admiring her, I suppose. The gallery was a large high white room with a glass front. She was leaning against a desk with a sheaf of papers in her hand, reading. She wore a white dress. Her hair, bleached silver by the sun, was done in a complicated fashion, with a single heavy braid hanging down at her shoulder. She might have been a piece on show, standing there so still in that tall, shadowless light behind sun-reflecting glass. I went in and spoke to her, admiring again that long, slightly off centre, melancholy face with its close-set grey eyes and florentine mouth. I remembered the two tiny white spots on the bridge of her nose where the skin was stretched tight over the bone. She was friendly, in her distant way. She watched my lips as I talked. On the walls there were two or three vast canvases, done in the joky, minimalist style of the time, hardly distinguishable in their pastel bareness from the blank spaces surrounding them. I asked her if she was thinking of buying something. This amused her. I work here, she said, pushing back the blonde braid from her shoulder. I invited her to lunch, but she shook her head. She gave me her telephone number. When I stepped out into the sunlit street a jet plane was passing low overhead, its engines making the air rattle, and there was a smell of cypresses and car exhaust, and a faint whiff of tear-gas from the direction of the campus. All this was fifteen years ago. I crumpled the file card on which she had written her phone number, and started to throw it away. But I kept it.

She lived in the hills, in a mock-Tyrolean, shingled wooden house which she rented from a mad widow. More than once on the way there I stood up to get off the bus and go home, bored and half-annoyed already at the thought of Anna's amused, appraising glance, that impenetrable smile. When I called her she had spoken hardly a dozen words, and twice she put a hand over the phone and talked to someone with her in the room. Yet that morning I had shaved with particular care, and put on a new shirt, and selected an impressive volume of mathematical theory to carry with me. Now, as the bus threaded its way up these narrow roads, I was assailed by a sense of revulsion, I seemed to myself an obscurely shameful, lewd object, exposed and cringing, with my palped and powdered flesh, my baby-blue shirt, the floppy book clutched in my hand like a parcel of meat. The day was overcast, and there was mist in the pines. I climbed a zigzag of damp steps to the door, looking about me with an expression of bland interest, trying to appear blameless, as I always seem to do when I am on unfamiliar territory. Anna wore shorts, and her hair was loose. The sight of her there suddenly in the doorway, ash-blonde, at ease, her long legs bare, caused an ache at the root of my tongue. The house was dim inside. A few books, prints on the wall, a straw hat on a hook. The widow's cats had left a trace of themselves on the carpets and the chairs, a sharp, citrus stink, not wholly unpleasant.

Daphne was sitting cross-legged in a canvas chair, shelling peas into a nickel bowl. She wore a bathrobe, and her hair was wrapped in a towel. Another coincidence, you see.

What did we talk about that day, the three of us? What did I do? Sat down, I suppose, drank a beer, stretched out my legs and leaned back, playing at being relaxed. I cannot see myself. I am a sort of floating eye, watching, noting, scheming. Anna came and went between the living-room and the kitchen, bringing cheese and oranges and sliced avocados. It was Sunday. The place was quiet. I watched through the window the mist moving among the trees. The telephone rang and Anna answered it, turning away and murmuring into the receiver. Daphne smiled at me. Her glance was unfocused, a kind of soft groping among the objects around her. She rose and handed me the bowl and the remaining unshelled peas, and went away upstairs. When she came back in a while she was dressed, her hair was dried and she was wearing her spectacles, and at first I did not recognise her, and thought she was yet another tenant of the house. It was only then that I realised it was she I had seen on the lawn that day at Professor Something's party. I started to tell her about it, about having seen her, but I changed my mind, for the same, unknown reason that

I had turned away that first time without speaking to her. She took the bowl of peas from me and sat down again. Anna answered another phonecall, murmuring, quietly laughing. It occurred to me that my presence was hardly impinging on their day, that they would have done just these same things if I were not there. It was a soothing thought. I had not been invited to dinner, but it seemed accepted that I would stay. After we had eaten we sat on at the table for a long time. The fog thickened, pressing against the windows. I see the two of them opposite me there in that milky twilight, the dark one and the fair: they have an air of complicity, of secret amusement, as if they are sharing a mild, not very unkind joke at my expense. How distant it all seems, an age away, when we were still innocent, if that is the word, which I doubt.

I was, I confess it, captivated by them, their looks, their composure, their casual selfishness. They embodied an ideal that I had not known I harboured until now. I was still working at my science in those days, I was going to be one of those great, cold technicians, the secret masters of the world. Now suddenly another future had opened up, as if these two had caused a whole rockface before me to fall away and reveal beyond the swirling dust a vast, radiant distance. They were splendid, at once languorous and dashing. They reminded me of a pair of adventuresses out of the last century. They had arrived in New York the previous winter, and drifted by stages across the country to this tawny, sunlit shore, where they were poised now, as if on tiptoe, hands joined and arms extended, with the Pacific all before them. Though they had been in this house nearly half a year their impress was so light, so fleeting, that the rooms had barely registered their presence. They seemed to have no belongings – even the straw hat hanging on the door had been left behind by a previous tenant. There must have been friends, or acquaintances at least – I'm thinking of those phonecalls – but I never met them. Once in a while their landlady would descend on them, a darkly dramatic person with soulful eyes and very black hair twisted tight into a bun and skewered with a carved wooden pin.

She dressed like an Indian squaw, festooning herself with beads and brightly coloured scarves. She would surge about the house distractedly, talking over her shoulder and trailing a dense, musky perfume, then fling herself with a balletic leap on to the couch in the living-room and sit for an hour telling of her woes – the result mostly of what with a throb in her voice she referred to as *man trouble* – meanwhile getting steadily, tearfully drunk on calvados, a supply of which she kept in a locked cupboard in the kitchen. A ghastly woman, I could not abide her, that leathery skin and daubed mouth, all that hysteria, that messy loneliness. The girls, however, found her greatly entertaining. They liked to do imitations of her, and made catchphrases of things she said. Sometimes, listening to them mimicking her, I wondered if perhaps, when I was not there, they treated *me* like this, lobbing remarks at each other in a comically solemn version of my voice and laughing softly, in that jaded way they had, as if the joke were not really funny, just ridiculous.

They thought the country, too, was a scream, especially California. We had a lot of fun together laughing at the Americans, who just then were entering that stage of doomed hedonistic gaiety through which we, the gilded children of poor old raddled Europe, had already passed, or so we believed. How innocent they seemed to us, with their flowers and their joss-sticks and their muddled religiosity. Of course, I felt a secret twinge of guilt, sneering at them like this. I had been captivated by the country when I first came there, now it was as if I had joined in mocking some happy, good-hearted creature, the fat girl at the party against whom only a moment ago I had been pressing myself, under cover of the general romp, in wordless, swollen ecstasy.

Perhaps contempt was for us a form of nostalgia, of homesickness, even? Living there, amid those gentle, paintbox colours, under that dome of flawless blue, was like living in another world, a place out of a storybook. (I used to dream of rain – real, daylong, Irish rain – as if it were something I had been told about but had never seen.) Or perhaps laughing at America was a means of defence? It's true, at times it crossed our minds, or it crossed *my* mind, at least, that we might be just the teeniest bit laughable ourselves. Was there not a touch of the preposterous about us, with our tweeds and our sensible shoes, our extravagant accents, our insolently polite manners? More than once I thought I detected a suppressed smile twitching the lips of some person who was supposed to be the unknowing butt of our ridicule. Even among ourselves there were moments of silence, of awkwardness, when a half-formed admission hovered between us, like a bad, embarrassing smell. A trio of expatriates meeting in this mellow playground – what could be more novelettish? We were a triangle, for God's sake!

We were a triangle. It happened, the inevitable, one afternoon a month or so after we met. We had been sitting on the porch at the back of the house drinking gin and smoking something with a horrid taste and the oddest effects. The day was hot and hazy. Above us a coin-coloured sun was stuck in the middle of a white sky. I was watching a cloud of hummingbirds sipping at a honeysuckle bush beside the porch steps. Daphne, in shorts and halter and high-heeled sandals, stood up, a little unsteadily, blinking, and wandered into the house. I followed her. I was not thinking of anything – I was fetching more ice, something like that. After the glare outside I could hardly see indoors, everywhere I turned the air had a huge dark hole in it. Idly I looked about for Daphne, following the sound of the ice tinkling in her glass, from the kitchen through the living-room to the bedroom. The blind was drawn. She was sitting on the side of the bed, gazing before her in the amber half-light. My head suddenly began to ache. She drained her drink in one long gulp, and was still holding the glass when we lay down together, and a bead of ice slid out of it and dropped into the hollow of my shoulder. Her lips were chill and wet. She began to say something, and laughed softly into my mouth. Our clothes seemed tight as bandages, I clawed at them, snorting. Then abruptly we were naked. There was a startled pause. Somewhere nearby children were playing. Daphne laid her hand on my hip. Her eyes were closed, and she was smiling with her eyebrows raised, as if she were listening to a distant, dreamy, and slightly funny melody. I heard a sound, and looked over my shoulder. Anna was standing in the doorway. I had a glimpse of myself as she would see me, my glimmering flanks and pale backside, my fish-mouth agape. She hesitated a moment, and then walked to the bed with her eyes on the ground, as if deep in thought, and sat down beside us and began to undress. Daphne and I lay quietly in each other's arms and watched her. She pulled her blouse over her head, and surfaced like a swimmer, tossing her hair. A metal clasp left its mauve imprint in the centre of her back. Why did she seem to me so much older now than us, world-weary, a little used, an adult joining tolerantly in a children's not quite permissible game? Daphne hardly breathed, her fingers steadily tightening on my hip. Her lips were parted, and she frowned a little, gazing at Anna's bared flesh, lost in a sort of vague amazement. I could feel her heartbeat, and my own. We might have been attending at a ritual disrobing.

A ritual, yes, that's how it was. We strove together slowly on the bed, the three of us, as if engaged in an archaic ceremonial of toil and worship, miming the fashioning and raising of something, a shrine, say, or a domed temple. How grave we were, how pensive, with what attentiveness we handled each other's flesh. No one spoke a word. The women had begun by exchanging a chaste kiss. They smiled, a little bashfully. My hands were trembling. I had felt this choking sense of transgression once before, long ago, when as a child I tussled with two girl cousins in the dark on the stairs one winter evening at Coolgrange – the same dread and incredulity, the same voluptuous, aching, infantile glee. Dreamily we delved and nuzzled, shivering, sighing. Now and then one of us would clutch at the other two with a child's impatient, greedy fervour and cry out softly, tinily, as if in pain or helpless sorrow. It seemed to me at times that there were not two women but one, a strange, remote creature, many-armed, absorbed behind an enamelled mask in something I could not begin to know. At the end, the final spasm gathering itself inside me, I raised myself up on trembling arms, with Daphne's heels pressed in the small of my back, and looked down at the two of them gnawing at each other with tender avidity, mouth on open mouth, and for a second, as the blood welled up in my eyes, I saw their heads merge, the fair one and the dark, the tawny and the panther-sleek. At once the shudder started in my groin, and I fell upon them, exultant and afraid.

But afterwards it was Daphne alone who lay in my arms, still holding me inside her, while Anna got up and walked to the window, and lifted the canvas blind at the side with one finger and stood gazing out into the hazy glare of afternoon. The children were still at play. There's a school, Anna murmured, up the hill. She laughed quietly and said, *But what do I know, I ask you?* It was one of the mad widow's catchphrases. Suddenly everything was sad and grey and waste. Daphne put her face against my shoulder and began to weep silently. I will always remember those children's voices.

*

It was a strange encounter, never to be repeated. I brood on it now, not for the obvious reasons, but because it puzzles me. The act itself, the troilism, was not so remarkable: in those days everyone was doing that sort of thing. No, what struck me then, and strikes me still, is the curious passiveness of my role in that afternoon's doings. I was the man among the three of us, yet I felt that it was I who was being softly, irresistibly penetrated. The wise will say that I was only the link along which the two of them had negotiated their way, hand over hand, into each other's arms. It may be true, but it is not of much significance, and certainly not the central thing. I could not rid myself of the feeling that a rite was being performed, in which Anna Behrens was the priestess and Daphne the sacrificial offering, while I was a mere prop. They wielded me like a stone phallus, bowing and writhing about me, with incantatory sighs. They were—

They were saying goodbye. Of course. It's just occurred to me. They were not finding each other, but parting. Hence the sadness and the sense of waste, hence Daphne's bitter tears. It was nothing to do with me, at all.

Well well. That's the advantage of jail, one has the time and leisure really to get to the heart of things.

The illusion of their melting into each other which I had experienced at the end of our bout on the bed that day was to last for a long time. Even yet when I think of them together it is a kind of double-headed coin that I see, on which are stamped their twin profiles, serene, emblematic, looking away, a stylised representation of paired virtues – Calm and Fortitude, let's say, or, better still, Silence and Sacrifice. I am remembering a certain moment, when Anna lifted her bruised, glistening mouth from between Daphne's legs and, glancing back at me with a complicitous, wry little smile, leaned aside so that I might see the sprawled girl's lap lying open there, intricate and innocent as a halved fruit. Everything was present, I see now, in that brief passage of renunciation and discovery. A whole future began just there.

I do not recall proposing to Daphne. Her hand, so to speak, had already been granted me. We were married one misty, hot afternoon in August. The ceremony was quick and squalid. I had a headache all through it. Anna and a colleague of mine from the university acted as witnesses. Afterwards the four of us went back to the house in the hills and drank cheap champagne. The occasion was not a success. My colleague made a limp excuse and departed after half an hour, leaving the three of us together in a restless, swirling silence. All sorts of unspoken things swam in the air between us like slithery, dangerous fish. Then Anna, with that smile, said she supposed we young things would want to be alone, and left. Suddenly I was prey to an absurd embarrassment. I jumped up and began collecting the empty bottles and the glasses, avoiding Daphne's eye. There was sun and mist in the kitchen window. I stood at the sink looking out at the blue-black ghosts of trees on the hillside, and two great, fat, inexplicable tears gathered on the rims of my eyelids, but would not fall.

I do not know that I loved Daphne in the manner that the

world understands by that word, but I do know that I loved her ways. Will it seem strange, cold, perhaps even inhuman, if I say that I was only interested really in what she was on the surface? Pah, what do I care how it seems. This is the only way another creature can be known: on the surface, that's where there is depth. Daphne walking through a room searching for her spectacles, touching things gently, quickly, reading things with her fingertips. The way she had of turning aside and peering into her purse, frowning, lips compressed, like a maiden aunt fetching up a shilling for sweets. Her stinginess, her sudden rushes of greed, childish and endearing. That time, years ago, I can't remember where, when I came upon her at the end of a party, standing by a window in a white dress in the half-light of an April dawn, lost in a dream — a dream from which I, tipsy and in a temper, unceremoniously woke her, when I could — dear Christ! — when I could have hung back in the shadows and painted her, down to the tiniest, tenderest detail, on the blank inner wall of my heart, where she would be still, vivid as in that dawn, my dark, mysterious darling.

We quickly agreed — tacitly, as always — to leave America. I gave up my studies, the university, my academic career, everything, with hardly a second thought, and before the year was out we had sailed for Europe.

MAOLSEACHLAINN MAC GIOLLA GUNNA, my counsel and, he insists, my friend, has a trick of seizing on the apparently trivial in the elaboration of his cases. Anecdotes of his methods circulate in the corridors of chancery, and around the catwalks in here. Details, details are his obsession. He is a large, lumbering, unhandy man – yards, literally yards of pinstripe – with a big square head and raggedy hair and tiny, haunted eyes. I think a life spent poking in the crevices of other people's nasty little tragedies has damaged something in him. He exudes an air of injured longing. They say he is a terror in court, but when he sits at the scarred table in the counsel room here, with his half-glasses hooked on that big head, crouched over his papers and writing out notes in a laborious, minute hand, panting a little and muttering to himself, I am reminded irresistibly of a certain fat boy from my schooldays, who was disconsolately in love with me, and whom I used to get to do my homework for me.

At present Maolseachlainn is deeply interested in why I went to Whitewater in the first place. But why should I not have gone there? I knew the Behrenses – or God knows I knew Anna, anyway. I had been away for ten years, I was paying a social call, as a friend of the family. This, however, is not good enough, it seems. Maolseachlainn frowns, slowly shaking his great head, and without realising it goes into his court routine. Is it not true that I left my mother's house in anger only a day after my arrival there? Is it not the case that I was in a state of high indignation because I had heard my father's collection of pictures had been sold to Helmut Behrens for what I considered a paltry sum? And is it not further the case that I had reason already to feel resentment against the man Behrens, who had attempted to cuckold my father in – But hold on there, old man, I said: that last bit only came to light later on. He always looks so crestfallen when I stop him in his tracks like this. All the same, facts are facts.

It is true, I did fight with my mother again, I did storm out of the house (with the dog after me, of course, trying to bite my heels). However, Binkie Behrens was not the cause of the row, or not directly, anyway. As far as I remember it was the same old squabble: money, betrayal, my going to the States, my leaving the States, my marriage, my abandoned career, all that, the usual – and, yes, the fact that she had flogged my birthright for the price of a string of plug-ugly ponies out of which she had imagined she would make a fortune to provide for herself in the decrepitude of her old age, the deluded bloody bitch. There was as well the business of the girl Joanne. As I was leaving I paused and said, measuring my words, that I thought it hardly appropriate for a woman of my mother's position in society – her position! – in society! – to be so chummy with a stable-girl. I confess I had intended to cause outrage, but I am afraid I was the one who ended up goggle-eyed. My mother, after a moment's silence, stared me straight in the face, with brazen insouciance, and said that Joanne was not a child, that she was in fact twenty-seven years of age. She is – with a pause here for effect – she is like a son to me, the son I never had. Well, I said, swallowing hard, I'm happy for you both, I'm sure! and flounced out of the house. On the drive, though, I had to stop and wait for my indignation and resentment to subside a little before I could get my breath back. Sometimes I think I am an utter sentimentalist.

*

I got to Whitewater that evening. The last leg of the journey I made by taxi from the village. The driver was an immensely tall, emaciated man in a flat cap and an antique, blue-flannel suit. He studied me with interest in the driving-mirror, hardly bothering to watch the road ahead of us. I tried staring back at him balefully, but he was unabashed, and only grinned a little on one side of his thin face with a peculiarly friendly air of knowing. Why do I remember people like this so vividly? They clutter my mind, when I look up from the page they are thronged around me in the shadows, silent, mildly curious – even, it might be, solicitous. They are witnesses, I suppose, the innocent bystanders who have come, without malice, to testify against me.

I can never approach Whitewater without a small, involuntary gasp of admiration. The drive leads up from the road in a long, deep, treeless curve, so that the house seems to turn, slowly, dreamily, opening wide its Palladian colonnades. The taxi drew to a stop on the gravel below the great front steps, and with the sudden silence came the realisation – yes, Maolseachlainn, I admit it – that I had no reasonable cause to be there. I sat for a moment looking about me in groggy consternation, like a wakened sleep-walker, but the driver was watching me in the mirror now with rapt expectancy, and I had to pretend to know what I was about. I got out of the car and stood patting my pockets and frowning importantly, but I could not fool him, his lopsided grin grew slyer still, for a second I thought he was going to wink at me. I told him brusquely to wait, and mounted the steps pursued by an unshakeable sensation of general mockery.

After a long time the door was opened by a wizened little angry man in what appeared at first to be a bus conductor's uniform. A few long strands of very black hair were plastered across his skull like streaks of boot polish. He looked at me with deep disgust. Not open today, he said, and was starting to shut the door in my face when I stepped smartly past him into the hall. I gazed about me, rubbing my hands slowly and smiling, playing the returned expatriate. Ah, I said, the old place! The great Tintoretto on the stairs, swarming with angels and mad-eyed martyrs, blared at me its vast chromatic chord. The doorman or whatever he was danced about anxiously behind me. I turned and loomed at him, still grinning, and said no, I wasn't a tripper, but a friend of the family – was Miss Behrens at home, by any chance? He dithered, distrustful still, then told me to wait, and scuttled off down the hall, splaying one flat foot as he went and carefully smoothing the oiled hairs on his pate.

I waited. All was silent save for the ticking of a tall, seventeenth-century German clock. On the wall beside me there was a set of six exquisite little Bonington watercolours, I could have put a couple of them under my arm there and then and walked out. The clock took a laboured breath and pinged the half-hour, and then, all about me, in farther and farther rooms, other clocks too let fall their single, silvery chimes, and it was as if a tiny tremor had passed through the house. I looked again at the Tintoretto. There was a Fragonard, too, and a Watteau. And this was only the hallway. What was going on, what had happened, that it was all left unattended like this? I heard the taximan outside sounding his horn, a tentative, apologetic little toot. He must have thought I had forgotten about him. (I had.) Somewhere at the back of the house a door banged shut, and a second later a breath of cool air brushed past my face. I advanced creakingly along the hall, a hot, almost sensuous thrill of apprehensiveness pulsing behind my breastbone. I am at heart a timid man, large deserted places make me nervous. One of the figures in the Fragonard, a silken lady with blue eyes and a plump lower lip, was watching me sidelong with what seemed an expression of appalled but lively speculation. Cautiously I opened a door. The fat knob turned under my hand with a wonderful, confiding smoothness. I entered a long, high, narrow, many-windowed room. The wallpaper was the colour of tarnished gold. The air was golden too, suffused with the heavy soft light of evening. I felt as if I had stepped straight into the eighteenth century. The furnishings were sparse, there were no more than five or six pieces – some delicate, lyre-backed chairs, an ornate sideboard, a small ormolu table – placed just so, in such a way that not the things but the space around them, the light itself, seemed arranged. I stood quite still, listening, I did not know for what. On the low table there was a large and complicated jigsaw puzzle, half-assembled. Some of the pieces had fallen to the floor. I gazed at them, sprinkled on the parquet like puddles of something that had spilled, and once again a faint shiver seemed to pass through the house. At the far end of the room a french window stood wide-open, and a gauze curtain billowed in the breeze. Outside there was a long slope of lawn, whereon, in the middle distance, a lone, heraldic horse was prancing. Farther off was the river bend, the water whitening in the shallows, and beyond that there were trees, and then vague mountains, and then the limitless, gilded blue of summer. It struck me that the perspective of this scene was wrong somehow. Things seemed not to recede as they should, but to be arrayed before me – the furniture, the open window, the lawn and river and far-off mountains – as if they were not being looked at but were themselves looking, intent upon a vanishing-point here, inside the room. I turned then, and saw myself turning as I turned, as I seem to myself to be turning still, as I sometimes imagine I shall be turning always, as if this might be my punishment, my damnation, just this breathless, blurred, eternal turning towards her.

You have seen the picture in the papers, you know what she looks like. A youngish woman in a black dress with a broad white collar, standing with her hands folded in front of her, one gloved, the other hidden except for the fingers, which are flexed, ringless. She is wearing something on her head, a cap or clasp of some sort, which holds her hair drawn tightly back from her brow. Her prominent black eyes have a faintly oriental slant. The nose is large, the lips full. She is not beautiful. In her right hand she holds a folded fan, or it might be a book. She is standing in what I take to be the lighted doorway of a room. Part of a couch can be seen, or maybe a bed, with a brocade cover. The darkness behind her is dense and yet mysteriously weightless. Her gaze is calm, inexpectant, though there is a trace of challenge, of hostility, even, in the set of her mouth. She does not want to be here, and yet cannot be elsewhere. The gold brooch that secures the wings of her wide collar is expensive and ugly. All this you have seen, all this you know. Yet I put it to you, gentle connoisseurs of the jury, that even knowing all this you still know nothing, next to nothing. You do not know the fortitude and pathos of her presence. You have not come upon her suddenly in a golden room on a summer eve, as I have. You have not held her in your arms, you have not seen her asprawl in a ditch. You have not – ah no! – you have not killed for her.

I stood there, staring, for what seemed a long time, and gradually a kind of embarrassment took hold of me, a hot, shamefaced awareness of myself, as if somehow I, this soiled sack of flesh, were the one who was being scrutinised, with careful, cold attention. It was not just the woman's painted stare that watched me. Everything in the picture, that brooch, those gloves, the flocculent darkness at her back, every spot on the canvas was an eye fixed on me unblinkingly. I retreated a pace, faintly aghast. The silence was fraying at the edges. I heard cows lowing, a car starting up. I remembered the taxi, and turned to go. A maid was standing in the open french window. She must have come in just then and seen me there and started back in alarm. Her eyes were wide, and one knee was flexed and one hand lifted, as if to ward off a blow. For a moment neither of us stirred. Behind her a sudden breeze burnished the grassy slope. We did not speak. Then slowly, with her hand still raised, she stepped backwards carefully through the window, teetering a little as her heels blindly sought the level of the paved pathway outside. I felt an inexplicable, brief rush of annoyance – a presentiment, perhaps, a stray zephyr sent ahead of the storm that was to come. A telephone was ringing somewhere. I turned quickly and left the room.

There was no one in the hall. The telephone rang and rang, with peevish insistence. I could still hear it going as I descended the front steps. The taxi had left, of course. I swore, and set off down the drive, hobbling over the stony ground in my thin-soled Spanish shoes. The low sun glared in my face. When I looked back at the house the windows were ablaze, and seemed to be laughing fatly in derision. I began to perspire, and that brought on the midges. I asked myself again what had possessed me to come to Whitewater. I knew the answer, of course. It was the smell of money that had attracted me, as the smell of sweat was attracting these damned flies. I saw myself, as if from one of those sunstruck windows, skulking along here in the dust, hot, disgruntled, overweight, head bowed and fat back bent, my white suit rucked at the armpits and sagging in the arse, a figure of fun, the punchline of a bad joke, and at once I was awash with self-pity. Christ! was there no one who would help me? I halted, and cast a troubled glance around me, as if there might be a benefactor lurking among the trees. The silence had a sense of muffled gloating. I plunged on again, and heard the sound of engines, and presently an enormous black limousine came around the bend, followed by a sleek red sportscar. They were going at a stately pace, the limousine bouncing gently on its springs, and for a second I thought it was a funeral. I stepped on to the grass verge but kept on walking. The driver of the limousine, a large, crop-headed man, sat erect and vigilant, his hands lightly cupped on the rim of the steering-wheel, as if it were a projectile he might pluck from its moorings and throw with deadly aim. Beside him there was a stooped, shrunken figure, as the car swished past I glimpsed a dark eye and a liver-spotted skull, and huge hands resting one upon the other on the crook of a stick. A blonde woman wearing dark glasses was driving the sportscar. We gazed at each other with blank interest, like strangers, as she went by. I recognised her, of course.

Ten minutes later I was trudging along the road with my thumb stuck out when I heard her pull up behind me. I knew it would be she. I stopped, turned. She remained in the car, her wrists folded before her on the steering-wheel. There was a brief, wordless tussle to see which one of us would make the first move. We compromised. I walked back to the car and she got out to meet me. I *thought* it was you, she said. We smiled, and were silent. She wore a cream suit and a white blouse. There was blood on her shoes. Her hair was yellower than I remembered, I wondered if she was dyeing it now. I told her she looked marvellous. I meant it, but the words sounded hollow, and I blushed. Anna, I said. I remembered, with a soft shock, how one day long ago I stole the envelope of one of her letters to Daphne, and took it into the lavatory and prised open the flap, my heart pounding, so that I might lick the gum where she had licked. The thought came to me: I loved her! and I gave a sort of wild, astonished laugh. She took off her sunglasses and looked at me quizzically. My hands were trembling. Come and see Father, she said, he needs cheering up.

She drove very fast, working the controls probingly, as if she were trying to locate a pattern, a secret formula, hidden in this mesh of small, deft actions. I was impressed, even a little cowed. She was full of the impatient assurance of the rich. We did not speak. In a moment we were at the house, and pulled up in a spray of gravel. She opened her door, then paused and looked at me for a moment in silence and shook her head. Freddie Montgomery, she said. Well!

As we went up the steps to the front door she linked her arm lightly in mine. I was surprised. When I knew her, all those years ago, she was not one for easy intimacies – intimacies, yes, but not easy ones. She laughed and said, God, I'm a little drunk, I think. She had been to the hospital in the city – Behrens had suffered some sort of mild attack. The hospital was in an uproar. A bomb had gone off in a car in a crowded shopping street, quite a small device, apparently, but remarkably effective. She had wandered unchallenged into the casualty ward. There were bodies lying everywhere. She walked among the dead and dying, feeling like a survivor herself. Good God, Anna, I said. She gave a tense little laugh. What an experience, she said – luckily Flynn keeps a flask of something in the glove compartment. She had taken a few good swigs, and was beginning to regret it now.

We went into the house. The uniformed doorman was nowhere to be seen. I told Anna how he had gone off and left me to wander at will about the place. She shrugged. She supposed everyone had been downstairs watching the news of the bombing on television. All the same, I said, anyone could have got in. Why, she asked, do you think someone might come and plant a bomb here? And she looked at me with a peculiar, bitter smile.

She led the way into the gold salon. The french window was still open. There was no sign of the maid. A sort of shyness made me keep my eyes averted from the other end of the room, where the picture leaned out a little from the wall, as if listening intently. I sat down gingerly on one of the Louis Quinze chairs while Anna opened the carved and curlicued sideboard and poured out two whopping measures of gin. There was no ice, and the tonic was flat, but I didn't care, I needed a drink. I was still breathless with the notion of having been in love with her. I felt excited and bemused, and ridiculously pleased, like a child who has been given something precious to play with. I said it to myself again – *I loved her!* – trying it out for the sound of it. The thought, lofty, grand, and slightly mad, fitted well with the surroundings. She was pacing between me and the window, clutching her glass tightly in both hands. The gauze curtain bellied lazily at the edge of my vision. Something in the air itself seemed to be shaking. Suddenly the telephone on the low table beside me sprang to life with a crashing noise. Anna snatched it up and cried yes, yes, what? She laughed. It's some taximan, she said to me, looking for his fare. I took the phone and spoke harshly to the fellow. She watched me intently, with a kind of avid amusement. When I put down the receiver she said gaily, Oh, Freddie, you've got so pompous! I frowned. I was not sure how to respond. Her laughter, her glazed stare, were tinged with hysteria. But then, I too was less than calm. Look at that, she said. She was peering in annoyance at her bloodstained shoes. She clicked her tongue, and putting down her glass she quickly left the room. I waited. All this had happened before. I went and stood in the open window, a hand in my pocket, swigging my gin. Pompous, indeed – what did she mean? The sun was almost down, the light was gathering in bundles above the river. I stepped out on to the terrace. A balm of soft air breathed on my face. I thought how strange it was to be here like this, glass in hand, in the silence and calm of a summer evening, while there was so much darkness in my heart. I turned and looked up at the house. It seemed to be flying swiftly against the sky. I wanted my share of this richness, this gilded ease. From the depths of the room a pair of eyes looked out, dark, calm, unseeing.

Flynn, the crop-headed chauffeur, approached me from the side of the house with an air of tight-lipped politeness which was somehow menacing, rolling on the balls of his disproportionately dainty feet. He sported a bandit's drooping blue-black moustache, trimmed close and squared off at the ends, so that it looked as if it had been painted on to his large, pasty face. I do not like moustaches, have I mentioned that? There is something lewd about them which repels me. I have no doubt the prison shrink could explain what such an aversion signifies – and I've no doubt, too, that in my case he would be wrong. Flynn's was a particularly offensive specimen. The sight of it gave me heart suddenly, cheered me up, I don't know why. I followed him eagerly into the house. The dining-room was a great dim cavern full of the glint and gleam of precious things. Behrens came in leaning on Anna's arm, a tall, delicate figure in rich tweeds and a bow-tie. He moved slowly, measuring his steps. His head, trembling a little, was smooth and steeply domed, like a marvellous, desiccated egg. It must have been twenty years since I had seen him last. I confess I was greatly taken with him now. He had the fine high patina of something lovingly crafted, like one of those exquisite and temptingly pocket-sized jade figurines which I had been eyeing only a moment ago on the mantelpiece. He took my hand and squeezed it slowly in his strangler's grip, looking deep into my eyes as if he were trying to catch a glimpse of someone else in there. Frederick, he said, in his breathy voice. So like your mother.

We dined at a rickety table in the bay of a tall window overlooking the garden. The cutlery was cheap, the plates mismatched. It was something I remembered about Whitewater, the makeshift way that life was lived in odd corners, at the edge of things. The house was not meant for people, all that magnificence would not tolerate their shoddy doings in its midst. I watched Behrens cutting up a piece of bleeding meat. Those enormous hands fascinated me. I was always convinced that at some time in the past he had killed someone. I tried to imagine him young, in flannels and a blazer, carrying a tennis racquet – *Oh look, here's Binkie!* – but it was impossible. He talked about the bombing. Five dead – or was it six by now? – from a mere two pounds of explosive! He sighed and shook his head. He seemed more impressed than shocked. Anna hardly spoke. She was pale, and looked tired and distracted. I noticed for the first time how she had aged. The woman I knew fifteen years ago was still there, but fixed inside a coarser outline, like one of Klimt's gem-encrusted lovers. I looked out into the luminous grey twilight, aghast and in an obscure way proud at the thought of what I had lost, of what might have been. Piled clouds, a last, bright strip of sky. A blackbird whistled suddenly. Someday I would lose all this too, I would die, and it would all be gone, this moment at this window, in summer, on the tender brink of night. It was amazing, and yet it was true, it would happen. Anna struck a match and lighted a candle on the table between us, and for a moment there was a sense of hovering, of swaying, in the soft, dark air.

My mother, I said to Behrens, and had to stop and clear my throat – my mother gave you some pictures, I believe. He turned his raptor's gaze on me. *Sold,* he said, and it was almost a whisper, sold, not gave. He smiled. There was a brief silence. He was quite at ease. He was sorry, he said, if I had come in the hope of seeing the pictures again. He could understand that I might be attached to them. But he had got rid of them almost at once. He smiled again, gently. There were one or two quite nice things, he said, but they would not have been comfortable, here, at Whitewater.

There you are, father, I thought, so much for your connoisseur's eye.

I wanted to do something for your mother, you see, Behrens was saying. She had been ill, you know. I gave her much more than the market value – you mustn't tell her that, of course. She wanted to set up in business of some kind, I think. He laughed. Such a spirited woman! he said. There was another silence. He fiddled with his knife, amused, waiting. I realised, with some astonishment, that he must have thought I had come to demand the return of the collection. Then, of course, I began to wonder if despite his protestations he had cheated on the price. The notion bucked me up immensely. Why, you old scoundrel, I thought, laughing to myself, you're just like all the rest of us. I looked at Anna's profile faintly reflected in the window before me. What was she, too, but an ageing spinster, with her wrinkles and her dyed hair – probably Flynn serviced her once a month or so, between hosing down the car and taking his moustache to the barber's for a trim. Damn you all! I poured myself a brimming glass of wine, and spilled some on the tablecloth, and was glad. Oh dark, dark.

I expected to be asked to stay the night, but when we had drunk our coffee Anna excused herself, and came back in a minute and said she had phoned for a taxi. I was offended. I had come all this way to see them and they would not even offer me a bed. An ugly silence fell. Behrens at my prompting had been talking about Dutch painters. Did I imagine it, or did he glance at me with a sly smile when he asked if I had been into the garden room? Before I realised it was the gilded salon that he meant he had passed on. Now he sat, head trembling, his mouth open a little, staring dully at the candle-flame. He lifted a hand, as if he were about to speak again, but let it fall slowly. The lights of a car swept the window and a horn tooted. Behrens did not get up. So good to see you, he murmured, giving me his left hand. So good.

Anna walked with me to the front door. I felt I had somehow made a fool of myself, but could not think how, exactly. In the hall our footsteps sounded very loud, a confused and faintly absurd racket. It's Flynn's night off, Anna said, or I would have had him drive you. I said stiffly that was quite all right. I was asking myself if we could be the same two people who had rolled with Daphne naked on a bed one hot Sunday afternoon on the other side of the world, on the other side of time. How could I have imagined I had ever loved her. Your father seems well, I said. She shrugged. Oh, she said, he's dying. At the door, I don't know what I was thinking of, I fumbled for her hand and tried to kiss her. She stepped back quickly, and I almost fell over. The taxi tooted again. Anna! I said, and then could think of nothing to add. She laughed bleakly. Go home, Freddie, she said, with a wan smile, and shut the door slowly in my face.

I knew who would be driving the taxi, of course. Don't say anything, I said to him sternly, not a word! He looked at me in the mirror with a mournful, accusing eye, and we lumbered off down the drive. I realised I had nowhere to go.

It is September. I have been here now for two months. It seems longer than that. The tree that I can glimpse from the window of my cell has a drab, dusty look, it will soon begin to turn. It trembles, as if in anticipation, at night I fancy I can hear it, rustling excitedly out there in the dark. The skies in the morning are splendid, immensely high and clear. I like to watch the clouds building and dispersing. Such huge, delicate labour. Today there was a rainbow, when I saw it I laughed out loud, as at a wonderful, absurd joke. Now and then people pass by, under the tree. It must be a shortcut, that way. At nine come the office girls with cigarettes and fancy hairdos, and, a little later, the dreamy housewives lugging shopping bags and babies. At four every afternoon a schoolboy straggles by, bearing an enormous satchel on his back like a hump. Dogs come too, walking very fast with an air of determination, stop, give the tree a quick squirt, pass on. Other lives, other lives. Lately, since the season began to change, they all seem to move, even the boy, with a lighter tread, borne up, as if they are flying, somehow, through the glassy blue autumnal air.

At this time of year I often dream about my father. It is always the same dream, though the circumstances vary. The person in it is indeed my father, but not as I ever knew him. He is younger, sturdier, he is cheerful, he has a droll sense of humour. I arrive at a hospital, or some such large institution, and, after much searching and confusion, find him sitting up in bed with a steaming mug of tea in his hand. His hair is boyishly rumpled, he is wearing someone else's pyjamas. He greets me with a sheepish smile. On impulse, because I am flustered and have been so worried, I embrace him fervently. He suffers this unaccustomed display of emotion with equanimity, patting my shoulder and laughing a little. Then I sit down on a chair beside the bed and we are silent for a moment, not quite knowing what to do, or where to look. I understand that he has survived something, an accident, or a shipwreck, or a hectic illness. Somehow it is his own foolhardiness, his recklessness (my father, reckless!), that has got him into danger, and now he is feeling silly, and comically ashamed of himself. In the dream it is always I who have been responsible for his lucky escape, by raising the alarm, calling for an ambulance, getting the lifeboat out, something like that. My deed sits between us, enormous, unmanageable, like love itself, proof at last of a son's true regard. I wake up smiling, my heart swollen with tenderness. I used to believe that in the dream it was death I was rescuing him from, but lately I have begun to think that it is, instead, the long calamity of his life I am undoing at a stroke. Now perhaps I'll have another, similar task to perform. For they told me today my mother has died.

*

By the time the taxi got me to the village the last bus to the city had left, as my driver, with melancholy enjoyment, had assured me would be the case. We sat in the darkened main street, beside a hardware shop, the engine purring. The driver turned around in his seat, lifting his cap for a rapid, one-finger scratch, and settled down to see what I would do next. Once again I was struck by the way these people stare, the dull, brute candour of their interest. I had better give him a name – it is Reck, I'm afraid – for I shall be stuck with him for a while yet. He would be happy, he said, to drive me into the city himself. I shook my head: it was a good thirty miles, and I already owed him money. Otherwise, he said, with an awful, ingratiating smile, his mother might put me up – Mrs Reck, it seemed, ran a public house with a room upstairs. The idea did not appeal to me, but the street was dark and grimly silent, and there was something very depressing about those tools in that shop window, and yes, I said faintly, with a hand to my forehead, yes, take me to your mother.

77

But she was not there, or asleep or something, and he led me up the back stairs himself, going on tiptoe like a large, shaky spider. The room had a little low window, one chair, and a bed with a hollow in the middle, as if a cadaver had lately been removed from it. There was a smell of piss and porter. Reck stood smiling at me shyly, kneading his cap in his hands. I bade him a firm goodnight, and he withdrew, lingeringly. The last I saw of him was a bony hand slowly pulling the door closed behind him. I walked back and forth once or twice gingerly, the floorboards creaking. Did I wring my hands, I wonder? The low window and the sagging bed gave me a vertiginous sense of disproportion, I seemed too tall, my feet too big. I sat on the side of the bed. A faint radiance lingered in the window. If I leaned down sideways I could see a crooked chimney pot and a silhouette of trees. I felt like the gloomy hero in a Russian novel, brooding in my bolthole above the dramshop in the village of Dash, in the year Dot, with my story all before me, waiting to be told.

I did not sleep. The sheets were clammy and somehow slippery, and I was convinced I was not the first to have tossed and turned between them since their last laundering. I tried to lie, tensed like a spring, in such a way that as little of me as possible came in contact with them. The hours were marked by a distant churchbell with a peculiarly dull note. There was the usual barking of dogs and bellowing of cattle. The sound of my own fretful sighs infuriated me. Now and then a car or a lorry passed by, and a box of lighted geometry slid rapidly over the ceiling and down the walls and poured away in a corner. I had a raging thirst. Waking dreams assailed me with grotesque and bawdy visions. Once, on the point of sleep, I had a sudden, dreadful sense of falling, and I sprang awake with a jerk. Though I tried to put her out of my mind I kept returning to the thought of Anna Behrens. What had happened to her, that she should lock herself away in that drear museum, with only a dying old man for company? But perhaps nothing had happened, perhaps that was it. Perhaps the days just went by, one by one, without a sound, until at last it was too late, and she woke up one morning and found herself stuck fast in the middle of her life. I imagined her there, sad and solitary, bewitched in her magic castle, year after year, and – oh, all sorts of mad notions came into my head, I am too embarrassed to speak of them. And as I was thinking these things, another thought, on another, murkier level, was winding and winding its dark skein. So it was out of a muddled conflation of ideas of knight errantry and rescue and reward that my plan originated. I assure you, your honour, this is no sly attempt at exoneration: I only wish to explain my motives, I mean the deepest ones, if such a thing is possible. As the hours went on, and stars flared in the little window and then slowly faded again, Anna Behrens merged in my mind with the other women who were in some way in my care – Daphne, of course, and even my mother, even the stable-girl, too – but in the end, when the dawn came, it was that Dutch figure in the picture in the garden room who hovered over the bed and gazed at me, sceptical, inquisitive and calm. I got up and dressed, and sat on the chair by the window and watched the ashen light of day descend upon the rooftops and seep into the trees. My mind was racing, my blood fizzled in my veins. I knew now what I would do. I was excited, and at the same time I had a deep sense of dread. There were stirrings downstairs. I wanted to be out, out, being and doing. I started to leave the room, but paused and lay on the bed for a moment to calm myself, and fell at once into a profound and terrible sleep. It was as if I had been struck down. I cannot describe it. It lasted no more than a minute or two. I woke up shaking. It was as if the very heart of things had skipped a beat. So it was that the day began, as it would continue, in the horrors.

Mrs Reck was tall and thin. No, she was short and fat. I do not remember her clearly. I do not wish to remember her clearly. For God's sake, how many of these grotesques am I expected to invent? I'll call her for a witness, and you can do the job yourselves. At first I thought she was in pain, but it was only a terrible, tongue-tied shyness that was making her duck and flinch. She fed me sausages and rashers and black pudding in the parlour behind the bar (it was the executioner who ate a hearty breakfast).

An intricate silence filled the room, I could hear myself swallow. Shadows hung down the walls like fronds of cobweb. There was a picture of Jesus with his dripping heart on show, done in thick shades of crimson and cream, and a photograph of some pope or other blessing the multitudes from a Vatican balcony. A feeling of gloom settled like heartburn in my breast. Reck appeared, in his braces and shirt-sleeves, and asked coyly if everything was all right. Grand, I said stoutly, grand! He stood and gazed at me, smiling tenderly, with a sort of happy pride. I might have been something he had left to propagate overnight. Ah, these poor, simple lives, so many, across which I have dragged my trail of slime. He had not once mentioned the monies I owed him – even on the phone he had apologised for not waiting for me. I rose and edged past him in the doorway. Just popping out for a moment, I said, get a breath of air. I could feel my horrible smile, like something sticky that had dripped on to my face. He nodded, and a little flicker of sadness passed over his brow and down his sheep's muzzle. You knew I was going to do a flit, didn't you? Why did you not stop me? I don't understand these people. I have said it before. I don't understand them.

The sun was shining through a thinning haze. It was still impossibly early. I walked down one side of the main street and up the other, twitching with impatience. Few people were about. Where did the notion come from that country folk are early risers? A van passed by, towing a trailer with a pig in it. At the end of the street there was a bridge over a shallow brown stream. I sat on the parapet and watched the water for a while. I needed a shave. I thought of going back to Reck's and borrowing a razor from him, but even I was not ruffian enough for such effrontery. The day was growing hot already. I began to feel light-headed there in the sun, watching the water squiggle and gulp below me. Presently a large, ancient man came along and began to address me earnestly. He wore sandals, and a torn mackintosh slung like a kern's tartan over one shoulder, and carried a thick ash stave. His hair was long, his beard matted. For some reason I found myself picturing his head borne aloft on a platter. He spoke calmly, in a loud, strong voice. I could not understand a word he said – he seemed to have lost the power of articulation – yet I found something oddly affecting in the way he stood there, leaning on his ashplant, with one knee flexed, his eyes fixed on me, speaking out his testament. I watched his mouth working in the thicket of his beard, and nodded my head slowly, seriously. Madmen do not frighten me, or even make me uneasy. Indeed, I find that their ravings soothe me. I think it is because everything, from the explosion of a nova to the fall of dust in a deserted room, is to them of vast and equal significance, and therefore meaningless. He finished, and continued regarding me in silence for a moment. Then he nodded gravely, and, with a last, meaningful stare, turned and strode away, over the bridge.

Your honour, I know I have spoken of having a plan, but it was a plan only in the broadest sense. I have never been much good at details. In the night, when the egg hatched and the thing first flexed its sticky, brittle wings, I had told myself that when morning came and real life started up again I would laugh at such a preposterous notion. And I did laugh, even if it was in a thoughtful sort of way, and I believe, I really do, that if I had not been stranded in that hole, with nothing to pass the time except my own dark thoughts, none of this would have happened. I would have gone to Charlie French and borrowed some money from him, and returned to the island and paid my debt to Señor Aguirre, and then I would have taken my wife and child and come home, to Coolgrange, to make my peace with my mother, and settle down, and become a squireen like my father, and live, and be happy. Ah—

What was I saying? My plan, yes. Your lordship, I am no mastermind. The newspapers, which from the start have been quite beside themselves – it was the silly season, after all, and I gave them a glorious, running story – have portrayed me both as a reckless thug and a meticulous, ice-cool, iron-willed blond beast. But I swear, it was all just drift, like everything else. I suppose at first I played with the idea, telling it to myself as a sort of story, as I lay there, the sleepless prince, in Mother Reck's gingerbread house, while the innocent stars crowded silently in the window. In the morning I rose and held it up to the light, and already it had begun to harden, to set. Strangely, it was like the work of someone else, which had been given to me to measure and to test. This process of distancing seems to have been an essential preliminary to action. Perhaps this accounts for the peculiar sensation which came over me there on the bridge above that gurgling river. It's hard to describe. I felt that I was utterly unlike myself. That is to say, I was perfectly familiar with this large, somewhat overweight, fair-haired man in a wrinkled suit sitting here fretfully twiddling his thumbs, yet at the same time it was as if I – the real, thinking, sentient I – had somehow got myself trapped inside a body not my own. But no, that's not it, exactly. For the person that was inside was also strange to me, stranger by far, indeed, than the familiar, physical creature. This is not clear, I know. I say the one within was strange to *me*, but which version of *me* do I mean? No, not clear at all. But it was not a new sensation. I have always felt – what is the word – bifurcate, that's it. Today, however, this feeling was stronger, more pronounced than usual. Bunter was restive, aching to get out. He had been shut up for so long, burbling and grumbling and taunting in there, and I knew that when he burst out at last he would talk and talk and talk. I felt dizzy. Grey nausea made my insides cringe. I wonder if the court appreciates what a state my nerves were in, not just that day, but throughout that period? My wife and child were being held hostage by wicked people, I was practically broke, my quarterly allowance from the pittance left me by my father was not due for another two months, and here I was, after a ghastly night, red-eyed, unshaven, stranded in the middle of nowhere and contemplating desperate actions. How would I not have been dizzy, how would I not have felt sick to my guts?

Eventually I sensed the village behind me coming sluggishly to life, and I walked back along the main street, keeping an eye out in case I should encounter an importunate Reck or, worse, Reck's mother. The morning was sunny and still, dew-laden, and a little dazed, as if drunk on its own newness. There were patches of damp on the pavements. It would be a glorious day. Oh yes, glorious.

I did not know until I found it that I was looking for the hardware shop where Reck had stopped the taxi the night before. My arm reached out and pushed open the door, a bell pinged, my legs walked me inside.

Gloom, a smell of paraffin and linseed oil, and clusters of things pendent overhead. A short, stout, elderly, balding man was sweeping the floor. He wore carpet slippers, and a cinnamon-coloured shopcoat such as I had not seen since I was a child. He smiled and nodded at me, and put aside his brush. He would not speak, however – professional etiquette, no doubt – until he had taken up position behind the counter, leaning forward on his arms with his head cocked to one side. Wire-rimmed glasses, I thought, would have completed the effect. I liked him straight away. Good day to you, sir, he said, in a cheery, hand-rubbing sort of voice. I felt better already. He was polite to just the correct degree, without undue subservience, or any hint of nosiness. I bought a ball of twine and a roll of brown wrapping-paper. Also a hank of rope – coiled, I recall, in a tight cylinder, very like a hangman's knot – good hard smooth hemp, not that modern plastic stuff. I had little notion of what I intended to do with these things. The rope, for instance, was pure indulgence. I didn't care. It was years – decades! – since I had experienced such simple, greedy pleasure. The shopman placed my purchases lovingly before me on the counter, crooning a little under his breath, smiling, pursing his lips approvingly. It was playtime. In this pretend-world I could have anything I wanted. A tenon-saw, for instance, with rosewood stock. A set of brass fire-irons, their handles made in the shape of crouching monkeys. That white enamelled bucket, with a delicate, flesh-blue shadow down one side. Oh, anything! Then I spotted the hammer. One moulded, polished piece of stainless steel, like a bone from the thigh of some swift animal, with a velvety, black rubber grip and a blued head and claw. I am utterly unhandy, I do not think I could drive a nail straight, but I confess I had always harboured a secret desire to have a hammer like that. More laughter in court, of course, more ribald guffaws from the wiseacres in the gallery. But I insist, your honour, gentle handymen of the jury, I insist it was an innocent desire, a wish, an ache, on the part of the deprived child inside me – not Bunter, not him, but the true, lost ghost of my boyhood – to possess this marvellous toy. For the first time my fairy-godfather hesitated. There are other models, he ventured, less – a hurried, breathy whisper – less expensive, sir. But no, no, I could not resist it. I must have it. That one. Yes, that one, there, with the tag on it. Exhibit A, in other words.

I stumbled out of the shop with my parcel under my arm, bleared and grinning, happy as a drunken schoolboy. The shop-keeper came to the door to watch me go. He had shaken hands with me in an odd, cryptic manner. Perhaps he was a mason, and was testing to see if I too might be a member of the brotherhood? – but no, I prefer to think he was merely a decent, kindly, well-meaning man. There are not many such, in this testimony.

I felt by now that I knew the village. I felt in fact that I had been here before, and even that I had done all these things before, walked about aimlessly in the early morning, and sat on the bridge, and gone into a shop and purchased things. I have no explanation: I only felt it. It was as if I had dreamed a prophetic dream and then forgotten it, and this was the prophecy coming true. But then, something of that sense of inevitability infected everything I did that day – inevitable, mind you, does not mean excusable, in my vocabulary. No indeed, a strong mixture of Catholic and Calvinist blood courses in my veins.

It came to me suddenly, with happy inconsequentiality, that it was midsummer day.

This is a wonderful country, a man with a decent accent can do almost anything. I thought I was heading for the bus-stop, to see if there was a bus to the city, but instead – more inevitability – I found myself outside a tumbledown garage in the village square. A boy in filthy overalls a number of sizes too small for him was heaving tyres and whistling tunelessly out of the side of his face. A rusty tin sign nailed to the wall above his head proclaimed: *Melmoth's ar Hire*. The boy paused and looked at me blankly. He had stopped whistling, but kept his lips puckered. Car? I said, pointing to the sign, for hire, yes? I jiggled an invisible steering wheel. He said nothing, only frowned in deep puzzlement, as if I had asked for something utterly outlandish. Then a stout, big-bosomed woman came out of the cash office and spoke to him sharply. She wore a crimson blouse and tight black trousers and high-heeled, toeless sandals. Her hair, black as a crow's wing, was piled up in a brioche shape, with ringlets trailing down at the sides. She reminded me of someone, I could not think who. She led me into the office, where with a lurch I spied, among a cluster of gaudy postcards tacked to the wall behind her desk, a view of the island, and the harbour, and the very bar where I had first encountered Randolph the American. It was unnerving, an omen, even a warning, perhaps. The woman was studying me up and down with a sort of smouldering surmise. With another shock I realised who it was she reminded me of: the mother of the squalling baby in Señor Aguirre's apartment.

The car was a Humber, a great, heavy, high model, not old enough to be what they call vintage, just hopelessly out of fashion. It seemed to have been built for a simpler, more innocent age than this, one peopled by a species of big children. The upholstery had a vaguely fecal smell. I drove sedately through the village in third gear, perched high above the road as if I were being borne along on a palanquin. The engine made a noise like muffled cheering. I had paid a deposit of five pounds, and signed a document in the name of Smyth (I thought the *y* a fiendishly clever touch). The woman had not even asked to see a driving licence. As I say, this is a wonderful country. I felt extraordinarily light-hearted.

*

Speaking of jaunts: I went to my mother's funeral today. Three plain-clothes men took me in a closed car, I was very impressed. We sped through the city with the siren hee-hawing, it was like my arrest all over again, but in reverse. A lovely, sunny, crisp morning, pale smoke in the air, a few leaves down already on the pavements. I felt such a strange mingling of emotions – a certain rawness, of course, a certain pain, but elation, too, and something like grief that yet was not without sweetness. I was grieving not for my mother only, perhaps not for her at all, but for things in general. Maybe it was just the usual September melancholy, made unfamiliar by the circumstances. We drove by the river under a sky piled high with bundles of luminous Dutch clouds, then south through leafy suburbs. The sea surprised me, as it always does, a bowl of blue, moving metal, light rising in flakes off the surface. All three detectives were chain-smokers, they worked at it grimly, as if it were a part of their duties. One of them offered me a cigarette. Not one of my vices, I said, and they laughed politely. They seemed embarrassed, and kept glancing warily out the windows, as if they had been forced to come on an outing with a famous and disreputable relative and were afraid of being spotted by someone they knew. Now we were in the country, and there was mist on the fields still, and the hedges were drenched. She was buried in the family plot in the old cemetery at Coolgrange. I was not allowed to leave the car, or even to open a window. I was secretly glad, for somehow I could not conceive of myself stepping out suddenly like this, into the world. The driver parked as near as possible to the graveside, and I sat in a fug of cigarette smoke and watched the brief, hackneyed little drama unfold beyond the fogged glass, among the leaning headstones. There were few mourners: an aunt or two, and an old man who had worked years ago for my father in the stables. The girl Joanne was there, of course, red-eyed, her poor face blotched and swollen, dressed in a lumpy pullover and a crooked skirt. Charlie French stood a little apart from the rest, with his hands awkwardly clasped. I was surprised to see him. Decent of him to come, courageous, too. Neither he nor the girl looked in my direction, though they must have felt the pressure of my humid gaze. The coffin seemed to me surprisingly small, they got it down into the hole with room to spare. Poor Ma. I can't believe that she's gone,

I mean the fact of it has not sunk in yet. It is somehow as if she had been bundled away to make room for something more important. Of course, the irony of the situation does not escape me: if I had only waited a few months there would have been no need to – but no, enough of that. They'll read the will without me, which is only right. The last time I saw her I fought with her. That was the day I left for Whitewater. She did not visit me in jail. I don't blame her. I never even brought the child for her to see. She was not as tough as I imagined. Did I destroy her life, too? All these dead women.

When the ceremony was over Charlie walked past the car with his head down. He seemed to hesitate, but changed his mind and went on. I think he would have spoken to me, had it not been for the presence of the detectives, and my aunts agog behind him, and, oh, just the general awfulness of everything.

So I am driving away from the village, in the Humber Hawk, with a foolish grin on my face. I felt, for no good reason, that I was escaping all my problems, I pictured them dwindling in space and time like the village itself, a quaint jumble of things getting steadily smaller and smaller. If I had stopped for a moment to think, of course, I would have realised that what I was leaving behind me was not my tangled troubles, as I fondly imagined, but, on the contrary, a mass of evidence, obvious and unmistakable as a swatch of matted hair and blood. I had skipped Ma Reck's without paying for my lodgings, I had bought a burglar's kit in the village shop, and now I had as good as stolen a car – and all this not five miles from what would soon come to be known as the scene of the crime. The court will agree, these are hardly the marks of careful premeditation. (Why is it that every other thing I say sounds like the sly preamble to a plea of mitigation?) The fact is, I was not thinking at all, not what could really be called thinking. I was content to sail through sun and shade along these dappled back roads, one hand on the wheel and an elbow out the window, with the scents of the countryside in my nostrils and the breeze whipping my hair. Everything would be well, everything would work itself out. I do not know why I felt so elated, perhaps it was a form of delirium. Anyway, I told myself, it was only a madcap game I was playing, I could call it off whenever I wished.

Meanwhile here was Whitewater, rising above the trees.

An empty tour bus was parked at the gate. The driver's door was open, and the driver was lounging in the stepwell, sunning himself. He watched me as I swung past him into the drive. I waved to him. He wore tinted glasses. He did not smile. He would remember me.

Afterwards the police could not understand why I showed so little circumspection, driving up brazenly like that, in broad daylight, in that unmistakable motor car. But I believed, you see, that the matter would be entirely between Behrens and me, with Anna perhaps as go-between. I never imagined there would be anything so vulgar as a police investigation, and headlines in the papers, and all the rest of it. A simple business transaction between civilised people, that's what I intended. I would be polite but firm, no more than that. I was not thinking in terms of threats and ransom demands, certainly not. When later I read what those reporters wrote – the Midsummer Manhunt, they called it – I could not recognise myself in their depiction of me as a steely, ruthless character. Ruthless – me! No, as I drove up to Whitewater it was not police I was thinking of, but only the chauffeur Flynn, with his little pig eyes and his boxer's meaty paws. Yes, Flynn was a man to avoid.

Halfway up the drive there was

God, these tedious details.

Halfway up there was a fork in the drive. A wooden arrow with HOUSE written on it in white paint pointed to the right, while to the left a sign said STRICTLY PRIVATE. I stopped the car. See me there, a big blurred face behind the windscreen peering first this way, then that. It is like an illustration from a cautionary tract: the sinner hesitates at the parting of the ways. I drove off to the left, and my heart gave an apprehensive wallop. Behold, the wretch forsakes the path of righteousness.

I rounded the south wing of the house, and parked on the grass and walked across the lawn to the garden room. The french window was open. Deep breath. It was not yet noon. Far off in the fields somewhere a tractor was working, it made a drowsy, buzzing sound that seemed the very voice of summer, I hear it still, that tiny, distant, prelapsarian song. I had left the rope and the hammer in the car, and brought with me the twine and the roll of wrapping paper. It struck me suddenly how absurd the whole thing was. I began to laugh, and laughing stepped into the room.

The painting is called, as everyone must know by now, *Portrait of a Woman with Gloves*. It measures eighty-two centimetres by sixty-five. From internal evidence – in particular the woman's attire – it has been dated between 1655 and 1660. The black dress and broad white collar and cuffs of the woman are lightened only by a brooch and gold ornamentation on the gloves. The face has a slightly Eastern cast. (I am quoting from the guidebook to Whitewater House.) The picture has been variously attributed to Rembrandt and Frans Hals, even to Vermeer. However, it is safest to regard it as the work of an anonymous master.

None of this means anything.

I have stood in front of other, perhaps greater paintings, and not been moved as I am moved by this one. I have a reproduction of it on the wall above my table here – sent to me by, of all people, Anna Behrens – when I look at it my heart contracts. There is something in the way the woman regards me, the querulous, mute insistence of her eyes, which I can neither escape nor assuage. I squirm in the grasp of her gaze. She requires of me some great effort, some tremendous feat of scrutiny and attention, of which I do not think I am capable. It is as if she were asking me to let her live.

She. There is no she, of course. There is only an organisation of shapes and colours. Yet I try to make up a life for her. She is, I will say, thirty-five, thirty-six, though people without thinking still speak of her as a girl. She lives with her father, the merchant (tobacco, spices, and, in secret, slaves). She keeps house for him since her mother's death. She did not like her mother. Her father dotes on her, his only child. She is, he proclaims, his treasure. She devises menus – Father has a delicate stomach – inspects the kitchen, she even supervises his wine cellar. She keeps an inventory of the household linen in a little notebook attached to her belt by a fine gold chain, using a code of her own devising, for she has never learned to read or write. She is strict with the servants, and will permit no familiarities. Their dislike she takes for respect. The house is not enough to absorb her energies, she does good works besides: she visits the sick, and is on the board of visitors of the town's almshouse. She is brisk, sometimes impatient, and there are mutterings against her among the alms-folk, especially the old women. At times, usually in spring and at the beginning of winter, everything becomes too much for her. Notice the clammy pallor of her skin: she is prey to obscure ailments. She takes to her bed and lies for days without speaking, hardly breathing, while outside in the silvery northern light the world goes about its busy way. She tries to pray, but God is distant. Her father comes to visit her at evening, walking on tiptoe. These periods of prostration frighten him, he remembers his wife dying, her terrible silence in the last weeks. If he were to lose his daughter too— But she gets up, wills herself to it, and very soon the servants are feeling the edge of her tongue again, and he cannot contain his relief, it comes out in little laughs, roguish endearments, a kind of clumsy skittishness. She considers him wryly, then turns back to her tasks. She cannot understand this notion he has got into his head: he wants to have her portrait painted. I'm old, is all he will say to her, I am an old man, look at me! And he laughs, awkwardly, and avoids her eye. My portrait? she says, mine? – I am no fit subject for a painter. He shrugs, at which she is first startled, then grimly amused: he might at least have attempted to contradict her. He seems to realise what is going through her mind, and tries to mend matters, but he becomes flustered, and, watching him fuss and fret and pluck at his cuffs, she realises with a pang that it's true, he has aged. Her father, an old man. The thought has a touch of bleak comedy, which she cannot account for. You have fine hands, he says, growing testy, annoyed both at himself and her, your mother's hands – we'll tell him to make the hands prominent. And so, to humour him, but also because she is secretly curious, she goes along one morning to the studio. The squalor is what strikes her first of all. Dirt and daubs of paint everywhere, gnawed chicken bones on a smeared plate, a chamber-pot on the floor in the corner. The painter matches the place, with that filthy smock, and those fingernails. He has a drinker's squashed and pitted nose. She thinks the general smell is bad until she catches a whiff of his breath. She discovers that she is relieved: she had expected someone young, dissolute, threatening, not this pot-bellied old soak. But then he fixes his little wet eyes on her, briefly, with a kind of impersonal intensity, and she flinches, as if caught in a burst of strong light. No one has ever looked at her like this before. So this is what it is to be known! It is almost indecent. First he puts her standing by the window, but it does not suit, the light is wrong, he says. He shifts her about, grasping her by the upper arms and walking her backwards from one place to another. She feels she should be indignant, but the usual responses do not seem to function here. He is shorter than her by a head. He makes some sketches, scribbles a colour note or two, then tells her to come tomorrow at the same time. And wear a darker dress, he says. Well! She is about to give him a piece of her mind, but already he has turned aside to another task. Her maid, sitting by the door, is biting her lips and smirking. She lets the next day pass, and the next, just to show him. When she does return he says nothing about the broken appointment, only looks at her black dress – pure silk, with a broad collar of Spanish lace – and nods carelessly, and she is so vexed at him it surprises her, and she is shocked at herself. He has her stand before the couch. Remove your gloves, he says, I am to emphasise the hands. She hears the note of amused disdain in his voice. She refuses. (*Her* hands, indeed!) He insists. They engage in a brief, stiff little squabble, batting icy politenesses back and forth between them. In the end she consents to remove one glove, then promptly tries to hide the hand she has bared. He sighs, shrugs, but has to suppress a grin, as she notices. Rain streams down the windows, shreds of smoke fly over the rooftops. The sky has a huge silver hole in it. At first she is restless, standing there, then she seems to pass silently through some barrier, and a dreamy calm comes over her. It is the same, day after day, first there is agitation, then the breakthrough, then silence and a kind of softness, as if she were floating away, away, out of herself. He mutters under his breath as he works. He is choleric, he swears, and clicks his tongue, sending up sighs and groans. There are long, fevered passages when he works close up against the canvas, and she can only see his stumpy legs and his old, misshapen boots. Even his feet seem busy. She wants to laugh when he pops his head out at the side of the easel and peers at her sharply, his potato nose twitching. He will not let her see what he is doing, she is not allowed even a peek. Then one day she senses a kind of soundless, settling crash at his end of the room, and he steps back with an expression of weary disgust and waves a hand dismissively at the canvas, and turns aside to clean his brush. She comes forward and looks. For a second she sees nothing, so taken is she by the mere sensation of stopping like this and turning: it is as if – as if somehow she had walked out of herself. A long moment passes. The brooch, she says, is wonderfully done. The sound of her own voice startles her, it is a stranger speaking, and she is cowed. He laughs, not bitterly, but with real amusement and, so she feels, a curious sort of sympathy. It is an acknowledgement, of – she does not know what. She looks and looks. She had expected it would be like looking in a mirror; but this is someone she does not recognise, and yet knows. The words come unbidden into her head: Now I know how to die. She puts on her glove, and signals to her maid. The painter is speaking behind her, something about her father, and money, of course, but she is not listening. She is calm. She is happy. She feels numbed, hollowed, a walking shell. She goes down the stairs, along the dingy hall, and steps out into a commonplace world.

Do not be fooled: none of this means anything either.

I had placed the string and the wrapping-paper carefully on the floor, and now stepped forward with my arms outstretched. The door behind me opened and a large woman in a tweed skirt and a cardigan came into the room. She halted when she saw me there, with my arms flung wide before the picture and peering wildly at her over my shoulder, while I tried with one foot to conceal the paper and the ball of twine on the floor. She had blue-grey hair, and her spectacles were attached to a cord around her neck. She frowned. You must stay with the party, she said loudly, in a cross voice – really, I don't know how many times

I have to say it. I stepped back. A dozen gaudily dressed people were crowding in the doorway behind her, craning to get a look at me. Sorry, I heard myself say meekly, I got lost. She gave an impatient toss of the head and strode to the middle of the room and began at once to speak in a shouted singsong about Carlin tables and Berthoud clocks, and weeks later, questioned by the police and shown my photograph, she would deny ever having seen me before in her life. Her charges shuffled in, jostling surreptitiously in an effort to stay out of her line of sight. They took up position, standing with their hands clasped before them, as if they were in church, and looked about them with expressions of respectful vacancy. One grizzled old party in a Hawaiian shirt grinned at me and winked. I confess I was rattled. There was a knot in the pit of my stomach and my palms were damp. All the elation I had felt on the way here had evaporated, leaving behind it a stark sense of foreboding. I was struck, for the first time, really, by the enormity of what I was embarked on. I felt like a child whose game has led him far into the forest, and now it is nightfall, and there are shadowy figures among the trees. The guide had finished her account of the treasures in the room – the picture, *my* picture, was given two sentences, and a misattribution – and walked out now with one arm raised stiffly above her head, still talking, shepherding the party behind her. When they had gone I waited, staring fixedly at the doorknob, expecting her to come back and haul me out briskly by the scruff of the neck. Somewhere inside me a voice was moaning softly in panic and fright. This is something that does not seem to be appreciated – I have remarked on it before – I mean how timorous I am, how easily daunted. But she did not return, and I heard them tramping away up the stairs. I set to work again feverishly. I see myself, like the villain in an old three-reeler, all twitches and scowls and wriggling eyebrows. I got the picture off the wall, not without difficulty, and laid it flat on the floor – shying away from that black stare – and began to tear off lengths of wrapping-paper. I would not have thought that paper would make so much noise, such scuffling and rattling and ripping, it must have sounded as if some large animal were being flayed alive in here. And it was no good, my hands shook, I was all thumbs, and the sheets of paper kept rolling back on themselves, and I had nothing to cut the twine with, and anyway the picture, with its thick, heavy frame, was much too big to be wrapped. I scampered about on my knees, talking to myself and uttering little squeaks of distress. Everything was going wrong. Give it up, I told myself, oh please, please, give it up now, while there's still time! but another part of me gritted its teeth and said, no you don't, you coward, get up, get on your feet, do it. So I struggled up, moaning and snivelling, and grasped the picture in my arms and staggered with it blindly, nose to nose, in the direction of the french window. Those eyes were staring into mine, I almost blushed. And then – how shall I express it – then somehow I sensed, behind that stare, another presence, watching me. I stopped, and lowered the picture, and there she was, standing in the open window, just as she had stood the day before, wide-eyed, with one hand raised. This, I remember thinking bitterly, this is the last straw. I was outraged. How dare the world strew these obstacles in my path. It was not fair, it was just not fair! Right, I said to her, here, take this, and I thrust the painting into her arms and turned her about and marched her ahead of me across the lawn. She said nothing, or if she did I was not listening. She found it hard going on the grass, the picture was too heavy for her, and she could hardly see around it. When she faltered I prodded her between the shoulder-blades. I really was very cross. We reached the car. The cavernous boot smelled strongly of fish. There was the usual jumble of mysterious implements, a jack, and spanners and things – I am not mechanically minded, or handed, have I mentioned that? – and a filthy old pullover, which I hardly noticed at the time, thrown in a corner with deceptive casualness by the hidden arranger of all these things. I took out the tools and threw them behind me on to the grass, then lifted the painting from the maid's arms and placed it face-down on the worn felt matting. This was the first time I had seen the back of the canvas, and suddenly I was struck by the antiquity of the thing. Three hundred years ago it had been stretched and sized and left against a lime-washed wall to dry. I closed my eyes for a second, and at once I saw a workshop in a narrow street in Amsterdam or Antwerp, smoky sunlight in the window, and hawkers going by outside, and the bells of the cathedral ringing. The maid was watching me. She had the most extraordinary pale, violet eyes, they seemed transparent, when I looked into them I felt I was seeing clear through her head. Why did she not run away? Behind her, in one of the great upstairs windows, a dozen heads were crowded, goggling at us. I could make out the guide-woman's glasses and the American's appalling shirt. I think I must have cried aloud in rage, an old lion roaring at the whip and chair, for the maid flinched and stepped back a pace. I caught her wrist in an iron claw and, wrenching open the car door, fairly flung her into the back seat. Oh, why did she not run away! When I got behind the wheel, fumbling and snarling, I caught a whiff of something, a faint, sharp, metallic smell, like the smell of worn pennies. I could see her in the mirror, crouched behind me as in a deep glass box, braced between the door and the back of the seat, with her elbows stuck out and fingers splayed and her face thrust forward, like the cornered heroine in a melodrama. A fierce, choking gust of impatience surged up inside me. Impatience, yes, that was what I felt most strongly – that, and a grievous sense of embarrassment. I was mortified. I had never been so exposed in all my life. People were looking at me – she in the back seat, and the tourists up there jostling at the window, but also, it seemed, a host of others, of phantom spectators, who must have been, I suppose, an intimation of all that horde who would soon be crowding around me in fascination and horror. I started the engine. The gears shrieked. In my agitation I kept getting ahead of myself and having to go back and repeat the simplest actions. When I had got the car off the grass and on to the drive I let the clutch out too quickly, and the machine sprang forward in a series of bone-shaking lurches, the bonnet going up and down like the prow of a boat caught in a wash and the shock absorbers grunting. The watchers at the window must have been in fits by now. A bead of sweat ran down my cheek. The sun had made the steering-wheel almost too hot to hold, and there was a blinding glare on the windscreen. The maid was scrabbling at the door handle, I roared at her and she stopped at once, and looked at me wide-eyed, like a rebuked child. Outside the gate the bus driver was still sitting in the sun. When she saw him she tried to get the window open, but in vain, the mechanism must have been broken. She pounded on the glass with her fists. I spun the wheel and the car lumbered out into the road, the tyres squealing. We were shouting at each other now, like a married couple having a fight. She pummelled me on the shoulder, got a hand around in front of my face and tried to claw my eyes. Her thumb went up my nose, I thought she would tear off the nostril. The car was going all over the road. I trod with both feet on the brake pedal, and we sailed in a slow, dragging curve into the hedge. She fell back. I turned to her. I had the hammer in my hand. I looked at it, startled. The silence rose around us like water. Don't, she said. She was crouched as before, with her arms bent and her back pressed into the corner. I could not speak, I was filled with a kind of wonder. I had never felt another's presence so immediately and with such raw force. I saw her now, really saw her, for the first time, her mousy hair and bad skin, that bruised look around her eyes. She was quite ordinary, and yet, somehow, I don't know – somehow radiant. She cleared her throat and sat up, and detached a strand of hair that had caught at the corner of her mouth.

You must let me go, she said, or you will be in trouble.

It's not easy to wield a hammer in a motor car. When I struck her the first time I expected to feel the sharp, clean smack of steel on bone, but it was more like hitting clay, or hard putty. The word *fontanel* sprang into my mind. I thought one good bash would do it, but, as the autopsy would show, she had a remarkably strong skull – even in that, you see, she was unlucky. The first blow fell just at the hairline, above her left eye. There was not much blood, only a dark-red glistening dent with hair matted in it. She shuddered, but remained sitting upright, swaying a little, looking at me with eyes that would not focus properly.

Perhaps I would have stopped then, if she had not suddenly launched herself at me across the back of the seat, flailing and screaming. I was dismayed. How could this be happening to me – it was all so *unfair*. Bitter tears of self-pity squeezed into my eyes. I pushed her away from me and swung the hammer in a wide, backhand sweep. The force of the blow flung her against the door, and her head struck the window, and a fine thread of blood ran out of her nostril and across her cheek. There was blood on the window, too, a fan-shaped spray of tiny drops. She closed her eyes and turned her face away from me, making a low, guttural noise at the back of her throat. She put a hand up to her head just as I was swinging at her again, and when the blow landed on her temple her fingers were in the way, and I heard one of them crack, and I winced, and almost apologised. Oh! she said, and suddenly, as if everything inside her had collapsed, she slithered down the seat on to the floor.

There was silence again, clear and startling. I got out of the car and stood a moment, breathing. I was dizzy. Something seemed to have happened to the sunlight, everywhere I looked there was an underwater gloom. I thought I had driven only a little way, and expected to see the gates of Whitewater, and the tour bus, and the driver running towards me, but to my astonishment the road in both directions was empty, and I had no idea where I was. On one side a hill rose steeply, and on the other I could see over the tops of pine trees to far-off, rolling downs. It all looked distinctly improbable. It was like a hastily painted backdrop, especially that smudged, shimmering distance, and the road winding innocently away. I found I was still clutching the hammer. With a grand sweep of my arm I flung it from me, and watched it as it flew, tumbling slowly end over end, in a long, thrilling arc, far, far out over the blue pine-tops. Then abruptly I bent forward and vomited up the glutinous remains of the breakfast I had consumed an age ago, in another life.

I crawled back into the car, keeping my eyes averted from that crumpled thing wedged behind the front seat. The light in the windscreen was a splintered glare, I thought for a second the glass was smashed, until I put a hand to my face and discovered I was crying. This I found encouraging. My tears seemed not just a fore-token of remorse, but the sign of some more common, simpler urge, an affect for which there was no name, but which might be my last link, the only one that would hold, with the world of ordinary things. For everything was changed, where I was now I had not been before. I trembled, and all around me trembled, and there was a sluggish, sticky feel to things, as if I and all of this – car, road, trees, those distant meadows – as if we had all a moment ago struggled mute and amazed out of a birthhole in the air. I turned the key in the ignition, bracing myself, convinced that instead of the engine starting something else would happen, that there would be a terrible, rending noise, or a flash of light, or that slime would gush out over my legs from under the dashboard. I drove in second gear along the middle of the road. Smells, smells. Blood has a hot, thick smell. I wanted to open the windows, but did not dare, I was afraid of what might come in – the light outside seemed moist and dense as glair, I imagined it in my mouth, my nostrils.

I drove and drove. Whitewater is only thirty miles or so from the city, but it seemed hours before I found myself in the suburbs. Of the journey I remember little. That is to say, I do not remember changing gears, accelerating and slowing down, working the pedals, all that. I see myself moving, all right, as if in a crystal bubble, flying soundlessly through a strange, sunlit, glittering landscape. I think I went very fast, for I recall a sensation of pressure in my ears, a dull, rushing blare. So I must have driven in circles, round and round those narrow country roads. Then there were houses, and housing estates, and straggling factories, and supermarkets big as aircraft hangers. I stared through the windscreen in dreamy amazement. I might have been a visitor from another part of the world altogether, hardly able to believe how much like home everything looked and yet how different it was. I did not know where I was going, I mean I was not going anywhere, just driving. It was almost restful, sailing along like that, turning the wheel with one finger, shut off from everything.

It was as if all my life I had been clambering up a steep and difficult slope, and now had reached the peak and leaped out blithely into the blue. I felt so free. At the first red traffic light the car drifted gently to a stop as if it were subsiding into air. I was at the junction of two suburban roads. On the left there was a little green rise with a chestnut tree and a neat row of new houses. Children were playing on the grassy bank. Dogs gambolled. The sun shone. I have always harboured a secret fondness for quiet places such as this, unremarked yet cherished domains of building and doing and tending. I leaned my head back on the seat and smiled, watching the youngsters at play. The lights changed to green, but I did not stir. I was not really there, but lost somewhere, in some sunlit corner of my past. There was a sudden rapping on the window beside my ear. I jumped. A woman with a large, broad, horsy face – she reminded me, dear God, of my mother! – was peering in at me and saying something. I rolled down the window. She had a loud voice, it sounded very loud to me, at any rate. I could not understand her, she was talking about an accident, and asking me if I was all right. Then she pressed her face forward and squinnied over my shoulder, and opened her mouth and groaned. Oh, she said, the poor child! I turned my head. There was blood all over the back seat now, far too much, surely, for just one person to have shed. For a mad instant, in which a crafty spark of hope flared and died, I wondered if there *had* been a crash, which somehow I had not noticed, or had forgotten, if some overloaded vehicle had ploughed into the back of us, flinging bodies and all this blood in through the rear window. I could not speak. I had thought she was dead, but there she was, kneeling between the seats and groping at the window beside her, I could hear her fingers squeaking on the glass. Her hair hung down in bloodied ropes, her face was a clay mask streaked with copper and crimson. The woman outside was gabbling into my ear about telephones and ambulances and the police – the police! I turned to her with a terrible glare. Madam! I said sternly (she would later describe my voice as *cultured* and *authoritative*), will you please get on about your business! She stepped back, staring in shock. I confess I was myself impressed, I would not have thought I could muster such a commanding tone. I rolled up the window and jammed the car into gear and shot away, noticing, too late, that the lights had turned to red. A tradesman's van coming from the left braked sharply and let out an indignant squawk. I drove on. However, I had not gone more than a street or two when suddenly an ambulance reared up in my wake, its siren yowling and blue light flashing. I was astonished. How could it have arrived so promptly? In fact, this was another of those appalling coincidences in which this case abounds. The ambulance, as I would later learn, was not looking for me, but was returning from – yes – from the scene of a car crash, with – I'm sorry, but, yes – with a dying woman in the back. I kept going, haring along with my head down, my nose almost touching the rim of the wheel. I do not think I could have stopped, locked in fright as I was. The ambulance drew alongside, swaying dangerously and trumpeting like a frenzied big beast. The attendant in the passenger seat, a burly young fellow in shirt-sleeves, with a red face and narrow sideburns, looked at the blood-streaked window behind me with mild, professional interest. He conferred briefly with the driver, then signalled to me, with complicated gestures, nodding and mouthing, to follow them. They thought I was coming from the same crash, ferrying another victim to hospital. They surged ahead. I followed in their wake, befuddled with alarm and bafflement. I could see nothing but this big square clumsy thing scudding along, whooshing up dust and wallowing fatly on its springs. Then abruptly it braked and swung into a wide gateway, and an arm appeared out of the side window and beckoned me to follow. It was the sight of that thick arm that broke the spell. With a gulp of demented laughter I drove on, past the hospital gate, plunging the pedal to the floor, and the noise of the siren dwindled behind me, a startled plaint, and I was free.

I peered into the mirror. She was sitting slumped on the seat with her head hanging and her hands resting palm upwards on her thighs.

Suddenly the sea was on my left, far below, blue, unmoving. I drove down a steep hill, then along a straight cement road beside a railway track. A pink and white hotel, castellated, with pennants flying, rose up on my right, enormous and empty. The road straggled to an end in a marshy patch of scrub and thistles, and there I stopped, in the midst of a vast and final silence. I could hear her behind me, breathing. When I turned she lifted her sibyl's fearsome head and looked at me. *Help me*, she whispered. *Help me*. A bubble of blood came out of her mouth and burst. *Tommy!* she said, or a word like that, and then: *Love.* What did I feel? Remorse, grief, a terrible— no no no, I won't lie. I can't remember feeling anything, except that sense of strangeness, of being in a place I knew but did not recognise. When I got out of the car I was giddy, and had to lean on the door for a moment with my eyes shut tight. My jacket was bloodstained, I wriggled out of it and flung it into the stunted bushes – they never found it, I can't think why. I remembered the pullover in the boot, and put it on. It smelled of fish and sweat and axle-grease. I picked up the hangman's hank of rope and threw that away too. Then I lifted out the picture and walked with it to where there was a sagging barbed-wire fence and a ditch with a trickle of water at the bottom, and there I dumped it. What was I thinking of, I don't know. Perhaps it was a gesture of renunciation or something. Renunciation! How do I dare use such words. The woman with the gloves gave me a last, dismissive stare. She had expected no better of me. I went back to the car, trying not to look at it, the smeared windows. Something was falling on me: a delicate, silent fall of rain. I looked upwards in the glistening sunlight and saw a cloud directly overhead, the merest smear of grey against the summer blue. I thought: I am not human. Then I turned and walked away.

II

ALL MY ADULT LIFE I have had a recurring dream (yes, yes, dreams again!), it comes once or twice a year and leaves me disturbed for days afterwards. As usual it is not a dream in the ordinary sense, for not much happens in it, really, and nothing is explicit. There is mainly an undefined but profound and mounting sensation of unease, which rises at the end to full-fledged panic. A long time ago, it seems, I have committed a crime. No, that is too strong. I have done something, it is never clear what, precisely. Perhaps I stumbled upon something, it may even have been a corpse, and covered it up, and almost forgot about it. Now, years later, the evidence has been found, and they have come to question me. As yet there is nothing to suggest that I was directly involved, not a hint of suspicion attaches to me. I am merely another name on a list. They are mild, soft-spoken, stolidly deferential, a little bored. The young one fidgets. I respond to their questions politely, with a certain irony, smiling, lifting an eyebrow. It is, I tell myself smugly, the performance of my life, a masterpiece of dissembling. Yet the older one, I notice, is regarding me with deepening interest, his shrewd eyes narrowing. I must have said something. What have I said? I begin to blush, I cannot help it. A horrible constriction takes hold of me. I babble, what is intended as a relaxed little laugh turns into a strangled gasp. At length I run down, like a clockwork toy, and sit and gape at them helplessly, panting. Even the younger one, the sergeant, is interested now. An appalling silence descends, it stretches on and on, until at last my sleeping self makes a bolt for it and I start awake, aghast and sweating. What is peculiarly awful in all this is not the prospect of being dragged before the courts and put in jail for a crime I am not even sure I have committed, but the simple, terrible fact of having been found out. This is what makes me sweat, what fills my mouth with ashes and my heart with shame.

And now, as I hurried along the cement road, with the railway track beside me and the sea beyond, I had that same feeling of ignominy. What a fool I had been. What trouble there would be in the days, the weeks, the years ahead. Yet also there was a sensation of lightness, of buoyancy, as if I had thrown off an awkward burden. Ever since I had reached what they call the use of reason I had been doing one thing and thinking another, because the weight of things seemed so much greater than that of thoughts. What I said was never exactly what I felt, what I felt was never what it seemed I should feel, though the feelings were what felt genuine, and right, and inescapable. Now I had struck a blow for the inner man, that guffawing, fat foulmouth who had been telling me all along I was living a lie. And he had burst out at last, it was he, the ogre, who was pounding along in this lemon-coloured light, with blood on his pelt, and me slung helpless over his back. Everything was gone, the past, Coolgrange, Daphne, all my previous life, gone, abandoned, drained of its essence, its significance. To do the worst thing, the very worst thing, that's the way to be free. I would never again need to pretend to myself to be what I was not. The thought made my head spin and my empty stomach heave.

I was prey to a host of niggling worries. This pullover was smelly, and too tight for me. The knee of my left trouser-leg had a small rip in it. People would notice that I had not shaved today. And I needed, I positively longed, to wash my hands, to plunge up to the elbows in scalding suds, to sluice myself, to drench, rinse, scour – to be clean. Opposite the deserted hotel there was a jumble of grey buildings that had once been a railway station. Weeds were growing on the platform, and all the windows in the signal box were smashed. A pockmarked enamel sign with a lovingly painted pointing hand indicated a cement blockhouse set at a discreet distance down the platform. A clump of purple buddleia was flourishing by the doorway of the gents. I went into the ladies – there were no more rules, after all. The air here was chill and dank. There was a quicklime smell, and something green and glistening was growing up the walls. The fittings had been ripped out long ago, even the stall doors were gone. It was apparent from the state of the floor, however, that the place was still in frequent use. In a corner there was a little heap of stuff – used condoms, I think, discoloured wads of cotton, even bits of clothing – from which I quickly averted my eyes. A single tap on a green copper pipe stuck out of the wall where the handbasins had been. When I turned the spigot there was a distant groaning and clanking, and presently a rusty dribble came out. I washed my hands as best I could and dried them on the tail of my shirt. Yet when I had finished, and was about to leave, I discovered a drop of blood between my fingers. I don't know where it came from. It may have been on the pullover, or even in my hair. The blood was thick by now, dark, and sticky. Nothing, not the stains in the car, the smears on the windows, not her cries, not even the smells of her dying, none of it affected me as did this drop of brownish gum. I plunged my fists under the tap again, whining in dismay, and scrubbed and scrubbed, but I could not get rid of it. The blood went, but something remained, all that long day I could feel it there, clinging in the fork of tender flesh between my fingers, a moist, warm, secret stain.

I am afraid to think what I have done.

For a while I sat on a broken bench on the platform in the sun. How blue the sea was, how gay the little flags fluttering and snapping on the hotel battlements. All was quiet, save for the sea-breeze crooning in the telegraph wires, and something some-where that creaked and knocked, creaked and knocked. I smiled. I might have been a child again, daydreaming here, in these toy surroundings. I could smell the sea, and the sea-wrack on the beach, and the cat-smell of the sand. A train was on the way, yes, a puff-puff, the rails were humming and shivering in anticipation. Not a soul to be seen, not a grown-up anywhere, except, away down the beach, a few felled sunbathers on their towels. I wonder why it was so deserted there? Perhaps it wasn't, perhaps there were seaside crowds all about, and I didn't notice, with my inveterate yearning towards backgrounds. I closed my eyes, and something swam up dreamily, a memory, an image, and sank again without breaking the surface. I tried to catch it before it was gone, but there was only that one glimpse: a doorway, I think, opening on to a darkened room, and a mysterious sense of expectancy, of something or someone about to appear. Then the train came through, a slow, rolling thunder that made my diaphragm shake. The passengers were propped up in the wide windows like manikins, they gazed at me blankly as they were borne slowly past. It occurred to me I should have turned my face away: everyone was a potential witness now. But I thought it did not matter. I thought I would be in jail within hours. I looked about me, taking great breaths, drinking my fill of the world that I would soon be losing. A gang of boys, three or four, had appeared in the grounds of the hotel. They straggled across the unkempt lawns, and stopped to throw stones at a for-sale sign. I rose, with a leaden sigh, and left the station and set off along the road again.

*

I took a bus into the city. It was a single-decker, on an infrequent route, coming from far out. The people on it all seemed to know each other. At each stop when someone got on there was much banter and friendly raillery. An old chap with a cap and a crutch was the self-appointed host of this little travelling club. He sat near the front, behind the driver, his stiff left leg stuck out into the aisle, and greeted each newcomer with a start of feigned surprise and a rattle of his crutch. Oh! watch out! here he comes! he would say, mugging at the rest of us over his shoulder, as if to alert us to the arrival of some terrible character, when what had appeared up the step was a ferret-faced young man with a greasy season-ticket protruding from his fist like a discoloured tongue. Girls provoked gallantries, which made them smirk, while for the housewives off to town to do their shopping there were winks and playful references to that stiff limb of his. Now and again he would let a glance slide over me, quick, tentative, a little queasy, like that of an old trouper spotting a creditor in the front row. It struck me, indeed, that there was something faintly theatrical about the whole thing. The rest of the passengers had the self-conscious nonchalance of a first-night audience. They too had a, part of sorts to play. Behind the chatter and the jokes and the easy familiarity they seemed worried, their eyes were full of uncertainty and tiredness, as if they had got the text by heart but still were not sure of their cues. I studied them with deep interest. I felt I had discovered something significant, though what it was, or what it signified, I was not sure. And I, what was I among them? A stage-hand, perhaps, standing in the wings envying the players.

When we reached town I could not decide where to get off, one place seemed as good as another. I must say something about the practicalities of my situation. I should have been shaking in fear. I had a five-pound note and some coins – mostly foreign – in my pocket, I looked, and smelled, like a tramp, and I had nowhere to go. I did not even have a credit card with which to bluff my way into a hotel. Yet I could not worry, could not make myself be concerned. I seemed to float, bemused, in a dreamy detachment, as if I had been given a great dose of local anaesthetic. Perhaps this is what it means to be in shock? No: I think it was just the certainty that at any moment a hand would grasp me by the shoulder while a terrible voice boomed out a caution. By now they would have my name, a description would be in circulation, hard-eyed men in bulging jackets would be cruising the streets on the look-out for me. That none of this was so is still a puzzle to me. The Behrenses must have known at once who it was that would take that particular picture, yet they said nothing. And what about the trail of evidence I left behind me? What about the people who saw me, the Recks, the señorita at the garage, the man in the hardware shop, that woman who looked like my mother who came upon me sitting like a loon at the traffic lights? Your lordship, I would not wish to encourage potential wrongdoers, but I must say, it is easier to get away with something, for a time at least, than is generally acknowledged.

Vital days – how easily one slips into the lingo! – *vital days* were to pass before they even began to know who it was they were after. If I had not continued to be as rash as I was at the start, if I had stopped and taken stock, and considered carefully, I believe I might not be here now, but in some sunnier clime, nursing my guilt under an open sky. But I did not stop, did not consider. I got off the bus and set off at once in the direction in which I happened to be facing, since my fate, I was convinced, awaited me all around, in the open arms of the law. Capture! I nursed the word in my heart. It comforted me. It was the promise of rest. I dodged along through the crowds like a drunk, surprised that they did not part before me in horror. All round me was an inferno of haste and noise. A gang of men stripped to the waist was gouging a hole in the road with pneumatic drills. The traffic snarled and bellowed, sunlight flashing like knives off the windshields and the throbbing roofs of cars. The air was a poisonous hot blue haze. I had become unused to cities. Yet I was aware that even as I struggled here I was simultaneously travelling smoothly forward in time, it seemed a kind of swimming without effort. Time, I thought grimly, time will save me. Here is Trinity, the Bank. Fox's, where my father used to come on an annual pilgrimage, with great ceremony, to buy his Christmas cigars. My world, and I an outcast in it. I felt a deep, dispassionate pity for myself, as for some poor lost wandering creature. The sun shone mercilessly, a fat eye stuck in the haze above the streets. I bought a bar of chocolate and devoured it, walking along. I bought an early edition of an evening paper, too, but there was nothing in it. I dropped it on the ground and shambled on. An urchin picked it up – Eh, mister! – and ran after me with it. I thanked him, and he grinned, and I almost burst into tears. I stood there, stalled, and looked about me blearily, a baffled hulk. People crowded past me, all faces and elbows. That was my lowest point, I think, that moment of helplessness and dull panic. I decided to give myself up. Why had I not thought of it before? The prospect was wonderfully seductive. I imagined myself being lifted tenderly

and carried through a succession of cool white rooms to a place
of calm and silence, of luxurious surrender.

In the end, instead, I went to Wally's pub.

*

It was shut. I did not understand. At first I thought wildly that it
must be something to do with me, that they had found out I had
been there and had closed it down. I pushed and pushed at the
door, and tried to see through the bottle-glass of the windows,
but all was dark inside. I stepped back. Next door there was a
tiny fashion boutique where a pair of pale girls, frail and blank as
flowers, stood motionless, staring at nothing, as if they were
themselves a part of the display. When I spoke they turned their
soot-rimmed eyes on me without interest. Holy hour, one said,
and the other giggled wanly. I retreated, simpering, and went to
the pub and pounded on the door with renewed force. After some
time there were dragging footsteps inside and the sound of locks
being undone. What do you want, Wally said crossly, blinking in
the harsh sunlight slanting down from the street. He was wearing
a purple silk dressing-gown and shapeless slippers. He looked me
up and down with distaste, noting the stubble and the filthy
pullover. I told him my car had broken down, I needed to make
a phonecall. He gave a sardonic snort and said, A phonecall! as if
it were the richest thing he'd heard in ages. He shrugged. It was
nearly opening time anyway. I followed him inside. His calves
were plump and white and hairless, I wondered where I had seen
others like them recently. He switched on a pink-shaded lamp
behind the bar. There's the phone, he said with a wave, pursing
his lips derisively. I asked if I could have a gin first. He sniffed,
his sceptic's heart gratified, and permitted himself a thin little
smile. Have a smash-up, did you? he said. For a second I did not
know what he was talking about. Oh, the car, I said, no, no it
just – stopped. And I thought, with bleak amusement: There's
the first question answered and I haven't lied. He turned away to
make my drink, priest-like in his purple robe, then set it before

me and propped himself on the edge of his stool with his fat arms folded. He knew I had been up to something, I could see it from the look in his eye, at once eager and disdainful, but he could not bring himself to ask. I grinned at him and drank my drink, and gleaned a grain of enjoyment from his dilemma. I said it was a good idea, wasn't it, the siesta. He raised an eyebrow. I pointed a finger at his dressing-gown. A nap, I said, in the middle of the day: good idea. He did not think that was funny. From somewhere in the shadowy reaches behind me a tousle-haired young man appeared, clad only in a drooping pair of underpants. He gave me a bored glance and asked Wally if the paper was in yet. Here, I said, take mine, go ahead. I must have been twisting it in my hands, it was rolled into a tight baton. He prised it open and read the headlines, his lips moving. Fucking bombers, he said, fucking lunatics. Wally had fixed him with a terrible glare. He threw the paper aside and wandered off, scratching his rump. I held out my glass for a refill. We still charge for drinks, you know, Wally said. We'll accept money. I gave him my last fiver. A thin blade of light had got in through a chink in a shutter somewhere and stood at a slant beside me, embedded in the floor. I watched Wally's plump back as he refilled my glass. I wondered if I might tell him what I had done. It seemed perfectly possible. Nothing, I told myself, nothing shocks Wally, after all. I could almost believe it. I imagined him looking at me with a twist of the mouth and one eyebrow arched, trying not to leer as I recounted my horrid tale. The thought of confessing gave me a little lift, it was so splendidly irresponsible. It made the whole thing seem no more than a spot of high jinks, a jape that had gone wrong. I chuckled mournfully into my glass. You look like shit, Wally said complacently. I asked for another gin, a double this time.

Distinctly in my head her voice again said: Don't.

The boy with the curls came back, now wearing tight jeans and a shiny tight green shirt. He was called Sonny. Wally left him in charge of the bar and waddled off to his quarters, his dressing-gown billowing behind him. Sonny poured a generous measure of crème de menthe into a tumbler and filled it up with ice cubes, then perched himself on the stool, squirming his narrow little nates, and examined me without much enthusiasm. You're new, he said, making it sound like an accusation. No I'm not, I said, you are, and I smirked, pleased with myself. He made a wide-eyed face. Well excuse me, he said, I'm sure. Wally came back, dressed and coiffed and reeking of pomade. I had another double. My face was growing taut, it felt like a mud mask. I had reached that stage of inebriation where everything was settling into another version of reality. It seemed not drunkenness, but a form of enlightenment, almost a sobering-up. A crowd of theatre people came in, prancing and squawking. They looked at my appearance and then at each other, brimming with merriment. Talk about rough trade, one said, and Sonny tittered. And I thought, that's what I'll do, I'll get one of them to take me home and hide me, Lady Macbeth there with the mascara and the blood-red nails, or that laughing fellow in the harlequin shirt – why not? Yes, that's what I should do, I should live henceforth among actors, practise among them, study their craft, the grand gesture and the fine nuance. Perhaps in time I would learn to play my part sufficiently well, with enough conviction, to take my place among the others, the naturals, those people on the bus, and all the rest of them.

It was only when Charlie French came in that I realised it was for him I had been waiting. Good old Charlie. My heart flooded with fondness, I felt like embracing him. He was in his chalkstripes, carrying a battered, important-looking briefcase. Although he had seen me three days ago he tried at first not to know me. Or perhaps he really didn't recognise me, in my dishevelled, wild-eyed state. He said he had thought I was going down to Coolgrange. I said I had been there, and he asked after my mother. I told him about her stroke. I laid it on a bit, I think – I may even have shed a tear. He nodded, looking past my left ear and jingling the coins in his trouser pocket. There was a pause, during which I snuffled and sighed. So, he said brightly, you're off on your travels again, are you? I shrugged. His car's broke down, isn't it, Wally said, and expelled an unpleasant little chuckle. Charlie assumed a sympathetic frown. Is that right? he said slowly, with a dreamy lack of emphasis. The crowd of actors behind us suddenly shrieked, so piercingly that glasses chimed, but he might not have heard them, he did not even blink. He had perfected a pose for places and occasions such as this, by which he managed to be at once here and not here. He stood very straight, his black brogues planted firmly together and his briefcase leaning against his leg, with one fist on the bar – oh, I can see him! – and the other hand holding his whiskey glass suspended halfway to his lips, just as if he had stumbled in here by mistake and was too much the gentleman to cut and run before partaking of a snifter and exchanging a few civilities with the frantic denizens of the place. He could maintain this air of being just about to leave throughout a whole night's drinking. Oh yes, Charlie could act them all into a cocked hat.

The more I drank the fonder I became of him, especially as he kept paying for gins as fast as I could drink them. But it was not just that. I was – I am – genuinely fond of him, I think I have said so already. Did I mention that he got me my job at the Institute? We had kept in touch during my years in college – or at least *he* had kept in touch with *me*. He liked to think of himself as the wise old family friend watching over with an avuncular eye the brilliant only son of the house. He took me out for treats. There were teas at the Hibernian, the odd jaunt to the Curragh, the dinner at Jammet's every year on my birthday. They never quite worked, these occasions, they smacked too much of contrivance. I was always afraid that someone would see me with him, and while I squirmed and scowled he would sink into a state of restless melancholy. When we were ready to part there would be a sudden burst of hearty chatter which was nothing but relief badly disguised, then we would each turn and slink away guiltily. Yet he was not deterred, and the day after my return with Daphne from America he took me for a drink in the Shelbourne and suggested that, as he put it, I might like to give the chaps at the Institute a hand. I was still feeling groggy – we had made a hideous winter crossing, on what was hardly more than a tramp steamer – and he was so diffident, and employed such elaborate depreciations, that it was a while before I realised he was offering me a job. The work, he assured me hurriedly, would be right up my street – hardly work at all, and to such as I, he fancied, more a form of play – the money was decent, the prospects were limitless. I knew at once, of course, from his suppliant, doggy manner, that all this was at my mother's prompting. Well, he said, showing his big yellow teeth in a strained smile, what do you think? First I was annoyed, then amused. I thought: why not?

If the court pleases, I shall skim lightly over this period of my life. It is a time that is still a source of vague unease in my mind, I cannot say why, exactly. I have the feeling of having done something ridiculous by taking that job. It was unworthy of me, of course, of my talent, but that is not the whole source of my sense of humiliation. Perhaps that was the moment in my life at which – but what am I saying, there are no moments, I've said that already. There is just the ceaseless, slow, demented drift of things. If I had any lingering doubts of that the Institute extinguished them finally. It was housed in a great grey stone building from the last century which always reminded me, with its sheer flanks, its buttresses and curlicues and blackened smoke-stacks, of a grand, antiquated ocean liner. No one knew what exactly it was we were expected to achieve. We did statistical surveys, and produced thick reports bristling with graphs and flow-charts and complex appendices, which the government received with grave words of praise and then promptly forgot about. The director was a large, frantic man who sucked fiercely on an enormous black pipe and had a tic in one eye and tufts of hair sprouting from his ears. He plunged about the place, always on his way elsewhere. All queries and requests he greeted with a harsh, doomed laugh. Try that on the Minister! he would cry over his shoulder as he strode off, emitting thick gusts of smoke and sparks in his wake. Inevitably there was a high incidence of looniness among the staff. Finding themselves with no fixed duties, people embarked furtively on projects of their own. There was an economist, a tall, emaciated person with a greenish face and unruly hair, who was devising a foolproof system for betting on the horses. He offered one day to let me in on it, clutching my wrist in a trembling claw and hissing urgently into my ear, but then something happened, I don't know what, he grew suspicious, and in the end would not speak to me, and avoided me in the corridors. This was awkward, for he was one of a select band of savants with whom I had to treat in order to gain access to the computer. This machine was at the centre of all our activities. Time on it was strictly rationed, and to get an uninterrupted hour at it was a rare privilege. It ran all day and through the night, whirring and crunching in its vast white room in the basement. At night it was tended by a mysterious and sinister trio, a war criminal, I think, and two strange boys, one with a damaged face. Three years I spent there. I was not violently unhappy. I just felt, and feel, as I say, a little ridiculous, a little embarrassed. And I never quite forgave Charlie French.

*

It was late when we left the pub. The night was made of glass. I was very drunk. Charlie helped me along. He was worrying about his briefcase, and clutched it tightly under his arm. Every few yards I had to stop and tell him how good he was. No, I said, holding up a hand commandingly, no, I want to say it, you're a good man, Charles, a good man. I wept copiously, of course, and retched drily a few times. It was all a sort of glorious, grief-stricken, staggering rapture. I remembered that Charlie lived with his mother, and wept for that, too. But how is she, I shouted sorrowfully, tell me, Charlie, how is she, that sainted woman? He would not answer, pretended not to hear, but I kept at it and at last he shook his head irritably and said, She's dead! I tried to embrace him, but he walked away from me. We came upon a hole in the street with a cordon of red and white plastic ribbon around it. The ribbon shivered and clicked in the breeze. It's where the bomb in the car went off yesterday, Charlie said. Yesterday! I laughed and laughed, and knelt on the road at the edge of the hole, laughing, with my face in my hands. Yesterday, the last day of the old world. Wait, Charlie said, I'll get a taxi. He went off, and I knelt there, rocking back and forth and crooning softly, as if I were a child I was holding in my arms. I was tired. It had been a long day. I had come far.

I woke in splintered sunlight with a shriek fading in my ears. Big sagging bed, brown walls, a smell of damp. I thought I must be at Coolgrange, in my parents' room. For a moment I lay without moving, staring at sliding waterlights on the ceiling. Then I remembered, and I shut my eyes tight and hid my head in my arms. The darkness drummed. I got up and dragged myself to the window, and stood amazed at the blue innocence of sea and sky. Far out in the bay white sailboats were tacking into the wind. Below the window was a little stone harbour, and beyond that the curve of the coast road. An enormous seagull appeared and flung itself on flailing pinions at the glass, shrieking. They must think you are Mammy, Charlie said behind me. He was standing in the doorway. He wore a soiled apron, and held a frying-pan in his hand. The gulls, he said, she used to feed them. At his back a white, impenetrable glare. This was the world I must live in from now on, in this searing, inescapable light. I looked at myself and found I was naked.

*

I sat in the vast kitchen, under a vast, grimy window, and watched Charlie making breakfast in a cloud of fat-smoke. He did not look too good in daylight, he was hollow and grey, with flakes of dried shaving soap on his jaw and bruised bags under his phlegm-coloured eyes. Besides the apron he wore a woollen cardigan over a soiled string vest, and sagging flannel trousers. Used to wait till I was gone, he said, then throw the food out the window. He shook his head and laughed. A terrible woman, he said, terrible. He brought a plate of rashers and fried bread and a swimming egg and set it town in front of me. There, he said, only thing for

118

a sore head. I looked up at him quickly. *A sore head?* Had I blurted something out to him last night, some drunken confession? But no, Charlie would not make that kind of joke. He went back to the stove and lit a cigarette, fumbling with the matches.

Look, Charlie, I said, I may as well tell you, I've got into a bit of a scrape.

I thought at first he had not heard me. He went slack, and a dreamy vacancy came over him, his mouth open and drooping a little on one side and his eyebrows mildly lifted. Then I realised that he was being tactful. Well, if he didn't want to know, that was all right. But I wish to have it in the record, m'lud, that I would have told him, if he had been prepared to listen. As it was I merely let a silence pass, and then asked if I might borrow a razor, and perhaps a shirt and tie. Of course, he said, of course, but he would not look me in the eye. In fact, he had not looked at me at all since I got up, but edged around me with averted gaze, busying himself with the teapot and the pan, as if afraid that if he paused some awful awkward thing would arise which he would not know how to deal with. He suspected something, I suppose. He was no fool. (Or not a great fool, anyway.) But I think too it was simply that he did not quite know how to accommodate my presence. He fidgeted, moving things about, putting things away in drawers and cupboards and then taking them out again, murmuring to himself distractedly. People did not come often to this house. Some of the weepy regard I had felt for him last night returned. He seemed almost maternal, in his apron and his old felt slippers. He would take care of me. I gulped my tea and gloomed at my untouched fry congealing on its plate. A car-horn tooted outside, and Charlie with an exclamation whipped off his apron and hurried out of the kitchen. I listened to him blundering about the house. In a surprisingly short time he appeared again, in his suit, with his briefcase under his arm, and sporting a raffish little hat that made him look like a harassed bookie. Where are you based, he said, frowning at a spot beside my left shoulder, Coolgrange, or—? I said nothing, only looked at him appealingly, and he said, Ah, and nodded slowly, and slowly withdrew. Suddenly, though, I did not want him to go – alone, I would be alone! – and I rushed after him and made him come back and tell me how the stove worked, and where to find a key, and what to say if the milkman called. He was puzzled by my vehemence, I could see, and faintly alarmed. I followed him into the hall, and was still talking to him as he backed out the front-door, nodding at me warily, with a fixed smile, as if I were – ha! I was going to say, a dangerous criminal. I scampered up the stairs to the bedroom, and watched as he came out on the footpath below, a clownishly foreshortened figure in his hat and his baggy suit. A large black car was waiting at the kerb, its twin exhaust pipes discreetly puffing a pale-blue mist. The driver, a burly, dark-suited fellow with no neck, hopped out smartly and held open the rear door. Charlie looked up at the window where I stood, and the driver followed his glance. I saw myself as they would see me, a blurred face floating behind the glass, blear-eyed, unshaven, the very picture of a fugitive. The car slid away smoothly and passed along the harbour road and turned a corner and was gone. I did not stir. I wanted to stay like this, with my forehead against the glass and the summer day all out there before me. How quaint it all seemed, the white-tipped sea, and the white and pink houses, and the blurred headland in the distance, quaint and happy, like a little toy world laid out in a shop window. I closed my eyes, and again that fragment of memory swam up out of the depths – the doorway, and the darkened room, and the sense of something imminent – but this time it seemed to be not my own past I was remembering.

The silence was swelling like a tumour at my back.

Hurriedly I fetched my plate with the fried egg and greying rashers from the kitchen, taking the stairs three at a time, and came back and opened the window and clambered on to the narrow, wrought-iron balcony outside. A strong, warm wind was blowing, it startled me, and left me breathless for a moment. I picked up the pieces of food and flung them into the air, and watched the gulls swooping after the rich tidbits, crying harshly in surprise and greed. From behind the headland a white ship glided soundlessly into view, shimmering in the haze. When the food was gone I threw the plate away too, I don't know why, skimmed it like a discus out over the road and the harbour wall. It slid into the water with hardly a splash. There were strings of lukewarm fat between my fingers and egg-yolk under my nails. I climbed back into the room and wiped my hands on the bed-clothes, my heart pounding in excitement and disgust. I did not know what I was doing, or what I would do next. I did not know myself. I had become a stranger, unpredictable and dangerous.

I explored the house. I had never been here before. It was a great, gaunt, shadowy place with dark drapes and big brown furniture and bald spots in the carpets. It was not exactly dirty, but there was a sense of staleness, of things left standing for too long in the same spot, and the air had a grey, dull feel to it, as if a vital essence in it had been used up long ago. There was a smell of must and stewed tea and old newspapers, and, everywhere, a flattish, faintly sweet something which I took to be the afterglow of Mammy French. I suppose there will be guffaws if I say I am a fastidious man, but it's true. I was already in some distress before I started poking among Charlie's things, and I feared what I might find. His sad little secrets were no nastier than mine, or anyone else's, yet when here and there I turned over a stone and they came scuttling out, I shivered, and was ashamed for him and for myself. I steeled myself, though, and persevered, and was rewarded in the end. There was a rolltop desk in his bedroom, which took me ten minutes of hard work with a kitchen knife to unlock, squatting on my heels and sweating beads of pure alcohol. Inside I found some banknotes and a plastic wallet of credit cards. There were letters, too – from my mother, of all people, written thirty, forty years before. I did not read them, I don't know why, but put them back reverently, along with the credit cards, and even the cash, and locked the desk again. As I was going out I exchanged a shamefaced little grin with my reflection in the wardrobe mirror. That German, what's his name, was right: money is abstract happiness.

The bathroom was on the first-floor return, a sort of wooden lean-to with a gas geyser and a gigantic, clawfooted bath. I crouched over the handbasin and scraped off two days' growth of stubble with Charlie's soap-encrusted razor. I had thought of growing a beard, for disguise, but I had lost enough of myself already, I did not want my face to disappear as well. The shaving-glass had a concave, silvery surface in which my magnified features – a broad, pitted jaw, one black nose-hole with hairs, a single, rolling eyeball – bobbed and swayed alarmingly, like things looming in the window of a bathysphere. When I had finished I got into the tub and lay with my eyes shut while the water cascaded down on me from the geyser. It was good, at once a solace and a scalding chastisement, if the gas had not eventually gone out I might have stayed there all day, lost to myself and everything else in that roaring, tombal darkness. When I opened my eyes tiny stars were whizzing and popping in front of me. I padded, dripping, into Charlie's room, and spent a long time deciding what to wear. In the end I chose a dark-blue silk shirt and a somewhat louche, flowered bow-tie to go with it. Black socks, of course – silk again: Charlie is not one to stint himself – and a pair of dark trousers, baggy but well cut, of a style which was antique enough to have come back into fashion. For the present I would do without underwear: even a killer on the run has his principles, and mine precluded getting into another man's drawers. My own clothes – how odd they looked, thrown on the bedroom floor, as if waiting to be outlined in chalk – I gathered in a bundle, and with my face averted carried them to the kitchen and stuffed them into a plastic garbage bag. Then I washed and dried the breakfast things, and was standing in the middle of the floor with a soiled tea-towel in my hand when the image of her bloodied face shot up in front of me like something in a fairground stall, and I had to sit down, winded and shaking. For I kept forgetting, you see, forgetting all about it, for quite long periods. I suppose my mind needed respite, in order to cope. Wearily I looked about the big dank kitchen. I wondered if Charlie would notice there was a plate missing. Why did I throw it into the sea, why did I do that? It was not yet noon. Time opened its black maw in my face. I went into one of the front rooms – net curtains, vast dining-table, a stuffed owl under glass – and stood at the window looking out at the sea. All that blue out there was daunting. I paced the floor, stopped, stood listening, my heart in my mouth. What did I expect to hear? There was nothing, only the distant noise of other lives, a tiny ticking and plinking, like the noise of an engine cooling down. I remembered days like this in my childhood, strange, empty days when I would wander softly about the silent house and seem to myself a kind of ghost, hardly there at all, a memory, a shadow of some more solid version of myself living, oh, living marvellously, elsewhere.

I must stop. I'm sick of myself, all this.

Time. The days.

Go on, go on.

*

Disgust, now, that is something I know about. Let me say a word or two about disgust. Here I sit, naked under my prison garb, wads of pallid flesh trussed and bagged like badly packaged meat. I get up and walk around on my hind legs, a belted animal, shedding an invisible snow of scurf everywhere I move. Mites live on me, they lap my sweat, stick their snouts into my pores and gobble up the glop they find there. Then the split skin, the cracks, the crevices. Hair: just think of hair. And this is only the surface. Imagine what is going on inside, the purple pump shuddering and squelching, lungs fluttering, and, down in the dark, the glue factory at its ceaseless work. Animate carrion, slick with gleet, not ripe enough yet for the worms. Ach, I should—

Calm, Frederick. Calm.

*

My wife came to see me today. This is not unusual, she comes every week. As a remand prisoner I have the right to unrestricted visiting, but I have not told her this, and if she knows it she has said nothing. We prefer it this way. Even at its most uneventful the Thursday visiting hour is a bizarre, not to say uncanny ritual. It is conducted in a large, square, lofty room with small windows set high up under the ceiling. A partition of plywood and glass, an ugly contraption, separates us from our loved ones, with whom we converse as best we can by way of a disinfected plastic grille. This state of virtual quarantine is a recent imposition. It is meant to keep out drugs, we're told, but I think it is really a way of keeping *in* those interesting viruses which lately we have begun to incubate in here. The room has a touch of the aquarium about it, with that wall of greenish glass, and the tall light drifting down from above, and the voices that come to us out of the plastic lattices as if bubbled through water. We inmates sit with shoulders hunched, leaning grimly on folded arms, wan, bloated, vague-eyed, like unhoused crustaceans crouching at the bottom of a tank. Our visitors exist in a different element from ours, they seem more sharply defined than we, more intensely present in their world. Sometimes we catch a look in their eyes, a mixture of curiosity and compassion, and faint repugnance, too, which strikes us to the heart. They must feel the force of our longing, must hear it, almost, the mermen's song, a high needle-note of pure woe buzzing in the glass that separates us from them. Their concern for our plight is not a comfort, but distresses us, rather. This is the tenderest time of our week, we desire tranquillity, decorum, muted voices. We are constantly on edge, worried that someone's wife or girlfriend out there will make a scene, jump up and shout, pound her fists on the partition, weep. When such a thing does happen it is awful, just awful, and afterwards the one that it happened to is an object of sympathy and awe amongst us, as if he had suffered a bereavement.

No fear of Daphne making a scene. She maintains an admirable poise at all times. Today, for instance, when she told me about the child, she spoke quietly, looking away from me with her usual air of faint abstraction. I confess I was annoyed at her, I couldn't hide it. She should have told me she was having him tested, instead of just presenting me with the diagnosis out of the blue like this. She gave me a quizzical look, tilting her head to one side and almost smiling. Are you surprised? she said. I turned my face away crossly and did not answer. Of course I was not surprised. I knew there was something wrong with him, I always knew – I told her so, long before she was ready to admit it. From the start there was the way he moved, warily, quaking, on his scrawny little legs, as if trying not to drop some large, unmanageable thing that had been dumped into his arms, looking up at us in bewilderment and supplication, like a creature looking up out of a hole in the ground. Where did you take him, I said, what hospital, what did they say exactly? She shrugged. They were very nice, she said, very sympathetic. The doctor talked to her for a long time. It is a very rare condition, somebody's syndrome, I have forgotten the name already, some damn Swiss or Swede – what does it matter. He will never speak properly. He'll never do anything properly, it seems. There is something wrong with his brain, something is missing, some vital bit. She explained it all to me, repeating what the doctor told her, but I was only half-listening. A sort of weariness had come over me, a sort of lethargy. Van is his name, have I mentioned that? Van. He's seven. When I get out he will probably be, what, thirty-something? Jesus, almost as old as I am now. A big child, that's what the country people will call him, not without fondness, at Coolgrange. A big child.

*

I will not, I will not weep. If I start now I'll never stop.

*

In the afternoon I broke into Charlie's desk again, and took some cash and ventured out to the newsagent's on the harbour. What a strange, hot thrill of excitement I felt, stepping into the shop, my stomach wobbled, and I seemed to be treading slowly through some thick, resistant medium. I think a part of me hoped – no, expected – that somehow I would be saved, that as in a fairy tale everything would be magically reversed, that the wicked witch would disappear, that the spell would be lifted, that the maid would wake from her enchanted sleep. And when I picked up the papers it seemed for a moment as if some magic had indeed been worked, for at first I could see nothing in them except more stuff about the bombing and its aftermath. I bought three mornings, and an early-evening edition, noting (is this only hindsight?) the hard look that the pimpled girl behind the counter gave me. Then I hurried back to the house, my heart going at a gallop, as if it were some choice erotica I was clutching under my arm. Indoors again, I left the papers on the kitchen-table and ran to the bathroom, where in my agitation I managed to pee on my foot. After a lengthy, feverish search I found a quarter-full bottle of gin and took a good slug from the neck. I tried to find something else to do, but it was no good, and with leaden steps I returned to the kitchen and sat down slowly at the table and spread out the papers in front of me. There it was, a few paragraphs in one of the mornings, squeezed under a photograph of a bandaged survivor of the bombing sitting up in a hospital bed. In the evening edition there was a bigger story, with a photograph of the boys I had seen playing in the hotel grounds. It was they who had found her. There was a photograph of her, too, gazing out solemn-eyed from a blurred background, it must have been lifted from a group shot of a wedding, or a dance, she was wearing a long, ugly dress with an elaborate collar, and was clutching something, flowers, perhaps, in her hands. Her name was Josephine Bell. There was more inside, a file picture of Behrens and a view of Whitewater House, and an article on the Behrens collection, littered with mis-spellings and garbled dates. A reporter had been sent down to the country to talk to Mrs Brigid Bell, the mother. She was a widow. There was a photograph of her standing awkwardly in front of her cottage, a big, raw-faced woman in an apron and an old cardigan, peering at the camera in a kind of stolid dismay. Her Josie, she said, was a good girl, a decent girl, why would anyone want to kill her. And suddenly I was back there, I saw her sitting in the mess of her own blood, looking at me, a bleb of pink spittle bursting on her lips. *Mammy* was what she said, that was the word, not Tommy, I've just this moment realised it. *Mammy*, and then: *Love*.

I THINK THE TIME I spent in Charlie French's house was the strangest period of my life, stranger even and more disorienting than my first days here. I felt, in the brownish gloom of those rooms, with all that glistening marine light outside, as if I were suspended somehow in mid-air, in a sealed flask, cut off from everything. Time was split in two: there was clock time, which moved with giant slowness, and then there was that fevered rush inside my head, as if the mainspring had broken and all the works were spinning madly out of control. I did sentry-go up and down the kitchen for what seemed hours on end, shoulders hunched and hands stuck in my pockets, furiously plotting, unaware how the distance between turns was steadily decreasing, until in the end I would find myself at a shuddering stop, glaring about me in bafflement, like an animal that had blundered into a net. I would stand in the big bedroom upstairs, beside the window, with my back pressed to the wall, watching the road, for so long, sometimes, that I forgot what it was I was supposed to be watching for. There was little traffic in this backwater, and I soon got to recognise the regular passers-by, the girl with the orange hair from the flat in the house next door, the smooth, shady-looking fellow with the salesman's sample-case, the few old bodies who walked their pugs or shuffled to the shops at the same hour every day. Anyway, there would be no mistaking the others, the grim ones, when they came for me. Probably I would not even see them coming. They would surround the house, and kick in the door, and that would be the first I would know of it. But still I stood there, watching and watching, more like a pining lover than a man on the run.

Everything was changed, everything. I was estranged from

myself and all that I had once supposed I was. My life up to now had only the weightless density of a dream. When I thought about my past it was like thinking of what someone else had been, someone I had never met but whose history I knew by heart. It all seemed no more than a vivid fiction. Nor was the present any more solid. I felt light-headed, volatile, poised at an angle to everything. The ground under me was stretched tight as a trampoline, I must keep still for fear of unexpected surges, dangerous leaps and bounces. And all around me was this blue and empty air.

I could not think directly about what I had done. It would have been like trying to stare steadily into a blinding light. It was too big, too bright, to contemplate. It was incomprehensible. Even still, when I say *I did it*, I am not sure I know what I mean. Oh, do not mistake me. I have no wish to vacillate, to hum and haw and kick dead leaves over the evidence. I killed her, I admit it freely. And I know that if I were back there today I would do it again, not because I would want to, but because I would have no choice. It would be just as it was then, this spider, and this moonlight between the trees, and all, all the rest of it. Nor can I say I did not mean to kill her – only, I am not clear as to when I began to mean it. I was flustered, impatient, angry, she attacked me, I swiped at her, the swipe became a blow, which became the prelude to a second blow – its apogee, so to speak, or perhaps I mean perigee – and so on. There is no moment in this process of which I can confidently say, there, that is when I decided she should die. Decided? – I do not think it was a matter of deciding. I do not think it was a matter of thinking, even. That fat monster inside me just saw his chance and leaped out, frothing and flailing. He had scores to settle with the world, and she, at that moment, was world enough for him. I could not stop him. Or could I? He is me, after all, and I am he. But no, things were too far gone for stopping. Perhaps that is the essence of my crime, of my culpability, that I let things get to that stage, that I had not been vigilant enough, had not been enough of a dissembler, that I left Bunter to his own devices, and thus allowed him, fatally, to understand that he was free, that the cage door was open, that nothing was forbidden, that everything was possible.

After my first appearance in court the newspapers said I showed no sign of remorse when the charges were read out. (What did they expect, that I would weep, rend my garments?) They were on to something, in their dimwitted way. Remorse implies the expectation of forgiveness, and I knew that what I had done was unforgivable. I could have feigned regret and sorrow, guilt, all that, but to what end? Even if I had felt such things, truly, in the deepest depths of my heart, would it have altered anything? The deed was done, and would not be cancelled by cries of anguish and repentance. Done, yes, finished, as nothing ever before in my life had been finished and done – and yet there would be no end to it, I saw that straight away. I was, I told myself, responsible, with all the weight that word implied. In killing Josie Bell I had destroyed a part of the world. Those hammer-blows had shattered a complex of memories and sensations and possibilities – a life, in short – which was irreplaceable, but which, somehow, must be replaced. For the crime of murder I would be caught and put away, I knew this with the calmness and certainty which only an irrelevance could inspire, and then they would say I had paid my debt, in the belief that by walling me up alive they had struck a sort of balance. They would be right, according to the laws of retribution and revenge: such balance, however, would be at best a negative thing. No, no. What was required was not my symbolic death – I recognised this, though I did not understand what it meant – but for her to be brought back to life. That, and nothing less.

*

That evening when Charlie returned he put his head cautiously around the door as if he feared there might be a bucket of water balanced on it. I leered at him, swaying. I had finished the gin, and moved on, reluctantly, to whiskey. I was not drunk, exactly, but in a kind of numbed euphoria, as if I had just come back from a lengthy and exquisitely agonising visit to the dentist.

Under the new buzz the old hangover lurked, biding its time. My skin was hot and dry all over, and my eyes felt scorched. Cheers! I cried, with a fatuous laugh, and the ice cubes chuckled in my glass. Charlie was darting sidelong looks at my outfit. Hope you don't mind, I said. Didn't think we'd be the same size. Ah, he said, yes, well, I've shrunk in my old age, you see. And he gave a graveyard laugh. I could see he had been hoping I would be gone when he came home. I followed him out to the hall, where he took off his bookie's titfer and put it with his briefcase on the bog-oak hallstand. He went into the dining-room and poured himself a modest whiskey, adding a go of flattish soda from a screw-top bottle. He took a sip, and stood for a little while as if stalled, with a hand in his pocket, frowning at his feet. My presence was interfering with his evening rituals. He put away the whiskey bottle without offering me a refill. We traipsed back to the kitchen, where Charles donned his apron and rooted about in cupboards and on murky shelves for the makings of a stew. While he worked he talked distractedly over his shoulder, with a cigarette hanging from a corner of his lopsided mouth and one eye screwed shut against the smoke. He was telling me about a sale he had made, or a picture he had bought, or something like that. I think he only spoke for fear of the prospect of silence. Anyway I was not really listening. I watched him glugging the better half of a fifty-pound bottle of Pommerol into the stew. An inch of cigarette ash went into the pot as well, he tried vainly to fish it out with a spoon, clucking in annoyance. You can imagine what it's like for me, he said, actually parting with pictures! I nodded solemnly. In fact, what I was imagining was Charlie in his poky gallery, bowing and scraping and wringing his hands in front of some fur-coated bitch reeking of face-powder and perspiration, whose hubby had given her the money to bag a bauble for her birthday. I was depressed suddenly, and suddenly tired.

He served up the stew, spilling some on the floor. He was not good with implements, they tended to turn treacherous in his hands, to wobble and veer and let things slither off. We carried our plates into the dining-room and sat down at the table under the stuffed owl's virulent, glassy stare. We drank the rest of the Pommerol, and Charles fetched another bottle. He continued to make an elaborate business of avoiding my eye, smiling about him at the floor, the furniture, the fire-irons in the grate, as if the commonplace had suddenly presented itself to his attention with a new and unexpected charm. The lowering sun was shining full upon me through the tall window at my back. The stew tasted of burnt fur. I pushed my plate aside and turned and looked out at the harbour. There was a shimmering flaw in the window-pane. Something made me think of California, something about the light, the little yachts, the gilded evening sea. I was so tired, so tired, I could have given up then and there, could have drifted out into that summer dusk as easily as a breeze, unknown, planless, free. Charlie squashed out a sodden fag-end on the rim of his plate. Did you see that thing about Binkie Behrens in the paper? he said. I poured myself another fill of wine. No, I said, what was that, Charles?

By the by, what would I have done in all this affair without the solace of drink and its deadening effect? I seem to have got over those days in a series of quaking lunges from one brief state of drunken equilibrium to another, like a fugitive fleeing across a zigzag of slimed stepping-stones. Even the colours, gin-blue and claret-red, are they not the very emblems of my case, the court-colours of my testimony? Now that I have sobered up forever I look back not only on that time but on all my life as a sort of tipsy but not particularly happy spree, from which I knew I would have to emerge sooner or later, with a bad headache. This, ah yes, this is hangover time with a vengeance.

The rest of that evening, as I recall it, was a succession of distinct, muffled shocks, like falling downstairs slowly in a dream. That was when I learned that my father had kept a mistress. I was first astonished, then indignant. I had been his alibi, his camouflage! While I sat for hours in the back of the car above the yacht club in Dun Laoghaire on Sunday afternoons, he was off fucking his fancy-woman. Penelope was her name – Penelope, for God's sake! Where did they meet, I wanted to know, was there a secret love-nest where he kept her, a bijou little hideaway with roses round the door and a mirror on the bedroom ceiling? Charlie shrugged. Oh, he said, they used to come here. At first I could not take it in. Here? I cried. Here? But what about—? He shrugged again, and gave a sort of grin. Mammy French, it seems, did not mind. On occasion she even had the lovers join her for tea. She and Penelope exchanged knitting patterns. You see, she knew – Charlie said, but stopped, and a spot of colour appeared in the cracked skin over each cheekbone, and he ran a finger quickly around the inside of his shirt collar. I waited. She knew I was fond of your – of Dolly, he said at last. By now I was fairly reeling. Before I could speak he went on to tell me how Binkie Behrens too had been after my mother, how he would invite her and my father to Whitewater and ply my father with drink so he would not notice Binkie's gamy eye and wandering hands. And then my mother would come and tell Charlie all about it, and they would laugh together. Now he shook his head and sighed. Poor Binkie, he said. I sat aghast, lost in wonderment and trying to hold my wine-glass straight. I felt like a child hearing for the first time of the doings of the gods: they crowded in my buzzing head, these tremendous, archaic, flawed figures with their plots and rivalries and impossible loves. Charlie was so matter-of-fact about it all, half wistful and half amused. He spoke mostly as if I were not there, looking up now and then in mild surprise at my squeaks and snorts of astonishment. And you, I said, what about you and my—? I could not put it into words. He gave me a look at once arch and sly.

Here, he said, finish the bottle.

I think he told me something more about my mother, but I don't remember what it was. I do remember phoning her later that night, sitting cross-legged in the dark on the floor in the hall, with tears in my eyes and the telephone squatting in my lap like a frog. She seemed immensely far away, a miniature voice booming at me tinily out of a thrumming void. Freddie, she said, you're drunk. She asked why had I not come back, to collect my bag if for nothing else. I wanted to say to her, Mother, how could

I go home, now? We were silent for a moment, then she said Daphne had called her, wondering where I was, what I was doing. Daphne! I had not thought of her for days. Through the doorway at the end of the hall I watched Charlie pottering about in the kitchen, rattling the pots and pans and pretending he was not trying to hear what I was saying. I sighed, and the sigh turned into a thin little moan. Ma, I said, I've got myself into such trouble. There was a noise on the line, or maybe it was in my head, like a great rushing of many wings. What? she said, I can't hear you – what? I laughed, and two big tears ran down the sides of my nose. Nothing, I shouted, nothing, forget it! Then I said, Listen, do you know who Penelope is – was – do you know about her? I was shocked at myself. Why did I say such a thing, why did I want to wound her? She was silent for a moment, and then she laughed. That bitch? she said, of course I knew about her. Charlie had come to the doorway, and stood, with a rag in one hand and a plate in the other, watching me. The light was behind him, I could not see his face. There was another pause. You're too hard on yourself, Freddie, my mother said at last, in that reverberant, faraway voice, you make things too hard on yourself. I did not know what she meant. I still don't. I waited a moment, but she said nothing more, and I could not speak. Those were the last words we would ever exchange. I put down the receiver gently, and got to my feet, not without difficulty. One of my knees was asleep. I limped into the kitchen. Charlie was bent over the sink doing the washing-up, with a cigarette dangling from his lip, sleeves rolled, his waistcoat unbuckled at the back. The sky in the window in front of him was a pale shade of indigo, I thought I had never seen anything so lovely in my life.

Charlie, I said, swaying, I need a loan.

I had always been a weeper, but now any hint of kindness could make me blub like a babe. When there and then he sat down at the kitchen table and wrote out a cheque – I have it still: spidery black scrawl, an illegible signature, a stewy thumb-print in one corner – I tried to seize his liver-spotted hand, I think I meant to kiss it. He made a little speech, I don't remember it well. My mother figured in it, Daphne too. I think even Penelope's name was mentioned. I wonder if he was drunk? He kept looming into focus and fading out again, yet I felt this was less an effect of my blurred vision than of a sort of tentativeness on his part. Oh, Charlie, you should have heeded that niggle of suspicion, you should have thrown me out that night, fuddled and defenceless though I was.

The next thing I recall is being on my knees in the lavatory, puking up a ferruginous torrent of wine mixed with fibrous strands of meat and bits of carrot. The look of this stuff gushing out filled me with wonder, as if it were not vomit, but something rich and strange, a dark stream of ore from the deep mine of my innards. Then there is an impression of everything swaying, of glistening darkness and things in it spinning past me, as though I were being whirled round and round slowly on a wobbly carousel made of glass. Next I was lying on my back on the big, disordered bed upstairs, shivering and sweating. There was a light on, and the window was a box of deep, glistening darkness. I fell asleep, and after what seemed a moment woke again with the sun shining in my face. The house was silent around me, but there was a thin, continuous ringing which I seemed to feel rather than hear. The sheets were a sodden tangle. I did not want to move, I felt as fragile as crystal. Even my hair felt breakable, a shock of erect, minute filaments bristling with static. I could hear the blood rushing along my veins, quick and heavy as mercury. My face was swollen and hot, and strangely smooth to the touch: a doll's face. When I closed my eyes a crimson shape pulsed and faded and pulsed again on the inside of my lids, like the repeated after-image of a shell bursting in blackness. When I swallowed, the ringing in my ears changed pitch. I dozed, and dreamed I was adrift in a hot lake. When I woke it was afternoon. The light in the window, dense, calm, unshadowed, was a light shining straight out of the past. My mouth was dry and swollen, my head seemed packed with air. Not since childhood had I known this particular state of voluptuous distress. It was not really illness, more a kind of respite. I lay for a long time, hardly stirring, watching the day change, listening to the little noises of the world. The brazen sunlight slowly faded, and the sky turned from lilac to mauve, and a single star appeared. Then suddenly it was late, and I lay in a sleepy daze in the soft summer darkness and would not have been surprised if my mother had appeared, young and smiling, in a rustle of silk, with a finger to her lips, to say goodnight to me on her way out for the evening. It was not Maman who came, however, but only Charlie, he opened the door cautiously on its wheezy hinges and peered in at me, craning his tortoise neck, and I shut my eyes and he withdrew softly and creaked away down the stairs. And I saw in my mind another doorway, and another darkness – that fragment of memory, not mine, yet again – and waited, hardly breathing, for something or someone to appear. But there was nothing.

*

I think of that brief bout of ague as marking the end of an initial, distinct phase of my life as a murderer. By the morning of the second day the fever had abated. I lay in a clammy tangle of sheets with my arms flung wide, just breathing. I felt as if I had been wading frantically through waist-high water, and now at last I had gained the beach, exhausted, trembling in every limb, and yet almost at peace. I had survived. I had come back to myself. Outside the window the seagulls were crying, looking for Mammy French, they rose and fell with stiff wings spread wide, as if suspended on elastic cords. I rose shakily and crossed the room. There was wind and sun, and the sea glared, a rich, hazardous blue. Below in the little stone harbour the yachts bobbed and slewed, yanking at their mooring-ropes. I turned away. There was something in the gay, bright scene that seemed to rebuke me. I put on Charlie's dressing-gown and went down to the kitchen. Silence everywhere. In the calm matutinal light everything stood motionless as if under a spell. I could not bear the thought of food. I found an open bottle of Apollinaris in the refrigerator and drank it off. It was flat, and tasted faintly of metal. I sat down at the table and rested my forehead in my hands. My skin felt grainy, as if the surface layer had crumpled to a sort of clinging dust. Charlie's breakfast things were still on the table, and there was spilled cigarette ash and a saucer of crushed butts. The newspapers I had bought on Thursday were stuffed in the rubbish bin. This was Saturday. I had missed, what, nearly two days, two days of accumulating evidence. I looked for the plastic bag in which I had put my clothes, but it was gone. Charlie must have put it out for the binmen, it would be on some dump by now. Perhaps at this very moment a rag-picker was rummaging in it. A spasm of horror swarmed over me. I jumped up and paced the floor, my hands clasped together to keep them from shaking. I must do something, anything. I ran upstairs and swept from room to room like a mad king, the tail of the dressing-gown flying out behind me. I shaved, glaring at myself in the fish-eye mirror, then I put on Charlie's clothes again, and broke into his desk and took his cash and his wallet of credit cards, and went down the stairs three at a time and stormed out into the world.

And paused. Everything was in its place, the boats in the harbour, the road, the white houses along the coast, the far headland, those little clouds on the horizon, and yet – and yet it was all different somehow from what I had expected, from what something inside me had expected, some nice sense of how things should be ordered. Then I realised it was I, of course, who was out of place.

I went into the newsagent's, with the same cramp of fear and excitement in my breast as I had felt the first time. When I picked up the papers the ink came off on my hands, and the coins slipped in my sweaty fingers. The girl with the pimples gave me another look. She had a curious, smeared sort of gaze, it seemed to pass me by and take me in at the same time. Pre-menstrual, I could tell by her manner, that tensed, excitable air. I turned my back on her and scanned the papers. By now the story had seeped up from the bottom of the front pages like a stain, while reports on the bombing dwindled, the injured having stopped dying off. There was a photograph of the car, looking like a wounded hippo, with a stolid guard standing beside it and a detective in wellington boots pointing at something. The boys who had found it had been interviewed. Did they remember me, that pallid stranger dreaming on the bench in the deserted station? They did, they gave a description of me: an elderly man with black hair and a bushy beard. The woman at the traffic lights was sure I was in my early twenties, well-dressed, with a moustache and piercing eyes. Then there were the tourists at Whitewater who saw me make off with the painting, and Reck and his ma, of course, and the idiot boy and the woman at the garage where I hired the car: from each of their accounts another and more fantastic version of me emerged, until I became multiplied into a band of moustachioed cut-throats, rushing about glaring and making threatening noises, like a chorus of brigands in an Italian opera. I nearly laughed. And yet I was disappointed. Yes, it's true, I was disappointed. Did I want to be found out, did I hope to see my name splashed in monster type across every front page? I think I did. I think I longed deep down to be made to stand in front of a jury and reveal all my squalid little secrets. Yes, to be found out, to be suddenly pounced upon, beaten, stripped, and set before the howling multitude, that was my deepest, most ardent desire. I hear the court catching its breath in surprise and disbelief. But ah, do you not also long for this, in your hearts, gentlepersons of the jury? To be rumbled. To feel that heavy hand fall upon your shoulder, and hear the booming voice of authority telling you the game is up at last. In short, to be unmasked. Ask yourselves. I confess (I confess!), those days that passed while I waited for them to find me were the most exciting I have ever known, or ever hope to know. Terrible, yes, but exciting too. Never had the world appeared so unstable, or my place in it so thrillingly precarious. I had a raw, lascivious awareness of myself, a big warm damp thing parcelled up in someone else's clothes. At any moment they might catch me, they might be watching me even now, murmuring into their handsets and signalling to the marksmen on the roof. First there would be panic, then pain. And when everything was gone, every shred of dignity and pretence, what freedom there would be, what lightness! No, what am I saying, not lightness, but its opposite: weight, gravity, the sense at last of being firmly grounded. Then finally I would be me, no longer that poor impersonation of myself I had been doing all my life. I would be real. I would be, of all things, human.

I took the bus to town, and got off at a street where I used to live years ago, when I was a student, and walked along by the railings of the park in the warm wind under the seething trees, my heart filled with nostalgia. A man in a cap, with terrible, soiled eyes, stood on the pavement shaking a fist in the air and roaring obscene abuse at the cars passing by. I envied him. I would have liked to stand and shout like that, to pour out all that rage and pain and indignation. I walked on. A trio of light-clad girls came tripping out of a bookshop, laughing, and for a second I was caught up in their midst, my side-teeth bared in a frightful grin, a beast among the graces. In a bright new shop I bought a jacket and trousers, two shirts, some ties, underwear, and, in a flourish of defiance, a handsome but not altogether unostentatious hat. I thought I detected a slight stiffening of attention when I produced Charlie's credit cards – my God, did they know him, did he shop here? – but I turned up my accent to full force and dashed off his signature with aplomb, and everyone relaxed. I was not really worried. In fact, I felt ridiculously excited and happy, like a boy on a birthday spree. (What is it about the mere act of buying things, that it can afford me so much simple pleasure?) I seemed to swim along the street, upright as a sea-horse, breasting the air. I think I must have been feverish still. The people among whom I moved were strange to me, stranger than usual, I mean. I felt I was no longer of their species, that something had happened since I had last encountered a crowd of them together, that an adjustment had occurred in me, a tiny, amazingly swift and momentous evolutionary event. I passed through their midst like a changeling, a sport of nature. They were beyond me, they could not touch me – could they see me, even, or was I now outside the spectrum of their vision? And yet how avidly I observed them, in hunger and wonderment. They surged around me at a sort of stumble, dull-eyed and confused, like refugees.

I saw myself, bobbing head and shoulders above them, disguised, solitary, nursing my huge secret. I was their unrecognised and their unacknowledged dream – I was their Moosbrugger. I came to the river, and dawdled on the bridge, among the beggars and the fruit-sellers and the hawkers of cheap jewellery, admiring the wind-blurred light above the water and tasting the salt air on my lips. The sea! To be away, out there, out over countless fathoms, lost in all that blue!

I went – everything was so simple – I went into a bar and bought a drink. Each sip was like a sliver of metal, chill and smooth. It was a cavernous place, very dark. The light from the street glared whitely in the open doorway. I might have been somewhere in the south, in one of those dank, tired ports I used to know so well. At the back, in a lighted place like a stage, some youths with shaven heads and outsize lace-up boots were playing a game of billiards. The balls whirred and clacked, the young men softly swore. It was like something out of Hogarth, a group of wigless surgeons, say, intent over the dissecting table. The barman, arms folded and mouth open, was watching a horse-race on the television set perched high up on a shelf in a corner above him. A tubercular young man in a black shortie overcoat came in and stood beside me, breathing and fidgeting. I could tell from the tension coming off him that he was working himself up to something, and for a moment I was pleasurably alarmed. He might do anything, anything. But he only spoke. *I've lived here thirty-three years*, he said, in a tone of bitter indignation, *and everyone is afraid*. The barman glanced at him with weary contempt and turned back to the television. Blue horses galloped in silence over bright-green turf. *I* am afraid, the young man said, resentful now. He gave a tremendous twitch, hunching his shoulders and ducking his head and throwing up one arm, as if something had bitten him on the neck. Then he turned and went out hurriedly, clutching his coat around him. I followed, leaving my drink half-finished. It was blindingly bright outside. I spotted him, a good way off already, dodging along through the crowds with his elbows pressed to his sides, taking tight, swift little steps,

nimble as a dancer. Nothing could stop him. In the thickest surge
of bodies he would find a chink at once, and swivel deftly from
the waist up and dive through without altering his pace. What
a pair we would have made, if anyone had thought to link us, he
in his tight shabby coat and I with my fancy hat and expensive clutch of carrier bags. I could hardly keep up with him, and
after a minute or two I was puffing and in a sweat. I had an
unaccountable sense of elation. Once he paused, and stood glaring
into the window of a chemist's shop. I waited, loitering at a bus-
stop, keeping him in the corner of my eye. He was so intent, and
seemed to quiver so, that I thought he was going to do something
violent, turn and attack someone, maybe, or kick in the window
and stamp about among the cameras and the cosmetic displays.
But he was only waiting for another shudder to pass through him.
This time when he flung up his arm his leg shot up as well, as if
elbow and knee were connected by an invisible string, and a
second later his heel came down on the pavement with a ringing
crack. He cast a quick look around him, to see if anyone had
noticed, and gave himself a casual little shake, as if by that he
would make the previous spasm appear to have been intentional
too, and then he was off again like a whippet. I wanted to catch
up with him, I wanted to speak to him. I did not know what I
would say. I would not offer him sympathy, certainly not. I did
not pity him, I saw nothing in him to merit my pity. No, that's
not true, for he was pathetic, a maimed and mad poor creature.
Yet I was not sorry for him, my heart did not go out to him in
that way. What I felt was, how shall I say, a kind of brotherly
regard, a strong, sustaining, almost cheerful sense of oneness with
him. It seemed the simplest thing in the world for me to walk up
now and put my hand on that thin shoulder and say: *my fellow
sufferer, dear friend, compagnon des misères!* And so it was with
deep disappointment and chagrin that at the next corner I stopped
and looked about me in the jostling crowd and realised that I had
lost him. Almost at once, however, I found a substitute, a tall fat
girl with big shoulders and a big behind, and big, tubular legs
ending in a pair of tiny feet, like a pig's front trotters, wedged

into high-heeled white shoes. She had been to the hairdresser's, her hair was cropped in a fashionable, boyish style that was, on her, grotesque. The stubbled back of her neck, with its fold of fat, was still an angry shade of red from the dryer, it seemed to be blushing for her. She was so brave and sad, clumping along in her ugly shoes, and I would have followed her all day, I think, but after a while I lost her, too. Next I took up with a man with a huge strawberry mark on his face, then a tiny woman wheeling a tiny dog in a doll's pram, then a young fellow who marched resolutely along, as if he could see no one, with a visionary's fixed glare, swinging his arms and growling to himself. In a busy pedestrian thoroughfare I was surrounded suddenly by a gang of tinker girls, what my mother would have called *big rawsies*, with red hair and freckles and extraordinary, glass-green eyes, who pushed against me in truculent supplication, plucking at my sleeve and whining. It was like being set upon by a flock of importunate large wild birds. When I tried to shoo them away one of them knocked my hat off, while another deftly snatched out of my hand the carrier bag containing my new jacket. They fled, shoving each other and laughing shrilly, their raw, red heels flying. I laughed too, and picked up my hat from the pavement, ignoring the looks of the passers-by, who appeared to find my merriment unseemly. I did not care about the jacket – in fact, the loss of it chimed in a mysteriously apt way with that of its discarded predecessor – but I would have liked to see where those girls would go. I imagined a lean-to made of rags and bits of galvanised iron on a dusty patch of waste ground, with a starving dog and snot-nosed infants, and a drunken hag crouched over a steaming pot. Or perhaps there was a Fagin somewhere waiting for them, skulking in the shadows in some derelict tenement, where the light of summer fingered the shutters, and dust-motes drifted under lofty ceilings, and the rat's claw in the wainscoting scratched at the silence, scratched, stopped, and scratched again. So I went along happily for a little while, dreaming up other lives, until I spotted a whey-faced giant with rubber legs clomping ahead of me on two sticks, and I set off after him in avid pursuit.

What was I doing, why was I following these people – what enlightenment was I looking for? I did not know, nor care. I was puzzled and happy, like a child who has been allowed to join in an adults' game. I kept at it for hours, criss-crossing the streets and the squares with a drunkard's dazed single-mindedness, as if I were tracing out a huge, intricate sign on the face of the city for someone in the sky to read. I found myself in places I had not known were there, crooked alleyways and sudden, broad, deserted spaces, and dead-end streets under railway bridges where parked cars basked fatly in the evening sun, their toy-coloured roofs agleam. I ate a hamburger in a glass-walled café with moulded plastic chairs and tinfoil ashtrays, where people sat alone and gnawed at their food like frightened children abandoned by their parents. The daylight died slowly, leaving a barred, red and gold sunset smeared on the sky, and as I walked along it was like walking under the surface of a broad, burning river. The evening crowds were out, girls in tight trousers and high heels, and brawny young men with menacing haircuts. In the hot, hazy dusk the streets seemed wiser, flattened, somehow, and the cars scudded along, sleek as seals in the sodium glare. I got back late to Charlie's house, footsore, hot and dishevelled, my hat awry, but filled with a mysterious sense of achievement. And that night I dreamed about my father. He was a miniature version of himself, a wizened child with a moustache, dressed in a sailor suit, his pinched little face scrubbed and his hair neatly parted, leading by the hand a great, tall, dark-eyed matron wearing Greek robes and a crown of myrtle, who fixed me with a lewd, forgiving smile.

I HAVE HAD A SHOCK. My counsel has been to see me today, bringing an extraordinary piece of news. Usually I enjoy our little conferences, in a lugubrious sort of way. We sit at a square table in a small airless room with no windows. The walls are painted filing-cabinet grey. Light from a strip of neon tubing above our heads sifts down upon us like a fine-grained mist. The bulb makes a tiny, continuous buzzing. Maolseachlainn at first is full of energy, rooting in his bag, shuffling his papers, muttering. He is like a big, worried bear. He works at finding things to talk to me about, new aspects of the case, obscure points of law he might bring up, the chances of our getting a sympathetic judge, that sort of thing. He speaks too fast, stumbling over his words as if they were so many stones. Gradually the atmosphere of the place gets in at him, like damp, and he falls silent. He takes off his specs and sits and blinks at me. He has a way of squeezing the bridge of his nose between two fingers and a thumb which is peculiarly endearing. I feel sorry for him. I think he truly does like me. This puzzles him, and, I suspect, disturbs him too. He believes he is letting me down when he runs out of steam like this, but really, there is nothing left to say. We both know I will get life. He cannot understand my equanimity in the face of my fate. I tell him I have taken up Buddhism. He smiles carefully, unsure that it is a joke. I divert him with tales of prison life, fleshing them out with impersonations – I do our governor here very convincingly. When Maolseachlainn laughs there is no sound, only a slow heaving of the shoulders and a stretched, shiny grin.

By the way, what an odd formulation that is: to get life. Words so rarely mean what they mean.

Today I saw straight away he was in a state about something. He kept clawing at the collar of his shirt and clearing his throat, and taking off his half-glasses and putting them back on again. Also there was a smeary look in his eye. He hummed and hawed, and mumbled about the concept of justice, and the discretion of the courts, and other such folderol, I hardly listened to him. He was so mournful and ill at ease, shifting his big backside on the prison chair and looking everywhere except at me, that I could hardly keep from laughing. I pricked up my ears, though, when he started to mutter something about the possibility of my making a guilty plea – and this after all the time and effort he expended at the beginning in convincing me I should plead not guilty. Now when I caught him up on it, rather sharply, I confess, he veered off at once, with an alarmed look. I wonder what he's up to? I should have kept at it, and got it out of him. As a diversionary measure he dived into his briefcase and brought out a copy of my mother's will. I had not yet heard the contents, and was, I need hardly say, keenly interested. Maolseachlainn, I noticed, found this subject not much easier than the previous one. He coughed a lot, and frowned, and read out stuff about gifts and covenants and minor bequests, and was a long time getting to the point. I still cannot credit it. The old bitch has left Coolgrange to that stable-girl, what's-her-name, Joanne. There is some money for Daphne, and for Van's schooling, but for me, nothing. I suppose I should not be surprised, but I am. I was not a good son, but I was the only one she had. Maolseachlainn was watching me with compassion. I'm sorry, he said. I smiled and shrugged, though it was not easy. I wished he would go away now. Oh, I said, it's understandable, after all, that she would make a new will. He said nothing. There was a peculiar silence. Then, almost tenderly, he handed me the document, and I looked at the date. The thing was seven, nearly eight years old. She had cut me out long ago, before ever I came back to disgrace her and the family name. I recalled, with shocking clarity, the way she looked at me that day in the kitchen at Coolgrange, and heard again that cackle of raucous laughter.

Well, I'm glad she enjoyed her joke. It's a good one. I find a surprising lack of bitterness in my heart. I am smiling, though probably it seems more as if I am wincing. This is her contribution to the long course of lessons I must learn.

Maolseachlainn stood up, assuming his heartiest manner, as always, in an attempt to disguise his relief at the prospect of getting away. I watched him struggle into his navy-blue overcoat and knot his red woollen muffler around his neck. Sometimes, when he first arrives, his clothes give off little wafts and slivers of the air of outdoors. I snuff them up with surreptitious pleasure, as if they were the most precious of perfumes. What's it like, outside? I said now. He paused, and blinked at me in some alarm. I think he thought I was asking him for an overall picture, as if I might have forgotten what the world looked like. The day, I said, the weather. His brow cleared. He shrugged. Oh, he said, grey, just grey, you know. And I saw it at once, with a pang, the late November afternoon, the dull shine on the wet roads, and the children straggling home from school, and rooks tossing and wheeling high up against ragged clouds, and the tarnished glow in the sky off behind bare, blackened branches. These were the times I used to love, the weather's unconsidered moments, when the vast business of the world just goes on quietly by itself, as if there were no one to notice, or care. I see myself as a boy out there, dawdling along that wet road, kicking a stone ahead of me and dreaming the enormous dream of the future. There was a path, I remember, that cut off through the oak wood a mile or so from home, which I knew must lead to Coolgrange eventually. How green the shadows, and deep the track, how restless the silence seemed, that way. Every time I passed by there, coming up from the cross, I said to myself, Next time, next time. But always when the next time came I was in a rush, or the light was fading, or I was just not in the mood to break new ground, and so I kept to the ordinary route, along the road. In the end I never took that secret path, and now, of course, it is too late.

*

I have been doing calculations in my head – it keeps my mind off other things – and I find to my surprise that I spent no more than ten days in all at Charlie's house, from midsummer day, or night, rather, until the last, momentous day of June. That *is* ten, isn't it? Thirty days hath September, April, June – yes, ten. Or is it nine. It's nine nights, certainly. But where does the day end and the night start, and vice versa? And why do I find the night a more easily quantifiable entity than day? I have never been any good at this kind of thing. The simpler the figures the more they fox me. Anyway. Ten days, thereabouts, more or less, is the length of my stay with Charlie French, whose hospitality and kindness I did not mean to betray. It seemed a longer time than that. It seemed weeks and weeks. I was not unhappy there. That's to say, I was no more unhappy there than I would have been somewhere else. Unhappy! What a word! As the days went on I grew increasingly restless. My nerves seethed, and there was a permanent knot of pain in my guts. I suffered sudden, furious attacks of impatience. Why didn't they come for me, what were they doing? In particular I resented the Behrenses' silence, I was convinced they were playing a cruel game with me. But all the time, behind all these agitations, there was that abiding, dull, flat sensation. I felt disappointed. I felt let down. The least I had expected from the enormities of which I was guilty was that they would change my life, that they would make things happen, however awful, that there would be a constant succession of heart-stopping events, of alarms and sudden frights and hairbreadth escapes. I do not know how I got through the days. I awoke each morning with an anguished start, as if a pure, distilled drop of pain had plopped on my forehead. That big old house with its smells and cobwebs was oppressive. I drank a lot, of course, but not enough to make myself insensible. I tried to achieve oblivion, God knows, I poured in the booze until my lips went numb and my knees would hardly bend, but it was no good, I could not escape myself. I waited with a lover's rapt expectancy for the evenings, when I would put on my hat and my new clothes – my new mask! – and step forth gingerly, a quavering Dr Jekyll, inside whom that other, terrible creature chafed and struggled, lusting for experience. I felt I had never until now looked at the ordinary world around me, the people, places, things. How innocent it all seemed, innocent, and doomed. How can I express the tangle of emotions that thrashed inside me as I prowled the city streets, letting my monstrous heart feed its fill on the sights and sounds of the commonplace? The feeling of power, for instance, how can I communicate that? It sprang not from what I had done, but from the fact that I had done it and *no one knew*. It was the secret, the secret itself, *that* was what set me above the dull-eyed ones among whom I moved as the long day died, and the streetlights came on, and the traffic slid away homeward, leaving a blue haze hanging like the smoke of gunfire in the darkening air. And then there was that constant, hot excitement, like a fever in the blood, that was half the fear of being unmasked and half the longing for it. Somewhere, I knew, in dayrooms and in smoke-filled, shabby offices, faceless men were even now painstakingly assembling the evidence against me. I thought about them at night, as I lay in Charlie's mother's big lumpy bed. It was strange to be the object of so much meticulous attention, strange, and not entirely unpleasant. Does that seem perverse? But I was in another country now, where the old rules did not apply.

It was hard to sleep, of course. I suppose I did not want to sleep, afraid of what I would encounter in my dreams. At best I would manage a fitful hour or two in the darkness before dawn, and wake up exhausted, with an ache in my chest and my eyes scalding. Charlie too was sleepless, I would hear at all hours his creaking step on the stair, the rattle of the teapot in the kitchen, the laborious, spasmodic tinkle as he emptied his old man's bladder in the bathroom. We saw little of each other. The house was big enough for us both to be in it at the same time and yet feel we were alone. Since that first, drunken night he had been avoiding me. He seemed to have no friends. The phone never rang, no one came to the house. I was surprised, then, and horribly alarmed, to come back early one evening from my rambles in town and find three big black cars parked on the road, and a uniformed guard loitering in the company of two watchful men in anoraks at the harbour wall. I made myself walk past slowly, an honest citizen out for a stroll at end of day, though my heart was hammering and my palms were damp, and then skipped around the back way and got in through the mews. Halfway up the jungly garden I tripped and fell, and tore my left hand on a rose-bush that had run wild. I crouched in the long grass, listening. Smell of loam, smell of leaves, the thick feel of blood on my wounded hand. The yellow light in the kitchen window turned the dusk around me to tenderest blue. There was a strange woman inside, in a white apron, working at the stove. When I opened the back door she turned quickly and gave a little shriek. Holy God, she said, who are you? She was an elderly person with a henna wig and ill-fitting dentures and a scattered air. Her name, as we shall discover presently, was Madge. They're all upstairs, she said, dismissing me, and turned back to her steaming saucepans.

There were five of them, or six, counting Charlie, though at first it seemed to me there must be twice that number. They were in the big, gaunt drawing-room on the first floor, standing under the windows with drinks in their hands, ducking and bobbing at each other like nervous storks and chattering as if their lives depended on it. Behind them the lights of the harbour glimmered, and in the far sky a huge bank of slate-blue cloud was shutting down like a lid on the last, smouldering streak of sunset fire. At my entrance the chattering stopped. Only one of them was a woman, tall, thin, with foxy red hair and an extraordinary stark white face. Charlie, who was standing with his back to me, saw me first reflected in their swivelling glances. He turned with a pained smile. Ah, he said, there you are. His winged hair gleamed like a polished helm. He was wearing a bow-tie. Well, I heard myself saying to him, in a tone of cheery truculence, well, you might have told me! My hands were trembling. There was a moment of uncertain silence, then the talk abruptly started up again. The woman went on watching me. Her pale colouring and vivid hair and long, slender neck gave her a permanently startled look, as if at some time in the past she had been told a shocking secret and had never quite absorbed it. Charlie, mumbling apologetically, had put a shaky old hand under my elbow and was gently but firmly steering me backwards out of the room. The fear I had felt earlier had turned into annoyance. I felt like giving him a clout, and putting a dent in that ridiculous praetorian helmet of hair. Tell Madge, he was saying, tell Madge to give you something to eat, and I'll be down presently. He was so worried I thought he was going to weep. He stood on the top step and watched me make my way downstairs, as if he were afraid I would come scampering back up again if he took his eye off me, and only when I had safely reached the bottom and was heading for the kitchen did he turn back to the drawing-room and his guests.

The kitchen was filled with steam, and Madge, her wig awry, looked even hotter and more harassed than before. This place, she said bitterly, honest to God! She was, as she picturesquely put it, Mr French's occasional woman, and came in when there were dinner parties, and that. This was interesting. Dinner parties, indeed! I helped her by opening the wine, and sat down at the table with a bottle for myself. I had drunk half of it when there was a loud knock at the front door that set my heart thumping again. I went into the hall, but Charlie was already rattling hurriedly down the stairs. When he opened the door I could see the two anoraks outside, guarding the way for a burly man and a tall, sleek woman, as they advanced at a regal pace into the hall. Ah, Max, Charlie said, and stepped forward with clumsy eagerness. The woman he ignored. Max shook hands with him briefly, and then took back his hand and ran it upwards quickly over his low, truculent brow. Christ, he said, you're far enough out, I thought we were never going to get here. They moved towards the stairs, Charlie and Max in front and the woman behind them. She wore an ugly blue gown and a triple rope of pearls. She glanced along the hall and caught my eye, and held it until I looked away. Madge had come out of the kitchen, and hovered at my shoulder. There's his nibs, she whispered, and the missus too.

I waited a while after they had gone up, and when Madge

returned to her cooking I followed them, and slipped into the drawing-room again. Charlie and Max and Mrs Max were standing at one of the windows admiring the view, while the others bobbed and ducked and tried not to stare too openly in their direction. I seized an armful of bottles from the mantelpiece and passed among them, topping up their glasses. The men had a scrubbed, eager, slightly anxious air, like that of big, blue-suited schoolboys on their first adult outing, except for one old chap with a nose like a blood-orange and stains down the front of his waistcoat, who stood to one side all on his own, glazed and dejected. The others carefully looked through me, but he brightened up at once, and was ready for a chat. What do you think, anyway, he said loudly, will we win, will we? I understood it to be a rhetorical question. We will, I said stoutly, and gave him a broad wink. He raised his eyebrows and stepped back a pace, however, peering at me doubtfully. By God, he said, I don't know, now. I shrugged, and passed on blandly. Charlie had caught sight of me, and was smiling fixedly in alarm. Mine was a vodka, Mrs Max said coldly when I offered her gin. My attention was on her husband. He had a raw, scrubbed look to him, as if he had been exposed for a long time to some far rougher form of light and weather than the others in the room had ever known. His movements, too, the way he held himself, the slow, deliberate way he turned his glance or lifted his hand to his brow, all these bore a unique stamp, and were weighted with a kind of theatrical awareness. His voice was slow and guttural, and he had a violent manner of speaking that was impressive, and even, in an odd way, seductive. It was the voice of a man moving inexorably forward through a forest of small obstacles. I imagined him carelessly crunching things underfoot, flowers, or snails, or the insteps of his enemies. Well, Charlie, he was saying, still buying cheap and selling dear? Charlie blushed, and glanced at me. That's right, Mrs Max said, embarrass everyone. She spoke loudly, with a dull emphasis, and did not look at him. It was as if she were lobbing remarks past his shoulder at a sardonic ally listening there. Nor did he look at her, it might have been a disembodied voice that had spoken. He laughed harshly. Have you acquired that Dutch job for me yet? he said. Charlie, grinning in anguish, shook his head, speechless. His left eyelid began to flutter, as if a moth had suddenly come to life under it. I proffered the whiskey bottle but he put a hand quickly over his glass. Max also waved me away. The woman with the foxy hair had come up behind me. Your hand, she said, you've cut it. For a moment we all stood in silence, Max and his missus, and Charlie and Foxy and me, contemplating the beaded scratch across my knuckles. Yes, I said, I fell over a rose-bush. I laughed. That half-bottle of wine had gone straight to my head. Charlie was shifting stealthily from foot to foot, afraid, I suppose, that I was about to do something outrageous. It struck me for the first time how frightened of me he was. Poor Charlie. A lighted yacht was gliding silently across the inky harbour. Lovely view, Max said grimly.

In the dining-room the stuffed owl looked out of its bell-jar at the company with an expression of surprise and some dismay. By now Patch, I mean Madge, was in a state of panic. I carried plates for her, and serving-dishes, and plonked them down on the table with extravagant waiterly flourishes. I confess, I was enjoying myself. I was light-headed, brimming with manic glee, like a child in a dressing-up game. I seemed to move as if under a magic spell, I do not know how it worked, but for a while, for an hour or two, posing as Charlie's factotum, I was released from myself and the terrors that had been pursuing me relentlessly for days. I even invented a history for myself as I went along, I mean I – how shall I express it – I fell into a certain manner that was not my own and that yet seemed, even to me, no less authentic, or plausible, at least, than my real self. (My real self!) I became Frederick the Indispensable, Mr French's famous man, without whom that crusty, moneyed old bachelor would not be able to survive. He had rescued me from uncongenial circumstances when I was a young man – tending the bar, say, in some sleazy downtown pub – and now I was devoted to him, and loyal to the point of ferocity. I bullied him too, of course, and could be a terror when he had people in. (Jealousy? Acquaintances did sometimes speculate among themselves, but no, they decided, Charlie was not that way inclined: remember that horsy woman down the country, the lost love of his life?) Really, we were like father and son, except that no son would be so steadfast, and no father so forgiving of my little ways. At times it was hard to tell which was master and which the man. Tonight, for instance, when the main course was finished, I sat myself down among the guests and poured a glass of wine as if it were the most natural thing in the world. A silence fell, and Charlie frowned, and rolled a breadcrumb about on the tablecloth, pretending he was thinking about something else, and Max stared balefully out the window at the harbour lights while his henchmen around him fidgeted and glanced at each other nervously, and at last I took up my glass, and rose and said, Well! I suppose us ladies better withdraw, and fairly flounced out of the room. In the hall, of course, I leaned against the wall and laughed. All the same, my hands were shaking. Stage fright, I suppose. What an actor the world has lost in me!

Now what shall I do?

I went upstairs to the drawing-room. No, I went into the kitchen. Madge: wig, false teeth, white apron, I have done all that. Out again. In the hall I found Foxy. She had wandered out of the dining-room. Under the stairs was a dark place, there we met. I could see her face in the gloom, her eyes watching me, so solemn and fearful. Why are you sad? I said, and for a moment she did not know what to do with her hands, then she put them behind her back, and flexed one knee and briefly swayed her shoulders and her hips, like a schoolgirl playing the coquette. Who says I'm sad? she said. I'm not sad. And I thought she was going to cry. Did she see it in me, the terror and the shame, had she seen it from the first? For she had sought me out, I knew that. I reached behind her and opened a door, and we stepped suddenly on to bare floorboards in an empty room. There was a smell, dry and oniony, that was the smell of a certain attic room at Coolgrange. A parallelogram of moonlight was propped against one wall like a broken mirror. I am still holding these damned plates. I put them on the floor at our feet, and while I was still bending she touched my shoulder and said something which I did not catch. She laughed softly, in surprise, it seemed, as if the sound of her own voice were unexpected. Nothing, she said, nothing. She shook in my arms. She was all teeth, breath, clutching fingers. She held my head between her hands as if she would crush it. She had kicked off her shoes, they clattered where they fell. She raised one foot behind her and pressed it against the door, pressed, and pressed. Her thighs were cold. She wept, her tears fell on my hands. I bit her throat. We were like – I don't know. We were like two messengers, meeting in the dark to exchange our terrible news. O God, she said, O God. She put her forehead against my shoulder. Our hands were smeared with each other. The room came back, the moonlight, the oniony smell. No thought, except: her white face, her hair. Forgive me, I said. I don't know why I laughed. Anyway, it wasn't really a laugh.

*

How peaceful the days are now, here at the dead end of the year. Sitting in the fastness of this grey room I sometimes imagine I am utterly alone, that there is no one around me for miles and miles. It is like being in the deep hold of a great grey ship. The air is heavy and still, it presses in my ears, on my eyes, on the base of my skull. A trial date has been fixed at last. I know this should concentrate my mind, give me a purpose and so on, make me excited, or afraid, but it does not. Something has happened to my sense of time, I think in aeons now. The days, the weeks of this banal little courtroom drama will register as no more than a pinprick. I have become a lifer.

Again today Maolseachlainn brought up the topic of how I should plead. I let him maunder on for a while, then I got fed up and told him I would dispense with his services if he did not come straight out and say whatever it was he had on his mind. This was disingenuous of me, for I had realised, of course, since his last visit, that he was hinting at the possibility of an arrangement – I understand, from the conversations I have had in here, that there is hardly a sentence handed down that has not been prearranged among counsel. I was curious to know what the court could want from me. Now, as I watched poor old Mac squirm and sweat, I thought I had it: Charlie, of course, they were trying to salvage something of Charlie's reputation. (How could I have imagined they would care a fig for Charlie, or his reputation?) I would do all I could for him, that went without saying, though it seemed to me a bit late now. All right, Mac, I said, holding up a hand, I'll plead guilty – and what then? He gave me one of his over-the-spectacles looks. Then it'll be an open-and-shut case, won't it? he said. This, I realised after a moment, was intended as a witticism. He grinned dolefully. What he meant was that the trial would open, I would deny the charges as stated, plead guilty to manslaughter or something, the judge would pass sentence, with a bit lopped off in return for my co-operation, and then, presto, it would all be over, the hearing would end, the case would be closed. He could guarantee nothing, he said, but he had a duty to his client to try to secure the best judgment that was possible within the law. He is very charming when he waxes pompous like this. What's the point, I said, what's the trick? He shrugged. The trick is that no evidence will be heard. Simple as that. For a moment we were silent. And will that work, I said, will that save him? He frowned in puzzlement, and at once I saw I had been wrong, that Charlie and his embarrassment were not the subject here. I laughed. I've said it before, sometimes I think I am hopelessly innocent. Maolseachlainn glanced over his shoulder – he did, he really did – and leaned across the table conspiratorially. No one is worrying about Charlie French, he said, no one is worrying about *him*.

Your honour, I do not like this, I do not like this at all. I'll plead guilty, of course – haven't I done so all along? – but I do not like it that I may not give evidence, no, that I don't like. It's not fair. Even a dog such as I must have his day. I have always seen myself in the witness box, gazing straight ahead, quite calm, and wearing casual clothes, as the newspapers will have it. And then that authoritative voice, telling my side of things, in my own words. Now I am to be denied my moment of drama, the last such, surely, that I'll know in this life. No, it's not right.

Look, the fact is I hardly remember that evening at Charlie French's. I mean, I remember the evening, but not the people, not with any clarity. I see far more vividly the lights on the water outside, and the last streak of sunset and the dark bank of cloud, than I do the faces of those hearty boy-men. Even Max Molyneaux is not much more, in my recollection, than an expensive suit and a certain sleek brutishness. What do I care for him and his ilk, for God's sake? Let them keep their reputations, it's nothing to me, one way or the other, I have no interest in stirring up scandal. The occasion passed before me in a glassy blur, like so much else over those ten days. Why, even poor Foxy was hardly more substantial to me in my frantic condition than a prop in a wet dream. No, wait, I take that back. However much they may hoot in ribald laughter, I must declare that I remember her clearly, with tenderness and compassion. She is, and will most likely remain, the last woman I made love to. Love? Can I call it that? What else can I call it. She trusted me. She smelled the blood and the horror and did not recoil, but opened herself like a flower and let me rest in her for a moment, my heart shaking, as we exchanged our wordless secret. Yes, I remember her. I was falling, and she caught me, my Gretchen.

In fact, her name was Marian. Not that it matters.

They stayed very late, all except Mrs Max, who left directly dinner was over. I watched as she was driven away, sitting up very straight in the back of one of the black limousines, a ravaged Nefertiti. Max and his pals went upstairs again, and caroused until the dawn was breaking. I spent the night in the kitchen playing cards with Madge. Where was Marian? I don't know – I got blotto, as usual. Anyway, our moment was over, if we were to encounter each other now we would only be embarrassed. Yet I think I must have gone to look for her, for I recall blundering about upstairs, in the bedrooms, and falling over repeatedly in the dark. I remember, too, standing at a wide-open window, very high up, listening to the strains of music outside on the air, a mysterious belling and blaring, that seemed to move, to fade, as if a clamorous cavalcade were departing into the night. I suppose it came from some dancehall, or some nightclub on the harbour. I think of it, however, as the noise of the god and his retinue, abandoning me.

NEXT DAY THE WEATHER BROKE. At mid-morning, when my hangover and I got up, the sun was shining as gaily and as heartlessly as it had all week, and the houses along the coast shimmered in a pale-blue haze, as if the sky had crumbled into airy geometry there. I stood at the window in my drawers, scratching and yawning. It struck me that I had become almost accustomed to this strange way of life. It was as if I were adapting to an illness, after the initial phase of frights and fevers. A churchbell was ringing. Sunday. The strollers were out already, with their dogs and children. Across the road, at the harbour wall, a man in a raincoat stood with his hands clasped behind his back, gazing out to sea. I could hear voices downstairs. Madge was in the kitchen doing last night's washing-up. She gave me a peculiar glance. I was wearing Charlie's dressing-gown. How is it, I wonder, that I did not catch it then, that new, speculative note in her voice, which should have alerted me? She had a helper with her this morning, her niece, a dim-looking child of twelve or so with – with what, what does it matter what she had, what she was like. All these minor witnesses, none of whom will ever be called now. I sat at the table drinking tea and watched them as they worked. The child I could see was frightened of me. Fe fi fo fum. He's gone out, you know, Madge said, her arms plunged in suds, Mr French, he went out as I was coming in. Her tone was unaccountably accusing, as if Charlie had fled the house because of me. But then, he had.

In the afternoon a huge cloud grew up on the horizon, grey and grainy, like a deposit of silt, and the sea swarmed, a blackish blue flecked with white. I watched an undulant curtain of rain sweep in slowly from the east. The man at the harbour wall buttoned his raincoat. The Sunday morning crowd was long gone, but he, *he* was still there.

*

Strange how it felt, now that it was here at last. I had expected terror, panic, cold sweat, the shakes, but there was none of that. Instead, a kind of wild-eyed euphoria took hold of me. I strode about the house like the drunken captain of a storm-tossed ship. All sorts of mad ideas came into my head. I would barricade the doors and windows. I would take Madge and her niece hostage, and barter them for a helicopter to freedom. I would wait until Charlie came back, and use him as a human shield, marching him out ahead of me with a knife at his throat – I even went down to the kitchen to find a blade for the purpose. Madge had finished the washing-up, and was sitting at the table with a pot of tea and a Sunday tabloid. She watched me apprehensively as I rummaged in the cutlery drawer. She asked if I would be wanting my lunch, or would I wait for Mr French. I laughed wildly. Lunch! The niece laughed too, a little parrot squawk, her top lip curling up to reveal a half-inch of whitish, glistening gum. When I looked at her she shut her mouth abruptly, it was like a blind coming down. Jacintha, Madge said to her sharply, you go home. Stay where you are! I cried. They both flinched, and Jacintha's chin trembled and her eyes filled up with tears. I abandoned the search for a knife, and plunged off upstairs again. The man in the mackintosh was gone. I gave a great gasp of relief, as if I had been holding my breath all this time, and slumped against the window-frame. The rain teemed, big drops dancing on the road and making the surface of the water in the harbour seethe. I heard the front door open and bang shut, and Madge and the girl appeared below me and scampered away up the street with their coats over their heads. I laughed to see them go, the child leaping the puddles and Madge wallowing in her wake. Then I spotted the car, parked a little way up the road, on the other side, with two dim, large, motionless figures seated in the front, their faces blurred behind the streaming windscreen.

I sat in a chair in the drawing-room, gazing before me, my hands gripping the armrests and my feet placed squarely side by side on the floor. I do not know how long I stayed like that, in that glimmering, grey space. I have an impression of hours passing, but surely that cannot be. There was a smell of cigarettes and stale drink left over from last night. The rain made a soothing noise. I sank into a kind of trance, a waking sleep. I saw myself, as a boy, walking across a wooded hill near Coolgrange. It was in March, I think, one of those blustery, Dutch days with china-blue sky and tumbling, cindery clouds. The trees above me swayed and groaned in the wind. Suddenly there was a great quick rushing noise, and the air darkened, and something like a bird's vast wing crashed down around me, thrashing and whipping. It was a branch that had fallen. I was not hurt, yet I could not move, and stood as if stunned, aghast and shaking. The force and swiftness of the thing had appalled me. It was not fright I felt, but a profound sense of shock at how little my presence had mattered. I might have been no more than a flaw in the air. Ground, branch, wind, sky, world, all these were the precise and necessary co-ordinates of the event. Only I was misplaced, only I had no part to play. And nothing cared. If I had been killed I would have fallen there, face down in the dead leaves, and the day would have gone on as before, as if nothing had happened. For what would have happened would have been nothing, or nothing extraordinary, anyway. Adjustments would have been made. Things would have had to squirm out from under me. A stray ant, perhaps, would explore the bloody chamber of my ear. But the light would have been the same, and the wind would have blown as it had blown, and time's arrow would not have faltered for an instant in its flight. I was amazed. I never forgot that moment. And now another branch was about to fall, I could hear that same rushing noise above me, and feel that same dark wing descending.

The telephone rang, with a sound like glass breaking. There was a hubbub of static on the line. Someone seemed to be asking for Charlie. No, I shouted, no, he's not here! and threw down the receiver. Almost at once the thing began to shrill again. Wait, wait, don't hang up, the voice said, this *is* Charlie. I laughed, of course. I'm down the road, he said, just down the road. I was still laughing. Then there was a silence. The guards are here, Freddie, he said, they want to speak to you, there's been some sort of misunderstanding. I closed my eyes. Part of me, I realised, had been hoping against hope, unable quite to believe that the game was up. The hum in the wires seemed the very sound of Charlie's anxiety and embarrassment. Charlie, I said, Charlie, Charlie, why are you hiding in a phone-box, what did you think I would do to you? I hung up before he could answer.

I was hungry. I went down to the kitchen and made an enormous omelette, and devoured half a loaf of bread and drank a pint of milk. I sat hunched over the table with my elbows planted on either side of the plate and my head hanging, stuffing the food into myself with animal indifference. The rain-light made a kind of dusk in the room. I heard Charlie as soon as he entered the house – he never was very good at negotiating his way around the furniture of life. He put his head in at the kitchen door and essayed a smile, without much success. I motioned to the chair opposite me and he sat down gingerly. I had started on the cold remains of last night's boiled potatoes. I was ravenous, I could not get enough to eat. Charles, I said, you look terrible. He did. He was grey and shrunken, with livid hollows under his eyes. The collar of his shirt was buttoned though he wore no tie. He ran a hand over his jaw and I heard the bristles scrape. He had been up early, he said, they had got him up and asked him to go to the station. For a second I did not understand, I thought he meant the train station. He kept his eyes on my plate, the mess of spuds there. Something had happened to the silence around us. I realised that the rain had stopped. God almighty, Freddie, he said softly, what have you done? He seemed more bemused than shocked. I fetched another, half-full bottle of milk from the back of the fridge. Remember, Charlie, I said, those treats you used to stand me in Jammet's and the Paradiso? He shrugged. It was not clear if he was listening. The milk had turned. I drank it anyway. I enjoyed them, you know, those occasions, I said, even if I didn't always show it. I frowned. Something wrong there, something off, like the milk. Mendacity always makes my voice sound curiously dull, a flat blaring at the back of the throat. And why resurrect now an ancient, unimportant lie? Was I just keeping my hand in, getting a bit of practice for the big tourney that lay ahead? No, that's too hard. I was trying to apologise, I mean in general, and how was I supposed to do that without lying? He looked so old, sitting slumped there with his head drooping on its stringy neck and his mouth all down at one side and his bleared eyes fixed vaguely before him. Oh, fuck it, Charlie, I said. I'm sorry.

Was it coincidence, I wonder, that the policeman made his move just at that moment, or had he been listening outside the door? In films, I have noticed, the chap with the gun always waits in the corridor, back pressed to the wall, the whites of his eyes gleaming, until the people inside have had their say. And this one was, I suspect, a keen student of the cinema. He had a hatchet face and lank black hair and wore a sort of padded military jacket. The sub-machine gun he was holding, a blunt squarish model with only about an inch of barrel, looked remarkably like a toy. Of the three of us he seemed the most surprised. I could not help admiring the deft way he had kicked in the back door. It hung quivering on its hinges, the broken latch lolling like a hound's tongue. Charlie stood up. It's all right, officer, he said. The policeman advanced into the doorway. He was glaring at me. You're fucking under arrest, you are, he said. Behind him, in the yard, the sun came out suddenly, and everything shone and glittered wetly.

More policemen came in then by the front way, there seemed to be a large crowd of them, though they were in fact only four. One of them was the fellow I had seen standing at the harbour wall that morning, I recognised the raincoat. All were carrying guns, of assorted shapes and sizes. I was impressed. They ranged themselves around the walls, looking at me with a kind of bridling curiosity. The door to the hall stood open. Charlie made a move in that direction and one of the policemen in a flat voice said: Hang on. There was silence except for the faint, metallic pattering of police radios outside. We might have been awaiting the entrance of a sovereign. The person who came in at last was a surprise. He was a slight, boyish man of thirty or so, with sandy hair and transparent blue eyes. I noticed at once his hands and feet, which were small, almost dainty. He approached me at an angle somehow, looking at the floor with a peculiar little smile. His name, he said, was Haslet, Detective Inspector Haslet. (Hello, Gerry, hope you don't mind my mentioning your dainty hands – it's true, you know, they are.) The oddness of his manner – that smile, the oblique glance – was due, I realised, to shyness. A shy policeman! It was not what I had expected. He looked about him. There was a moment of awkwardness. No one seemed to know quite what to do next. He turned his downcast eyes in my direction again. Well, he said to no one in particular, are we right? Then all was briskness suddenly. The one with the machine gun – Sergeant Hogg, let's call him – stepped forward and, laying his weapon down on the table, deftly clapped a pair of handcuffs on my wrists. (By the way, they are not as uncomfortable as they might seem – in fact, there was something about being manacled that I found almost soothing, as if it were a more natural state than that of untrammelled freedom.) Charlie frowned. Is that necessary, Inspector? he said. It was such a grand old line, and so splendidly delivered, with just the right degree of solemn hauteur, that for a second I thought it might elicit a small round of applause. I looked at him with renewed admiration. He had thrown off that infirm air of a minute or two ago, and looked, really, quite impressive there in his dark suit and silver wings of hair. Even his unshaven cheeks and tieless collar only served to give him the appearance of a statesman roused from his bed to deal with some grave crisis in the affairs of the nation. Believe me, I am sincere when I say I admire his expertise as a quick-change artist. To place all faith in the mask, that seems to me now the true stamp of refined humanity. Did I say that, or someone else? No matter. I caught his eye, to show him my appreciation, and to ask him – oh, to ask some sort of pardon, I suppose. Afterwards I worried that my glance might have seemed to him more derisive than apologetic, for I think I must have worn a smirk throughout that grotesque kitchen comedy. His mouth was set grimly, and a nerve was twitching in his jaw – he had every right to be furious – but in his eyes all I could see was a sort of dreamy sadness. Then Hogg prodded me in the back, and I was marched quickly down the hall and out into the dazzling light of afternoon.

There was a moment of confusion as the policemen milled on the pavement, craning their stumpy necks and peering sharply this way and that about the harbour. What did they expect, a rescue party? I noticed that they all wore running shoes, except Haslet, the good country boy, in his stout brown brogues. One of his men bumped into him. Too many cops spoil the capture, I said brightly. No one laughed, and Haslet pretended he had not heard. I thought it was awfully witty, of course. I was still in that mood of mad elation, I cannot explain it. I seemed not to walk but bound along, brimful of tigerish energy. Everything sparkled in the rinsed sea-air. The sunlight had a flickering, hallucinatory quality, and I felt I was seeing somehow into the very process of it, catching the photons themselves in flight. We crossed the road. The car I had seen from the upstairs window was still there, the windscreen stippled with raindrops. The two figures sitting in the front watched us with cautious curiosity as we went past. I laughed – they were not police, but a large man and his large missus, out for a Sunday spin. The woman, chewing slowly on a sweet, goggled at the handcuffs, and I raised my wrists to her in a friendly salute. Hogg poked me again between the shoulder-blades, and I almost stumbled. I could see I was going to have trouble with him.

There were two cars, unmarked and nondescript, a blue one and a black. The comedy of car-doors opening, like beetles' wings. I was put into the back seat with Sergeant Hogg on one side of me and a big, baby-faced bruiser with red hair on the other. Haslet leaned on the door. Did you caution him? he enquired mildly. There was silence. The two detectives in the front seats went very still, as if afraid to stir for fear of laughing. Hogg stared grimly before him, his mouth set in a thin line. Haslet sighed and walked away. The driver carefully started up the engine. You have the right to remain silent blah blah blah, Hogg said venomously, without looking at me. Thank you, Sergeant, I said. I thought this another splendid bit of repartee. We took off from the kerb with a squeal, leaving a puff of tyre-smoke behind us on the air. I wondered if Charlie was watching from the window. I did not look back.

*

I pause to record that Helmut Behrens has died. Heart. Dear me, this is turning into the Book of the Dead.

*

How well I remember that journey. I had never travelled so fast in a car. We fairly flew along, weaving through the sluggish Sunday traffic, roaring down the inside lanes, taking corners on two wheels. It was very hot, with all the windows shut, and there was a musky, animal stink. The atmosphere bristled. I was entranced, filled with terror and a kind of glee, hurtling along like this, packed in with these big, sweating, silent men, who sat staring at the road ahead with their arms tightly folded, clasping to them their excitement and their pent-up rage. I could feel them breathing. Speed soothed them: speed was violence. The sun shone in our eyes, a great, dense glare. I knew that at the slightest provocation they would set on me and beat me half to death, they were just waiting for the chance. Even this knowledge, though, was bracing. I had never in my life been so entirely the centre of attention. From now on I would be watched over, I would be tended and fed and listened to, like a big, dangerous babe. No more running, no more hiding and waiting, no more decisions. I snuggled down between my captors, enjoying the hot chafe of metal on my wrists. Yet all the while another part of my mind was registering another version of things – was thinking, for instance, of all that I was losing. I looked at the streets, the buildings, the people, as if for the last time. I, who am a countryman at heart – yes, yes, it's true – and never really knew or cared for the city, even when I lived here, had come to love it now. Love? That is not a word I use very often. Perhaps I mean something else. It was the loss, yes, the imminent loss of – of what, I don't know. I was going to say, *of the community of men*, something solemn and grand like that, but when was I ever a part of *that* gathering? All the same, as we travelled along, some deep cavern of my heart was filling up with the grief of renunciation and departure. I recall especially a spot, near the river, where we were held up for a minute by a faulty traffic light. It was a street of little houses wedged between grey, featureless buildings, ware-houses and the like. An old man sat on a window sill, an infant played in the gutter with a grimy pup. Lines of brilliant washing were strung like bunting across an alleyway. All was still. The light stayed red. And then, as if a secret lever somewhere had been pressed, the whole rackety little scene came slowly, shyly to life. First a green train passed over a red metal bridge. Then two doors in two houses opened at once, and two girls in their Sunday best stepped out into the sunlight. The infant crowed, the pup yapped. A plane flew overhead, and an instant later its shadow skimmed the street. The old man hopped off the window-sill with surprising sprightliness. There was a pause, as if for effect, and then, with a thrilling foghorn blast, there glided into view above the rooftops the white bridge and black smokestack of an enormous, stately ship. It was all so quaint, so innocent and eager, like an illustration from the cover of a child's geography book, that I wanted to laugh out loud, though if I had, I think what would have come out would have sounded more like a sob. The driver swore then, and drove on through the red light, and I turned my head quickly and saw the whole thing swirling away, bright girls and ship, child and dog, old man, that red bridge, swirling away, into the past.

The police station was a kind of mock-Renaissance palace with a high, grey, many-windowed stone front and an archway leading into a grim little yard where surely once there had been a gibbet. I was hauled brusquely out of the car and led through low doorways and along dim corridors. There was a Sunday-afternoon air of lethargy about the place, and a boarding-school smell. I confess I had expected that the building would be agog at my arrival, that there would be clerks and secretaries and policemen in their braces crowding the hallways to get a look at me, but hardly a soul was about, and the few who passed me by hardly looked at me, and I could not help feeling a little offended. We stopped in a gaunt, unpleasant room, and had to wait some minutes for Inspector Haslet to arrive. Two tall windows, extremely grimy, their lower panes reinforced with wire mesh, gave on to the yard. There was a scarred desk, and a number of wooden chairs. No one sat. We shuffled our feet and looked at the ceiling. Someone cleared his throat. An elderly guard in shirt-sleeves came in. He was bald, and had a sweet, almost childlike smile. I noticed he was wearing a pair of thick black boots, tightly laced and buffed to a high shine. They were a comforting sight, those boots. In the coming days I was to measure my captors by their footwear. Brogues and boots I felt I could trust, running shoes were sinister. Inspector Haslet's car arrived in the yard. Once again we stood about awaiting his entrance. He came in as before, with the same diffident half-smile. I stood in front of the desk while he read out the charges. It was an oddly formal little ceremony. I was reminded of my wedding day, and had to suppress a grin. The bald old guard typed out the charge sheet on an ancient upright black machine, as if he were laboriously picking out a tune on a piano, the tip of his tongue wedged into a corner of his mouth. When Inspector Haslet asked if I had anything to say I shook my head. I would not have known where to begin. Then the ritual was over. There was a kind of general relaxing, and the other detectives, except Hogg, shuffled out. It was like the end of Mass. Hogg produced cigarettes, and offered the grinning packet to Haslet and the guard at the typewriter, and even, after a brief hesitation, to me. I felt I could not refuse. I tried not to cough. Tell me, I said to Haslet, how did you find me? He shrugged. He had the air of a schoolboy who has scored an embarrassingly high mark in his exams. The girl in the paper shop, he said. You never read only the one story, every day. Ah, I said, yes, of course. It struck me, however, as not at all convincing. Was he covering up for Binkie Behrens, for Anna, even? (He wasn't. They kept silent, to the end.) We smoked for a while, companionably. Twin shafts of sunlight leaned in the windows. A radio was squawking somewhere. I was suddenly, profoundly bored.

Listen, Hogg said, tell us, why did you do it?

I stared at him, startled, and at a loss. It was the one thing I had never asked myself, not with such simple, unavoidable force. Do you know, sergeant, I said, that's a very good question. His expression did not change, indeed he seemed not to move at all, except that his lank forelock lifted and fell, and for an instant I thought I had suffered a seizure, that something inside me, my liver, or a kidney, had burst of its own accord. More than anything else I felt amazement – that, and a curious, perverse satisfaction. I sank to my knees in a hot mist. I could not breathe. The elderly guard came from behind the desk and hauled me to my feet – did he say Oops-a-daisy, surely I imagine it? – and led me, stumbling, through a door and down a corridor and shoved me into a noisome, cramped lavatory. I knelt over the bowl and puked up lumps of egg and greasy spuds and a string of curdled milk. The ache in my innards was extraordinary, I could not believe it, I, who should have known all about such things. When there was nothing left to vomit I lay down with my arms clasped around my knees. Ah yes, I thought, this is more like it, this is more what I expected, writhing on the floor in a filthy jakes with my guts on fire. The guard knocked on the door and wanted to know was I done. He helped me to my feet again and walked me slowly back along the corridor. Always the same, he said, in a chatty tone, stuff comes up that you think you never ate.

Hogg was standing at the window with his hands in his pockets, looking out at the yard. He glanced at me over his shoulder. Better now? he said. Inspector Haslet sat in front of the desk, wearing a faraway frown and drumming his fingers on a jumble of papers. He indicated the chair beside him. I sat down gingerly. When he turned sideways to face me our knees were almost touching. He studied a far corner of the ceiling. Well, he said, do you want to talk to me? Oh, I did, I did, I wanted to talk and talk, to confide in him, to pour out all my poor secrets. But what could I say? What secrets? The bald guard was at his typewriter again, blunt fingers poised over the keys, his eyes fixed on my lips in lively expectation. Hogg too was waiting, standing by the window and jingling the coins in his trouser pocket. I would not have cared what I said to them, they meant nothing to me. The inspector was a different matter. He kept reminding me of someone I might have known at school, one of those modest, inarticulate heroes who were not only good at sport but at maths as well, yet who shrugged off praise, made shy by their own success and popularity. I had not the heart to confess to him that there was nothing to confess, that there had been no plan worthy of the name, that I had acted almost without thinking from the start. So I made up a rigmarole about having intended to make the robbery seem the work of terrorists, and a lot of other stuff that I am ashamed to repeat here. And then the girl, I said, the woman — for a second I could not think of her name! — and then *Josie*, I said, had ruined everything by trying to stop me taking the picture, by attacking me, by threatening to to to — I ran out of words, and sat and peered at him helplessly, wringing my hands. I so much wanted him to believe me. At that moment his credence seemed to me almost as desirable as forgiveness. There was a silence. He was still considering the corner of the ceiling. He might not have been listening to me at all. Jesus, Hogg said quietly, with no particular emphasis, and the guard behind the desk cleared his throat. Then Haslet stood up, wincing a little and flexing one knee, and ambled out of the room, and shut the door softly behind him. I could hear him walk away along the corridor at the same leisurely pace. There were voices faintly, his and others. Hogg was looking at me over his shoulder in disgust. You're a right joker, aren't you, he said. I thought of answering

him, but decided on prudence instead. Time passed. Someone
laughed in a nearby room. A motorcycle started up in the yard. I
studied a yellowed notice on the wall dealing with the threat of
rabies. I smiled, Mad-dog Montgomery, captured at last.

Inspector Haslet came back then, and held open the door and
ushered in a large, red-faced, sweating man in a striped shirt, and
another, younger, dangerous-looking fellow, one of Hogg's breed.
They gathered round and looked at me, leaning forward intently,
breathing, their hands flat on the desk. I told my story again,
trying to remember the details so as not to contradict myself. It
sounded even more improbable this time. When I finished there
was another silence. I was becoming accustomed already to these
interrogative and, as it seemed to me, deeply sceptical pauses. The
red-faced man, a person of large authority, I surmised, appeared
to be in a rage which he was controlling only with great difficulty.
His name will be – Barker. He looked at me hard for a long
moment. Come on, Freddie, he said, why did you kill her? I
stared back at him. I did not like his contemptuously familiar
tone – *Freddie*, indeed! – but decided to let it go. I recognised in
him one of my own kind, the big, short-tempered, heavy-
breathing people of this world. And anyway, I was getting tired
of all this. I killed her because I could, I said, what more can I
say? We were all startled by that, I as much as they. The younger
one, Hickey – no, Kickham, gave a sort of laugh. He had a thin,
piping, almost musical voice that was peculiarly at odds with his
menacing look and manner. What's-his-name, he said, he's a
queer, is he? I looked at him helplessly. I did not know what he
was talking about. Pardon? I said. French, he said impatiently, is
he a fairy? I laughed, I could not help it. I did not know whether
it was more comic or preposterous, the idea of Charlie prancing
into Wally's and pinching the bottoms of his boys. (It appears
that Wally's creature, Sonny of the emerald hues, had been telling
scurrilous lies about poor Charlie's predilections. Truly, what a
wicked world this is.) Oh no, I said, no – he has an occasional
woman. It was just nervousness and surprise that made me say it,
I had not meant to attempt a joke. No one laughed. They all just

went on looking at me, while the silence tightened and tightened like something being screwed shut, and then, as if at a signal, they turned on their heels and trooped out and the door slammed behind them, and I was left alone with the elderly guard, who smiled his sweet smile at me and shrugged. I told him I was feeling nauseous again, and he went off and fetched me a mug of sticky-sweet tea and a lump of bread. Why is it that tea, just the look of it, always makes me feel miserable, like an abandoned waif? And how lost and lonely everything seemed, this stale room, and the vague noises of people elsewhere going about their lives, and the sunlight in the yard, that same thick steady light that shines across the years out of farthest childhood. All the euphoria I had felt earlier was gone now.

Haslet returned, alone this time, and sat down beside me at the desk as before. He had removed his jacket and tie and rolled up his sleeves. His hair was tousled. He looked more boyish than ever. He too had a mug of tea, the mug looking enormous in that small, white hand. I had an image of him as a child, out on some bog in the wastes of the midlands, stacking turf with his da: quake of water in the cuttings, smell of smoke and roasting spuds, and the flat distances the colour of a hare's pelt, and then the enormous, vertical sky stacked with luminous bundles of cloud.

Now, he said, let's start again.

We went on for hours. I was almost happy, sitting there with him, pouring out my life-story, as the shafts of sunlight in the windows lengthened and the day waned. He was infinitely patient. There seemed to be nothing, no detail, however minute or enigmatic, that did not interest him. No, that's not quite it. It was as if he were not really interested at all. He greeted everything, every strand and knot of my story, with the same passive air of toleration and that same, faint, bemused little smile. I told him about knowing Anna Behrens, and about her father, about his diamond mines and his companies and his priceless art collection. I watched him carefully, trying to judge how much of this was new to him, but it was no good, he gave nothing away. Yet he must have spoken to them, must have taken statements and all the rest of it. Surely they would have told him about me, surely they were not protecting me still. He rubbed his cheek, and gazed again into the corner of the ceiling. Self-made man, is he, he said, this Behrens? Oh Inspector, I said, aren't we all? At that he gave me a peculiar look, and stood up. I noticed again that brief grimace of pain. Bad knee. Footballer. Sunday afternoons, the shouts muffled in grey air, the flat thud of leather on leather. Now what, I said, what happens now? I did not want him to leave me yet. What would I do when the darkness came? He said I should give the guard my solicitor's name, so he could be told I was here. I nodded. I had no solicitor, of course, but I felt I could not say so – everything was so relaxed and chummy, and I did not want to create any awkwardnesses. Anyway, I was fully intending to conduct my own defence, and already saw myself making brilliant and impassioned speeches from the dock. Is there anything else I should do, I said, frowning up at him seriously, is there anyone else I should tell? (Oh, I was so good, so compliant, what a warm thrill of agreeableness I felt, deferring like this to this good chap!) He gave me that peculiar look again, there was irritation and impatience in it, but a certain ironic amusement too, and even a hint of complicity. What you can do, he said, is get your story straight, without the frills and fancy bits. What do you mean, I said, what do you mean? I was dismayed. Bob Cherry had suddenly turned harsh, had almost for a moment become Mr Quelch. You know very well what I mean, he said. Then he went off, and Hogg came back, and he and the elderly guard – oh, call him something, for God's sake – he and Cunningham, old Cunningham the desk sergeant, took me down to the cells.

Am I still handcuffed?

I do not know why I say they took me *down* (well, I do, of course) for we simply walked a little way along a corridor, past the lavatory, and through a steel gate. I confess I felt a qualm of fear, but that was quickly replaced by surprise: it was all just as I expected! There really are bars, there really is a bucket, and a pallet with a striped, lumpy mattress, and graffiti on the scarred walls. There was even a stubbled old-timer, standing white-knuckled at the door of his cell, who peered out at me in wordless, angry derision. I was given a piece of soap and a tiny towel and three pieces of shiny toilet-paper. In return I surrendered my belt and shoelaces. I saw at once the importance of this ritual. Cowering there, with the tongues of my shoes hanging out, clutching in one hand the waistband of my trousers and holding in the other, for all to see, the fundamental aids to my most private functions, I was no longer wholly human. I hasten to say this seemed to me quite proper, to be, indeed, a kind of setting to rights, an official and outward definition of what had been the case, in my case, all along. I had achieved my apotheosis. Even old Cunningham, even Sergeant Hogg seemed to recognise it, for they treated me now, brusquely, with a sort of truculent, abstracted regard, as if they were not my jailers, but my keepers, rather. I might have been a sick old toothless lion. Hogg put his hands in his pockets and went off whistling. I sat down on the side of the cot. Time passed. It was very quiet. The old boy in the other cell asked me my name. I did not answer him. Well fuck you, then, he said. Dusk came on. I have always loved that hour of the day, when that soft, muslin light seeps upward, as if out of the earth itself, and everything seems to grow thoughtful and turn away. It was almost dark when Sergeant Hogg came back, and handed me a grubby sheet of foolscap. He had been eating chips, I could smell them on his breath. I peered in bafflement at the ill-typed page. That's your confession, Hogg said. Feel like signing it? The lag next door cackled grimly. What are you talking about? I said. These are not my words. He shrugged, and belched into his fist. Suit yourself, he said, you'll be going down for life anyway. Then he went off again. I sat down and examined this strange document. Oh, well-named Cunningham! Behind the mask of the bald old codger a fiendish artist had been at work, the kind of artist I could never be, direct yet subtle, a master of the spare style, of the art that conceals art. I marvelled at how he had turned everything to his purpose, mis-spellings, clumsy syntax, even the atrocious typing. Such humility, such deference, such ruthless suppression of the ego for the sake of the text. He had taken my story, with all its –

what was it Haslet said? – with all its frills and fancy bits, and
pared it down to stark essentials. It was an account of my crime I
hardly recognised, and yet I believed it. He had made a murderer
of me. I would have signed it there and then, but I had nothing
to write with. I even searched my clothing for something sharp,
a pin or something, with which to stick myself, and scrawl
my signature in blood. But what matter, it did not require my
endorsement. Reverently I folded the page in four and placed it
under the mattress at the end where my head would be. Then I
undressed and lay down naked in the shadows and folded my
hands on my breast, like a marble knight on a tomb, and closed
my eyes. I was no longer myself. I can't explain it, but it's true.
I was no longer myself.

*

That first night in captivity was turbulent. I slept fitfully, it was
not really sleep, but a helpless tossing and sliding on the surface
of a dark sea. I could sense the deeps beneath me, the black,
boundless deeps. The hour before dawn was, as always, the
worst. I masturbated repeatedly – forgive these squalid details –
not for pleasure, really, but to exhaust myself. What a motley
little band of manikins I conjured up to join me in these melancholy frostings. Daphne was there, of course, and Anna Behrens,
amused and faintly shocked at the things I was making her do,
and poor Foxy as well, who wept again in my arms, as I, silent
and stealthy about my felon's work, pressed her and pressed her
against that door in the empty, moonlit room of my imagination.
But there were others, too, whom I would not have expected:
Madge's niece, for instance – remember Madge's niece? – and the
big girl with the red neck I had followed through the city streets
– remember *her*? – and even, God forgive me, my mother and
the stable-girl. And in the end, when they all had come and gone,
and I lay empty on my prison bed, there rose up out of me again,
like the spectre of an onerous and ineluctable task, the picture of
that mysterious, dark doorway, and the invisible presence in it,
yearning to appear, to be there. To live.

MONDAY MORNING. Ah, Monday morning. The ashen light, the noise, the sense of pointless but compulsory haste. I think it will be Monday morning when I am received in Hell. I was wakened early by a policeman bearing another mug of tea and lump of bread. I had been dozing, it was like being held fast in the embrace of a large, hot, rank-smelling animal. I knew at once exactly where I was, there was no mistaking the place. The policeman was young, an enormous boy with a tiny head, when I opened my eyes first and looked up at him he seemed to tower above me almost to the ceiling. He said something incomprehensible and went away. I sat on the edge of the cot and held my head in my hands. My mouth was foul, and there was an ache behind my eyes and a wobbly sensation in the region of my diaphragm. I wondered if this nausea would be with me for the rest of my life. Wan sunlight fell at a slant through the bars of my cage. I was cold. I draped a blanket around my shoulders and squatted over the bucket, my knees trembling. I would not have been surprised if a crowd had gathered in the corridor to laugh at me. I kept thinking, yes, this is it, this is how it will be from now on. It was almost gratifying, in a horrible sort of way.

Sergeant Cunningham came to fetch me for the first of that day's inquisitions. I had washed as best I could at the filthy sink in the corner. I asked him if I might borrow a razor. He laughed, shaking his head at the idea, the richness of it. He thought I really was a card. I admired his good humour: he had been here all night, his shift was only ending now. I shuffled after him along the corridor, clutching my trousers to keep them from falling down. The dayroom was filled with a kind of surly pandemonium. Typewriters clacked, and short-wave radios snivelled in adenoidal

174

bursts, and people strode in and out of doorways, talking over their shoulders, or crouched at desks and shouted into telephones. A hush fell when I came through – no, not a hush, exactly, but a downward modulation in the noise. Word, obviously, had spread. They did not stare at me, I suppose that would have been unprofessional, but they took me in, all the same. I saw myself in their eyes, a big, confused creature, like a dancing bear, shambling along at the steel-tipped heels of Cunningham's friendly boots. He opened a door and motioned me into a square, grey room. There was a plastic-topped table and two chairs. Well, he said, I'll be seeing you, and he winked and withdrew his head and shut the door. I sat down carefully, placing my hands flat before me on the table. Time passed. I was surprised how calmly I could sit, just waiting. It was as if I were not fully there, as if I had become detached somehow from my physical self. The room was like the inside of a skull. The hubbub in the dayroom might have been coming to me from another planet.

Barker and Kickham were the first to arrive. Barker today wore a blue suit which had been cut in great broad swathes, as if it were intended not for wearing, but to house a collection of things, boxes, perhaps. He was red-faced and in a sweat already. Kickham had on the same leather jacket and dark shirt that he was wearing yesterday – he did not strike me as a man much given to changing his clothes. They wanted to know why I had not signed the confession. I had forgotten about it, and left it under the mattress, but I said, I don't know why, that I had torn it up. There was another of those brief, stentorian silences, while they stood over me, clenching their fists and breathing heavily down their nostrils. The air rippled with suppressed violence. Then they trooped out and I was left alone again. Next to appear was an elderly chap in cavalry twill and a natty little hat, and a narrow-eyed, brawny young man who looked like the older one's disgruntled son. They stood just inside the door and studied me carefully for a long moment, as if measuring me for something. Then Detective Twill advanced and sat down opposite me, and crossed his legs, and took off his hat, revealing a flattish bald head, waxen and peculiarly pitted, like that of an ailing baby. He produced a pipe and lighted it with grave deliberation, then recrossed his legs and settled himself more comfortably, and began to ask me a series of cryptic questions, which after some time I realised were aimed at discovering what I might know about Charlie French and his acquaintances. I answered as circumspectly as I could, not knowing what it was they wanted to know – I suspect they didn't, either. I kept smiling at them both, to show how willing I was, how compliant. The younger one, still standing by the door, took notes. Or at least he went through the motions of writing in a notebook, for I had an odd feeling that the whole thing was a sham, intended to distract or intimidate me. All that happened, however, was that I grew bored – I could not take them seriously – and got muddled, and began to contradict myself. After a while they too seemed to grow discouraged, and eventually left. Then my chum Inspector Haslet came sidling in with his shy smile and averted glance. My God, I said, who were they? Branch, he said. He sat down, looked at the floor, drummed his fingers on the table. Listen, I said, I'm worried, my wife, I – He wasn't listening, wasn't interested. He brought up the matter of my confession. Why hadn't I signed it? He spoke quietly, he might have been talking about the weather. Save a lot of trouble, you know, he said. Suddenly I flew into a rage, I don't know what came over me, I banged my fist on the table and jumped up and shouted at him that I would do nothing, sign nothing, until I got some answers! I really did say that: *until I get some answers*! At once, of course, the anger evaporated, and I sat down again sheepishly, biting on a knuckle. The ruffled air subsided. Your wife, Haslet said mildly, is getting on a plane – he consulted his watch – just about now. I stared at him. Oh, I said. I was relieved, of course, but not really surprised. I knew all along Señor what's-his-name would be too much of a gentleman not to let her go.

*

It was noon when Maolseachlainn arrived, though he had the rumpled air of having just got out of bed. He always looks like that, it is another of his endearing characteristics. The first thing that struck me was how alike we were in build, two big soft broad heavy men. The table groaned between us when we leaned forward over it, the chairs gave out little squeaks of alarm under our ponderous behinds. I liked him at once. He said I must be wondering who had engaged him on my behalf. I nodded vigorously, though in truth no such thought had entered my head. He grew shifty then, and mumbled something about my mother, and some work he claimed to have done for her in some unspecified period of the past. It was to be a long time before I would discover, to my surprise and no little dismay, that in fact it was Charlie French who arranged it all, who called my mother that Sunday evening and broke the news to her of my arrest, and told her to contact straight away his good friend Maolseachlainn Mac Giolla Gunna, the famous counsel. It was Charles too who paid, and is paying still, Mac's not inconsiderable fees. He puts the money through the bank, and my mother, or it must be that stable-girl, now, I suppose, sends it on as if it were coming from Coolgrange. (Sorry to have kept this bit from you, Mac, but it's what Charlie wanted.) You made some sort of confession, Maolseachlainn was saying, is that right? I told him about Cunningham's marvellous document. I must have grown excited in the telling, for his brow darkened, and he closed his eyes behind his halfglasses as if in pain and held up a hand to silence me. You'll sign nothing, he said, nothing – are you mad? I hung my head. But I'm guilty, I said quietly, I *am* guilty. This he pretended not to hear. Listen to me, he said, listen. You will sign nothing, say nothing, do nothing. You will enter a plea of not guilty. I opened my mouth to protest, but he was not to be interrupted. You will plead not guilty, he said, and when I judge the moment opportune you will change your submission, and plead guilty to manslaughter. Do you understand? He was looking at me coldly over his glasses. (This was early days, before he had become my friend.) I shook my head. It doesn't seem right, I said. He gave a sort of laugh. Right! he said, and did not add: that's rich, coming from you. We were silent for a moment. My stomach made a pinging sound. I felt sick and hungry at the same time. By the way, I said, have you spoken to my mother, is she coming to see me? He pretended not to hear. He put away his papers, and took off his glasses and squeezed the bridge of his nose. Was there anything I wanted? Now it was my turn to snicker. I mean is there any thing I can have them get for you, he said, in a primly disapproving tone. A razor, I said, and they could give me back my belt, I'm not going to hang myself. He stood up to leave. Suddenly I wanted to detain him. Thank you, I said, so fervently that he paused and stared at me owlishly. I meant to kill her, you know, I said, I have no explanation, and no excuse. He just sighed.

*

I was brought to court in the afternoon. Inspector Haslet and two uniformed guards accompanied me. My hand where I had caught it on the rose-bush had become infected. O Frederick, thou art sick. I have a strangely hazy recollection of that first appearance. I had expected the courtroom to be rather grand, something like a small church, with oaken pews and a carved ceiling and an air of pomp and seriousness, and I was disappointed when it turned out to be little more than a shabby office, the kind of place where obscure permits are issued by incompetent clerks. When I was led in, there was a sort of irritable flurry of activity which I took to be a general making-ready, but which was, as I discovered to my surprise, the hearing itself. It cannot have lasted more than a minute or two. The judge, who wore an ordinary business suit, was a jolly old boy with whiskers and a red nose. He must have had a reputation as a wit, for when he fixed me with a merry eye and said, Ah, Mr Montgomery, the whole place fairly rocked with amusement. I smiled politely, to show him I could take a joke, even if I did not get it. A guard prodded me in the back, I stood up, sat down, stood up again, then it was over. I looked about me in surprise. I felt I must have missed something. Maolseachlainn was asking for bail. Judge Fielding gently shook his head, as if he were reproving a forward child. Ah no, he said, I think not, sir. That provoked another tremor of merriment in the court. Well, I was glad they were all having such a good time. The guard behind me was saying something, but I could not concentrate, for there was a horrible, hollow sensation in my chest, and I realised that I was about to weep. I felt like a child, or a very old man. Maolseachlainn touched my arm. I turned away helplessly. Come on now, the guard said, not unkindly, and I blundered after him. Everything swam. Haslet was behind me, I knew his step by now. In the street a little crowd had gathered. How did they know who I was, which court I would be in, the time at which I would appear? When they caught sight of me they gave a cry, a sort of ululant wail of awe and execration that made my skin prickle. I was so confused and frightened I forgot myself and waved – I waved to them! God knows what I thought I was doing. I suppose it was meant as a placatory gesture, an animal sign of submission and retreat. It only made them more furious, of course. They shook their fists, they howled. One or two of them seemed about to break from the rest and fly at me. A woman spat, and called me a dirty bastard. I just stood there, nodding and waving like a clockwork man, with a terrified grin fixed on my face. That was when I realised, for the first time, it was *one of theirs* I had killed. It had rained while I was inside, and now the sun was shining again. I remember the glare of the wet road, and a cloud stealthily disappearing over the rooftops, and a dog skirting the angry crowd with a worried look in its eye. Always the incidental things, you see, the little things. Then the blanket was thrown over me and I was pushed head-first into the police car and we sped away, the tyres hissing. Hee-haw, hee-haw. In the hot, woolly darkness I wept my fill.

*

179

Prison. This place. I have described it already.

*

My first visitor was a surprise. When they told me it was a woman I expected Daphne, straight from the airport, or else my mother, and at first when I came into the visiting-room I did not recognise her. She seemed younger than ever, in her shapeless pullover and plaid skirt and sensible shoes. She had the unformed, palely freckled look of a schoolgirl, the dullard of the class, who cries in the dorm at night and is mad on ponies. Only her marvellous, flame-coloured hair proclaimed her a woman. Jenny! I said, and she blushed. I took her hands in mine. I was absurdly pleased to see her. I did not know then that she would soon prove my usurper. Joanne, actually, she mumbled, and bit her lip. I laughed in embarrassment. Joanne, I said, of course, forgive me, I'm so confused just now. We sat down. I beamed and beamed. I felt light-hearted, almost skittish. I might have been the visitor, an old bachelor friend of the family, come to see the poor duckling on the school open day. She had brought my bag from Cool-grange. It looked strange to me, familiar and yet alien, as if it had been on an immense, transfiguring voyage, to another planet, another galaxy, since I had seen it last. I enquired after my mother. I was tactful enough not to ask why she had not come. Tell her I'm sorry, I said. It sounded ridiculous, as if I were apologising for a broken appointment, and we looked away from each other furtively and were silent for a long, awkward moment. I have a nickname in here already, I said, they call me Monty, of course. She smiled, and I was pleased. When she smiles, biting her lip like that, she is more than ever like a child. I cannot believe she is a schemer. I suspect she was as surprised as I when the will was read. I find it hard to see her as the mistress of Coolgrange. Perhaps that is what my mother intended – after *her*, the drip. Ah, that is unworthy of me, my new seriousness. I do not hate her for disinheriting me. I think that in her way she was trying to teach me something, to make me look more closely at things, perhaps, to pay more attention to people, such as this poor clumsy girl, with her freckles and her timid smile and her almost invisible eyebrows. I am remembering what Daphne said to me only yesterday, through her tears, it has lodged in my mind like a thorn: *You knew nothing about us, nothing!* She's right, of course. She was talking about America, about her and Anna Behrens and all that, but it's true in general – I know nothing. Yet I am trying. I watch, and listen, and brood. Now and then I am afforded a glimpse into what seems a new world, but which I realise has been there all along, without my noticing. In these explorations my friend Billy is a valuable guide. I have not mentioned Billy before, have I? He attached himself to me early on, I think he is a little in love with me. He's nineteen – muscles, oiled black hair, a killer's shapely hands, like mine. Our trials are due to open on the same day, he takes this as a lucky omen. He is charged with murder and multiple rape. He insists on his innocence, but cannot suppress a guilty little smile. I believe he is secretly proud of his crimes. Yet a kind of innocence shines out of him, as if there is something inside, some tiny, precious part, that nothing can besmirch. When I consider Billy I can almost believe in the existence of the soul. He has been in and out of custody since he was a child, and is a repository of prison lore. He tells me of the various ingenious methods of smuggling in dope. For instance, before the glass screens were put up, wives and girlfriends used to hide in their mouths little plastic bags of heroin, which were passed across during lingering kisses, swallowed, and sicked-up later, in the latrines. I was greatly taken with the idea, it affected me deeply. Such need, such passion, such charity and daring – when have I ever known the like?

What was I saying. I am becoming so vague. It happens to all of us in here. It is a kind of defence, this creeping absentmindedness, this torpor, which allows us to drop off instantly, anywhere, at any time, into brief, numb stretches of sleep.

Joanne. She came to see me, brought me my bag. I was glad to have it. They had confiscated most of what was in it, the prison authorities, but there were some shirts, a bar of soap – the scented smell of it struck me like a blow – a pair of shoes, my books. I clutched these things, these icons, to my heart, and grieved for the dead past.

But grief, that kind of grief is the great danger, in here. It saps the will. Those who give way to it grow helpless, a wasting lethargy comes over them. They are like mourners for whom the period of mourning will not end. I saw this danger, and determined to avoid it. I would work, I would study. The theme was there, ready-made. I had Daphne bring me big thick books on Dutch painting, not only the history but the techniques, the secrets of the masters. I studied accounts of the methods of grinding colours, of the trade in oils and dyes, of the flax industry in Flanders. I read the lives of the painters and their patrons. I became a minor expert on the Dutch republic in the seventeenth century. But in the end it was no good: all this learning, this information, merely built up and petrified, like coral encrusting a sunken wreck. How could mere facts compare with the amazing knowledge that had flared out at me as I stood and stared at the painting lying on its edge in the ditch where I dropped it that last time? That knowledge, that knowingness, I could not have lived with. I look at the reproduction, pinned to the wall above me here, but something is dead in it. Something is dead.

It was in the same spirit of busy exploration that I pored for long hours over the newspaper files in the prison library. I read every word devoted to my case, read and reread them, chewed them over until they turned to flavourless mush in my mind. I learned of Josie Bell's childhood, of her schooldays – pitifully brief – of her family and friends. Neighbours spoke well of her. She was a quiet girl. She had almost married once, but something had gone wrong, her fiancé went to England and did not return. First she worked in her own village, as a shopgirl. Then, before going to Whitewater, she was in Dublin for a while, where she was a chambermaid in the Southern Star Hotel. The Southern Star! – my God, I could have gone there when I was at Charlie's, could have taken a room, could have slept in a bed that she had once made! I laughed at myself. What would I have learned? There would have been no more of her there, for me, than there was in the newspaper stories, than there had been that day when I turned and saw her for the first time, standing in the open french window with the blue and gold of summer at her back, than there was when she crouched in the car and I hit her again and again and her blood spattered the window. This is the worst, the essential sin, I think, the one for which there will be no forgiveness: that I never imagined her vividly enough, that I never made her be there sufficiently, that I did not make her live. Yes, that failure of imagination is my real crime, the one that made the others possible. What I told that policeman is true – I killed her because I could kill her, and I could kill her because for me she was not alive. And so my task now is to bring her back to life. I am not sure what that means, but it strikes me with the force of an unavoidable imperative. How am I to make it come about, this act of parturition? Must I imagine her from the start, from infancy? I am puzzled, and not a little fearful, and yet there is something stirring in me, and I am strangely excited. I seem to have taken on a new weight and density. I feel gay and at the same time wonderfully serious. I am big with possibilities. I am living for two.

*

I have decided: I will not be swayed: I will plead guilty to murder in the first degree. I think it is the right thing to do. Daphne, when I told her, burst into tears at once. I was astonished, astonished and appalled. What about me, she cries, what about the child? I said, as mildly as I could, that I thought I had already destroyed their lives, and that the best thing I could do was to stay away from them for as long as possible – forever, even – so that she might have the chance to start afresh. This, it seems, was not tactful. She just cried and cried, sitting there beyond the glass, clutching a sodden tissue in her fist, her shoulders shaking. Then it all came out, the rage and the shame, I could nor make out the half of it through her sobs. She went back over the years. What I had done, and not done. How little I knew, how little I understood. I sat and gazed at her, aghast, my mouth open. I could not speak. How was it possible, that I could have been so wrong about her, all this time? How could I not have seen that behind her reticence there was all this passion, this pain? I was thinking about a pub I had passed by late on one of my night rambles through the city in that week before I was captured. It was in, I don't know, Stoney Batter, somewhere like that, a working-class pub with protective steel mesh covering the windows and old vomit-stains around the doorway. As I went past, a drunk stumbled out, and for a second, before the door swung shut again, I had a glimpse inside. I walked on without pausing, carrying the scene in my head. It was like something by Jan Steen: the smoky light, the crush of red-faced drinkers, the old boys propping up the bar, the fat woman singing, displaying a mouthful of broken teeth. A kind of slow amazement came over me, a kind of bafflement and grief, at how firmly I felt myself excluded from that simple, ugly, roistering world. That is how I seem to have spent my life, walking by open, noisy doorways, and passing on, into the darkness. – And yet there are moments too that allow me to think I am not wholly lost. The other day, for instance, on the way to yet one more remand hearing, I shared the police van with an ancient wino who had been arrested the night before, so he told me, for killing his friend. I could not imagine him having a friend, much less killing one. He talked to me at length as we bowled along, though most of what he said was gibberish. He had a bloodied eye, and an enormous, weeping sore on his mouth. I looked out the barred window at the city streets going past, doing my best to ignore him. Then, when we were rounding a sharp bend, he fell off his seat on top of me, and I found myself holding the old brute in my arms. The smell was appalling, of course, and the rags he wore had a slippery feel to them that made me clench my teeth, but still I held him, and would not let him fall to the floor, and I even – surely I am embroidering – I think I may even have clasped him to me for a moment, in a gesture of, I don't know, of sympathy, of comradeship, of solidarity, something like that. Yes, an explorer, that's what I am, glimpsing a new continent from the prow of a sinking ship. And don't mistake me, I don't imagine for a second that such incidents as this, such forays into the new world, will abate my guilt one whit. But maybe they signify something for the future.

Should I destroy that last paragraph? No, what does it matter, let it stand.

Daphne brought me one of Van's drawings. I have pinned it up on the wall here. It is a portrait of me, she says. One huge, club foot, sausage fingers, a strangely calm, cyclopean eye. Quite a good likeness, really, when I think about it. She also brought me a startling piece of news. Joanne has invited her and the child to come and live at Coolgrange. They are going to set up house together, my wife and the stable-girl. (How quaintly things contrive to make what seems an ending!) I am not displeased, which surprises me. Apparently I am to live there also, when I get out. Oh, I can just see myself, in wellingtons and a hat, mucking out the stables. But I said nothing. Poor Daphne, if only – ah yes, if only.

Maolseachlainn too was horrified when I told him of my decision. Don't worry, I said, I'll plead guilty, but I don't want any concessions. He could not understand it, and I had not the energy to explain. It's what I want, that's all. It's what I must do. Apollo's ship has sailed for Delos, the stern crowned with laurel, and I must serve my term. By the way, Mac, I said, I owe a plate to Charlie French. He did not get the joke, but he smiled anyway. She wasn't dead, you know, when I left her, I said. I wasn't man enough to finish her off. I'd have done as much for a dog. (It's true – is there no end to the things I must confess?) He nodded, trying not to show his disgust, or perhaps it was just shock he was hiding. Hardy people, he said, they don't die easily. Then he gathered up his papers and turned to go. We shook hands. The occasion seemed to require that small formality.

*

Oh, by the way, the plot: it almost slipped my mind. Charlie French bought my mother's pictures cheap and sold them dear to Binkie Behrens, then bought them cheap from Binkie and sold them on to Max Molyneaux. Something like that. Does it matter? Dark deeds, dark deeds. Enough.

*

Time passes. I eat time. I imagine myself a kind of grub, calmly and methodically consuming the future, what the world outside calls the future. I must be careful not to give in to despair, to that aboulia which has been a threat always to everything I tried to do. I have looked for so long into the abyss, I feel sometimes it is the abyss that is looking into me. I have my good days, and my bad. I think of the monsters on whose side my crime has put me, the killers, the torturers, the dirty little beasts who stand by and watch it happen, and I wonder if it would not be better simply to stop. But I have my task, my term. Today, in the workshop, I caught her smell, faint, sharp, metallic, unmistakable. It is the smell of metal-polish – she must have been doing the silver that day. I was so happy when I identified it! Anything seemed possible. It even seemed that someday I might wake up and see, coming forward from the darkened room into the frame of that doorway which is always in my mind now, a child, a girl, one whom I will recognise at once, without the shadow of a doubt.

It is spring. Even in here we feel it, the quickening in the air. I have some plants in my window, I like to watch them, feeding on the light. The trial takes place next month. It will be a quick affair. The newspapers will be disappointed. I thought of trying to publish this, my testimony. But no. I have asked Inspector Haslet to put it into my file, with the other, official fictions. He came to see me today, here in my cell. He picked up the pages, hefted them in his hand. It was to be my defence, I said. He gave me a wry look. Did you put in about being a scientist, he said, and knowing the Behrens woman, and owing money, all that stuff? I smiled. It's my story, I said, and I'm sticking to it. He laughed at that. Come on, Freddie, he said, how much of it is true? It was the first time he had called me by my name. True, Inspector? I said. All of it. None of it. Only the shame.

GHOSTS

I

HERE THEY ARE. There are seven of them. Or better say, half a dozen or so, that gives more leeway. They are struggling up the dunes, stumbling in the sand, squabbling, complaining, wanting sympathy, wanting to be elsewhere. That, most of all: to be elsewhere. There is no elsewhere, for them. Only here, in this little round.

'List!'

'Listing.'

'Leaky as a—'

'So I said, I said.'

'Everything feels strange.'

'That captain, so-called.'

'I did, I said to him.'

'Cythera, my foot.'

'Some outing.'

'Listen!'

Behind them the boat leans, stuck fast on a sandbank, canted drunkenly to starboard, fat-bellied, barnacled, betrayed by a freak wave or a trick of the tide and the miscalculations of a tipsy skipper. They have had to wade through the shallows to get to shore. Thus things begin. It is a morning late in May. The sun shines merrily. How the wind blows! A little world is coming into being.

Who speaks? I do. Little god.

*

Licht spied them from afar, with his keen sight. It was so long since he had seen their like that for a moment he hardly knew what they were. He flew to the turret room at the top of the house where the Professor increasingly spent his time, brooding

by himself or idly scanning the horizon through the brass telescope mounted on his desk. Inside the door Licht stopped,
irresolute suddenly. It is always thus with him, the headlong rush
and then the halt. The Professor turned up his face slowly from
the big book open in front of him and stared at Licht with such
glassy remoteness that Licht grew frightened and almost forgot
what he had come to say. Is this what death is like, he wondered,
is this how people begin to die, swimming a little farther out each
time until in the end the land is out of sight for good? At last the
Professor returned to himself and blinked and frowned and pursed
his lips, annoyed that Licht had found him there, lost like that.
Licht stood panting, with that eager, hazy smile of his.

'What?' the Professor said sharply. 'What? Who are they?'

'I don't know,' Licht answered breathlessly. 'But I think
they're coming here, whoever they are.'

Poor Licht. He is anything from twenty-five to fifty. His
yellow-white curls and spindly little legs give him an antique look:
he seems as if he should be got up in periwig and knee-breeches.
His eyes are brown and his brow is broad, with two smooth dents
at the temples, as if whoever moulded him had given his big head
a last, loving squeeze there between finger and thumb. He is never
still. Now his foot tap-tapped on the turret floor and the fist he
had thrust into his trousers pocket flexed and flexed. He pointed
to the spyglass.

'Did you see them?' he said. 'Sheep, I thought they were.
Vertical sheep!'

He laughed, three soft, quick little gasps. The Professor turned
away from him and hunched a forbidding black shoulder, his
sea-captain's swivel chair groaning under him. Licht stepped to
the window and looked down.

'They're coming here, all right,' he said softly. 'Oh, I'm sure
they're coming here.'

He shook his head and frowned, trying to seem alarmed at the
prospect of invasion, but had to bite his lip to keep from grinning.

*

Meanwhile my foundered creatures have not got far. They have not lost their sea-legs yet and the sand is soft going. There is an old boy in a boater, a pretty young woman, called Flora, of course, and a blonde woman in a black skirt and a black leather jacket with a camera slung over her shoulder. Also an assortment of children: three, to be precise. And a thin, lithe, sallow man with bad teeth and hair dyed black and a darkly watchful eye. His name is Felix. He seems to find something funny in all of this, smiling fiercely to himself and sucking on a broken eye-tooth. He urges the others on when they falter, Flora especially, inserting two long, bony fingers under her elbow. She will not look at him. She has a strange feeling, she says, it is as if she has been here before. He wrinkles his high, smooth forehead, gravely bending the full weight of his attention to her words. Perhaps, he says after a moment, perhaps she is remembering childhood outings to the seaside: the salt breeze, the sound of the waves, the cat-smell of the sand, that sun-befuddled, sparkling light that makes everything seem to fold softly into something else.

'What do you think?' he said. 'Might that be it?'

She shrugged, smiled, tossed her hair, making an end of it. She thought how quaint yet dangerous it sounded when a person spoke so carefully, with such odd emphasis.

Softly.

The boys – there are two of them – watched all this, nudging each other and fatly grinning.

'So strange,' Flora was saying. 'Everything seems so . . .'

'Yes?' Felix prompted.

She was silent briefly and then shivered.

'Just . . . strange,' she said. 'I don't know.'

He nodded, his dark gaze lowered.

Felix and Flora.

The dunes ended and they came to a flat place of dark-green sward where the sandy grass crackled under their tread, and there were tiny, pink-tipped daisies, and celandines that blossom when the swallows come, though I can see no swallows yet, and here and there a tender violet trembling in the breeze. They paused in vague amaze and looked about, expecting something. The ground was pitted with rabbit-burrows, each one had a little pile of diggings at the door, and rabbits that seemed to move by clockwork stood up and looked at them, hopped a little way, stopped, and looked again.

'What is that?' said the blonde woman, whose name is Sophie. 'What is that noise?'

All listened, holding their breath, even the children, and each one heard it, a faint, deep, formless song that seemed to rise out of the earth itself.

'Like music,' said the man in the straw hat dreamily. 'Like . . . singing.'

Felix frowned and slowly turned his head this way and that, peering hard, his sharp nose twitching at the tip, birdman, raptor, rapt.

'There should be a house,' he murmured. 'A house on a hill, and a little bridge, and a road leading up.'

Sophie regarded him with scorn, smilingly.

'You have been here before?' she said, and then, sweetly: 'Aeaea, is it?'

He glanced at her sideways and smiled his fierce, thin smile. They have hardly met and are old enemies already. He hummed, nodding to himself, and stepped away from her, like one stepping slowly in a dream, still peering, and picked up his black bag from the grass. 'Yes,' he said with steely gaiety, 'yes, Aeaea: and you will feel at home, no doubt.'

She lifted her camera like a gun and shot him. I can see from the way she handles it that she is a professional. In fact, she is mildly famous, her name appears in expensive magazines and on the spines of sumptuous volumes of glossy silver and black prints. Light is her medium, she moves through it as through some fine, shining fluid, bearing aloft out of the world's reach the precious phial of her self.

Still they lingered, looking about them, and all at once, unaccountably, the wind of something that was almost happiness wafted through them all, though in each one it took a different form, and all thought what they felt was singular and unique and so were unaware of this brief moment of concord. Then it was gone, the god of inspiration flew elsewhere, and everything was as it had been.

I must be in a mellow mood today.

*

The house. It is large and of another age. It stands on a green rise, built of wood and stone, tall, narrow, ungainly, each storey seeming to lean in a different direction. Long ago it was painted red but the years and the salt winds have turned it to a light shade of pink. The roof is steep with high chimneys and gay scalloping under the eaves. The delicate octagonal turret with the weather-vane on top is a surprise, people see its slender panes flashing from afar and say, Ah! and smile. On the first floor there is a balcony that runs along all four sides, with french windows giving on to it, where no doubt before the day is done someone will stand, with her hand in her hair, gazing off in sunlight. Below the balcony the front porch is a deep, dim hollow, and the front door has two broad panels of ruby glass and a tarnished brass knocker in the shape of a lion's paw. Details, details: pile them on. The windows are blank. Three steps lead from the porch to a patch of gravel and a green slope that runs abruptly down to a stony, meandering stream. Gorse grows along the bank, and hawthorn, all in blossom now, the pale-pink and the white, a great year for the may. Behind the house there is a high ridge with trees, old oaks, I think, above which seagulls plunge and sway. (Oaks and seagulls! Picture it! Such is our island.) This wooded height lowers over the scene, dark and forbidding sometimes, sometimes almost haughty, almost, indeed, heroic.

The house is a summer house; at other seasons, especially in autumn, it wheezes and groans, its joints creaking. But when the weather turns warm, as now, in May, and the fond air invades even the remotest rooms, something stirs in the heart of the house, like something stirring out of a long slumber, unfolding waxen wings, and then suddenly everything tends upwards and all is ceilings and wide-open windows and curtains billowing in sea-light. I live here, in this lambent, salt-washed world, in these faded rooms, amidst this stillness. And it lives in me.

Sophie pointed her camera, deft and quick.

'Looks like a hotel,' she said.

'Or a guesthouse, anyway,' said Croke, doubtfully.

It is neither. It is the home of Professor Silas Kreutznaer and his faithful companion, Licht. Ha.

They had come to the little wooden bridge but there they hesitated, even Felix, unwilling to cross, they did not know why, and looked up uncertainly at the impassive house. Croke took off his boater; or do I mean panama, yes, Croke took off his panama and mopped his brow, saying something crossly under his breath. The hat, the striped blazer and cravat, the white duck trousers, all this had seemed fine at first, a brave flourish and just the thing for a day-trip, but now he felt ridiculous, ridiculous and old.

'We can't stand here all day,' he said, and glared accusingly at Felix, as if somehow everything were all his fault. 'Will I go and see?'

He looked about at the rest of them but all wanly avoided his eye, indifferent suddenly, unable to care.

'I'm hungry,' Hatch said. 'I want my breakfast.'

Pound the bespectacled fat boy muttered in agreement and cast a dark look at the adults.

'Where's that picnic that was promised us?' Croke said testily.

'Fell in the water, didn't it,' Hatch said and snickered.

'Pah! Some bloody outing this is.'

'Listen to them,' Felix said softly to Flora, assuming the soft mask of an indulgent smile. 'Rhubarb rhubarb.'

His smile turned fawning and he inclined his head to one side as if imploring something of her, but she pretended to be distracted and frowned and looked away. She felt so strange.

Sophie turned with an impatient sigh and took Croke's arm.

'Come,' she said. 'We will ask.'

And they set off across the bridge, Sophie striding and the old boy going carefully on tottery legs, trying to keep up with her, the soaked and sand-caked cuffs of his trousers brushing the planks. The stream gurgled.

*

Licht in the turret window watched them, the little crowd hanging back – were they afraid? – and the old man and the woman advancing over the bridge. How small they seemed, how distant and small. The couple on the bridge carried themselves stiffly, at a stately pace, as if they suspected that someone, somewhere, was laughing at their expense. He was embarrassed for them. They were like actors being forced to improvise. (One of them is an actor, is improvising.) He pressed his forehead to the glass and felt his heart racing. Since he had first spotted them making their meandering way up the hillside he had warned himself repeatedly not to expect anything of them, but it was no use, he was agog. Somehow these people looked like him, like the image he had of himself: lost, eager, ill at ease, and foolish. The glass was cool against his forehead, where a little vein was beating. Silence, deep woods, a sudden wind. He blinked: had he dropped off for a second? Lately he had been sleeping badly. That morning he had been awake at three o'clock, wandering through the house, stepping through vague deeps of shadowed stillness on the stairs, hardly daring to breathe in the midst of a silence where others slept. When he looked out he had seen a crack of light on the leaden horizon. Was it the day still going down or the morning coming up? He smiled sadly. This was what his life was like now, this faint glimmer between a past grown hazy and an unimaginable future.

The woman on the bridge stumbled. One moment she was upright, the next she had crumpled sideways like a puppet, all arms and knees, her hair flying and her camera swinging on its strap. Licht experienced a little thrill of fright. She would have fallen had not the old boy with surprising speed and vigour caught her in the crook of an arm that seemed for a second to grow immensely long. His hat fell off. A blackbird flew up out of a bush, giving out a harsh repeated warning note. The woman, balancing on one leg, took off her sodden shoe and looked at it: the heel was broken. She kicked off the other shoe and was preparing to walk on barefoot when Felix, as if he had suddenly bethought himself and some notion of authority, put down his bag and fairly bounded forward, shot nimbly past her and set off up the slope, buttoning the jacket of his tight, brown suit.

'Who is that,' the Professor said sharply. 'Mind, let me see.'

Licht turned, startled: he had forgotten he was not alone. The Professor had been struggling with the telescope, trying in vain to angle it so he could get a closer look at Felix coming up the path. Now he thrust the barrel of the instrument aside and lumbered to the window, humming unhappily under his breath. When Licht looked at him now, in the light of these advancing strangers, he noticed for the first time how slovenly he had become. His shapeless black jacket was rusty at the elbows and the pockets sagged, his bow-tie was clumsily knotted and had a greasy shine. He looked like a big old rain-stained statue of one of the Caesars, with that big balding head and broad pale face and filmy, pale, protruding eyes. Licht smiled to himself hopelessly: how could he leave, how could he ever leave?

Felix was mounting the slope swiftly, swinging out his legs in front of him and sawing the air with his arms.

'Look at him,' Croke said, chuckling. 'Look at him go.'

From the bridge it seemed as if he were swarming along on all fours. The nearer he approached to the house the more it seemed to shrink away from him. Licht was craning his neck. The Professor turned aside, patting his pockets, still humming tensely to himself.

Below, the lion's peremptory paw rapped once, twice, three-four times.

Here it is, here is the moment where worlds collide, and all I can detect is laughter, distant, soft, sceptical.

*

At that brisk and gaily syncopated knock the house seemed to go still and silent for a moment as if in alarmed anticipation of disturbances to come. Licht lingered dreamily at the turret window, watching the others down at the bridge. Then another knock sounded, louder than before, and he started and turned and pushed past the Professor and rattled down the stairs in a flurry of arms and knees. In the hall he paused, seeing Felix's silhouette on the rubyglass of the door, an intent and eerily motionless, canted form. When the door was opened Felix at once produced a brilliant smile and stepped sideways deftly into the hall, speaking already, his thin hand outstretched.

'. . . Shipwrecked!' he said, laughing. 'Yes, cast up on these shores. I can't tell you!' Licht in his agitation could hardly understand what he was saying. He fell back a pace, mouthing helplessly and nodding. Felix's sharp glance flickered all around the hall. 'What a charming place,' he said softly, and threw back his head and smiled foxily, showing a broken eye-tooth. He had a disjointed, improvised air, as if he had been put together in haste from disparate bits and pieces of other people. He seemed full of suppressed laughter, nursing a secret joke. With that fixed grin and those glossy, avid eyes he makes me think of a ventriloquist's dummy; in his case, though, it would be he who would do the talking, while his master's mouth flapped open and shut like a broken trap. 'Yes, charming, charming,' he said. 'Why, I feel almost at home already.'

Afterwards Licht was never absolutely sure all this had happened, or had happened in the way that he remembered it, at least. All he recalled for certain was the sense of being suddenly surrounded by something bright and overwhelming. It was not just Felix before whom he fell back, but the troupe of possibilities that seemed to come crowding in behind him, tumbling and leaping invisibly about the hall. He saw himself in a dazzle of light, heroic and absurd, and the hallway might have been the pass at Roncesvalles. I should not sneer: I too in secret have always fancied myself a hero, dying with my face to Spain, though I suspect no ministering angel or exaltation of saints will come to carry me off as I cough out my heart's last drops of blood.

Felix was describing how the boat had run aground. Daintily

with finger and thumb he hoisted skirt-like the legs of his trousers to show a pair of skinny, bare, blue-white ankles and his shoes dark with wet. Head on one side, and that comical, self-disparaging grin.

'Professor Kreutznaer,' Licht said in a sort of hapless desperation, 'Professor Kreutznaer is . . . busy.'

Felix was regarding him keenly with an eyebrow lifted.

'Busy, eh?' he said softly. 'Well then, we shall not disturb him, shall we?'

*

The others had shuffled across the bridge by now, dragged forward reluctantly in the wake of Felix's rapid ascent to the house, as if they were attached to him at a distance somehow; they loitered, waiting for a sign. Sophie sat down on a rock and kneaded the foot she had twisted. Hatch was clutching his stomach and rolling his eyes in a dumbshow demonstration of hunger, while Pound snickered and Alice smiled doubtfully. Have we met Alice? She is eleven. She wears her hair in a shiny, fat, brown braid. She is not pretty. Sophie considered the elfin Hatch without enthusiasm, his narrow, white face and red slash of a mouth; there is one clown in every company.

'After the war,' she said to him, 'when I was younger than you are now, we had no food. Every day for months, for months, I was hungry. My mother rubbed the top of the stove with candle grease—' with one hand she smoothed large, slow circles on the air '—and fried potatoes in it, and when the potatoes were eaten she fried the peelings and we ate those, too.'

Hatch with a tragic look embraced himself and did a dying fall on to the grass and lay there twitching.

'Oh, leave them alone, Countess,' Croke said waggishly, wagging his head at her. 'This is not old Vienna.'

She eyed him coolly. When he grinned he showed a large set of yellowed, horsey teeth, and the skin over his cheekbones tightened and the skull under the taut skin seemed to grin as well, but in a different way. Countess: he had started calling her that last night in the hotel bar when he was tipsy, winking at her and trying to get her drunk; she suspected gloomily it would stick.

'So funny you are,' she said. 'All of you, so funny.'

The boys laughed – how quickly the grown-ups could irritate each other today! – but they were uneasy, too. Sophie already was an object of deep and secret speculation to them, this moody woman in black who was as old as a mother would be but unlike any mother they had ever known, the hungry way she smoked cigarettes, the way she sat with her knees apart, like a man, not caring (Hatch on the ground was trying to look up her skirt), the fascinating tang of sweat she left behind her on the air when she passed by.

Croke, still leering at her toothily, sang under his breath, in a quavery voice:

Wien, Wien, nur du allein!

When he laughed he coughed, a string of phlegm twanging in his throat, and Alice glared at him. She disapproved of Croke, because of his coarseness, and because he was old.

'I am not even Viennese,' Sophie said ruefully, frowning at her foot.

'But you should be, Countess,' Croke said, with what he thought was gallantry. 'You should be.'

Flora had moved away carefully with her eyes lowered. Sophie watched her narrowly. Flora was wearing an affected, far-off look, as if she thought there might be unpleasantness that she would have to pretend not to notice. How beautiful she was, like one of Modigliani's girls, with that heavy black hair, those tilted eyes, that hesitant, slightly awkward, pigeon-toed grace. Sophie suspected she had been with Felix last night. Sanctimonious little twat.

Vienna. God! She lit a cigarette. Her foot was callused and the nail on the little toe had almost disappeared into the flesh. She closed her eyes. She was sick of herself. Why had she said that nonsense about the potato peelings? For whom was she playing this part that she had to keep on making up as she went along?

A comedy, of course, all a horrible comedy. Out there in the flocculent, moth-laden darkness an invisible audience was splitting its sides at her. She rose, suddenly angry, at herself and everything else, and, carrying her shoes and stepping warily, set off up the pathway to the house, where Felix had reappeared and was waiting for them on the porch with a proprietorial air, his hands like a brahmin's joined before him, a man brimming with secrets, smiling.

*

He might have been master of the house so warmly did he welcome them, touching an elbow here, patting a shoulder-blade there, winking gaily at the boys, who had carried up his black bag between them. And to their surprise as he ushered them in they all, even Sophie, felt a rush of gratitude for his ministering presence; they remembered the awful, sickening lurch when the boat had keeled over, things falling and a big crate sliding off the deck into the water and the drunken skipper cursing, and it came to them that after all they were survivors, in a way, despite the festive look that everything insisted on wearing, and suddenly they were full of tenderness for themselves and pity for their plight. Licht hovered in the dimness of the doorway, smiling helplessly, nodding to them and mouthing wordless greetings as they entered.

'Hello, Harpo,' Hatch said brightly, and Pound behind him spluttered.

The hall was wide and paved unevenly with black and white tiles. There was a pockmarked mirror in a gilt frame and an umbrella stand with an assortment of walking canes and a broken shooting-stick. The walls up to the dado were clad with embossed wallpaper to which repeated layers of varnish had imparted a thick, clammy, toffee-coloured texture, while above the rail stretched shadowy grey expanses that had once, long ago, been white. There was a smell of apples just starting to rot. And an air now of polite shock, of a hand put to mouth in amazement at all this noise, this intrusion. Licht was beside himself.

They stood uneasily in a huddle and did not know what to do next.

And then something happened, I am not sure what it was. They were all crowded together there, uncertain whether to advance or wait, and this uncertainty produced a ripple amongst them, a restless stirring, as when the day darkens suddenly and a gust of wind from nowhere blows through the trees, shaking them. Nice touch of the Virgilian, that. Croke, squinting up at something on the ceiling, stepped backwards and trod on Sophie's foot, the one that she had twisted. She shrieked, and her shriek brought an immediate and solemn silence and everyone went as still as a statue. I could leave them there, I could walk away now and leave them there forever. The silence lasted for the space of half a dozen heartbeats and then slowly, as if she were slowly falling, Alice began to cry.

'Oh,' Licht said in distress, 'my poor . . . my dear . . .'

He touched a tremulous hand to her shoulder but she twisted away from him violently with a great slack sob. She did not know what was the matter with her. The boys stared at her with frank interest.

'Christ,' Pound said in happy disgust, 'there she goes.'

Alice cries easily.

Licht led them into the kitchen, a big, high-ceilinged room with a scrubbed pine table and mismatched wooden chairs and a jumble of unwashed crockery in the sink. An enormous, gruel-coloured stove with a black chimney squatted in a blackened recess. The window looked out on sloped fields and the tree-clad rise, so that they had a curious sense of submersion, and felt as if they were looking up through the silvery water-light of a deep, still pool. Licht leaned down at the stove and opened the little door of the firebox and looked inside.

'Out, of course,' he said disgustedly and shouted: 'Stove!' but no one answered. He turned up to them an apologetic smile. 'Are you wet?'

They were wet. They were tired. They said nothing. They had got on board a boat at first light to take a little pleasure trip and now here they were stranded in a strange house on this island in the middle of nowhere.

Licht was still leaning at the stove gazing up at them, the smile forgotten on his face. They might have walked straight out of his deepest longings. Days he had dreamed of an invasion just such as this, noise and unfamiliar voices in the hall and the kitchen full of strangers and he amongst them, grinning like a loon. He left the stove and busied himself with making them sit and taking their wet shoes and offering them tea, scurrying here and there, hot with happy fear that they might at any moment prove a figment after all and vanish. Sophie was asking him something about the ruins in the hills, but he could not concentrate, and kept saying yes, yes, and smiling his unfocused, flustered smile. When Flora at the table looked up at him weakly and handed him her wet, warm shoes he felt a sort of plunge inside him, as if something had dropped in the hollow of his heart and hung there bobbing lightly on its elastic. She felt strange, she told him, strange and sort of shivery. Her voice was soft. She looked at him from under her long lashes, helpless and at the same time calculating, he could see it, how she was measuring him; he did not care, except he wished that he were younger, taller, altogether different. He stood before her holding her shoes, one in each hand, and a swarm of impossible yearnings rose up in him drunkenly. He brought her upstairs to rest and lingered in the doorway of the bedroom, twisting and twisting the doorknob in his hand. She sat down slowly on the side of the bed and folded her arms tightly around herself and looked emptily at the floor.

'Are you on a holiday?' he said tentatively.

'What?' She continued to stare before her in dull bewilderment, frowning. She roused herself a little and shook her head. 'No. I'm taking care of them.' She gestured disdainfully in the direction of downstairs. 'Supposed to be, anyway.' She gave a soft snort.

'Oh?'

She glanced up at him impatiently.

'The children,' she said. 'It's only a summer job, at the hotel.'
She bit her lip and looked sullen.

'Ah,' he said. Some sort of skivvy, then; he felt encouraged.
He waited for more, but in vain. 'Did that boat,' he said after a
moment, 'did that boat really run aground?'

She did not seem to be listening. She was staring blankly at
the floor again. Behind her an enormous, lead-blue cloud was
edging is way stealthily into the window, humid and swollen, the
very picture of his own muffled desires. She was so lovely it made
him ache to look at her, with her slender, slightly turned-in feet
and enormous eyes and faint hint of moustache. A memory stirred
in his mind, the sense of something sleek and smooth and faintly,
tenderly repulsive. Yes: the hare's nest in the grass that he had
found one day on the dunes when he was a child, the two baby
hares in it lying folded around each other head to rump like
an heraldic emblem. He had brought them home under his coat
but his mother would not let him keep them. How tinily their
hearts had ticked against his own suddenly heavy heart! That was
him all over, always on the look-out for something to love that
would love him in return and never finding it. Or hardly ever.
Poor mama. When he went back to look for the nest he could
not find it and had to leave the leverets under the shelter of a
rock, with leaves to lie on and grass and dandelion stalks to eat.
Next day they were gone. Not a trace. The stalks untouched.
Gone. And yet how little he had cared, standing there in the grey
of morning contemplating that absence, while the sea beyond the
dunes muttered and the wind polished the dark grass around him.
Now he sighed, baffled at himself, as always.

'I think I want to lie down,' Flora said.

'Of course, of course.'

'Just for a little while.'

'Of course.'

He was torn between staying there, leaning sleepless on his
shield, and rushing downstairs again to reassure himself that the
others had not disappeared. Instead, when she had stretched
herself out on the bed, yawning and sighing, and he had shut the

door behind him lingeringly, he found himself wandering in a sort of aimless, apprehensive rapture about the upper storeys, stopping now and then to listen, he was not sure for what: for the crackle of wing-cases, perhaps, for the sounds of the new life breaking out of its cocoon. From the stairs he caught a glimpse through the half-closed lavatory door of Sophie sitting straight-backed on the stool with her skirt hiked up and her pants around her knees, gazing before her with a dreamy, stern stare as her water tinkled freely into the bowl beneath her. He hurried past with eyes averted, red-faced, smiling madly in embarrassment, muttering to himself.

Oh, agog, agog!

THE SEAGULLS wake me early. I hear them up on the chimney-pots beating their wings and uttering strange, deep-throated cries. They sound like human babies. Perhaps it is the young I am hearing, not yet flown from the nest and still demanding food. I never was much of a naturalist. How lovely the summer light is at this time of morning, a seamless, soft grey shot through with water-glints. I lie for a long time thinking of nothing. I can do that, I can make my mind go blank. It is a knack I acquired in the days when the thought of what was to be endured before darkness and oblivion came again was hardly to be borne. And so, quite empty, weightless as a paper skiff, I make my voyage out, far, far out, to the very brim, where a disc of water shimmers like molten coin against a coin-coloured sky, and everything lifts, and sky and waters merge invisibly. That is where I seem to be most at ease now, on the far, pale margin of things. If I can call it ease. If I can call it being.

An island, of course. The authorities when they were releasing me had asked in their suspicious way where I would go and I said at once, Oh, an island, where else? All I wanted, I assured them, was a place of seclusion and tranquillity where I could begin the long process of readjustment to the world and pursue my studies of a famous painter they had never heard of. It sounded surprisingly plausible to me. (Oh yes, guv, says the old lag, standing before the big desk in his arrowed suit and twisting his cap in his hands, this time I'm going straight, you can count on it, I won't let you down!) There is something about islands that appeals to me, the sense of boundedness, I suppose, of being protected from the world – and of the world being protected from me, there is that, too. They approved, or seemed to, anyway; I have a notion they were relieved to get rid of me. They treated me so tenderly, were so considerate of my wishes, I was amazed. But that is how it had been all along, more or less. They had worse cases than me on their hands, fellows who in a less squeamish age would have been hanged, drawn and quartered for their deeds, yet they seemed to feel that I was special. Perhaps it was just that I had confessed so readily to my crime, made no excuses, even displayed a forensic interest in my motives, which were almost as mysterious to me as they were to them. For whatever reason, they behaved towards me as if I had done some great, grave thing, as if I were a messenger, say, come back from somewhere immensely difficult and far, bringing news so terrible it made them feel strong and noble merely to be the receivers of it. It may be, of course, that this solemn mien was only a way of hiding their hatred and disgust. I suspect they would have done violence to me but that they did not wish to soil their hands. Maybe they had been hoping my fellow inmates would mete out to me the punishments they were loth to administer themselves? If so, they were disappointed; I was a man of substance in there, ranging freely as I might among that hobbled multitude. And now I had done my time, and was out.

I was not at all the same person that I had been a decade before (is the oldster in his dotage the same that he was when he was an infant swaddled in his truckle bed?). A slow sea-change had taken place. I believe that over those ten years of incarceration – life, that is, minus time off for good, for exemplary, behaviour – I had evolved into an infinitely more complex organism. This is not to say that I felt myself to be better than I had been – the doctrine of penal rehabilitation broke against the rock of my inexpungible guilt – nor did it mean I was any worse, either: just different. Everything had become more intricate, more dense and pensive. My crime had ramified it; it sat inside me now like a second, parasitic self, its tentacles coiled around my cells. I had grown fat on my sin; I seemed to myself to wallow along, bloated and empurpled, like a mutated species of jellyfish stuffed full with

poison. Soft, that is, formless, malignant still, yet not so fierce
as once I had been, not so careless, or so cold. Puzzled, too,
of course, still unable to believe that I had done what I did do.
I make no pleas; it is the only thing I can boast of, that I never
sought to excuse myself for my enormities. And so I had come to
this penitential isle (there are beehive huts in the hills), seeking
not redemption, for that would have been too much to ask,
but an accommodation with myself, maybe, and with my poor,
swollen conscience.

They tell me I am too hard on myself; as if such a thing were
possible.

I was brought, or perhaps transported is a better word: yes, I
was transported here by boat. It was charming. I had expected to
find myself standing outside the gates some desolate grey morning
with a brown-paper parcel under my arm, whey-faced and baffled
before a prospect of enormous streets, yet here I was, skimming
gaily over the little waves with the breeze in my face and the tarry
smell of the sea in my nostrils. The morning was sunny and
bright, the light like glass. Shadows of clouds raced towards us
across the water, darkened the air around us for a second, and
swept on. When we got into the lee of the island the breeze
dropped and the skipper cut the engine and we glided smoothly
forward into a vast, flat silence. The water with the sun on it was
wonderfully clear, I could see right down to the bottom, where
there were green rocks and opulent, coffee-coloured weeds, and
shoals of darting fish, mud-grey, with now and then a flash of
platinum-white. The little jetty was deserted, the strand, too, and
the green hill behind. On the quayside there was a jumble of
tumbledown stone houses with holes in the roofs; at the sight
of them, I do not know why, I experienced one of my moments
of black fright. I have almost got used to these attacks, these little
tremors. They last only an instant. There are times, especially at
night, when I mistake them for stabs of physical pain, and wonder
if something inside me is diseased, not a major organ, not heart
or liver, but the spleen, perhaps, or the gall-bladder, something

like that, some bruised little purple plum or orchidaceous fold of malignant tissue that might one day be the thing that would do me in to the accompaniment of exquisite torments.

I heard then for the first time that strange, soft, bellowing sound the island makes, it came to me clearly across the water, a siren voice.

'Like music,' I said. 'Like . . . singing.'

When I asked the skipper what it was he shrugged.

'Ah, don't mind that,' he said. 'There must be an old blowhole somewhere that the tide pushes out the air through. Don't mind that, at all.'

Then that teetering moment of slide and sway and the soft bump of the boat against the dock: landfall.

*

I liked the island straight away, finding its bleakness congenial. It suits me well. It is ten miles long and five miles wide (or is it five miles long and ten miles wide? – this matter of length and breadth has always puzzled me), with cliffs on one side and a rocky foreshore on the other. The seas round about are treacherous, running with hidden currents and rip-tides, so that yachts and pleasure boats for the most part steer clear of us, with the happy result that we are not troubled by day-trippers, or hearty people in caps and rugged jumpers tramping about the harbour demanding grog and talking incomprehensibly about jibs and mizzens and all the rest of it. The place overall is gratifyingly lacking in the picturesque. It is true, there are whitewashed cottages and dry-stone walls, and sheep, and even here and there a tweed-clad shepherd. We have the bigger stuff as well, the rolling hills and ocean views and shimmering, lavender distances, and at night there is the light-thronged firmament. What is missing is that look of stony fortitude – storms withstood, privations endured – which a real island turns upon the outside world and which fills the casual visitor with an equal mixture of awe and irritation. The fact is, the place is not like an island at all, more like a bit of the mainland that has recently come adrift. There are patches of waste ground, and mysterious, padlocked sheds smelling of diesel oil, and tarred roads that set off determinedly into the hills as if great highways awaited them out there like destiny. The village, though it lies no more than a mile inland from the harbour, hidden in the fold of a hill, has the forlorn look of a place lost in the midst of the plains. It seems to be inhabited entirely by idiots. (I should move there, I could be the village savant; imagine a mournful chuckle.) There is a shop, a post office, and a pub the door of which I do not darken. It is mostly the old who live here now, the young having fled to what I suppose they imagined would be the easier life of the mainland. I had thought, when I first arrived, of opening a little school, like poor Ludwig on the Snow Mountain, to teach the few children that remain, but nothing came of it, as was the case with so many of my projects. I, a schoolteacher! What an idea. Still, the thought was benevolent, I do not have many such. The island services in general are meagre. The nearest doctor is a slow and sometimes erratic boat-journey away on the mainland. So when I arrived I felt at once as if somehow I had come home. Will that seem strange, to say I felt at home in such seemingly uncongenial surroundings? But the poverty, you see, the dullness and lack of emphasis, these might have been a form of subtlety, after all. Drama was the last thing I wanted, unless it be seagulls wheeling above oaks, or a boat stuck on a sandbank, or a woebegone band of strangers struggling up the dunes one day and spying an old house standing on the side of a hill.

From my copious reading – what else had I to do, in those first days of so-called freedom, except to read and dream? – I gleaned the following: *I have an habitual feeling of my real life having passed, and that I am leading a posthumous existence.* I had burned my boats, the years were strewn like ashes on the water. I was at rest here, in the calm under the great wave of the world. Yes, I felt at home – I, who thought never again to feel at home anywhere. This does not mean I did not at the same time feel myself to be an outsider. The place tolerated me, that's all. I had the impression of a certain disdain, of everything leaning carefully away from me with averted gaze. The house especially had a frowning, tight-lipped aspect. Or perhaps I am wrong, perhaps what I detected was not contempt, or even disapproval, but something quite other: tactfulness, for instance – inanimate objects seem ever anxious not to intrude – or just a general wish to preserve the forms. Yet wherever I went, even when I walked into an empty room, I had an uncanny sense of things having fallen silent at my approach. I know, of course, that this was all foolishness, that the place did not care a damn about me, really, that I could have vanished into the air with a *ping*! and everything would have gone on in its own sweet way as if nothing had happened. Yet I could not rid myself of the conviction that somehow I was – how shall I put it? – required.

And I was alone, despite the presence of the others. How to be alone even in the midst of the elbowing crowd, that is another of those knacks that the years in captivity had taught me. It is a matter of inward stillness, of hiding inside oneself, like an animal in cover, while the hounds go pounding past. Oh, I know only too well how this will seem: that I had retreated into solitude, that I was living in a fantasy world, a world of pictures and painted figures and all the rest of it. But that is not it, no, that is not it at all. It is only that I was trying to get as far away as possible from everything. I had tried to get away from myself, too, but in vain. The Chinese, or perhaps it was the Florentines of Dante's day – anyway, some such fierce and unforgiving people – would bind a murderer head and toe to the corpse of his victim and sling this terrible parcel into a dungeon and throw away the key. I knew something of that, here in my oubliette, lashed to my ineluctable self, not to mention . . . well, not to mention. What I was striving to do was to simplify, to refine. I had shed everything I could save existence itself. Perhaps, I thought, perhaps it is a mistake: perhaps I should be shouldering the emcumbrances of life instead of throwing them off? But no, I wanted not to live – I would have others to do that for me – but only endure. True, there is no getting away from the passionate attachment to self, that I-beam set down in the dead centre of the world and holding the whole rickety edifice in place. All the same, I was determined at least to try to make myself into a – what do you call it? – a monomorph: a monad. And then to start again, empty. That way, I felt, I might come to understand things, in however rudimentary a fashion. Small things, of course. Simple things.

But then, there are no simple things. I have said this before, I shall say it again. The object splits, flips, doubles back, becomes something else. Under the slightest pressure the seeming unit falls into a million pieces and every piece into a million more. I was myself no unitary thing. I was like nothing so much as a pack of cards, shuffling into other and yet other versions of myself: here was the king, here the knave, and here the ace of spades. Nor did it seem possible to speak simply. I would open my mouth and a babble would come pouring out, a hopeless glossolalia. The most elementary bit of speech was a cacophony. To choose one word was to exclude countless others, they thronged out there in the darkness, heaving and humming. When I tried to mean one thing the buzz of a myriad other possible meanings mocked my efforts. Everything I said was out of context, necessarily, and every plunge I made into speech inevitably ended in a bellyflop. I wanted to be simple, candid, natural – I wanted to be, yes, I shall risk it: I wanted to be *honest* – but all my striving provoked only general hoots of merriment and rich scorn.

My case, in short, was what it always had been, namely, that I did one thing while thinking another and in this welter of difference I did not know what I was. How then was I to be expected to know what others are, to imagine them so vividly as to make them quicken into a sort of life?

Others? Other: they are all one. The only one.

Not to mention.

*

And yet it all went on, went on without stop, and every moment of it had to be lived, used up, somehow; not a lapse, not the tiniest falter in the flow; a life sentence. Even sleep was no escape. In the mornings I would get up exhausted, as if part of me had been out all night roving in the dark like a dog in rut. Such dreams I had, immense elaborations, they wore me out. What were they for, I wondered? They were like alibis, fiendishly intricate versions of an event the true circumstances of which I dared not admit, even to myself, that I remembered. To whom was I offering these implausible farragos, before what judge was I arraigned? Not that I imagined I was innocent, only I would have liked to see the face of my oneiric accusers. I remember the first dream I had, the very first night I slept here. I have no idea what it signified, if it signified anything. I was somewhere in the Levant, at the gates of a vast, grey, crumbling city, at evening, with my mother. She was nothing at all like her real self as I recalled it, but very brisk, very much the intrepid traveller, rigged out in tweeds and a broad-brimmed hat and wielding a stout stick. She kept stopping and hectoring me, the laggard son stumbling at her heels in his city shoes and sag-arsed trousers, overweight and sweating and risibly middle-aged. When we entered the city we found ourselves at once in a high, narrow alleyway lined with stalls. There were many people and a great hubbub of voices and eastern music and the mellifluous shrillings of merchants crying their wares. This is the gold market, my mother said to me, speaking very loudly close to my ear. There was a sumptuous shine in the air, as if the light were coming not from the sky but rising spontaneously from the countless precious things laid out around us, the ornaments and piled plates and great beaten bowls. We pressed on through the winding streets, into the heart of the town. There were mosques and minarets and arched gateways and houses with latticed windows giving on to courtyards where lemon trees grew in enormous stone pots. Everything was made of the same grey stone, a sort of pumice only darker, which was wrong, it should have been something hard and smooth and almost precious, like marble, or porphyry, whatever that is. Evening was coming on, and now there was no one to be seen, and our footsteps echoed along the little streets. It is Ramadan, my mother said softly. At that moment suddenly under a dim archway before us two boys appeared, slender, barefoot, honey-skinned, wearing faded robes that swirled about them loosely as they moved. They crossed the archway at a dancing run from left to right, lithe and swift as monkeys, bearing above their heads a gleaming shell of beaten gold the size and shape of an inverted coracle but so delicate and light it seemed to float on the tips of their fingers. They laughed, making soft, trilling noises deep in their throats. Were they playing a game, or was it some marvellous, ritual task they were performing? I saw them only for a second and then they were gone, and my mother too was gone from my side, and it was all so real, so fraught with mysterious significance, that I began to cry in my sleep, and woke up sobbing my heart out, like a child.

There are the nightmares too, of course, the recurring ones, lit with a garish, unearthly glow, in which the dead speak to me: flesh, burst bone, the slow, secret, blue-black ooze. I shall not try to recount them, these bloodstained pageants. They are no use to me. They are only a kind of lurid tinkering that my fancy indulges in, the crackles and jagged sparks thrown off by the spinning dynamo of my overburdened conscience. It is not the dead that interest me now, no matter how piteously they may howl in the chambers of the night. Who, then? The living? No, no, something in between; some third thing.

*

Dreams, then waking. At times it was hard to tell the difference; I would drift out of riotous slumber and get up and walk around in a hazy, shallow state that seemed only a calmer, less tormented form of sleep than that which had gone before. I tramped the roads in the chill of dawn while a white sun came up tremblingly out of the sea. Everything is strange at that hour, stranger than usual, I mean: the world looks as I imagine it will look after I am dead, wide and empty and streaked with long shadows, shocked somehow and not quite solid, all odd-angled light and shifting façades. These open vistas – so much sky! – alarmed me. I was permanently dizzy, clinging for dear life to our flying island, and there was constantly a sort of distant ringing in my ears. It felt like early morning all day long, there was that fizzing in the blood, that taste of metal in the mouth. The days hung heavy, falling towards night. We watched in silence the unremitting, slow advance of time. Here on Devil's Island we are not allowed the illusion of highs and troughs, of sudden speedings up, of halts and starts. There is only the steady, glacial creep that carries all along with it. Sometimes I fancied I could feel the planet itself hurtling ponderously through space in its bubble of bright air. I had my moments of rebellion, of course, when I would scramble up from the slimed flagstones and rattle my shackles in rage, shouting for the non-existent jailer. Mostly, though, I was content, or calm, at least, with the febrile calm of the chronic invalid. That's it, that's what this place is most like, not a prison or a pilgrimage isle, but one of those sanatoriums that were so numerous when I was a child and half the world had rotting lungs. Yes, I see myself up here in those first weeks and months immured behind a wall of glass, peering out in a feverish daze over serried blue pines while a huge sun declined above a distant river valley. Heights, I have always sought the heights, physical if not moral. It is not grandeur I crave, not the mossy crag or soaring peak, but the long perspective, the distance, the diminution of things. I had hardly arrived here before I found myself tramping up the fields behind the house to the oak ridge. Wonderful prospect from this lofty crest, the near green and the far blue and that strip of ash-white beach holding up an enormity of sea and sky, the whole scene clear and delicate, like something by Vaublin himself, a background to one of his celebrated *pélerinages* or a delicate *fête galante*. From this vantage I could make out in the fields around me a curious, ribbed pattern in the turf. I wondered if vines perhaps had grown here once (vines, in these latitudes! – what an ignoramus I am), but the spinster who runs the post office in the village put me right. 'Potato drills,' she told me, shouting because for some reason she took me for a foreigner (which, when I think of it, I suppose I am). 'From before the famine times, that was.' A thousand souls lived here then. I picture them, in their cawbeens and their shawls, straggling down the path to the beach and the waiting black ship, the men fixed on something distant and the women looking back out of huge, stricken eyes. Cythera, my foot. Such suffering, such grief: unimaginable. No, that's not right. I can imagine it. I can imagine anything.

I bring the household rubbish up here on to the ridge to burn it. I like burning things, paper especially. I think fire must be my element; I relish the sudden flare and crackle, the anger of it, the menace. I stand leaning on my pitchfork (a wonderful implement, this, the wood of the shaft silky from use and the tines tempered by flame to a lovely, dark, oily opalescence), in my boots and my old hat, chewing the soft inside of my cheek and thinking of nothing, and am excited and at the same time strangely at peace. At times I become convinced I am being watched, and turn quickly to see if I can catch a glimpse of a foxy face and glittering, mephitic eye among the leaves; I tell myself I am imagining it, that there is no one, but I am not persuaded; I suppose I want him to be here still, someone worse than me, feral, remorseless, laughing at everything. The heat shakes the air above the fire and makes the trees on the far side of the clearing seem to wobble. Between the trunks I can see the sea, deep-blue, unmoving, flecked with white. The stones banked around the fire hum and creak, big russet shards with threads of yellow glitter running through them. I recall as a child melting lumps of lead in a tin can, the way the lead trembled inside itself and abruptly the little secret shining worm ran out. I used to try to melt stones, too, imagining the seams of ore in them were gold. And when they would not break nor the gold melt I could not understand it, and would fly into a rage and want to set fire to everything, burn everything down. Timid little boy though I was, I harboured dreams of irresistible destruction. I imagined it, the undulating sheets of flame, the red wind rushing upwards, the rip and roar. Fire: yes, yes.

I have other chores. I draw wood, of course, and tend the stove, and check that the water pump is running freely and that the septic tank is functioning. These used to be Licht's jobs; he took a great satisfaction in handing them over to me as soon as I arrived. I had not the heart to let him see how I enjoyed the work that he thought would be a burden. I could rhapsodise about this kind of thing – I mean the simple goodness of the commonplace. Jail had taught me the quiet delights of drudgery. Manual work dulls the sharp edges of things and sometimes can deflect even the arrows of remorse. Not that convicts are required any more to do what you would call hard labour. I have a theory, mock me if you will, that modern penal practice aims not to punish the miscreant, or even to instil in him a moral sense, but rather seeks to emasculate him by a process of enervation. I know I had ridiculously old-fashioned notions of what to expect from prison, picked up no doubt from the black-and-white movies of my childhood: the shaved blue heads, the manacled, ragged figures trudging in a circle in the exercise-yard, the fingernails destroyed, like poor Oscar's, from picking oakum – why, even leg-irons and bread and water would not have surprised me – instead of which, what we had was ping-pong and television and the ever-springing tea-urn. I tell you, it would soften the most hardened recidivist. (Perhaps when I am finished with Vaublin I shall produce a monograph on prison reform: here as elsewhere, though it may be slower, the spread of liberal values goes unchecked and cannot but do harm to the moral fibre of the race, which needs its criminals, just as it needs its sportsmen and its butchers, for that vital admixture of strength, cunning and freedom from squeamishness.) Of course, in prison there were deprivations, and they were hard to bear, I will not deny it. I had thought it would be women I would want when I got out, women and silk suits and crowded city streets, all that rich world from which I had been isolated for so long, but here I was, pottering about in this rackety house on a crop of rock in the midst of a waste of waters. I had my books, my papers, my studies, playing the part of Professor Kreutznaer's amanuensis, supposedly aiding him in the completion of his great work on the life and art of Jean Vaublin for which the world, or that part of it that cares about such things, has grown weary of waiting. The fiction that I was no more than his assistant was one that, for reasons not wholly clear to me, it suited us both to maintain; the truth is, before I knew it he had handed over the task entirely to me. I was flattered, of course, but I did not deceive myself as to his opinion of my abilities; it is true, I have a capacity to take pains, learned in a hard school, but I am no scholar. It was not regard for me but a growing indifference to the fate of his life's work that led the Professor to abdicate in my favour. No, that's not right. Rather it was, I think, an act of expiation on his part. He like me had sins to atone for, and this sacrifice was one of the ways he chose. Or was it, on the contrary, as the weasel of doubt sometimes suggests to me, was it his idea of a joke? Anyway, no matter, no matter. My name will not appear on the title page; I would not want that. A brief acknowledgment will do; I look forward to penning it myself, savouring in advance the reflexive thrill of writing down my own name and being, even if only for a moment, someone wholly other. If, that is, it is ever to be finished. I am happy at my labours, happier than I expected or indeed deserve to be; I feel I have achieved my apotheosis. My time is wonderfully balanced between the day's rough chores and those scrupulosities and fine discriminations that art history demands, this saurian stillness before the shining objects it is my task to interrogate. In these soft, pale nights, while a grey-blue effulgence lingers in the window, I work at the kitchen table at the centre of a vast and somehow, attentive silence, doing my impression of a scholar, sorting through sources, reading over the Professor's material, in Licht's exuberant typewriting, and writing up my own notes; collating, imbricating, advancing by a little and a little. It is a splendid part, the best it has ever been my privilege to play, and I have played many. I am in no hurry; the lamplight falls upon me steadily, my bent head and half a face, my hand inching its way down the pages. Now and then I pause and sit motionless for a moment, a watchman testing the night. I have a gratifying sense of myself as a sentinel, a guardian, a protector against that prowler, my dark other, whom I imagine stalking back and forth out there in the dark. Where can he be hiding, if he is still here? Could he have got back into the house, could he be skulking somewhere, in the attic, or in some unused room, nibbling scraps purloined from the kitchen and watching the day gradually decline towards darkness, biding his time? Is he in the woodpile, perhaps? If he is here it is the girl he is after. He shall not have her, I will see to that.

So anyhow: I came here, and I settled down, if that is the way to put it. I was content. This was a place to be. I did not travel to the mainland. No one had said I might not do so, but I seemed to feel an unspoken interdiction. If there was such a rule it must have been of my own making, for I confess I had no desire to realight from Laputa into the land of giants and horses. Yes, I was happy to bide here, with my catalogues and my detailed reproductions, polishing my *galant* style in preparation for the great work that lay before me impatient for my attentions. Ah, the little figures, I told myself, how convincingly, how gaily they shall strut!

Did I pin too many of my hopes on this work, I wonder? Could I really expect to redeem something of my fouled soul by poring over the paintings – over the reproductions of the paintings – of a long-dead and not quite first-rate master? We know so little of him. Even his name is uncertain: Faubelin, Vanhoblin, van Hobelijn? Take your pick. He changed his name, his nationality, everything, covering his tracks. I have the impression of a man on the run. There is no early work, no juvenilia, no remnants of his apprenticeship. Suddenly one day he starts to paint. Yes, a manufactured man. Is that what attracts me? Something in these dreamy scenes of courtly love and melancholy pantomime appeals to me deeply, some quality of quietude and remoteness, that sense of anguish they convey, of damage, of impending loss. The painter is always outside his subjects, these pallid ladies in their gorgeous gowns – how he loved the nacreous sheen and shimmer of those heavy silks! – attended by their foppish and always slightly tipsy-looking gallants with their mandolins and masks; he holds himself remote from these figures, unable to do anything for them except bear witness to their plight, for even at their gayest they are beyond help, dancing the dainty measures of their dance out at the very end of a world, while the shadows thicken in the trees and night begins its stealthy approach. His pictures hardly need to be glazed, their brilliant surfaces are themselves like a sheet of glass, smooth, chill and impenetrable. He is the master of darkness, as others are of light; even his brightest sunlight seems shadowed, tinged with umber from these thick trees, this ochred ground, these unfathomable spaces leading into night. There is a mystery here, not only in *Le monde d'or*, that last and most enigmatic of his masterpieces, but throughout his work; something is missing, something is deliberately not being said. Yet I think it is this very reticence that lends his pictures their peculiar power. He is the painter of absences, of endings. His scenes all seem to hover on the point of vanishing. How clear and yet far-off and evanescent everything is, as if seen by someone on his deathbed who has lifted himself up to the window at twilight to look out a last time on a world that he is losing.

*

Twice a week I report to Sergeant Toner, the island's only civic guard, a taciturn and stately figure. His dayroom in the barracks reminds me strangely of the schoolrooms of my childhood: the dusty floorboards, the inky smell, the woodframed clock up on the wall ticking away the slow, sunstruck afternoons. Sergeant Toner moves with vast deliberation, rising from his desk in a rolling motion, as if he were shouldering great soft weights, nodding to me in sober salutation. A kind of monumental decorum marks these occasions. We speak, when we speak, mainly of the weather, its treacheries and unexpected beneficences. The Sergeant leans at his counter, his meaty shoulders hunched and his pink scalp gleaming through the stubble of his close-cropped, sandy hair, and writes my name into the daybook with the stub of a plain, sweat-polished pencil tethered to the counter on a piece of string; that pencil must have been here since the days when he was still a recruit. He breathes heavily, so heavily that once in a while, seemingly without his noticing it, a slurred word will surface, a fragment of his inner musings which he involuntarily extrudes in a sort of rasping sigh. *Ah, dear Christ*, he will murmur, or *Wednesday*, or, on one memorable occasion, *Puddings* . . . He honours the niceties of our predicament, maintaining a careful distance between us. In the beginning I had worried that he would be impressed with me, in a professional way, that he might look on me as a sort of celebrity to be watched over and shown off – after all, it is not every day a man of my notoriety swims into his ken – but the very first time when, nervous as a schoolboy, I came to report to him, he repeated my name to himself thoughtfully a couple of times and then – though he had been expecting me, of course, and knew all about me, having been thoroughly briefed, as they say, by the authorities – he asked gently, with that fastidiousness and sense of tact which I have come so much to admire in him, if I would please spell it for him. When I had done so, and he had carefully written it into his book, we observed a brief silence, with eyes downcast, in acknowledgment I suppose of the solemnity of the occasion. 'Ah yes,' he said then with a sigh, 'yes: life means life, right enough.' This is something that has been dinned into me over the years, yet coming from him, and the way that he put it, it had a certain weight, a certain grandeur, even, and for a moment I saw myself as a person of consequence; a serious person, deeply flawed and irremediably damaged, it is true, but someone, all the same: definitely someone.

I need these people, the Sergeant, and Mr Tighe the shopman in the village, even Miss Broaders, she of the pink twinsets and tight mouth, who presides over the post office. I needed them especially in the early days. They had substance, which was precisely what I seemed to lack. I held on to them as if they were a handle by which I might hold on to things, to solid, simple (yes, simple!) things, and to myself among them. For I felt like something suspended in empty air, weightless, transparent, turning this way or that in every buffet of wind that blew. At least when I was locked away I had felt I was definitively there, but now that I was free (or at large, at any rate) I seemed hardly to be here at all. This is how I imagine ghosts existing, poor, pale wraiths pegged out to shiver in the wind of the world like so much insubstantial laundry, yearning towards us, the heedless ones, as we walk blithely through them.

*

Time. Time on my hands. That is a strange phrase. From those first weeks on the island I recall especially the afternoons, slow, silent, oddly mysterious stretches of something that seemed more than clock time, a thicker-textured stuff, a sort of sea-drift, tidal, surreptitious, deeper than the world. Look at this box-kite of sunlight sailing imperceptibly across the floor, listen to the scrape of the curtain as it stirs in the breeze, see that dazed green view framed in the white window, the far, narrow line of the beach and beyond that the azure sea, unreal, vivid as memory. This is a different way of being alive. I thought sometimes at moments such as this that I might simply drift away and become a part of all that out there, drift and dissolve, be a shimmer of light slowly fading into nothing. It was coming into the season of white nights, I found it hard to sleep. Extraordinary the look of things at dusk then, it might have been another planet, with that pale vault of sky, those crouched and hesitant, dreamy distances. I wandered about the house, going softly through the stillness and shadows, and sometimes I would lose myself, I mean I would flow out of myself somehow and be as a phantom, a patch of moving dark against the lighter darkness all around me. The night seemed something on the point of being spoken. This sense of immanence, of things biding their time, waiting to occur, was it all just imagination and wishful thinking? Night-time always seems peopled to me; they throng about me, the dead ones, yearning to speak.

*

The house has a nautical feel to it. Sea breezes make the timbers shift and groan, and the blue, salt-laden light in the windows is positively oceanic. The air reeks of brine and the floors when the sun comes in give off a tang of pitch. Then there is that faint smell of rancid apples everywhere: I might be Jim Hawkins, off on a grand venture. When I came down at last on that morning of their arrival the kitchen was like a ship's cabin. I felt at first a certain sullen indignation, tinged with fear: this was my place and they were invading it. And yet, although I had only been here a few weeks, like Licht I too was eager already for change, for disorder, for the mess and confusion that people make of things. It was simple, you see, no matter how much of a mystery I may make the whole thing seem. Company, that was what we wanted, the brute warmth of the presence of others to tell us we were alive after all, despite appearances. They were crowded at the long pine table nursing mugs of the tea that Licht had made for them and looking distinctly queasy. Their shoes were lined up on top of the stove to dry. It was still early, and outside a flinty sun was shining and piled-up vastnesses of luminous silver and white clouds were sailing over the oak ridge. When I came in from the hall the back door flew open in the wind and everything flapped and rattled and something white flew off the table, and poor Licht waded forward at an angle with one arm outstretched and his coat-tails flying and slammed the door, and all immediately subsided, and our galleon ploughed serenely on again.

'This milk is sour,' said Pound.

I forget: is he the comedian or the fat one with the specs? I can see I shall have trouble with these two.

You would think I would have asked myself questions, as characters such as I are expected to do: for instance, Who can they be? or, What are they doing here? or, What will this mean to me? But no, not à bit of it. And yet I must have been waiting all along for them, or something like them, without knowing it, perhaps. Biding my time, that is the phrase. It has always been thus with me, not knowing myself or my velleities, drifting in ignorance. Now as I stood there gazing at them in dull wonderment, with that eerie sense of recognition that only comes in dreams, a memory floated up – though memory is too strong a word, and at the same time not strong enough – of a room in the house where I was born. It is a recurring image, one of a handful of emblematic fragments from the deep past that seem mysteriously to constitute something of the very stuff of which I am made. It is a summer afternoon, but the room is dim, except where a quartered crate of sunlight, seething with dustmotes, falls at a tilt from the window. All is coolness and silence, or what passes for silence in summer. Outside the window the garden stands aghast in a tangle of trumpeting convolvulus. Nothing happens, nothing will happen, yet everything is poised, waiting, a chair in the corner crouching with its arms braced, the coiled fronds of a fern, that copper pot with the streaming sunspot on its rim. This is what holds it all together and yet apart, this sense of expectancy, like a spring tensed in mid-air and sustained by its own force, exerting an equal pressure everywhere. And I, I am there and not there: I am the pretext of things, though I sport no thick gold wing or pale halo. Without me there would be no moment, no separable event, only the brute, blind drift of things, That seems true; important, too. (Yes, it would appear that after all I am indeed required.) And yet, though I am one of them, I am only a half figure, a figure half-seen, standing in the doorway, or sitting at a corner of the scrubbed pine table with a cracked mug at my elbow, and if they try to see me straight, or turn their heads too quickly, I am gone.

'That skipper,' Felix was saying. 'What a fellow! *Listing?* I said to him, *listing?* More like we are in danger of turning tortoise, I believe!' And he laughed his laugh.

I was thinking how strangely matters arrange themselves at times, as if after all there were someone, another still, whose task it is to set them out just so.

Licht from across the room gave me one of his mournfully accusing glares.

'It's all right,' he called out loudly, 'it's all right, don't trouble yourself, I'll light the stove.'

PROFESSOR KREUTZNAER in his eyrie sat for a long time without stirring, hearing only the slow beat of his own blood and the spring wind gusting outside and now and then the hoarse baby-cry of a gull, startlingly close. Strain as he might he could hear nothing from downstairs. What were they doing? They had not left, he would have seen them go. He pictured them standing about the dim hallway, magicked into immobility, glazed and mute, one with a hand raised, another bending to set down a bag, and Licht before them, stalled at the foot of the stairs, nodding and twitching like a marionette, as usual.

He fiddled with the telescope and sighed. Surely he had been mistaken, surely it was not who he thought it was?

He went to the door. It had a way of sticking and was hard to open quietly. Sure enough it gave its little *eek*! and shuddered briefly on its hinges. A flare of irritation made his heart thud hotly. He stood a moment on the landing with an ear cocked. Not a sound. Out here, though, he could feel them, the density of their presence, the unaccustomed fullness in the air of the house. His heart quietened, settling down grumpily in his breast like a fractious babe. The stairs at this level were narrow and uncarpeted. On the return a little circular window, greyed with dust and cobwebs, looked out blearily on treetops and a bit of brilliant blue, it might be sea or sky, he could never decide which. Again he found himself listening to his own heartbeat, with that occasional delicate tripping measure at the systole that made him think of rippling silk. If he were to pitch headlong down these stairs now would he feel it, his face crumpling, knees breaking, his breastbone bumping from step to step, or would he be gone already, a bit of ectoplasm floating up into the dimness under the

226

ceiling, looking back with detached interest at this sloughed slack bag of flesh slithering in a comic rush on to the landing? When he was young he had thought that growing old would be a process of increasing refinement by which the things that mattered would fall away like little lights falling dark one by one, until at last the last light winked out. And it was true, things that had once seemed important had faded, but then others had taken their place. He had never paid much attention to his body but now it weighed on him constantly. He felt invaded by his own flesh, squatted upon by this ailing ape with its pains and hungers and its traitorous heart. And he was baffled all the time, baffled and numb.

He began cautiously to descend the stairs, wincing on each step as the boards squeaked. If it was Felix, how had he found his way here? Chance? He smiled to himself bitterly. Oh, of course – pure chance. He could feel the past welling up around him, a smoking, sulphurous stuff.

At the window on the first-floor landing he paused again and looked out at the distant sea. How clear it was today: he could see the burnished tufts of grass on the slopes of the dunes tossing in the wind. He liked mornings, the cold air and immensities of light, the raw, defenceless feel of things. This was the time to work, when the brain was still tender from the swoons and mad alarms of sleep and the demon flesh had not yet reasserted its foul hegemony. Work. But he no longer worked. He could feel the wind pummelling the house, pounding softly on the window-panes. On the sill a fly was buzzing itself to death, fallen on its back and spinning madly in tiny, spiralling circles. He leaned against the window-frame and at once the old questions rose again, gnawing at him. How can these disparate things – that wind, this fly, himself brooding there – how can they be together, continuous with each other, in the same reality? Incongruity: disorder and incongruity, the grotesqueries of the always-slipping mask, these were the only constants he had ever been able to discern. He closed his eyes for a moment, taking a tiny sip of darkness. Stay here, never stir again, gradually go dry and hollow, turn into a brittle husk a breath of wind would blow away. He imagined it, everything quiet and the light slowly changing and evening coming on, then the long dark, then rain at dawn and the gull's wing, then shine again, another bright day declining towards dusk, then another night, endlessly.

Suddenly there was a muffled cataclysm and the door behind him opened and Flora came out. At first he saw her only as a silhouette against a haze of white light in the lavatory window at her back. She shimmered in the doorway as if enveloped in some dark, flowing stuff, an angled shape flexing behind her shoulder like a wing being folded.

'Oh,' she said, and, so it seemed to him, laughed.

She closed the door behind her with one hand while with the other she held up her long hair in a bundle at the nape of her neck. He touched a hand to his crooked bow-tie. A hairpin fell to the floor and she crouched quickly to retrieve it. He looked down at her knees pressed tightly together, pale as candle-wax, and saw the outlines of the frail bones packed under the skin and caught for a second her warm, dark, faintly urinous smell. She was barefoot. As she was rising she swayed a little and he put out a hand to steady her, but she pretended not to notice and turned from him with a blurred, stiff smile, murmuring something, and went away quickly down the stairs, still holding up the flowing bundle of her hair. When she was gone the only trace of her was the borborygmic grumbling of the cistern refilling, and for a moment he wondered if he might have dreamed her. Suddenly the image of his mother rose before him. He saw her as she had been when he was a child, turning from shadow into light, a slight, small-boned woman in a black dress with a bodice, her heavy dark hair, which gave her so much trouble and of which she was so vain, done up in two braided shells over her ears and parted down the middle with such severity he used to think it must hurt her, the white weal scored from brow to nape like a bloodless wound. *Das Mädel*, his father used to call her, with a bitter, mocking smile, *das kleine Mädel*. Father in his white suit standing under the arbour of roses, idly drawing figures on the pathway with the tip of his cane, gay and disappointed and dreamily sinister, like a character out of Chekhov. Where was that? Up on the Baltic, the summer house. In the days when they had a summer house. The past, the past. He faltered, as if he had been struck a soundless blow, and closed his eyes briefly and pressed his fingertips to the window-sill for support, and a sort of hollow opened up inside him and he could not breathe.

Licht came up the stairs. 'What's wrong?' he said, sounding annoyed. 'What's wrong with you?'

The Professor blinked. 'What?'

'She said you were . . .'

They looked at each other. Licht was the first to turn away his eyes.

'Who is that,' the Professor said after a pause.

'Who?'

'That girl.'

Licht shrugged and hummed a tune under his breath, tapping one foot. The Professor lifted his weary eyes to the window and the shining day outside. The wind was still blowing, the fly still buzzed. He turned to Licht again.

'What did you say to them?' he said. 'Have they asked to stay?'

Licht frowned blandly and went on humming as if he had not heard, picking with a fingernail at a patch of flaking paint on the wall in front of him. The Professor descended a step towards him menacingly and paused. He could feel it suddenly, no mistaking it, the tiny but calamitous adjustment that had been made in their midst.

Felix, then: it must be Felix.

Licht spoke a word under his breath.

'What?' the Professor said.

'Flora,' Licht answered and looked up at him defiantly. 'That's her name. Flora.' Then he turned and skipped off swiftly down the stairs.

*

The room that Flora found herself in was small and had a low ceiling; everything in it seemed made on a miniature scale, so that she felt huge, with impossible hands and feet. Also the floor sloped; when she got up from the bed and walked to the window it was as if she were toppling backwards in slow motion. One of the panes in the little window was broken and a piece of cardboard was wedged in its place. Down in the sunlit yard a few scrawny chickens were picking half-heartedly in the dust and a fat old dog was asleep under a wheelbarrow. When she leaned down she could see fields and, beyond them, that sort of long ridge with trees on it. There was a fire going up there, weak flitters of white smoke were whipping in the wind above the treetops. She waded back to the narrow bed and sat down carefully with her arms pressed to her sides and her hands gripping the edge of the mattress. She could still feel the sway of the sea, a flaccid, teetering sensation, as if her limbs were brim-full of some heavy, sluggish liquid. She was not well, she did not want to be in this house, on this island. When Licht had brought her up here the bed had still been warm from someone sleeping in it. She had lain on top of the covers – a fawn blanket with a suspicious-looking stain in the middle of it and a sheet made, she was convinced, from old flour sacks – not daring to pull them back. The mattress sagged in the middle as if a heavy corpse had been left lying on it for a long time. On the little pine dressing-table there was a hairbrush with a few thin strands of reddish hair tangled in the bristles. A speckled mirror leaned from the wall at a watchful angle, reflecting a mysterious shimmer of grey and blue. She thought of searching the chest of drawers – she liked to poke about in other people's stuff – but she had not the energy. A coloured reproduction of a painting torn from a book was tacked to the wall beside the mirror. She looked at it dully. Strange scene; what was going on? There was a sort of clown dressed in white standing up with his arms hanging, and people behind him walking off down a hill to where a ship was waiting, and at the left a smirking man astride a donkey.

Felix opened the door stealthily and put in his narrow head and smiled, showing a glint of jagged tooth.

'Are you decent?'

She did not answer. She felt detached from things. Everything around her was sparklingly clear – the tilted mirror, the window with its sunny view, that little brass globe on the bedpost – but it was all somehow small and far away. She might have been standing at the back of a deep, narrow tunnel, looking out. Felix closed the door behind him and moved in that sinuous way of his to the window, seeming not to touch the floor but rather to clamber smoothly along the wall. He did not look at her but kept smiling to himself with a show of ease. Why had she let him into her room last night? She knew nothing about him, nothing; he had just turned up, suddenly there, like someone she had known once and forgotten who now had come back. That was the strange thing, that there had seemed nothing strange about it when he smiled at her in the hotel corridor and put a hand on the door to stop her shutting it and glanced all around quickly and stepped into the room sideways with a finger to his lips. He could have been anyone: anything could have happened. He was horrible with his clothes off, all skin and bone and sort of stretched, like a greyhound standing up on its hind legs. How white he had looked in the dark, coming towards her, glimmering, with that huge thing sticking up sideways like something that had burst out of him, blunt head bobbing and one slit eye looking everywhere for a way in again. He had squirmed and groaned on top of her, jabbing at her as if it were a big blunt knife he was sticking into her. When she moaned and rolled up her eyes she had felt him stop for a second and look down at her and give a sort of snicker and she knew he knew she was pretending. His hair down there was copper-coloured and crackly, like little tight coils of copper wire.

'Nice view,' he said now and for some reason laughed. 'Lovely prospect. Those trees.'

He came towards her, and his reflection, curved and narrow

and tinily exact, slid abruptly over the rim of the polished brass ball on the bedpost beside her. She sat without moving and looked at him and a pleasurable surge of fear made her throat thicken; it was like the panicky excitement she would feel as a little girl when in a game of hide-and-seek some surly, bull-faced boy was about to stumble on her in her hiding-place. She saw that Felix was going to try to kiss her and she stood up quickly, lithe as a fish suddenly, and twisted past him.

'It's hot,' she said loudly. 'Isn't it hot?'

Her voice had a quaver in it. He would think she was frightened of him. A voice said mockingly in her head, *You are, you are*. She leaned down and tried to open the little window. He came up behind her and tapped the frame with his knuckles.

'Painted shut,' he said. 'See?' She could feel him thinly smiling and could smell his grey breath. He reached up and deftly plucked out a hairpin and her hair fell down; he took a thick handful of it and tugged it playfully and put his mouth to her ear. 'Poor Rapunzel,' he whispered. 'Poor damsel.'

She closed her eyes and shivered.

'Are you frightened?' he whispered. 'You must not be frightened. There is no danger. Everything is safe and sound. We have fallen flat on our feet here.'

In the yard the chickens scratched among the cobbles, stopped, stepped, scratched again. The dog was gone from under the wheelbarrow. Felix breathed hotly on her neck. Everything felt so strange. Her skin was burning.

'Hmm?'

'So strange,' she said. 'As if I . . .'

He let fall her hair and, suddenly full of tense energy, turned away from her and paced the little room, head down, his hands clasped behind his back.

'Yes yes,' he said impatiently. 'Everyone feels they have been here before.'

She heard the dog somewhere nearby barking half-heartedly.

'That man,' she said. 'I thought he was going to . . .'

'Who?'

'That old man.'

He laughed silkily.

'Ah, you have met the Professor, have you?' he said. 'The great man?'

'He was standing on the stairs. He—'

'Do you know who he is?' He smiled; he seemed angry; she was frightened of him.

'No,' she said faintly. 'Who?'

'Ah, you would like to know, now, wouldn't you.' He glanced at her slyly. 'He is famous.'

'Is he?'

'Or was, at least,' he said and laughed. 'I could tell you a secret about him, but I do not choose to.'

She pressed her back against the window-frame and folded her arms, cradling herself, and watched him where he paced. Yes, he would do anything, be capable of anything. She wanted him to hit her, to beat her to the floor and fall on her and feed his fill on her bleeding mouth. She pictured herself dressed in white sitting at a little seafront café somewhere in Italy or the south of France, where he had brought her, the hot wind blowing and the palms clattering and the sea a vivid blue like in those pictures, and she so cool and pale, and people glancing at her, wondering who she was as she sat there demurely in her light, expensive frock, squirming a little in tender pain, basking in secret in the slow heat of her hidden bruises, waiting for him to come sauntering along the front with his hands in his pockets, whistling.

Then somehow she was sitting on the bed again looking at her bare feet on the blue and grey rug on the floor and Felix was sitting beside her stroking her hand.

'I can give you so much,' he was saying fervently, in a voice thick with thrilling insincerity. 'You understand that, don't you?'

She sighed. She had not been listening.

'What?' she said. 'Yes.' And then, more distantly: 'Yes.'

What was he talking about? Love, she supposed; they were always talking about love. He smiled, searching her eyes, scanning her face all over. Behind his shoulder, like another version of him in miniature in a far-off mirror, the man on the donkey in the picture grinned at her gloatingly.

'Will you be my slave, then, and do my bidding?' he said with soft playfulness. He lifted a hand and gently cupped her breast, hefting its soft weight. 'Will you, Flora?' His dark eyes held her, lit with merriment and malice. It was as if he were looking down at her from a little spyhole, looking down at her and laughing. He had not said her name before. She nodded in silence, with parted lips. 'Good, good,' he murmured. He touched his mouth to hers. She caught again his used-up, musty smell. Then, as if he had tested something and was satisfied, he released her hand and stood up briskly and moved to the door. There he paused. 'Of course,' he said gaily, 'where there is giving there is also taking, yes?'

He winked and was gone.

She looked at her hand where he had left it lying on the blanket. Her breast still felt the ghost of his touch. She shivered, as if a cold breeze had blown across her back, her shoulder-blades flinching like folded wings. The day around her felt like night. Yes, that was it: a kind of luminous night. And I am dreaming. She smiled to herself, a thin smile like his, and pulled back the covers and laid herself down gently in the bed and closed her eyes.

*

When Professor Kreutznaer came down to the kitchen at last the stove was going and Licht was frying sausages on a blackened pan. The Professor stopped in the doorway. The blonde woman sat with her black jacket thrown over her shoulders and an elbow on the table and her head on her hand, regarding him absently, her camera on the table before her. A cloud of fat-smoke tumbled slowly in mid-air. The smaller of the boys was gnawing a crust of bread, the little girl sat red-eyed with her hands in her lap. And that ancient character in the candy-striped coat, what was he? What were they all? A travelling circus? Felix had outdone himself this time. Licht was saying something to him but he took no notice and advanced into the room and sat down frowningly at a corner of the table. The one in the striped blazer cleared his throat and half rose from his chair.

'Croke's the name,' he said heartily, then faltered. 'We . . .' He looked at Sophie for support. 'Damn boat ran aground,' he said. 'That captain, so-called.'

The Professor considered the raised whorls of grain in the table and nodded. The silence whirred.

'We were in a boat,' Sophie said loudly, as if she thought the Professor might be deaf. 'It got stuck on something in the harbour and nearly capsized.' She pointed to their shoes on the stove. 'We had to walk through the water.'

The Professor nodded again without looking at her. He appeared to be thinking of something else.

'Yes,' he said. 'The tides hereabouts are treacherous.'

'Yes.' She caught Croke's eye and they looked away from each other quickly so as not to laugh.

Licht brought the pan from the stove and forked the charred sausages on to their plates, smiling nervously and nodding all around and making as much clatter as he could. He did not look at the Professor. There was a smell of boiled tea.

Felix came bustling in, rubbing his hands and smiling, and sat down beside Pound and picked up a sausage from the boy's plate and bit a piece off it and put it back again.

'Yum yum,' he said, chewing. 'Good.'

Something tilted wildly for a second. All waited, looking from Felix to the Professor and back again, feeling the air tighten between them across the table. The Professor, frowning, did not lift his eyes. Pound regarded his bitten sausage with sullen indignation.

'Well,' Sophie said to break the silence, 'how is Beauty?'

Felix looked blank for a moment and then nodded seriously.

'She is not well,' he said. 'She has an upset head. A certain dizziness, you know.'

Croke nudged Sophie under the table and whispered hoarsely into her ear:

'Struck down by our friend Poison-Prick.'

Sophie let her lids droop briefly and she faintly smiled.

Suddenly, as if he had been rehearsing it in his head, Felix jumped up and leaned across the table and thrust out his hand to the Professor.

'So good of you to take us in,' he said with a breathy laugh, avoiding the Professor's eye, 'so good, yes, thank you.' The old man looked without expression at the hand that was offered him and after a second Felix snapped it shut like a jack-knife and withdrew it. 'May I introduce—? This is Mr Croke, and Sophie here, and little Alice, and Patch—'

'Hatch,' said Hatch.

'Hatch I mean. Ha ha! And Pound – Pound? Yes.' A mumbling, a shuffling of feet. He sat down. 'Ouf! what a business,' he said. 'I believe that captain was drunk. I said to him, I did, I said to him, *You will be responsible, remember!* A tour of the islands, we were told; a pleasure cruise. What pleasure, I ask, what cruise? Look at us: we are like the Swiss family Robertson!' He laughed excessively, his shoulders shaking, and paused for a moment, licking his lips with a glistening tongue-tip. 'This house, sir,' he said softly, in an almost confidential voice, 'the garden, those trees up there,' pointing, 'I have to tell you, it is all very handsome, very handsome and agreeable. I hope we do not inconvenience you. We shall be here only for a very little time. A day. Less than a day. An afternoon. Perhaps an evening, no more. Dusk, I always think, is so lovely in these latitudes: that greying light, those trembling shadows. I am reminded of my favourite painter, do you know the one I mean?' He mused a moment, smiling upwards, displaying his profile, then looked at the Professor again and smiled. 'You will hardly know we are here at all, I think. Our wings—' he made an undulant movement with his hands '—our wings will scarcely stir the air.'

Another silence settled and all sat very still again, waiting for the Professor to speak. But the Professor said nothing, and Felix shrugged and winked at Sophie and made a face of comic helplessness. Licht turned to the stove with a wincing look, his shoulders hunched, as if something had fallen and he were waiting for the crash. A little leftover breathy sob took Alice by surprise and she gulped, and glanced at Hatch quickly and blushed. Felix drummed his fingertips on the table and softly sang:

> *Din din!*
> *Don don!*

The sun shone in the window, the wind rattled the back door on its latch.

'This milk *is* sour,' Pound said. 'Jesus!'

*

The lounge, as it is called, is a long, narrow, low-ceilinged, cluttered room with windows looking out to sea. It smells like the railway carriages of my youth. Here, in the unmoving, brownish air, big, indistinct lumps of furniture live their secret lives, sprawled armchairs and an enormous, lumpy couch, a high, square table with knobbled legs, a roll-top desk sprouting dog-eared papers so that it looks as if it is sticking out a score of tongues. Everything is stalled, as though one day long ago something had happened and the people living here had all at once dropped what they were doing and rushed outside, never to return. Still the room waits, poised to start up again, like a stopped clock. I have my place to sit by the window while I drink my morning tea, wedged in comfortably between a high bookcase and a little table bearing a desiccated fern in a brass pot; behind me, above my head, on a bureau under a glass dome, a stuffed owl is perched, holding negligently in one mildewed claw a curiously unconcerned, moth-eaten mouse. From where I sit I can see a bit of crooked lawn and a rose bush already in bloom and an old rain barrel at the corner of the house.

I think to myself, *My life is a ruin, an abandoned house, a derelict place.* The same thought, in one form or another, has come to me at least once a day, every day, for years; why then am I surprised anew by it each time?

I have my good days and my bad. Guess which this one is.

Tea. Talk about tea. For me, the taking of tea is a ceremonial and solitary pleasure. I prefer a superior Darjeeling; there was a firm of merchants in Paris, I remember – what were they called? – who did a superb blend, an ounce or two of which they would part with in exchange for a lakh of rupees. Otherwise a really fine Keemun is acceptable, at a pinch. Then there is the matter of the cup: even the worst of Licht's stewed sludge will taste like something halfway decent if it is served in, say, an antique fluted gold-rimmed piece of bird's-egg-blue Royal Doulton. I love bone china, the very idea of it, I want to take the whole thing, cup and saucer and all, into my mouth and crack it lingeringly between my teeth, like meringue. Tea tastes of other lives. I close my eyes and see the pickers bending on the green hillsides, their saffron robes and slender, leaf-brown hands; I see the teeming docks where half-starved fellows with legs like knobkerries sticking out of ragged shorts heave stencilled wooden chests and call to each other in parrot shrieks; I even see the pottery works where this cup was spun out of cloud-white clay one late-nineteenth-century summer afternoon by an indentured apprentice with a harelip and a blind sister waiting for him in their hovel up a pestilential back lane. Lives, other lives! a myriad of them, distilled into this thimbleful of perfumed pleasure—

Oh, stop.

The philosopher asks: *Can the style of an evil man have any unity?*

The lounge.

The day outside was darkening. A bundled, lead-coloured cloud burning like magnesium all along its edge had reared up in the window. A crepitant stillness gathered, presaging rain. I wonder what causes it, this expectant hush? I suppose the air pressure alters, or the approaching rain damps down the wind somehow. I should have studied meteorology, learned how it all works, the chaotic flood and flow of things, air currents, wind, clouds, these vast nothingnesses tossing to and fro over the earth.

Flora is dreaming of the golden world.

Worlds within worlds. They bleed into each other. I am at

once here and there, then and now, as if by magic. I think of the stillness that lives in the depths of mirrors. It is not our world that is reflected there. It is another place entirely, another universe, cunningly made to mimic ours. Anything is possible there; even the dead may come back to life. Flaws develop in the glass, patches of silvering fall away and reveal the inhabitants of that parallel, inverted world going about their lives all unawares. And sometimes the glass turns to air and they step through it without a sound and walk into *my* world. Here comes Sophie now, barefoot, still with her leather jacket over her shoulders, and time shimmers in its frame.

She stopped inside the door and looked about her at the big dark pieces of furniture huddled in the brownish gloom, and immediately there started up in her head the rattly music of a barrel organ and she saw a little girl standing at a window above a wide avenue, with grey light like this lingering and dead leaves in the wind stealthily scurrying here and there over the pavement. Assailed, she sank down into a corner of the sagging couch, drawing up her legs and folding them under her and gingerly massaging her bruised instep. There were so many things she was tired of remembering, the happy as well as the bad. The apartment on Kirchenallee, the upright piano by the window where she practised scales through the endless winter afternoons, her fingers stiff from the cold and her kneecaps numb. Smell of almonds and ersatz coffee, of the dust in the curtains where she leaned her head, looking down on the people passing by on the broad, bare pavements of the ruined city, hunched and hurrying, carrying bags or clutching parcels under their arms, like people in a newsreel. Her mother in the kitchen selling silk stockings and American cigarettes from a suitcase open on the table, talking and talking in that high, fast voice that sounded always as if at any moment it might break and fly off in pieces like a shattering lightbulb. The customers were furtive, timid, resentful, Frau Müller who limped, the sweaty, grey-faced man in the tight suit, that skinny girl from the café across the street. They glanced at her guiltily with weak, somehow beseeching smiles as they crossed the living room, hiding their purchases; how quietly, how carefully they would shut the door behind them, as if they were afraid of breaking something. She had thought she had managed to forget all that, she had thought she had banished it all, and now here it was again. The past mocked her with its simplicities, its completedness.

You see how for them too the mirror turns transparent and that silver world advances and folds them in its chill embrace?

She longed to be in her darkroom, in that dense, red, aortic light, watching the underwater figures darken and take shape, swimming up to meet her. Things for her were not real any longer until they had been filtered through a lens. How clear and small and perfectly detailed everything looked inside that little black box of light!

Humbly the first drops of rain tapped on the window.

All out there, oh, all out there.

What if, I ask myself, what if one day I were to wake up so disgusted with my physical self that my flesh should seem no longer habitable? Such torment that would be: a slug thrashing in salt.

Sophie looked at her hands and sighed and closed her eyes for a second. She felt dizzy. There was a sort of whirring in her head. It was as if she had been spinning in a circle and had suddenly stopped. When she was a little girl her father would take her hands and whirl her round and round in the air until her feet seemed to fill with lead and her wrists creaked. It was like flying in a dream. Afterwards, when he let go of her and she stood swaying and hiccuping, everything would keep on lurching past her like a vast, ramshackle merry-go-round. And sometimes she grew frightened, thinking it was the movement of the earth she was seeing, the planet itself, spinning in space. She had never really lost it, that fear of falling into the sky. There were still moments when she would halt suddenly, like an actor stranded in the middle of the stage, lines forgotten, staring goggle-eyed and making fish-mouths. She took a cigarette from the packet in the pocket of her leather jacket and struck a match. She paused, watching the small flame creep along the wood, seeing the tiny tremor in her hand. Corpsing: that was the word. She imagined being in bed here, in an anonymous little room up at the very top of the house, just lying at peace with her hands resting on the cool, turned-down sheet, looking at the sea-light in the salt-rimed windows and the gulls wheeling and crying. To be there, to be inconsequential; to forget herself, even for a little while; to stop, to be still; to be at peace.

She entertained the notion that her father was alive somewhere, a fugitive in the tropic south, on some jungly islet, perhaps; she pictured him, immensely old by now, shrivelled and wickedly merry, sitting at his ease in the shade outside an adobe shack, tended hand and foot by a flat-nosed Indian woman while naked children brown and smooth as mud gambolled at his feet, with the broad, cocoa-coloured river at his back, and beyond that the enormous forest wall, screeching, green-black, impenetrable. She wanted him to have been important, terrible, a hunted man; it was her secret fantasy. They had waited for him day after day in the icy apartment (strange how heavy the cold felt, a sort of invisible, stony substance standing motionless in the air), then week after week, then the weeks became months, the months years, and he did not come. She thought of him as she had seen him for the last time, going down the stairs with a kit-bag on his shoulder. She could not remember his face now, but she recalled how lightly he had skipped down the steps, whistling, his head with its oiled hair and neat white parting sinking from sight. The pain, the outrageous pain of being abandoned had surprised her, the way all pain always surprised her in those days, like news from another world, the big, the real one, where she did not want to go but to which each day brought her a little closer. She was six years old when he left. Her mother lay in bed at night and cried; night after night, Sophie could hear her from across the hall, moaning and gulping, stuffing the pillow into her mouth, trying to stop herself, trying not to be heard, as if it were something shameful she was doing, some shameful act.

There was a scrabbling at the door and Croke came in

cautiously, first a big, liver-spotted paw, then bigger head, then knees, then last of all the bowed back. He glanced about the room and did not see her curled up in the shadowed corner of the sofa. He advanced to the window, stepping over the carpet with a camel's ponderous slouch, seeming to lag half a pace behind his legs, his long head swaying on its drooped stalk. The rain was coming down heavily now, like a fall of dirty light. He stood with his hands behind his back and stared out bleakly, his loose lips pursed as if he were trying to remember how to whistle.

'The golden world!' he muttered, in a tone of deep disgust.

He farted, closing one eye and scrunching up his face at the side. At Sophie's soft laugh he started in fright and peered wildly at her over his shoulder.

'Jesus!' he cried. 'Do you want to kill me?' He waggled his fingers at her as if he were sprinkling water. 'Sitting there like a ghost!'

She laughed again. He was a game old brute: when she had stumbled on the bridge and he caught her his big hands had been all over her. She shivered, remembering the feel of his old man's arm, the slippery, fishy flesh inside the sleeve and beneath it the bone hard and sharp as an ancient weapon. Now he paced agitatedly in a little circle, mumbling to himself and shaking his head. He halted, looking down at his feet.

'My shoes are wringing still,' he said and did his phlegmy laugh. 'Leaky as an unstanched wench. Ha!' He peered at her but she said nothing and he resumed his pacing. He stopped at the window and looked out again balefully at the rain. The world out there had turned to an undulant grey blur.

Silence. Picture them there, two figures in rainlight. Something, something out of childhood.

'I was trying to think,' Croke said, 'of the name of that thing they keep the host in to show it at Benediction. What do they call that? The thing shaped like the sun that the priest holds up. Did you ever see it? What is it, now. I've been trying to remember all morning.' He sighed. 'And I was an altar boy, you know.' He turned to her stoutly, expecting her to laugh. 'I was.'

But she was not listening. She sat and rocked herself in her arms, her eyes fixed on the floor. Croke shrugged and turned away and fiddled with the knobs of a huge, old-fashioned radio standing on a low table beside the window. The green tuning light came on, a pulsing eye, and as the valves warmed up a distant crackling swelled, as if it were the noise of the past itself that was trapped in there among the coils and the glowing filaments. He spun the dial, and out of the crackling a faint voice emerged, speaking incomprehensible words, distantly. Croke listened slack-eyed for a moment and then switched it off.

Felix came in. When he saw Sophie he hesitated and let his gaze go blank and wander about the room. Croke he ignored.

'What a place!' he said. 'You know there is no telephone?'

She watched him, her eyes narrowed against the smoke of her cigarette. She had heard him creeping about in the hotel corridor last night, until that little bitch had let him in, she was sure of it. She had been using her cupped hand as an ashtray and now she held the swiftly-smoking stub of her cigarette aloft and looked about her with a frown. Felix stepped smartly to the mantelpiece and found a saucer there and brought it to her. He watched with what seemed almost fondness as she leaned forward and crushed out the butt. The last, acrid waft of smoke was like something swift and bitter being said. She raised her eyes briefly and then looked away.

'You know who he is,' he said, 'the Professor? You recognised him?' She shrugged, and he shook his head at her reprovingly. 'O, Fama . . .!' He heaved a histrionic sigh.

'Tell me, then,' she said, stung. 'Tell me who he is.'

'Someone famous. A famous man.'

She looked sceptical.

'Oh yes?'

He nodded with mock solemnity and laid a finger to the side of his nose. She felt herself flush. She said brusquely:

'Should you not go and see if the Princess is sleeping soundly?'

Still he leaned above her in his buttoned brown suit and stringy tie, a pent-up, parcelled man, his smile twitching and one eyebrow arched, studying her. She drew the collar of her jacket tight about her throat.

'Am I,' he said, 'the charming Prince, I wonder, or the Beast?' She did not answer and he advanced his smiling face close to hers and softly asked: 'Are you jealous?'

She laughed out loud.

'What, of her?'

He shook his head once.

'I meant of me,' he said.

She opened wide her eyes and looked at him steadily with a formless smile and said nothing. Croke stood motionless with his head lifted as if he were listening to something in the distance, an echo of that voice out of the ether. (That gold thing, like a sort of sunburst, with the big gold knobs on the handle and the big square base, and the price tag still on the instep of the priest's shoe when he genuflected; smell of incense and of candle-grease, the fleshy stink of lilies – *what* was it called?) There was a gust of wind, and the rain whispered softly like blown sand against the glass. Felix turned from Sophie with a flourish and strolled up the room and down again at an equine prance, seeming pleased with himself, humming lightly under his breath and smirking. He stopped to examine the stuffed owl, his narrow head lifted at an angle and his lips pursed. A spot of silver light gleamed in the hollow of his temple. He took a dented, flat gold case from his breast pocket and extracted from it a black cheroot and lit it carefully, holding it clipped between the second and third fingers of his left hand.

'I see you kept your baccy dry, anyhow,' Croke at the window said, and still was ignored.

'We have not had a real talk, you and I,' Felix said to Sophie over his shoulder, making a frowning face at the owl. A ribbon of harsh smoke trickled out at the corners of his mouth. The bird stared back at him with apoplectic fixity. 'We should, I think, don't you?'

Abruptly the rain stopped and the sun came out shakily and everything outside shimmered and dripped.

'Talk?' Sophie said. 'Talk about what?'

'Oh, anything. Everything. I am trying to be friendly, you see.'

Sophie considered his narrow back for a moment thoughtfully.

'Who is he?' she said. 'That old man.'

'What? I told you: a famous person. From the past. A professor of fine arts.' He seemed to find that very funny. 'Oh yes,' he said, laughing without sound, one bony shoulder shaking, 'a great appreciator of the fine arts!'

She studied him with her head held on one side.

'Is that why you came here,' she said, 'because of him?'

He laughed almost shyly this time and touched a hand to his dyed hair.

'No, no,' he murmured happily. 'Chance – pure chance!'

She nodded, not believing him.

'He does not seem to have heard of *you*,' she said.

'He has – oh, he has. But perhaps he prefers to forget.' He cast a smiling glance at her. 'Maybe you will make him famous again?' He took the cheroot from his lips and lifted an invisible camera to his eye. 'Snap-snap, yes? *The great man at his desk.*' He was mimicking her accent.

She rose from the couch, smoothing the lap of her dress, and crossed the room and stood with one hand on the doorknob and the other still holding her jacket closed at her throat.

'What a fraud you are,' she said.

'A fake, yes,' he answered swiftly, pouncing, with his fierce, tight-lipped smile, 'but not a fraud. Ask the Professor: he knows about such things.' He advanced a step towards her eagerly and stopped and stood with his hands in the pockets of his jacket and his head thrown back, looking at her along his nose and smiling genially, the cheroot held in his teeth and his curved mouth oozing smoke. 'What do you say,' he said, 'shall we fight?'

She hesitated, her eyes lowered, looking at the spot where he was standing. She pictured herself striding forward without a word and beating him to his knees, could almost see the blood-dark shadow in her head and feel the irresistible exultation shake her heart; she would cross the space between them at a run, one arm drawn back like a bow, fleet-footed, winged, taking a little skipping step halfway, the floor like firm air under her tread, and then feel the crack of fist on flesh and hear his laughter and his cries as he fell in a clatter with limbs askew, like a wooden doll. She trembled, and turned abruptly and went out, letting the door shut behind her with a ragged click.

Felix turned to Croke with eyebrows raised and empty palms helplessly upturned and lifted his shoulders and sighed.

'Listen,' Croke said, 'you look like a man that would know: that thing at Benediction that the priest holds up, what is that called?'

He demonstrated, lifting clasped hands aloft. Felix studied him carefully and then slowly smiled and wagged a finger in his face.

'Aha,' he said, with a reproving laugh, 'trying to pull the wool from under my feet, eh?'

*

Flora's dream has darkened. She wanders now in a wooded place at evening. The trees encircle her, stirring their branches and murmuring among themselves like masked attendants at a ceremony. Above her the sky is bright, lit with the smoke-blue, tender glow of springtime, but all is dimness and false shadow where she walks, circling the circle of trees, searching in vain for a way out. People are indistinctly present, posed like statues, Sophie and the children, old Croke in his straw hat, and someone else whose face she cannot see, who stands in the centre of the clearing, motionless and hanging somehow, as if suspended from invisible strings, a glimmering figure clad in white, grief-stricken and in pain, who does not stir or speak. Felix approaches her astride a pantomime donkey, stumping along on his own legs with the stuffed animal clamped between his knees. He puts his face close to hers and laughs and crosses his eyes and flaps his pink, pointed tongue suggestively. She notices that the donkey, though it is made of some sort of thick, furred stuff, is alive; it looks up at her pleadingly and she recognises Licht, sewn up tight inside the heavy fur. She flees, but there is no way out, and she hears Felix at her heels, his laughter and the jingling of buckles and poor Licht's harsh gasps of complaint. At last she runs behind the motionless, white-clad figure and finds that it has turned into a hollow tube of heavy cloth, and there is a little ladder inside it that she climbs, pulling the heavy, stiff tunic shut behind her. There is a musty smell that reminds her of childhood. In the dark she climbs the little steps and reaches the hollow mask that is the figure's face and fits her own face to it and looks out through the eyeholes into the broad, calm distances of the waning day and understands that she is safe at last.

*

I walked up the fields to the oak ridge. I noticed that my hands were shaking; nothing like a visitation to set the adrenalin coursing through the blood. The rain had stopped but the grass was thick with wet. Another dark cloud stood hugely above the trees like an ogre with arms outstretched. The little wood was green as green, and there were bluebells and wild garlic and even a nosegay of primroses here and there, nodding on a mossy bank or lurking coyly in the rotted bole of a storm-felled oak. The trees were lacily in leaf, at just that stage when Corot loved to capture them. All very pretty, and plausible too, yet I could not help thinking how all of it seemed laid on for someone else, someone milder than I, less tainted, without that whiff of brimstone that I suspect precedes me wherever I go. In the clearing my fire of yesterday was smouldering still; I soon got it back to life. Presently the rain started up again, tentatively at first, pattering on the dead leaves above me and then coming down in whitish swathes, billowing brightly through the trees and hissing in the fire. I stood with my head bowed and my arms hanging at my sides and the rain ran over my scalp and into my eyebrows and trickled down my face like tears and fell in heavy drops from my chin.

Sometimes I like to abandon myself to the elements like this. I have never been one to worship nature, yet I recognise a certain therapeutic value in the contemplation of natural phenomena; I believe it has to do with the world's indifference, I mean the way the world does not care about us, about our happiness, or how we suffer, the way it just bides there with uplifted glance, murmuring to itself in a language we shall never understand. Even such a one as I might learn humility from that unfailing example of endurance and small expectations. Nothing surprises nature; terrible deeds, the most appalling crimes, leave the world unmoved, as I can attest. Some find this uncanny, I know, and lash out all round them, raging for a response, though nothing avails, not even the torch. I, on the other hand, take comfort from this universal dispassion—

But stop, stop; I have begun to generalise again. That is what the philosophic mode will do to you. Nature did not exist until we invented it one eighteenth-century morning radiant with Alpine light.

Anyway, I am standing in the rain with my head bowed, in my penitential pose. All at once, though I had noticed no flash, a terrible crack of thunder sounded directly above my head, making the trees rattle. It gave me a dreadful fright. What a thing that would be, to be struck down by a bolt out of the blue, or the grey, at least. So much for the world's indifference then; that would be what you might call a pathetic fallacy, all right. Or perhaps lightning would galvanise me into life, poor inert monster that I am? Then, by God, the world would want to watch out, oh yes.

The rain crashed down and almost at once began to ease. A storm in May; how well that sounds, to say it. I thought how my life is like a little boat and I must hold the tiller steady against the buffeting of wind and waves, and how sometimes, such as this morning, I lose my hold somehow and the sail luffs helplessly and the little vessel wallows, turning this way and that in the swell. Such formulations please me, as if to picture the world in this way were somehow to subdue it. (Subdue? Did I say subdue? Perhaps I am not so insouciant in the face of nature's heedlessness after all.) Yes, a little skiff, and I in it, out over depthless waters.

When the shower had passed and the sun came out again I took off my shirt and strung it between two sticks by the fire to dry. The breeze fingered my bared back, giving me gooseflesh. I looked at myself; I noticed that I was beginning to develop breasts; I laughed, and hunkered down by the fire for warmth. The flames faltered among the wet wood and the smoke stung my eyes. When Hatch and Pound came upon me even Hatch hung back at first, uncertain of this big, half-naked, red-eyed, dripping creature, the wildman of the woods, squatting with his arms wrapped round his knees and watching them from under half-closed lids. Circumspectly then they advanced and stood beside me and we stared all three into the fire. Around us the wind swept wetly through the trees and the leaves dripped and the damp sunlight flickered. Each fresh gust brought with it faintly the sound of the sea: the far, faint thud of waves and the hiss of water running on the shingle. I closed my eyes and the past was like a melody I had lost that was starting to come back, I could hear it in my mind, a tiny, thin, heartbreaking music.

'What's this place called?' Hatch asked.

'The Land of Nod,' I said, and they laughed without conviction and then lapsed again into silence.

I studied them with covert attention. Hatch was sly and unhappy and Pound was sharper than he looked. Pound's mother was supposed to have accompanied them on the boat trip but something had come up. He frowned into the fire, gnawing his lip. I wondered what his mammy would say if she knew her plump little boy was consorting unchaperoned with the ogre himself in the wild wood now. Sometimes I wonder if it was wise of the authorities to free me like this. But perhaps they knew me better than I know myself? I am harmless, I'm sure. Fairly harmless. No longer dangerous, anyway. Or not very.

Hatch said nothing; Hatch had no mother.

A strong gust shook the trees and the wet leaves clattered.

'This is worse than at home,' Pound said with sudden vehemence and kicked the embers at the fire's margin. 'Nothing to bloody do.'

I remembered suddenly how when I was young like them I sat in a hazel wood one winter Sunday by a damply smoking fire like this one as night came on and a boy whose name I cannot recall (Reck, I think it was, or Rice) arrived and told us a woman had been beaten to death in her sweetshop down a lane. I pictured the scene, distorted, wavering, the colours seeping into each other, as if I were looking at it all through bottle-glass, and felt fearful and inexplicably guilty. I have never forgotten that moment, that sudden, blood-boltered vision, intense as if I had been there myself. First such stain on my life.

The boys watched me uncertainly, waiting for me to speak. I said nothing. They must have thought I was cracked. I am, a little. I must be, surely. It would be a comfort to think so.

A squashy, wet, warm smell rose from the greenery around us as the sun dried out the rain, and suddenly summer stood up out of the undergrowth like a gold man, dripping and asinine. Between the trees the lapis glint of sea. The air was gaudy with birdsong.

I left them and made my way down the hillside, carrying a stick; my shirt, still damp, clung to my back. The wind had grown gay and the sun was hot. The house stood below me, closed on itself. I sat down on a rock under a flowering thorn bush. There are times when my mind goes dead, as if something had switched itself off in my head. Some mornings when I wake I do not remember who I am or what it is I have done. I will lie there for a minute or more, unwilling to stir, basking in the anaesthetic of forgetfulness. It is like being new-born. At such moments I glimpse a different self, as yet unblackened, ripe with potential, a sort of radiant big infant swaddled in shining light. Then it all comes seeping back, spreading like a slow, thick liquid through my mind. Yet sometimes even when I am fully awake, in the middle of the day, I will imagine for a second, as if I were walking in a dark place and suddenly stepped through a patch of sunlight, that none of it had happened, that I am what I might have been, an innocent man, though I know well I have never been innocent, nor, for that matter, have I ever been what could properly be called a man. Still the dream persists, suppressed but always there, that somehow by some miraculous effort of the heart what was done could be undone. What form would such atonement take that would turn back time and bring the dead to life? None. None possible, not in the real world. And yet in my imaginings I can clearly see this cleansed new creature streaming up out of myself like a proselyte rising drenched from the baptismal river amid glad cries.

While I sat there on my hard rock under the may-tree the house below me as I watched over it began to come alive. Licht appeared in the yard with slops for the chickens, and above him, on the first floor, the french windows opened with theatrical suddenness and Sophie stepped out into the sunlight on the balcony with her camera. Dimly at a high-up window I could see Felix loitering, his long swarth face and glittering eye. Alice was climbing the stairs, I saw her on successive landings, a small, solemn figure resolutely ascending, first to the right, then to the left, and then the frosted glass of the lavatory window whitened briefly as she entered there and shut the door behind her. The Professor was pacing the turret room, a moving darkness against the light of the windows all around him, and now, as he turned, the weathervane on the roof turned with him in the breeze, and I smiled at this small coincidence that only I had seen.

It was Flora I was vainly watching for, of course, the rest of them might have been so many maggots in a cheese for all I cared. Oh yes, I had spotted her straight away, with my gimlet eye, the moment I had walked into the kitchen and seen them sitting there barefoot with their mugs of tea. She sprang out from their midst like the Virgin in a busy Annunciation, calm as Mary and nimbed with that unmistakable aura of the chosen. What did I hope for, what did I expect? Not what you think. I have never had much interest in the flesh. I used to be as red-blooded, or red-eyed, at least, as the next man, but for me that side of things was always secondary to something else for which I cannot find an exact name. Curiosity? No, that is too weak. A sort of lust for knowledge, the passionate desire to delve my way into womanhood and taste the very temper of its being. Dangerous talk, I know. Well, go ahead, misunderstand me, I don't care. Perhaps I have always wanted to be a woman, perhaps that's it. If so, I have reached the halfway stage, unsexed poor androgyne that I am become by now. But the girl had nothing to do with any of this. (By the way, why so coy about using her name? Want to rob her of her individuality, eh? – want to turn her into *das Ewig-Weibliche* that will lead you on to salvation, is that it, you sly old Faustus? . . . What have I said?) Sophie would have been more my vintage, with her camera and her fags and her tragic memories, but it was the girl I singled out. It was innocence I was after, I suppose, the innocent, pure clay awaiting a grizzled Pygmalion to inspire it with life. It is as simple as that. Not love or passion, not even the notion of the radiant self rising up like flame in the mirror of the other, but the hunger only to have her live and to live in her, to conjugate in her the verb of being.

Leave me there on my rock, leaning on my staff under may blossom in the rinsed air of May, a figure out of Arcady. Give me this moment.

*

The Professor paced the narrow round of his glass tower and considered the ruins of his life. When he sat down in his sea-captain's chair the things on the desk before him would not be still, pencils, papers, a teacup in its saucer, all trembled faintly; it puzzled him, until he realised that it was he, his tremulous presence, that was making everything quake like this. He was breathless and a little dazed, as if at the start of a large and perilous exploit. He felt excited, foolish, aghast at himself, as always, at the preposterousness of all that he was and did. Felix. It was Felix, bringing it all back. He seemed to hear the squeal of pipes and the rattle of timbrels, a raucous clamour rising through the bright air; was it the god departing, or returning a last time, to deliver him a last blow to the heart?

'Am I disturbing you?'

Sophie made a show of hesitating on the threshold, leaning against the door-frame, regarding him with a small, false, enquiring smile. He said nothing, merely looked at her, and she advanced, still smiling. She smelled of smoke and perfume and something sweetly dirty. The expanse of skin above her collarbone was mottled and there were hairline cracks in the make-up around her eyes. Stop at the window, consider the view. The sun shines on a glitter of green and summer strides up the hillside. He watched her where she stood with her back to him and her arms folded, as if she were holding another, slighter self clasped tightly to her. He noticed her poor bare feet with their stringy tendons and the scribble of purplish veins at the backs of her ankles. Once the world had seemed to him a rich, a coloured place, now all he saw was the poverty of things.

'Felix says you are famous,' she said without turning.

'What?'

He was not sure if he had spoken or only imagined that he had. He had got out of the habit of speech.

'He seems to know you,' she said.

He nodded absently, frowning, glancing here and there about the desk as if he were trying to calculate its dimensions.

'That girl,' he said, 'what is her name—?'

'Flora.'

'Yes. She reminds me of someone.'

'Oh,' she said blankly. 'Who?'

'From long ago.'

A ravelled silence.

'I know what you mean,' she said.

He lifted his head, frowning. 'What?'

'Faces,' she said. 'There are not many; five or six, I think, no more than that.'

He nodded; he had not been listening.

'Dead,' he said. He cleared his throat and gave himself a sort of heave as if he were shifting a weight from one shoulder to the other. Dead, yes; her cold hand in his, like a little bundle of brittle twigs wrapped in tissue paper; how much smaller than herself she had seemed, like a carved figurine, a memento of herself she had left behind. 'My mother,' he said. Sophie turned her face to the view again and stood still. 'A long time ago.' He nodded slowly, thinking. 'Remarkable, that girl . . .'

Another silence, longer this time. With the covert flourish of a conjuror she produced her camera from somewhere under her arm. He fidgeted, and she laughed.

'Don't worry,' she said, 'I have not come to photograph people, only ruins.' She focused on his desk, the back of his chair, the window-sills. He listened with faint pleasure to the repeated grainy slither of the shutter working. 'I am making a book,' she said. '*Tableaux morts*: that is the title. What do you think?'

He had stopped listening again.

'Have you known him for a long time?' he said.

She glanced at him, then shook her head.

'He was at the hotel last night,' she said, 'and afterwards on the boat. Why?'

He shrugged.

'I thought you knew him,' he said. 'I thought . . .'

'No,' she said. 'I do not know him.'

Thus they converse, haltingly, between long pauses. Behind the language that they speak other languages speak in silence, ones that they know and yet avoid, the languages of childhood and of loss. This reticence seems imperative. Both are thinking how strange it is to be here and at the same time to be conscious of it, seeing themselves somehow reflected in each other. That must be how it is with humans, apart and yet together, in their world, their human world.

*

Far thunder at dead of night, I wake to it, a low rumble along the horizon, the air crumpling. I imagine what it must be like out there, out beyond the land, where the humped sea hugely heaves, black as oilskin, under a bulging, clay-dark sky; I imagine it, and I am there. In these waters there are dolphins, I have seen them; uncanny creatures, with their rubbery grins and little mewling cries. It is said they save men from drowning. Would they save me, I wonder, if I came plummeting down and disappeared under the waves with a hiss? I live amongst ghosts and absences. A nightbird flies past, I hear the rapid whirr of wings, and down in the direction of the stream suddenly something gallops away. A horse? There are no horses here. A donkey, perhaps. I hear it, clear as anything, the unmistakable sound of hoofbeats. Who is the horseman?

Life, life: being outside.

Night and silence and

Oh life!

And I in flames.

I HAD HARDLY been a week on the island before I found myself a widow-woman. At least, I am sure that is how they told it hereabouts, where it seems every other cottage harbours a canny bachelor on the look-out for a secondhand mate, one already well accustomed to the bit, as Mr Tighe the shopman put it to me wheezily the other day, leaning over his counter on one elbow and giving me a large, lewd wink. My widow even had a few acres of land. She lived above us here on the ridge, in a rain-coloured cottage backed up crookedly against the messy dark-nesses of the oak wood. She kept chickens, and a goat tethered to a post in the front yard. Odd objects lay here and there about the place, as if they had become bogged down on their way elsewhere. There was a bright-red plastic baby-bath, a car tyre, a rusty mangle, and something that looked like a primitive version of a washing machine. The first time I went up there it was a brumous evening, more like November than May, with a solid blare of wind out of the west and the sea lying flat in the distance like a sheet of rippled steel. The front door stood open but there was no one to be seen. I approached cautiously, unnerved by the look of that dark doorway; I am always wary of strange houses. The goat, chewing on something with a rapid, sideways motion, eyed me with what seemed a sardonic smirk, while the chickens gave their goitrous croaks of complaint. I knocked and waited, and had to knock again, and at last there was a scuffling sound and she appeared, rising up suddenly in the dim doorway with her medusa-head of tangled hair and her unnerving, bleached-blue eyes. She said nothing, but stood with her hand on the latch and looked at me with a sceptical air, as if she did not really believe I could be real. She was a tall, spare figure with arthritic hands and a fine, long, ravaged face, handsome and yet curiously indistinct: when I think of her I always see her in profile, upright, archaic, noble, as if on the side of a worn silver coin. Everything about her was faded, her skin, her old skirt, her bird's nest of ash-coloured hair, and I had the notion that if I reached out to touch her my hand would encounter only shadowed air. For a moment I could think of nothing to say, then asked lamely if she would let me have a few eggs, since that was mainly what we were living on here at Château d'If and the hens that week had taken it into their heads to stop laying. She waited a moment, pondering, and then turned without a word and went away to the back of the house. I peered greedily through the open doorway: that's me always, hungering after other worlds, the drabber and more desolate the better, God knows why: so that I can fill them up, I suppose, with my imaginings. There was a table with a plain cloth, a rocking chair, a black stove; the walls and the concrete floor were bare. At the back dimly I could see a lean-to kitchen, with a roof of transparent corrugated plastic from which there sifted down an incongruously lovely, peach-coloured light such as might bathe a domestic interior by one of the North Italian masters. When she returned with the eggs in a paper bag I offered to pay for them but she shrugged and said she had more of them than she could use. Her voice was so distant and light I could hardly hear it, a sort of dry, papery rustling. I was halfway down the hill again before her accent registered.

*

She was not a native of these parts. Her name was Mrs Vanden. The islanders called her the Dutchwoman, but she might have been South African; I never did find out what her true nationality was. She had lived in many places abroad – her husband had been a colonial official of some sort. She rarely talked about the past, and when she did her voice took on a weary and faintly irritated edge, as if she were a historian describing an important but not very interesting period of antiquity. The late Mr Vanden hardly figured in this all-but-vanished age, and perhaps it was because

I know so little about him that he has assumed in my imagination the outlines of a legendary figure, a Stanley or a Mungo Park, with pith helmet and swagger stick and enormous moustaches. How his widow ended up here I do not know. When I ventured to ask her, she said she had come to the island to get away from the noise; I presume she meant noise in general, the hubbub of the world. She was a great one for silence; it seemed a form of sustenance for her, she fed on it, like a patient on a drip. Sometimes when I visited her, as I did with increasing and, it strikes me now, surprising frequency over the weeks that I knew her, she hardly spoke a word. Perhaps Mr Vanden had been a talker? They did not seem rude, these silences. Rather, I took them as a mark of, not friendliness, perhaps – I would not describe our relations as friendly, no matter how close they might have been – but of toleration. She suffered me as she did those things in the yard, the odds and ends that just happened to have come to rest there. I suspect she never did manage to believe that I was entirely real. At times, if I were to say something after a long pause, or otherwise make my presence unexpectedly felt, a look of startlement tinged with dismay would cross her face, as if some comfortably inanimate presence had suddenly sprung to troublesome life before her eyes.

I met her a second time one evening in the oak wood. I had the fire going there; in fact, it was her fire I had taken over, as she had taken it over from some previous tender of the flame; I see a line of us, with our flints and pitchforks, stretching back to the time of the druids. She came wandering through the trees with her head down, in that distracted way she had, weaving a little, as if she were searching for something on the ground. I confess I was not greatly pleased to see her; a good bonfire, like so many things for me in those days, from sex to tea, was best enjoyed in solitude. She did not look at me, and even when she had drifted to a stop by the fire I was not sure if she was fully aware of me. She wore wellingtons and a crooked skirt and a battered hat that surely had seen duty on the veldt. The evening was grey and greyly warm. We stood gazing into the flames. Then she cast a thoughtful, sideways glance at my feet and invited me to come to her house and take tea. I was too surprised to refuse.

Her kitchen smelled of cooking fat and bottled gas and old water. I sat warily at the bare deal table and watched her. She reminded me of a piece of polished bone, or a stick of driftwood, thinned and hardened by the action of the years. I looked for her marks on the room, the impress of her solitary life here, but could find none. Plain chairs, plain pots, plain delft on the dresser. On a nail above my head hung one of Mr Tighe's advertising calendars with a photo on it of an outmoded bathing beauty. My attention was caught briefly by an electric Sacred Heart lamp on a wooden socket fixed to the wall, pink as an iced lolly and tremulously aglow, but when she saw me looking at it she smiled drily and shook her head: it had been here, she said, when she came to the house, and she had not known how to disconnect it.

We ate in ruminant silence. The slow day died and the sun went down in the kitchen window in a gradual catastrophe of reds and golds. As the dusk advanced we talked desultorily of this and that. It was not exactly a conversation, more a sort of laborious, intermittent batting; we were like a pair of decrepit tennis players having a game at close of day, lobbing slow balls high up to and fro through the darkening air. The name Dickie kept coming up, and Mrs Vanden grew almost animated: Dickie was this, and Dickie had done that, and oh, Dickie did have such a fine seat on a horse. I took it she was speaking of her late husband, but when my mistake became apparent an awkward silence fell and she looked at me directly, for the first time, it seemed, with those blank, impenetrable eyes, and it was as if I had come to a stumbling stop on the very lip of a precipice with nothing before me but the vast and depthless sky. No, she said, Dickie was her daughter, her only child, dead this twenty years. I was flustered, and could think of nothing to say, and looked down in confusion at my plate. I ask myself now, did I miss a real opportunity on that occasion? For what? Well, I might for instance have found out all sorts of things about her and her travels with the intrepid Mr Vanden. Perhaps I might even have let my own dead walk abroad for a bit, they who are as palpably present to me as Dickie the phantom horsewoman was to her. But the moment passed and already it was night, and I stood up fumblingly from the table and thanked her and hurried off down the hill through the immense, soft darkness;

How courtly we were, how correctly we conducted ourselves. I think that even if she had been fifty years younger there would have been no more between us than there was. And yet I believe that what there was was much. Does that make sense? There are certain people who seem to know me better than I know myself. To some, I realise, this would be an uncomfortable intrusion on their privacy and their sense of themselves, and it is true, there were occasions when in her presence I was acutely conscious of the pressure upon me of the sagging and unmanageable weight of all she must have known about me and did not say; mostly, though, I felt, well, lightened, somehow, as if I had been given permission to set down for a moment my burden – the burden of my self, that is – and stand breathing, unrequired briefly, in some calm, wide place. There was nothing filial in all of this, and certainly, I am sure of it, nothing maternal – no mother of mine was ever remotely like Mrs Vanden, apart from the Dutch blood – yet there was in it something that must have been very like that tentative, unspoken complicity, that feeling of basking in the knowledge of a secret agreement, that I am told exists between sons and mothers. This is perilous territory, I know; any minute now Bigfoot will come clumping on to the scene, with his sockets streaming. But I don't care, you can do all the cheap psychologising you want, I will still say that I felt when I was with her that I was protected, shielded somehow from at least some of the things that the world had it in mind to do to me; the smaller things, the quotidian inflictions. It is what I had always wanted, someone strong and mute and unknowable behind whose skirts I could hide. Wait, that's a surprise; do I mean that? Sometimes my pen just goes prattling along all by itself and the strangest things come out, things I did not know I was aware of, or of which I would prefer not to be made aware, or not to hear expressed, anyway.

Mute, now, *unknowable*: is that what I really want, a sort of statue, one of those big Mooreish pieces, all scooped-out hollows and cuppable curves, faceless and tightly swathed, like a bronze mummy (oops! – what a treacherously ambiguous medium our language is)? I was content, at any rate, to be adrift in Mrs Vanden's company, if that is what it can be called, incurious as to the nature of her inner life, her thoughts, her opinions, if shep had any. I should berate myself for my selfishness, I suppose, my incurable solipsism, yet I cannot do it, with any conviction. I have the notion – I hesitate to speak of it, really, knowing how it will sound – that what we achieved, that what we began to achieve, Mrs V. and I, was a new or at least rare form of relation, one that, I realise, I had been aiming for for longer than I can remember. I do not know what to call it, how to describe it; words such as *reticent, respectful, calm*, these do not begin to suffice. There are men, I know, who prowl the world in search of an ideal woman, one who will indulge their darkest desires and slake for them the hot, half-formed urgings of the blood; I am like that, except that what I lust after is not some sly-eyed wanton but a being made up of stillnesses; not inert, not lifeless, only quiet, like me – yes, quiet, I am quiet, in spite of all this gabble – a pale pool in a shaded glade in which I might bathe my poor throbbing brow and cool its shamefaced fires (I know, I know: the pool, and the lover leaning over it, I too caught that echo). Forgiveness, I suppose; it all seems to come down to that, in the end, though I hate these big words. Forgiveness not for the things I have done, but for the thing that I am. That is the toughest one to absolve: what they used to call, if I remember rightly, a reserved sin.

Anyway, one day a couple of weeks after our first meeting I went up to the cottage and she did not answer my knock, though the door stood open as always, and when, with my heart in my mouth, I had climbed the stairs to what I knew was her bedroom, I found her lying neatly on her back in the narrow bed with the blanket pulled to her chin and her eyes open and all filmed over and a cocky fly strolling across her cold forehead. At first, in my

surprise and numbed dismay, I had the crazy thought that it was
not she at all, but an effigy of herself she had left behind her to
fool me while she made good her escape. (I was not too far off
the mark, I suppose.) The fly on her forehead stopped and wrung
its hands as if in energetic dismay and then flew off in a bored
sort of way, and I leaned over her and closed her eyes – now *there*
is a creepy sensation – and quietly withdrew. I discovered that I
was holding my breath. At the front door I debated with myself
whether or not to shut it, but decided in the end to leave it open,
since that was her way; besides, it is the practice in these parts,
when someone dies, for the house to be left open to all-comers.
Do I imagine it, or did the goat give me a soulful, commiserating
look as I walked off down the path?

*

What I felt most strongly was resentment. It was as if she had
played a tasteless practical joke on me, had tricked me, first luring
me on and then abruptly vanishing. I had needed her, and she
had let me down. But what had I needed her *for*? I brooded on
the question without really wanting to find the answer, touching
it gingerly, with the barest tips of thought, as if it were one of
those lethal lumps the precise depth and dimensions of which I
would not care to discover. Forgiveness, as I've said, absolution,
I was aware of all that; but that was what I had wanted, not
what I had wanted her to represent, as a being separate from me.
(Oh God, this is all so murky and confused!) Look, here, let me
come clean: I could not rid myself of the belief that she had
seemed some sort of hope, not just for me, but for – well, I don't
know. Hope. I am well aware how foolhardy it is to say such
things, but there you are: it's true, it's what I felt. The trouble
with death, I realised, is that it is really not an ending at all; it
leaves so much unfinished, and so much unassuaged. You keep
thinking that the one who died has just gone away, has walked
off in the middle of things and will come back presently and take
up where you both left off. I cursed myself for not having
searched her house that last day, when I had the opportunity; no

one would have known, I could have delved into every corner, investigated every last cranny in the place. However, I know in my heart that I would have found nothing, no cache of family papers, no eyebrow-raising diaries, no bundle of dusty letters done up in a blue ribbon. She had jettisoned everything but the barest essentials. Compared to hers my life was still awash with the flotsam of former, sunken lives. I entertained the hope that someone would turn up and surprise us at the funeral, a leathery old colonial, say, who would talk about kaffirs and gin slings and that time that new chap went mad and shot himself on the steps of the club, but in vain; Sergeant Toner and I were the only mourners. As the priest droned the prayers and shook holy water on her coffin I realised with a start that I had not even known her Christian name.

*

Another dead one; dear Jesus, I do keep on adding to them, don't I? Well, that's life, I suppose. I think of them like the figures in one of Vaublin's twilit landscapes, placed here and there in isolation about the scene, each figure somehow the source of its own illumination, aglow in the midst of shadows, still and speechless, not dead and yet not alive either, waiting perhaps to be brought to some kind of life. That's it, let us have a disquisition, to pass the time and keep ourselves from brooding. Think of a topic. Ghosts, now, why not. I have never been able to understand why ghosts should be considered something to be afraid of; they might be troublesome, a burden to us, perhaps, pawing at us as we try to get on with our poor lives, but not frightening, surely. Yet, though the fresh-made widow weeps and tears her breast, if she were to come home from the cemetery in her weeds and veil and find her husband's spirit sitting large as life in his favourite armchair by the fire she would run into the street gibbering in terror. It makes no sense. I can think of times and circumstances when even the ghosts of complete strangers, no matter how horrid, would be welcomed. The prisoner held in solitary confinement, for instance, would be grateful surely to wake up some fevered night and find a troupe of his predecessors come walking through the wall in their rags and beards and clanking their chains, while Saint Teresa would have been tickled, I suspect, to receive a visit to her interior castle from some long-dead hidalgo of Old Castile. And what of our friend Crusoe in his hut, would he not have been happy to be haunted by the spirits of his drowned shipmates? The ship's doctor could have advised him on his ague, the carpenter on his fencing, while the cabin boy, no matter how fey, surely would have afforded a welcome change of fare from Friday's dusky charms.

There are ghosts and ghosts, of course. Banquo was a dampener on the king's carousings, and Hamlet's father made what I cannot but think were excessive calls on filial piety. Yet, for myself, I know I would be grateful for any intercourse with the dead, no matter how baleful their stares or unavoidable their pale, pointing fingers. I feel I might be able, not to exonerate, but to explain myself, perhaps, to account for my neglectfulness, my failures, the things left unsaid, all those sins against the dead, both of omission and commission, of which I had been guilty while they were still in the land of the living. But more than that, more important than the desire for self-justification, is the conviction that I have, however preposterous it may sound, that there is an onus on us, the living, to conjure up our particular dead. I am certain there is no other form of afterlife for them than this, that they should live in us, and through us. It is our duty. (I like the high moral tone. How dare I, really!)

Let us take the hypothetical case of a man surprised by love, not for a living woman – he has never been able to care much for the living – but for the figure of a woman in, oh, a painting, let's say. That is, he is swept off his feet one day by a work of art. It happens; not very often, I grant you, but it does happen. The fact that the subject is a female perhaps is not of such significance, although it should be perfectly possible to 'fall in love', as they like to put it, with a painted image; after all, what is it lovers ever love but the images they have of each other? Freud himself remarked that in the passionate encounter of every couple there are four people involved. Or should it be six? – the two so-called real lovers, plus the images they have of themselves, plus the images that they have of each other. What a tangled web Eros weaves! Anyhow. This man, this hypothetical man, finds himself one day in the house of a rich acquaintance, where he is confronted by a portrait of a woman and knows straight away that at once and by whatever means he must possess it. That is what they mean by love, surely? It is not, mark you, that the woman is beautiful; in fact, the model was evidently a plain, pinched person with fishy eyes and a big nose and too much flesh about the lips. But ah, in her portrait she has presence, she is unignorably *there*, more real than the majority of her sisters out here in what we call real life. And our Monsieur Hypothesis is not used to seeing people whole, the rest of humanity being for him for the most part a kind of annoying fog obscuring his view of the darkened shop-window of the world and of himself reflected in it. He tells himself he will steal the picture and hold it for ransom, but really that is just for the purposes of the plot. His true and secret desire – secret even from himself, perhaps – is to have this marvellous object, to have and to hold it, to bathe in the brightness of its perfected, still and immutable presence. He is, or at least has been, let us say, a man of some learning, trained to reason and compute, who in the face of a manifestly chaotic world has lost his faith in the possibility of order. He drifts. He has no moral base. Then suddenly one midsummer day he comes upon this painting and is smitten. Some other object might have done as well, a statue, for example (I feel we shall have something to say on the subject of statues before long; yes, definitely I feel that topic coming on), or a beautiful proposition in mathematics, or even, who knows, a real, walking-and-talking, peeing-and-pouting, big live pink mama-doll. Obviously the need was there all along, awaiting its fulfilment in whatever form chance might provide. It is *being* that he has encountered here, the thing itself, the pure unmediated essence, in which, he thinks, he will at last find himself and his true home, his place in the world. Impossible, impossible dreams, but for a moment he allows himself to believe in them. He takes the painting.

Here the plot does not so much thicken as coagulate.

He is an inept thief, our lovelorn hypothetical hero. He comes along bold as brass in broad daylight and lifts the lady off the wall, then turns and is confronted at once by a living, flesh-and-blood person (oh yes, lots of flesh, lots of blood), a maidservant, perhaps (pretend this is olden times, when domestics were readily available, not to say expendable), who by bad luck happens at that moment to walk into the room. Well, to shorten a long and grisly tale, without ado he bashes in the maid's head, not because she is a threat to him, really, but because, well, because she is there, or because she is there and he does not see her properly, or – or whatever, what does it matter, for Christ's sake! He kills her, isn't that enough? And he makes his get-away. Such things were commonplace in olden times. Suddenly, however, to his intense surprise and deep chagrin, he discovers that the picture has lost its charm for him. Ashes. Daubs. Mere paint on a piece of rag. He tosses it aside as if it were a page of yesterday's newspaper. What interests him now, of course, is the living woman that he so carelessly did away with. He recalls with fascination and a kind of swooning wonderment the moments before he struck the first blow, when he looked into his victim's eyes and knew that he had never known another creature – not mother, wife, child, not anyone – so intimately, so invasively, to such indecent depths, as he did just then this woman whom he was about to bludgeon to death. Well, he was shocked. Guilt, remorse, fear of capture and disgrace, he had expected these things, welcomed them, indeed, as a token that he had not entirely relinquished his claim to be considered human, but this, this sudden access to another's being, this astonished and appalled him. How, with such knowledge, could he have gone ahead and killed? How, having seen straight down through those sky-blue, transparent eyes into the depths of what for want of a better word I shall call her soul, how could he destroy her?

And how, having done away with her, was he to bring her back? For that, he understood, was his task now. Prison, punishment, paying his debt to society, all that was nothing, was merely how he would pass the time while he got on with the real business of atonement, which was nothing less than the restitution of a life. *Restitution*, that was the word, he remembered it from when he was a child at school and they told him what the thief must do, which is *to make proper restitution*.

Of course, he did not know how to do it, where to begin. He stood aghast before the prospect, baffled and helpless. That moment of ineffable knowing when he had turned on her with the weapon raised was no help to him here, that was a different order of knowledge, the stuff of life, so to speak, while what he needed now was the art of necromancy. The question was how to put into place another's life, but how could he answer, he who hardly knew how to live his own? A life! with all its ragged complexities, its false starts and sudden closures, the summer solitudes and winter woes, the inexplicable exaltations in April weather, the meals to be eaten, the sleeps to be slept, the blood in its courses, the coat that will go one more season, the new shoes, the old shoes, the afternoons, the nights, the bird-thronged dawns, the old dying and the new ones being born, the prime and then in a twinkling the autumnal shadows, then age, and then the proper death. That was what he had taken from her, and now must restore. He would need help. Oh, he would need help. And so he waits for the rustle in the air, for the moment of sudden cold, for the soundless falling into step beside him that will announce the presence of the ghost that somehow he must conjure.

As I say, merely a hypothesis.

*

Last night I had a dream about my father. This is an unusual occurrence. I rarely think of him, never mind entertain him in my dreams. My mother was a dreadful old brute but we were fond of each other, I believe, in our violent, unforgiving way. For my father, however, I seem never to have felt anything stronger than distaste. I mean, I probably loved him, as sons do love fathers, biologically, as it were, but I had as little to do with him as I could. He was a fearsome little fellow, a constant complainer and prone to sudden, ungovernable rages. I always think of him, God forgive me, as Mr Hyde, in his too-big tweeds, stumping along and snorting and stabbing at things with his stick. He died badly, rotting away before our eyes, shrinking to nothing as if he were consuming himself in his own anger. In my dream we were walking together through a huge and echoing administrative building, a place out of my childhood, a town hall or public library or something, I don't know. Anyway, the light in the dream was the light of childhood, steady and clear and dense with its own insubstantial vastness. Though I could see no one, I could hear distinctly the sounds of the place: the brittle clacking of a typewriter, the laughter of a fellow and a girl larking somewhere, and someone with squeaky shoes walking away very businesslike down a long corridor. Father and I were climbing an interminable, shallow staircase with many turns: I could feel the clammy sheen of the banister rail under my hand and sense the high, domed ceiling far above me. The old man was stamping along at a great rate, a pace in front of me, as usual, head down and elbows going like pistons. Suddenly he faltered, and I, not noticing, came up behind him and collided with him, or perhaps it was that he fell against me, I do not know which it was. Anyway, for an amazing moment I thought he was assaulting me. What I noticed most strongly was his smell, of hair oil and serge and cigarette smoke, and something else, something intimate and sour and wholly, shockingly other. He clung to me for a second to steady himself, fixing iron fingers on my wrist in a grip at once infirm and fierce, and I seemed to feel a sort of oscillation start up suddenly, as if some enormous, general and hitherto unnoticed equilibrium had collapsed. A clerk put his sleek head out of an office doorway below us and quickly withdrew it again. My father thrust me aside with what seemed revulsion. *I tripped!* he snarled, as if expecting to be contradicted, and glared at the banister, white with fury. He searched his pockets and produced a hand-kerchief and wiped his hands. We stood panting, as if we had indeed been engaged in a scuffle. A telephone rang nearby, a raucous jangling, like metallic laughter, and someone picked it up and began to speak at once in a low voice, urgently, as if trying to placate the machine itself. And I realised that what we had come there for was my father's death certificate; this seemed perfectly natural, of course, as such things do in dreams. We went on up the long stairs, and he was very brisk now, cheery, almost, in a pitiful sort of way, trying to pretend nothing of any note was happening, and I was embarrassed for him because I understood that he had already started to die and that death was something that would be shameful for him as a man, like being cuckolded, or going bankrupt. I was hoping that no one would see us there together, for if we got away without being seen we could pretend I did not know that he was doomed and that way he would save face. Then came a confused and hectic digression which I shall not bother with: how strange, the people that pop up in dreams, like the figures that loom at the shrieking travellers in a ghost train, springing out of the surrounding murk for a gesticulating, mad moment before being jerked away again on their strings. Anyway, after that wild interval my father and I found ourselves presently in an enormous room full of people rushing about in all directions, shouting, waving bits of paper at each other, demanding, beseeching, cursing. Father plunged at once, terrier-like, into the thick of this mêlée, shoving and shouting with the best of them, with me after him, desperately trying to keep up. He was outraged that the officials among the throng were not marked off somehow from the rest, and he kept stopping random passers-by, grasping them by the upper arms and rising on tiptoe and roaring in their faces. You don't understand, he would yell at them, I'm here for my chit, dammit, I'm here for my chit! But no one listened, or even looked at him, so busy were they craning to look past him, trying to glimpse whatever it was they were searching for with such fierce determination. Somehow I lost him, and now I in my turn found myself running here and there in desperation, shouting out his name and plucking at people and demanding if they had seen him. And then all at once, like smoke clearing, the crowd dispersed and I was left alone in the enormous room. After a long, panicky search I found a litttle door built flush to the wall and so well camouflaged that it could hardly be distinguished from the panelling, though by some means I knew it had been there for me to find. When I went through I was in another, much smaller room, with a barred window looking out on a sunlit, classical landscape of meadows and hills and bosky glades, dotted about with statuary and marble follies and dainty, sparkling waterfalls. My father was sitting crookedly on a chair in the middle of the bare floor with an air of bewilderment, stooped and crumpled, peering up fearfully as if expecting a blow; it was obvious that he had been thrust hurriedly on to the chair as I was about to enter. Behind him a group of silent men in starched high collars and black morning-coats and striped trousers stood about in attitudes of stern pensiveness, frowning at their finger-nails, or gazing fixedly out of the window. Father had been weeping, his face was blotched and his nose was runny. All his fierceness was gone. It's *you*, he said to me, in a mixture of accusation and pleading, *you* have to serve your term before they'll do anything! At that the group of gentlemen behind him sprang at once into action and came forward hurriedly and picked him up, still seated, and bustled him chair and all out of the room, negotiating the narrow door with difficulty, muttering directions to each other and tut-tutting irritably. When I opened my eyes and sat up in the dawn light I was lost for a moment in that half-world between sleep and waking, and was convinced I had not been dreaming at all, but remembering; all day there has lingered the uneasy sense of an opportunity missed, of some large signifi-cance left unacknowledged. Certain dreams do that, they seem to darken the very air, crowding it with the shadows of another world.

Dreams bring remembrance, too; perhaps that is what they are for, to force us to dredge up those dirty little deeds and dodges we thought we had succeeded in forgetting. These half-involuntary memories are a terrible thing. There are days like this when they course through me from morning until night like pure pain. They leave me gasping, even the seemingly happy ones, as if they were the living record of heinous yet immensely subtle sins I had thought were covered up forever. And always, of course, there is the unexpected: although last night's dream was about my father, all day today I have been thinking mainly of my mother. After Father died I was surprised by the depth of her grief. It made of her something ancient and elemental, a tribal figure, sitting dry-eyed draped in black, bereft, unmoving, monumentally silent, like a pelt-clad figure in a forest clearing watching over the smouldering ashes of a funeral pyre. Had I misjudged her, thinking she was made of sterner stuff? I believe that was for me the beginning of maturity, if that is the word, the moment when I realised it was too late to readjust my notions of her; too late for atonement, too (there is that word again). I tiptoed around her, not knowing what to say, fearful of intruding on this primitive rite. The house wore the startled, doggy air of having been undeservedly rebuked. I knew the feeling.

INHABITANTS OF THIS PLACE. What a peculiar collection we must seem, the Professor and Licht, the girl and I, disparates that we are, thrown together here on this rocky isle. The girl has complicated everything, of course. Before her coming things had settled down nicely; even Licht, who at first had been so resentful of me, had reconciled himself to my presence. Yes, without her we might have pottered along indefinitely, I at my art history and Licht at his schemes – he is a great one for schemes – and the Professor doing whatever it is the Professor does. Now we have grown restless, and chafe under the imposed languor of these summer days; time, that before seemed such a calm medium, has grown choppy as a storm-threatened sea. If the others had remained, I mean Sophie and Croke and the children, if they too had stayed behind they might have become a little community, might have formed a little fold, and I could have been the shepherd, guarding them against the prowling wolf. Idle fancies; forgive me, I get carried away sometimes.

Inevitably of course there has grown up a half-acknowledged divide, with the Professor and Licht on one side, the girl and I on the other, and behind that again there is yet another grouping in which the girl stands between Licht and me, a pair of ragged old rats scrabbling in the dirt and showing each other our sharpest teeth. Licht thinks he is in love with her, of course, and resents what he considers the excessive attentions I pay to her. Her silences torment him and strike him mute in his turn; he creeps up and stands behind her tongue-tied and quivering, or sits and stares at her across the dinner table, rabbit-eyed, his pink-rimmed nostrils flared and his hands trembling. He devises sly, round-about ways of talking about her, deprecating as Mr Guppy,

introducing her name with elaborate casualness into the most
unlikely topics and employing laboriously cunning circumlocu-
tions. He is heartsick, mooning about the house with the agonised
look of a man nursing an unassuageable toothache. At least it has
made him smarten himself up a bit. He runs a comb now and
then through that fright-wig of hair, and bathes more frequently
than he used to, if my nose is any judge. I suppose she has
become associated in his mind with the dream he has of leaving
here and finding some more fulfilling life elsewhere; I see them,
as in one of those old silent films, in a bare room with a square
table, he sitting head in hands and she smiling her Lulu smile at
the mustachioed and leering landlord who beckons to her suggestively from the doorway.

She is a singular creature, or seems so to me, at any rate. She
claims to be twenty-one but I think she is no more than eighteen
or nineteen. She will not tell me about her life, or at least does
not: I mean maybe if I knew how to ask, if I knew the codes that
everyone else has been privy to since the cradle, she would prattle
away non-stop about her mammy and her daddy and schooldays
and the job she did at the hotel and all the rest of it. As it is she
wears the dulled, frowning air of an amnesiac. There are times
when I catch her studying me with that remote stare that she has
as if I were something that had suddenly appeared in her path,
like a rock, or a fallen branch, or an unfordable blank span of
water. Probably she finds me as baffling a phenomenon as I find
her, my songless Mélisande. She trails about the house in an
old raincoat of Licht's that she uses for a dressing-gown, with
her lank hair and wan cheeks. I am startled anew each time
I encounter her. I am like an anthropologist studying the last
surviving specimen of some delicate, elusive species long thought
extinct. I am assembling her gradually, with great care, starting at
the extremities; I ogle her bare feet – the little toe is curled under
its neighbour like a baby's thumb – her hard little hands, the
vulnerable, veined, milk-blue backs of her knees. Sometimes at
night she comes and sits in the kitchen while I work. I do not
know if she is lonely, or afraid, or if the kitchen is just one of a

series of stopping-places in her fitful wanderings; she has a way of touching things as she passes them by, tapping them lightly with her fingertips, like a child touching the markers of a secret game. She is tense, restless, preoccupied, always poised somehow, as if at any moment she might unfurl a set of hidden wings and take flight out of the window into the darkness and be gone. It will happen; some morning I will wake and know at once that she has flown, will feel her absence like a jagged hole in the air through which the wind pours without a sound. What shall I do then, when my term is ended?

Felix she does not mention.

I tell her about the painter Vaublin, what little is known of him. She listens, large-eyed, nodding faintly now and then, taking it all in or thinking of something else, I do not know which. Perhaps I am talking to myself, telling myself the same story all over again. Listen—

*

Who does not know, if only from postcards or the lids of superior chocolates boxes, these scenes suffused with tenderness and melancholy that yet have something harsh in them, something almost inhuman? *Le monde d'or* is one of those handful of timeless images that seem to have been hanging forever in the gallery of the mind. There is something mysterious here beyond the inherent mysteriousness of art itself. I look at this picture, I cannot help it, in a spirit of shamefaced interrogation, asking, What does it mean, what are they doing, these enigmatic figures frozen forever on the point of departure, what is this atmosphere of portentousness without apparent portent? There is no meaning, of course, only a profound and inexplicable significance; why is that not enough for me? Art imitates nature not by mimesis but by achieving for itself a natural objectivity, I of all people should know that. Yet in this picture there seems to be a kind of valour in operation, a kind of tight-lipped, admirable fortitude, as if the painter knows something that he will not divulge, whether to deprive us or to spare us is uncertain. Such stillness; though the scene moves there is no movement; in this twilit glade the helpless tumbling of things through time has come to a halt: what other painter before or after has managed to illustrate this fundamental paradox of art with such profound yet playful artistry? These creatures will not die, even if they have never lived. They are wonderfully detailed figurines, animate yet frozen in immobility: I think of the little manikins on a music-box, or in one of those old town-hall clocks, poised, waiting for the miniature music that will never start up, for the bronze bell that will not peal. It is the very stillness of their world that permits them to endure; if they stir they will die, will crumble into dust and leave nothing behind save a few scraps of brittle lace, a satin bow, a shoe buckle, a broken mandolin.

I admire the faint but ever-present air of concupiscence that pervades all of this artist's work. Viewed from a certain angle these polite arcadian scenes can seem a riotous bacchanal. How lewdly his ladies look out at us, their ardent eyes shiny as marbles, their cheeks pinkly aglow as if from a gentle smacking. Even the props have something tumescent about them, these smooth pillars and thick, tall trees, these pendulous and smoothly rounded clouds, these mossy arbours from within which there seem to issue the sighs and soft laughter of breathless lovers. Even in *Le monde d'or*, apparently so chaste, so ethereal, a certain hectic air of expectancy bespeaks excesses remembered or to come. The figure of Pierrot is suggestively androgynous, the blonde woman walking away on the arm of the old man – who himself has a touch of the roué – wears a wearily knowing air, while the two boys, those pallid, slightly ravaged putti, seem to have seen more things than they should. Even the little girl with the braided hair who leads the lady by the hand has the aura of a fledgling Justine or Juliette, a potential victim in whom old men might repose dark dreams of tender abuse. And then there is that smirking Harlequin astride his anthropomorphic donkey: what sights he seems to have seen, what things he knows!

*

I pause to record an infestation of flies, minute, glittering black creatures with disproportionately large yet impossibly delicate wings shaped like sycamore seeds. I think they must be newly hatched. What is a blow-fly? That is what I thought when I saw them: blow-flies. Is there something dead around here that has not yet begun to stink? I cannot discover where they are coming from; they just appear in the light of the lamp, attracted by the warmth, I suppose, and fly up against the bulb and then drop stunned on the table and flop about groggily until I sweep them away with my sleeve. They have got into my papers, too, I lift a page and find them squashed flat there, tiny black and crimson bursts of blossom stuck with wing-petals. It is eerie, even a bit alarming, yet I am almost charmed. It is like something out of the Bible. What does it portend? I have become superstitious, the result no doubt of living for so long with ghosts. Down here in the underworld things give the uncanny impression of being other things, all these Pierrots and Colombines in their black masks, and even flies, looked at in a certain light, can seem celestial messengers. When they first began to appear I did not feel repugnance, only a sort of pleased surprise. I sat for a long time watching them, head on hand, lost to myself and inanely smiling, like one of those bewhiskered dreamers fluttered about by fairies in a Victorian engraving. I know that the reality they inhabit is different from mine, that for them this world they have blundered into is all struggle and pain and sudden, inexplicable fire – they are only flies after all, and I am only I – yet as they rise and fall, fluttering in the light, they might be a host of shining seraphim come to comfort me.

*

Today in my reading I chanced upon another jewel: *Hard beside the woe of the world, and often upon its volcanic soil, man has laid out his little garden of happiness.* Yes, you have guessed it, I have taken up gardening, even in the shadow of my ruins. It is a relaxation from the rigours of scholarship. (Scholarship!) But no, no, it is more than that. Out here among these greens, in this clement weather, I have the irresistible sensation of being in touch with something, some authentic, fundamental thing, to which a part of me I had thought atrophied responds as if to a healing and invigorating balm. So many things I have missed in my life; there are moments, rare and brief, when I think it might not be too late after all to experience at least some of them. My needs are modest; a spell of husbandry will do, for now. (Later will there come the tree of knowledge, Eve, the fatal apple, and all the rest of it, Cain included?) Perhaps I shall make a little statue of myself and grind it up and mix it with the clay, as the philosopher so charmingly recommends, and that way come to live again through these growing things.

I found down at the side of the house the remains of what must once have been a kitchen garden. Everything was choked with weeds and scutch grass, but the outlines of bed and drill were still there. I cleared the ground and found good black soil and put in vegetables – runner beans, mainly, I'm afraid, for I love their scarlet flowers. Already the first fruits have appeared (shall I hear the voice of the turtle, too?). I cannot express the excitement I felt when these tender seedlings began to come up. They were so fragile and yet so tenacious, so – so valiant. I have a great fondness for the stunted things, the runts, the ones that fail to flower and yet refuse to die, or are beaten down by the wind and still put out blossoms on the fallen stems. I have the notion, foolish, I know, that it is because of me that they cling on, that my ministrations, no, simply my presence gives them heart somehow, and makes them live. Who or what would there be to notice their struggles if I did not come out and walk among them every day? It must mean something, being here. I am the agent of individuation: in me they find their singularity. I planted them in neat rows, just so, and gave each one its space; without me only the madness of mere growth. Not a sparrow shall fall but I . . . how does it go? I have forgotten the quotation, the misquotation. Just as well, I am getting carried away; next thing

I shall be hearing voices. It is just that there are days when, like Rameau's nephew, I have to reflect: it is an affliction that must run its course.

Where was I? My garden, yes. I entertain high hopes of a bumper crop. What shall I do with such abundance, though? Perhaps Mr Tighe will take some of it to sell in his shop? If not, what matter. Let it all go to waste. Life, growth, this tender green fighting its way up through the dirt, that's all that interests me. Obvious, of course, but what do I care about that? The obvious is fine, for me. Sometimes, anyway.

And then there are the weeds; I know that if I were a real gardener I would do merciless and unrelenting battle against weeds, but the fact is I cherish them. They seem to me even more fiercely alive than the planted things they flourish among. Cut them down today and tomorrow they will be back; tear them out of their holes and leave the merest thread of root behind and they will come shouldering their way up again, stronger than ever. Compared to these ruffians even my hardiest cabbages are namby-pambies. How cunning they are, too, how cleverly they choose their spot, growing up slyly beside those cultivated plants they most resemble. Against whom are they adopting this camouflage? Pests do not seem to eat them, having my more tender produce to gorge upon, and birds leave them alone. Is it me they fear? Do they see me coming, with my boots and blade? I wonder if they feel pain, experience terror, if they weep and bleed, in their damp, vermiculate world, just as we do, up here in the light? I look at the little sprigs of chickweed trembling among the bean shoots and I am strangely moved. Such steadfastness, such yearning! They want to live too. That is all they ask: to have their little moment in the world.

A robin comes to forage where I dig, a tough-looking type. It watches me with a glint and darts under my feet after its prey. Seagulls swoop and blackbirds fly up at a low angle, fluting shrilly. This morning when I was hoeing between the potato beds a rat appeared, nosing along under the whitewashed wall that separates my garden from the yard. It must have been sick: when it saw me it did not run away, only sat up on its hunkers and looked at me in weary surprise. (Where is that dog?) I thought of Alba Longa, of course, of Carthage in flames, all that. What a mind I have, stuffed with lofty trivia! After a moment or two the thing turned and made off, going at a sort of sideways wallow and dragging its fat pink tail over the clay. Trust me: the quick all around and I find myself face to face with a rat dying of decrepitude. I suppose I should have killed it. I am not so good at killing things, any more. Will it come back? In dreams, perhaps.

All this, the garden and so on, why does it remind me so strongly of boyhood days? God knows, I was never a tow-haired child of nature, ensnared with flowers and romping on the grass. Cigarettes and dirty girls were my strongest interests. Yet when I trail out here with my hoe I feel the chime of an immemorial happiness. Is it that the past has become pastoral, as much a fancy as in my mind this garden is, perpetually vernal, aglow with a stylised, prelapsarian sunlight such as that which shines with melancholy radiance over Vaublin's pleasure parks? That is what I am digging for, I suppose, that is what I am trying to uncover: the forfeited, impossible, never to be found again state of simple innocence.

So picture me there in this still-springlike early summer weather, in my peasant's blouse and cracked brogues, delving among the burdocks, an unlikely Silvius, striving by harmless industry to do a repair job on what remains of my rotten soul. The early rain has ceased and the quicksilver air is full of flash and chill fire; a surprise, really, this drenched brilliance. There is a sort of ringing everywhere and everything is damp and silky under a pale, nude sky. We had a wet winter, summer has made a late start, and the clay is sodden still, a rich, dark stuff that heaves and slurps when I plunge my blade into it. All moves slowly, calmly, at a mysteriously ordained, uniform pace; I have the sense of a vast clock marking off the slow strokes, one by one by one. I pause and lean on the handle of the hoe with my face lifted to the light, ankles crossed and feet in the clay (which is their true medium, after all) and think of nothing. There is a tree at the corner of the garden, I am not sure what it is, a beech, I believe, I shall call it a beech – who is to know the difference? – a wonderful thing, like a great delicate patient animal. It seems to look away, upward, carefully, at something only it can see. It makes a restless, sibilant sound, and the sunlight trapped like bright water among its branches shivers and sways. I am convinced it is aware of me; more foolishness, I know. Yet I have a sense, however illusory, of living among lives: a sense, that is, of the significance, the ravelled complexity of things. They speak to me, these lives, these things, of matters I do not fully understand. They speak of the past and, more compellingly, of the future. They are urgent at times, at times so weary and faded I can scarcely hear them.

*

I have discovered the source of those flies: a bunch of flowers that lovelorn Licht left standing for too long on the window sill above the sink. Another attempt to brighten the place; that is his great theme these days, the need to 'brighten up the place'. Chrysanthemums, they were, blossoms of the golden world. Among the petals there must have been eggs that hatched in the sun. The water they were standing in has left behind a sort of greeny, fleshy smell. But imagine that: flies from flowers! Ah Charles, Charles – wait, let me strike an attitude: there – Ah, Charles, *mon frère mélancolique*! You held that genius consists in the ability to summon up childhood at will, or something like that, I can't remember exactly. I have lost mine, lost it completely. Childhood, I mean. Versions of it are all I can manage. Well, what did I expect? Something had to be forfeited, for the sake of the future; that is where I am pinning my hopes now. The future! Ah.

*

Flora is sleeping on her side with one glossy knee exposed and an arm thrown out awkwardly, her hand dangling over the side of the bed. See the parted lips and delicately shadowed eyelids, that strand of damp hair stuck to her forehead. A zed-shaped line of sunlight is working its imperceptible way towards her over the crumpled sheet. She murmurs something and frowns.

'Are you all right?' Alice says softly and touches her lolling arm.

'What?' Flora sits up straight and stares about her blankly with wide eyes. 'What?'

'Are you all right?' People waking up frighten Alice, they look so wild and strange. 'They sent me up to see if you were better.'

Flora closed her eyes and plunged her hands into her hair. She was hot and damp and her hair was hot and damp and heavy. She took a deep breath and held it for a moment and then sighed.

'I'm not better,' she said. 'I feel shivery still. I must have got a chill. Will you bring me a drink of water?'

She flopped back on the bed and stared vexedly at the ceiling, her dark hair strewn on the pillow and her arms flung up at either side of her face. The undersides of her wrists are bluish white.

'It was raining but it's lovely now,' Alice said.

'Is it?' Flora answered from the depths. She was trying to remember her dream. Something about that picture: she was in that picture. 'Yes,' she said, staring at the print pinned on the wall beside her, that strange-looking clown with his arms hanging and the one at the left who looked like Felix, grinning at her.

Alice had the feeling she often had, that she was made of glass, and that anyone who looked at her would see straight through and not notice her at all. She is in love with Flora; in her presence she has a sense of something vague and large and bright, a sort of painful rapture that is all the time about to blossom yet never does. She wished now she could think of something to say to her, something that would make her start up in excitement and dismay. She could hear the wind thrumming in the chimneys and the gulls crying like babies. She thought of her mother. A cloud switched off the sunlight. In the sudden gloom she began to fidget.

'That man made sausages for us,' she said.

A faint smell of frying lingered.

'Who?' Flora said. Not that she cared. She lifted her knees

under the blanket and hugged them; she reclined there, coiled around the purring little engine of herself, with the restless and faintly aggrieved self-absorption of a cat. Suddenly she sat up and laughed. 'What?' she said, 'Did *he* cook – Felix?'

Alice put her hands behind her back and swivelled slowly on one heel.

'No,' she said witheringly. 'The one that lives here. That little man.'

The sunlight came on again and everywhere there was a sense of running, silent and fleet. Flora pulled the coarse sheet over her breast and snuggled down in the furry hollow of the mattress, inhaling her own warm, chocolatey smells. She no longer cared whose bed it was, what big body had slept here before her. Blood beat along her veins sluggishly like oil.

'Tell them I'm all right,' she said. 'Tell them I'm asleep.' The soft light in the window and the textured whiteness of the pillow calmed her heart. She was sick and yet wonderfully at ease. She closed her eyes and listened to the sounds of the day around her, birdsong and far calls and the wind's unceasing vain attempt to speak. She was a child again, adrift in summer. She saw the sun on the convent wall and the idiot boy on the hill road making faces at her, and below her the roofs shimmering, the harbour beyond, and then the sea, and then piled clouds like coils of dirty silver lying low on the hot horizon. 'Tell them I . . .'

*

Outside the door Alice paused. Through the little window above the landing she could see the shadows of clouds skimming over the distant sea and the whitecaps that from here looked as if they were not moving at all. Outside the window on the next landing there was a big tree that shed a greenish light on the stairs. She glanced down through the shifting leaves and thought she saw someone in the garden looking up at her and she turned hot with fright. Hatch had said this place was surely haunted. She hurried on.

The kitchen had the puzzled, lost look of a place lately

abandoned. Only Licht was there, sitting at the strewn table with his head lifted, dreaming up into the wide light from the window. At first when he saw her he did not stir, then blinked and shook himself and sat upright.

'She said to say that she's asleep,' she said. He nodded pleasantly and smiled, quite baffled. 'Flora,' she said with firmness.

'Ah. Flora.' Nodding. 'Yes.' His gaze shied uncertainly. He was thinking there was something he should think. The noise of the wind had made him feel dizzy, as if a crowd had been shouting in his ear for hours, and he could not clear that awful buzzing sensation in his head. For an instant he saw himself clearly, sitting here in the broad, headachey light of morning, an indistinct, frail figure. Over the oak wood a double rainbow stood shimmering, one strong band and, lower down, its fainter echo. 'Flora,' he said again. Dimly in the dark of his mind the lost thought swirled.

Alice imagined taking him by the shoulders and shaking him; she wondered if his head would rattle.

'She said to say she's still not well,' she said.

'Oh?' Childe Someone to the dark tower came. 'I hope she . . .'

The unwashed crockery was still in the sink, the breakfast things were on the table.

'Will we wash up?' Alice said.

Licht shook his head.

'No,' he said, 'leave that, that's someone else's job.' He looked at her sidelong with a crafty smile. 'We had a maid one time who had a dog called Water, and when my mother complained that the plates were dirty, Mary always said, *Well, ma'am, they're as clean as Water can make them.*' He laughed, a sudden, high whoop, and slapped the table with the flat of his hand and then grew solemn. 'Poor mama,' he murmured. He stood up. Hop, little man, hop. 'Come,' he said, 'I'll show you something.'

The rainbows were fading already in the window.

The house was quiet as they climbed up through it and she imagined figures lurking unseen all around her with their hands pressed to their mouths and their eyes slitted, trying not to let her hear them laughing. She walked ahead of Licht and had a funny sensation in the small of her back, as if she had grown a little tail there. She could hear him humming busily to himself. The thought of her mother was like a bubble inside her ready to burst. Everything was so awful. On the boat that morning Pound had come into the lavatory when she was there and offered her sweets to pull down her pants and let him look at her. She was a little afraid of him, but she felt sorry for him; too, the way he bared his front teeth when he frowned and had to keep pushing his glasses up on his sweaty nose. His breath smelled of cheese.

On the first landing Licht stopped and cocked his head and listened, his smile fixed on nothing. Who did he look like, in that long sort of frock-coat thing and those tight trousers? 'All clear!' he whispered, and winked and shooed her on. The White Rabbit? Or was it the March Hare. For she was Alice, after all.

'Tell me,' he said, 'was the boat trip nice?'

She was not sure what she should answer. She thought he might be making fun of her. He was walking beside her now, leaning around so that he could look into her face. There were little webs of wrinkles at the corners of his mouth and eyes, very fine, like cracks in china.

'It was all right,' she said carefully. 'Then it ran on to that sandbank thing and we all fell down. I think—'

'Ssh!'

They crept past the room where Flora was asleep. He wondered if she had taken off her clothes. A slow, dull ache of longing kindled itself anew in his breast.

Again he stopped and listened.

All clear.

They gained the topmost storey.

In the turret room Alice stood with her hands clasped before her and her lips pressed shut. Everything tended upwards here. The windows around her had more of sky in them than earth and huge clouds white as ice were floating sedately past. Something wobbled. She had a sense of airy suspension, as if she were hovering a foot above the floor. She imagined that as well as a tail she had sprouted little wings now, she could almost feel them, at ankle and wrist, little feathery swift wings beating invisibly and bearing her aloft in the glassy air. She could see all around, way off to the sea in front and behind her up to the oak wood. It seemed to her she was holding something in her hands, a sort of bowl or something, that she had been given to mind.

'This is Professor Kreutznaer's room,' Licht said, with a hand on his heart, panting a little after the climb. 'This is his desk, see – and his stuff, his books and stuff.'

She advanced a step and bent her eyes dutifully to the muddle of yellowed papers with their scribbled hieroglyphs and the big books lying open with pictures of actors and musicians and ladies in gold gowns. It all seemed set out, arranged like this, for someone to see. There was dust on everything.

'Does he look at the stars?' she said.

'What?' He had turned his head and was gazing out of the windows into the depths of the sky.

'The stars,' she said, louder. 'At night.'

Reluctantly he came back from afar. Alice pointed to the telescope.

'I suppose so,' he said. 'And the sea.' He gestured vaguely. 'The clouds.'

She stood before him, blank and attentive, waiting. He touched a fingertip to the back of the swivel chair and it flinched.

'He used to only look at pictures,' he said, frowning. 'He was an expert on provenance.'

She nodded.

'Providence,' she said. 'Yes.'

'No no: *provenance.* Where a painting comes from, who owned it, and so on. You have to know that sort of thing to prove it's not a fake. The painting, I mean.'

'Oh.'

A helpless silence fell. Faintly from the garden below came the sound of voices; in a rush both stepped at once to the window and peered down, their foreheads almost touching. The boys were down there, wrestling half-heartedly on the grass.

'Look at them,' said Alice softly, with soft contempt.

Licht from the corner of his eye studied her in sudden wonderment. He had not been able to look at her this closely before now. She might have been a new species of something that had alighted at his side. He could hear her breathing. Each time that she blinked, her eyelashes rested for an instant on the soft rise of her cheek. She had a smell like the mingled smell of milk and pencil shavings. Distinctly they heard Hatch say, *Oh, fuck!* Silence, dark woods, that wind again, like a river running through the glimmering leaves. He closed his eyes. A nerve was twitching in his jaw.

'Do you ever think,' he said softly, 'that you are not here? Sometimes I have the feeling that I have floated out of myself, and that what's here, standing, talking, is not me at all.' He turned his troubled eyes away from her and bit his lip. Alice gazed intently down through the glass, hardly breathing. Something swayed between them and then gently settled. He sighed. Of late he had been experiencing the strangest things, all sorts of strange noises and reverberations in his head, pops and groans and sudden, sharp cracks, as if the world were surreptitiously disintegrating around him. One night when he was on the very brink of sleep something had gone off with a bang and a flash of white light, like a pistol being fired inside his skull, and he had started awake in terror but there was nothing, not the faintest sound or echo of a sound. 'I wonder,' he said, 'I wonder is there something the matter with my brain.' He saw himself elsewhere, running down a street, or crouched at a school desk in dusty sunlight under a ponderously ticking clock. 'Do you think we just die, Alice?' he murmured. 'That everything just . . . ends?'

The shadow of a bird, stiff-winged and plunging, skimmed slantwise across the window.

'I think that captain really was drunk,' she said suddenly, still looking down through the glass.

'What?'

'The captain of the boat. He had a bottle under a shelf. First he cursed and then laughed and told that Felix fellow to go to hell.'

She sighed.

'Is that right?' he said. He watched her as she stood on tiptoe peering down through the window, the shell-pink rim of one ear showing through her hair and a tongue-tip touching her upper lip.

'I'm staying in a hotel, you know,' she said. She gestured in the direction where she thought the mainland lay. 'My mammy . . .'

A tremulous frown passed over her face and he was afraid she was going to cry again.

'Come on,' he said.

Outside the turret room three deep steps led up to a door so low that even Alice had to stoop going through it. Here is the attic, a long, broad, tent-shaped, shadowed place with a dazzling pillar of sunlight suspended at an angle from a grimy mansard window in the roof. Smell of dust and apples and the sweetish stink of decaying timbers. It is hot up here under the roof and the air is thick. There were things piled everywhere, bits of furniture, old bottles, croquet mallets, an antique black bicycle, all standing like their own ghosts under a soft, furry outline of dust. 'The Emperor Rudolf,' Licht was saying, 'the Emperor Rudolf . . .' but the odd acoustics of the place took the rest of his words and made of them an unintelligible booming. They stood a moment, struck, listening to the echoes ricochet and fall like needles. A draught came in from the stairs and a door somewhere cried tinily on its hinges. The heat pressed on their eardrums. Unseen pigeons murmured lasciviously in the eaves and a mouse under the floorboards softly scurried. I have been here before.

'A great collector,' Licht said softly, as if someone else might be listening. 'Did you ever hear of him?'

Alice glanced sideways worriedly at his knees. 'I don't think so,' she said slowly.

'He had such things! – a magic statue, for instance, that sang a kind of song when the sun shone on it.' He looked uncertain for a moment. 'At least, that's what I read in a book somewhere.'

She turned and took a step away from him carefully, teetering. The thing she seemed to be holding in her hands now felt as if it were brimming over with some precious, volatile stuff. Suddenly he laughed behind her and the echoes flew up.

'Listen,' he said, 'listen,' and came forward with a finger lifted. 'What shape is a dead parrot?' She made a pretence of thinking hard. He watched her gloatingly, nodding, his eyebrows rising higher and higher. 'Give up?' She got ready to laugh. 'A polygon!' He quivered with glee, teeheeing soundlessly. She smiled as hard as she could, nodding. She had heard it before.

In a corner the floor was strewn with shrivelled apples. When his eye fell on them Licht grew morose.

'My pippins,' he said. 'I forgot about them.' He picked one up and sniffed it wistfully. 'Gone.' He gave her a mournful smile. 'Like poor Polly.'

He knelt before a brassbound chest. There were costumes in it, he told her, fancy-dress things from long ago, ball-gowns and helmets and an officer's uniform with a cocked hat. He tugged at the catches but could not get them undone. After a brief effort he gave up; leave them, leave them there, the gaudy centuries. He sat down on the lid of the chest and rocked himself back and forth, hugging one knee, while Alice stood, swaying a little, looking away. Another cloud swept over and the sunlight in the window above their heads died abruptly with a sort of click.

'He was famous, you know,' Licht said. 'Oh yes. He was in books, and people came from all over the world to get his opinion on pictures.' His face darkened and he looked like a vexed child. 'Then they said that he—' He paused and lifted a warning finger, listening.

Eek.

The sunlight returned. Distantly they heard again from the garden the raucous voices of the boys.

'Where was he emperor of?' Alice said.

Licht looked at her and blinked. 'Eh? No, no, not him – I mean Professor Kreutznaer.'

'Oh.'

He looked more vexed than ever. He stood up from the chest and paced the floor moodily with his hands at his back and the corners of his mouth pulled down. Alice felt the invisible bowl tilting in her hands.

'I was his assistant, you know,' he said airily, pointing to the papers on the desk. 'I used to type up what he wrote.' He waggled his fingers, tapping invisible keys. 'I was the only one who could read his handwriting.'

He stood and frowned, scratching his head with one finger.

'Did they write about you in the books, too?' she asked.

He glanced at her sharply. 'Of course not!' he snapped, and she felt the ghost of a quicksilver splash fall at her feet. He broke off and lifted a hand again, frowning, his rabbity nostrils flared. A stair creaked; then silence. (The Professor is out there, poised like a voyeur, listening.) I watch them, outlined in dusty sunlight against the soft dark, an emblem of something, and my heart contracts.

'What is it?' Alice whispered.

'What? Oh, I thought I heard – ssh!'

They listened. No sound. Licht shrugged and started to speak, but suddenly Alice turned to him and said:

'I'm afraid!'

And as soon as it was said it ceased to be true. Licht stepped back, staring, cradling in his startled palms the invisible vessel she had handed him.

*

When Alice had run off down the stairs and Licht came stooping through the little doorway Professor Kreutznaer was there at the landing window with his fists sunk in the sagging pockets of his old black jacket. Licht flushed angrily.

'What are you doing?' the Professor said.

'Nothing!' Licht cried. It came out as a squeak. He cleared his throat and tried again. 'Nothing. What do you mean? Are you spying on me?'

From below came the abrupt thud of the front door slamming; the house quivered and after a second a ghostly draught came wafting up the stairs.

'I told you you shouldn't let them stay,' the Professor said. 'Why did you let them in?'

Licht strode past him to the window and stood looking out. Tears of anger and resentment welled up in his eyes.

'Why do you blame me?' he cried. 'You blame me for everything, and spy on me, creeping around and listening at doors. It's you they're after, it's you that fellow came to find!' How gay and carefree everything outside seemed, the sun on the dunes and the grass waving and the unreal blue of the sea in the distance. At moments such as this he felt the world was rocking with laughter, jeering at him. He beat his fists softly on the window-sill and wept, his shoulders shaking. 'I have to get away from here,' he said as if to himself and heaved a juicy sob, shaking his head slowly from side to side, and a big bubble of spit formed on his blubby lips and burst with a tiny plop. 'I have to get away!'

The Professor regarded him in silence, frowning. Licht, pawing at his eyes and muttering something, pushed past him and blundered away down the stairs.

The front door banged again and the Professor felt the tiny tremor under his feet. He waited and presently he heard another sound, closer at hand, and when he looked over the banisters he saw Felix on the landing below, leaning at the door of the bedroom there with one hand in the pocket of his jacket and his head inclined, smiling to himself, listening for a sound from within. The Professor drew back quickly, his heart joggling, but too late. For a moment there was silence and then from below he heard Felix laugh softly and softly sing up the stairwell:

'Helloo-oo!' Pause. 'Professor?' Pause; again a laugh. 'Are you there, Truepenny?'

The Professor closed his eyes briefly and sighed. There were things he did not wish to recall. Black nights by the river, the

lamps on the quayside shivering in the wind and the gulls wheeling in the darkness overhead like big, blown sheets of paper, and the boys standing in the shadows, all silk and sheathed steel, shuffling their feet in the cold, the tips of their cigarettes flaring and their soft cat-voices calling to him as he walked past them on the pavement for the third or fourth time, trying to appear distracted, trying to look like what at other times he thought himself to be. *How are you, hard? Are you looking for it, are you?* They all had the same, quick eyes, like the eyes of half-tamed animals. He was frightened of them. And yet behind all the toughness and the insolent talk how tentative they were; alone with him at last in a dark doorway or down a back lane they laughed self-consciously and ducked their heads, avoiding his furtive, beseeching eyes, pretending not to be there, just like him. It was that mixture of menace and vulnerability he found irresistible. And then stumbling away through the rain-slimed streets, light-headed, shaking with a sort of sated glee. Never again! he would cry out in his heart, never, I swear it! addressing a phantom version of himself that stood over him with arms folded and lips shut tight in terrible accusal. And Felix there always, lord of the streets, popping up out of nowhere, horribly knowing, making little jokes and smiling his malign, insinuating smile. They all knew Felix, with his cartons of contraband cigarettes off the boats and his little packets of precious powder. *The Pied Piper, Professor, that's me.* And that laugh.

'Coo-ee!' he called now, in soft singsong. He was leaning out over the banisters, his face upturned, with a wide, lipless grin. '*There* you are. Don't be shy, Professor, it's only me.'

Professor Kreutznaer slowly descended the stairs; Felix, still grinning, stood and watched him approach, beating out a little rhythm on the banister rail with his fingertips. How silent the house seemed suddenly.

'What—' the Professor said, and had to clear his throat and start again. 'What are you doing here?'

Felix expelled a gasp of laughter and pressed spread fingers to his breast and assumed an expression of startled innocence.

'You mean here?' he said, pointing to the floor under his feet. 'Why, nothing. Loitering without intent.'

'I mean on the island,' the Professor said.

Felix merely smiled at that and moved to the window and leaned there looking out brightly at the sunlit scene: the sloped lawn and the bridge over the stream and the grassed-over dunes in the distance and the far strip of sea. He sighed. 'What a pleasant place you have here,' he said. 'So peaceful.' He glanced over his shoulder and winked. 'Not like the old days, eh? Although I suppose there is the odd fisher-lad to bring you up your kippers.' He took out his dented gold case and lit a cheroot and placed the spent match carefully on the window-sill. He nodded thoughtfully, smoking. 'Yes,' he said, 'a spot like this would do me very nicely, I must say.'

The Professor stood and listened to the unsteady beating of his heart, thinking how fear always holds at its throbbing centre that little, thin, unquenchable flame of pleasure.

'Why have you come here,' he said.

Felix blew a big stream of smoke and shook his head in rueful amusement.

'I told you,' he said. 'The captain was drunk, our boat ran aground. We are castaways!' And lightly laughed. 'It's true, really. A happy chance. Are you not pleased to see me?'

The Professor continued to fix him with a dull glare.

'How did you know where to find me?' he said.

Felix clicked his tongue in mock annoyance.

'Really,' he said, 'I don't know why you won't believe me!' He chuckled. 'Have I ever lied to you?'

At that the Professor produced a brief bark of what in him passed for laughter. They eyed each other through a swirl of lead-blue smoke. The Professor raised his eyes and Felix touched a hand shyly to his dyed hair.

'I thought you'd never notice,' he said and put on a coy look and batted his eyelashes. 'You know me, Professor, mutability is my middle name.'

'What do you want from me?' the Professor said.

CROKE, NOW, try Croke, he is the real thing, the *homo verus* of myth and legend. He stepped out on the sunlit porch and stopped with a sour look and sniffed the day. Sea stink and the thick pungency of drenched grass and a sort of buttery smell that he supposed must be the smell of gorse. He did not much care for the countryside, trees and weather and suchlike. He was a city man, born and bred. A walk by the canal of an October morning, swans gliding on their own reflections and the sun on the gasworks and the air delicately blued with petrol fumes, that was enough of outdoors for him. He descended the porch steps and turned right along the flagged path past the rose bush and the rain barrel and the bluebottle-coloured mound where the coal-ash from the kitchen stove is dumped. Stunted apple trees grow here, standing in lush grass, and there are fruit bushes and a thick clump of nettles jostling greenly to attention, their webbed ears pricked up. Smell of roses, then of lilac, then of something sweetly dead. A cloud abruptly palmed the sun. Water was dripping nearby, or was it a bird, making that *plip, plip* noise? He arrived at the iron gate that led from the corner of the lawn into the yard behind the house. The cobbles were still wet in patches. He watched his hand grasp the bar of the gate and for a moment he was held, staring at that withered claw he could hardly believe was his. Nowadays he avoided looking at himself too closely, not caring to see the dewlapped neck and grizzled chest, the sagging tits, the quaking, varicosed legs. The years had worn his skin to a thin, translucent stuff, clammy and smooth, like waxed paper, a loose hide within which his big old carcass slipped and slid. He would not need a shroud, they could just truss him up in himself like a turkey and fold over the flaps and tie a final knot. He smiled grimly and the gate opened before him with a clang. A wash of sunlight swept the yard and as he stepped forward falteringly into this sudden weak blaze the god unseen anointed him and he felt for a moment an extraordinary happiness.

A hen was picking over bits of straw, sharp eye agleam, looking for something among the slimed cobbles. It paused thoughtfully and dropped behind it a little twirled mound of shit, chalk-white and olive-green. Croke stared in mild disgust: what in the name of God is it they eat? The dog emerged from its bed under the wheelbarrow and advanced lopsidedly a pace or two and halted, gasping. 'Here, old fellow,' Croke said and was startled at the loudness of his voice, how hollow it sounded, how unconvincing. He saw himself there, a comic turn, in his candy-stripes and sopping shoes and ridiculous straw hat. 'Here, boy,' he said gruffly. 'Here, old chap.'

The dog, a black and white spaniel with something awful coming out of its eyes, turned disdainfully and waddled back to its lair.

Croke walked on and came to another, wider iron gate. Beyond it were the fields sloping up to the oak ridge. He took off his hat and looked at it, feeling the air suddenly cool on his forehead.

What is it called, that thing, that gold thing?'

Under the gate there was a patch of churned-up mud (are there cows?) with little puddles of sky-reflecting water in it like shards of glass. He stepped across the mud-patch shakily but the ground beyond too was boggy and the wet grass clutched at his feet alarmingly. He kept going, though, clambering up the uneven slope and treading on his own squat shadow lurching along in front of him.

> *Unless to see my shadow in the sun,*
> *And* something *on mine own deformity.*

Not that he was ever let play the king. All he ever got to do was stand around in sackcloth trews and a tunic that smelled of someone else's sweat, trying not to yawn while a fat queer in a paper crown strode up and down, ranting. Pah. In his heart he despised the whole business, dressing up and pretending to be someone else. It was a pity no one did revues any more. He used to like revues, the old-fashioned kind, before everything got smart and smutty. He had been a great straight-man, because of his size, probably: a big, slow, shiny-faced gom with slicked-back hair standing up there in suit and tie with his brow furrowed while the little fellow ran rings around him, what could be funnier? Strange, he had never minded looking foolish like that. The funny men thought they were the ones in control; wrong, of course; that was the secret. Nasty little tykes, the lot of them, jealous, tightfisted, throbbing with grievances – and chasers too, God, yes, anything in a skirt.

He found himself thinking of Felix. He did not trust that joker, with his dyed hair and his dirty smile. Very sallow, too: was he a jewhoy? Got his hands on the girl straight away, of course. They always do. That girl, now—

Oh!

He reared back in fright as a bird of some sort flew up suddenly out of the grass with burbled whistlings and shot into the sky. A lark, was it? He stood with his head thrown back, leering from the effort, and watched the tiny creature where it hung above him, pouring out its thick-throated song. After a minute it got tired, or perhaps the song was finished, and it sank to earth in stages, dropping from one steep step of air to another, and disappeared into the grass again. Croke walked on. Long ago, when he was a child, someone had kept a canary; he remembered it, perched in its cage in a sunny window. Who was that, who would have kept a singing-bird? He could see it all clearly, the cage there, and the net curtain pulled back, and the window with the little panes and the yellow light streaming in. He sighed. Melancholy, thick and sweet as treacle, welled up in his heart.

He went on, up the slope. This last part was steep and there was mud and dead leaves to make the going treacherous. He smelled wet smoke. Above him the trees were making a troubled, rushing sound. He paused to rest for a moment, leaning forward with his hands on his knees and breathing with his mouth open. His lungs pained him. What was he doing, climbing up here, what craziness had got hold of him? He could die like this, keel over like a tree and die, be here for days and no one would find him. He turned his darkening gaze to the fields falling away behind him, to the house down there, to the beach and the distant sea. White clouds sailed above his head. He seemed for a moment to be airborne, and he felt light-headed. Behind him someone started to sing.

> *Oh*
> *He came off twice*
> *In a bowl of rice*
> *And called it tapioca*

It was one of the boys. He was squatting in the middle of a clearing beside the remains of a fire, poking at the smouldering embers with a stick. He looked up at Croke without surprise. His no-colour hair was wet and plastered to his skull. His eyes were an eerie, washed-out shade of blue.

'Which one are you?' Croke said, still wheezing from the climb. 'Are you Hatch?' It occurred to him he should carry a cane, it would lend him authority, pointing with it and so on. Hatch went on looking at him with detachment; he might have been looking in through the bars of a cage. Croke, disconcerted by the child's unwavering regard, tried another tack and pointed to the fire. 'Go out on you?' he said.

Hatch shrugged. 'Pound pissed on it.'

'I did not,' Pound said, stepping out of the trees. Pound was the fat one: glasses, cowlick, shoes like boats. 'He pissed on it himself.'

Unnerved, Croke grinned weakly. He opened his mouth but could think of nothing to say, and stood irresolute, feeling exposed and somehow mocked. He was secretly a little afraid of these two. Hatch in particular alarmed him, with his pixie's face and violet eyes and pale little clawlike hands.

Pound came and stood by the fire and kicked at the ashes

with the toe of his shoe. He cast a sidelong glance in Croke's direction. 'He must be gone,' he said to Hatch. 'I can't see him.'

'Gone to ground,' Hatch said and laughed.

A gust of wind blew across the clearing, lifting dry husks and the lacy skeletons of last year's leaves. In the silence Croke had a dreamy sense of slow, weightless toppling.

'Someone up here, was there?' he said.

Hatch stuck his stick into the ashes.

'That fellow,' he said.

'Which fellow?'

'Tarzan the apeman.'

This time Pound laughed, a fat bark. Croke looked from one of them to the other, the fey one squatting on the ground and fatty with his swollen cheeks and infant's pasty brow. He tried again to think of something to say that would confound them, something harsh and funny, but in vain, and turned instead with an angry gesture and walked away, willing himself to saunter, the back of his neck on fire. Children and animals, children and animals: he should have known better.

He came to the edge of the trees and had to scramble down the first few yards of the slope at a crouch. He felt odd: *wall-falling*, his father used to say: *I'm wall-falling*. The ground seemed more uneven than it had when he was coming up, and the grass hid holes in which he was afraid he would twist an ankle (there must be cows, then – or horses, perhaps there are horses, after all). The house was clear to see below him but somehow he kept listing away from it, as if there were a hidden tilt to things, and when he got down to level ground the roof and even the little turret sank from view off to the left behind a steep, grassy bank riddled with rabbit-burrows and he found himself toiling along a broad, sandy path with high dunes on either side.

The sea was before him, he could hear it, the hiss and rush of it and the gritty crash of the waves collapsing on the shingle. The sun shone upon him thickly. He stopped and stood there dully in the sun, his head bowed. What had happened to him? He could not understand it. A minute ago he had been up there on the ridge and now he was down here, sunk in this hot hollow. He looked about. The boys were behind him, standing on a dune, watching him. He could not see them very well; were they laughing? He felt dizzy again and something was buzzing in his head.

He went on. Sweat dimmed his sight. The band of his hat was greasy and hot and there was sand in his waterlogged shoes, hard ridges of it under his arches and wedged against his toes, making his corns pain him. The way grew steeper, the smooth slope rising before him like a wall; up there on the crest of the rise the wind was lifting fine swirls of sand and the sky beyond was a surprised, dense blue. A thick stench assailed him. A dead sheep lay crumpled in the sand, the head twisted sideways and the dainty black hoofs splayed. It must have lost its footing and tumbled down the dunes and broken its neck. Something had eaten out the hindquarters; the empty fleece, still intact, flapped in the wind, so that the dead thing seemed to be shuddering in pain and struggling to yank itself to its feet. He passed it by, trying not to breathe the smell, and caught the shine of a glazed muzzle and the black hole of an eye-socket. He coughed, spat, groaned. He hardly knew where he was any more, there was only this slope and the dazzling glitter of sunlight and the burning sand squirming under his feet. He wanted to get to the sea; he would be all right if only he could get to the sea. He heard the music the island makes, the deep song rising out of the earth, and thought he must be imagining it. He stumbled on, his heart wobbling in its cage and the salt air rasping in his lungs. After a dozen paces he halted again and turned. The boys were still behind him, keeping their distance. They stopped when he stopped and stood impassive, watching him. He shouted and shook his fist at them. Why would they not help him? Surely they could see he was in need of help. He was frightened. He thought he was going to cry. There was sand in his mouth now. What is that word? Anabasis. No. Descant. No, no, that thing, that gold thing, what is it! As if in a dream he watched his leaden feet slog through the sand, one sinking as the other rose, then that one sinking in its turn. How had he come to this, what had gone wrong, and so quickly? He saw the canary again, the light in the window of the cramped front room and the old man in the big high bed. Yes, yes, that was it, she had bought the bird for him at the end, to keep him company – *To pipe me out!* the old man would shout, laughing and coughing, amused and furious. He heard again the harsh laugh and the voice weary with contempt: *My son, the comedian.* Down the narrow stairs, the years falling away and suddenly he was a child again, the hall with the lino gleaming and that worn quarter-circle inside the door where the flap dragged, and out into the square, hand in her hand, the drinking trough and the cherry trees in blossom in their wire cages, and then the big, wide, echoing corridor ablaze with grainy light and the tall nun's rapid step on the bumpy tiles – never see their feet – and her thin, high voice saying something about prayers and being good.

Mother! Hold me!

He gained the crest of the slope and stood for a moment swaying, looking out in slack-jawed amazement over the beach and the blue-green vasts of water, smelling the stink of sand and wrack. The wind blew his hat off and bowled it down the slope behind him. He set off across the beach at a stumbling run, yearning towards the ocean, his long arms swinging and his knees going out sideways. At the margin of the waves he halted. Above him the sun was a wafer of white gold shaking and slipping at the centre of the huge blue. He stretched out his arms. He was laughing or crying, he did not know which.

That gold

That thing that gold

He shut his eyes and it was as if a door had slammed shut inside his head.

The boys appeared over the brow of the dunes in time to see him rise up slowly on one leg, like a big old dying bird, his arms clutching helplessly at hoops of air. He wavered a moment, then slowly toppled over and collapsed full-length upon the sand.

*

I dreamed last night that— No, no, I can't. Some dreams are too terrible to be told.

*

Pain in my breast suddenly. Ah! it pains. Perhaps I am the one who is dying of his heart. That would be a laugh, for me to die and leave them there, trapped, the tide halted, the boat stuck fast forever. End it all, space and time, one huge flash and then darkness and a blessed silence as the babble stops. Serve them right. Serve us all right. We are the dangerous ones, no other species like us, all of creation cowering before us, the death-dealers. I see a forked beast squatting on the midden of the world, red-eyed, regardant, gnawing on a shinbone: poor, dumb destroyer. Better without us, better the nothing than this, this shambles we have raised. Yes, have done with it all: one universal neck and I the hangman. In the end. Not yet. In the end.

*

Vaublin's double. Curious episode. (See how quicky I recover my poise?) All the experts, Professor Kreutznaer included, agree that it was all a delusion, a phantasm spawned by fever and exhaustion in that last, desperate summer of the painter's brief life. I am not so sure. The deeper I look into the matter the stranger it becomes. He was living on the Île de la Cité, last resting place in his fitful wanderings at the end, in big rooms high above the Seine. He was thirty-seven; his lungs were ruined. The paintings from that period, hurried dreamscapes bathed in an eerie, lunar radiance, have a shocked look to them, the motionless, inscrutable figures scattered about the canvas like the survivors of a vast calamity of air and light. What he is seeking here is something intangible, some pure, distilled essence that perhaps is not human at all. He speaks in one of his last letters of coming to the realisation that the centre of a painting, that packed point of equilibrium out of which every element of the composition flows and where at the same time everything is ingathered, is never where it seems it should be, is never central, or obviously significant, but could be a patch of sky, the fold of a gown, a dog scratching its ear, anything. The trick is to locate that essential point and work outwards from it. By now he had given himself up entirely to theatricality. The actors from the Comédie-Française sat for him in costume, all the leading figures, Paul Poisson, La Thorillière, the tragedienne Charlotte Desmares, Biancolelli whose Pierrot was the talk of the season. They were perfect for his purposes, all pose and surface brilliance. They would strike an attitude and hold it for an hour without stirring, in a trance of self-regard. He was drawing too on his memories of the *fêtes* and staged *spectacles* years before in the great gardens of the city. Those green and umber twilights of which he was so fond are surely recollections of the Duchesse de Maine's *grandes nuits* at Sceaux, the soft shadows among the trees, the music on the water, the masked figures strolling down the long lawns as the last light of evening turned to blackening dusk and the little bats came out and flittered in the darkening air. The melancholy that was always his mark is mingled in these final scenes with a kind of shocked hilarity. The luminance in which they are bathed seems always on the point of being extinguished, as if it had its source in the little palpitant flame of the painter's own enfeebled, failing life.

When the notion came to him of a shadowy counterpart stalking him about the city he thought the thing must be a joke, an elaborate hoax got up perhaps by someone with a grudge against him – he had always been of a suspicious nature. In the street an acquaintance would stop and stare in surprise, saying he had seen him not five minutes ago walking in the opposite direction and wearing a black cloak. He was not amused. Then he began to notice the pictures. There were *fêtes galantes* and *amusements champêtres*, and even theatre scenes, his speciality, the figures in which seemed to look at him with suppressed merriment, knowingly. They were executed in a style uncannily like his own, but in haste, with technical lapses and scant regard for quality of surface. This slapdash manner seemed a gibe aimed directly at him and his pretensions, mocking his lapses in concentration, the shortcuts and the technical flaws that he had thought no one would notice. When he tried to get a close look at this or that piece somehow he was always foiled. He would glimpse a *Récréation galante* being carried between two aproned porters out of a dealer's shop, or a gold and green *Île enchantée*, which for a dizzy second seemed surely his own work, hanging over the fireplace of a fashionable salon just as he was being ushered from the room. Who was this prankster who could dash off imitation Vaublins with such assurance, who knew his secret flaws, who could imitate not only his strengths but his weaknesses too, his evasions, his failures of taste and technique? He tells in a letter to his friend and obituarist, the collector Antoine de La Roque, of having a feeling constantly of being hindered; some days, he says, he has almost to fight his way to the easel, as if indeed there were an invisible double there before him, crowding him aside, and when he steps to the canvas another, heavier arm seems to lift alongside his. *I seem to hear mocking laughter*, he wrote, *and someone is always standing in the corner behind me, yet when I turn there is no one there.*

He had begun work on *Le monde d'or*, hastening while his strength lasted. The summer was hot. I see him aloft in his attic rooms, all doors and windows open to the air and the noises of the city, the breezes and sudden smells and shimmering waterlights. His hands shake, everything shakes, flapping and straining as if the house were a great, lumbering barquentine in full sail. He tells La Roque, *I have embarked for the golden world.* He wants to confess to something but cannot, something about a crime committed long ago; something about a woman.

STEALTHILY THE DAY BURGEONS, climbing towards noon. The wind has died. On the ridge the oaks are motionless, dark with heat, and the air above the fields undulates like a blown banner. The hens have departed from the yard, fleeing the sun, the old dog is asleep again under the wheelbarrow. The beech tree at the corner of the garden stands unmoving in the purple puddle of its own shadow. Something squeaks and then is still. Hushed, secret world! The back door is open, an up-ended box of soft black darkness; glide through here, light as a breeze, touch this and that, these dim things, with a blindman's feathery touch. The narrow passageway beside the stairs smells of lime, the hall is loud with light. Voices. Upstairs a door opens and rapid footsteps sound. Listen! they are living their little lives.

In the kitchen Sophie stood with one haunch perched on the edge of the table taking photographs of Alice, who sat before her on a chair with her little wan face meekly lifted up to the lens, intent and motionless, like a flower holding itself up to the light. Felix came in from the hall, with Licht, rabbit-eyed and shaky, trotting worriedly at his heels. Sophie held up a hand to them and they stopped in the doorway, watching.

'Don't move,' she said to Alice softly and with soft intentness turned the camera this way and that, softly crushing the shutter-button.

Felix came up behind her and she lowered the camera but did not turn to him. Alice smiled up at her anxiously.

'I thought you only take pictures of things that are dead,' Felix murmured.

Sophie did not reply. She could feel the faint heat of his presence behind her; she put down the camera and rose abruptly and crossed to the window and stood with her hands braced on the cool, fat rim of the sink. She looked down at her face in the bit of broken mirror propped on the window-sill and hardly recognised her own reflection, all glimmering throat and hooded, unfamiliar eyes, like a burnished metal mask. When she turned back Felix was looking at her knowingly, with sly amusement, his head on one side and his lips pursed, and she felt herself flinch, as if she had brushed against some thrillingly loathsome, lewd and cloying thing.

A shadow fell in the doorway and Croke came in blunderingly, carrying his straw hat and laughing in distress.

'Jesus!' he said.

He stood swaying and looked about him in a kind of wonderment, smiling dazedly, his mouth open. The brim of his hat was crushed on one side and there were patches of wet sand on his blazer and his white trousers were stained and wet again at the cuffs. Hatch and Pound appeared behind him, one on either side, with the cerulean air of noon between them, bored and dully frowning. 'What?' Croke said sharply, as if someone had spoken. He shook his head and lumbered forward and sat down heavily at the table beside Alice. He seemed to have aged and yet at the same time looked impossibly young, with his face lifted listeningly and his hands hanging between his knees, a big, ancient, bewildered babe. His sunken jaw was stubbled and there were flecks of spit at the corners of his mouth; his hair stood up in a cowlick over one ear, when he tried to smooth it flat it sprang up again.

'Fell down,' he said, gesturing. 'Like that: bang, down on my arse.'

He shook his head, bemused and laughing; he picked up a fork from the table and fiddled with it distractedly and put it down again. The boys sidled in and he heaved himself round on his chair and pointed a quivering finger at them accusingly. 'And as for these two—!' He laughed again and coughed and thumped himself in the chest with his fist, then turned back to the table and frowned, licking salt-cracked lips. The world was luminous around him. Everything shone out of itself, shaking in its own radiance. There was movement everywhere; even the most solid objects seemed to seethe, the table under his hands, the chair on which he sat, the very walls themselves. And he too trembled, as if his whole frame had been struck like a tuning fork against the hard, bright surface of things. The others looked at him, stilled for a moment, staring. He imagined himself as they would see him, a shining man, floating in the midst of light. He turned his head quickly and peered up, thinking he had heard a voice behind him call out his name. No one was there.

'Jesus!' he said again softly, with a soft, whistling sigh.

Licht went to the stove and pushed the pots and pans this way and that. A spill of sunlight from the window wavered in the murky recess above the stove, a roiling, goldened beam. He closed his eyes for a second and saw himself free, flying up without a sound into the blue, the boundless air. He crossed to the meat-safe on the wall and took out a white dish on which was draped a scrawny, plucked chicken with rubber-red wattles and scaly, yellow claws.

'Look at that,' he said in disgust. 'Tighe didn't clean it again.'

He put the bird on the table and took off his coat.

'When my father died,' Croke said to no one in particular, 'he was younger than I am now.'

He looked about him with an empty smile, his clouded stare sliding loosely over everything. Alice stared with faint revulsion into the whorl of his huge, hairy ear. She thought of a picture she had seen when she was little of an old beggarman standing at a street corner and a tall angel with long golden hair and broad gold wings bending over him solicitously. She wondered idly if Croke was dying. She did not care. She picked up Sophie's camera and was surprised by its weight. She liked the feel of it, its hard heaviness and leathery, stippled skin, the silky coolness of its steel underparts. She pictured the film rolled up tight inside, with her face printed on it over and over, dozens of miniature versions of her, with ash-white hair and black skin, strangely staring out of empty eye-sockets, and she shivered and felt something approach in the shadowed, purplish air and touch her.

'So he breaks into the laundry,' Hatch was saying furtively, 'and fucks them all and then runs off, and the headline in the paper next day says: *Nut Screws Washers and Bolts.*' He laughed wheezily, his colourless lips drawn back and his sharp little teeth on show. He cocked an eye at Licht and said: ''At'sa some joke, eh, boss?'

Licht pretended not to hear; Hatch turned to Alice.

'I suppose you don't get it,' he said.

Pound, slumped at the table with his chin on his fat hands, snorted. Light flashed on his glasses and made it seem as if he had no eyes. Hatch kicked him casually under the table and said:

'How's your diet?' He winked at Alice. 'His ma has him on a diet, you know.'

'Shut up,' Pound said listlessly. 'You eat your snot.'

Felix laughed and clipped the fat boy playfully on the ear and said:

'Bunter, you are a beast.'

'Ow!'

Hatch's violet eyes glittered and he kicked Pound again on the shin, harder this time.

'Damn you,' Licht said to the chicken through clenched teeth and hacked off its head.

Felix went and stood beside Sophie at the sink and peered at her closely, putting on a look of grave concern.

'You seem down in the doldrums, *contessa*. What is it — crossed in love?'

And he chuckled.

She studied his long, laughing face and merrily malicious eye. When he laughed he slitted his eyes and the pointed, pink, wet tip of his tongue came flicking out.

'Will the *principessa* be joining us?' she asked.

He shrugged.

'*Quella povera ragazza!*' he said, and shook his head and heaved a heavy sigh. 'She sleeps.'

'Yes,' Sophie said. 'I know.'

It took him a moment. He laughed, and wagged a finger at her playfully.

'*Ah, crudle!*' he trilled.

He went and stood in the back doorway and contemplated happily the sunlit yard, a hand inserted in the side pocket of his tight jacket and his narrow back twisted. A robin alighted at his feet.

'Oh!' Alice stood up quickly from the table. 'I was supposed to bring her a drink of water.'

She went hurriedly to the sink and rinsed a smeared glass and filled it under the tap. Felix produced a key from the pocket of his jacket and held it negligently aloft.

'You will need this,' he said. Sophie stared in scorn and he shrugged. 'A man must protect what is his,' he said, smirking.

Alice took the key and put it in the pocket of her dress and went out, holding the glass carefully in both hands and watching the water sway under its shining, tin-bright, tense meniscus, her grave little face inclined.

Without warning Hatch and Pound leaped up from the table, like a pair of leaping fish, and Hatch in an amazing rage went at the fat boy with fists flailing. Pound stood suspended like a punchbag, with a mild expression, almost diffident, frowning in a kind of puzzlement as the punches sank in. Hatch leaned against him with his head down, hitting and hitting, as if he were trying to fight his way into Pound's fat chest. The others looked on, mesmerised, until Croke struggled up and grasped Hatch by his skinny shoulders and lifted him into the air, where the boy, incoherently in tears, squirmed and swore, thrashing his arms and legs like a capsized beetle. Croke set him on his feet with a thump and the boy sat down and gathered himself into a huddle, biting his knuckles and furiously sobbing.

'I only said,' Pound said dully, 'I only said . . .'

Alice came back and sat down and folded her hands in her lap. Felix lifted an eyebrow at her.

'How is the patient?' he asked.

Alice did not look at him.

'She says she only wants to rest,' she said and pursed her lips.

Felix came and stood above her, a hand outstretched.

'The key?'

Alice looked sideways at his hand and considered.

'She has it,' she said and smiled a little smile of triumph and for a second she looked like a tiny wizened old woman.

Sophie laughed.

Felix hesitated, then shrugged and walked to the middle of the floor and stood with his feet together and his elbows pressed to his sides, smiling about him and bobbing gently on his toes, like a swimmer effortlessly treading water, borne up in his element. *'Ah, Mélisande, Mélisande!'* he sang softly in thin falsetto, turning heavenwards his stricken eyes. Then he cut a sudden caper, tip and toe, rolling his eyes and waggling his hands limply from the wrists.

The latch of the back door rattled and knuckles tentatively rapped.

Felix, crooning wordlessly and holding himself at breast and back in a tango-dancer's embrace, shimmied to the door and flung it wide. Light from the yard entered and along with it the smell of sun-warmed straw and hen droppings. Soft flurry of wings. A little breeze. The blue day shimmers.

A red-haired, buck-toothed boy in wellingtons stood on the step.

'Aha!' cried Felix, 'there you are! How fares *le bateau ivre*? Gone down, I trust, women and children in the boats, flag still flying and the captain saluting from the poop, all that?'

The boy squinted at him warily and said:

'The skipper says to say the tide will be up before long and youse are to be ready.'

Felix turned back to the room and opened wide his arms.

'Do you hear, gentles?' he said. 'The waters are rising.'

Sophie was winding the film in her camera.

'Are you not coming with us?' she asked.

But Felix only smiled.

*

Easing open the wooden gate Sergeant Toner paused a moment before tackling the steep path up to the house. He lifted his cap and scratched his head with middle and little finger and reset his cap at a sharper angle. The light had thickened to a hot haze over the fields. Housemartins skimmed here and there in the radiant air above him, shooting in swift loops in and out of their nests under the eaves. The Sergeant, a large, freckled, mild man, moved in his policeman's deliberate way, thoughtfully, with a sober and abstracted air. He climbed the steps to the porch and knocked loudly on the door and waited, and knocked again, but no one answered, and cupping his hands around his eyes he bent and peered through the ruby panels of the door but could see nothing except the claret-coloured shapes of hall table and umbrella stand and the tensed and somehow significantly unpeopled stairs. He descended the steps and stood with hands on hips and head thrown back and peered up frowningly at the upstairs windows. Behind sky-reflecting glass nothing moved. He turned and put his hands behind his back and with fist clasped in palm walked slowly around by the side of the house. In the yard a high-stepping hen stopped and looked at him sharply and the dog under the wheelbarrow growled but did not rise, thumping its tail half-heartedly in the dust. The back door was open; the kitchen was deserted. The Sergeant leaned in and rapped on the door with his knuckles and called out: 'Shop!' but no answer came except a tiny, ringing echo, like a stifled titter, of his own big voice. He stepped inside and stood a moment listening and then walked forward on creaking soles and pulled out a chair and sat down, removing his cap and setting it on the table beside his elbow, where the shiny dark-blue peak reflected in elongated form a squat milk-jug. He sighed. On the stove a big pot was making muffled eructations and there was the smell of chicken soup.

A shimmering blade of sunlight stood broken on the rim of the sink.

Somewhere in the house someone loudly sneezed.

A very large bumble-bee flew in through the back door and did a staggering circle of the room and settled on the window sill. Sergeant Toner studied it with interest as it throbbed there in its football jersey. He thought how it would feel to be a bee in summertime, drunk on the smell of clover and of gorse, and for a moment his mind reeled in contemplation of the prospect of other worlds.

Licht came hurrying in from the hall and skidded to a stop and stared at the Sergeant and sneezed.

'God bless you!' Sergeant Toner said largely, with broad good humour.

Blinking rapidly and gasping Licht fumbled in his trouser pocket and brought out a greyed handkerchief and stood with his mouth open weakly and his red-rimmed nose tilted back. 'Ah . . . ah . . . ahh,' he said expectantly on a rising scale, but this time nothing happened and amid a general sense of anti-climax he put away his handkerchief. 'Getting a cold,' he said thickly. He looked as if he had been weeping. He lifted the lid of the simmering pot on the stove and peered squintingly through the steam.

The bee with an angry buzzing rose up from the window sill and flew straight out the door and was gone.

'I was just passing by,' the Sergeant said, quite at his ease.

'Oh,' Licht said flatly and nodded, avoiding the other's eye. He sniffed. 'Will you take something?'

The Sergeant considered.

'Glass of water?' he said, without conviction.

Licht centred the big black kettle on the hob; a thread of steam was already rising from the spout. Sergeant Toner watched him as he had watched the bumble-bee, with interest, calmly. Licht's hands were unsteady. He let fall a spoon and tried to catch it and knocked over the tea caddy and spilled the tea. The spoon bounced ringingly on the tiles. The kettle came to the boil.

'I think we're in for a fine spell,' the Sergeant said.

Licht nodded distractedly. He paused with the grumbling kettle in his hand and frowned at the wall in front of him.

'I spend my life making tea,' he said darkly to himself.

Sergeant Toner nodded seriously but made no comment. Licht picked up the spoon from the floor and wiped it on his trousers and spooned the tea into the pot and poured the seething water over the leaves and banged the lid back on the pot, then carried pot and a cracked white mug to the table and set them down unceremoniously beside the Sergeant's hat. Milk, sugar, the same spoon. The Sergeant surveyed the table hopefully.

'A heel of bread would be the thing,' he said, 'if you had it.'

Licht, unseen by the Sergeant, cast his eyes to the ceiling and went to the sideboard and came back with a biscuit tin and opened it and put it on the table with a tinny thump. The fawn smell of biscuit-dust rose up warmly on the air. Sergeant Toner smiled and nodded thanks. Judiciously he poured the tea, raising and lowering the pot with a practised hand, watching with satisfaction the rich, dark flow and enjoying the joggling sound the liquid made filling up the mug. Licht fetched cutlery from a drawer and began to set out places at the table while the Sergeant looked on with placid gaze.

'Visitors?' he said. Licht did not answer. From the dresser he brought soup bowls and dealt them out. The Sergeant idly counted the places, his lips silently moving. 'Do you remember,' he said, 'the time we had the devil-worshippers?' He glanced up enquiringly. His white eyelashes were almost invisible. 'Do you remember that?'

Licht looked at him blankly in bafflement.

'What?' he said. 'No.'

'Your mother, God rest her, was still with us then.'

The Sergeant lifted the brimming mug with care and extended puckered lips to the hot brim and took a cautious slurp. 'Ah,' he said appreciatively, and took another, deeper draught and then put down the mug and turned his attention to the biscuit tin, rising an inch off the chair and peering into the mouth of the tin with lifted brows. 'A bad lot, they were,' he said. 'They used to cut up cats.'

Licht went to the sink, where the line of sunlight, thinned to a rapier now, smote him across the wrists. The sink was still piled with unwashed crockery; he stood and looked helplessly at the grease-caked plates and smeared cutlery.

'Locals, were they?' he said absently.

The Sergeant was biting gingerly on a ginger nut. 'Hmm?'

Licht sighed. 'Were they locals, these people?'

'No, no,' the Sergeant said. 'They used to come over on the boat from the mainland when their feast days or whatever they were were coming up. The solstices, or whatever they're called. They'd start off by making a big circle of stones down on the strand, that's how I'd know they were here. Oh, a bad crowd.'

Licht plunged his hands into the greasy water.

'Did you catch them?' he asked.

Sergeant Toner smiled to himself, drinking his tea.

'We did,' he said. 'We always get our man, out here.'

The Professor came in. Seeing the Sergeant he stopped and stood and all went silent. The Sergeant half rose from his chair in respectful greeting and subsided again.

'I was just telling Mr Licht here about the devil-worshippers,' he said equably.

The Professor stared.

'Devil-worshippers,' he said.

'They killed cats,' Licht said from the sink, and snickered.

'Oh, more than cats,' said the Sergeant, unruffled. 'More than cats.' He lifted the teapot invitingly. 'Will you join me in a cup of this tea, Professor?'

Licht came forward bustlingly and put the lid back on the biscuit tin, ignoring the Sergeant's frown of weak dismay.

'We're a bit busy,' Licht said pointedly. 'I'm making the lunch.'

Sergeant Toner nodded understandingly but made no move to rise.

'For your visitors,' he said. 'That's grand.'

For a moment all three were silent. Licht and the Professor looked off in opposite directions while the Sergeant thoughtfully sipped his tea.

'I seen the ferry out on the Black Bank, all right,' he said. 'Ran aground, did it?' He paused. 'Is that the way they came?' Then, softly: 'Your visitors?'

Licht lifted a streaming plate from the sink and rubbed it vigorously with a dirty cloth.

'The skipper was drunk, apparently,' he said. 'That ferry service is a joke. Someday somebody is going to be drowned.' It sounded a curiously false note; too many words. He rubbed the plate more vigorously still.

The Sergeant nodded, pondering.

'I was talking to him, to the skipper,' he said. 'The eyes were a bit bright, right enough.' He nodded again and then sat still, thinking, the mug lifted halfway to his mouth. 'And where would they be now, tell me,' he said, 'these castaways?'

Licht looked at the Professor and the Professor looked at the floor.

'Oh,' Licht said with a careless gesture, 'they're around the house, getting ready.'

The Sergeant frowned. 'Ready?'

'To leave,' Licht said. 'They're waiting for the tide to come up.'

He could feel his voice getting thick and his eyes prickling. He wished now they had never come, disturbing everything. Blast them all. He thought of Flora.

'Just over for the day, then, were they?' the Sergeant said.

Licht turned away and muttered something under his breath.

'Beg pardon?' Sergeant Toner said pleasantly, cupping a finger behind his ear.

'I said,' Licht said, 'maybe they came to say a black mass.'

A brief chill settled. Sergeant Toner was not a man to be mocked. Licht turned to the sink again, head down and shoulders hunched.

The Professor cleared his throat and frowned. The Sergeant with a musing air inspected a far corner of the ceiling.

'Was there a chap with them,' he said, 'thin chap, reddish sort of hair, foreign, maybe?'

Licht turned from the sink.

'Red hair?' he said. 'No, but—'

'No,' the Professor said heavily, and Licht glanced at him quickly, 'there was no one like that.'

Sergeant Toner nodded, still eyeing the ceiling. From outside came the faint buzz of a tractor at work far off in the fields. Licht dried his hands, not looking at anyone now. The Sergeant made a tube of his fist and confided to it a soft, biscuity belch, then poured himself another cup of tea. The sun had left the window but the room was still drugged with its heat.

'Grand day,' the Sergeant said. 'A real start to the summer.'

The Professor looked on as the Sergeant put two spoonfuls of sugar into his tea, hesitated, added a third, and picked up the mug in both large hands and leaned back comfortably on his quietly complaining chair. 'Did you ever wonder, Professor,' he said, 'why people do the things they do?' The Professor raised his eyebrows and said nothing. 'I see a lot of it,' the Sergeant went on, 'in my line of work.'

The Professor regarded him with a level stare.

'A lot of what?' he said.

'Hmm?' The Sergeant looked up at him smilingly with his head at an enquiring tilt. 'Oh, anything and everything.' He drank the last draught of tea and set down the mug firmly on the table and looked at it, smiling to himself. 'People think we're out of touch out here,' he said. 'That we don't know what's going on in the big world. But I'll tell you now, the fact is we're no fools at all.' He looked up laughing in silence. 'Isn't that so, Mr Licht?'

Licht, at the stove peering into the soup-pot, pretended not to hear.

The Professor turned aside slowly, like a stone statue turning slowly on a pivot. The Sergeant made a show of rousing himself. He slapped himself on the knees and took up his cap and stood up from the table.

'I'll be on my way now,' he said, firmly, as if someone were seeking to detain him. He walked heavily to the back door and paused to set his cap carefully on his large head. Before him the afternoon stood trembling in the yard. 'If you do see that chap,' he said, 'the one I mentioned, tell him I'm on the look-out for him.' He glanced back over his shoulder. 'You know the one I mean?'

The Professor was looking away at nothing. Licht turned from the stove and nodded and did not speak.

'Well,' the Sergeant said, hitching up his belt, 'good day to you both.'

He tipped a finger to the peak of his cap and made his way almost daintily down the back step. They listened to the noise of his boots crossing the yard. The dog growled.

*

Licht halted on the landing and sneezed hugely, bending forward at the waist and spraying his shoes with spit. 'Bugger!' he cried, fumbling for his handkerchief. He waited, peering slackly before him, hankie at the ready, and then sneezed again and shuddered. Perhaps it was Flora's cold he had caught. The thought brought him a crumb of melancholy comfort. Heavy footsteps sounded below him and presently the Professor appeared, rising up in the stairwell dark-browed and brooding, like an effigy, being borne aloft on unseen shoulders. When he saw Licht he stopped with his foot on the top step and they stood confronting each other with a sort of weary animosity. Suddenly Licht understood that something had happened, that something had shifted, that things would never be again as they had been before. He experienced a pang of regret. He had wanted change and escape but this felt more like an end than a beginning.

'Well,' he said, 'what was all that about?'

He could even hear the new note in his voice, that touch of imperiousness and impatience. The Professor turned aside and looked hard out of the window at the dunes and the far sea.

'I think I may have to leave,' he said, in a distant voice, as if in his mind he were already on his way.

'Yes?' Licht said, surprised at himself, at how cold his own voice sounded. The Professor opened his mouth to speak, fumbling the words as if they were coin, but in the end said nothing and shrugged and moved past Licht and went on up the stairs. Licht looked after him as he ascended, like a bundled, flying figure on a painted ceiling, and watched until he was gone from sight, and then listened until his footsteps were no longer to be heard, and even then he lingered, gazing upwards almost wonderingly, imagining the old man rising steadily through higher and still higher reaches of luminous, washed-blue air, and dwindling to a point, and vanishing.

*

Listening at the door of what already he thought of as Flora's room Licht could hear no sound. As the grave. The shadows on the landing seemed to gather about him like other, ghostlier listeners. He tried the doorknob; the tumblers played a sinister phrase on their tiny clavier: locked. He listened again and then tapped a knuckle gently on the wood. He wanted to say her name but did not dare. He knocked again and leaped in fright when at once a muffled voice spoke directly behind the door.

'Who's there?'

He looked about him wildly, thrilled with panic. It was as if he had put his hand into a trap and had been invisibly seized and held.

'It's me,' he said squeakily. 'Licht.' She said nothing. He stood listening to his heart beating itself against the bars of its cage. He felt foolish and at a loss, and inexplicably expectant. 'Are you all right?'

There came a sigh and then a faint, silky slithering; when she spoke, her voice was at the level of his knees; she must be sitting on the floor, or kneeling there, perhaps, with her forehead against the door.

'What do you want?' she said.

He squatted on his heels and lost his balance and had to steady himself. Clearly, yet with a curious, dreamy sense of inconsequence, and not for the first time, he saw his life for what it was. In the end nothing makes sense.

'There was a guard here,' he said.

Briefly he entertained an image of Sergeant Toner marching off down the hill, thumbs hitched in his belt and his big feet splayed, a wind-up, mechanical man with cheery painted cheeks and fixed grin and a huge key slowly rotating between his shoulder-blades.

'A guard?' Flora said dully through the door.

'Yes. A policeman. He was looking for . . . he was looking for someone.'

She said nothing for a long time. He waited and presently she asked him what time it was. He heard her sigh and rise and walk away from the door, her bare feet making a fat, slow little slapping patter on the floorboards, and then the mattress-springs jangled and after that there was stillness again. Shakily he stood up, stiff-kneed and grimacing. He listened for another moment, then sighed and went on down the stairs.

*

Everywhere was silence. She lay still and listened but could hear nothing except the far soft gasping of the sea and the gulls crying and that strange booming in the distance. The day glared with a brassy radiance. She felt shaky; her mind was vague yet she had an impression of openness and clarity, as of light falling into a vast, empty room. She remembered Licht coming to the door; was there another after him or had she dreamed it, the timid little knock, the whisperings, the soft noise of breathing as whoever it was stood out there, listening? Alice, was it, or someone else again? Now there was only this silence and a sort of hollowness everywhere. She had made a journey through a dark place: water, sea-surge and sway, a dull, repeated rhythm, then a reddening, and then the sudden astonishment of light. Sticky-eyed, with a coppery taste in her mouth and her skin smeared, she struggled from the bed and stood trembling, looking about her at nothing she could recognise, the hot key clutched in her damp hand.

Something was starting up, she could sense it. Someone was waiting for her, content to wait, biding his time. She unlocked the door and stepped on to the landing, a blanket clutched about her, and paused a moment to listen again. She heard a step below her on the stairs and drew back, waiting, half in fear and half in fascinated, breathless expectation.

*

Nothing could have prepared me for it. After all these weeks, out of nowhere, as if, as if, I don't know. This morning, not half an hour ago, I, that is Flora and I, that is Flora, when I . . . Easy. Go easy. What happened, after all, except that she began to talk? Yet it has changed everything, has transfigured everything, I don't know how. Let me try to paint the scene, paint it as it was and not as it seemed, in washes of luminous grey on grey. The kitchen, midsummer morning, eight o'clock. Grey is not the word, but a densened whiteness, rather, the sky all over cloud and the light not falling but seeming to seep out of things and no shadows anywhere. Think of the particular thick dulled shine on the cheek of a tin teapot. Breakfast time. Frail smoke of morning in the air and a sort of muffled hum that is not sound but is not silence either. An ordinary day. My mind does not work very well at that early hour; that is to say, it works, all right, but on its own terms, as if it were independent of me, as if in the night it had broken free of its moorings and I had not yet hauled it back to shore. So I am sitting there at the old pine table, in that light, with the breakfast things set out and a mug of strong tea in one hand and a book in the other and my mind rummaging idly through its own thoughts. Licht and the Professor are still abed – they are late risers – and I am, I suppose, enjoying this hour of solitude, if enjoyment is the word for such a neutral state of simple drift. Enter Flora. She was barefoot, with her shoulders hunched as usual and her hands buried deep in the pockets of Licht's old raincoat. She sat down at the table and in dumb show I offered her the teapot and she nodded and I poured her out a mug of tea. The usual. We often meet like this at breakfast time;

we do not speak at all. How eloquent at these times the sounds
that humble things make, the blocky slosh of tea being poured,
the clack and dulled bang of crockery, the sudden silver note of a
spoon striking the rim of a saucer. And then without warning she
began to talk. Oh, I don't know what about, I hardly listened
to the sense of it; something about a dream, or a memory; of
being a child and standing one summer afternoon on a hill road
under a convent wall and looking across the roofs of the town to
the distant sea while a boy who was soft in the head capered and
pulled faces at her. The content was not important – to either of
us, I think. What interested her was the same thing that interested
me, namely . . . namely what? How the present feeds on the past,
or versions of the past. How pieces of lost time surface suddenly
in the murky sea of memory, bright and clear and fantastically
detailed, complete little islands where it seems it might be possible
to live, even if only for a moment. And as she talked I found
myself looking at her and seeing her as if for the first time, not as
a gathering of details, but all of a piece, solid and singular and
amazing. No, not amazing. That is the point. She was simply
there, an incarnation of herself, no longer a nexus of adjectives
but pure and present noun. I noticed the little fine hairs on her
legs, a scarp of dried skin along the edge of her foot, a speck of
sleep in the canthus of her eye. No longer Our Lady of the
Enigmas, but a girl, just a girl. And somehow by being suddenly
herself like this she made the things around her be there too. In
her, and in what she spoke, the world, the little world in which
we sat, found its grounding and was realised. It was as if she had
dropped a condensed drop of colour into the water of the world
and the colour had spread and the outlines of things had sprung
into bright relief. As I sat with my mouth open and listened to
her I felt everyone and everything shiver and shift, falling into
vividest forms, detaching themselves from me and my conception of them and changing themselves instead into what they
were, no longer figment, no longer mystery, no longer a part of
my imagining. And I, was I there amongst them, at last?

II

LET US REGRESS. Imagine the poor old globe grinding to a halt and then with a cosmic creak starting up again but in the opposite direction. Events whizz past in reverse, the little stick figures hurrying backwards, the boat hauling itself off the sandbank with a bump and putting out stern-first to fasten the unzipped sea, the sun calmly sinking in the east. Halt again, and we all fall over a second time and then pick ourselves up, blinking. The fact is, I did find myself outside the gates one grey morning, I did have a brown-paper parcel under my arm. I had imagined this moment so often that now when it had arrived I could hardly believe in it. Everything looked like an elaborate stage-set, plausible but not real. It was early, there was no one about except a schoolboy, with satchel and one drooping sock, who gave me, the freed man, a resentful, murky stare and passed on. A harsh wind was blowing. I hesitated, uncertain which way to turn. It is a desolate spot, this cobbled sweep where the broad gates give on to the road. I suspect it was a site of execution in former times, it has the shuddery, awed air of a place that has known some dreadful dawns. Minor devils surely hang about here, on the look-out for likely lads. I, of course, am already spoken for, by the boss.

I felt, I felt – oh, what did I feel. Well, fearful, for a start, but in an odd, almost girlish way. For the first minute or two I kept my eyes lowered, shy of the big world. It is laughable, I know, but I was terrified someone would see me there, I mean someone from the old life who would recognise me. And then, my horizons had been limited for so long: high walls make the gaze turn inward. For years I had only been able to see beyond the confines of my sequestered world by looking up. I was the boy at the bottom of the well, peering aloft in awe at the daytime stars. In captivity I had got to know the sky in all its moods, the great, stealthy drifts of light, the pales and slow darkenings, the twilight shoals. Out here, though, this morning, all was wide air and flat, glimmering spaces, and the prospect before me looked somehow tilted, and for a moment I had a bilious sense of falling. A lead-grey plume of smoke flew sideways from a tall chimney and a flock of crows wheeled afar in the wind. I turned up the collar of my jacket and set off shakily down the hill, towards the quays.

Sartorially my situation left a lot to be desired; I had, unwisely, as it now turned out, garbed myself for the occasion in the white – by now off-white – linen suit I had been wearing on the day I was apprehended ten years before. It had seemed to me that a ceremonial robing was required, that my outfit should somehow both proclaim my shriven state and mark me out as a pariah, and this was the best I could do. I must have looked as if I had dropped from Mars, an alien trying to pass for human, in my out-of-season suiting, which probably was risibly out of fashion too by now. Also, there was a cutting wind off the river and it was bloody cold.

I have always loved the river, the grand sweep of it, that noble prospect. The tide was high today, the water shouldering along swiftly with a full, pewter shine. I leaned to gaze on the embankment, just breathing the dirty air, and sure enough my racing thoughts began to slow a little. There are certain harsh, knife-coloured mornings in springtime that are more plangently evocative than any leaf-blown autumn day. On the far bank the nine o'clock traffic flowed and stopped, flowed and stopped, the car-roofs darkly gleaming, humped like seals. By the river it is always the eighteenth century; I might have been Vaublin beside the Seine, I could see myself in a cloak and slouch hat, could almost smell the flowers and the excrement of Paris. The city, this dingy little city for which I have such a grim affection, seemed hardly changed. I scanned the skyline, looking for momentous gaps. A few landmarks had been taken away, a few incongruities added, but generally the view looked much as I remembered it. Strange to have been here all this time and yet not here at all. At dead of night I would lie awake in my cell, in that hour when the beast briefly ceased its bellowings, and try to hear the hum of life from beyond the walls; sometimes I would even get up, haggard with longing, and sit with my face pressed to the meshed window of my cell to catch the tiny vibrations in the glass, telling myself it was the noise of the great world I could feel beating there, its whoops and cries and crashes, that whole ragged, hilarious clamour, and not just the faint drumming of the prison generator.

I leaned out over the river wall and dropped my poor parcel of belongings into the oily water and watched it bob away. It was something I had planned to do, another ceremonial gesture; not very original, I suppose, but all the same a small sense of solemnity informed the occasion. The brown-paper wrapping came undone and rode the little waves like a sloughed skin, undulant and wrinkled. Here it is, I said to myself, here is where it really starts: my life. But I was not convinced.

By the window of a boarded-up shop two derelicts were having a confab. One was a tall, emaciated fellow with a woollen cap and matted beard and drooping, tragic eyes. It was he who caught my attention. I thought I remembered him, from former times; could that be, could he still be going about, haunting these streets the same as ever, after all these years? It seemed impossible, yet I felt sure I recognised him. A survivor, just like me! The idea of it was unwarrantedly cheering. His companion, in burst running-shoes and an outsize pair of maroon-coloured trousers, was short and rumpled-looking, with a babyish back to his head. He was doing most of the talking, jabbing a finger in the air and vigorously nodding agreement with himself, while the tall one just stood and stared bleakly into the middle distance, slowly champing his jaws, on the dim memory of his last square meal, probably, pausing now and then to drop in a considered word. Professional men, exchanging news of their world, its ups and downs. I wondered if I might become like them. I pictured myself falling through darker and darker air, tumbling slowly end over end, until the last, ragged net caught me. Down there in that shadowed, elemental state I would learn a new lingo, know all the dodges, be one of that band, one of the lost ones, the escapees. How restful it would be, traipsing the roads all day long, or skulking in rainstained doorways as evening came on, with nothing to think about but hunger and lice and the state of my feet.

While I lingered there, idly watching these two, I became aware that I too in my turn was being watched. On the humpbacked bridge over the river a man was standing, with one hand on the metal rail, a thin, black-haired, shabbily dressed man. This one also I seemed to know, though I could not say how, or from where; he might have been someone I had dreamed about, in a dream long forgotten. His face was lifted at an awkward angle and although his eyes were not directly on me there was no doubt that it was me he was regarding, with peculiar and unwavering interest. He was very still. There was an air about him that was at once sinister and jaunty: I had an impression of hidden laughter. Standing above me there against the whitening sky, nimbed with soiled light and with people passing to and fro behind him, he looked flat and one-sided, like a figure cut out of cardboard. We remained thus for a moment, he scrutinising me with his covert, angled glance and I staring back boldly, ready to challenge him, why, or for what, I could not say. Then he turned away swiftly and slipped into the crowd and was gone.

After this encounter, if that is what it can be called, I found myself going along with a lighter step, almost gaily, despite the bitter wind and the ashen light. It was as if I had been sent a signal, a message of encouragement, from my own kind. All at once the world about me seemed more vivid, more dangerous, shot through with secret laughter: my world, and I in it. This was not what I had expected, this sudden, unlooked-for lightening, this chipper step and brisk straightening of the shoulders. Surely it was not right, surely in common decency the least I could do would be to put my head down and creep away abjectly into some dark hole where the world would not have to look at me. Yet I could not help feeling that somehow something like a blessing had been bestowed on me here, in this moment by the river. Oh, not a real blessing, of course; the paraclete will never extend forgiving wings above my bowed head. No, this was a benison from somewhere else. The angels sing in hell, too, remember, as the prophet K. tells us – and ah, how sweetly they sing!

*

Billy was waiting for me in the Boatman. It is not the kind of place I would have frequented in the old days. A handful of drinkers were at it already despite the early hour, rough-looking, indeterminate types hunched over their pints in the furry grey gloom. The sour stench from the quays outside was mingled with the smells of stale beer and cigarette smoke. At that hour the atmosphere of the place was watchful and faintly piratical; I would not have been surprised to glimpse a peg-leg under a chair, or the flash of a cutlass. Whenever the door opened a whitish cloud of light from the river came in like ectoplasm, hovered a moment and then sank down among the scarred tables and the plastic stools. Billy sat on a bench seat with a glass of beer untouched before him, tense as a pointer, gazing up in rapt attention from under a fallen lock of oiled black hair at the busy television set above the bar. He had been out for six months. He was dressed in a crisp white shirt, with the cuffs buttoned, and very clean jeans and very shiny black shoes with thick leather soles. A fag-end smouldered in one fist, and with the other hand he was kneading pensively the bunched muscles of his upper arm. When he saw me he stubbed out the cigarette hastily and scrambled up. He shook my hand with violent energy, rolling his shoulders and frantically smiling. Behind him on the television screen a cartoon bulldog was holding aloft by the neck a cartoon cat and slapping it back and forth rapidly across the snout with grim gusto.

This, I told myself, this is a mistake.

Billy was blushing. He blushes easily. He went on pumping my hand as though afraid that if he let it go he would have to do something even more awkward and embarrassing. His hand was as hard as stone. He has the body of a boxer, short and broad and packed with muscle. He seems made not of flesh but of some more solid stuff, a sort of magma, pliant and weighty and warm; beside him I feel bloated and cheesy, a big, soft, wallowing hulk. He exuded a faint, plumbeous smell, like the smell of machine oil; there used to be talk, I remembered, of an enthusiasm for motorbikes: perhaps this whiff of hot oil was their ghostly afterburn. He must be, my God, he must be nearly thirty by now, though he looks about eighteen. He still had a trace of that washed-out, tombal pallor that I suppose our kind never lose. His eyes, though, brown as sea-snails, were clear and clean as ever. Billy the butcher, we used to call him; very handy with a flensing knife, our Billy, in his younger days.

We sat down at the table and there was an awful silence, like something tightening and tightening in the air between us. I wondered if I still smelled of prison: something musty and mildewed, with a hint of wet wool and old smoke and cold cocoa. Billy kept shooting his white cuffs and plucking at the knees of his jeans. I pictured the nerves fizzing and popping under his skin like bundles of electric wires. He had a bag between his feet. It was a very small bag, black, solid, and peculiarly dangerous-looking; all Billy's things give off an air of casual menace. When I pointed to it and asked him if he was going somewhere he shook his head. 'Just gear,' he said, mysteriously. Billy always seems on the point of departure. Even in our early days inside, when I was still in shock, searching for the first hand-holds on the ziggurat of my sentence, he had the air of an innocent confidently awaiting imminent release. He would sit on his bunk, braced to leap up, his legs folded under him like a complicated pair of springs, or stand at the cell door beating out tense little rhythms with his fingertips on the bars, as if it had not sunk in even yet that this was real, that they were not going to come pounding down the corridor any minute now, red-faced and apologetic, to tell him it was all a preposterous mistake and slap him on the back and let him go. Ah, Billy. His trial was held on the same day as mine (a perfunctory and dispiriting affair, I'm afraid, much as I expected), which made us natural chums; he was by then already an experienced jailbird, having passed his adolescence in a variety of correctional institutions between riotous and increasingly brief bouts of freedom, and he was a great help to me in there in those first months, poor fledgling jailbird that I was.

The shirt-sleeved barman came over, wiping his reddened paws on a filthy rag. I asked for tea and got a sour look.

'Not drinking?' Billy said, with a sly, sideways grin. He has an unshakeable notion of me as a terrible fellow.

The barman slouched off. Why do barmen wear such awful trousers, I wonder? I hate to generalise, as I have probably remarked already, but they do, it is a thing I have noticed. On the screen before us the incorrigible cat, having suffered another whacking, sat slumped and skew-eyed under a spinning halo of multi-coloured stars.

'Well, Billy,' I said, 'tell me, how do I look? Honestly, now.'

'You look great.'

'No, really.'

He rolled his shoulders again and squinted at me, biting his lip.

'You look like shit,' he said, with a crooked little apologetic smile.

I took a breath.

'Do you know, Billy,' I said, 'the last time I was in a pub, a very long time ago, someone said the same thing to me. Exactly the same thing. Isn't that an amazing coincidence?'

All at once I thought I was going to weep; I felt that tickle in my sinuses and the tears squeezing up into my eyes. I stood up hurriedly, fumbling in my pockets for a hankie and muttering under my breath, terrified of making a spectacle of myself. I could not start blubbing now. I had thought I was finished with all that. Prison is supposed to harden but I'm afraid it softened me. I am like one of those afflicted sinners in a medieval altarpiece, skulking under my own little personalised cloud that rains on me a steady drizzle of grief.

There was a telephone at the far end of the bar. I hurried to it. I had difficulty getting it to work; I was out of practice with such things. The drinkers looked up from their pints and watched me with sardonic interest. 'Them are the wrong coins,' one of them said, and the barman, waiting for the kettle to boil, snickered. It is by such little signs – outmoded width of the trouser-leg, sideburns cut too long or too short, a constant expression of surprise at the price of things – that the old lag betrays his provenance.

My wife answered. She took her time. I was convinced, mistakenly, I'm sure, that she had known it was me and had deliberately waited to pick up the receiver until I was about to hang up. Why do I think such things of her?

'You,' she said.

It was a bad connection, hollow and crackly and overlaid with an oceanic surge and slush, as if great waves were breaking in the distance across the line.

'Yes, me,' I said.

She was silent for so long I thought we had been cut off. I leaned my back against the wall, hearing myself breathe into the clammy hollow of the mouthpiece, and watched Billy where he sat with his legs crossed, lighting another cigarette, self-conscious and ill at ease, glancing about him with studied casualness as if he thought there might be someone watching, waiting to laugh at him. He caught my eye and smiled uneasily and then let his gaze drift, dismantling his smile awkwardly in a series of small, covert readjustments of his facial muscles. He had seemed so natural when we were inside, so sure of himself, in his affably menacing way, padding along the catwalks with feline grace. I am convinced there are people who are born to go to jail. It is not a fashionable notion, I know, but I believe it. And I, am I one of those fated malefactors, I wonder? Was it all determined from the start? How eagerly, quaking like a rickety hound, my poor old conscience leaps for the well-gnawed bone of mitigation.

'You could have told me it was today,' my wife said.

'I would have,' I said, 'but . . .'

'But?'

'But.' Amazing how we had fallen straight away into the old routine, the deadpan patter that used to seem so sophisticated, so worldly, in the days when we had a world in which to perform it. 'I'm sorry,' I said.

I pictured her standing in the hall, a big, dark, serious woman waylaid for a moment in the midst of her day, a day in which until now there had been nothing of me. My wife. What shall I call her this time – Judy? Perhaps she will not need to have a name. I have dragged her deep enough into the mire; let her be decently anonymous.

'I'd like to see you,' I said.

Again she was silent. I listened to the harsh susurrus on the line and thought myself sunk in the deeps of the sea.

'I don't think,' she said slowly then, in a toneless voice, 'I don't think I want you to come here. I don't think I want that.' This time I said nothing. 'I'm sorry,' she said.

'You don't sound sorry.' In fact, she did. 'I need my things,' I said. 'My clothes. My books. I have nothing.' I was feeling aggrieved by now, in a happily sorrowful, self-pitying sort of way.

'I'll send them to you,' she said. 'It's all packed up. I'll post it.'

'You'll post it.'

Silence.

One of the drinkers at the bar tranquilly raised his backside off the stool and farted.

'Very well,' I said. 'I'll stay away.' I waited. 'How are you—?'

'I'm fine,' she said, too quickly, and then paused; I could almost hear her biting her lip. 'I'm all right.'

'What do you mean, all right?'

'I mean I'm all right. How do you think I am?'

Was that a hint of tears in her voice? She does not weep easily, but when she does it is a terrible thing to see. I put a hand over my eyes. I felt weary all of a sudden. Come, I told myself, make an effort, this may be your last shot at what will be the nearest you will ever get to normal life. I still had hopes, you see, that the human world would take me back into its simple and forgiving embrace.

'Can't I see you?' I said plaintively.

She sighed; I imagined her tapping her foot impatiently. She is not unfeeling – far from it – but the spectacle of other people's sufferings always irritates her, she cannot help it.

'Someone was looking for you,' she said.

'What? Who?'

'On the phone. Foreign, by the sound of him. Or pretending to be. He seemed to think something was very funny—'

An angry bleating started up: my money was running out. I gave her the number and hung up and waited. She did not call back. The absence of that ringing still tolls faintly in my memory like a distant mourning bell.

My cup of tea was on the table, with one of those swollen brown bags submerged in it, its horribly limp string dangling suggestively over the rim. The tea was tepid by now. I put in four lumps of sugar and watched them slowly crumble. My sweet tooth: another vice I picked up in the clink.

'Everything all right?' Billy said.

'Oh, tip-top,' I said. 'Tip-top.'

He nodded seriously and took a sip of beer. How calm he is, how incurious! They expect so little from the world, these people. They just stand there quietly, looking at nothing and chewing the cud, until the bone-cart comes for them. Sometimes I think I must belong to a different species. Suddenly he brightened and reached down and unzipped his bag and brought out a bottle of gin and thrust it at me with another awkward dip of his shoulders and another embarrassed smile. A present! He had bought me a present! For a moment I could not speak, and sat, dumb with emotion, clutching the bottle in helpless hands and nodding gravely. I could feel him watching me.

'Is that kind all right?' he said anxiously. Billy does not touch spirits; he is quite the puritan, in his way. 'I got it from my brother-in-law.'

'It's splendid, Billy,' I said thickly. 'Really, splendid.' I was on the verge of tears again. Honestly, what a cry-baby I am.

Things improved after that. Billy became talkative and kept on laughing breathily in the enthusiasm of relief. He told me about his job. It seemed he delivered things, I cannot remember what they were supposed to be, for that brother-in-law, the gin merchant. It was all very vague. He had his own van. What he really wanted to do, though, was get into the army. He did not know if they would take him. He hesitated, sitting on his hands and gnawing the corner of his mouth, and then blurted it out: would I write a reference for him?

'You know,' he said excitedly, 'sort of a character reference.'

I laughed. That was a mistake. He looked away from me and brooded darkly, staring before him with narrowed eyes. There are moments, I confess, when I am a little afraid of him. Not that I think he might injure me – he would not dream of it, I know. I am just aware of a general uneasiness, a creeping sensation along the spine, the kind of thing I would feel walking past the cage of some crouched and simmering, green-eyed, big-shouldered animal. I wonder if others find me frightening in the same way? I can hardly credit it, yet it must be so, I suppose. Do they realise, I wonder, how afraid of them we are, on our side, for all our bruited ferocity, as we watch them sauntering abroad out there in the world, masters of the whip and chair?

A rain-shower clattered briefly against the window. Idly I watched the drinkers at the bar.

'Can they spot us, Billy, would you say?' I said.

He nodded. 'Oh, they can. They'd spot *us*, anyway.' He grinned and made a clockwork motion with his arm, wielding an invisible club. 'Two of a kind, you and me. Sort of a brother-hood, eh?'

A man with an orange face and desperate eyes and a mouth like a trap came on the television and began to tell jokes at breakneck speed, mugging and leering, mad as Mister Punch.

'Yes, Billy,' I said, 'that's right: sort of a brotherhood.'

Wind and smoke and scudding clouds and wan sunlight flickering on the rain-splashed pavements. The river surged, steely and aswarm. Billy strode forward muscularly with his hands stuck in the pockets of his jeans and his bag under his arm, fairly springing along on his stout leather soles, careless of the cold wind. I remembered the two tramps at their colloquy; we must look an odd pair too, Billy all brawn and youthful tension and I scurrying at his heels huddled around myself as if I were running in a sack-race. We passed by junk shops and bargain stores and flyblown windows with the names of solicitors painted on them in tarnished gold lettering. A plastic bag flew high up into the sky, slewing and snapping. These are the things we remember.

Billy's van was a ramshackle contraption with fringes of rust around the mudguards and a deep dent in one wing. In the back seat a spring stuck up at a comical angle through a hole in the upholstery. I could see he was anxious to get away from me, making a great show of looking for his keys and frowning like a man awaited importantly elsewhere. I did not blame him: I find myself creepy company, sometimes. When he bent forward to open the door I looked down at the crown of his head and the little white twirled patch there and without thinking I said:

'Listen, Billy, will you give me a lift somewhere?'

He looked up at me in alarm. 'What? Where?'

'Down south. I have to get a boat in the morning.'

His frown deepened slowly.

'You mean, now?' he said. 'You mean just . . . go?'

'Yes,' I said. 'Just go.'

He turned his troubled eyes to the river. There was his mam to think about, he said, she was expecting him home for his dinner, and he was supposed to see his girl tonight – and the day's deliveries, what about them? I said nothing, only waited. What was I thinking of, trying to hold on to him like that? Was it just that I did not want to travel alone, trapped with my haunted thoughts? Yes, that must have been it, I'm sure: I wanted company, I wanted to rattle along in Billy's banger with the wind whistling in the leaky doors and that spring waggling in the back seat like a broken jack-in-the-box. Loneliness: that, and no more. Sometimes it strikes me what a simple organism I must be, after all, without knowing it.

He gave in in the end. At first he drove hunched over the wheel, frowning worriedly out at the road, but as we got away from the city centre he cheered up. He has, like me, a fondness for the suburbs. What is it about these tidy estates, these little parks and shopping malls, that speaks so eloquently to us? What is still living there that in us is dead? The miniature trees were tenderly in leaf and the little clouds fleeted and the streets shimmered and swayed with pale swoops of sunlight. As we bowled along Billy talked, between long, thoughtful pauses, about his girl. She was, he confided, an apprentice hairdresser. She did not mind about his crimes, he said, even that rape business, regarding them it seemed as no more than the follies of youth. In fact, she rather fancied the idea of being a lifer's girl: Billy was a bit of a celebrity round their way, having cut out the tripes of a fellow on the street one night for making a remark about his sister. He was all for getting married right off, but she had said no, they should wait: when he got into the army they would have a place of their own at the camp and she would open a salon for the camp wives. I listened happily, slumped in my seat like a child at bedtime, as he filled in with loving strokes the colours – olive-drab, eiderdown-pink – of his dream of the future. This is how we used to while away the time inside, spinning each other stories of the life to come. In return now I told him my plans, how I was going to redeem myself through honest labour and all the rest of it; it must have sounded as much of a fairy tale to him as his talk of a rosy future seemed to me. I even showed him my letter of introduction to Professor Kreutznaer, written for me by a kindly and forgiving woman. I was troubled to see that although I had kept it carefully it had already taken on that grubby, greyed, dog-eared look that prison somehow imparts to all important papers; how many such tired documents have I handled – my opinion was much sought after, inside – while young bloods such as Billy sat on the edge of their bunks twisting their hands and watching me with eyes in which anxiety and hopefulness struggled for command. Believe me, you do not know the tenderness of things in there, the strange mingling of violence and sorrow and unshakeable optimism.

'Anna who?' Billy said, squinting at the letter where I held it out for his inspection.

'Behrens,' I said. 'An old friend. Her late father was a very rich man who collected pictures. I borrowed one of them, once.' Billy quietly sniggered. 'They were very understanding about it, I must say. Anna has quite forgiven me. See what she says: *Please give him any help you can as he has lost everything and wants to make a new start.* Isn't that fine of her? I call that very fine, I must say.'

The van rattled and shook, lurching to the left every time Billy pressed the brakes, yet it felt as if we were flying swiftly through the soft, spring air. I love to travel like this, it is one of my secret joys. Any motorised mode of conveyance will do, car, bus, van – black maria, even. It is not the speed or the womby seclusion that works the magic, I think, but the fact of being enclosed on all sides by glass. The windscreen is for me one of the happiest inventions of humankind. Looked at through this moulded curve of light the travelling world outside seems itself made of crystal, a toylike place of scattering leaves and skimming shadows, where trees flash past and buildings rise up suddenly and as suddenly collapse, and staring people loom, standing at a tilt, impossibly tall, like the startled manikins in the shop windows of my childhood. If I were to believe in the possibility of anything other than endless and unremitting torment in store for me after I die – if, say, a power struggle on Mount Olympus were to result in a general amnesty for mortal sinners, including even me – then this is how I see myself travelling into eternity, reclining like this, with my arms folded, in a sort of happy fuddlement, at the warm centre of this whirling, glassy globe.

It must have been Billy's talk of his girl that got me thinking about my wife again. Idly I pictured her there in the hall after I had been cut off, listening to the hum of the dead line and then putting down the receiver and standing with a hand to her face in that sombre way she has when something unexpected happens. This time, however, as she stood there in my musings, I gave her, without really intending it, a companion. He was indistinct at first, just a man-shape hovering at the edge of fancy, but as my imagination – bloodshot, prehensile – took hold of him in fierce scrutiny the current crackled in the electrodes and a shudder ran through him and at once he began to walk and talk, with awful plausibility. Where do they come from, these sudden phantoms that stride unbidden into my unguarded thoughts, pushy and smug and scattering cigarette ash on the carpet, as if they owned the place? Invented in the idle play of the mind, they can suddenly turn treacherous, can rear up in a flash and give a nasty bite to the hand that fashioned them. This one was taking on attributes by the instant. He was tall and lean, with lank fair hair and a square jaw, togged out in tweeds and a checked shirt and scuffed, oxblood brogues. He would have a pipe about him somewhere, and strong, coarse tobacco in a fine, soft pouch. He cultivates an air of faint disdain, behind which lurks a crafty-eyed watchfulness. There is a touch of the rake about him. He drives a sports car and rides a large horse. He is probably a Protestant. And he is fucking my wife.

I had forgotten about the gin but now with trembling hands I fished the bottle out of my jacket pocket hurriedly and got it open. I love that little click when the metal cap gives; it is like the noise of the neck of some small, toothsome creature being snapped. I took a swig and gasped at the chill scald of the liquor on my tongue and an entire world came flooding back, silvery-blue and icily atinkle. I felt immediately drunk, as if that first mouthful had stirred up a sediment left over in me from the gallons of the stuff I used to drink in the old days. Billy glanced at me with a deep frown of disapproval; I know what he is thinking – that a gent like me should not be seen rattling along in a rusty jalopy and slugging from the neck of a gin bottle at ten-thirty in the morning. I would be in spats and a monocle if he had his way.

We were in the country now, lurching down a leafy road, with a preposterously lovely view before us of rolling fields and silver streams and vague, mauve mountains. Not once in all the years I endured inside had it occurred to me to be jealous. Oh, I knew that most likely I had lost my wife, yet I had thought of her all along as somehow safe, chained to the rock of my absence, like one of those mysteriously afflicted, big-eyed Pre-Raphaelite maidens. The idea of her cavorting with some hard-faced horse-man of the kind who in the old days were always hanging around her struck me with the force of a blow to the heart. I sat aghast, hot all over, blushing in pain, and saw the whole thing. They are in a hotel on the market square of some small, nondescript midland town. The bedroom looks out on the square, where his roadster is discreetly parked under blossoming trees. Soft light of the deserted afternoon falls from the high window. She looks about her in faint surprise and a kind of amusement at the bed, the bureau, the worn rug on the floor: so, she thinks, what had seemed like accident was really something willed, after all, and here she is, on this blank Tuesday, in this anonymous room in a strange town miles away from her life. He stands awkwardly, not looking at her, a little nervous now despite all his easy talk on the way here, and takes things from his pockets and lines them up neatly on the bedside table: change, keys, that thing he uses to scrape the ash out of his pipe. The back of his neck is inflamed. The sight of that childish patch of pink makes something thicken in her throat. He turns to her, talking to cover his awkwardness, and stops and stares at her helplessly. She hears him swallow. They stand a moment, poised, listening to themselves, to that swelling inner buzz. Then a hand is lifted, a face touched, a breath indrawn. This is what shakes my heart, the thought of this wordless moment of surrender. All that will follow is terrible too – there is no stopping this imagination of mine – but it is here, when his fingers brush her cheek and her mouth softens and her eyes go vague, that my mind snags like a broken nail. Yet I know too there is something in me that wants it to have happened, wants to lean over them with face on fire and feed in sorrow on their embraces and drink deep their cries. What awful need is this? Am I the ghost at their banquet, sucking up a little of their life to warm myself? Her phantom lover is more real than I: when I look into that mirror I see no reflection. I am there and not there, flitting in panic this way and that in the torture chamber of my imaginings, poor, parched Nosferatu.

On a straight stretch Billy put his foot down and we fairly flew along. I sat watching the countryside rise up and rush to meet us and I drank more gin and felt faintly sick. She is a troubled sleeper, my wife, yet I always envied what seemed to me the rich drama of her nights, those fretful, laborious struggles through the dark from one shore of light to another. She would drop into sleep abruptly, often in the middle of a sentence, and lie prone on the knotted sheet with her face turned sideways and her mouth open and her limbs twitching, like a long-distance swimmer launching out flounderingly into icy black waters. She used to talk in her sleep too, in dim grumbles and sudden, sharp questionings. Sometimes she would cry out, staring sightlessly into the dark. And I would lie awake on my back beside her, stiff as a drifting spar, numb with that obscure anguish that wells up in me always when I am left alone with myself. Now I wondered if there was someone else who lay by her side at night with a dry throat and swollen heart, listening to her as she slept her restless sleep: not the prancing centaur of my inventing, but some poor solitary mortal just like me, staring sightlessly into the dark, still leaking a little, doing his gradual dying. I think I would have preferred the centaur.

'Stop here, Billy!' I cried. 'Stop here.'

I AM ALWAYS FASCINATED by the way the things that happen happen. I mean the ordinary things, the small occurrences that keep adding themselves on to all that went before in the running total of what I call my life. I do not think of events as discrete and discontinuous; mostly there is just what seems a sort of aimless floating. I am not afloat at all, of course, it only feels like that: really I am in free fall. And I come to earth repeatedly with a bump, though I am surprised every time, sitting in a daze on the hard ground of inevitability, like Tom the cat, leaning on my knuckles with my legs flung wide and stars circling my poor sore head. When Billy stopped the van we sat and listened for a while to the engine ticking and the water gurgling in the radiator, and I was like my wife in that hotel room that I had conjured up for her imaginary tryst, looking about her in subdued astonishment at the fact of being where she was. I had not intended that we should come this way, I had left it to Billy to choose whatever road he wished; yet here we were. Was it another sign, I asked myself, in this momentous day of signs? Billy looked out calmly at the stretch of country road before us and drummed his fingers on the steering wheel.

'Where's this?' he said.

'Home.' I laughed. The word boomed like a foghorn.

'Nice,' Billy said. 'The trees and all.' I marvelled anew at his lack of curiosity. Nothing, it seems, can surprise him. Or am I wrong, as I usually am about people and their ways? For all I know he may be in a ceaseless fever of amazement before the spectacle of this wholly improbable world. He twitches a lot, and sometimes he used to wake up screaming in his bunk at night; but then, we all woke up screaming in the night, sooner or later, so that proves nothing. All the same, I am probably underestimating him; underestimating people is one of my less serious besetting sins. 'Your family still here?' he said. 'Your mam and dad?'

He frowned. I could see him trying to imagine them, big, bossy folk with loud voices clattering down this road astride their horses, as outlandish to him as medieval knights in armour.

'No,' I said. 'All dead, thank God. My wife lives here now.'

I opened the door of the van and swung my legs out and sat for a moment with my head bowed and shoulders sagging and the gin bottle dangling between my knees. When I lifted my eyes I could see the roof of the house beyond the ragged tops of the hedge. I found myself toying with the notion that this was all there was, just a roof put up there to fool me, like something out of the *Arabian Nights*, and that if I stood up quickly enough I would glimpse under the eaves a telltale strip of silky sky and a shining scimitar of moon floating on its back.

'Did I ever tell you, Billy,' I said, still gazing up wearily at those familiar chimney-pots, 'about the many worlds theory?'

Of the few scraps of science I can still recall (talk about another life!), the many worlds theory is my favourite. The universe, it says, is everywhere and at every instant splitting into a myriad versions of itself. On Pluto, say, a particle of putty collides with a lump of lead and another, smaller particle is created in the process and goes shooting off in all directions. Every single one of those possible directions, says the many worlds theory, will produce its own universe, containing its own stars, its own solar system, its own Pluto, its own you and its own me: identical, that is, to all the other myriad universes except for this unique event, this particular particle whizzing down this particular path. In this manifold version of reality chance is an iron law. Chance. Think of it. Oh, it's only numbers, I know, only a cunning wheeze got up to accommodate the infinities and make the equations come out, yet when I contemplate it something stirs in me, some indistinct, fallen thing that I had thought was dead lifts itself up on one smashed wing and gives a pathetic, hopeful cheep. For is it not possible that somewhere in this crystalline multiplicity of worlds, in this infinite, mirrored regression, there is a place where the dead have not died, and I am innocent?

'What do you think of that, Billy?' I said. 'That's the many worlds theory. Isn't that something, now?'

'Weird,' he answered, shaking his head slowly from side to side, humouring me.

Spring is strange. This day looked more like early winter, all metallic glitters and smooth, silver sky. The air was cool and bright and smelled of wet clay. An odd, unsteady sort of cheerfulness was gradually taking hold of me – the gin, I suppose.

'What's the first thing you noticed when you got out, Billy?' I said.

He hardly had to think at all.

'The quiet,' he said. 'People not shouting all the time.'

The quiet, yes. And the breadth of things, the far vistas on every side and the sense of farther and still farther spaces beyond. It made me giddy to think of it.

I got myself up at last, feet squelching in the boggy verge, and walked a little way along the road. I had nothing particular in mind. I had no intention as yet of going near the house – the gate was in the other direction – for in my heart I knew my wife was right, that I should stay away. All the same, now that I was here, by accident, I could not resist looking over the old place one more time, trying my feet in the old footprints, as it were, to see if they still fitted. Yet I could not feel the way one is supposed to feel amid the suddenly rediscovered surroundings of one's past, all swoony and tearful, in a transport of ecstatic remembrance, clasping it all to one's breast with a stifled cry and a sudden, sweet ache in the heart, that kind of thing. No; what I felt was a sort of glazed numbness, as if I were suspended in some thin, transparent stuff, like one of those eggs my mother used to preserve in waterglass when I was a child. This is what happens to you in prison, you lose your past, it is confiscated from you, along with your bootlaces and your belt, when you enter through that strait gate. It was all still here, of course, the ancient, enduring world, suave and detailed, standing years-deep in its own silence, only beyond my touching, as if shut away behind glass. There were even certain trees I seemed to recognise; I would not have been surprised if they had come alive and spoken to me, lifting their drooping limbs and sighing, as in a children's storybook. At that moment, as though indeed this were the enchanted forest, there materialised before me on the road, like a wood-sprite, a little old brown man in big hobnailed boots and a cap, carrying, of all things, a sickle. He had long arms and a bent back and bandy legs, and progressed with a rolling gait, as if he were bowling himself along like a hoop. As we approached each other he watched me keenly, with a crafty, sidewise, leering look. When we had drawn level he touched a finger to his cap and croaked an incomprehensible greeting, peering up at me out of clouded, half-blind eyes. I stopped. He took in my white suit with a mixture of misgiving and scornful amusement; he probably thought I was someone of consequence.

'Grand day,' I said, in a loud voice hollow with false heartiness.

'But hardy, though,' he answered smartly and looked pleased with himself, as if he had caught me out in some small, deceitful stratagem.

'Yes,' I said, abashed, 'hardy indeed.'

He stood bowed before me, bobbing gently from the waist as if his spine were fitted with some sort of spring attachment at its base. The sickle dangled at the end of his long arm like a prosthesis. We were silent briefly. I considered the sky while he studied the roadway at my feet. I was never one for exchanging banter with the peasantry, yet I was loth to pass on, I do not know why. Perhaps I took him for another of this day's mysterious messengers.

'And are you from these parts yourself, sir?' he said, in that wheedling tone they reserve for tourists and well-heeled strangers in general.

For answer I made a broad, evasive gesture.

'Do you know that house?' I asked, pointing over the hedge.

He passed a hard brown hand over his jaw, making a sandpapery noise, and gave me a quick, sly look. His eyes were like shards from some large, broken, antique thing, a funerary jar, perhaps.

'I do,' he said. 'I know it well.'

Then he launched into a long rigmarole about my family and its history. I listened in awed astonishment as if to a tale of the old gods. It was all invention, of course; even the few facts he had were upside-down or twisted out of shape. 'I knew the young master, too,' he said. (*The young master?*) 'I seen him one day kill a rabbit. Broke its neck: like that. A pet thing, it was. Took it up in his hands and—' he made a crunching noise out of the side of his mouth '—kilt it. He was only a lad at the time, mind, a curly-headed little fellow you wouldn't think would say boo to a goose. Oh, a nice knave. I wasn't a bit surprised when I heard about what he done.'

What was this nonsense? I had never wrung the neck of any rabbit. I was the most innocuous of children, a poor, shivering mite afraid of its own shadow. Why had he invented this grotesque version of me? I felt confusion and a sort of angry shame, as if I had been jostled aside in the street by some ludicrously implausible imposter claiming to be me. The old man was squinting up at me with a slackmouthed grin, a solitary, long yellow tooth dangling from his upper gums. 'I suppose you're looking for him too, are you?' he said.

A cold hand clutched my heart.

'Why?' I said. 'Who else was looking for him?'

His grin turned slyly knowing. 'Ah,' he said, 'there's always fellows like that going around, after people.'

He winked and touched a finger to his cap again, with the smug, self-satisfied air of a man who has properly settled someone's hash, and bowled himself off on his way. I looked after him but saw myself, a big, ragged, ravaged person, flabby as a porpoise, standing there in distress on the windy road, dangling from an invisible gibbet in my incongruous white suit, arms limp, with my mouth open and my bell-bottoms flapping and the neck of the gin bottle sticking out of my pocket. I do not know why I was so upset. There came over me then that sense of dislocation I experience with increasing frequency these days, and which frightens me. It is as if mind and body had pulled loose from each other, or as if the absolute, essential *I* had shrunk to the size of a dot, leaving the rest of me hanging in enormous suspension, massive and yet weightless, like a sawn tree before it topples. I wonder if it is incipient epilepsy, or some other insinuating cerebral malady? But I do not think the effect is physical. Perhaps this is how I shall go mad in the end, perhaps I shall just fly apart like this finally and be lost to myself forever. The attack, if that is not too strong a word for it, the attack passed, as it always does, with a dropping sensation, a sort of general lurch, as if I had been struck a great, soft, padded punch and somehow had fallen out of myself even as I stood there, clenched in fright. I looked about warily, blinking; I might have just landed from somewhere entirely different. Everything was in its place, the roof beyond the hedge and the old man hobbling away and the back of Billy's seal-dark head motionless in the car, as though nothing had happened, as though that fissure had not opened up in the deceptively smooth surface of things. But I know that look of innocence the world puts on; I know it for what it is.

I found a gap in the hedge and pulled myself through it, my shoes sinking to the brim in startlingly cold mud. Twigs slapped my face and thorns clutched at my coat. I had forgotten what the countryside is like, the blank-faced, stolid malevolence of bush and briar. When I got to the other side I was panting. I had the feeling, as so often, that all this had happened before. The house was there in front of me now, quite solid and substantial after all and firmly tethered to its roof. Yet it seemed changed, seemed smaller and nearer to the road than it should be, and for a panicky moment I wondered if my memory had deceived me and this was not my house at all. (*My* house? Ah.) Mother's rose bushes were still flourishing under the big window at the gable end. They were in bud already. Poor ma, dead and gone and her roses still there, clinging on in their slow, tenacious, secret way. I started across the lawn, the soaked turf giving spongily under my tread. The past was gathering ever more thickly around me, I waded through it numbly like a greased swimmer, waiting to feel the chill and the treacherous undertow. I veered away from the front door – I do not naturally go in at front doors any more – and skirted round by the rose bushes, squinting up at the windows for a sign of life. How frowningly do empty windows look out at the world, full of blank sky and oddly arranged greenery. At the back of the house I skulked about for a while in the clayey dampness of the vegetable garden, feeling like poor Magwitch on the run. A few big stalks of last year's cabbages, knobbed like backbones, leaned this way and that, and there were hens that highstepped worriedly away from me in slow motion, or stood canted over on one leg with their heads inclined, shaking their wattles and uttering mournful croaks of alarm. (What strange, baroque creatures they are, hens; there is something Persian about them, I always feel.) I was not thinking of anything. I was just feeling around blindly, like a doctor feeling for the place that pains. I would have welcomed pain. Dreamily I advanced, admiring the sea-green moss on the door of the disused privy, the lilac tumbling over its rusted tin roof. A breeze swooped down and a thrush whistled its brief, thick song. I paused, light-headed and blinking. At last the luminous air, the bird's song, that particular shade of green, all combined to succeed in transporting me back for a moment to the far, lost past, to some rain-washed, silver-grey morning like this one, forgotten but still somehow felt, and I stood for a moment in inexplicable rapture, my face lifted to the light, and felt a sort of breathlessness, an inward staggering, as if an enormous, airy weight had been dropped into my arms. But it did not last; that tender burden I had been given to hold, whatever it was, evaporated at once, and the rapture faded and I was numb again, as before.

I put my face to the kitchen window and peered inside. I could see little except shadows and my own eyes reflected in the glass, fixed and hungry, like the eyes of a desperate stranger. Crouched there with my breath steaming the pane and the bilious smell of drains in my nostrils, I felt intensely the pressure of things behind me, the garden and the fields and the far woods, like an inquisitive crowd gathering at my back, elbowing for a look. I am never really at ease in the open; I expect always some malignity of earth or air to strike me down or, worse, to whirl me up dizzyingly into the sky. I have always been a little afraid of the sky, so transparent and yet impenetrable, so deceptively harmless-looking in its bland blueness.

The back door was locked. I was turning to go, more relieved I think than anything else, when suddenly, in a sudden swoon of anger, or proprietorial resentment, or something, I don't know what, I turned with an elbow lifted and bashed it against one of the panes of frosted glass in the door. These things are not as easy as the cinema makes them seem: it took me three good goes before I managed it. The glass gave with a muffled whop, like a grunt of laughter, guttural and cruel, and the splinters falling to the floor inside made a sinister little musical sound, a sort of elfin music. I waited, listening. What a connoisseur of silences I have become over the years! This one had astonishment in it, and warm fright, and a naughty child's stifled glee. I took a breath. I was trembling, like a struck cymbal. How darkly thrilling it is to smash a pane of glass and reach through the jagged hole into the huge, cool emptiness of the other side. I pictured my hand pirouetting all alone in there, in that shocked space, doing its little back-to-front *pas de deux* with the key. The door swung open abruptly and I almost fell across the threshold; it was not so much the suddenness that made me totter but the vast surprise of being here. For an instant I saw myself as if lit by lightning, a stark, crouched figure, vivid and yet not entirely real, an emanation of myself, a hologram image, pop-eyed and flickering. Shakily I stepped inside, and recalled, with eerie immediacy, the tweedy and damply warm underarm of a blind man I had helped across a street somewhere, in some forgotten city, years ago.

I shut the door behind me and stood and took another deep breath, like a diver poised on the springboard's thrumming tip. The furniture hung about pretending not to look at me. Stillness lay like a dustsheet over everything. There was no one at home, I could sense it. I walked here and there, my footsteps falling without sound. I had a strange sensation in my ears, a sort of fullness, as if I were in a vessel fathoms deep with the weight of the ocean pressing all around me. The objects that I looked at seemed insulated, as if they had been painted with a protective coating of some invisible stuff, cool and thick and smooth as enamel, and when I touched them I could not seem to feel them. I thought of being here, a solemn little boy in a grubby jersey, crop-headed and frowning, with inky fingers and defenceless, translucent pink ears, sitting at this table hunched over my homework on a winter evening and dreaming of the future. Can I really ever have been thus? Can that child be me? Surely somewhere between that blameless past and this grim present something snapped, some break occurred without my noticing it in the line I was paying out behind me as I ran forward, reaching out an eager hand towards all the good things that I thought were waiting for me. Who was it, then, I wonder, that picked up the frayed end and fell nimbly into step behind me, chuckling softly to himself?

I went into the hall. There was the telephone she had delayed so long before answering. The machine squatted tensely on its little table like a shiny black toad, dying to speak, to tell all, to blurt out everything that had been confided to it down the years. Where had everyone gone to? Had they fled at the sound of my voice on the line, had she dropped everything and bundled the child in her arms and run out to the road and driven away with a shriek of tyres? I realised now why it was I could touch nothing, could not feel the texture of things: the house had been emptied of me; I had been exorcised from it. Would she know I had been here? Would she sense the contamination in the air? I closed my eyes and was assailed anew by that feeling of both being and not being, of having drifted loose from myself. I have always been convinced of the existence somewhere of another me, my more solid self, more weighty and far more serious than I, intent perhaps on great and unimaginable tasks, in another reality, where things are really real; I suppose for him, out there in his one of many worlds, I would be no more than the fancy of a summer's day, a shimmer at the edge of vision, something half-glimpsed, like the shadow of a cloud, or a gust of wind, or the hover and sudden flit of a dragonfly over reeded, sun-white shallows. And now as I stood in the midst of my own absence, in the birthplace that had rid itself of me utterly, I murmured a little prayer, and said, Oh, if you are really there, bright brother, in your more real reality, think of me, turn all your stern attentions on me, even for an instant, and make *me* real, too.

(Of course, at times I think of that other self not as my better half but my worse; if he is the bad one, the evil, lost twin, what does that make me? That is an avenue down which I do not care to venture.)

I climbed the stairs. I felt oddly, shakily buoyant, as if there were springs attached to the soles of my shoes and I must keep treading down heavily to prevent them from bouncing me over the banisters. On the first landing I stopped and turned from side to side, poor baffled minotaur, my head swinging ponderously on its thick tendons, a bullish weight, my humid, blood-dark glower groping stubbornly for something, for some smallest trace of my past selves lurking here, like the hidden faces in a comic-book puzzle. As a child I loved to be alone in the house; it was like being held loosely in the friendly clutches of a preoccupied, mute and melancholy giant. Something now had happened to the light, some sort of gloom had fallen. It was not raining. Perhaps it was fog; in these parts fog has a way of settling without warning and as quickly lifting again. At any rate I recall a clammy and crepuscular glow. I walked down the corridor. It was like walking in a dream, a sort of slow stumbling, weightless and yet encumbered. At the end of the corridor there was an arched window with a claret-coloured pane that had always made me think of cold churches and the word *litany*. The door to one of the bedrooms was ajar; I imagined someone standing behind it, breathless and listening, just like me. I hesitated, and then with one finger pushed the door open and stepped in sideways and stood listening in the softly thudding silence. The room was empty, a large, high, white chamber with a vaulted ceiling and one big window looking out into the umbrage of tall trees. There was no furniture, there were no pictures on the walls, there was nothing. The floorboards were bare. Whose room had this been? I did not remember it; that elaborate ceiling, for instance, domed and scooped like the inner crown of a priest's biretta: there must have been a false ceiling under it in my time that now had been removed. I looked up into the soft shadows and felt everything fall away from me like water. How cool and calm all was, how still the air. I thought how it would be to live here in this bone-white cell, in all this emptiness, watching the days ascend and fall again to darkness, hearing faintly the wind blow, seeing the light edge its way across the floor and die. And then to float away, to be gone, like dust, dispersed into the vast air. Not to be. Not to be at all. Deep down, deep beyond dreaming, have I ever desired anything other than that consummation? Sometimes I think that satyr, what's-his-name, was right: better not to have been born, and once born to have done with the whole business as quick as you can.

A bird like a black bolt came flying straight out of the trees and dashed itself with a bang against the window-pane.

Something jogged my memory then, the bird, perhaps, or the look of those trees, or that strange, misty light in the glass: once, when I was sick, they had moved me here from my own room, I cannot think why – for the view, maybe, or the elevation, I don't know. I saw again the bed at the window, the tall, fluted half-columns of the curtains rising above me, the tops of the autumnal trees outside, and the child that I was then, lying quietly with bandaged throat, grey-browed and wan, my hands resting on the turned down sheet, like a miniature warrior on his tomb. How strangely pleasurable were the illnesses of those days. Afloat there in febrile languor, with aching eyes and leaden limbs and the blood booming in my ears, I used to dream myself into sky-bound worlds where metallic birds soared aloft on shining loops of wire and great clouded glass shapes sailed ringingly through the cool, pellucid air. Perhaps this is how children die; perhaps still pining somehow for that oblivion out of which they have so lately come they just forget themselves and quietly float away.

A faint reflection moved on the glass before me and I turned to find my son standing in the doorway, watching me with a placid and enquiring smile. I thought, *I met Death upon the road.* I sat down on the window-sill. I felt feeble suddenly.

'Van!' I said and laughed breathlessly. 'How you've grown!'

Did he know me, I wonder? He must be seventeen now, or eighteen – in my confusion I could not remember his birthday, or even what month it falls in. I had not seen him for ten years. Would it upset him to come upon me suddenly here like this? Who knows what upsets him. Maybe nothing does, maybe he is perfectly at peace, locked away inside himself. I picture a far, white country, everything blurred and flat under a bleached sky, and, off on the horizon, a bird, perhaps, tiny as a toy in all that distance, flying steadily away. But how huge he was! – I could do nothing at first except sit leaning forward with my hands on my knees, gaping at him. He was a good half head taller than I, with a barrel chest and enormous shoulders and a great, broad brow, incongruously noble, like that of a prehistoric stone statue standing at an angle on a hillside above the shore of some remote, forgotten island. The blond curls that I remembered had grown thick and had turned a rusty shade of red; that is from me. He had his mother's dark colouring, though, and her dark, solemn eyes. His gaze, even at its steadiest, kept pulling away distractedly to one side, which created a curious, flickering effect, as if within that giant frame a smaller, frailer version of him, the one that I remembered, were minutely atremble. In my imagination I got up out of myself, like a swimmer clambering out of water, and took a staggering step towards him, my arms outstretched, and pressed him to my breast and sobbed. Poor boy, my poor boy. This is awful. In reality I am still sitting on the window-sill, with my hands with their whitened knuckles clamped on my knees, looking up at him and inanely, helplessly smiling; I never was one for embraces. He made a noise deep in his throat that might have been a chuckle and walked forward with a sort of teetering and unexpectedly light, almost dancing step, and peered at the stunned blackbird perched outside on the sill, glazed and motionless and all puffed up around its puzzlement and pain. It kept heaving shuddery little sighs and slowly blinking. There was blood on its beak. What a shock the poor thing must have had when what looked like shining air turned suddenly to solid glass and the world snapped shut. Is that how it is for my boy all the time, a sort of helpless blundering against darkly gleaming, impenetrable surfaces? He pointed to the bird and glanced at me almost shyly and did that chuckle again. He had a musty, faintly sweet smell that made me think of wheelchairs and those old-fashioned, cloth-padded wooden crutches. He was always fascinated by birds. I remembered, years ago, when he was a child, walking with him one blustery autumn day through the grounds of a great house we had paid a shilling to see. There was a peacock somewhere, we could hear its uncanny, desolate cry above the box hedges and the ornamental lawns. Van was beside himself and kept running agitatedly back and forth with his head lifted in that peculiar, angled way that he had when he was excited, looking to see what could be making such extravagant sounds. But we never did find the peacock, and now the day came back to me weighted with that little absence, that missed, marvellous bird, and I felt the pang of it, distant and piercing, like the bird's cry itself.

'Are you all right?' I said to him. That curious, dense light was in the trees and pressing like gauze against the windowpanes. 'Are you happy?'

What else could I say? His only response was a puzzled, fleeting frown, as if what he had heard was not my voice but only a familiar and yet as always incomprehensible, distant noise, another of the squeaks and chirrups thronging the air of his white world. I have never been able to rid myself of the notion that his condition was my fault, that even before he was born I damaged him somehow with my expectations, that my high hopes made him hang back inside himself until it was too late for him to come out properly and be one with the rest of us. And no matter what I may tell myself, I did have hopes. Of what? Of being saved through him, as if the son by his mere existence might absorb and absolve the sins of the father? Even that grandiloquent name I insisted on hanging around his neck – Vanderveld! for God's sake, after my mother's people – even that was a weight that must have helped to drag him down. When he was still an infant I used to picture us someday in the far future strolling together down a dappled street in the south somewhere, he a grown man and I still miraculously youthful, both of us in white, my hand lightly on his shoulder and him smiling: father and son. But while I had my face turned away, dreaming of that or some other, equally fatuous idyll, the Erl King got him.

Suddenly, as if nothing at all had happened, the blackbird with a sort of clockwork jerk rose up and flexed its wings and flew off swiftly into the cottony white light. Van made a little disappointed mewling noise and pressed his face to the glass, craning to see the last of the bird, and for a second, as he stood with his face turned like that, I saw my mother in him. Dear Jesus, all my ghosts are gathering here.

Things are sort of smeared and splintery after that, as if seen through an iridescent haze of tears. I walked here and there about the house, with Van going along softly behind me with that dancer's dainty tread. I poked about in bedrooms and even looked through drawers and cupboards, but it was no good, I could make no impression. Everything gave before me like smoke. What was I looking for, anyway? Myself still, the dried spoor of my tracks? Not to be found here. I gathered a few bits of clothes together and took down from the top of a wardrobe an old cardboard suitcase to put them in. The clasps snapped up with a noise like pistol shots and I opened the lid and caught a faint smell of something that I almost recognised, some herb or fragrant wood, a pallid sigh out of the past. When I looked over my shoulder Van was gone, leaving no more than a fading shimmer on the air. I saw myself, kneeling on the floor with the case open before me, like a ravisher hunched over his splayed victim, and I stuffed in the last of my shirts and shut the lid and rose and hurried off down the stairs. In the kitchen the back door with its broken pane still stood open; it had a somehow insolent, insinuating look to it, like that of a tough lounging with his elbow against the wall and watching me with amusement and scorn. I went out skulkingly, clutching my suitcase and flushed with an inexplicable shame. I shall never, not ever again, go back there. It is lost to me; all lost. As I emerged from the gap in the hedge I felt myself stepping out of something, as if I had left a part of my life behind me, snagged on the briars like an old coat, and I experienced a spasm of blinding grief; it was so pure, so piercing, that for a moment I mistook it for pleasure; it flooded through me, a scalding serum, and left me feeling almost sanctified, holy sinner.

I was surprised to find Billy still waiting for me. After all I had been through I thought he would be gone, taken by the whirlwind like everything else I seemed to have lost today. Someone was leaning in the window of the van, talking to him, a thin, black-haired man who, seeing me approach, straightened up at once and legged it off around the bend in the road, stepping along hurriedly in a peculiarly comic and somehow ribald way, one arm swinging and the other hand inserted in his jacket pocket and the cuffs of his trousers flapping.

The air in the van was thick with cigarette smoke.

'Who was that?' I said.

Billy shrugged and did not look at me. 'Some fellow,' he said. He threw his fag-end out of the window and started up the engine and we lurched on our way. When we drove around the bend there was no sign of the black-haired man.

'See the family?' Billy asked.

'I told you,' I said, 'I have no family. I had a son once, but he died.'

I THINK OF THAT TRIP SOUTH as a sort of epic journey and I an Odysseus, homeless now, setting out once more, a last time, from Ithaca. The farther we travelled the lighter I felt, the more insubstantial, as if I were steadily throwing out bits of ballast as we went along. The van kept breaking down, and Billy, shaking his head in rueful amusement, would get out and hammer at something under the bonnet while I leaned across and pumped the pedals at his shouted command. It was strange, sitting there in the sudden quiet in the middle of nowhere. The countryside around wore a look of surprise and tight-lipped disapprobation, as if by these unexpected stops we were flouting some general rule of decorum; deep silence stood over the fields and the trees stirred restlessly, rustling their silks in the soft, varnished air. This lovely world, and we the only blot on the landscape. We, or just me? Sometimes I think I can feel the world recoiling from me, as if from the touch of some uncanny, cold and sticky thing. I recall one day when I was a child walking with my mother into a hotel in town, one of those shabby, grand places that are gone now, and halting on the threshold of the lounge as all the people there in the midst of their afternoon tea fell silent suddenly. It was only a coincidence, of course, it just happened that everyone had stopped talking at the same moment, but I was convinced it was because of me this dreadful hush had fallen, that somehow I had infected the air and struck the people dumb, and I stood there hot with shame and terror as stout matrons paused with teapots lifted and rheumy old men looked about them in startlement and blinked, until the next moment the whole thing calmly started up again, and my mother took my hand and gave me an impatient shake, and I trailed dully after her, stumbling in all that noise and light.

An early dusk was falling when we got to Coldharbour, a humped little town clinging to a rocky foreland facing the Atlantic. The houses shone whitely in the failing light and smoke swirled up from chimney-pots, mussel-blue against the paler blue of evening, and beyond the harbour wall the thick sea heaved like a jumble of big, empty iron boxes bobbing and jostling. I seemed to hear melodeon music and smell kippers being smoked. Billy parked outside a large pub that looked like a ranch and we went in for a drink. We sat before a turf fire in a low room with fake rafters and smoked yellow walls and listened to the wireless muttering to itself. Horse-brasses, plastic ivy, an astonished, stuffed fish in a glass case. We were the only customers. The publican was a big, slow man; he stood behind the bar ruminatively polishing a pint glass, frowning vacantly as if he were trying in vain to remember something very important. What did he make of us, I wonder? He seemed a decent sort. (Mind you, there are probably times when even I seem a decent sort.) His daughter, a skinny little thing with a pinched face and bitten fingernails and his eyes, came down from upstairs, still in her green school uniform, and said he was to help her with her sums, her mammy had said so. While he muttered over her jotter, a fat tongue-tip stuck in the corner of his mouth, she leaned against the bar and hummed a tune whiningly and made a great show of not looking in our direction. He showed her the solved sums and spoke to her softly, teasing her, and she kept saying: 'Oh, da!' and sighing, throwing up her eyes and making an El Greco face. We crouched over our grog, Billy and I, and watched them covertly, our noses pressed to the briefly lit window of all we had forfeited, and Billy, prompted I suppose by something in the example of this little familial scene, suddenly launched into a halting confession, keeping his head down and speaking in a stumbling monotone. He had no girl, he said. He had made it all up, the hairdressing salon, the wedding plans, everything. There was no job, either, no iffy brother-in-law in the delivery business; he had been on the dole since he got out. Even the stuff about his mam was an invention: she had not been at home keeping his dinner hot for him, she was in the hospital, dying of a rotted liver. And now his parole officer would be after him for leaving the city without telling him.

We were silent for a long time, as if listening to the reverberations after an enormous crash, and then I heard myself in a flat voice say:

'Where did you get the gin?'

Hardly what you would call an adequate response, I know, but it was an awkward moment. Billy shrugged.

'Robbed,' he said.

'Ah. I see.'

I was not surprised by all this – I think in my heart I had known all along that the whole thing was a fantasy – and certainly I did not disapprove: after all, why shouldn't he make up a life for himself? I confess, though, that I was cross, not because he had lied to me but, on the contrary, precisely because he had changed his mind and owned up, damn it. Had I asked for honesty? I had not. In my opinion the truth, so called, is a much overrated quantity. The trouble with it is that it is closed: when you tell the truth, that's the end of it; lies, on the other hand, ramify in all sorts of unexpected directions; complicating things, knotting them up in themselves, thickening the texture of life. Lying makes a dull world more interesting. To lie is to create. Besides, fibs are more fun, and liars, I am convinced, live longer. Yes, yes, I am an enthusiastic advocate of the whopper. But now bloody Billy had developed scruples and what on earth were we to do? From some things there is no going back. We sat and stared solemnly into the fireplace for a while, slumped in another horrible silence, and the publican's daughter went back upstairs and the publican returned to his glasses, and then – oh, my God, it was appalling! – Billy began to cry. In all the years we had spent together in the jug I had never once seen him shed a tear, even on his worst days. And this was not even proper crying, he did not blub or wail, as I would have made sure to do, but just sat there with his head bowed and the water squeezing out of his eyes and his shoulders shaking. The embarrassment of it! – I was thankful the place was deserted. I glanced at the publican but he was carefully looking the other way, his lips pursed, whistling without sound. I cannot imagine what he thought we were or what was happening. I had been sure it was I who would be the one to do the weeping today. I touched Billy's shoulder, less to console, I'm afraid, than as a signal to him that really I thought it was time for him to get a grip on himself, but I snatched away my hand at once, for the feel of that warmly quivering flesh brought back disturbing echoes of old intimacies: behind bars, Eros finds his comforts where he can. I finished my drink and stood up, clearing my throat, and said, still in that toneless voice that I hardly recognised as my own, that I had to go outside for a minute. Billy nodded but did not look up, and I walked away from him almost on tiptoe, a craven Captain Oates, and went through the lavatory and across a yard and came out in a lane at the back of the pub and stood for a little while in the marine darkness with my eyes closed, breathing deep the stink of another dirty little betrayal.

I got my suitcase out of the van and set off in the direction of the harbour. It was black night by now and I had nothing to guide me but the starshine on the cobbles and an occasional, dim streetlamp shivering in the wind. I seemed to be going somewhere. My steps took their own way, down a sloping street and along by the sea wall and on to the pier. A few dim boats reared at anchor out on the jostling water, their mast-ropes tinkling. Have I mentioned My Search For God? Every lifer sooner or later sets out on that quest; I have seen the hardest inmates, fellows who would slit your throat before you could say knife, kneeling meek as toddlers beside their bunks before lights-out, their fingers clasped and eyes shut tight and lips moving in silent communion with the Lord. I am glad to say I managed to hold out for what I consider was a creditably long time. I had never really thought about religion and all that; this world had always been enough of a mystery for me without my needing to invent implausible hereafters (the adjective is redundant, I know). True, I had, and have still, off and on, a hazy sort of half belief in some general force, a supreme malignancy in operation behind the apparent chaos and contingency of the world. There are times, indeed, when I even entertain the notion of a personal deity, a God out of the old books, He that laughs, the *deus ridens*. I remember, when I was a young man and tenderly impressionable, reading in some book of an event in the history of the Xhosa people of the eastern Cape Province. Do you know about the Xhosa? They were a proud and sophisticated race, and great warriors, too, yet unaccountably, for nigh on a hundred years, they had been losing battle after battle against the armies of the white settlers. Again and again they had stormed across the veldt and hurled themselves with perfect confidence against the bullets and the bayonets of these grub-coloured pygmies in their scarlet tunics and were repulsed every time, suffering terrible losses. Then one day in a vision a young girl whose name was Nongqawuse was instructed by the voices of her ancestors to inform her people that they must slaughter all their cattle and give up all forms of agriculture, after which sacrifices the tribe's ancestral dead would return to life, bringing with them great new herds and boundless supplies of corn, to form a ghostly, invincible army that would drive the white man into the sea. The tribal elders conferred and decided that the people must do as they were bidden; even the wise king Sandili (see, I have even remembered the names), who had been sceptical at first, in the end declared himself a believer in the New People. The livestock was slaughtered, the fields were laid waste, and the tribe settled down in confidence to await the day of days, which came and went, of course, without the appearance of a single phantom warrior. Nothing happened. The sun did not stand still in the sky, no great herds came thundering out of the dust, not a grain of corn appeared in the emptied bins. In that year of 1857 alone seventy thousand of the Xhosa died of starvation. Clearly I remember letting the book fall from my hand and staring before me with the mad light of the convert shining for a moment in my eyes and thinking yes, yes, there must be a God, if such things can happen! And I pictured Him, a rascally old boy with a tangled yellow beard and a drinker's nose, reclining on a woolly cloud with his chin on his fist and chuckling to himself as that proud people walked out in solemn ritual into the fields and butchered their cattle and burned their crops. Probably by the time the famine came He had lost interest, had turned his attention somewhere else entirely, leaving the Xhosa to die alone, huddled and speechless, on the parched savannah. In time, of course, I lapsed from my faith in this prankster God, preferring to believe in the Great Nothing instead, which when you think about it is itself a kind of force. However, the moment came one impossible night in prison when I felt so far from everything, so lost in fear and anguish, that I found myself reaching out, like an abandoned baby reaching out its arms beseechingly from the cold cot, for someone or something to comfort me, to save me from these horrors. There was no one there, of course, or not for me, anyway. It was like coming to in the dark on the battlefield amid the cries and the flying cannon-smoke and feeling around for a limb that had been shot off. I had never known a blackness so vast and deep as that which my groping soul encountered that night. Almost as bad as the emptiness, though, was the fact of the need itself, that bleeding stump I could not bring myself to touch. And now as I stood on the pier, whirled about by the night wind, I felt pressing down on me the weight of another vast darkness and another unassuageable need, for what, I could not say precisely. I looked back at the town; how far off it seemed, how distant its little lights, as if I had already embarked and my voyage were under way. It came to me that I had reached the end of something, that this long day drawing to a close was the last of its kind I would know. What next, then? The voices spoke to me out of the wind, the dead voices. I stood above the black, heaving water and imagined how it would be, the blundering leap and then the plunge and the sudden, bulging silence as I sank. And in the morning they would find my suitcase standing on the pier, unique and incongruous, a comic prefiguration of my tombstone. Strange: I never seriously considered doing away with myself, even in prison, where regularly fellows were found strung up by ropes of knotted bedsheets from the waterpipes in their cells. But what did I have to lose now, that I had not lost already, except life itself, and what was that worth, to me? Cowardice, of course, plain funk, that was a stalwart that could be counted on to keep me dragging along, but there are times when even cowardice must and does give way to stronger, irresistible forces. Yet I knew I would not do it; not even for a moment did I think I might. Was it that in a way I was already dead, or was I waiting for some new access of life and hope? Life! Hope! And yet it must have been something like that that kept me going. Unfinished business, a debt not paid – yes, that too, of course, of course, we know all about that. But beyond even that there was something more, I did not know what. I felt that whatever it was – is! – it must be simple but so immense I cannot see it, as immense as air: that secret everyone is in on, except me. When I look back all seems inevitable, as if under everything there really were a secret structure, held immovably in place by an unknown and unknowable force. Every tiniest action I ever took was a grain of sand in the flow of things tapering towards that moment when I let go of myself, when with a great *Tarraa*! I flung open the door of the cage and let the beast come bounding out. Now I am condemned to sit here in my filthy straw and sift through the bones of it all over again. Eternal recurrence! That is what I realised that night, standing in the blackness at the end of the pier above the roiling, seductive sea: there was to be no end of it, for me; my term was just beginning. But what I was sentenced to this time was freedom. Freedom! What a thought! The very word gave me the shivers. Freedom, formless and ungraspable, yes, that was the true nature of my sentence. For ten terrible years I had yearned to be free, I had eaten, slept, drunk the thought of it, lain in my bunk at night, heart racing and eyes popping, panting like a decrepit masturbator towards that fantastic moment when the gates would swing open and I would be released, and now it had arrived and I was appalled at the prospect. I am free, I told myself, but what does it signify? This objectless liberty is a burden to me. Forget the past, then, give up all hope of retrieving my lost selves, just let it go, just let it all fall away? And then be something new, a sticky, staggering thing with myriad-faceted eyes and wet wings, an astonishment standing up in the world, straining drunkenly for flight. Was that it, that I must imagine myself into existence before tackling the harder task of conjuring another? I closed my eyes. My poor brain throbbed. I did not know what to do, whether to go on or go back or just stay here, somehow, forever. Presently I turned and retraced my steps to the town, ploddingly, confused as always, lost, and alone.

*

Statues. I am thinking of statues. I have always found something uncanny about these sudden, frozen figures, the way they stand so still among moving leaves, or off at the end of an avenue, watching something that is not us, that is beyond us, some endless, transfixing spectacle only they can see. Time for them moves as slow as mountains. I am remembering, for instance, that great photographer old Père Atget's matutinal studies at Versailles and St Cloud of rainstained Venuses and laughing fauns, Vertumnus removing his winter mask, that rapt Diana with her bow starting out of the shrubbery into the sunlight beside the motionless pond; how vivid and rounded his lens makes them seem, how immanent with intent, these bleached, impetuous creatures poised as if to leap down from their plinths and stride away, trailing storms of dust behind them. Diderot developed a theory of ethics based on the idea of the statue: if we would be good, he said, we must become sculptors of the self. Virtue is not natural to us; we achieve it, if at all, through a kind of artistic striving, cutting and shaping the material of which we are made, the intransigent stone of selfhood, and erecting an idealised effigy of ourselves in our own minds and in the minds of those around us and living as best we can according to its sublime example. I like this notion. There is something grand and tragic in it, and something of essential gaiety, too. Diderot himself had great reverence for statues; he thought of them as living, somehow: strange, solitary beings, exemplary, aloof, closed on themselves and at the same time yearning in their mute and helpless way to step down into our world, to laugh or weep, know happiness and pain, to be mortal, like us. *Such beautiful statues*, he wrote in a letter to his mistress Sophie Volland, *hidden in the remotest spots and distant from one another, statues which call to me, that I seek out or that I encounter, that arrest me and with which I have long conversations* . . . I like to picture him, that cheerful *philosophe*, at St Cloud or Marly or the great park at Sceaux, talking to the cherubs on a carved vase or lecturing a stone Pygmalion on the hegemony of the senses.

What statue of myself did I erect long ago, I wonder? Must have been a gargoyle.

Here's a story. Chap I knew in Spain once, in a previous life, painter, not very good, got a commission to do a portrait of a local bigwig in the village where we were both scraping a living at the time. My pal would go to the old boy's house in the mornings and work on the canvas for an hour or so while it was still cool; he had not much Spanish and anyway in those parts they spoke an incomprehensible dialect, so conversation was at a minimum. For a long time the work did not go well. It was very hard to fix a likeness. The mayor, I think he was the mayor, an ugly old peasant with enormous hands and a simian brow, would sit very stiffly in his best blue suit in a white room staring fixedly before him with a hunted look, as if, said my friend, he were at the oncologist's waiting to hear the worst. Some subjects, my friend explained, simply do not look like themselves; shyness, embarrassment, self-consciousness, something compels them to put on a mask and hide behind it; they will look like their mothers, their siblings, complete strangers, even, but not themselves. With such sitters the painter must coast along, biding his time, waiting for them to relax and forget themselves for long enough to be themselves. The mayor was such a one. He just sat there like a stuffed barbary ape, blank, featureless, folded up in himself. Until one morning my friend arrived and found him transformed; he was no more animated than at other times, but suddenly at last his face was open, the mask cast aside, his character – violent, rapacious, fearful, melancholy – legible in every wrinkle and mole and ill-shaved whisker. Well, the portrait was finished within the hour – and damned good it was, too, according to my friend – yet still the mayor sat there, gazing before him with a pensive and faintly puzzled look. You know of course what had happened, you saw it coming, didn't you: the old man was dead, had died calmly of a stroke a few minutes before the painter arrived. You see, you see what I mean? To thine own self be true, they tell you; well, I allowed myself that luxury just once and look what happened. No, no, give me the mask any day, I'll settle for inauthenticity and bad faith, those things that only corrode the self and leave the world at large unmolested.

I am reading Diderot on actors and acting, too. He knew how much of life is a part that we play. He conceived of living as a form of necessary hypocrisy, each man acting out his part, posing as himself. It is true. What have I ever been but an actor, even if a bad one, too much involved in my role, not detached enough, not sufficiently cold. Yes, yes, it's so. You think me cold? I am not. Harsh, perhaps, uncaring of the proprieties, too apt to make poor jokes, but not cold, no. Quite the opposite, in fact, hot and sweating in my doublet and hose, trying not to see the upturned faces beyond the footlights, the eyes greedy for disaster fixed on me as I stumble among my fellow players, stammering out my implausible lines and corpsing at all the big moments. This is why I have never learned to live properly among others. People find me strange. Well, I find myself strange. I am not convincing, somehow, even to myself. *The man who wishes to move the crowd must be an actor who impersonates himself.* Is that it, is that really it? Have I cracked it? And there I was all that time thinking it was *others* I must imagine into life. Well well. (To act is to be, to rehearse is to become: Felix *dixit*, or someone like him.) This has the feel of a great discovery. I'm sure it must be a delusion.

*

Do you notice how the gull's cry echoes through these pages, sounding its note of hunger and harsh beseeching? It is my emblem; my watermark. Next morning it was everywhere around me, a disembodied keening in the calm, white air. The wind had died and there was a kind of luminous, faint fog. I walked along the pier again, carrying my suitcase, but in daylight now, the scene a developed print of last night's heartsick negative. The boat was a blunt vessel with a rusted chimney and a limp flag dangling in the cordage. When I arrived it was already loaded up with a cargo of tomatoes and potato crisps and bales of toilet paper and mysterious, complicated machine parts, all gleamingly, implausibly new. The skipper, a big-bellied man with a red face, stood in the wheelhouse and yawned. (If I were a visitor from another planet – but then, am I not a visitor from another planet? – I think that of all the earthlings' quirks it is the act of pandiculation that would surprise and fascinate me most, that slow stretch and then the soundless ape-howl, in which they indulge themselves with such languorous relish.) There was a boy also, a nimble, bow-legged fellow with red hair and buck-teeth; he did all the work, scurrying about the deck and cursing violently to himself while Bulkington in the wheelhouse watched him with amusement and a kind of fond contempt, taking a quick nip now and then from a secret bottle stowed under a shelf behind the wheel. I seemed to be the only passenger. As soon as the cargo was loaded we got under way. I always feel a childish surge of excitement when the last mooring rope is cast off and the boat backs away shudderingly from the dock. We swerved into the middle of the harbour and swung about smartly and headed out past the lighthouse into the open sea. I stood in the bow and watched Coldharbour turn into a miniature of itself, complete with smoking chimneys and bristling masts and tiny figures moving on the quayside. I spotted Billy's van, still parked outside the pub. Probably he had slept in it last night, huddled on the back seat with that wobbly spring sticking up and his knees in his chest. I, of course, had passed the hours of darkness in my accustomed fashion, hanging upside down under the tavern eaves wrapped in my leathern wings.

The morning was extraordinarily still under a sky of pure pearl. The coast dwindled behind us; when I looked out from the prow we might have been a thousand leagues from land. The sea stretched away empty save for a white ship far off on the high horizon, unmoving, it seemed, impossibly tall and lit somehow from below, a glimmering, ghostly vessel. I like the sea; I am afraid of it, but all the same I like it, its strangeness, its indifferent thereness; in all that space I can forget for a while who and what I am. A pair of dolphins broke the surface and swam with us, criss-crossing our bows and gambolling in the wash, seeming emblematic of something, and now and then long-necked brown birds appeared out of nowhere, singly, flying low and straight at great speed above the water. The skipper kept to the wheelhouse and the boy sat on the deck with a transistor radio pressed to his ear, dead-eyed and rhythmically twitching. Soon the sky cleared and a delicate wind sprang up and the water turned to splintered sapphire. I lay and drowsed on a pile of tarpaulins, lapped about by sea-sounds and cool zephyrs. I slept briefly and dreamed that I was back in prison and could not understand why the floor of my cell was swaying; then a warder wearing a seaman's cap at a jaunty angle came and told me not to worry, that I would soon be let out, and laughed extravagantly, pointing a finger at me through the bars.

I woke with a start and struggled groggily to my feet, rubbing my eyes. It was as though I had fallen asleep in one world and woken up in another. The air seemed brisker, the sky bluer. The boat fairly skimmed along, tensed in every timber, eager and light, as if at any moment it might take to the air in a great, groaning leap. I felt light-headed; when I looked out to the horizon it seemed it was not the boat but rather the sea itself that was swaying. Despite the early hour I brought out the gin bottle and took a steely swallow straight from the neck and walked to the bow-rail and stood and watched our wake unfurling behind us. Cloud-shadows, whale-blue and swift, skimmed the glittering surface of the sea. Have I said all this already? Suddenly there came to me the memory of a day when I was a boy and I cycled across country to the coast with my friend Horse. My friend; I had not many such, and those that I had did not last long, and nor did Horse. But that day our friendship was still at the tremulous, solemn stage that I sometimes think is all I have ever known of what they seem to mean when they chatter about love. We left our bikes hidden in a ditch and made our way through a little, dense dark wood and came out on the river estuary and found moored in the shallows among the reeds the punt that Horse's father kept there for duck shooting. A keen hunter, Horse's father, I remember him, a big, slow-moving, smooth-faced man, which Horse in his turn must be by now, I imagine. Horse undid the mooring rope and pushed us out of the reeds with a negligent deftness that filled me with envy and made me feel proud to be his pal. How lightly, with hardly a sound, the white punt glided over the water, seeming barely to touch the swiftly running surface. Horse stood above me in the bow and plied the scull, his eye fixed on a far horizon. We saw not a soul; we might have been alone in the world. For a mile or two we went along close to the river bank and then all at once sky and sea opened before us and we crossed a broad reach and came in sight of a long, low, khaki-coloured shore. I can see it, I can see it all, as clear as day, the white punt and that sunlit shoreline and the two of us there, Horse and me. It must have been a place where the river waters met the open sea, or perhaps it was something to do with the currents, or the tide was turning – I do not understand these things – but for a minute we were halted and held motionless on the unmoving water in the midst of a golden calm. The burnished surface of the sea was high and heavy and smooth as metal, and a small, repeated wave gambolled like an otter along the margin of the shore. The sun was hot. Nothing happened. We just stayed there for that minute, poised between sea and sky, suspended somehow as if in air, no, not air, but some other, unearthly element, and it seemed to me I had never known such happiness, and never would again, though happiness is not the word, not the word at all. That is where I would like to live, on some forgotten strip of sandy shore, with my back to the land, facing out into the limitless ocean. That would be freedom, watching in solitude the days pass, marking the seasons, observing the spring tides and the autumn auroras, weathering the summer sun and the storms of winter. Pure existence, pure existence and nothing else.

Now, a grown-up, so-called, I stood there in the bows, for how long I do not know, watching the white waters purling behind us and the little clouds flying overhead, and then all at once I heard that soft, roaring noise coming to us across the water and I turned, startled, and there it was, the island, looming up in front of us, with sheep-strewn hill and tiny trees and the narrow road winding away, as if it had been conjured up that moment out of sea and clouds. We chugged into the deserted harbour past jagged, chocolate-coloured rocks such as the Italian masters liked to set at the backs of their madonnas. Red-headed Pip had put aside his radio and was furiously at work again with ropes and winches while the skipper in the wheelhouse, his bottle empty, plied the wheel with ample and unsteady grapplings. I took another drink of gin and looked about me brightly at the harbour and the hill as they disposed themselves glidingly like well-oiled stage machinery around our smooth advance.

We docked. Everything went quiet suddenly. The skipper came out of the wheelhouse and spat over the side. The boy was already on the pier, winding a rope around a bollard. When I stepped up after him on to dry land the world went on moving under my feet. Hyperborean Apollo, I prayed, make haste to help me! Mr Tighe's van came bumping along the pier and drew to a shuddering halt at the dockside where the boy was unloading the cargo from the deck. How vivid and gay everything seemed to my gin-tinted gaze, the acid-green hill and the opalescent water shimmering under a lemon light. I set off up the hill and presently Mr Tighe in his laden van drew level with me and offered me a lift which I declined, making large gestures of thanks. He nodded in friendly fashion and drove on, the van farting petrol-blue billows of exhaust smoke. Shall we describe him now? I think not. Mr Tighe, and that old dog that comes and goes, and the horse I am supposed to have heard but never saw: holes in the backdrop, through which the bare sky twinkles. When I looked back from the last bend of the road the boat was already under way again, veering out past the jetty like an offer of reprieve being unceremoniously withdrawn. What had I done, coming to this far-flung place? Yet how light I felt, how fleet, as if I were aloft on wings! I went on and soon spotted the house, perched in its solitude under the oak ridge. The hawthorn was in blossom. Here is the little bridge. Wind, shine, clouds, the unwarranted yet irrepressible expectancies of the heart. I am arrived.

I MUST HAVE LOOKED LIKE something out of a Bible story, toiling up that stony track in my soiled suit with my cardboard suitcase in my hand and my collar turned up against the wind. I should have been on my knees, of course, or, better still, barefoot, with staff and falcon, like the penitent pilgrim I was pretending to be. I could still feel the sway of the sea, and of that other sea of gin sloshing around inside me, and the ground kept rearing up under my feet in the most alarming way, like a carpet with the wind under it; I stumbled more than once, making the stones fly and getting grit in my shoes. I could hear myself breathing. I always know I am drunk when I can hear myself breathing; it sounded as if I were carrying a large, fat, winded man on my back. At the gate I paused to gather my wits but that only made my head spin; I set off again sternly, marching up the path to the front door like a wooden man, snorting and muttering, with my head thrown back and swinging my free arm. I rapped the knocker smartly and turned and surveyed the scene before me, chest out and nostrils flared, snuffing up the air.

I had to knock a second and then a third time before Licht came at last. He opened the door a crack and stuck out his little face and peered crossly past my shoulder, the tip of his sharp little nose twitching. I told him my name and he pursed his lips and sniffed.

'Oh, it's you, is it,' he said. I thought he might shut the door on me, but after a moment of sullen indecision he stood aside grudgingly and motioned me in. 'I'm Licht. The Professor said you were coming.'

He sniffed again.

The hallway was high and hung with shadows. I experienced

a mysterious shock of recognition: it was as if I had stepped inside myself, into the shadowed vault of my own skull.

'He's working,' Licht said truculently. 'There's a room ready for you.' That seemed to amuse him.

He shut the door, fussing with the lock. I stood breathing; I could feel a horrible, tipsy leer slipping and sliding uncontrollably about my face. I seemed to be floating in some heavy, sluggish substance, a Dead Sea of the mind. I had a sense of vague, violent hilarity, and there was an inner roll and lurch as if something inside me had come loose and was yawing wildly from side to side. Licht still would not look directly at me but eyed vexedly a patch of the floor between us with his mouth pursed and a hand twitching in his pocket and one leg jigging. Never still, never still. I did not know what to say to him. At bottom I am a shy soul – yes, yes, I am, really. My kind always are. When I hear on the wireless a report of some grimy little atrocity – the bloodstained body discovered in the wood, the pensioner beaten to death in his bed, the mother-in-law dismembered and packed in a trunk and sent off on the night mail to Dundee – I think at once not of the victim, as I know I should, but of the other one, the poor, shivering, dandruffy, whey-faced fellow in his sleeveless pullover and cheap shoes, with his shaking hands and haunted eyes, caught there, frozen in the spotlight, realising with a falling sensation in the pit of his stomach that he will never again have a moment's privacy, never a second he can call his own, that they will poke at him and probe him and ask endless questions and then put him in the dock to be gawped at and then send him for life – life! – to that panopticon where he will not even be able to void his bowels without an audience looking on. This is how you lose yourself, this is how they wrench you out of what you thought you were and hang you up by the hair and invite the world to gather round and point and laugh and take a shy at you for free. And all the time of course you know you deserve it, deserve it all, and more.

'You look awful,' Licht said with satisfaction and grinned uncontrollably and bit his lip. 'Were you seasick?'

'No, no,' I said. 'Just a little, just a little . . . tired.'

I tramped behind him up the stairs. The upper flights grew progressively narrower and our footsteps thudded ringingly on the uncarpeted boards. My room was cramped and low, with peeling wallpaper and a tilted floor. I could see why Licht had been amused. There was a rush-bottomed chair – a relic of St Vincent – and a pine dressing-table and a coffin-sized wardrobe. On the floor beside the bed there was a worn, blue and grey rug. (How many more such cells must I invent?) One of the panes in the little window was broken and someone had mended it by wedging a bit of cardboard in the hole. Pigeons had got in, there were droppings on the sill and down the wall, hardened to a whitish stuff, like coral. The window framed a three-quarters view of indistinct greenery and the corner of a sloped field. I put my suitcase on the bed and looked about me. There was a steady, pulsing hum in my head as if a delicately balanced pinion spinning in there had developed a wobble.

Licht hovered on the threshold with a hand on the doorknob, frowning hard at the wardrobe.

'So,' he said, 'you're another expert, are you?'

'An expert?' I said blearily.

'On art.' His lip curled on the word.

'Oh no,' I said, 'no, not at all.'

'Good,' he said. 'One is enough.'

We stood a moment saying nothing, each thinking his own thoughts. I felt a weight in my jacket pocket and brought out the half-empty gin bottle. We both looked at it dully.

'How is the Professor?' I said.

He glanced at me sharply.

'He's all right,' he said. 'Why?' I had no answer to that. He looked away from me again and nibbled the nail of his little finger. 'So you were in jail,' he said and tittered, and then quickly recomposed his sullen glare. 'What was it like?'

'Like hell,' I said. 'Very warm and crowded.'

He nodded, thinking, still chewing his fingernail. We might have been talking about the weather.

'I wouldn't like that,' he said, 'jail.'

'No,' I said.

He slid a rapid glance across the floor and let it settle somewhere near my feet.

'Bad, was it, yes?'

I said nothing. Still he waited, eyes aglitter with eager malice, hoping for the worst, I suppose, for some tearful cry or terrible, blurted confession. The wind in the chimneys, the gulls, all that: the strangeness of things. The strangeness of being here – of being anywhere.

'When did you get out?' he asked.

'Yesterday,' I said, and thought: Yesterday!

Licht nodded.

'I'll tell Professor Kreutznaer you're here,' he said. 'We have our tea at five o'clock.'

He tarried a moment more, then muttered something under his breath and abruptly withdrew, shutting the door behind him with a soft bang.

I sat down on the side of the bed with my hands on my knees, gazing at the floor between my feet and sighing the while, in a kind of weary and not wholly unpleasant dejection. Thus the prodigal son must have felt – shaky, dazed, a little hollow – as the haunch of veal was wheeled in and the infuriate brother slunk away gnawing his knuckles.

*

Professor Kreutznaer did not fall upon my neck. The first thing that struck me about him was how plausible he appeared, how authentic, at least when looked at from a decent distance; compared to him I seemed to myself a thing of rags and smoke, flapping helplessly this way and that at the mercy of every passing breeze. I had met him once before, many years ago, in a golden world now gone. He had hardly changed at all; I do not imagine he has ever been much different from what he is now. I see receding versions of him – young man, boy, babe in arms – all nestling inside each other, each one smaller than the next and yet all the same, with the same big bloodless head and filmy stare and that same air of standing somehow sideways to the world. He is calm, remote, taciturn, possessed of a faintly shabby imperium; he is, or was, at least, a legend in the world of art, foremost authority on Vaublin, frequent guest at I Tatti in the great days, co-author with the late Keeper of the Queen's Pictures of that controversial monograph on Poussin, consultant for the great galleries of the world and valued adviser to private collectors on however many continents there are. It used to be said that a Thyssen or a Helmut Behrens would not lift a finger in the auction room without first consulting Kreutznaer. Yet when Licht ushered me at last into his presence and left me there, the thing I felt most strongly was the urge to laugh. Yes, laugh, as I want to laugh for instance in the concert hall when the orchestra trundles to a stop and the virtuoso at his piano, hunched like a demented vet before the bared teeth of this enormous black beast of sound, lifts up deliquescent hands and prepares to plunge into the cadenza. I was immediately ashamed of myself, of course, convinced this tickle of raucous glee must be the self-protective reflex of the second-rater before the spectacle of excellence, the guffaw of the half-educated in the presence of the scholar. I thought of a monkey leaping among the palms, pointing and shrieking and hilariously hurling excrement as the famous naturalist in his baggy shorts comes tramping down the jungle track on the heels of his burdened bearers, his nose buried in his field-notes. It has always been thus with me. Even in what I like to think of now as the renaissance period of my life, when my interests were catholic and everything was a matter of perspective, I always worried that I would burst into shrieks of laughter in the face of this or that grand savant and so show myself up for the hopelessly shallow creature that I am. But then sometimes too I comfort myself with the thought that, as someone or other has rightly pointed out, shallowness has no bottom. Is it any wonder I went to the bad?

So there we are in the turret room, with the transparent sky of morning all around us, he seated in his sea-captain's chair and I standing meekly before him, exchanging solemnities with him and trying to keep a straight face while with protruding lower lip he read over yet again my letter of introduction from the administrator of the Behrens Collection. I was still three-quarters drunk, but the hot, brassy taste of gathering sobriety was in my mouth and I could hear in the distance the dull tom-tom beat of an approaching headache. It was like being up before the beak – and I should know, after all. Presently, however, and most unexpectedly, another sensation came over me, a sort of burning flush, which it took me a moment to identify. It was shame. I mean the real thing, the sear, the scald, the pure, fat, fiery stuff itself: shame. Do you know what it is to feel like that, to cringe and writhe inside yourself as if your flesh were on fire? It is not given to every man to know without the shadow of a doubt that he is a scoundrel. (It takes more courage than you think to name yourself as you should be named. You do not know what it costs to bring yourself to that pass, I can tell you.) I wanted to abase myself before him, to cast myself down at his feet with cries and imprecations, drumming my fists and weeping, or wrap my arms around his knees and cry my sins aloud and beg forgiveness. Oh, I was in a transport. In the end, however, I only put my head back and snuffled up a deep breath, like a diver surfacing, and brought out with a certain ceremonial air the fact of our previous meeting, as if it were the broken half of the precious amulet that would identify me as the long-lost son of the palace, despite my rags and sores. He stiffened, I thought, and rolled his soft-boiled eyes at me suspiciously.

'We met?' he said. 'Where was that?'

'At Whitewater,' I said. 'Oh, twenty years ago. We were house-guests there one weekend. We walked together in the gallery, I remember; you spoke of Vaublin.'

Talk about another life! The windows of the great house filled with greenish summer light and the pictures on the walls like high doorways opening on to other, luminously peopled worlds. The Professor wore black that day, too; for all I know it may have been the same outfit as the one he was wearing now, the same rusty velvet jacket and tubular trousers and boots so old the uppers looked as if they were made of crêpe paper. He had reminded me, I remember, with his big body and little legs and great, round, suet-coloured head, of one of the mighty Germans, Hegel, perhaps, someone like that, someone solemn and ponderous and faintly, unconsciously ridiculous. It struck me how he managed to be both abstracted and sharply watchful. What did we talk about as we paced the polished timbers of that long, high gallery, stepping through blocks of sunlight streaming in the immense windows? I can't remember, though I can see us there, clear as anything. The Professor, however, was firmly sceptical.

'No no,' he said brusquely, 'you have mistaken me for someone else.'

I persisted gently, determined to establish my connection, however tenuous, with the great days of Whitewater when Helmut Behrens was still alive and I had not yet forfeited my place in the realm of light. I should have married his daughter, I would be master there now, would even have a Vaublin of my very own. Whitewater! I think of permed girls in old-fashioned tennis shoes and pleated skirts and slacks – remember slacks? – and the grass green as it only can be in memory, and gin-and-tonics on the terrace and everyone smoking, and all day long that general air of idleness shot through with languid lusts. When I conjure up those days I feel like old Adam pausing in anguish in the midst of the stony fields, mattock in hand, pierced by paradisal visions of a past now hardly to be believed in. The more I insisted, the more firmly the Professor denied we had ever met; a sort of tussle resulted, elaborately polite, of course, I pushing and he pulling, our teeth gritted. It was all very awkward and in the end embarrassing. We fell into a rueful silence and looked out of the windows for a while, he fiddling with things on his desk and I standing behind him with my hands plunged in the pockets of my jacket; we must have looked like something out of one of Munch's more melancholic studies. A sea-fret had blurred the far dunes and clouds the colour of wood-smoke were piling up from the horizon, and as we watched, two thick, butter-coloured pillars of sunlight stepped slowly over the far, unmoving waves; sometimes even Dame Nature overdoes her effects. The Professor cleared his throat, huffing and frowning. He dropped Anna Behrens's letter on the desk and sat brooding, palping his lower lip with a thumb and forefinger.

'A very great collection,' he said.

'Yes, wonderful, wonderful,' I said, with what I suppose must have seemed a horribly suggestive, pushy coyness. 'There is that Vaublin, for instance.'

He shot me a rapid, sideways glance and cleared his throat. What had I said? His chair gave a stifled cry of protest under him as he rose. He walked heavily to the window and stood looking out, hunched and motionless, his fat, bloodless little hands clasped tight behind his back, the two stubby thumbs busily circling each other. Whenever I think of him this is how I see him, in the act of turning away from me like this, in the furtive way that he has, with one fat shoulder lifted and that great, round head bowed, like a man anticipating a hail of brickbats. Outside, rain fell glittering through sunlight.

'Miss Behrens speaks highly of you,' he said, and directed at me over his shoulder a sort of fishy rictus.

'She's very kind,' I said. 'We have known each other a long time.'

'Ah.' He sniffed.

'I would like to have seen *Le monde d'or*,' I said. 'It is the centrepiece of the collection, as you know.' A definite plumminess was creeping into my tone; I was beginning to sound like the suave cat-burglar in the old movies – where was my silver cigarette case, my patent-leather pumps, my cummerbund? The Professor sniffed again, louder than before. 'Of course,' I said, 'I would not go to Whitewater now. It would hardly be . . .' I could not think of the word; the language is not commodious enough to encompass the notion of a return by me to – well, yes, to the scene of the crime. 'I can't go home either,' I said and essayed a light, melancholy laugh. 'I have burnt my boats, I'm afraid.'

He did not seem to be listening, standing motionless at the window with his back firmly set against me. At length he turned, frowning abstractedly at the floor between us.

'There is a lot to be done,' he said. 'Papers, notes . . .' He waved a hand over the disorder on his desk. 'Secretarial work, really. Licht does what he can, but of course . . .' He shrugged.

'Then I can stay?' I said.

It came out like a whoop. He flinched, as if he had been pounced upon by something large and heavy.

'Yes,' he said, shrugging his shoulders again, trying to extricate himself from the woolly embrace of my enthusiasm, 'yes, I suppose you . . . I suppose . . .'

I thanked him. There was a catch in my voice, thick as it was with the pent of unshed tears; had I let them flow they would have come out forty per cent proof. Feeling the unabating waft of my gratitude he blinked and gave me one of his consternated, slow stares and turned away from me again uneasily. You must understand, this was a fraught moment for me, the commencement of my return from the wilderness into the place of humankind. I had come prepared to throw myself at his feet and here I was, still standing. Conceive of my joy, spiced though it was, I confess, with the actor's secret triumph at having moved the house to tears (I have said it before, I shall say it again, the stage has lost a star in me). I went down the stairs and locked myself in the lavatory on the landing and sat on the bowl and gazed at the space between my knees, swaying a little and humming to myself, lost in a euphoric, unfocused introspection. I brought out my broad-shouldered comforter and took another good stiff nip of gin. My nose was running. Here I was, hardly a day out of prison and already a hand had come down from the clouds to haul me up to celestial heights. Why then, behind the euphoria, did I have the impression that something was being palmed off on me? Was there, I asked myself, a trace of dirt under the fingernails of that helping hand? Oh, not the greasy black stuff flecked with blood and hair that is lodged immovably under my splintered nails, but just the ordinary grime, the stuff that humans naturally accumulate as they claw their way through this filthy world. Would the Professor draw me up out of myself, or was I to help him to descend?

*

Thus I had alighted at last in what I suppose I may as well call my destination. I had a feeling of weightlessness, a floating sensation, which I recognised; I always feel like this when I first come to a new place, as if something of me were lagging behind the physical arrival, some part of myself hanging back, out on the ocean, or in the air, dazed by speed and change. Thus the angel when he came to Mary must have felt, trembling on one knee with his wings still spread in this other, denser azure, stammering out his amazing message. But what annunciation did I bring, what grotesque incarnation did I herald? What word? What flesh?

*

We ate our tea in the kitchen, the Professor frowning at his plate and Licht eyeing me narrowly and saying things under his breath. I felt like the interloper that I was. Interloper: what an apt word: as if I had run up quietly and pressed myself between them. I had an awkward sense of myself caught up in a sort of antique dance, smiling and wincing and mouthing excuse-me's as together they trod out the measures of their ancient minuet, their eyes fixed on something elsewhere and their feet dragging leadenly.

Licht could not contain himself.

'Why don't we open a hostel?' he said at last, loudly, his voice shaking.

The room cringed. The Professor put on a bland expression and did not lift his eyes, and Licht, white-faced and furious, glared across the table at his inclined, broad bald pate. 'Why not turn the place into a doss-house?' he cried. 'We could take in every tinker and drunkard that happens to be passing by.'

A long and weighty silence followed. Licht sat and stared

before him with livid fixity, his knife and fork clutched in his fists and his knuckles white and one leg going like a sewing-machine under the table, making the cruets rattle.

'How was the crossing?' the Professor enquired of me at last, in a resonantly courteous tone.

The effects of the gin were wearing off and the faint buzzing of a hangover had started up. My eyes felt as if they had been toasted and my breath came out in furnace blasts.

'There's the extra work,' Licht shouted. 'There's the cooking, for instance. Am I expected to do all that? – because I won't.' He beat a fist softly on the table; there were tears in his eyes, big, shining drops brimming on the lids. 'You never tell me anything!' he cried. 'You never consult me!'

Professor Kreutznaer fixed his eye on a patch of the tablecloth beside his plate and sighed.

I fell to quiet contemplation, as is my wont at times of social awkwardness such as this. How shyly chance portions of the world dispose themselves – a bit of yard spied through a doorway at evening, clouds crowding in the corner of a window – as if to say, Look at us! we mean something!

The dog came waddling in from the yard (yes, yes! – Mr Tighe will make a full appearance yet, arm in arm with Miss Broaders the postmistress, and a winged horse will put its head over the half-door, and there will be no mysteries left). Licht took our plates and set them on the floor for the beast to finish off the scraps. Its name was Patch; all dogs are Patch, to me. It had a bad case of pink-eye. As it gulped and gasped Licht talked to it loudly in angry good humour that was meant to sound a general rebuke, tousling its rank fur and slapping it on the rump, raising a cloud of brownish dust.

Another prison, I was thinking, its walls made of air, and the old self inside me still in its white cell snarling for release.

'Good dog,' Licht said heartily. 'Good old dog!'

That's me.

*

In time of course we got used to each other. Even Licht in the end reconciled himself, not without a lingering and occasionally eruptive resentment, to my invasion of his little world. What an oddly assorted trio we would have seemed anywhere else; the island, however, with its long tradition of inbreeding and recurring bouts of internecine strife, was well used to peculiar and contingent arrangements such as ours. We were like a family of orphaned, elderly siblings, the resentments and rivalries of childhood calcified inside us, like gallstones. When I think of it I am surprised at myself for the brazen way in which I insinuated myself here – it is not like me, really it's not – but the truth is I had nowhere else to go. The house, the Professor, the work on Vaublin, all this represented for me the last outpost at the border; beyond were the fiery, waterless wastes where no man or even monster could survive.

Eventually the house too in its haughty way accommodated itself to my coming, though there were still times when the whole place seemed to twang like a spider's web under the weight of my unaccustomed tread. I suspect it was not any noise that I made but on the contrary the uncanny quiet of my presence that was most unsettling. I have always moved gingerly, excessively so, perhaps, among the furniture of other people's lives, not for fear of disturbing things but out of an obscure terror of being myself somehow caught out, of being surprised among surprised surroundings, redhanded. At times I fancied I could hear everything going silent suddenly for no particular reason, listening for me, and then of course I too would stop and stand with held breath, straining to catch I knew not what, and so the silence would stretch and stretch until it could bear the strain no longer and snapped of its own accord when a floorboard groaned or a door banged in the wind. At moments such as that I sympathised with the aboriginal tenants as they too stood stock-still, Licht in the kitchen and the Professor in his tower, straining despite themselves to catch the faint, discordant note of my presence. It must have been as if some large and softly padding animal had got into the house and was hiding somewhere, in the dark under a bed, or behind a not quite closed door, breathing and waiting, half fierce and half afraid. Licht in particular seems unable to prevent himself from listening for me, from the moment I wake in the morning until I drag myself up to my room again at dead of night. He wants to ask me things, I know, but cannot formulate the questions. He is like a child longing to learn all the thrilling, dirty secrets of the big world. He listens to the beast stirring, and smells blood.

Poor Licht. I seem unable to utter his name without that adjective attached to it. He keeps himself busy; that is his aim, to keep busy, as if he fears dissolution, a general and immediate falling apart, should he stop even for a moment in his headlong stumble. He cleaves to the principle of the perfectability of man, and gives himself over enthusiastically to self-improvement programmes. He sends off for things advertised in the newspapers, kitchen utensils, hiking boots, patented remedies for this or that deficiency of the blood or brain; he possesses books and manuals on all sorts of matters – how to set up a windmill or grow mushrooms commercially, how to draw and paint, or do wickerwork; he has piles of pamphlets on bee-keeping, wine-making, home accountancy, all of them eagerly thumb-marked for the first few pages and in pristine condition thereafter. He writes letters to the newspapers, does football competitions, labours for days over prize crossword puzzles. Always busy, always in motion, frantically treading the rungs of his cage-wheel. Nor does he neglect the outer man: at morning and evening, unfailingly, he strips down to his vest and drawers and spends a quarter of an hour ponderously bending knees and flexing arms and touching fingertips to toes; on occasion, looking up from the garden, I catch a glimpse of him in his room engaged in these shaky callisthenics, his strained little face yo-yoing slowly behind the shadowed glass like a lugubrious moon. He aims to get in shape, he says – but what shape, I wonder, is that? I suspect that, like me, he is convinced that large adjustments need to be made before he can consider himself to have reached the stage of being fully human.

We each of us have our ceremonies. There is the Professor's

nightly bath, for instance, which has all the solemn trappings of a royal balneation. I hear him in the cavernous bathroom on the second-floor return, vigorously sluicing and sloshing; then for a long time all goes quiet except for an occasional aquatic heave or the sudden, echoing plop of a big drop falling from chin or lifted elbow. I picture him sitting up in the tub like a big, mottled frog, just sitting there with the steam rising around him, quite still, water-wrinkled, hardly breathing, the lids dropping abruptly now and then over those little bulging black eyes and as abruptly lifting again. Afterwards I discover his damp trail on the stairs, dumbbell-shaped footprints dark in the moonlight, at once comic and sinister, winding their splayed way upwards to the mysterious fastness of his bedroom.

Strange, now that I think of it, how many of the rituals of the house involve water; we are a little Venice here, all to ourselves. There are the plants to be watered, the kettle to be kept simmering on the stove for the endless pots of tea the house requires, the washings-up, the launderings. I do our clothes, the girl's and mine, in an old tin bath in the scullery; there is an antiquated washing-machine I could use, but like all lifers I am set in my ways. I used to hang the laundry in bits and pieces out of the window of my room to dry, until Licht complained ('We're not living in a tenement here, you know'), and then I rigged up a line in a corner of the garden. Still Licht was not pleased – he is pained I suppose by the sight of my flapping shirts excitedly embracing the girl's slip. I confess I derive a certain wan pleasure from annoying him; it is wrong of me, I know, but somehow he invites cruelty. He patronises me, seeing in my ruin an encourage-ment to lord it over me. I do not mind, moth eaten old lion that I am, and obligingly open wide my toothless jaws and let him put in his head as far and for as long as he likes. He confides in me, despite himself, under cover of a blustering anger that does not convince either of us, telling me how he loathes the life here, the harshness of it, the isolation. The villagers laugh at him, Mr Tighe cheats him on the grocery bill, Miss Broaders listens in when he goes to the post office to use the telephone. He professes to hate the house, too, speaking of it with deep disgust, in a furious, spitting undertone, as if he thinks the walls might be eavesdropping; it bears him along like a big old broken-down ship, its ancient timbers shuddering; he looks forward to the day when it will founder at last. He is convinced it plays tricks on him. Inanimate things rear up at him, trip him up, give way under his feet, fall on his head. He will put down something and return an hour later and find it gone. Door handles come away in his hand, curtains when he tries to draw them will collapse suddenly in a muffled cascade of dust and jangling brass rings. He retaliates, letting the rain come in through open windows, allowing filth to gather in hidden corners of the kitchen, neglecting things until they break, or get scorched, or overflow. He dreams of escape, of getting up one morning before dawn and sneaking off like a hotel guest doing a flit. He has no idea where he would go to, yet flight, just flight itself, is a constant theme, a kind of hazy, blue and gold background to everything he does. I could tell him about freedom, but I have not the heart; let him dream, let him dream.

How at a word things shift suddenly, the whole pattern falling apart and reassembling itself in a new way out of the old pieces. I had been here some time before I discovered that it is not Professor Kreutznaer who owns the house, but Licht. This was a great surprise. I had, naturally, I believe, taken it for granted that the Professor was the man of property and Licht his vassal, but not so; in fact, the Professor is as much the parvenu as I am. Licht has lived here since he was a child – he may even have been born here. I would not have thought of him as a native, mind you, he is not exactly the craggy, weatherbeaten type one would expect an islandman to be. His mother it seems was a widow of many years; I pictured her as a scattered, birdlike creature with wild white hair and demented eyes, a sort of anile, genderless version of her son, but then Licht showed me a picture of her and she was nothing like my imagining, but a big strapping termagant with an implacable stare and a boxer's biceps. It is not clear when she died, or even that she did die; an inexplicably imperative sense of delicacy prevents me from enquiring too closely. He may have her in the cellar, or boarded up in the attic, for all I know. He speaks of her, on the rare occasions when he does speak of her, with the startled, heart-in-mouth air of a man stepping over a gaping crevice that has suddenly opened up before him in the pavement, frowning, his eyes cast down in alarmed despondency. I understand, however, that she had been long gone, by whatever means of departure she had chosen, by the time the Professor turned up, like me, looking for shelter. It seems he came over on the boat and climbed up here to enquire after lodgings and has been here ever since. In retirement from life, just like me.

*

Thus the days passed, the weeks. I walked the island, taking consolation from stray things, a red geranium in a blue window, a white sail in the bay, the suspense and then the sudden plummet of a hawk. In the evenings I lay on the frowsty bed in my room with my back against the wall and my hands behind my head and watched the dusk deepen in the window and the world out there fade from green to grey and turn at last to glossy black. I felt nothing, almost nothing. All my life I had been on my way elsewhere, despising the present, pressing always into the future, wanting the next thing, always the next thing; now at last I had come to rest, if that is what it can be called, as sometimes in my dreams I land with unexpected lightness after a long, tumbling, heart-stopping plunge through emptiness and dark air. I had sailed the sea and come to Cythera. That much I could say. Now I was waiting. The days would whiten and then flutter to the floor like so many leaves torn from a calendar; I would write my notes, do my chores, eat, sleep, be. And then one day, a day much like any other in that turning season between spring's breathless imminences and the first, gold flourishings of summer, I would look out the window and see that little band of castaways toiling up the road to the house and a door would open into another world. Oh, a little door, hardly high enough for me to squeeze through, but a door, all the same. And out there in that new place I would lose myself, would fade and become one of them, would be another person, not what I had been – or even, perhaps, would cease altogether. Not to be, not to be: the old cry. Or to be as they, rather: real and yet mere fancy, the necessary dreams of one lying on a narrow bed watching barred light move on a grey wall and imagining fields, oaks, gulls, moving figures, a peopled world. I think of a picture at the end of a long gallery, a sudden presence come upon unexpectedly, at first sight a soft confusion of greens and gilts in the calm, speechless air. Look at this foliage, these clouds, the texture of this gown. A stricken figure stares out at something that is being lost. There is an impression of music, tiny, exact and gay. This is the end of a world. Birds unseen are fluting in the trees, the sun shines somewhere, the distances of the sea are vague and palely blue, the galliot awaits. The figures move, if they move, as in a moving scene, one that they define, by being there, its arbiters. Without them only the wilderness, green riot, tumult of wind and the crazy sun. They formulate the tale and people it and give it substance. They are the human moment.

III

HE STANDS BEFORE US like our own reflection distorted in a mirror, known yet strange. What is he doing here, on this raised ground, in this gilded, inexplicable light? He is isolated from the rest of the figures ranged behind him, suspended between their world and ours, a man alone. Has he dropped from the sky or risen from the underworld? We have the sense of a mournful apotheosis. His arms hang loosely forward from his sides, his splayed feet are arranged in a parody of the mannered stance of prince or soldier posing for an heroic portrait. He seems trapped, held fast by invisible constraints. He might be in the stocks, or worse. We notice the pipe-clayed slippers tied with crimson ribbons in enormous, floppy bows, the broad satin trousers that are too short for him, the outsize coat of white twill, with its sixteen buttons, the rucked sleeves of which seem ample enough to accommodate the arms of an ape. Who has dressed him up in this clown's attire? For he has the look of having been bundled into his costume and thrust unceremoniously out of the wings to stand up here all alone, dumbfounded, mortified, afraid to move lest an unseen audience break into a storm of laughter; yet although for now he is lost for words, we have the feeling that at any moment he may burst out and talk and talk, unstoppably. He wears a limp ruff of white lace, a skullcap, or perhaps it is a headband, and a hat with a wide, circular brim pushed far back on his head. The head is oval, with a broad brow and receding chin. His gaze is at once remote and penetrating, his eyes are a greenish brown. His hair, what we can see of it, is black, or perhaps red. He seems weary. The eyelids, lips and nostrils are tinged with pink and appear to be inflamed; has he been weeping? Yet the corners of his fleshy mouth are dimpled in a sort of smile, distant, pained perhaps, without warmth. We have the impression of past suffering and a present numbness. Perhaps behind that pensive gaze he is laughing at us.

The X-rays show beneath his face another face which may be that of a woman. Pentimenti will out. (See fig. 1. Behrens Collection, recent acquisition.)

The figure of Pierrot derives from the Italian stock characters Pedrolino and the Neapolitan Pulcinella. These characters were introduced to the Paris Fairs by the King's Company of Italian Comedians towards the close of the 17th century and were transformed into the more familiar French form not long before Vaublin's arrival in Paris from his native Holland in the early 1700s; he would have seen the part played at the Comédie-Française by the great Biancolelli among others. Pierrot, disguised in outfit and in personality, is the childish man, the mannish child. Traditionally, as here, he wears a headband or skullcap and pleated ruff, broad silk trousers, a buttoned coat of silk or white twill with loose sleeves and white or black pumps. He appears in whiteface, though not always. Not always. In certain manifestations he is endowed with a humped back and a protruding chest, reminding us of his roots also in the character of Punch, that malign figure which itself dates from the time of the Roman circuses. He does not usually carry a club; in this instance, he does.

*

It is a large work, more than two metres high. Pierrot is slightly greater than lifesize. This disproportion, and the elevated placing – he seems somehow to hover in mid-air – lend a sense of lowering massiveness to an otherwise unremarkable, even absurd figure. Note too that Pierrot, for all his centrality in the design, is not centrally placed in the composition, but set a little way to the left; the small displacement creates an unsettling subliminal effect, which it is hard to believe is not intentional. Yes: a subtle harmonics is at work here, which plays upon our expectations of symmetry and balance; in the overall arrangement is there perhaps a sly parody of the rules of golden section? It is difficult to say which effects are intentional and which accidental.

The design of the work, the strange yet strangely pleasing asymmetry in the placing of the figures within the enveloping frame of trees and clouds and hazy, far-off sea, which strikes the viewer as at once arbitrary and inevitable, generates an air of mystery over and above the question of what it is that is happening and who or what the figures may be meant to represent – beyond, that is, their *commedia dell'arte* roles. Similar treatments of such subjects, by the same artist and others (Pater, Lancret, Watteau in particular), are equally baffling as to *plot*, if the term may be so employed, yet these works have not become the objects of unremitting, often ingenious yet for the most part futile speculation, as is the case with this work. Evidently there is an allegory here, and symbols seem to abound, yet the scene carries a weight of unaccountable significance that is disproportionate to any possible programme or hidden discourse. It is first of all a masterpiece of pure composition, of the architectonic arrangement of light and shade, of earth and sky, of presence and absence, and yet we cannot prevent ourselves asking what it is that gives the scene its air of mystery and profound and at the same time playful significance. Who are these people? we ask, for it seems to matter not what they may be doing, but what they are. Above all, who is this Pierrot? He is presented to us upright in darkening air, like a figure from the tarot pack, lost inside his too-large costume, mute and solitary, sorrowful, laughable perhaps, and yet unavoidable, hardly present at all and at the same time profoundly, palpably *there*, possessed it seems of a secret knowledge, our victim and our ineluctable judge.

Who is he? – we shall not know. What we seek are those evidences of origin, will and action that make up what we think of as identity. We shall not find them. This Pierrot, our Pierrot, comes from nowhere, from a place where no one else lives; nor is he on his way to anywhere. His sole purpose, it would appear, is to be painted; he is wholly pose; we feel ourselves to be the spectators at a melancholy comedy. See how strangely he fits into his costume; he seems not so much to be wearing it as standing behind it, like a cut-out paper doll. Notice the small size of the head in relation to the trunk, the unnatural length of the arms, the very broad hips, the oversized feet. He is almost deformed – almost, when we look long enough, a freak. He seems someone to whom something terrible has happened, or who has done some terrible thing, the effects of which upon his personality are suggested by these marked and at the same time subtle physical exaggerations. What is it he has done, what crime is he guilty of? And from whom is he hiding, if he is hiding? That smirking Harlequin mounted on the donkey seems to know the answers. Is it he who has lent Pierrot his club?

*

How deeply do we look into these depths? There is no end to what we may see. Consider this sky. Supposedly it is blue; we say, *Pierrot stands outlined against a blue sky*. In fact, what blue there is is more a faded, bluish green, and the effect is further softened by a scumbling of ochreous pinks; lower down, the shades range from turquoise through a watered mauve to deep indigo towards the barely discernible horizon of the sea; as is frequently the case in this master's work, evening is coming on, seeping up like a violet mist out of the earth. The cloud-mass on the right, behind the trees, is particulary well executed, a tarnished, whitish gold bundle, corpulent and dense. We might think that this is one of those high, smoky gold skies of early October, were it not for the tender foliage of the trees and the general sense of movement and expectancy. It is spring, surely, a cool, restless evening late in spring. We note the crepuscular, fulvous light, the softly thickening shadows; we feel the wind in the trees, in the clouds, and sense the stirring of the earth, the green shoots rising and the tight buds preparing to unfold. This is the springtime not of fêtes and fairs and gambolling milkmaids, but a more savage season, quick with a sense of the struggle in pain and darkness of things being born.

The crowded assortment of trees – oaks, poplars, umbrella pine – suggests a park or pleasure garden by the sea. Is this a calculated irony, a mocking gesture towards our feeble notions of pastoral? We have only to look more closely and the wildness of the scene becomes apparent. The wind blows, the clouds tumble, the trees shiver before the encroaching dark, while that statue of the scowling satyr – Pan, is it, or Silenus? – looks down stonily upon the action, his fleshy lips curled. Perhaps this tawny light is not the light of evening but of storm; if so, has the tempest passed, or is it only gathering? And whence comes this fierce luminescence falling full on Pierrot's breast, transforming his white tunic into a shining cuirass? It is as if some radiant being were alighting behind us from out of the sky and shedding upon him the glare of its shining wings.

*

The question has frequently been asked if the figures ranged behind Pierrot are the products of the artist's imagination or portraits of real people, actors from the Comédie-Française, perhaps, or the painter's friends and acquaintances, got up in the costumes of clowns and carnival types. They have a presence that is at once fugitive and fixed. They seem to be at ease, languorous almost, yet when we look close we see how tense they are with self-awareness. We have the feeling they are conscious of being watched, as they set off down the slope towards that magically insubstantial ship wreathed round with cherubs that awaits them on the amber shore with sails unfurled. The boy at the rear of the little procession is puzzled and frowning, while his slighter, somewhat wizened companion seems prey to a sort of angry longing. The woman dressed in black casts a backward glance that is at once wistful and resigned. The mood she suggests is a complex one; it is as if she were on her way to a sublimer elsewhere yet filled with regret for the creaturely world that she is leaving. There is about her a suggestion of the divine. If this is the Golden World, or the last of it, is she perhaps Astraea, regretfully withdrawing into the innocent sky? And is it Pierrot upon whom her last, lingering glance is fixed, or something or someone beyond him, which it is not our privilege to see?

The little girl with braided hair who leads the woman by the hand is eager to be away; what is Aphrodite's island to her, what does she know yet of the pains of love? At the other extreme of this little human chain of youth and age is the old man in the straw hat who looks away from us, over his shoulder, as if he has just now heard someone call to him from the shadows under the trees.

The presence of the donkey has puzzled many commentators. This creature is simultaneously one of the most mysterious and most immediate of the group, despite the fact that we see no more of it than a part of the head and one, pricked-up ear, and, of course, that single, soft, auburn, unavoidable eye. What is it that looks at us here? There is curiosity in its look, and apprehensiveness, and a kind of startled awe. We see in this unwavering gaze the windy stable and the stony road, the dawn-light in the icy yard and the rain-lashed corner of the field at evening; we feel the hunger and the beatings, the moment of brutish warmth in the byre, we taste the harsh straw of winter and the lush grass in the summer meadow. It is the eye of Nature itself, gazing out at us in a kind of stoic wonderment – at us, the laughing animal, the mad animal, the inexplicable animal.

Of that smirking Harlequin mounted on the donkey's back we shall not speak. No, we shall not speak of him.

*

At the window of that distant tower – we shall need a magnifying glass for this – a young woman is watching, waiting perhaps for some figure out of romance to come by and rescue her.

*

What happens does not matter; the moment is all. This is the golden world. The painter has gathered his little group and set them down in this wind-tossed glade, in this delicate, artificial light, and painted them as angels and as clowns. It is a world where nothing is lost, where all is accounted for while yet the mystery of things is preserved; a world where they may live, however briefly, however tenuously, in the failing evening of the self, solitary and at the same time together somehow here in this place, dying as they may be and yet fixed forever in a luminous, unending instant.

IV

I CONFESS I had avoided them all day. Oh, I know I pretended that I recognised in them what I had been waiting for since I first came here, the motley troupe who would take me into their midst and make a man of me, but the truth is I was afraid of them. I am not tough, not worldly-wise at all. It takes courage to expose yourself to the possibilities of the world and I am not a coura- geous man. I want only comfort, what little of it can be squeezed out of this life on a planet to which I have always felt ill-adapted. Their coming was a threat to the delicate equilibrium I had painstakingly established for myself. I was like a hungry old spider suddenly beset by a terrifying swarm of giant flying things. The web shook and I scuttled off into the foliage for shelter, legs flailing and eyes out on stalks. I saw old Croke walk up the hill and saw him too when he returned, staggering, from the beach where he had fallen, with the boys at his heels. I watched from hiding as Sophie set off into the hills to find the ruins she had come to photograph. I witnessed Felix pacing the lawn in the sun with a hand in his side pocket, smoking a cheroot. Oh yes, I skulked. And when late in the afternoon I screwed up my nerve and ventured back into the house it was I who seemed the intruder.

The kitchen was deserted. The debris of their lunch was still on the table, looking disturbingly like the remains of a debauch. I poured out the tepid dregs of Licht's chicken soup and ate it standing at the stove. I wanted one of them to come in and find me there. I would nod in friendly fashion and perhaps say something about the weather, claiming by this show of ease that I was the true inhabitant of the house while they were merely transients. No one came, however, and anyway, if someone had, probably I would have dropped my soup bowl and taken to my heels in a blue funk. I have always suffered from a tendency to generate panic out of my own fears and imaginings; I think it is a common weakness of the self-obsessed. There are moments of quiet and isolation when I can feel within me clearly the tiny, ceaseless tremor of impending hysteria that someday may break out and overwhelm me entirely. What is its source? It is the old emptiness, I suppose, the black vacuum the self keeps rushing into yet can never fill. I'm sure there is a formula for it, some elegant and simple equation balancing the void on one side and the endless inward spin of essence on the other. It is how I think of myself, eating myself alive, consuming myself always and yet never consumed.

Some incarnation this is. I have achieved nothing, nothing. I am what I always was, alone as always, locked in the same old glass prison of myself.

*

Why is it, I wonder, that silent, sunlit afternoons always remind me of childhood? Was there some marvellous moment of happiness that I have forgotten, some interval of stillness and radiance in which the enchanted child lingered on the forest path while his other self stepped out of him and blundered on oblivious into the dark entanglements of the future? I stood in the ancient light of the hallway for a long time, gazing up into the shadows thronging on the stairs, listening for them, for the sounds of their voices, for life going on. I do not know what I expected: cries, perhaps, arguments, sobs, wild laughter. I had got out of the way of ordinary things, you see; life, being what others did, must be all alarms and confrontations and matters coming to a head. I could hear nothing, or not nothing, exactly, only that faint, pervasive pressure in the air, that soundless hum that betrays the presence of humankind. How thoroughly the house had absorbed them, as if they really were the ones who belonged here; as if they had come home.

Flora was waiting on the landing, hanging back in the

shadowed corner between the window and the bedroom door. She had thrown a blanket over her shoulders, she clutched it about her like a shroud. The dark mass of her hair was tangled and damp and her eyes were swollen. Through the window beside her I could see far off in the fields a toy dog chivvying a toy flock of sheep. She had to clear her throat to speak.

'I thought you were Felix,' she said.

And almost smiled.

Licht had put her in my room; his idea of a joke, I suppose. Startling what a transformation her presence had wrought already; nothing was changed yet I would hardly have recognised the place as mine. The air was warm and thick with her smell, the musky smell of her hair and her hot skin. I shut the door behind me. She walked to the window and stood looking out at the dwindling afternoon, thick with slanted sunlight. Although she was on the far side of the room from me I had an extraordinarily vivid sense of her as she stood there with her arms folded around herself and her shoulder-blades unfurled, barefoot, in all her wan, popliteal frailty. I tend not to take much notice of other people – I have mentioned this before, it is one of my more serious failings – and on the rare occasions when I do put my head outside the shell and take a good gander at someone what strikes me as astonishing is not how different they are from me, but how similar, despite everything. I go along imagining myself to be unique, a sport of nature, a sort of tumour growing on the world, and suddenly I am brought up short: there it is, not I but another and yet made of skin, hair, clothed bone, just like me. This is a great mystery. Sex is supposed to solve it, but it doesn't, not in my experience, anyway (not that nowadays I have anything more than the haziest recollection of that universal palliative). Perhaps that is all I ever wanted to do, to break open the shell of the other and climb inside and slam it shut on myself, terrible spikes and all. What a way that would be to end it all.

'Have you lived here long?' Flora said.

I felt nauseous suddenly. My palms were clammy and my innards did a slow heave, as if there were something alive in there.

I had a teetering sensation, as if I had grown immensely tall, looming over the room, a great, fat, wallowing thing, a moving puffball stuffed with spores. I was frightened of myself. Not many people know the things they are capable of; I do. I wanted now to take this girl in my arms, to lift her up and hold her hotly to my heart, to feel the frail bones of her ankles and her wrists, to cup the delicate egg of her skull in my palm, to smell her blood and taste the silvery ichor of her sweat. How brittle she seemed, how easily breakable. This is what the poor giant in the old tales never gets to tell, that what is most precious to him in his victims is their fragility, the way they crack so tenderly between his teeth, giving up their little cries like lovers in the extremity of passion. He will never know what he yearns to know, how it feels to be little like them, gay and gaily vicious and full of fears and impossible plans. The human world is what he eats. It does not nourish him.

What she wanted, she was saying, was to stay here, on the island, just for a little while. She was sick, she was sure she was getting the flu. She stood for a moment frowning and biting her lip. The thing was, she said, she had made a mistake and now Felix had the wrong idea and she was afraid of him.

'He said he's going to stay on here,' she said. 'In this house. He knows something about that old man. He told me.'

Although her face was turned towards the window she was watching me. I still had that sensation of nausea. I felt shaky and almost tearful in what I imagined must be a womanly sort of way.

'Would he let *me* stay, do you think?' she said.

She meant the Professor.

'Yes,' I said, 'if I ask him.'

I meant Licht.

'If Felix was gone,' she said.

'Yes,' I said, so stoutly I surprised myself, 'yes, Felix will go.'

She nodded, still gnawing at her lip.

'I don't want to go back to that hotel,' she said, narrowing her eyes. 'They're not nice to me there. They boss me around. The parents expect me to do everything and the manageress is a bitch.'

Stop! I wanted to say, stop! you're ruining everything. I am told I should treasure life, but give me the realm of art anytime.

She went and sat down on the bed and hugged the blanket around her and stared at her bare feet. A girl, just a girl, greedy and dissatisfied, somewhat scheming, resentful of the world and all it would not give her. But that is not what I saw, that is not what I would let myself see.

Mélisande, Mélisande!

I still had, still have, much to learn. I am, I realise, only at the beginning of this birthing business.

I went downstairs, manoeuvring the way with difficulty in my newly swollen state, the gasping ogre, seeming to flop from step to step like an enormous bladder now, filled to the brim with slow, fat liquid. I was still queasy, still on the verge of tears, no, not tears, but a vast overflowing, an unstanchable flood of gall and gleet, my whole life oozing out of me in a final, foul regurgitation. I stopped at the window on the landing and rested a moment, leaning on the sill. How quickly the dusk was gathering, an oyster-grey stain spreading inland from the reaches of the sea, a darkness slowly, irresistibly descending.

Something had happened in that little room up there that before had been mine and now was hers, a solemn warrant had been issued on me, and I felt more than ever like the hero in a tale of chivalry commanded to perform a task of rescue and reconciliation. There they were, the old man in the tower with his books, the damsel under lock and key, and the dark one, my dark brother, waiting for me, the knight of the rosy cross, to throw down my challenge to him.

I laughed a soundless laugh and went on, down the stairs.

They were in the hall, ready to depart. They turned to look at me. What must I have seemed?

This toy dog, that toy flock.

*

We walked down the hill road in the blued evening under the vast, light dome of sky where Venus had risen. The fields were darkening on either side, the bay below us glistered. Everyone had acquired something. Croke his invisible companion that had risen with him from the sand at the sea's edge and walked at his shoulder now step for step, Sophie her photographs that tomorrow would swim into her red room like water sprites, the boys that sly phantom that had run up swiftly and insinuated itself between them while they fought and would not go away, Alice her image of a girl reclining in a sunny bed.

A moth reeled out of the gloaming and there was a sense of something falling and failing and I seemed to feel the faint dust of wings sifting down. The god takes many forms.

We rounded a bend in the road where there was a little copse and a stream running by and found Felix sitting perched on a dry-stone wall in the dark with his arms around his knees and his face turned to the sky. The others walked on in calm procession, Sophie arm in arm with Croke and holding Alice by the hand and the boys trudging behind them, kicking stones. You see? They have their party favours and now they are going home, after the long day's doings, Sophie to her developments, Croke to die, the children to grow up and become other people. This is what happens. What seems an end is not an end at all.

'What a start you gave me,' Felix said to me amiably, 'rearing up out of the dark like that. I thought you were Old Nick.'

It was as if all along we had been walking side by side, with something between us, some barrier, thin and smooth and deceptive as a mirror, that now was broken, and I had stepped into his world, or he into mine, or we had both entered some third place that belonged to neither of us. He lit one of his cheroots, bending his narrow face to the flare of the match in his cupped hands. A flaw of smoke shaped like Africa assumed itself into the leaves above him. Behind the tobacco smell I caught a faint whiff of his own unsavoury, stale stink. I found it hard to keep a hold of him, somehow. He kept going in and out of focus, one minute flat and transparent, a two-dimensional figure cut out of grimed glass, the next an overpowering presence pressing itself against me in awful intimacy, insistently physical, all flesh and breath and that stale whiff of something gone rank. He began to sing to himself softly, in a jaunty voice, crowingly.

Allo, allo, who's yer laidy friend,
Who's 'at little girl I sawre yer wiv larst night?

He mused a while, gazing into the thickening shadows.

'I cannot set my foot on board a ship,' he said, 'without the memory coming back of sailing to the frozen northern pole. I wonder, have you ever been up there? The tundra and the towering bergs, the sun that never sets: such solitude! such cold! And yet how beautiful, this land of ice! We sailed out of Archangel and due north we ploughed our way, all day, and all the night, for weeks. And then one morning when I looked out from the deck I saw the strangest sight: a figure, in the distance, on a sled, a giant man, it seemed, with whip and dogs, at great speed travelling on the floes, due north, like us. And then another—' There he paused, and said: 'I think you know this story, though?'

A drowsy bird in the branches above us stirred a wing. The stream muttered to itself. Felix considered me with his head on one side.

'Tell me,' he said, 'don't I know you? I mean from somewhere else. Your face looks familiar.'

The last light was ascending in the zenith. Stars swarmed. A big white gloating moon had hoisted itself clear of the velvet heights behind us.

'Time to go, I think,' he said. 'I had thought of staying for a bit, but now you're here there is no need. Definitely *de trop*, what?' He lowered his lashes almost shyly and smiled a thin-lipped smile that made it seem as if he were nibbling a tiny seed between his teeth. 'Anyway, you're inviting me to leave, aren't you. *Luxe, calme et volupté*, eh?'

In the gathering dark the trees kept lisping the same slurred phrase over and over. Felix sighed and unwound his legs and nimbly scrambled down from the wall. 'Time to go, yes,' he said, brushing himself off, and linked his arm in mine and together we set off down the hill towards the bay. On the brow of the hill he paused and looked back and laughed and waved a hand and softly cried:

'Farewell, happy fields!'

None of it was as I had thought it would be. I do not know what I had expected – some sort of tussle, I suppose, a contest on the road, maybe even fisticuffs, and then me pushing him protesting down to the boat, his nose bleeding and his collar sticking up and his heels furrowing the dust. What did I think I was, the avenging angel of the Lord? No, Felix would not fight, he would go quietly, or pretend to. I know his type, I know it only too well.

'And you are going to stay here, are you?' he said. 'You have it all worked out?' He laughed in the dark. We could see below us now the lights of the harbour and the dark bulk of the waiting boat crouched at the jetty. We heard the noise that the island makes, that deep, dark note rising through the gloom. We paused to listen, and Felix struck a dramatic pose and inclined an ear and shouted out softly in a stage-actor's voice, making it seem uncannily as if it were someone calling to us from an immense distance:

'*Thamous! Thamous! The great god Pan is dead!*'

And laughed.

We walked on.

'You know I too knew the Professor, long ago?' he said. 'Oh, yes. As you are now so I was once, his friend, his confidant.' He squeezed my arm against his side and I felt the meagre armature of his ribs. 'Tell me,' he said in a confidential tone, 'do you respect him? I mean, is he a great man, do you think? I thought so, at first. Alas, we all have our weaknesses. You realise that painting is a fake? Yes, more of gilt in it than gold, I fear. Poor Miss Behrens was taken in. Do you know her too? What a coincidence! She does not know she bought a fake. I may tell her, or I may not. What do you think? Which is better, ignorance or enlightenment? The Professor was the one who verified it. And made a killing on it, of course. Not for the first time either.' He chuckled. 'Curious phrase, that, don't you think – a killing?'

We had reached the harbour, and walked out now along the

pier still arm in arm. The boat reared gently at its moorings, sending up a soft puttering of smoke from the rusted stack. The skipper was in his lighted wheelhouse, the others stood about the deck, dim shadows of themselves, like the Pequod's swarth phantoms, fading already. A storm lantern hanging in the bow shed a frail, apricot glow around which the night seemed to gather itself and find a brief definition. Felix stopped on the dockside and released my arm only to take my hand in both of his.

'I say, old chap,' he said in his actor's voice with a fake sob in it, 'look after the girl for me, will you? She likes a bit of rough stuff, but these things can go too far, as you well know.'

I should have seen him go. I should have waited until he was safely on board and the boat under way. When I had walked back along the pier and turned he was still standing where I had left him on the dock, waving one hand slowly, like a mechanical man. Was he smiling?

No riddance of him.

*

Flora has decided she is recovered. She is getting ready to leave, I can feel it, the change in her, like the season changing. She is ruffling her feathers, testing the buoyant air. I shall be glad to see her go – glad, that is, as the hand is glad when the arrow flies from the bow. If she were to remain I should only engrey her life. Better that, you will say, than if I had incarnadined it, but that is not the issue. There was never any question but that I would lift her up and let her go; what else have I been doing here but trying to beget a girl? Licht of course will be heartbroken. We shall stand on the windy headland, he and I, bereft together, and watch her skim away over the waves. The Professor will hardly notice she is gone. I think he is the one whose heart is really breaking. I make no mention to him of the Golden World and its clouded provenance; we have both made killings, he in his way, I in mine; there is no comparison. I am still puzzling over the problem: if this is a fake, what then would be the genuine thing? And if

Vaublin did not paint it, who did? Who was *his* dark double? Perhaps the Professor will tell me, in his own time; I think I detect a speculative something in his filmy glance these days; I fear a deathbed confession. Maybe he painted it himself? He does have a touch of the old master to him; I can just picture him in velvet cap and ruff, peering from under the murk of centuries, one bleared, pachydermous eye following the viewer round the room and out the gilded door: *Self-portrait in the Guise of a Dutchman*. Well. He does not mention Felix, any of that. Matters go on as before, as if nothing had happened. My writing is almost done: Vaublin shall live! If you call this life. He too was no more than a copy, of his own self. As I am, of mine.

No: no riddance.

ATHENA

to Anthony Sheil

MY LOVE. If words can reach whatever world you may be suffering in, then listen. I have things to tell you. At this muffled end of another year I prowl the sombre streets of our quarter holding you in my head. I would not have thought it possible to fix a single object so steadily for so long in the mind's violent gaze. You. You. With dusk comes rain that seems no more than an agglutination of the darkening air, drifting aslant in the lamplight like something about to be remembered. Strange how the city becomes deserted at this evening hour; where do they go to, all those people, and so suddenly? As if I had cleared the streets. A car creeps up on me from behind, tyres squeaking against the sides of the narrow footpaths, and I have to stop and press myself into a doorway to let it pass. How sinister it appears, this sleek, unhuman thing wallowing over the cobbles with its driver like a faceless doll propped up motionless behind rain-stippled glass. It shoulders by me with what seems a low chuckle and noses down an alley-way, oozing a lazy burble of exhaust smoke from its rear end, its lollipop-pink tail-lights swimming in the deliquescent gloom. Yes, this is my hour, all right. Curfew hour.

Three things the thought of you conjures up: the gullet of a dying fish into which I have thrust my thumb, the grainy inner lining of your most secret parts, ditto, and the tumescent throb in the throat of some great soprano – who? – on the third, held note of the second alleluia of Schubert's *Die junge Nonne* (O night! O storm!). Much else besides, of course, but these textures persist above all, I do not know why, I mean why these three in particular. (I apologise, by the way, for associating you with that fish; I caught it when I was a boy and never caught another, but I remember it, the poor creature hauled out of its element, shuddering as it drowned in air.) I hardly dare think what form of me you would recall: an eyed unipod heaving and slithering towards you across the floor, something like that, no doubt. Yet what a thing we made there in that secret white room at the heart of the old house, what a marvellous edifice we erected. For this is what I see, you and me naked and glistening in the mirror-coloured light of an October afternoon, labouring word-lessly to fashion our private temple to the twin gods watching over us. I remember Morden telling me the story of a builder of his acquaintance demolishing a folly down the country some-where and finding a centuries-old chapel concealed inside the walls. *Tight as an egg*, he said. *Amazing*. And laughed his laugh. I thought of us.

*

We had our season. That is what I tell myself. We had our season, and it ended. Were you waiting all along to go, poised to leap? It seems to me now that even while I held you clasped in my appalled embrace you were already looking back at me, like one lingering on the brink of departure, all that you were leaving already fading in your glance, becoming memory even as it stood before you. Were you part of the plot, a party to it? I would like to know. I think I would like to know. Would we have been left free and undisturbed, left entirely to our own charming devices, as we were, had someone not decided it should be so? Before such little doors of doubt can open more than a crack my mind jumps up in panic and slams them shut. Yet reason with a scoffing laugh insists that you were in on it, as they say, that you must have been; but what does reason know except itself? Nowadays I prefer the murk and confusion of the lower brain, the one that used to go by the name of heart. Heart, yes; not a word you will have heard me employ very often up to now. I feel as I have not felt since I was a lovelorn adolescent, at once bereft and lightened, giddy with relief at your going – you were too *much* for me – and yet assailed by a sorrow so weighty, of so much more consequence than I seem to myself to be, that I stand, no, I kneel before it, speechless in a kind of awe. Even at those times when, sated with its pain, my mind briefly relinquishes the thought of you the sense of loss does not abate, and I go about mentally patting my pockets and peering absently into the shadowed corners of myself, trying to identify what it is that has been misplaced. This is what it must be like to have a wasting illness, this restlessness, this wearied excitation, this perpetual shiver in the blood. There are moments – well, I do not wish to melodramatise, but there are moments, at the twin poles of dusk and dawn especially, when I think I might die of the loss of you, might simply forget myself in my anguish and agitation and step blindly off the edge of the earth and be gone for good. And yet at the same time I feel I have never been so vividly alive, so quick with the sense of things, so exposed in the midst of the world's seething play of particles, as if I had been flayed of an exquisitely fine protective skin. The rain falls through me silently, like a shower of neutrinos.

*

The murders seem to have stopped. The police have not turned up a body now for weeks. I find this disturbing. The killings started about the time we met and now that you are gone they have come to an end. It is foolish, I know, but I cannot help wondering if there was a connection. I don't mean a direct link, of course, but could it be that we disturbed something with our wantonness, upset some secret balance in the atmosphere and thus triggered a misfire deep in the synapse maze of that poor wretch, whoever he is, and sent him ravening out into the night with his rope and knife? Foolish, as I say. I am convinced that I have seen him, the killer, without realising it, that somewhere in my prowlings I have stumbled across him and not recognised him. What a thought.

My headaches too have stopped. Pains in the head, murders in the night. If I tried I could connect everything in a vast and secret agenda. If I tried.

*

Aunt Corky left me all her money. (You see? – a lost love, a locked room, and now a will: we are in familiar territory after all.) There was a great deal more of it than I ever imagined there could be. Her last flourish, the sly old thing. I wonder if she thought it was her money I was after? I hope not. Sticking with her through all those long, last weeks of her dying was, I see now, the one unalloyed good deed I could point to in my life, the thing I thought might go some way towards balancing my account in the recording angel's big black book. Still, I won't pretend I am not glad to have the dough, especially as Morden despite his trumpetings about probity and fair dealing (and to think I believed him!) somehow managed to forget to recompense me for my troubles before he did a flit. My troubles . . . Funny thing, money; when you haven't got any you think of almost nothing else, then you get some and you can't understand why it ever seemed important. Aunt Corky at a stroke (to coin a phrase) has solved my life, or the getting and spending part of it, anyway. I feel light-headed and sort of wobbly; it is an odd sensation, like that flutter that lingers in the muscles when you put down a heavy load you have been carrying for a long time.

It's ironic, really: Aunt Corky was the one who was forever urging me to take up work and do something with my life, but now I have her money and will never again need to go out and earn a crust. What was she thinking of? I suppose it was me or the Cats and Dogs Home. 'You are a no-good,' she would say cheerfully in her deliberately fractured English, 'a no-good, yes, just as your father was.' She was given to such franknesses, they were not intended to wound – in fact, that mention of my father denotes rueful approval, for I know she had a soft spot for the old boy. What she meant was that he and I were wastefully dilettantish, even if to her eye we did have a certain style. She was not wrong, about the waste, I mean. I have frittered away the better part of my life. I did it all backwards, starting out an achiever and then drifting into vagueness and crippling indecision. Now, becalmed in the midst of my decidedly unroaring forties, I feel I have entered already if not my second childhood then certainly my second adolescence – look at all this love stuff, this gonadal simpering and sighing; I shall break out in a rash of pimples yet.

Now that I think of it, it was largely Aunt Corky's workward urgings, as well, of course, as my own natural (or should that be unnatural?) curiosity, that led me to Morden and his hoard of pictures. I am still not sure exactly how he came to know of me, for I have changed my name (by deed poll: yes, there really is such a process), along with everything else that was changeable; it was his man Francie who ran me to ground in the end, by God knows what devious channels. Morden had a touching fondness for secrecy and sudden pouncings, I noticed that about him right away; he loved to lead . . . his victims, I was about to say; he loved to lead people on by a show of seeming ignorance and then reveal with a flourish that he had known all along all there was to know about them. For all his moneyed look and the sense of menace he gave off, there wafted around him a definite air of the mountebank. The occasion of our first meeting retains in my memory a sort of lurid, phosphorescent glow; I have an impression of a greenish light and dispersing stage smoke and the sudden swirl and crack of a cloak and a big voice booming out: *Tarraa!*

It was the first time I had been in that quarter of the city, or at least the first time I noticed myself being there. September, one of those slightly hallucinatory, dreamy afternoons of early autumn, all sky and polished-copper clouds and thin, petrol-blue air. The river still had a summery stink. How much larger, higher, wider the world appears at that time of year; today even the bellowing traffic seemed cowed by this suddenly eminent new season rearing above the clanging streets. I crossed out of sunlight at the entrance to Swan Alley, dodging a charging bus that mooed at me angrily, and found myself at once plunged in shadow thin and chill, like watered ink, and had to stop a moment to let my eyes become accustomed to the gloom. When I think of the place now I always see it caught like this in a sort of eclipse; even your presence in my mental picture of these little streets and cobbled alleyways cannot disperse the glimmering, subfusc atmosphere with which my memory suffuses them.

The house was in ... what shall I call it? Rue Street, that sounds right. The house was in Rue Street. It looked derelict and I thought at first I must have the wrong address. Big gaunt grey townhouse with rotting windows and a worn step and a broad black door sagging on its hinges. I pressed the bell and heard no sound and knocked the dull knocker and imagined I could detect a muffled tittering from within. I waited, putting on that abstracted, mild look that waiting at doors always demands – or always demands of me, anyway. Next the obligatory ritual: step back, scan the upstairs windows, frown at the pavement, then scan the windows a second time while slowly assuming a querulous expression. Nothing. On the left there was a fenced-off site with rubble and empty crisp packets and a flourishing clump of purple buddleia, on the right a dim little flyblown shop that seemed to have its shoulders hunched. I went into the shop. It smelled of cat and stewed tea. Do we really need all this, these touches of local colour and so on? Yes, we do. The usual crone peered at me over the usual bottles of boiled sweets, at her back a dim doorway leading down to hell. Before I could ask her anything there was a light, syncopated step behind me and I turned. This is how things begin. A blue cloud of cigarette smoke coming at me like a claw opening and behind his shoulder the honeyed sunlight in the street and a diagonal shadow by de Chirico sharp as the blade of a guillotine. Francie. Francie the fixer: an S-shaped, shabby, faintly grinning, glitter-eyed, limping character, tallish, thin, concave of chest, with scant reddish hair under a flat cap, face like a chisel, and a fag-end with a drooping inch of ash attached to a bloodless, hardly existent thin long line of lower lip. I had never set eyes on him before yet felt I had known him always; or at least – I can't explain it – that he had known me. 'Mr Morrow!' he said, in the tone of a hunter claiming his bag, pointing a finger pistol-wise at my breast. Morrow: yes, that is my name, now; have I mentioned it before?

I chose it for its faintly hopeful hint of futurity, and, of course, the Wellsian echo. Finding a first name was more difficult. I toyed with numerous outlandish monikers: Feardorcha, for instance, which in our old language means man of darkness; also Franklin, the freeman, and Fletcher, a famous islander; Fernando, with its insinuation of stilettos and the poison cup; and even Fyodor, though the overtones of that were too obvious even for me. In the end what I settled for seemed just the thing. But I confess I have not yet accustomed myself to this new identity – or identification, at least – and there is always a hesitation when I am thus addressed. Francie I could see had caught that telltale lapse; Francie was a man who noticed such things. 'Come on along with me now, will you,' he said. I followed him out, and had a picture of the shopwoman standing there forever behind the counter with her pinched old face vaguely, patiently lifted, unable to stir, stricken into a statued trance for all eternity, waiting for the banal question I had left unasked.

On the sunny pavement Francie looked sideways at my legs and smiled with pursed lips as if something funny had occurred to him. 'We watched you from on high,' he said, pointing at the upper windows. 'I couldn't get down fast enough for you. Patience, they tell me, is a great thing.' The faint smile turned to a grin, his thin mouth seeming to stretch from ear to ear.

A large dog with bristling, shiny black fur and pricked-up, pointed ears had appeared from nowhere and was loping silently at our heels.

We stopped at the house and Francie flicked away his cigarette butt and produced a great key and jiggled it in the keyhole. He pushed open the sagging black door and waved me in with an elaborate sweep of his arm. High white shadowy hallway paved unevenly with sandstone flags. The door shutting produced a shiver of tiny echoes that fell plinkingly about us. Smell of distemper and ancient plaster and crumbling stone. A delicate staircase with a banister rail moulded into a sinuous, rising curve – I think of that part of your arm between the elbow and the wrist – ascended airily toward a soft glare of white light falling from tall windows high above. Echoingly we climbed. The dog, ignored, followed after us, claws clicking on the bare boards. 'These stairs,' Francie said, 'are a killer,' though I was the one who was panting. He turned suddenly and made a feint at the dog and roared merrily, '*Prince you bugger get out to hell out of that!*' The dog only looked at him adoringly and grinned, its pink-fringed, glistening jaws agape.

On the top floor we stopped under a peeling plaster dome. I could feel Francie eyeing me still with that expression of subdued mirth. I squared my shoulders and pretended interest in the architecture. There was a circular, railed balcony with white doors giving off it, all shut. I felt like the last Mrs Bluebeard. Francie walked ahead of me. That walk: a kind of slack-heeled, undulating lope, as if he belonged to a species that had only lately begun to go about upright. The limp seemed not to trouble him, seemed, in fact, to confer agility, less a limp than a spring in his step. He opened one of the white doors and again stood aside and waved me forward. 'Here we are, friend,' he said jauntily, and made an insolent, clicking noise out of the side of his mouth. *Now listen here, my man*, I said . . . No, of course I didn't. I stepped past him. I could sense the dog at my heels and hear its rapid breathing, like the sound of a soft engine hard at work. I do not like dogs.

There are certain moments in life when—

But no, no. We shall dispense with the disquisition on fate and the forked paths that destiny sets us upon and all such claptrap. There are no moments, only the seamless drift; how many times do I have to tell myself this simple truth? That day I could no more have prevented myself from stepping through that doorway than I could have made my heart stop beating or the lymph halt in its courses through my glands. I do not mean to imply there was coercion involved, that, fixed in Francie's amused, measuring gaze, I had been robbed of all volition; if it were so, how much easier everything would seem. No, what I mean simply is that I did not stop, did not turn aside, but went on, and so closed off all other possibilities. Things happen, therefore they have happened. If there are other worlds in which the alternatives to our actions are played out we may know nothing of them. Even if I had felt a spider's web of foreboding brush against my face I would have been drawn irresistibly through it by the force of that linked series of tiny events that began the instant I was born, if not before, and that would bundle me however unceremoniously through today's confrontation, just as it will propel me on to others more or less fateful than that one until at last I arrive at the last of all and disappear forever into the suddenly shattered mirror of myself. It is what I call my life. It is what I imagine I lead, when all the time it is leading me, like an ox to the shambles.

The corridor in which I found myself was low and broad and cluttered with stuff. White walls again, the peculiar, tired, parched yellowish-white that was the overall no-colour of the interior of the house. Of the same shade and texture, at least in my first vague awareness of them, were the nameless things piled everywhere, the litter of decades – of centuries – resembling, to my eyes, big bundles of slightly soiled clouds or enormous, dried-up blobs of papier mâché. As I picked my way through them I had the impression that they were more than merely rubbish that had been dumped and left here over the years, that they were, rather, a kind of detritus extruded by the place itself, a solidified spume that the walls by some process of slow internal decomposition had spontaneously precipitated. And even later on, when I came to rummage through these recrements, they retained for me something of this desiccated, friable texture, and there were times when I fancied that I too from prolonged contact with them was beginning to moulder and would steadily crumble away until nothing remained of me but a shapeless heap of unidentifiable odds and ends. Behind me Francie swore lightheartedly and kicked a cardboard box out of his way. 'Heavenly Christ,' he said with a sigh, 'this place, this place.'

The corridor before me curved a little – the house was all bends and droops and sudden inclines, the result of subsidence, according to Morden, who managed to give the word an infernal

resonance – and suddenly I came up against another door, this
one open an inch or two. Doors standing ajar like that have
always filled me with unease; they seem so knowing and somehow
suggestive, like an eye about to wink or a mouth opening to
laugh. A strange, intense white light was coming from behind it,
spilling through the crack as if a great flare of magnesium were
burning in the room beyond. It was only daylight, however,
falling from two tall and, so it seemed to me at first, slightly
canted, overhanging windows. The room, very high and airy, had
the look of an atelier. A thing made of poles and pulleys, like a
rack for drying washing, was suspended by ropes from the ceiling,
and a large, dirty white sheet that seemed as if it had been
stretched right across the room and had fallen down at one side
was draped in a diagonal sweep from the corner of a window-
frame to the floor, making a dramatic effect that was oddly
and unaccountably familiar; the whole thing – the high room,
the massed, white light, that cascading sash – might have been
a background to one of Jacques Louis David's revolutionary
group portraits. Morden followed my glance and said, 'The
Tennis Court Oath eh?,' and threw me a sharp, ironical look,
his great head thrown back. Thus at the very outset we had a
demonstration of his divinatory powers. I took a step backwards,
shocked, as if one of the floorboards had sprung up under my
foot and smacked me bang on the nose. I could see he was pleased
with himself. 'Yes,' he said, 'the place is that old, to the very year;
amazing, isn't it?'

He had the look himself of a somewhat later vintage, less
David's Robespierre than Rodin's Balzac, standing in the middle
of the empty floor wrapped in his long coat with his arms folded
high up on his massive chest and looking askance at me down his
boxer's big, splayed nose. The eyes – ah, the eyes! That panther
glance! I realised two things simultaneously, that he was younger
than me by a good ten years, and that I was afraid of him; I did
not know which of these two facts I found the more disturbing.
I heard Francie moving about softly behind me and for a mad
moment I had the notion that he was positioning himself to

tackle me, like a henchman in the movies who will suddenly yank the victim's jacket back and pinion his arms so that the boss in his camel-hair coat and raked fedora may step forward smilingly at his leisure and deliver the hapless hero a haymaker into the breadbasket. After an interval of compressed silence Morden, still fixing me with that glossy black stare, seemed to come to a decision and nodded and muttered, 'Yes indeed, yes indeed,' and put on a look that was partly a grin and partly a scowl and turned and paced slowly to the window and stood in silence for a long moment contemplating the building opposite. That coat, though, he cannot have been wearing that greatcoat yet, the weather was still too warm; if I have got that detail wrong what else am I misremembering? Anyway, that is how I see him that day, posed there in the light under those beetling windows with his arms still folded and one leg thrust forward from the skirts of his coat, a big, deep-chested, brooding man with flattened features and a moneyed suntan and a lovingly barbered thick long mane of lustreless red-brown hair.

'So: here you are,' he said, as if to set aside what had gone before and start all over again. Already I felt out of breath, as if I were being forced to scramble after him back and forth across a steep incline. 'Yes, here I am,' I said, not knowing what else to say. Morden looked past me at Francie and raised his eyebrows and said, 'Hark: he speaks!' Then he fixed his level, measuring gaze on me once more. Behind me Francie laughed quietly. Another silence. Prince the dog sat in the doorway, tongue lolling, watching us attentively, its vulpine ears erect and faintly twitching.

I'm sure none of this is as it really happened.

'I think that you can help me,' Morden said briskly. 'I hear you are a man a man might trust.' He seemed to find that briefly amusing and turned aside a faint smirk. His voice was large, resonating in that big chest, and weighted with odd emphases, deliberately running on and falling over itself as if he wanted to make it known that he had not the time or patience to say all he had to say and therefore the words themselves must work over-time; a manufactured voice. He said he had lately acquired the

house – I liked that word, acquired – and added, 'For development,' waving a beringed and strangely bloated, bloodless hand.
'Development, preservation, the two in one; big plans, we have;
yes, big plans.' Now it was Francie's turn to smirk. Oh, they were
having a rollicking time, the two of them. Morden nodded in
happy satisfaction, contemplating the future and breathing deep
through those wide nostrils as if he were snuffing up the heady
smells of fresh-cut timber, bricks and mortar. Then he roused
himself and turned from the window, suddenly, energetically
cheery. 'And now, I think, a little toast,' he said. 'Francie?'

Francie hesitated and for a moment there was rebellion in the
air. I turned and together Morden and I looked at him. In
the end he shrugged and gave his side teeth a disdainful suck and
slouched off with the dog following close behind him. Morden
laughed. 'He's a bit of an artist himself, you know, is old Francie,'
he said confidingly.

I felt something relax in me with a sort of creak, as if the pawl
and ratchet of a suspended, spring-loaded mechanism in my chest
had been eased a notch. Morden went back to his silent contemplation at the window. It was very quiet; we might have been in
a lift together, the two of us, soundlessly ascending towards I
knew not what. I could hear my heart beating; the rate seemed
remarkably slow. Strange, the moments like that when everything
seems to break free and just drift and anything might happen; it
is not like life at all, then, but some other state, conscious and yet
dreamy, in which the self hangs weightless in a sort of fevered
stillness. Perhaps there is a kind of volition, after all (involuntary
volition? – could there be such a thing?), and perhaps it is in
intervals such as this one that, unknowingly, we make our
judgments, arrive at decisions, commit ourselves. If so, everything I have ever believed in is wrong (belief in this sense is of
course a negative quality). It is an intensely invigorating notion.
I do not really credit it; I am just playing here, amusing myself
in this brief intermission before everything starts up again.

Presently Francie returned with a bottle of champagne and
three wine glasses greyed with dust. Morden took the bottle and

removed the foil and the wire cap and gave the cork a peremptory twist; I thought of a hunter putting some plump, sleek creature out of its misery. There was an unexpectedly feeble pop and a limp tongue of froth lolled from the neck. The wine was pink and tepid. Francie got none. Morden clinked his dusty glass against mine. 'To art!' he said. I drank but he did not, only raised the glass to his lips in dry dumbshow.

We tramped up and down the house, Morden ahead of me swinging the champagne bottle by the neck and his coat billowing and Francie in the rear going along softly at his syncopated slouch with the dog loping close behind him. This forced march had something violent and at the same time faintly preposterous about it. I had a sense of impending, laughable collapse, as in one of those burlesque dreams in which one finds oneself scampering trouserless through a convulsed crowd of hilariously pointing strangers. Solemnly we processed through high rooms with flaking plaster and torn-up floorboards and windows below which the sunlight's geometry was laid out in complicated sections. Everywhere there was a sense of the place's mute embarrassment at being seen like this, in such disarray.

'. . . A person by the name of Marbot,' Morden was saying, 'Josiah Marbot, esquire, gent. of this ward. Great traveller, great builder, great collector, confidant to the King of Naples, guest of Marie Antoinette at the palace of Versailles (they say she had a clitoris as thick as your thumb, did you know that?). There are letters to him from Madame de Somebody, King Whatsit's mistress. He made his fortune early, in the linen trade: flax from Flanders, hemp from Ghent, weavers from Bayeux. He paddled around the Low Countries picking up whatever he could find; oh yes, a fine eye for a bargain. He never married, and left his fortune to the Anti-Slavery Society or somesuch. Quaker he was, I believe. A real eighteenth-century type.' He halted abruptly and I almost walked into him. He smelled of shaving balm and the beginnings of gum disease. He was still carrying his glass of champagne untouched. Mine he refilled. 'At the end, of course, he went peculiar.' He held the bottle tilted and fixed me with a beadily playful stare, his eyebrows twitching. 'Shut himself away here in the house, only a manservant for company, years and years, then died. It's all written up, I've read it. Amazing.'

While he spoke my attention was diverted to something behind him that he did not see. We had come to what seemed the dead-end of a corridor with a narrow, tall blank wall before us and no doors visible. The arrangement struck me as peculiar. The dead-end wall was a lath and plaster affair, and in one place, low down, the plaster had crumbled in a big, jigsaw-puzzle shape through which I could see to the other side: daylight and bare floorboards, and something black: black material, velvet, perhaps, which I took to be a curtain or a narrow screen of some sort until suddenly it moved and I glimpsed the flash of a stockinged leg and the spiked heel of a slender black shoe. The dog moaned softly. 'Now watch this,' Morden said, and turned to the blind wall, and, pressed his fingers to a hidden switch or something, and with a click the narrow wall turned into a door and swung open on creaking hinges. What a childish thrill it was to see it, a wall opening! I felt like one of RLS's plucky boy heroes. Beyond was a triangular room with a low, grimed window looking across the street to a brick parapet over the top of which I could see the city's domed and spiked skyline dusted with September sunlight. The furnishings consisted of a single spindle-backed chair left there by someone and forgotten, and a broad, prolapsed chaise-longue that presented itself to our gaze with an air of elephantine suggestiveness. Stacked against the wall and draped with a mildewed dustsheet were what could only be framed pictures, half a dozen or so (eight, in fact; why this coyness?). I peered about: no one, and nothing, save a tang of perfume that was already so faint it might have been only in my imagination. Morden walked forward with an impresario's swagger and whisked the dustsheet from the stacked pictures. 'Have a look,' he said, gesturing at them with the champagne bottle, swinging it like an Indian club. 'Just have a look!' While Francie leaned in the doorway with his hands in his pockets and winked at me, dropping with practised ease a lizard's leathery eyelid.

1. Pursuit of Daphne ca. 1680

Johann Livelb (1633–1697)

Oil on canvas, 26½ × 67 in. (67.3 × 170.2 cm.)

A product of this artist's middle age, the *Pursuit of Daphne* is a skilfully executed, poised yet vigorous, perhaps even somewhat coarse work with uncanny and disturbing undertones. The brooding light which throws the central figures into high relief and bathes the background distances in an unearthly glimmer produces a spectral and almost surreal quality which constitutes what some critics consider the picture's chief interest. The dimensions of the canvas, a lengthy rectangle, would suggest the painting was commissioned for a specific site, perhaps above a couch or bed; certainly the atmosphere of unrestrained though polished lewdness informing the scene supports the contention (cf. Popov, Popham, Pope-Hennessy) that the work was painted for the boudoir. As always, Livelb adapts his vision to the dictates of available form, and here has used the dimensions of his long, low panel to create a sense of headlong dash appropriate to the theme while yet maintaining a kind of ersatz classical repose, an enervated stillness at the heart of seeming frenzy. The action, proceeding from left to right, strikes the viewer as part of a more extended movement from which the scene has suddenly burst forth, so that the picture seems not quite complete in itself but to be rather the truncated, final section of a running frieze. The artist reinforces the illusion of speed by having the wind blow – and a strong wind it is – not in the faces of pursuer and pursued, as we might expect, but from behind them, as if Aeolus himself had come to urge Apollo on in the chase. Despite this following wind, Daphne's hair, bound in a purple ribbon, flows back from her shoulders in long, rippling tresses, a sinuous movement that finds an echo in the path of the river Peneus meandering through the distant landscape of the background like a shining, silver serpent. The figure of Cupid with his bow, hovering at the extreme left of the picture, has the aspect less of a god than of a gloating satyr, and there is in his terrible smile not only the light of revenge but also a prurient avidity: he intends to enjoy the spectacle of the rape that he believes he is about to witness. Apollo, love's bolt buried to the gilded fletching in his right shoulder-blade, cuts a somewhat sorry figure; this is not the lithe ephebe of classical depiction but, probably like the painter himself at the time, a male in his middle years, slack-limbed, thick-waisted, breathing hard, no longer fit for amorous pursuit (there have been suggestions that this is a self-portrait but no evidence has been adduced to support the theory). If Daphne is suffering a transformation so too is the god. We see in the expression of his eyes – how well the painter has captured it! – the desperation and dawning anguish of one about to experience loss, not only of this ravishing girl who is the object of his desire but along with her an essential quality of selfhood, of what up to this he believed he was and now knows he will not be again. His sinewed hand that reaches out to grasp his quarry will never find its hold. Already Daphne is becoming leaf and branch; when we look closely we see the patches of bark already appearing through her skin, her slender fingers turning to twigs, her green eyes blossoming. How swooningly the laurel tree leans over her, each fringed leaf (*wie eines Windes Lächeln*, as Rilke so prettily puts it) eager to enfold her in a transfiguring embrace. We could have done without that indecent pun between the cleft boughs of the tree and the limbs of the fleeing girl. Here as in so much of Livelb's work the loftiness of the classical theme is sacrificed for the sake of showiness and vulgar effects, and in the end the picture lacks that nobility of purpose and simplicity of execution that a greater artist would have brought to it. To quote the critic Erich Auerbach writing in a different context, what we have here is 'a highly rhetorical style in which the gruesomely sensory has gained a large place; a sombre and highly rhetorical realism which is totally alien to classical antiquity.'

AUNT CORKY was not in fact my aunt but a cousin on my mother's side so far removed that by her time the bloodline must have become thinned to about the thickness of a corpuscle. She claimed to be Dutch, or Flemish when she thought that sounded fancier, and it is true, I believe, that her people originated in the same hunched hamlet in the Pays-Bas from which my mother's ancestors had emigrated centuries ago (I see it by Hobbema, of course: a huddle of houses with burnt-sienna roofs, a rutted road and a man in a hat walking along, and two lines of slender poplars diminishing into a dream-blue distance), but she had lived in so many places, and had convinced herself that she had lived in so many more, that she had become blurred, like a statue whose features time has abraded, her self-styled foreignness worn down to a vague, veiled patina. All the same, in places the original lines still stood out in what to me seemed unmistakable relief: she had the Lowlander's broad, bony forehead and high cheekbones (cf. Dürer's dauntless drawing of his mother, 1514), and her voice even had a faint, catarrhal catch on certain tricky consonants. When I was a child she was to me completely the continental, a product of steepled towns and different weather and a hotchpotch of impossible languages. Though she was probably younger than my parents, in those days she looked ancient to me, I suppose because she was so ugly, like the witch in a fairy-tale. She was short and squarely built, with a prize-fighter's chest and big square hands with knotted veins; with her squat frame and spindly legs that did not meet at the knees and her always slightly crooked skirts she had the look of an item of furniture, a sideboard, perhaps, or a dining-room table with its flaps down. She carried off her ugliness with a grand hauteur. She was said to have lost a husband in the war; her tragedy was always referred to by this formula, so that I thought of him as not dead but misplaced, a ragged, emaciated figure with desperate eyes wandering amidst cannon-smoke through the great forests and shattered towns of Europe in search of my Aunt Corky (her real name, by the way, was an unpronounceable collision of consonants interspersed with i's and y's). She had suffered other things during the war that were referred to only in hushed hints; this was a matter of deep and strangely exciting speculation to me in my fumbling pre-adolescence, and I would picture her bound and splayed in the dank cellar of a barracks in a narrow street beside a canal while a troupe of swastikaed squareheads approached her and . . . but there, unfed by experience or, as yet, by art, my imagination faltered.

I am still not sure which one of Aunt Corky's many versions of her gaudy life was true, if any of them was. Her papers, I have discovered, tell another story, but papers can be falsified, as I know well. She lied with such simplicity and sincere conviction that really it was not lying at all but a sort of continuing reinvention of the self. At her enraptured best she had all the passion and rich inventiveness of an *improvisatrice* and could hold an audience in a trance of mingled wonder and embarrassment for a quarter of an hour or more without interruption. I remember when I was very small listening to her recount to my mother one day the details of the funeral of the young wife of a German prince she claimed to have witnessed, or perhaps even to have taken part in, and I swear I could see the coffin as it was borne down the Rhine on the imperial barge, accompanied only by *seine königliche Hoheit* in his cream and blue uniform and plumed silver helmet while his grieving subjects in their thousands looked on in silence from the river banks. As so often, however, Aunt Corky went too far, not content until narrative had been spun into yarn: the barge passed under a bridge and when it came out the other side the coffin, bare before, was suddenly seen to be heaped with white roses, hundreds of them, in miraculous profusion. 'Like that,' she said, making hooped gestures with her big hands, piling imaginary blossoms higher and higher, her eyes shining with unshed tears, 'so many, oh, so many!'

How did she come to have all that money when she died? It is a mystery to me. She never had a job, that I know of, and had seemed to live off the charity of a network of relatives here and abroad. There was a prolonged liaison with an Englishman, a lugubrious and decidedly shifty character with a penchant for loud ties and two-tone shoes; he strikes me as an unlikely provider of wealth; rather the opposite, I should say. They married, I think – Aunt Corky's morals were a subject our family passed over in tight-lipped silence – and she moved with him to England where they travelled about a lot, mainly in the Home Counties, living in genteel boarding houses and playing a great deal of whist. Then something went wrong and Basil – that was his name, it's just come back to me – Basil was dismissed, never to be spoken of again, and Aunt Corky returned to us with another weight added to her burden of sorrows, and whenever there was talk of England or things English she would flinch and touch a hand to her cheek in a gesture at once tragic and resigned, as if she were Dido and someone had mentioned the war at Troy. I was not unfond of her. From those early days I remembered her curious, stumping walk and parroty laugh; I could even recall her smell, a powerful brew of cheap scent, mothballs and a dusty reek the source of which I was never able to identify but which was reminiscent of the smell of cretonne curtains. And cigarette smoke, of course; she certainly had the true continental's dedication to strong tobacco, and wherever she went she trailed an ash blue cloud behind her, so that when I thought of her from those days I saw a startlingly solid apparition constantly stepping forth from its own aura. She wore sticky, peach-coloured make-up, and rouge, and painted her large mouth, always slightly askew, with purplish lipstick; also she used to dye her hair a brassy shade of yellow and have it curled and set every Saturday morning.

How pleasant it is, quietly turning over these faded album leaves.

I don't know why I allowed myself to go and to see her after all those years. I shy from the sickroom, as who does not, and so much had happened to me and to my life since those by now archaic days that I was not sure I would still speak a language comprehensible to this fading relic of a lost age. I had assumed that she was already dead; after all, everyone else was, both of my parents, and my . . . and others, all gone into the ground, so how should she, who seemed ancient when they were young, be surviving still? Perhaps it was merely out of curiosity then that I—

Ah, what a giveaway it is, I've noticed it before, the orotund quality that sets in when I begin consciously to dissemble: *and so much had happened to me and to my life since those by now archaic days* – dear, oh dear! Whenever I employ locutions such as that you will know I am inventing. But then, when do I not use such locutions? (And I said that Aunt Corky was a liar!)

She was living, if that is the way to put it, in a nursing home outside the city called The Cypresses, a big pink and white gazebo of a place set in a semi-circle of those eponymous, blue-black, pointy trees on the side of a hill with a sweeping and slightly vertiginous view of the sea right across to the other side of the bay. There was a tall, creosote-smelling wooden gate with one of those automatic locks with a microphone that squawked at me in no language that I recognised, though I was let in anyway. Tarmac drive, shrubs, a sloping lawn, then suddenly, like an arrow flying straight out of the past, the sharp, prickly smell of something I knew but could not name, some tree or other, eucalyptus, perhaps, yes, I shall say eucalyptus: beautiful word, with that goitrous upbeat in the middle of it like a gulp of grief. I almost stumbled, assailed by the sweetness of forgotten sorrows. Then I saw the house and wanted to laugh, so delicate, spindly and gay was it, so incongruous, with its pillared arches and filigree ironwork and glassed-in verandah throwing off a great reflected sheet of afternoon sunlight. Trust Aunt Corky to end up here! As I followed the curve of the drive the sea was below me, far-off, blue, unmoving, like something imagined, a sea of the mind.

The verandah door was open and I stepped inside. A few

desiccated old bodies were sunning themselves in deckchairs among the potted palms. Rheumed yellowish eyes swivelled and fixed on me. A door with glass panels gave on to an interior umber dimness. I tapped cautiously and waited, lightly breathing. 'You'll have to give that a good belt,' one of the old-timers behind me said quaveringly, and coughed, making a squelching sound like that of a wellington boot being pulled out of mud. There was a pervasive mild smell of urine and boiled dinners. I knocked again, more forcefully, making the panes rattle, and immediately, as if she had been waiting to spring out at me, a jolly, fat girl with red hair threw open the door and said, 'Whoa up there, you'll wake the dead!' and grinned. She was dressed in a nurse's uniform, with a little white cap and those white, crêpe-soled shoes, and even had a wristwatch pinned upside down to her breast pocket (why do they do that?), but none of it was convincing, somehow. She had a faint air of the hoyden, and reminded me of a farm girl I knew when I was a child who used to give me piggyback rides and once offered to show me what she called her thing if I would first show her mine (nothing came of it, I'm afraid). I asked for Aunt Corky and the girl looked me up and down with an eyebrow arched, still grinning sceptically, as if she in her turn suspected me of being an impostor. A blue plastic tag on her collar said her name was Sharon. 'Are you the nephew?' she asked, and I answered stoutly that I was. At that moment there materialised silently at my side a plump, soft, sandy-haired man in a dowdy, pinstriped dark suit who nodded and smiled at me in a wistfully familiar way as if we were old acquaintances with old, shared sorrows. I did not at all like the look of him or the sinister way he had crept up on me. 'That will be all right, Sharon,' he murmured in a low and vaguely ecclesiastical-sounding voice, and the girl shrugged and turned and sauntered off whistling, her crêpe soles squeaking on the black-and-white tiled floor. 'Haddon is the name,' the pinstriped one confided, and waited a beat and added, 'Mr Haddon.' He slipped a hand under my arm and directed me towards a staircase that ascended steeply to a landing overhung by a broad window with gaudily coloured panes that seemed to me somehow menacing. I had begun to feel hindered, as if I were wading through thick water; I also had a sense of a suppressed, general hilarity of which I felt I was somehow the unwitting object. As I was about to mount the stairs I caught a flurry of movement from the corner of my eye and flinched as a delicate small woman with the face of an ancient girl came scurrying up to me and plucked my sleeve and said in a flapper's breathless voice, 'Are you the pelican man?' I turned to Haddon for help but he merely stood gazing off with lips pursed and pale hands clasped at his flies, biding and patient, as if this were a necessary but tiresome initiatory test to which I must be submitted. 'The pelican man?' I heard myself say in a sort of piteous voice. 'No, no, I'm not.' The old girl continued to peer at me searchingly. She wore a dress of dove-grey silk with a gauzy silk scarf girdling her hips. Her face really was remarkable, soft and hardly lined at all, and her eyes glistened. 'Ah,' she said, 'then you are no good to me,' and gave me a sweetly lascivious smile and wandered sadly away. Haddon and I went on up the stairs. 'Miss Leitch,' he murmured, as if offering an explanation. When we reached the landing he stopped at a door and tapped once and inclined his head and listened for a moment, then nodded to me again and mouthed a silent word of encouragement and softly, creakingly, descended the stairs and was gone. I waited, standing in a lurid puddle of multi-coloured light from the stained-glass window behind me, but nothing happened. I became at once acutely aware of myself, as if another I, mute and breathing, had sprouted up out of the balding carpet to loom over me monstrously. I put my face to the door and whispered Aunt Corky's name and immediately seemed to feel another heave of muffled laughter all around me. There was no response, and in a sudden bluster of vexation I thrust open the door and was blinded by a glare of light.

By now I had begun seriously to regret having breached this house of shades, and would have been thankful if Mr Haddon or some other guardian of the place had come and stepped firmly in front of me and shut the door and ushered me down the stairs and out into the day, saying, *There there, it is all a mistake, you have come to the wrong place, and besides your aunt is dead.* I thought with panicky longing of the blue sea and the sky out there, those swaying, sentinel trees. That's me all over, forever stepping unwillingly into one place while wishing for another. I had the impression, and have it still despite the evidence of later experience, that the room was huge, a vast, white, faintly humming space at the centre of which Aunt Corky lay tinily trapped on the barge of a big high bed, adrift in her desuetude. She had been dozing and at my approach her eyes clicked open as if the lids were controlled by elastic. In my first glimpse of her she did that trick that people do when you have not seen them for a long time, thrusting aside a younger and now not very convincing double and slipping deftly into its place. She lay still and stared at me for a long moment, not knowing, I could see, who I was or whether I was real or a figment. In appearance she seemed remarkably little changed since the last time I had seen her, which must have been thirty years before. She was wrinkled and somewhat shrunken and had exchanged her dyed hair for an even more startlingly lutescent wig but otherwise she was unmistakably Aunt Corky. I don't know why this should surprise me but it did, and even made me falter for a second. Without lifting her head she suddenly smiled and said, 'Oh, I would not have recognised you!' Did I ever describe to you Aunt Corky's smile? She opened her eyes wide and peeled her lips back from a set of dentures that would have fitted a small horse, while her head very faintly trembled as if she were quaking from the strain of a great though joyous physical effort. A mottled hand scrabbled crabwise across the sheet and searched in space for mine; I grasped her hooked fingers and held her under the elbow – what a grip she had: it was like being seized on by a branch of a dead tree – and she hauled herself upright in the bed, grunting. I did the usual business with pillows and so on, then brought a chair and sat down awkwardly with my hands on my knees; is there any natural way to sit beside a sickbed? She was wearing a not very clean white smock with short sleeves, the kind that patients are made to don for the operating theatre; I noticed bruises in the papery skin of the crook of her arm where blood must have been put in or taken out. She sat crookedly with her mouth open and gazed at me, panting a little, her unsteady smile making it seem as if she were shaking her head in wonderment. Two big tears brimmed up in her eyes and trembled on the lower lids. As ever in the presence of the distress of others I found myself holding my breath. I asked her how she was and without a trace of irony she answered, 'Oh, but wonderful, wonderful – as you see!'

After that, conveniently enough, there are gaps in my memory, willed ones, no doubt. I suppose we must have talked about the past, the family, my so-called life – God knows, Aunt Corky was not one to leave any chink of silence unstopped – but what I best recall are things, not words: that white smock, for instance, bleached by repeated use (how many had died in it, I wondered), an overflowing tinfoil ashtray on the bedside table, the livid smear of lipstick she hastened to put on with an unsteady hand. She was a little dazed at first, but as the anaesthetic of sleep wore off she became increasingly animated. She was annoyed to be discovered in such a state of disarray, and kept making furtive adjustments – that lipstick, a dab of face powder, a rapid tongue-test of the state of her dentures – assembling herself in flustered stages, a prima donna preparing for the great role of being what she imagined herself to be. And as the physical she became firmly established so too the old manner strongly reasserted itself, as she sat there, fully upright now, smoking and complaining, at once haughty, coquettish and put-upon. Aunt Corky had an intimately dramatic relationship with the world at large; no phenomenon of history or happenstance was so momentous or so trivial that she would not see it as an effect directed solely at her. In her version of it the most recent world war had been an act of spite got up to destroy her life, while she would look out at a rainy day with a martyr's sorrowing gaze and shake her head as if to say, *Now look what they have sent to try me!* But a moment later she would shrug and gamely tip her chin (each whisker sprouting on it dusted with a grain or two of face powder) and flash that equine smile that never failed to make me think of the talking mule in those films from my childhood, and be her usual, chirpy self again. Always she bobbed up, pert and bright and full of jauntiness, a plucky swimmer dauntlessly breasting a sea of troubles.

But none of this was as I had expected it would be. After all, they had summoned me to what I had assumed would be a deathbed scene, with my aunt, a serene and quietly breathing pre-corpse, arranged neatly among the usual appurtenances (crisp linen, tweed-suited doctor, and in the background the wordless nurse with glinting kidney-dish), instead of which here she was, as talkative and fantastical as ever. She was frail, certainly, and looked hollow, as old people do, but far from being on her last legs she seemed to me to have taken on a redoubled energy and vigour. The Aunt Corky of my memories of her had by now dwindled so far into the past that I could hardly make her out any more, so vivid was this new, wizened yet still spry version before me. The room too seemed to diminish in size as she grew larger in it, and the glare of sea-light abated in the window, dimmed by the smoke of her cigarettes.

'Of course, these are forbidden,' she said, tapping the barrel of her fag with a scarlet fingernail, and added darkly, 'They are telling me all the time to stop, but I say, what concern is it of theirs?'

The bed, the chair, the little table, the lino on the floor, how sad it all seemed suddenly, I don't know why, I mean why at just that moment. I rose and walked to the window and looked down over the tilted lawn to the sea far below. A freshening wind was smacking the smoke-blue water, leaving great slow-moving prints, like the whorls of a burnisher's rag on metal. Behind me Aunt Corky was talking of the summer coming on and how much she was looking forward to getting out and about. I had not the heart to remind her that it was September.

'They are all so kind here,' she said, 'so good. And Mr Haddon – you have met him, I hope? – he is a saint, yes, a saint! Of course, he is trained for it, you know, he has diplomas. I knew the moment I saw him that he was an educated man. I said to him, I said, *I recognise a person of culture when I meet him.* And do you know what he did? He bowed, and kissed my hand – yes, kissed my hand! *And I,* he said, in that very quiet voice he has, *I, dear madam, I too recognise breeding when I see it.* I only smiled and closed the conversation; it does not do to be too much familiar. He sees to everything himself, everything. Do you know—' she twisted about to peer at me wide-eyed where I stood by the window '—do you know, he even makes out the menus? This is true. I complimented him one day on a particularly good ragout – I think it was a ragout – and he became so embarrassed! Of course, he reddens easily, with that fair colouring. *Ah, Miss Corky,* he says – that is what he calls me – *ah, I can have no secrets from you!*' She paused for a moment thoughtfully, working at her cigarette with one eye shut and her mouth pursed and swivelled to one side. 'I hope I do not go too far,' she murmured. 'Sometimes these people . . . But—' with an airy toss of the head that made the gilded curls of her wig bounce '—what can I do? After all, since I am here I must—'

The door opened with a bang and Sharon the child-nurse stuck in her carroty head and said, 'Do you want the pot?' Aunt Corky was scrabbling to stub out her cigarette. She shook her head furiously with lips shut tight. 'Right-o,' Sharon said and withdrew, then popped back again and nodded at the bristling ashtray and said cheerfully, 'I'm telling you, them things will be the death of you.'

When she had gone I returned to the chair beside the bed and sat down. Aunt Corky, mortified, avoided my eye, breathing heavily through flared nostrils and casting about her indignantly with birdlike movements of her head. In the embarrassment of the moment I was holding my breath again; I felt like the volunteer in a levitation act, suspended horizontally on empty air and not daring to move a muscle. Aunt Corky with quivering hands lit another cigarette and blew a defiant trumpet of smoke at the ceiling. 'Of course,' she said bitterly, '*she* is nothing like *him.* She has I think no training, and certainly no feeling for things, no – no *finesse.* Where he got her no one can say.' I said vaguely, 'Well, she's young, after all . . .' Aunt Corky stared at me. 'Young?' she cried, a high, soft shriek, 'young – that one?' and began to cough. 'No, no,' she said impatiently, waving a hand and weaving a figure eight of smoke, 'not the nurse, I mean *her* – the wife.' A poisonous grimace. 'Mrs Haddon.' Whom, if I have the energy for the task, we shall be meeting presently. Aunt Corky got out her cartridge of lipstick again and with broad strokes moodily retouched the stylised pair of lips smeared over the ruined hollow where her mouth used to be, sighing and frowning; with the lipstick revivified she looked as if a tropical insect had settled on her face.

Was it on that visit or later, I wonder, that I told her about Morden and his pictures? Had I even gone to see him at that stage? See how you have loosened my grasp on chronology. I get as mixed up as a dotard. Things from long ago seem as if they had happened yesterday while yesterday itself grows ancient before today has waned. Once I used to date events from before and after the moment when you first confronted me on the corner of Ormond Street; then the day of your going became the pivot on which the eras turned; now all is flux. I feel as the disciples must have felt in the days of desolation between Calvary and the rolling aside of the sepulchre stone. (Dear God, where did that come from? Am I getting religion? Next thing I'll be seeing visions.) Anyway, anyway, whatever day it was, that first or another, when I told her about my new venture, Aunt Corky went into raptures. 'Art!' she breathed, clapping a hand to her breastbone and putting on a Rouault face. 'Art is prayer!' At once I was sorry I had mentioned the subject at all and sat and looked gloomily at my hands while she launched into one of her rhapsodies, at the end of which she reached out a shaky claw again and grasped my wrist and said in a fervent whisper, 'What a chance for you, to make of yourself something new!' I sat back and stared at her but she continued to gaze at me undaunted, still holding on to my wrist and nodding her head slowly, solemnly. 'Because, you know,' she said, with a sort of reproachful twinkle, 'you have been very naughty; yes, yes, very naughty.' I would not have been surprised if she had reached up and tweaked my ear; I may even have blushed. Somehow I had imagined she would know no more of my doings in the years since I had seen her than I knew of hers. Infamy, however, is a thing that gets about. Aunt Corky let go of my wrist and patted me on the hand and lit yet another cigarette. 'Death is nothing,' she said with vague inconsequence, and frowned; 'nothing at all.' She gave a fluttery sigh and sat for a moment looking about her blankly and then slowly subsided against the dented pillows at her back and closed her eyes. I stood up quickly and leaned over her in consternation, but it was all right, she was still breathing. I prised the cigarette cautiously from her fingers and crushed it in the ashtray. Her hand fell away limply and settled palm upward on the sheet. She began to say something but instead her mouth went slack and she suddenly emitted a loud, honking snore and her legs twitched under the bedclothes.

I am never at ease in the presence of sleeping people – that is, I am even less at ease with them than I am when they are awake. When I was married, I mean when I still had a wife and all that, I would have preferred to spend my nights alone, though of course I had not the nerve to say so. It is not so much the uncanny element of sleep that disturbs me, though that is disturbing enough, but the particular kind of solitude to which the sleeper at my side abandons me. It is so strange, this way of being alone: I think of Transylvania, voodoo, that sort of thing. There I sit, or, worse, lie, in the dark, in the presence of the undead, who seem to have attained a state of apotheosis, who seem so *achieved*, resting in this deeply breathing calm on a darkened plain between two worlds, here and at the same time infinitely far removed from me. It is at such moments that I am most acutely aware of my conscious self, and feel the electric throb and tingle, the flimsiness and awful weight, of being a living, thinking thing. The whole business then seems a scandal, or a dreadful joke devised by someone who has long since gone away, the point of which has been lost and at which no one is laughing. My wife, now, was a prompt if restless sleeper. Her head would hit the pillow and swish! with a few preparatory shudders she was gone. I wonder if it was her way of escaping from me. But there I go, falling into solipsism again, my besetting sin. God knows what it was she was escaping. Just everything, I suppose. If escape it was. Probably she was in the same fix as me, wanting a lair herself to lie down in and not daring to say so. To be alone. To be at one. Is that the same? I don't think so. To be at one: what a curious phrase, I've never understood exactly what it means. And I, what must I be like when I sleep, as I occasionally do? Something crouched, I imagine, crouched doggo and ready to spring out of the dark, fangs flashing and eyes greenly afire. No, no, that is altogether too fine, too sleek: more like a big, beached, blubbery thing, cast up out of the deeps, agape and gasping.

What was I . . .? Aunt Corky. Her room. Afternoon sunlight. I am there. The cigarette I had crushed in the ashtray was still determinedly streaming a thin, fast, acrid waver of blue smoke. I waited for a while, watching her sleep, my mind empty, and then with leaden limbs and pressing my hands hard against my knees I rose and lumbered quakingly from the room and closed the door without a sound behind me. By now the patch of part-coloured light from the big window on the landing had moved a surprising distance and was inching its way up the wall. It is odd how the exact look of that afternoon glares in my memory, suffused with a harsh, Hellenic radiance that is sharper and more brilliant, surely, than a September day in these latitudes could be expected to furnish. Probably I am not remembering at all, but imagining, which is why it seems so real. Haddon was waiting for me at the foot of the stairs, stooped and unctuous and at the same time sharply watchful. 'She is a handful, yes,' he said as we walked to the door. 'We were forced to confiscate her things, I'm afraid.' 'Things,' I said, 'what things?' He smiled, a quick little sideways twitch. 'Her clothes,' he said; 'even her nightdress. She had us demented, walking out of the place at all hours of the day and night.' I smiled what must have been a sickly smile and nodded sympathetically, craven as I am, and thought with a shiver, *Imagine, just imagine being him.*

It was a surprise, when I stepped out into the world again, how bright and gay everything seemed, the sun, the gleaming grass, those Van Gogh trees, and the big, light sky with its fringe of coppery clouds; I felt as if I had been away on a long journey and now all at once had arrived back home again. I legged it down the drive as fast as I could go, but when the gate had shut itself behind me I paused and pressed the bell again and the hidden speaker squawked at me as before. But I don't know what it was I had thought I would say, and after some moments of impatient, metallic breathing the voice-box clicked off, and in the sudden silence I felt foolish and exposed again and turned and skulked away down the hill road.

As I went along under the beneficence of the September afternoon's blue and deepening gold my heart grew calm and I felt another pang like the one that had pierced me when I smelled the eucalyptus at the gate. What paradisal longings are these that assail me at unconsidered moments when my mind is looking elsewhere? They are not, I think, involuntary memories such as those the celebrated madeleine is supposed to have invoked, for no specific events attach to them, no childhood landscapes, no beloved figures in rustling gowns or top-hats; rather they seem absences, suddenly stumbled upon, redolent of a content that never was but was only longed for, achingly. This mood of vague, sad rapture persisted even when I got back to the city and my steps took me unresisting and only half aware along the river and down Black Street in the direction of Morden's house. Some part of me must have been brooding on him and his secret trove of pictures stacked in that sealed room. The street was quiet, one side filled with the calm sunlight of late afternoon and the other masked in shadow drawn down sharply like a deep awning. The Boatman's double doors stood open wide and from the cavernous gloom of the interior a beery waft came rolling. A three-legged dog passed by and bared its side-teeth silently at me in a perfunctory way. Someone in an upstairs room nearby was listlessly practising scales on an out-of-tune piano. Thus does fate, feigning unconcern, arrange its paltry props, squinting at the sky and nonchalantly whistling. I stood on the corner and looked up along Rue Street at the house with its blank windows and broad black door. I was not thinking of anything in particular, just loitering. Or maybe in that impenetrable maze I call my mind I was turning over Morden's proposition, maybe that was the moment when I decided, in the dreamy, drifting way that in me passes for volition, to take on the task of evaluating and cataloguing his cache of peculiar pictures. (There it is again, that notion of volition, intention, decisiveness; am I weakening in my lack of conviction?) Suddenly the door opened and a young woman dressed in black stepped out and paused a moment on the pavement, checking in her purse – money? a key? – then turned and set off briskly in the direction of Ormond Street. I know you always insisted you saw me there, skulking on the corner, but that's how I remember it: the door, stop and peer into purse, then turn on heel without a glance and go, head down, and my heart quailing as if it knew already what was in store for it.

I am not naturally curious about people – too self-obsessed for that – but sometimes when my attention is caught I will go to extraordinary lengths to make the most banal discoveries about total strangers. It's crazy, I know. I will get off a bus miles before my own stop so I can follow a secretary coming home from the office to see where she lives; I will traipse through shopping malls – ah, those happy hunting-grounds! – just to find out what kind of bread or cabbages or toilet rolls a burdened housewife with two snotty kids in tow will buy. And it is not just women, in case some bloodhound's nostrils are starting to twitch: I follow men, too, children, anyone. No doubt a first-year psychiatry student could put a name to this mild malady. It's harmless, like picking my nose or biting my nails, and affords me a certain wan pleasure. I am saying all this in my defence (though who my accusers might be I do not know): when I set off that day in surreptitious pursuit of that young woman, a perfect (oh, perfect!) stranger, I had no object in mind other than to know where she was going. I am aware how strident and implausible these protestations of blamelessness sound. Certainly someone observing us making our way along that street, she in sun and I slinking after her on the other, shadowed side, might well have pondered the advisability of alerting a policeman. She was dressed in a short-sleeved black dress and impossible high heels, on which she teetered along at a remarkably swift pace, her purse clasped to her breast and her slender neck thrust forward and her head bent, so that as she clicked along she seemed to be all the while peering over the edge of a precipice that was steadily receding before her. Very pale, with black hair cut short in page-boy style (my Lulu!) and high, narrow shoulders and very thin legs; even at this distance I could see her little white hands with their pink knuckles and ill-painted nails bitten to the quick. On this calm, bright day she looked odd in her black dress and those black silk seamed stockings and gleaming black stilettos; a new-made widow, I thought, off to hear the reading of the will. When she came to the corner of Ormond Street she paused again, daunted, it seemed, by the crowd and the noise and the stalled herds of rush-hour traffic throbbing in the sun. She glanced over her shoulder (*that* was when you saw me) and I turned away quickly and peered into a shop window, my throat thick with fright and gleeful panic, for this is how I get, all hot and fluttery, when I am in full pursuit and my quarry hesitates as if sensing a waft of my hot breath on her neck. After a moment I noticed that the shop I had stopped in front of was derelict and that the cobwebbed window in which I was feigning such interest was empty. When I turned to look for her again she was gone. I hurried to the corner but there was no sign of her. As always when the object of my morbid interest eludes me like this I felt a flattish sensation, a mixture of disappointment and not quite comprehensible relief. With a lighter step I turned to go back the way I had come – and there she was right in front of me, so close that I almost collided with her, standing motionless in a plum-coloured pool of shadow with her purse still primly clutched to her breast. She was older than I had at first supposed (her age, I have just counted it on the calendar, was twenty-seven years, four months, eleven days and five hours, approximately). The glossy crown of her head came up to the level of my Adam's apple. Hair really very black, blue-black, like a crow's wing, and a violet shading in the hollows of her eyes. Identifying marks. Dear God. Absurdly, I see a little black pillbox hat and a black three-quarters veil – a joke, surely, these outlandish accessories, on the part of playful memory? Yet she did reach up to adjust something, a strand of hair or a stray eyelash, I don't know what, and I noticed the tremor in her hand and the nicotine stains on her fingers. With her small, pale, heart-shaped face averted she was frowning into the middle distance, and when she spoke I was not sure that it was me she was addressing.

2. The Rape of Proserpine 1655

L. van Hobelijn (1608–1674)

Oil on canvas, 15 × 21½ in. (38.1 × 53.3 cm.)

Although the grandeur of its conception is disproportionate to its modest dimensions, this is van Hobelijn's technically most successful and perhaps his finest work. The artist has set himself the task of depicting as many as possible of the elements of the myth of the abduction of Demeter's daughter by the god of the underworld, and the result is a crowded, not to say cluttered, canvas which with its flattened surface textures and uncannily foreshortened perspectives gives more the impression of a still life than the scene of passionate activity it is intended to be. The progression of the seasons, the phenomenon which lies at the heart of this myth, is represented with much subtlety and inventiveness. The year begins at the left of the picture in the vernal meadow by lake Pergus – note the opalescent sheen of water glimpsed through the encircling, dark-hued trees – where Prosperpine's companions, as yet all unaware of what has befallen her, wander without care amidst the strewn violets and lilies that were let drop from the loosened folds of the girl's gown when the god seized her. In the foreground the great seated form of Demeter presides over the fertile summer fields, her teeth like barley pearls (or pomegranate seeds?) and with cornstalks wreathed in her hair: a grotesque, Arcimboldoesque figure, ancient yet commanding, the veritable mother of the mysteries. To her left, at the right of the picture, the trees that fringe the headlands above the narrow

449

inlet of the sea have already turned and there is an autumnal smokiness in the air. Sunk here to her waist in the little waves the nymph Cyane, cursed by the god of death, is dissolving in her own bitter tears, while at her back the waters gape where Pluto has hurled his sceptre into the depths. On the surface of the water something floats which when we take a glass to it reveals itself to be a dark-blue sash: it is Proserpine's girdle, the clue that will lead her grief-demented mother to the underworld in pursuit of her lost daughter. The placing of the girdle in the sea is one of van Hobelijn's temporal jests, for when we examine the figure of Proserpine suspended above the waves we note that the girdle in fact has not yet fallen from her waist: in this painted world all time is eternally present, and redeemable. With what consummate draughtsmanship has the painter positioned in the pale, marine air the flying chariot with its god and girl. The arrangement of vehicle, horses and passengers measures no more than five centimetres from the flared nostrils of the leading steed to the tips of Proserpine's wind-rippled hair, yet we feel with overwhelming immediacy the full weight of this hurtling mass of iron and wood and flesh that is about to plunge into the gaping sea. With its sense of suspended yet irresistible violence the moment is an apt prefigurement of the rape shortly to take place in Tartarus. The god's swarth features are set in a grimace of mingled lust and self-loathing and his upraised arm wielding the great black whip forms a gesture that is at once brutal and heavy with weariness. Proserpine, a frail yet striking figure, intensely realised, seems strangely unconcerned by what is occurring and gazes back over her shoulder, out of the frame, with an air of languid melancholy, caught here as she is between the bright world of the living and the land of the dead, in neither of which will she ever again be wholly at home. Beyond her, in the background at the top of the picture, Mount Etna is spewing fire and ash over a wintry landscape laid waste already by the wrath of grief-stricken Demeter. We see the broken ploughshare and the starving oxen and the farmer lamenting for his fields made barren by the goddess in her rage at an ungrateful earth that will not give up to her the secret of her daughter's fate. And so the round of the seasons is completed. We think of other paintings with a seasonal theme, the *Primavera*, for example, but van Hobelijn is not that 'Botticelli of the North' some critics claim him to be, and his poor canvas with its jumbled perspectives and heavy-handed symbolism is utterly lacking in the poise, the celestial repose, the sense of unheard music sounding through its pellucid airs, that make of the Italian painter's work a timeless and inexhaustible masterpiece. However, *The Rape of Proserpine* wields its own eerie yet not inconsiderable power, fraught as it is with presentiments of loss and disaster, and acknowledging as it does love's destructiveness, the frailty of human wishes and the tyrannical and irresistible force of destiny.

I KNOW NOW I should have told her who I was, should have admitted I had been to the house already, had met Morden and seen the pictures. In other words, I should have come clean, but I did not, and so the whole thing started off in a fog of ambiguity and dissimulation. On the other hand, you, I mean she (I must try to stick to the third person, which is after all what you turned out to be), she too it seems was less than candid, for although she treated me that day as if I were no more than an amiable stranger whose burden of solitude she was prepared to lighten for an hour, she insisted later that she had known very well who I was, or that at least – her version of the matter varied – she had known that I was someone who was involved with Morden and the house. Why else would she have accosted me on the street like that, she demanded, in the chalk-on-blackboard shriek by which now and then she betrayed herself; did I think she was in the habit of picking up strange men? I did not answer that but instead diffidently made mention of Cupid and his arrow, which caused her to snort. Anyway, if I had owned up that first day it would have destroyed the clandestine intensity of the occasion. I believe the tone of all that was to happen between us was set in that first encounter with its sustained, hot hum of mendacity and secret knowing.

It was odd to be shown the house for a second time in the same week. Everything was different, of course. This time the emphases fell on the off-beats. I followed her up the stairs through the cool stillness of afternoon and tried to keep my eyes off her narrow little rump joggling in front of me in its tight sheath of black silk; for reasons that were and continue to be obscure I felt it was incumbent on me not to acknowledge the possibilities of

452

the situation. I think that despite everything I must be at heart a gentleman of the old school. I take this opportunity, before I have put both feet on the slippery slope and can still articulate a balanced sentence (there will be a lot of heavy breathing later on), to state that when it comes to what is called love and all that the word entails I am a dolt. Always was, always will be. I do not understand women, I mean I understand them even less than the rest of my sex seems to do. There are times when I think this failure of comprehension is the prime underlying fact of my life, a blank region of unknowing which in others is a lighted, well-signposted place. Here, in me, in this Bermuda Triangle of the soul, the fine discriminations that are a prerequisite for moral health disappear into empty air and silence and are never heard of again. I could blame the women I have consorted with – my mother, for instance – and of course my sometime wife, could accuse them of not having educated me properly, of not inducting me into at least the minor mysteries of their sorority, but to what avail? None. The lack was in me from the start. Maybe a chromosome went missing in the small bang out of which I was formed. Perhaps that's it, perhaps that's what I am, a spoilt woman, in the way that there used to be spoilt priests. That would explain a lot. But no, that is too easy; even if it should be the case, there is too much the possibility of exoneration in it. No, it is not the anima lost in me that I am after, but the ineffable mystery of the Other (I can hear your ribald snigger); that is what all my life long I have plunged into again and again as into a choked Sargasso Sea wherein I can never find my depth. In you I thought my feet at last would reach the sandy floor where I could wade weightlessly with bubbles kissing my shins and small things skittering under my slow-motion tread. Now it seems I was wrong, wrong again.

We stopped on the circular landing at the top of the house and she lit a cigarette. She kept frowning about her in a vague, vexed sort of way, as if she thought she had lost something but did not know what it could be. Abstract: that is the word I always associate with her: abstract, abstracted, abstractedly, and then the variants, such as absently, and absent-minded, and now, of course, in this endless aftermath, with the clangour of a wholly new connotation, just: absent. She smoked with a schoolgirl's amateurish swagger, dragging on the cigarette swiftly with hissing intakes of breath and puffing out big clouds of uninhaled blue smoke. Above us in the tall windows sunlight stood in blocks that looked as solid as blond stone. An aeroplane flew over, making the panes vibrate tinily, and as if in sympathy my diaphragm fluttered and with a faint shock I realised that what I was feeling most strongly was fear: not only of Morden and of being discovered here by him or his man or his man's black dog, but of her, too, and of the house itself – of everything. Yet I do not know if fear is the right word. Something less definite, then? Alarm? Apprehension? Whatever it was it was a not unpleasurable sensation; there was something of childhood in it, of games played with giddy girls in the groin-warm glow of firelit parlours on winter Sunday evenings long ago. Yes, this is what struck me that first time, this sense of having been transported back to some gropingly tentative, confused and expectant stage of life. For you see, I did not know what was happening, why she had brought me here or who she was or why she was dressed in these slinky, silken weeds (come to think of it, I never did discover the explanation for that outlandish costume; was it your seduction suit?), and I was as wary and uncertain as an adolescent, and as sweatily excited. No, I did not know what was going on, but being essentially a trusting type I was content to assume that someone did.

A., I shall call her. Just A. I thought about it for a long time. It's not even the initial of her name, it's only a letter, but it sounds right, it feels right. Think of all the ways it can be uttered, from an exclamation of surprise to a moan of pleasure or pure pain. It will be different every time I say it. A. My alpha; my omega.

Her manner was a mixture of curiosity and impatience and a kind of defiant offhandedness, like that of a spoiled, dissatisfied, far too clever twelve-year-old. She seemed to – how shall I say? –

to fluctuate, as if we were engaged in an improvised dance my part in which was to stand still while she flickered and shimmered in front of me, approaching close up and at once retreating, watching me covertly from behind that black veil which my overheated imagination has placed before her face. Then the next moment she would go limp and stand gawkily with one foot out of her shoe and pressed on the instep of the other, gazing down in a sort of stupor and holding a bit of her baby-pink lower lip between tiny, wet, almost translucent teeth. It was as if she were trying out alternative images of herself, donning them like so many slightly ill-fitting gowns and then taking them off again and dispiritedly casting them aside. It was not the house she had been showing me but herself – herselves! – moving against this big, blank-white, sombre background, successive approximations of an ultimate self that would, that must, remain forever hidden. And now, blood thudding in my ears with a jungle beat and my clenched palms beginning to sweat, I was waiting for her to make the final revelation, to let fall the final veil, and take me into the secret room. For I knew it must have been she I had glimpsed through the crumbling wall the first time I came here. Would she open that last door and let me in? I saw myself standing there, suspended in the slanted sunlight at the top of the stairs, and everything was shifting and shaking and thrummingly taut, as if the house were a ship running before the wind with all sails spread. I was, I realised, embarked on an adventure, no less.

All this in my recollection of it takes place in a kind of ringing silence, but in fact she had kept a commentary going in her unfocused, smoky voice the whole way up through the house. I don't recall the words. Her tone was vague yet touched with an odd, displaced vehemence; always it was to be like this with her, everything she said seemed no more than a way of not saying what she was thinking. Does that make sense? It does to me. Now and then she would pause and stand listening intently, not to the sounds of the world about her but as if to a voice coming from a great distance inside her own head, telling her things, advising her, upbraiding her. I remember her saying to me one

day – I think of it as much later, in another age, but it can only
have been a matter of weeks – I remember her saying how
sometimes she got frightened when she thought about her mind
and how she could not stop it working. In the toils of lovemaking
we had rolled from the lumpy chaise-longue on to the floor and
were lying quietly now watching rain-clouds progressing like
noble wreckage across the jumbled rooftops of the city. How
sweetly poignant were those silent autumn afternoons with their
quicksilver sheen and somehow friendly chilliness and the country
smells of leaf and loam and wood-smoke that penetrated even
here, in the depths of the city. She lay on her stomach with the
moth-eaten blanket pulled to her shoulders and a cigarette trembling in her incongruously plump, pale fingers with their reddened knuckles. There was a smudge of lipstick like a fresh bruise
at the corner of her mouth. What frightened her, she said, was
the way it all kept spinning, just spinning and spinning, even
when she was asleep, like a motor that could not be switched off
even for an instant because if it was it would never start up again.
She spoke as if she were alone in this predicament, as if it were
only her mind that was perpetually in motion while the rest of us
could turn ourselves into zombies whenever we felt like it. That
was the way she conceived of everything to do with herself; all
her experiences were unique. It wasn't egotism, I believe, or even
the kind of rueful self-absorption that I so often lose myself in;
she simply could not imagine that the rest of humankind lived
as she was forced to do, in such solitude, locked inside this racing,
unstoppable consciousness; if it were so, surely something would
have been done about it long ago? For unlike me she was a great
believer in progress, and was firmly of the opinion that everything
was improving all the time – for others, that is.

Anyway, that first day, while we dawdled there on the landing,
I convinced myself that I could sense her debating whether or not
to betray what she must think was still Morden's secret and show
me the white room and the stacked pictures, but in the end she
turned, regretfully, so I imagined, and led the way downstairs
again. I felt a sort of slackening then, a general relaxation of flesh

and fancy, and all at once I was impatient to be away from her and from the house, to be alone again, to be on my own: always it is there, you see, the yearning for solitude, for the cell. Then like a blow to the temple it struck me: it was Morden, of course, who had set her on to me (I was wrong, he had not), had led her to one of these high windows and pointed me out to her as I was passing by in the street below, a foreshortened, waddling figure, and said to her, *Look, that's him, go down there and do your stuff.* Oh, the pander! Now in a rush I recalled him casually mentioning his wife, with an ironical twist of the lips (*My wife, you know, my beautiful wife!*), and chuckling. She, I told myself now, she was the final part of the deal, after the free hand and the cut of the profits he had offered me; she was the clincher. (Was he somewhere in the house even now, spying on us?) Oh, I had it all worked out in a flash. As I descended the stairs behind her, my gaze, heavy now with rekindled tumescence, fastened to the back of her neck with its straight-cut fringe and tapering wisp of dark down the shape of an inverted candle-flame, I was working up a fine head of indignation at Morden's wiliness (by now I had conjured up his big face with its Cheshire Cat grin suspended before us in the stairwell), while in another, altogether shadier part of the forest something that had drunk the magic bottle was getting bigger and bigger as my mind, by itself, as it were, speculated in dark excitement on how broad might be the brief that he had given her. But at the same time I kept telling myself it was all nonsense, a fantasy made up out of my head and one or two other areas of my ice-encased anatomy, a story to tell myself to light the drabness in which I was sunk; if she had known who I was it was probably just boredom, or curiosity, or an impulsive wish to meddle in Morden's affairs that had prompted her to address me there in the sun and shadow on that noisy street-corner where I stood dithering in gloomy, middle-aged dishevel-ment. Yet abruptly now, as if she had heard the rusty cogwheels of my long-disused libido squeakingly engage, she stopped and turned with one hand on the banister rail (I notice, by the way, that she has acquired elbow-length black gloves to match the little black hat and veil I have already imagined for her) and looked up at me from under her painted, sootblack lashes with a smile of complicity that fell upon those labouring meshed gears of mine like a warmed drop of amber oil, and it was as if it were we, and not Morden, who were the conspirators in some double double-cross too complicated to be grasped by my poor overburdened understanding.

'Come on,' she said, 'I want to show you something.'

How can I communicate the strangeness, the thrilling incongruity of that first hour with her? It was as if we were aloft on an ill-strung net which she was negotiating with careless ease while I was in danger of losing my footing at any moment and ending up in a hopeless tangle of trapped, flailing limbs. I kept waiting with foreboding for her to tell me why we were here and what it was she supposed we were doing (why, I wonder, did I assume that an explanation would inevitably mean disappointment?), but I waited in vain. She just went along in her flitting, abstracted way, pointing out this or that wholly unremarkable feature of the empty house, as if everything had already been understood and settled between us. She was half tour guide and half the bored madam welcoming an unprepossessing new client to this gaunt bordello. She made no mention of Morden (but then, did she ever speak of him directly, in so many words, in all the time I knew her?), didn't tell me her name or ask mine. *Did* she know who I was? Perhaps when I saw her through that hole in the false wall she in turn caught a glimpse of me and wondered who and what I was and determined to find out. How calmly I pose these questions, yet what a storm of anxiety and pain they provoke in me — for I shall never know the answers for sure, no matter how long I brood on it all, no matter how many obsessed hours I spend turning over the scraps of evidence you left behind. Anyway, for her purposes, whatever they were, probably someone else would have done just as well as I, some needy other who, I suddenly realise, from this moment on will always be with me, now that I have conceived of him, a hopeful phantom lingering just beyond seeing in the corner of my mind's jealous eye. I do not think she was lying, I mean I believe that as time went on she became convinced that of course she had known who I was, whether she had or not. (I am so confused, so confused!) Things like that got lost in her, dates, events, the circumstances of certain meetings, decisive conversations and their outcomes, they just dropped away silently into empty air and were gone; useless to dispute with her – if she believed something had been so then that was how it had been and that was that. Such conviction could make me doubt the simplest of simple facts, and when I had at last given in she would turn away, mollified, with a small, hard look of satisfaction. So now like an anxious naturalist unable to trust his luck I shuffled behind her down those endless, echoing stairs, watching the wing-cases of her shoulder-blades flexing under the brittle stuff of her dress, noting the fish-pale backs of her knees and the fine hairs pressed flat under her nylons like black grass splayed by rain, wincing at the state of her poor heels where those intolerable shoes had chafed them, and I felt myself carried off to other times and other, imaginary places: a spring day in Clichy (I have never been in Clichy), a hot, thundery evening on a road somewhere in North Africa (never been there, either), a great, high, panelled room in an ancient château with straw-coloured sunlight on the faded tapestries and someone practising on a spinet (though I have never seen a spinet or heard one played). Where do they come from, these mysterious, exalted flashes that are not memories yet seem far more than mere imaginings? You believed, you said, that we have all lived before; perhaps you were right. *Are* right; *are*. I cling to the present tense as to a sheer cliff's last hand-hold.

When we came to the ground floor she led me along the hall to the rear of the house. I thought she was taking me into the garden – in the barred glass of the low back door viridian riot was briefly visible – but instead she turned down yet another flight of stairs, this one narrow and made of black stone. I clattered after her. At the bottom was a dank, flagstoned basement passageway dimly illumined from the far end by a high lunette through which I could see the oddly mechanical-looking legs of people passing by outside in a sunlit street that from here seemed a place on another planet. The air was chilly and damp and smelled strongly of lime. In the suddenly attentive silence A. slipped her arm through mine and I felt with a soft detonation along my nerves her wrist's cool silkiness and the intricate bones of her elbow pressing against my ribs. Behind the spice of her perfume I detected a sharp, faint, foxy tang of sweat, and when she leaned her shoulder into the protection of my arm the low neck of her dress fell forward and revealed to me (picture an eyeball swivelling downward wildly, the bloodshot white showing) a glimmering pale slope of skin and a deckled edging of lace. I felt so large beside her, so unwieldy, a big, shambling, out-of-breath baboon. I imagined myself picking her up in my hooped, hairy arms and making off with her into the undergrowth, hooting and gibbering. We came to a door and she stopped, and a tiny tremor ran through her like the passage of an arrow through air, and she laughed softly. 'Here,' she whispered, 'here it is.'

All I saw was a cellar, long and low with a vaulted brick ceiling criss-crossed by a network of wiring from which were suspended a dozen or more naked light bulbs, which despite their profusion shed only a sullen, sulphurous glow that trickled away into corners thick with blackness and died. Along one wall there was a workbench with old wooden planes and mitre boxes and other such stuff, and a battery of powerful electric lamps, turned off, that struck me as vaguely minatory, leaning there ranked and hooded in an attitude of silent alertness. A. began to say some-thing, too loudly, and stopped and laughed again and put a hand to her mouth as the echoes flittered up like bats into the vault of shadows above us. There was a smell, a mixture of sawdust and glue and pungent oil, that seemed familiar, though I could not identify it. Is it hindsight that has conferred on the place a pent-up, mocking air? I felt a silent breeze from somewhere on the back of my neck and I turned to speak to A. only to find that she was no longer there. I was about to call out to her when I heard the sound of clicking claws rapidly approaching along the passageway outside and my heart gave a sort of sideways lurch and then righted itself with a frightening thump. The clicking ceased and Prince the dog appeared soundlessly in the doorway and looked at me, jaws agape and red tongue softly throbbing. A moment passed. I spoke to the creature in a hoarse, high voice and put out a cautious hand. I felt an equal mixture of anger and alarm; how had I allowed myself to be lured into this trap? For this was what I had been expecting for the past half hour, to be discovered like this, caught in surprise and dismay and unaccountable guiltiness. A bead of sweat slid down between my shoulder-blades cold and quick as the point of a knife. Then Francie with his hands in his pockets materialised beside the dog and eyed me smilingly and sucked his teeth and said, 'Private view, eh?' He scanned the cellar with a swift, sharp glance and dog and master delicately sniffed the air: A.'s perfume; I could smell it too. Francie ambled forward and picked up a miniature hammer from the workbench and turned to me and—

Enough of this. I do not like it down here! I do not like it at all. A wave of my wand and *pop*! here we are magically at street level again.

Francie invited me to go with him to The Boatman for a drink, hunching his shoulders and looking away and smiling to himself. We walked along Fawn Street through the hazy, brazen light of early evening with the low sun in our faces. The dog kept close behind us, head down and sharp ears flattened along its skull. The office crowds were hurrying homeward; buses reared, bellowing, cars coughed and fumed. I thought of A., her pale face and vivid lips, the leaf-rustle of her silk dress. Spindly girls dressed all in black with stark white make-up passed us by, hanging on the arms of enchained, bristled young men; they glanced at Francie and nudged each other. He was in his usual outfit: threadbare tweed suit of a peculiar, gingery shade, a flat cap and collarless shirt and cracked brown sharp shoes curling up at the toes. He had the look of one of those characters who used to appear now and then at our door when I was a child, itinerant knife-sharpeners, rag-and-bone men, tinkers selling cans: timeless figures of uncertain origin who went as silently as they had come, and who afterwards would appear along the margins of my dreams.

We turned into Hope Alley and came upon Quasimodo – remember him? – singing *The Green Hills of Antrim Are Calling Me Home* and waggling an empty plastic cup at passers-by. I had been noticing him about the streets for some time, and took an interest in him. Down-and-outs have always appealed to me, for reasons that should be obvious. This was a new and fallen state for him; the last time I had seen him he was working as a signboard man for a jeweller's shop tucked up a laneway off Arcade Street. Those must have been his salad days, perched on a high stool at the sunny corner of the lane with flask of tea and mighty sandwich and the newspaper to read. His sign had borne the ambiguous legend, *The Bijou – Home of Happy Rings*, in front of which was painted a stylised hand with rigid index finger imperiously pointing up Tuck Lane. He was a little nut-brown fellow with curiously taut, shiny skin and a smear of oily black hair plastered to his skull as if he had just taken off a tight-fitting cap. His hump was not very pronounced, more hunch than hump, really; seen from the front, with his tortoise's flattish head thrust forward and that fixed, worried grin that he always wore (was it a tic?), he seemed to be flinching from a playful blow constantly expected but never delivered. I felt proprietorial about him, and I was not pleased when Francie pointed at him now with his chin and snickered and said, 'He's come down in the world. It will be the knacker's for him next.' We drew level with the hunchback and Francie stopped and set himself squarely before him with hands in pockets, feigning enthusiastic appreciation, swaying his head in time to the poor fellow's tuneless bellowing. Quasimodo, alarmed by this unexpected attention, roared all the louder and looked rapidly from one of us to the other in mulish panic, showing the yellowed whites of his eyes. I was wondering where he lived, what hovel sheltered him, and thinking in that slow, amazed way that one does that he would have had a mother once. I tried to picture him as a suckling babe, but failed. At last the song warbled to a close and he wrapped himself in his old grey coat and sidled off, glancing back at us over his hump. Francie watched him go and said, 'Off for a bracer, I don't doubt.' We walked on. Francie was laughing softly to himself again and shaking his head. 'Have you heard this one? Raggedy old geezer staggers into a chemist's shop. *Bottle of meths, please, miss.* Girl brings the bottle, old boy feels it, hands it back. *Have you got one chilled, my dear? – it brings out the bouquet, you know.*'

I must say something about Francie's laugh, though I am not sure laugh is the right word. With eyes slitted and his upper lip curled at one side to reveal a wax-coloured canine, he would produce a low, rasping, squeezed-out sound in falling triplets, a sort of repeated nasal wheeze, while his shoulders faintly shook. It was a guarded, costive sort of laugh, as if he were enjoying too much the world's side-splitting ridiculousness to let others in on the fun and thus risk diminishing it for himself. Even when, as now, he told the joke himself there was the suspicion that it was only a blind and that what was really amusing him was something else altogether that only he was privy to. He gave the impression always of a sort of surreptitious squirming, of slipping and ducking in and out of view. He was like the trickster who comes up silently at your left shoulder and taps you on the right, and when you spin around you think no one is there until you hear his soft chuckle on the other side of you.

The Boatman was loud with nine-to-fivers released for the day, callow young men in cheap sharp suits and watchful girls with crinkled hair and baked-chicken skin. We sat on stools at the bar and Francie took off his cap and set it on his knee and leaned back against a partition with a mirror in it in which I could see reflected the two taut strings at the back of his neck and one of his uncannily flat ears; I was there, too, or half of me: an oddly startled eye and gloomy jowl and one side of a mouth fixed in a sort of rictus over which I seemed to have no control. I drank gin while Francie toyed with a glass of thin beer; he would suck up a mouthful and strain it back and forth through his teeth and then let half of it wash back fizzing into the glass, so that after a while a clouded, stringy deposit that I tried not to look at gathered at the bottom of the glass. One of my headaches was coming on. Even with his eyes fixed on mine Francie gave the impression of looking me up and down with a sort of muffled amusement.

'And you've got down to it already,' he said and gave a low whistle. 'Well, there's eager!' For a moment I thought he was talking about A. and I experienced a hot heave in the region of the solar plexus, sure he must have seen into my mind, where the image of her supple young silken back was still before me, climbing the steps of a steadily ascending scale of speculation. He was watching me with a narrowed eye, and I caught something, like the flash of a weasel's tooth down in the dark of the burrow. 'So what do you think?' he said.

A tall young woman with naked shoulders and extraordinary, glaucescent eyes bumped into me and apologised and immediately burst out laughing and passed on.

What did I think? I thought I should keep mum. Give him the slightest sign and next thing we'd be plotting to make off with Morden's pictures and split the take between us. Not such a bad idea, I suppose. The trouble with Francie was that he was not really real for me. He seemed made-up, a manufactured man, in whose company (if that is the word for what it was to be with him) credence was not required. And this air of fakery that he carried with him infected even his surroundings. Take this day, now. The whole thing had a contrived look to it, the pub, the girl with the grey eyes, the crowd of over-acting extras around us, that theatrically thick yellow beam of sunlight slanting down through the window and lighting up the bottles behind the bar, and Francie himself, sitting in the middle of it all with his cap on his knee, reciting his lines with the edgy, unconvinced air of an actor who knows he is not going to get the part. Why do I allow myself to become involved with such people? (I should talk; who is the real actor here?) I have – I admit it – I have a lamentable weakness for the low life. There is something in me that cleaves to the ramshackle and the shady, a crack somewhere in my make-up that likes to fill itself up with dirt. I tell myself this vulgar predilection is to be found in all true connoisseurs of culture but I am not convinced. I present myself here as a sort of Candide floundering amidst a throng of crooks and sirens but I fear the truth (the truth!) is different. I wanted Morden and his dodgy pictures and all the rest of it, even including Francie, longed for it as the housewife longs for the brothel. I am not good, I never was and never will be. Hide your valuables when I am around, yes, and lock up your daughters, too. I am the bogey-man you dream of as you toss in your steamy beds of a night. That soft step you hear, that's me, prowling the unquiet dark where the light of the watchfire fails. Your sentries are asleep, the guard at your gate is drunk. I have done terrible things, I could do them again, I have it in me, I—

Stop.

Francie was about to speak again but

Was about to speak again but then a change occurred, and he went still and sat at an angle looking at his drink with a fixed, unfocused smile.

Christ, look at me, I'm sweating, my hands are shaking; I shouldn't, I really should not let myself get so worked up.

When Morden arrived I did not hear but rather sensed him behind me. He leaned down to my ear and with mock-menace softly said:

'You're under investigation, you are.'

Today he wore an expensive, ash-grey, double-breasted suit the jacket of which was wrapped around and buttoned tightly under his big bull chest like a complicated sling, so that he seemed even more top-heavy than usual, set down on those thick, short legs and small, incongruously dainty feet. He was not tall, you know; big and wide, but not tall; I must have had at least a couple of inches on him. Not that it made any difference, I was still afraid of him (I know, I know, afraid is not the word, but it will have to do). It would always be thus, I realised, in an odd sort of musing way which must have been partly an early effect of the gin; even if I were to get the better of him in some worldly

dealing I would still quail inwardly before him. He made me feel
off-balance, as if in his presence everything were pitched at an
angle and I must keep constantly at a tilt in order to stay upright.
But then, that was the way I felt with all three of them, more or
less. I was, I *was* Candide. I made my way amongst them in a
daze of uncertainty, looking the wrong way and tripping over
myself, picking my shaky steps, as in a panic dream, athwart the
treacherous slope of their unnervingly knowing regard. What a
dolt I was. Morden must have loved me for it; I was his
entertainment, his straight-man, his – what do they call it? –
his patsy. Why do I not think more harshly of him than I do?
Because – it has just come to me this moment – because he
reminded me of myself. Well, that's a surprise; I shall return to it
when I've given it some thought. Meanwhile he is standing in his
Rodin pose with a hand in his pocket and his head thrown back,
looking at me down the sides of his broad nostrils and smiling in
his glintingly jovial way.

'Yes,' he said almost gaily, 'we're running a few checks on
you. A few scans. Francie here thinks you may not be the thing
at all. He thinks he's come across you somewhere before, in
another life. Don't you, Francie? There's talk—' lowering his
voice to a conspiratorial growl '—there's talk of serious misde-
meanours, of grave misdeeds.'

And he laughed, still eyeing me merrily, as if it were all a
grand joke. Francie said nothing and sat with lowered gaze,
sucking his teeth and turning and turning his beer glass slowly in
its own puddle on the bar top. I want you to see the scene:
evening, the crowded, chattering pub, smoke and dust motes
coiling in the last, thick rays of sunlight slanting down over the
roofs of Gabriel Street, and the three of us there in that little pool
of stillness, Francie and me facing each other perched on our
stools with our knees almost touching and Morden standing at
his ease between us with a hand in the pocket of his jacket as if
he were cradling a gun, admiring his reflection in the flyblown
mirror behind the bar. You were there too, of course, I could feel
your presence vividly, the ghostly fourth of our quartet. Already,

you see, I was carrying you with me, my phantom, my other self. And nothing else mattered very much.

'What do you say?' Morden said to Francie in the mirror. 'Is he the real thing or not? Because if he's not . . .' He took his hand out of his pocket and with finger and cocked thumb shot me silently and grinned. 'Bang. You're dead.'

I am always surprised and gratified by the composure I am capable of in the face of shocks and sudden perils. Morden in his menacingly playful way had brought my past, my buried past, sitting bolt upright out of its coffin, wide-eyed and hideously grinning, and there I was sipping my drink and looking at the ceiling with what I considered an admirable show of unconcern. It is not always thus, of course, but when it is it's wonderfully convincing, I believe. At least, I hope it is. Francie still had not spoken and Morden nudged me and said, 'Sherlock is silent.' He waved a hand in which a glass had suddenly appeared: mineral water – he does not drink, remember? 'Well, in that case, case dismissed,' he said and tapped the base of his glass gavel fashion on the bar. The dog is there too, lying on the floor beside its master's stool with front paws extended and ears pricked up, doing its Anubis impression. Francie scowls. Everything seems small and distant in the tremulous, gin-blue air. For no reason at all I felt suddenly, fatuously, cheerful. Morden put his gun-hand on my shoulder; extraordinary grip, have I said that already? 'Listen,' he said into my ear with mock-sincerity, 'don't worry, I like a self-made man.'

Now everything shifts again, the false panels and secret compartments slide this way and that with an oiled, surreptitious smoothness, and it is another day and we are somewhere else, and the sun is shining steadily as before but from a different angle and not thick but piercing in white-gold filaments through shutters, is it? or wooden blinds? We must be having an Indian summer. Morning, I believe, calm and bright, with that clear-edged, headachy look to things as if they were exhibits set out under polished sheets of glass. We are in the lounge of one of those imitation grand hotels that had begun to spring up on the edge of the quarter, all chrome and honey-coloured wood and the woolly smell of expensive bad dinners. I was delivering a small, well-rounded lecture on the pictures, sitting with my hands clasped between my knees and frowning at the floor. Morden was in a restless mood and had begun to fidget, shifting massively in his chair and casting about him with impatient sighs. 'Yes yes,' he kept saying, trying to silence me, 'that's fine, fine,' and puffing on a vast cigar and clawing angrily at the smoke as though it were a tangle of cobwebs in front of his face. I kept on imperturbably, undeterred. It will not be news to you, I suppose, but I have come to realise that there is a strain of pedantry in me which I enjoy, in a quiet way. It dulls the senses, soothes the heart. It is satisfying to set out things just so, the facts on one side, speculation on the other, the strategies, the alternatives, the possible routes toward a desired conclusion. Perhaps there really is a scholar lost in me. (Need I add that I never believe a word I hear myself saying?) There in the flocculent hush of that hotel lounge I expounded on Josiah Marbot's bizarre collection in what used to be called measured tones, and was aware of a familiar calm descending on me at the centre of which there flickered a pilot-light of unemphatic happiness. And as I talked I listened to myself in mild surprise and admiration. It might have been another voice that was speaking for which I was only the medium. That is all I ever want, in a way, to be here and not here: a living absence. Sometimes in public places I fancy that if I were to stop and stand quite still people would be able to walk through me. I imagine them, that woman with the shopping bag, that girl on her bike, faltering for a second on the other side of me and frowning and giving an involuntary shiver, thinking someone had walked over their grave, while I, the invisible man, smile on them and hold my breath.

'Look,' Morden said, pressing his elbows down on the arms of his chair and squirming forward with knees splayed and ankles crossed, 'all we want to know is, are they genuine?' He waited, squatting before me like an ill-humoured frog. I paused for effect and then quietly pointed out, in my coolest, primmest tone, that the pictures were signed. He flexed an eyebrow; I could hear him breathing, a low, stertorous roar down those big nostrils. 'Which means,' I went on, 'that they are either genuine, or fakes.'

He opened his mouth and laughed, a short, sharp bark. 'What else would they be?' he said.

A large part of the pleasure of pedantry, I have discovered, is to pretend there is no pleasure in it at all. The low monotone, the neutral gaze, the faint edge of impatience and, of course, the touch of condescension, these are the things to cultivate. A picture done in the style of Vaublin, I explained slowly, even if it were a direct copy, does not pretend to be a Vaublin unless it is signed. 'For, you see, the signature—' I sketched a flourish on the air between us '—the signature is everything.'

He scowled. I found them odd and disconcerting, these looks of almost loathing he would fix on me. Now, of course, I suspect they were his way to keep from laughing. What a show it was, and what fun he must have had, playing the bluff businessmen with an eye for beauty and all the rest of it, that whole travesty.

'No,' he said, hawking up the word like phlegm, 'I'll tell you what everything is: everything is when you go to flog a fake and *say* that it's the real thing.'

He kept his scowling stare fixed on me for a moment, nodding his big bull-head, then flopped back in the armchair and stuck the cigar in his mouth and studied a far corner of the room through a rich flaw of smoke.

'Anyway, I'll probably give them away,' he said carelessly. 'To some gallery, maybe.' At the thought of it a brief spark lit his sullen eye: The Morden Collection! 'It's just that I'm . . .' He gestured impatiently and took a sip of his mineral water – no, I mean a puff of his cigar. 'I'm just . . .' He scowled again. There was a wrathful silence. The dog watched him keenly, expecting him, it seemed, to do something marvellous and mad at any moment.

'Curious,' Francie said flatly, and Morden and I turned and stared at him as if he were a foreigner who had suddenly spoken to us in our own language. He looked back at us with that air of boredom and wearied disenchantment, a cigarette dangling from his lip. Francie and his fags, his cap, his dog. Morden cleared his throat and said loudly, 'Yes, that's right, I'm curious.' He glared at me again as if he thought I might attempt to contradict him. 'I want to *know*, that's all,' he said. 'If they're fake they're fake.'

Did I believe him? It was a question that I used to put to myself over and over again, rolling on the floor of the prison cell of my anguish and shame, in the first days after the gimcrack edifice had all come crashing down. Futile, of course; it was never a matter of believing or disbelieving. Belief, trust, suspicion, these are chimeras that arise in hindsight, when I look back from the sad eminence of the knowledge of having been deceived. At the time I just tottered along as usual, like a drunk on a tightrope, trying to concentrate on the business in hand and not fall off despite the buzz of distractions around me, those trapeze artists whizzing past and the clowns cavorting down in the ring. Oh, of course, I must have known from the start that there was something fishy going on – but when is there not? Stick your nose into anything and you will get a whiff of brine and slime. I would catch one or other of them, even the dog, looking at me in what must have been incredulous wonderment, holding their breath, waiting for me to twig what was afoot. It was as if I had surprised them in the midst of a drunken carouse and now, sobered for a second, they were standing about and keeping a straight face, lips shut tight and cheeks bulging, trying not to catch each other's eye for fear of bursting out in guffaws. Sometimes, when I walked out of a room where they were, I would have an uneasy vision, which I would immediately dismiss, of them throwing their arms about each other's shoulders and collapsing into helpless mirth . . . But why do I torment myself like this, what does it matter any more? Is the loss of you not flame enough, that I must keep scorching myself over these embers? Yet I have nothing else, no packet of letters, no locket of bright hair, only these speculations that I turn over endlessly in my head like things on a spit. (*Ich brenne in dir . . .*) And I feel so foolish and pathetic, poor Mr

Punch with his black eye and broken heart and his back humped with shame. I think of myself there in that hotel or wherever it was that day, talking about provenance and dating techniques and the history of oil-based pigments and the necessity for a detailed comparison of brushstrokes, and I squirm like a slug in salt. How could I allow myself to be so easily taken in? And the answer comes of course as pat as you please: because I wanted to be. Bang! go my fists on the cell floor, and bang! my forehead too, between them. Bang! Bang! Bang!

How I talked in those days; when I think back I am aware of a ceaseless background buzz that is the noise of my own voice going on and on. Guilt, I mean the permanent, inexpungible, lifetime variety, turns you into a kind of earnest clown. They speak of guilt as something heavy, they talk about the weight of it, the burden, but I know otherwise; guilt is lighter than air; it fills you up like a gas and would send you sailing into the sky, arms and legs flailing, an inflated Grock, if you did not keep a tight hold on things. For years now talk had been my tether and my bags of ballast. Once I got going on the autodidact's monody there was no stopping me. Art history, the lives of the painters, the studio system in the seventeenth century, there was no end to the topics at my command. And all for no purpose other than to keep suppressed inside me that ever-surging bubble of appalled, excoriating, sulphurous laughter, the cackle of the damned. That's why I was so easily fooled, that's how I could be so easily taken in: because I was always thinking of other things, struggling inwardly with those big burdensome words that had I had the nerve to speak them would have made you stare first and then laugh. Atonement. Redemption. That kind of thing. I was still in hell, you see, or purgatory, at least, and you were one of the elect at whom I squinnied up yearningly as you paced the Elysian fields in golden light.

Yet wait. That is not quite right, or not complete, at least, and gives altogether too worthy an impression. Those big words . . . Oh, leave it, I can't be bothered.

Suddenly, with a violent turn of the wrist, Morden crushed

out his three-quarters unsmoked cigar and stood up briskly, startling the dog, and said, 'Come on, we'll go for a drive.' I looked at Francie but he only shrugged and rose with an air of weary resignation and followed Morden, who was already halfway across the lobby. The girl with the grey eyes gave me a distracted smile and turned away. Here is the door of the pub, I mean the hotel, the revolving door of the St Gabriel Hotel which with a violent sigh deposited me on the sunlit pavement in the middle of a crisp September morning.

Morden's car, a low-slung black beast, was parked on a double yellow line in a street behind the hotel loud with the archaic voices of delivery men. There was a parking ticket clipped to the windscreen. Morden crushed it in his fist and tossed it into the gutter, from where Francie dutifully retrieved it. This little exchange had the look of an established routine. 'I'll drive,' Morden said, and had the engine going before we were inside the car. I sat in the front while Francie lounged in the back with Prince beside him on the seat, ears up and breathing down the back of my neck. We travelled at high speed through the flashing streets. Morden drove with absent-minded violence, wrenching the wheel and stamping his foot furiously between the accelerator and the brakes. The river, then leafy avenues, then the canal, and then a broad cement road describing a long curve between acres of grim housing. Morden waved a hand. 'All this was fields in my day,' he said. We sped on in silence and sunlight over that sad, peopled plain under a high, thin blue sky. Behind me the dog moaned softly to itself, watching all that freedom flying past.

We were almost in the country when Morden slowed abruptly and turned into a drab estate. He negotiated a bewildering maze of streets at high speed and at last stopped at a place where the road dipped between a fenced-off terrace of identical houses on one side and on the other a stark grey school building fastened to a bleak field. A wind had sprung up and the sunlight had taken on a milky tinge. No one spoke. Morden, slumped in his seat, gazed out morosely upon the scene. Houses, and more houses, rank upon mean rank. The dog licked its chops and trembled in

how little I know of what they call the real world. 'Ten or
years ago it was,' he said. 'Anyone remember?'
pt my eyes on the passing streets. I have such a hunger in
the mundane.
ne name beginning with M,' Francie said and his shoulders

t's right,' Morden said. 'Montagu, or Montmorency,
ng like that.' He tapped me lightly on the knee. 'Do you
Io? You were away, maybe – you've been away for a long
ven't you?' He brooded, pretended to brood. 'A Vermeer,
r a Metsu? One of those. *Portrait of a Woman.* Lovely
it her on the head with a hammer, whack, like that.' He
me again. 'Ever been to Whitewater House, the Behrens
e said. 'Magnificent. The pictures! You should go. Take
. Do you good.' He heaved himself up until he was
leways on the seat and examined me critically. 'You're
you know,' he said. 'Cooped up too much, that's your

n to talk about Aunt Corky, her history and present
nursing home, the Haddons. Babblebabblebabble. Why
y? I have few topics, when all is said and done. Morden
on and when I had straggled to a stop he sat up and
hands and said he wanted to meet her. 'Francie,' he
the car, turn the car!' He waved aside my weak-voiced
e was enjoying himself. Soon we were bowling north-
g the coast road. The tide was out and the sun was
on the mudflats and the verdant algae. A heron stood
spar with wings spread wide. 'Flasher,' Morden said
l. Presently his mood turned again and he became
'I have no family, you know,' he said. 'I mean real
, uncles, brothers, that kind of thing.' He turned and
seized me by the wrist and peered searchingly into
ve you a brother?' he said. I looked away from him.
me, a sentimentalist and a bully. This was awful.
down the window and leaned out his elbow and
istle. The car climbed the hill road and at last we

anticipation and at last Francie leaned over with a grunt and
opened the door and the animal bounded out and was off across
the school field, going at a swift lope with its nose to the ground.
Morden got out too and stood squinting about him. I made to
follow but Francie from the back seat put a hand on my arm and
said, 'Hold on.' We sat and listened to the wind in the overhead
wires and the jumbled crackle and thrum of a distant radio.
Morden crossed the road and walked a little way along by the
houses and stopped at one and went in at the garden gate and
knocked on the narrow, frosted-glass door. The door opened
immediately, as if by remote control. He glanced about him once
and stepped inside. I got out of the car, unhindered this time,
and stood as Morden had stood, shading my eyes against the
light. The air hereabouts had that particular smell that poverty
generates, a mingling of unwashed clothes and peed-on mattresses
and sodden tea-leaves. On the other side of the road a toddler on
a tricycle came to the edge of the footpath and toppled slowly,
shakily into the gutter. An upstairs window opened and a raw-
faced woman leaned out and looked at me with interest, challeng-
ingly. The infant in the gutter began to cry, producing a curiously
detached, ratcheted little whimpering noise. Behind me Francie
got out and lounged against the bonnet of the car with his arms
and ankles crossed. The door where Morden had entered opened
again and a short, hard-looking young man with Popeye muscles
and bandy arms and legs appeared and ambled down the garden
path. He had cropped red hair and a pushed-in face, and wore a
vest and army trousers and lace-up boots and sported a single
gold earring in the shape of a crucifix. He stopped at the garden
gate and folded his stubby arms and gave me a cold stare. I turned
away and went into the school yard. The gin had produced in me
a fluctuating, tottery sensation. From within the school I could
hear a class raggedly chanting the two-times table. How affecting
and lonely it is to loiter like that where children are at their
lessons; nowhere emptier than a playground during school hours.
The field rose before me, humped and high, the dark grass wind-
bent and greyly burnished in the bruised sunlight. Far off I could

see Prince ranging in wide loops, and farther off again a boy galloping bareback in slow motion on a piebald pony. Presently without a sound Morden appeared at my side – how quietly he could move, for all his bulk – and stood rocking pensively on his heels with his face lifted and nostrils flared as if to catch some faint fragrance, the smell of the past, perhaps. I asked him, for the sake of saying something, if this was the place where he was born. He stared at me and laughed. 'Here?' he said. 'No!' He laughed again, skittishly. 'I wasn't born anywhere!' And still laughing to himself he turned and set off back to the car with that curiously dainty, shuffling walk that he had, head down and hands in pockets, his trouser legs flapping in the wind. I lingered a while, gazing off across the field and thinking of nothing. The boy on the pony was gone. Behind me Francie gave a long, trilling whistle and the dog immediately ceased its circlings and came loping back, passing me by without a glance. A cloud covered the sun and a rippling shadow raced across the field towards me and all at once I was frightened, I don't know why, exactly; it was just the look of things, I think, the vastness of the world, that depthless sky and the cloud-shadow running towards me, intangible, unavoidable, like fate itself. It is not the big occasions that terrify me most, when the car goes out of control or a wheel drops off the aeroplane, but the ordinary moments, like this one, when suddenly I lose my hold on things and the ground drops away from under me and I find myself staring aghast into empty air, like a character in a cartoon film who runs straight off the edge of a cliff and does not fall until he notices there is nothing under his feet but the long plunge to the canyon floor far below. Hurriedly I turned back towards the car and was almost running by the time I reached it. The tough at the gate had been joined now by a fat, unhealthy-looking fellow got up outlandishly in pink carpet slippers and a sort of kilt and a tasselled shawl that was wrapped tightly around his big belly and slung over his shoulder like an ancient Roman's robe. He seemed to be studying me in particular, thoughtfully, with an eyebrow cocked, and as the car pulled away he drew a plump hand from

under the shawl and lifted an index fi gesture, a sort of cautionary farewell, w Francie acknowledged. 'Master of disgu did his costive chuckle. I asked who wa no one answered, and Morden glared knees with an expression of angry beside its upturned tricycle, still whing

This time Francie drove, with th and Morden and me in the back. himself with his chin on his chest ar if he were strapped into a strait-jacke Still nothing. Is that not strange? I capacity for passive participation, if if just being there were itself a fo requiring only my presence for it this flow of happenings that was c the flood I would have had to stop picture altogether and stand back dean platform in space and view whole. But nothing is complete, that is why deep down I have in reality as it is described by moments of motionless and luci to take a cross-section of the n glass slides and study it in per flux and flow, unstoppable, th think of it. Yet more terrifyin behind. Talk is one way of doing? If I were to stop I'd stop

On a newsagent's stand t inches deep, were announcing

'Look at that,' Morden sa He sat back in the seat and 'Who was that chap,' he sai Behrens and killed the maid shops with delivery vans, d

were pulling up at the gate of The Cypresses. 'This it?' Morden said, peering. I was picturing Mr Haddon's face as Morden strode in shouting for Aunt Corky. But Morden had lost interest in my aunt and had already plunged back into himself again and sat looking off, dead-eyed and frowning. Then as I was starting to get out of the car he reached forward quickly and caught me by the wrist again and again demanded to know if I had a brother. No, I told him, eager to be away, no, I had no family. Searchingly he gazed into my eyes. 'A sister?' he said. 'No one?' He slowly nodded. 'Same as me,' he said; 'an orphan.' Then he let go of me with a wave and I stumbled out on to the road and the car roared away. I stood blinking. I felt as if I had been picked up and shaken vigorously before being tossed negligently aside.

Aunt Corky had got religion. In her hospital clouts she sat up in bed in her big room and talked ecstatically of God and salvation and Father Fanning (I suppose we shall have to meet him, too, before long). I did not mind. Her voice was a soothing noise. I wanted to crawl under the covers with her and beg her protection. I was shaky and breathless and my legs felt wobbly, as if I had scampered the last few yards of the tightrope and were clinging now to the spangled pole in a sweat of rubber-kneed relief with the vast, dusty darkness yawning beneath me; presently I would have to retrace my quaking steps, back, back to where Morden stood waiting for me in his tights and his acrobat's boots, grinning his dare-devil grin; but not yet. Aunt Corky's breakfast tray was on the bedside locker: a porridge bowl with bent spoon, a smeared cup and mismatched saucer, a charred crust of toast. When she stopped talking I hardly noticed. How tired I was suddenly. She peered at me closely, frowning. 'You,' she said, and poked me in the chest, 'what is the matter with you? You look as if you have seen a ghost.' She was right; an all too familiar revenant, the ghost of an old self, had risen up before me again. If only there were a deed poll by which past deeds might be changed.

3. **Pygmalion** (*called* **Pygmalion and Galatea**) 1649

Giovanni Belli (1602–1670)

Oil on canvas, 23 × 35 in. (58.4 × 89 cm.)

Belli is unusual in that he represents a reversal of the traditional direction of artistic migration, being an Italian who moved north. Born in Mantua, he is known to have studied for a time in Rome as a young man, probably as a pupil of Guido Reni (1575–1642), whose influence – less than benign – is clearly detectable in the works of the younger painter. We next hear of Belli in the year 1640 in a catalogue entry by the dealer Verheiden of The Hague, where he is referred to as *'Joh. Belli ex Mantova, habit. Amstelo-dam'*. Why this quintessentially Italian (southern, Catholic, death-obsessed) painter should have settled in the Low Countries is not clear. Certainly, from the evidence of his work, with its highly worked, polished textures and uncanny, one might almost say macabre, atmosphere, it seems it was not admiration for the serene genius of Dutch painting in the Golden Age that drew him northwards. He is an anachronistic, perhaps even faintly absurd figure, displaced and out of step with his time, an exile in an alien land. His work is marked by the inwardness and isolation of a man who has distanced himself from the known, the familiar, and betrays a hopeless yearning for all that has been lost and abandoned. His concern with the theme of death – or, rather, what one critic has called 'life-in-death' – is manifest not only in his characteristically morbid choice of subject matter but in the obsessive pursuit of stillness, poise, and a kind of unearthly splendour; a pursuit which, paradoxically, imparts to his work a restless, hectic quality, so that the epithet most often applied to it – inaccurately, of course – is 'Gothic'. This constant effort of transcendence results in a mannered, overwrought style; what Gombrich summarises as critical attitudes to Guido Reni might also be applied to Reni's pupil, that his work is 'too self-conscious, too deliberate in its striving for pure beauty'. In the *Pygmalion* this self-consciousness and desire for purity, both of form and expression, are the most obvious characteristics. We are struck at once by the remarkable daring of the angle at which the couch is placed upon which Pygmalion and his awaking statue-bride recline. This great crimson parallelogram lying diagonally across the painting from the lower right to upper left corners gives a sense of skewed massiveness that is almost alarming to the viewer, who on a first encounter may feel as if the room in which he is viewing the picture has tilted suddenly. Against the blood-hued brocade of the couch the ivory pallor of the awaking statue seems a token of submissiveness: here 'Galatea' (the name does not occur in any version of the myth in classical literature and in this context is probably an invention of Renaissance mythographers) is more victim than love-object. How strikingly this figure displays itself, at once demure and abandoned, sprawled on its back with left knee flexed to reveal where the smooth ivory of the lap has dimpled into a groove, and the right arm with its still bloodless, slender hand flung out; is it the goddess's inspiration of life that is convulsing these limbs, or are these the paroxysms of fleshly pleasure that the half-incarnate girl is experiencing already and for the first time? And is Pygmalion leaning over her the better to savour her sighs, or is he drawing back in consternation, appalled at the violence of this sudden passion he has kindled? The shocking gesture of his hand seizing upon the girl's right breast may as easily be a token of his fear as of his desire. Likewise, the gifts of shells and pebbles, dead songbirds, painted baubles and tear-shaped drops of ambergris that lie strewn in a jumble before the couch seem less 'the kind of presents,' as Ovid says, 'that girls enjoy' than votive offerings laid at the altar of an implacable deity.

With what obsessive exactitude has the artist rendered these trifles, as if they are indeed a sacrifice that he himself is making to Venus, whose great, smooth, naked form hovers above the two figures on the couch, dwarfing them. In this portrayal of the goddess – impassive, marmoreal, lubriciously maternal – can clearly be seen the influence of the mannerists, in particular the Bronzino of such works as *Venus, Cupid, Folly and Time*. The overall tone of ambiguous sexuality is slyly pointed up by the triple dancing tongues of flame rising from the sacrificial pyre that burns on the little moss-grown mound visible in the middle distance in the upper right-hand corner of the scene. However questionable they may be in terms of taste, it is in such subtle touches rather than in the larger gestures of this phantasmal and death-drunk work that, to quote Gombrich again, Belli's 'quest for forms more perfect and more ideal than reality [is] rewarded with success.'

WHAT AFFECTS ME most strongly and most immediately in a work of art is the quality of its silence. This silence is more than an absence of sound, it is an active force, expressive and coercive. The silence that a painting radiates becomes a kind of aura enfolding both the work itself and the viewer as in a colour-field. So in the white room when I took up Morden's pictures and began to examine them one by one what struck me first of all was not colour or form or the sense of movement they suggested but the way each one suddenly amplified the quiet. Soon the room was athrob with their mute eloquence. Athrob, yes, for this voluminous, inaudible din with which they filled the place, as a balloon is filled with densened air, did not bring calm but on the contrary provoked in me a kind of suspenseful agitation, a tremulous, poised expectancy that was all the more fraught because there seemed nothing to expect. As I worked I talked to myself, only half aware that I was doing so, putting on voices and playing out dialogues under my breath, so that often when I finished for the day my head resonated with a medleyed noise as if I had been since morning in the company of a crowd of garrulous, mild lunatics. The room too was disorienting, with its cramped wedge shape and single, disturbingly square window and invisible door. It's a wonder I did not go off my head in that first period of solitude and unremitting concentration (perhaps I did?). I could have worked elsewhere in the house, for the place had many big empty airy rooms, but it never occurred to me to shift. I had Francie help me (he was less than gracious) to carry up an old pine table from the kitchen on which I set out my reference books, my powders and potions and glass retorts (I exaggerate), and unfolded on their green oilskin cloth the tools of my craft: the tweezers, scrapers, scalpels, the fine sable brushes, the magnifying glass and jeweller's monocle; some other time, perhaps, I shall essay a little paean of praise to these beautiful artefacts which are an enduring source of quiet pleasure and consolation to me. So see me at play there just as in the days of my glowing if not quite gilded youth when it pleased me to pretend to be a scholar. Then it was science, now it is art.

I have considered many things since your going, and I have come to some conclusions. One is, that I was lost that radiant Florentine morning in the infancy of the *quattrocento* when the architect Brunelleschi disclosed to his painter colleagues the hitherto unrealised laws of perspective. Morally lost, I mean. The thousand years or so before that epochal event I think of as a period of deep and dreamless slumber, when everything moved in enfolding curves at a glacial pace and the future was no more than a replay of the past; a long, suspended moment of stillness and circularity between the rackety end of the classical world and the first, fevered thrashings of the so-called Renaissance. I picture a kind of darksome northern Arcady, thick-forested, befogged and silent, lost in the glimmering, frost-bound deeps of immemorial night. What calm! What peace! Then came that clarion dawn when the architect threw open his box of tricks and Masaccio (known to his contemporaries, with prescient and to me gratifying accuracy, as Clumsy Tommaso) and his henchmen clapped palms to foreheads in disbelief at their own short-sightedness and got down to drawing receding lines and ruined everything, spawning upon the world the chimeras of progress and the perfectibility of man and all the rest of it. Illusion followed rapidly by delusion: that, in a nutshell, is the history of our culture. Oh, a bad day's work. And as for the Enlightenment . . .! How, fed on these madnesses, could a man such as I be expected to keep his head?

Anyway.

In the first days in that secret room I was happier than I can remember ever having been before, astray in the familiar other-where of art. Astray, yes, and yet somehow at the same time more keenly aware, of things and of myself, than in any other of the periods of my life that have printed themselves with particular significance on my memory. Quick, is the word: everything, myself included, was quick with import and intent. I was like some creature of the so-called wild poised on open ground with miraculously refined senses tuned to the weather of the world. Each painting that I lifted up and set under my enlarging glass was a portent of what was coming. And what was coming, though I did not know it yet, was you, and all that you entailed.

Or did I know? Perhaps when I peered into those pictures what I was looking for was always and only the prospect of you, a speck of radiance advancing towards me from the vanishing-point.

At heart I am a hopeless romantic: I wished to believe in Josiah Marbot, that staid adventurer and beady-eyed snapper-up of unconsidered treasures. As I got to know the pictures I was convinced I was coming to know him, too (perhaps it was with him my phantom dialogues were conducted?), his bitter sense of humour, his taste for the grotesque, the diffident manner masking the ruthlessness of the dedicated collector. I could almost see him, a thin old tall figure in frock-coat and stock making his slow way up through the house at nightfall, leaning on a pearl-handled cane, one arm behind him with fist pressed to the small of his bent back, the arthritic fingers curled. His rheumed eyes are still sharp, the corners of his mouth turn down (the teeth are long gone); his nose is thin and pointed and bloodlessly white, dry white, like these desiccated walls. He pauses at a window, his man with candle going on ahead capered about by shadows, and looks down into the narrow street; drizzle greases the cobbles; a carriage clops and creaks past, the nag's head hanging; he is remembering an alleyway on the Île de la Cité thirty years before, the darkness coming on as now, and a half-drunk fat dealer under a low, smoke-blackened ceiling bringing out a package wrapped in dirty rags and crooning and kissing bunched fingers as if it were one of his daughters he was offering the rich milord: *Vaublin, m'sieur – un vrai Vaublin!* I thought of his passion for pictures, or at least for collecting them, as somehow indecent, a secret vice.

I imagined him haunting the showrooms, as he might have the great brothels of the time, in a subdued fever of longing and shame, stammering out his desire for something different, something special ... Certainly his taste was for the louche and the deformed, yet the sports he possessed himself of looked perfectly proper – I mean, insofar as technique was concerned – like so many humpbacked, three-breasted whores tricked out in silks and crinolines.

But what exactly did I make of these paintings, what exactly did I feel for them? (I am sitting here, by the way, with a pitying half smile on my face, like a magistrate listening to a doltish accused stumbling through his earnest and self-condemning testimony.) How can I say for certain what I felt or did not feel? The present modifies the past, it is a continuing, insidious process. That time, though it is only a little while ago, seems to me now impossibly distant, a prelapsarian era bathed in a tawny light and filled with the slow music of solitude. Did I give myself to the pictures with that sensation of inward falling that great art is supposed to provoke? Probably I did. True, I found them uncanny; they stared at me from across the room, remote and motionless, like a row of propped-up catatonics. But you see, I had never before been in such proximity to works of art, had never been allowed such freedoms, had never been permitted to take such liberties. It was like suddenly breaking through to a different version of reality, a new and hitherto undreamed-of dimension of a familiar world. It was like – yes, it was like what they seem to mean when they talk of love. To place one of these extraordinary artefacts before me on the little table in the white room and go to work on it with my tweezers and my magnifying glass was to be given licence to enter the innermost secret places of a sacred object. This was the surface the painter had worked in, I kept telling myself, these were the brushstrokes he had set down; still lodged in the paint would be a few stray atoms the creator had breathed out as he leaned rapt before his canvas three and a half centuries ago in a leaky garret on some back street of Antwerp or Utrecht under a sky piled high with gigantic clouds.

That was how it seemed to me, that was how I thought; no wonder when I stood back and rubbed my eyes I could not focus on what was before me. I was like a lover who gazes in tongue-tied joy upon his darling and sees not her face but a dream of it. You were the pictures and they were you and I never noticed. All this I understand now – but *then*; ah, my dear, *then*! You see my difficulty: a grotesque among grotesque things, I was content there and wanted nothing but that this peaceful and phantasmally peopled solitude should continue without disturbance; content, that is, until you became animate suddenly and stepped out of your frame.

Here is what happened. This is what happened, the first time. Not the first first time but the first time that you that I that we . . . Here it is.

And yet, what did happen? Nothing, to speak of, nothing that can be spoken of, in words, adequately. Morning. The autumn was really under way by now, with sunlight the colour of brass on the faces of the houses and the sense of a silent, continuous slippage in the full, still, shining air. Very quiet, too, only the odd blare of a bus engine revving on the quays and, farther off, a tipsy jangling of bells from the cathedral where what must have been an apprentice campanologist was practising his scales. I am at my table, poring over my catalogue of the big Vaublin show in Washington, the pages lying open at a rather muddy reproduction of the *Flaying of Marsyas*: peasants having a carouse in the foreground while the bad business is done in miniature in a bosky grove off in the middle distance. I have a headache, it is beating away in there, a slow, soft, silent pounding. I lift my gaze. A great chubby silver-white cloud by Magritte is standing upright in the window in front of me, opening its arms. You appear out of silence. That is how I think of it, as if the silence in the room had somehow materialised you and given you form. I felt you there before I heard your step. A sort of shift occurred, as if an engine somewhere had shunted silently, enormously, into another gear, and I looked up, puzzled. It is said that in the instant before lightning strikes you can feel the rocks and trees around you buzzing. You were wearing . . . what were you wearing? A light dress of linen, or cotton, with tiny flowers printed on it, tight-waisted with a full skirt; what was called in my day a summer frock, the weather was still just warm enough for it. And pumps, black pumps with a little pressed black satin bow on each instep. No make-up today, or none that I could detect, so that her features had a shimmery, ill-defined quality, as if I were seeing her through a fine, bright mist. What was surprising was that we were not surprised. We might have been meeting here like this every morning for months. When she leaned down at my shoulder I could hear the faint soft rasp of her breathing. And I could smell her. That was the first thing, really the first thing, her smell: at once staleish and tart, with a tang in it like a tang of nettles that made my saliva glands tingle. She smelled of childish things, of seasides, of schoolrooms, and of something else, I don't know, something chafed and raw – just flesh itself, maybe – and I thought at once, with a sort of startled, swollen avidity, of sunburn, and chilblains, and the delicate, translucent pink rims of your nostrils when you caught that cold and would not let me touch you for three days (I know, I know, this is all out of sequence). Occasionally even still I am reduced on the spot to a state of slack-jawed inanity by an afterbreath of that mingled, carnal savour; there must be a whiff of it lodged somewhere in the caverns of my skull. If only I could isolate that trace, some fiendish savant might be able to culture out of it a genetic model of you perfect in every detail – except, that is, the only one that matters. She wanted to know what was happening in the picture on the page before me and when I told her she squared her mouth in disgust and made a retching noise. Poor Marsyas; they sing Apollo's praises but give me Dionysus any day. She walked to the window and put her face close to the glass and peered off sideways at something only she could see. That stillness, that feline concentration: where had I seen some other loved one stand in just that pose? Then she turned and sat down on the sill, leaning forward with elbows locked and the hollows of her arms turned inside out (those delicate blue veins, my God!) and her hands braced at her sides and one balletic toe pressed to the floor, while she slowly swung the other leg which at the apogee of each swing bared itself to glimmering mid-thigh. I cannot see a Balthus, any Balthus – those autumnal tones, that characteristic air of jaded lewdness – without thinking of A. sitting there that day, lips parted, faintly frowning, gazing into herself with that irresistibly vacant expression her face always took on in repose. What was I thinking now, what was I feeling? I was waiting, I did not know for what exactly, while the pendulum of that hypnotically swinging leg marked off the slow, swollen seconds. How pale she was. Her hair at the side hung away from her canted cheek like a cropped black gleaming wing. I could not see her face clearly with the light behind her. Had her gaze shifted, was she looking at me now? Time passed. We must have talked, or at least exchanged remarks, we cannot have sat in silence all that while, but if so I don't remember. I recall only the look of things: her print dress, that hanging wing of hair, the triangular shadow lengthening and contracting along her inner thigh as she swung her leg, the polar blue in the window behind her and that ogreish cloud at her back still stealthily spreading its icy arms. Or is it just that I want to linger here in this moment when everything was still to come, to preserve it in the crystal of remembrance like one of those little scenes in glass globes that I used to play with as a child, cottage and tree and robin redbreast on a twig and all swirled about with snowflakes? (I could weep a blizzard if I once got started.) Her face was unexpectedly cool under my hand. With a fingertip I traced the line of her jaw, her chin. She did not lift her head. Her leg had stopped swinging. How had I got from table to window? I imagine a great soft bound, a sort of slow-motion kangaroo hop that landed me grinning and atremble before her. I felt shaky and impossibly lofty, as if I were balancing precariously on stilts and ogling down at her with a clownish, protuberant eye. She was very still, a sleek, warm, watchful creature poised in wait for whatever was to happen. I took a deep breath that caught in my gullet and became a gulp, and in the would be no-nonsense voice of a workman rolling up his sleeves to tackle a tricky but attractive job I said, 'Well, this chance won't come again,' and unaccountably the taste of blackberries flooded up from the root of my tongue. She began to say something rapidly, I did not catch the words, and she laughed breathily into my mouth and I felt her lips slacken and slide sideways under my ill-aimed, glancing kiss. We kept our eyes wide open and gaped swimmingly at each other in a sort of amazement, then she drew her face away quickly, looking at once pleased and scornful, and made a circle of her lips and said softly, 'Poh!' A very long moment of absolute immobility, and then I have the impression of a complicated, awkward untangling, with clearings of throats and muttered apologies and the threat of ruinous laughter hanging over all. Then I swung about and walked to the table, stumping along on my invisible stilts, hot with thrilling terror and keeping my back firmly turned to her. I picked up something from the table, I don't know what, and began to discourse on it in a laughable attempt at nonchalance. And when I looked again she was gone.

That kiss. Well. The effect of it was to last for days – for weeks. I felt like something that had been shattered and yet was still of a piece, all run through with hairline cracks and fissures and rocking on my base, as if I were an effigy carved from ice and she had come running at me with a hammer and delivered me a ringing blow. I brooded ceaselessly on that brief contact in a state of gloomy joyfulness and misgiving, turning the memory of it this way and that, scrutinising it from every possible angle. At times I got myself into such a state of finicking speculation that I doubted it had happened at all. It was so long since I had kissed a woman I hardly knew how it should feel, and anyway I was always old-fashioned in these matters. Nowadays young people (I still thought her much younger than she was) seemed to kiss each other at the drop of a hat. Everywhere I looked they were at it, in the street, in motor cars, on bicycles, even. And it was not the demure, stiff-backed grappling of my day, but the real thing, open-mouthed, groin-grinding, noisy. I know. I watched them. (It is a wonder I wasn't arrested.) And of course

I could not believe it had meant as much to her as it had to me; the tongue of flame that had licked my middle-aged flesh and made it sizzle would hardly register, surely, on her hot young hide. Probably she was being kissed all the time and thought nothing of it. Yes, I would tell myself sternly, it was nothing at all to her, she hardly noticed it, and I would give myself a vigorous shake, like a dog out of water, and go on about my business, only to fall again immediately, with redoubled frenzy, into tormented, mad-eyed, hopeless speculation. Ice, did I say I was like shattered ice? – a mud pool, more like, hot and heaving, and the thought of her a bubble rising and steadily swelling and then breaking the surface and bursting with an awful plop while down in the depths another bleb of turbid speculation was already forming itself.

I should say that A. herself was almost incidental to these swoony ruminations, which at their most concentrated became entirely self-sustaining. After all, what did I know of her? This was only the second time I had seen her, not counting the jigsaw-puzzle glimpse through the crumbling plaster of the false wall that first day I entered the house, and even after I had kissed her I could not summon up her face in my memory except in a general way. I know what I am saying here, I know how thoroughly I am betraying myself in all my horrible self-obsession. But that is how it was, at the start: as if in an empty house, at darkest midnight, I had stopped shocked before a gleaming apparition only to discover it was my own reflection springing up out of a shadowy, life-sized mirror. It was to be a long time before the silvering on the back of that looking-glass began to wear away and I could look through it and see her, or that version of her that was all she permitted me to see.

I felt such a fool. I seemed to myself an absurd figure, something like a village idiot, sad and laughable and yet in a way pathetically endearing. My ribs ached from the effort of holding in check a constantly incipient cheer. The city opened like a rose under the steady radiance of my newfound euphoria. I found myself talking to people in the streets, complete strangers; I might have done anything, ordered drinks on the house in The Boatman or clapped Quasimodo on his hump and dragged him off to the St Gabriel to share a bottle of bubbly with me. And she was everywhere, of course, or phantom images of her, at least: a fleeting face in the crowd, a figure disappearing around a corner, or lone and motionless on the top deck of a bus and being borne away from me down the grey wastes of a broad, windy, leaf-strewn avenue. My powers of misrecognition were prodigious. I remember one occasion in particular, when in the street I ran up panting and clapped a hand on a black-clad shoulder I was certain was hers, only to find myself a moment later confusedly apologising to a short, fierce gentleman of military aspect with a waxed moustache. What strikes me now is how little of thought there was in all this. By thought I don't mean deep and sober consideration, a weighing of matters upon the balance, that kind of thing, but just ordinary, everyday thinking, the half-conscious drone of instruction and admonition that seems an echo of the voice of a parent long ago teaching me to stand, to walk, to talk. My mind now had become a quaking marsh where if I tried to wade out over what seemed the shallowest margins I would promptly sink up to my crotch. And this, mark you, all this on the strength of a single and wholly ambiguous kiss. Oh, yes, what a fool!

And yet you, she – both of you! – must have been in something at least of the same elated, twittery state of adolescent expectation and surmise that I was. Surely you were. Don't say it was all false, or even if it was, say it was only so at the start and became real later. Please, do not deprive me of my delusions, they are all I have.

Three days passed. I think of them as somehow glazed, the things and events in them fixed, unreal, glossily distinct, and me set down in their midst, stiff-gestured and madly, unstoppably smiling, a manikin in a shop-window display. (Ah, this plethora of metaphors! I am like everything except myself.) I was waiting for A. There was no sense of hurry, everything was proceeding at the heart's excited but steady pace under a mysterious and ineluctable influence working on us in secret, a kind of aerial geometry that would bend us inevitably towards each other like lines of light in space. I basked in this time out of time as in one of those long Saturday mornings of childhood. She would come. We would be there together. Everything would happen.

What came instead, however, was Aunt Corky.

In fact, now that I think of it, it was a Saturday morning when I got the call. It was early and I was bleared after a fitful night and at first I could not understand what was being said. 'This is Mrs Haddon at the home,' a stranger's shrill voice kept repeating, with a rising inflection of annoyance. All I could do was stand on the cold lino of the hall and nod dumbly into the receiver, as if it were the phone itself that was hectoring me. The letter box in the front door behind me opened with a clack and spat a sheaf of bills on to the mat; Hermes was having a busy morning. '*Hello hello, can you hear me?*' the voice cried. '*Your auntie has taken a turn!*' In the background I could hear a swooping, ululating noise, and the image came to me of Aunt Corky twirling like a dervish in that black-and-white tiled hallway at The Cypresses, her cerements flying. 'She's asking for you,' Mrs Haddon said stridently. 'She says she'll only talk to you.' The keening noise intensified and drowned her words; she seemed to be saying something about the sun. 'Sharon,' she shrieked, '*Sharon*, turn off that bloody thing!' and the noise stopped abruptly. 'I'll come,' I said, sounding to myself like a sulky child who has been summoned from play. 'Well, I think you had better,' Mrs Haddon said, in a bridling, head-tossing tone, as if to let me know she had the right to expect considerably more from me than mere acquiescence.

She was a darting, nervy woman, oddly formed: thick and rounded in the middle but with thin arms and unexpectedly shapely legs that suggested tennis parties and pleated skirts and pink gins on the lawn. Her face was sharp and pale with a curiously moist sheen, and her washed-blue eyes were prominent and faintly fishy, which gave her something of the goggling look of one of Fragonard's pop-eyed, milky-skinned ladies. While she talked she looked away fixedly and kept chafing her wrist with a finger and thumb as if she were giving herself a Chinese burn. She met me in the glassed-in porch with an air of angry reproach, and although I had come with all speed I found myself mumbling apologetically about traffic and the infrequency of the hill bus. 'She's a terror,' she said, cutting me off. 'We don't know what to do with her. And of course when she starts she gets the rest of them going. They're like children, the lot of them.' All this was delivered in a distracted mutter with her face firmly averted and her sharp white nose aquiver. She was so pale and unpronounced that she seemed to lack a dimension, and I had the impression that if she turned to me head-on she would contract into a vertical line, like a cardboard cut-out. She led me into the hall, where I spotted her other half, the ghostly Mr Haddon, heavy-jowled, stooped and circumspect, loitering in the shadows by a potted palm; he pretended not to see me and was in turn ignored by his wife. 'You are the son,' she said to me; it sounded more like an accusation than a question. When I denied it she tightened her lips, in deprecation, it seemed, not only of me but of my entire irresponsible and unsupportive family. 'Well,' she said with a sniff, 'she has been talking non-stop about him.'

That Aunt Corky had a son was news to me. As far as I was aware she was without issue, and the image of her dandling on her knee a small, male reproduction of herself smacked, I am afraid, of the comic. That day, however, what with the dizzy-making earliness of the hour and my mood of adolescent exaltation (that kiss still!), the notion seemed wonderfully piquant and right, somehow, and with a sort of bleary brightness I said, 'Yes, well well, her son, I see!' all the while grinning and nodding and making a sort of humming noise under my breath. Mrs Haddon, walking ahead of me up the stairs, threw back a dark and disapproving glance that landed in the region of my knees. As we reached Aunt Corky's room the door opened and an untidy young man slipped out; seeing us he hesitated and looked about him wildly, ready it seemed to take to his heels. This was Doctor Mutter – I never did catch his name. He need not detain us here, we shall be meeting him again. He reminded me vaguely of a character out of *Alice in Wonderland*, the Rabbit, perhaps, or the Mad Hatter. Mrs Haddon gave him a hard glare of dismissal and with an awkward nod he sidled off, evidently much relieved.

Aunt Corky was lying so still and flat on her big bed that at first I thought she was under restraint. She seemed perfectly calm, with her eyes closed, breathing lightly. Redheaded Sharon, today looking about twelve years old, sat beside the bed on a metal chair with her raw knees splayed, reading a comic-book (I caught a glimpse of the open page: slack blood-dark mouth and a big tear and a voice-bubble in the shape of a fat apostrophe: *Oh Darren!* . . . – such are the things gimlet-eyed Mnemosyne records). As I approached on tiptoe Sharon looked up at me and grinned and winked, and I noticed with a sharp tender shock my aunt's hand like a big bundle of withered twigs resting in the girl's extended, fat little paw. I must have looked like the smiling undertaker himself, with my pouched and shadowed eyes and deathbed leer and my mackintosh folded on my arm like a shroud. I leaned over the bed and at once, as on my first visit, Aunt Corky's elasticated eyelids snapped open and she sat up in her white habit like the Bride of Frankenstein (come to think of it, she did bear a passing resemblance to Elsa Lanchester) and cried, 'Oh, I've seen him, I've seen him!' and clutched at me wildly with one hand while the other twitched agitatedly in Sharon's clasp. It was a scene for one of the Victorian sentimentalists: *The Dream*, by Sir Somebody Somebody-Somebody: the stark old woman leaning forward in distress in her disordered bed and supported on one side by the smiling child-nurse, on the other by the ageing and faintly disreputable nephew, whose shabby coat and less than perfect linen bespeak an interest in the whereabouts of the will, while in the background hovers whey-faced Mistress Death. 'She's seeing things,' Sharon confided to me cheerfully, and gently rattled Aunt Corky's hand and shouted, 'Aren't you, love?' My aunt ignored her and dug her dry old fingers into my arm. 'He came to me,' she whispered in a stricken voice, 'he came to me and stood just there where you are standing now and looked at me. Oh, how he looked at me, with those eyes, his father's eyes!' There was a pause then, and something, a sort of shimmer, passed through the room, as if a light-reflecting surface somewhere had been tilted inwards suddenly. 'You were only dreaming,' Mrs Haddon shouted, and then, more loudly still, '*I say, you were only dreaming, that's all!*' Aunt Corky gave her the merest glance and looked at me again and shrugged. 'Of course it was a dream,' she said with airy disdain, and letting go of my hand she reached for her cigarettes on the bedside locker and brazenly lit up, releasing into the air in Mrs Haddon's direction a big, bold balloon of rolling smoke.

Yes, yes, there had been a child, so she insisted, a little boy. The story was confused, the details vague. He did not seem even to have had a name, this *Wunderkind*. She had lost him, she said. I took this to be a euphemism for another violent though unspecified removal such as had befallen her husband, but no, she meant it literally. One day, one terrible day in the midst of the exigencies of war, she had just lost him, his hand had slipped from hers and he was gone. 'Such things happened, then,' she said. 'Such things happened.' We were silent for a long moment, listening to the raucous cries of gulls and the soft, gastric gurgling of water in the radiator under the window. Sharon and Mrs Haddon had been dismissed so that Aunt Corky might make her confession in confidence. She sat before me wreathed in cigarette smoke with her face turned aside and the light of morning playing on her gilded wig, while I wrestled with the tricky question of how much, if anything, it might be possible to believe of this latest instalment in the convoluted tale of tragedy and loss that she claimed was her life. Would she, even she, invent such a tale? But then I thought, why not? I was in a tolerant mood; I felt positively parental. This was one of the effects that infatuation (for now, I shall put it no more strongly than that) was having on me, this feeling of being fully grown-up at last, an adult called in to deal with a world of children. Aunt Corky might have been a daughter whose cries in the night had summoned me to her bedside, so softly solicitous was my manner. I squeezed her hand,

I smiled at her soothingly and nodded, letting my eyelids gravely fall and pursing up my lips, in a travesty of sympathy, full of self-regard. Yes, self-regard, for as usual it was I who was the real object of all this attentiveness, the new-made, sticky-winged I who had stepped forth from the cocoon that A.'s kiss had cracked. Half-heeded, meanwhile, poor Aunt Corky was pouring out the story of her little lost boy. I could see him, all alone on a cratered road under a hare's-pelt sky in his ragged coat and too-big peaked cap, clutching a cardboard suitcase in his frightened hand. Those eyes, looking at me out of Europe. 'The dead do not forgive,' Aunt Corky said, shaking her head sadly and sighing. And then she smiled at me sweetly. 'But you know that, of course,' she said.

Mrs Haddon was waiting for me outside the door, her white hands clasped under her bosom. I wondered if she had been listening at the keyhole. With her prominent, shiny eyes fixed on my Adam's apple she said in a flat voice, 'She's very bad.' I did not know in what sense she was using the word and could not think how to frame the question, and so I just nodded vaguely and put on a troubled expression. In fact, in all those weeks with Aunt Corky I never did find out exactly what it was that ailed her. I think she was just dying of herself, if I can put it that way. I walked with Mrs Haddon in solemn silence down the stairs. I could feel her wrestling with something and at last she brought it out, though in a roundabout fashion. 'Have you a family?' she said. I was being asked that question with remarkable frequency these days. I shook my head vigorously, half realising, I suppose, what was coming. 'Your auntie needs a home,' she said, in the restrained tones of a great hostess whose patience is being sorely tried by a no longer welcome but distressingly tenacious house-guest. 'You wouldn't want her to die here.' This was a shock in more ways than one. It was the first time I had heard it said in so many words that the old girl was dying; if it was true, and these were her last days, I could not decide what was more significant for me, that it increased the burden of my responsibility or promised a quick release – for me, I mean. I said nothing. I had begun seriously to take fright. What had seemed a harmless indulgence on my part had sprouted tendrils that were already wrapped around my ankles. I wanted to say that I could think of no more fitting place to die than this, but instead I muttered that I was living alone, that I had very little space and few facilities for an invalid, and that really I could not think of, I could not manage to, it would be impossible for . . . I'm sure I was blushing, my face felt as if it were on fire and there was a horrible thickening in my throat.

Amazing how the world keeps on offering new opportunities for betrayal. I had thought I was finished with everything: desire and duty, compassion, the needs of others – in a word, life – yet here I was, mooning after a girl and lumbered with a dying relative, up to my oxters again in the whole bloody shenanigans. No wonder I was in a funk. Slope-shouldered in his funereal dark suit Mr Haddon was waiting for us at the foot of the stairs with a carefully detached look in his eye. Beside me his wife called out to him grimly, 'I was just saying to Mr Morrow that his auntie is in need of a home.' He glanced at me with what seemed a melancholy hint of fellow-feeling; we were both afraid of this woman with her pale fish-eyes and candle-grease skin and air of screwed-down hysteria. I trotted out for him the same set of excuses I had given her, and plunged for the door, talking over my shoulder and fighting my arms into my mackintosh as if it were a pair of recalcitrantly flaccid wings I was trying to put on.

Outside it was a silver day. My heart lifted, as it always did when I made good my escape from that place, but beneath that momentary exaltation I was still upset. There were things I did not want to think about. Aunt Corky's story had stirred the murky waters of remembrance. That's how it is, you tie a rock to things and sink them in the depths and then the first autumn storm breaks and they come bobbing up again with bloated limbs and filmed-over eyes that stare straight through you into eternity. But I did not blame her. Why should she not people her world with dramatic figments, if they brought her comfort, or amused her, or helped to pass the time? I am done with blaming people for their weaknesses. I am done with blaming anyone for anything. Except myself, that is. No, no end to that.

Home, after that unsettling venture into the haunted landscapes of Aunt Corky's past, was suddenly a tricky proposition, so
when I got off the bus I found myself turning, inevitably, in the
direction of Rue Street. A Saturday quiet reigned in the quarter.
Outside the house, on the opposite pavement, a man was loitering. He had a large, smooth, globular head, and was dressed in a
buttoned-up tweed jacket and too-tight trousers and very shiny
black brogues; he reminded me of those glossy wooden peg-
shaped toy soldiers I used to be given to play with as a child. As I
approached he shot me a peculiar, underhand sort of smile, as if
he knew me, and turned away. I had a key by now and could let
myself into the house. I shut the front door behind me and stood
for a moment in the lofty silence of the hall. Immediately, as if I
had entered a decompression chamber of the heart, the thought
of A. came bubbling along my veins and everything else fell away.

But what does it mean, what does it signify, to say: the
thought of A.? Was it her I was thinking of, or the idea of her?
That is another of the questions that torment me now. For, even
when she was still here, still with me, if I summoned her to mind
it was not she who came but only the vague, soft sense of her, a
sort of vaporous cloud through which her presence gleamed like
the sun unseen, gleaming through a mist at morning. Only once
or twice, towards the end, when she was in my arms, did I seem
to penetrate that cloud of unknowing and find what I told myself
must surely be the real she. I know, I know the objections, I have
read the treatises: there is no real she, only a set of signs, a series
of appearances, a grid of relations between swarming particles; yet
I insist on it: she was there at those times, it was she who clutched
me to her and cried out, not a flickering simulacrum foisted on
me by the stop-frame technique of a duplicitous reality. I had her.
I don't care about the deceit and the cruel tricks that were played
on me, I don't care about any of that. I had her, that is the thing.
And already I am forgetting her. Oh yes, that is another torment.
Every day she decays a little more in my memory as the ever-
returning tides wash away steadily at her image. I cannot even
remember exactly what colour her eyes were, are. This is part of

the price I must pay: in order to have had her I must lose her. Something amiss with the tenses there, I think. What would I do to divert myself if I had not language to play with?

I felt her presence in the house before I heard her. I climbed the stairs silently, rising in spirals like a suppliant soul making its slow ascent to Heaven. The secret door stood open and I could see her moving about in the room. I lingered in the corridor, watching her. It occurs to me that this moment of covert surveillance was the first, unacknowledged token of what was to come; do I imagine it or did I feel an anticipatory flick of pleasure's flame, as I skulked there, bloodshot and breathless, wrapped in my dirty old mac? We were well matched, the watcher and the watched. Perhaps she in turn knew that I was there, perhaps that was what gave her the idea of the spyhole (which will open its amazed eye presently). She was busy at something, walking in and out of my field of vision, her high heels clicking. Quicksilver noon in the window behind her and the first murmurs of rain on the glass. What shall I dress my dolly in today? Black, as usual, a black silk blouse and those stretched trousers that I disliked – in my day they were called ski pants – that hooked under her heels and made her legs look rubbery and kneeless, tapering sharply from hip to ankle. I shall have to look into this matter of clothes, learn the styles and so on, the names, remember not to call a skirt a dress, that sort of thing. (And what exactly, by the way, is a frock?) That will be another diversion, a harmless one. In a drapery store the other day I saw a quietly distraught, haggard young man at the knickers counter in earnest consultation with a surprisingly tolerant female shop assistant. Certainly times have changed – in the old days that chap would have got himself a cuff on the ear or even have been put into the hands of the police. A. was indulgent in this regard. Once when we were lying together and I got up the courage to ask her shamefacedly not to take off a last, flimsy covering, and mumbled an apology, she laughed her throatiest laugh and said she had always wanted to have a fetishist for a lover. Happy memories. Meanwhile I am loitering in the corridor as the soft rain of September comes on and A., bless her dear and on occasion shockingly practical heart, is making up a bed for me (for us, in the fullness of time) on the old, lumpy, uncomplaining and ever accommodating chaise-longue that thoughtful fate or the exigencies of art had placed at our disposal in that white room.

At length my knees began to tremble from the strain of keeping still and I coughed with theatrical loudness and sidled into the room, trying to look abstracted, as if I had not noticed her. If she was surprised to see me she did not show it, just gave me a glance and put a pillow into my arms and said, 'Hold that.' She was being quite the little home-maker, all bustle and frown. She wanted to know if I thought the couch was all right where it was, opposite the window. 'And I must get curtains,' she said, measuring the casement with a slitted eye. Oh yes, curtains, by all means, and a rocking chair and a cat, and slippers and pipe for me, and presently a cradle in the corner, too, why not? I stood with the pillow clasped to my chest and a simpleton's smile on my face, trying to decide which was more absurd, what she was doing, or me behaving as if it were the most natural thing in the world to come upon her in the empty house on a Saturday lunchtime turning this grim little room into a love nest. That was the last moment when I might have come to my senses, the final, clear-eyed recognition that what was happening was ridiculous, impossible, fraught with unspeakable perils. I would only have to tell her who and what I really was, I thought, and she would back out the door shaking her head with eyes like saucers and her mouth working in silent horror and disbelief. But I said nothing, only stood smiling and nodding like a brand-new hubby drunk on love, and when she briskly plucked the pillow from my embrace and bore it like a plump white baby to the bed I let my hands fall helplessly to my sides and realised that I was lost. I remember wondering, with stupendous irrelevance, if she dyed her hair, it was so glossy and black against the white of her brow, her virginal neck. Have I mentioned her paleness? There was nothing enervated or sickly about it. She was luminous, she shone within the taut, transparent sheathing of her skin. At times, at the start, when I held her naked in my arms I fancied it was a false covering that I touched, a sort of marvellously fine and supple carapace within which another, unreachable she lay in hiding. Did I really, ever, manage to break through that gauzy membrane? – Oh for Christ's sake, stop! It's always the same question, I am sick of it! And anyway I know the answer, so why keep asking? The rain on the window whispered to itself, agog to know what we would do next. The smell of fresh linen made me think, incongruously, of childhood. A. held the pillow tucked under her temporarily doubled chin and was shrugging it into its case. I stepped towards her as if wading through oil, walking my fingers along the edge of the work-table like a squad of quaking soldiers. She threw the pillow on to the bed and turned her head sideways and watched me approach, with a faint, calculating smile, as if she were counting the paces diminishing between us, her eyes narrowed. For a moment I was afraid she was going to laugh. I seemed to have at least three arms, all of them superfluous. I began to say something but she put a finger quickly to my lips and shook her head once. I took her hand in both of mine and remembered a bird once that I had caught and held like this; it must have been sick; it must have been dying. 'You are cold,' I said to her. This is not the theatre, these are the banalities that spring to the most eloquent lover's lips on such occasions. 'Oh no,' she answered, 'oh no, I'm not.'

Of all our sweet occasions of sin, I think this one, preliminary and practically blameless, is the one I recollect most vividly, with the sharpest and acutest pangs of pain. I remember that unwavering small smile with which she held me as slowly she undid the buttons of her blouse. She was sitting on the edge of the couch now, with me standing over her, still in my raincoat, mouth agape, I suppose, and breathing laboriously, like a staggered old bull. I remember the dips of shadow in the hollows of her shoulders, and her shoulders themselves, shapely and high, the right one stamped with a curved patch of eggshell sheen from the window, and her odd little knobbled breasts with their swollen, bruise-coloured aureoles, that always made her look,

God forgive me, as if she were holding her upraised clenched fists pressed against her chest. The waistband of her ski pants was hidden under a fold of pale flesh the line of which I wanted to trace with my tongue. She had kicked off her shoes and unhooked the heel-straps of her pants, and the elasticated material clung to her legs now like deflated balloon skins. Her miniature feet were of a reddish hue, and curiously splayed at the toes, betokening a barefoot childhood spent in some gaudy, aquatic region of mud and magnolia and bright, shrieking birds. Oh, my Manon, where are you? Where are you.

From below came a knock at the front door. (Perhaps this *is* the theatre, after all.) What a change it brought. We stared at each other, two guilty children caught doing naughty things, and I noticed the gooseflesh on her arms and her puckered nipples and the mauve strap-marks scored into her shoulders. Came another knock, not loud, and oddly diffident, though all the more imperative for that. My heart joggled, rearing on its tethers. 'Don't answer it,' A. whispered. She seemed more thoughtful than alarmed, frowning towards the window and gnawing on a thumbnail; this noise off had not been in the stage directions as she knew them. Absently she began to put her clothes back on. Despite my fright I admired with a sort of tumid wonderment the deft, clambering shrug with which she fitted her joggling breasts into their skimpy lace sling and then dived stiff-armed into her blouse, and as I turned and blundered from the room, rabbit-eyed and wiping the back of a hand across my dried-up mouth, I was in such a swollen state I thought I might have to negotiate the stairs on all fours. All fives.

The front door as I approached it across the hall had a pent-up, gloating aspect, as if it were just dying to fly open and unleash on me a shouting throng of accusers. What prophetic intuition was it that provoked in me such dread? When I opened the door (how eagerly it swung on its snickering hinges!) my first reaction was an inward whinny of relief, though who or what it was I had expected I don't know. On the step, tilted at an apologetic angle and with raindrops glistening on his already shiny brow, was the fellow with the big smooth head I had seen earlier loitering on the pavement opposite – remember him? His hand was lifted to knock a third time; hastily he let it fall and smiled beatifically and cleared his throat and said:

'Ah, Mr M. – the very man.'

4. Syrinx Delivered 1645

Job van Hellin (1598–1647)

Oil on canvas, 23⅝ × 31½ in. (60 × 80 cm.)

This painter, as is well known, served in the busy studio of Peter Paul Rubens for some ten years before the Flemish master's death in 1640; indeed, it is possible that sections, some of them large-scale, in Rubens's greatest paintings are in fact the work of van Hellin, who was one of the finest technicians in the Flanders of his day and seems to have enjoyed the complete trust of his teacher and mentor. In his letters van Hellin speaks of his deep respect for the older painter, and certainly in the pictures of his final years the influence of Rubens is clearly apparent, particularly in the vigorous brushwork and the painterly richness of their execution. However, as *Syrinx Delivered* attests, there is in van Hellin a coolness of approach – a coldness, some critics would say – which sets him apart from the majority of Rubens's pupils and followers. Here, a remoteness and classical stillness are reminiscent more of Poussin or Claude Lorrain than of the fleshly immediacy characteristic of the school of the great Flemish master. The statuesque repose – so at variance with the violent subject – that is achieved in this picture, along with the pastoral simplicity of the landscape with its wandering flocks and feathery, evanescent distances, are the marks of a more temperate, less Italianate style than that of his teacher; van Hellin was a Catholic in Catholic Flanders, yet in his mature work we detect what, with licence, we may call a Protestant restraint that seems to indicate the painter's consciousness of the political and religious tensions of the time. The landscape depicted here is not the Arcady of rock and olive tree and harsh, noonday light, but a peaceable northern plain untouched by the riotous passions of gods and heroes yet over which there hangs an atmosphere of indefinable unease. Mount Lycaeus shimmers in a blue miasmic mist, and the brown, somehow bulging surface of the river Ladon has a menacing sheen. Placed in the middle distance, the figures of god and nymph, caught in their little drama of desire and loss, seem almost incidental to the composition, which could easily stand without them as a self-contained landscape. The temple buildings on the right, tall and pale and set amongst dense greenery which in places is almost black, lend an air of solemn calm to the scene. They are the portals to that other world where the invisible Olympians sit in silent contemplation of the mortal sphere that fascinates and baffles them. Here, in this green and golden world, on this tawny afternoon, their black sheep Pan disports himself; with what skill the artist has depicted this figure, making it at once numinous, comic and terrifying. The god seems to run and dance at the same time, in mad pursuit of the nymph already lost to him amongst the leaning reeds. This Syrinx, who, with her white robe gathered above her knee, might be taken for Diana the huntress, is expressive both of great sorrow and a kind of languorous yearning for release from the human sphere that has become wearisome to her; she seems to long for that transfiguration into the world of nature that is imminent. The wind that blows against her, bending the reeds in the river's shallows and drawing out her long yellow hair, is indeed the wind of change. (What a pity the painter has seen fit to set so delicate a figure amidst these swarming and frankly phallic bulrushes.) She is the pivot of the picture, the fulcrum between two states of being, the representation of life-in-death and death-in-life, of what changes and yet endures; the witness that she offers is the possibility of transcendence, both of the self and of the world, though world and self remain the same. She is the perfect illustration of Adorno's dictum that

'In their relation to empirical reality works of art recall the theologumenon that in a state of redemption everything will be just as it is and yet wholly different.' I haven't even a reed pipe to play on in commemoration of you.

ALWAYS IT COMES BACK. I think of it as another story altogether but it is not. I delude myself that I have sloughed it all off and that I can walk on naked and unashamed into a new name, a new life, light and gladsome as a transmigrating soul, but no, it comes back dragging its boneless limbs through the muck and rears up at me grotesquely in the unlikeliest of shapes. Such as this fellow, for instance, with his extruded head balanced perilously on top of that cylindrical trunk – all three buttons of his tweed jacket were fastened – like a stone ball set on the pillar of a gate. I have never come across another such almost perfectly spherical head. The effect was emphasised by the oiled black hair parted just above his left ear and fanned out sideways across the dome of his bald skull like a tight-fitting, patent-leather cap. His eyes, also black, were very small and set very close together and slightly out of alignment, the left one higher than the right, which gave to his expression a quizzical cast I found both comic and disturbing. His smile, which he did with lips pressed shut and turned up at right angles at the corners, seemed less a mark of pleasure than discomfort, as if he were wincing at a twinge of indigestion or the pinching of a too-tight shoe. I had the impression of exceptional, fanatic cleanliness: he shone; he fairly glowed. I pictured him of a morning at a cracked sink in vest and drawers, vehemently ascrub, buffing himself to this high sheen. I knew straight away what, if not who, he was, and I felt a sort of soundless shock, and a shiver ran through me, as if I had been cloven clean in two from poll to fork by a blade of unimaginable fineness. Fright always has a flash of pleasure in it, for me.

He told me his name was Hackett. 'Do you not remember me?' he said, seeming genuinely crestfallen.

'Of course I do,' I said, lying.

Now, it is a curious thing, but really, I did not know him at all. My recollections of that time of crisis and disaster in my life – what is it, twelve, thirteen years ago? – have become blurred in certain aspects. No doubt memory, selective and indulgent record-keeper that it is, has seen fit to suppress this or that detail of my case, but I do not see how it could have erased entirely from the admittedly crowded picture of those fraught weeks a figure so memorable as Detective-Inspector Ambrose Hackett. Yet one of us was misremembering and it did not seem to be him. We stood in uncomfortable silence for a moment and he inserted a finger under his shirt-collar behind the fat knot of his tie and turned his head to the left with a quick little painful jerk, one of the many tics he had and which if I had already encountered them I would surely not have forgotten. Some more moments passed, marked by heartbeats. Among the few things I have learned over the years is that there is no occasion, no matter how weighty or terrible the circumstances, that is not susceptible to a merely social awkwardness. In my time I have known lawyers to go mute with embarrassment, judges to avoid my eye, jailers to blush. Surely it says something for our species, this sudden, helpless floundering when the universal code of manners fails us; surely the phenomenon bespeaks the soul's essential authenticity? Here we were, the detective and myself, caught in an impossible situation, me proprietorial at the door of someone else's uninhabited and unfurnished house, with a half-naked young woman upstairs eager for my imminent return, and him coatless on the step getting rained on and waiting with a wistful demeanour to be asked in.

I said that I had been doing some work; it was all I could think of that would be vague and businesslike at once. It sounded preposterous. My voice was abnormally loud and unconvincing, as if I were speaking for the benefit of some concealed eavesdropper. Hackett nodded in a thoughtful way. 'Yes,' he said, 'that was what I wanted to have a word about.'

This was a surprise. I had thought he was just another of the functionaries the authorities like to send periodically to remind me that I am not a free man (*life means life*: how often has that deceptively tautological-sounding caution rung in my ears).

I invited him to step into the hall and wait while I fetched my coat.

A. was gone from the room. I stood a moment gazing about the place in helpless distress, panting, then clattered down the stairs again, in a panic that Hackett would have started nosing about the place, though I'm sure I don't know what I feared he might uncover; his kind can turn the most trivial of things into a clue to a crime you were not even aware of having committed. I need not have worried, though; he was the soul of punctiliousness. I found him standing to attention in the hall with his hands clasped behind him, blamelessly smiling, like a big gawky schoolboy waiting at the side of the stage on prize-day.

We walked in the direction of the river. Hackett turned up the collar of his jacket against the drizzle. 'Forgot my mac,' he said ruefully; he had a way of injecting into everything he said a note of humorous apology.

I was in a strange state, unable fully to acknowledge the alarming potentials of this encounter. On the contrary, still swollen and hazy with the thought of A., I seemed to bounce along, like a dirigible come loose from its moorings and softly, hugely adrift, puffed up on heedless bliss. And there was something else, another access of almost-pleasure, which it took me a while to identify: it was relief. To harbour a secret is to have power, says the philosopher, but it is a burden, too. I had not realised, or had forgotten, that the effort of pretending to be someone other than I was was a great, an intolerable weight, one that I was glad to be allowed to put down, if only for a brief while, and by one who claimed to have been amongst those who had loaded it on to my back in the first place. When I told him I had changed my name he smiled indulgently and nodded. 'Oh, I know,' he said. 'But I don't mind that. Leopards and spots, Mr M., leopards and spots.'

The rain was intensifying, big drops were dotted like pearls on his glossy crown.

I suggested we might go for a drink, or was he on duty? He took this for a joke and laughed appreciatively, crinkling up his eyes. 'Still a card, I see,' he said.

His motor car, a dented red Facade with a nodding plastic dog in the back window, was parked up a narrow street behind the cathedral close. Hackett opened the door for me and we got in. Inside it smelled of pine air-freshener, synthetic leather, sweat; I have travelled many times in the back seats of cars like this, pinned between big, tense, heavy-breathing men in blazers and blue shirts. At once the sheep-stink of our wetted clothes overpowered the tang of pine and the windows began to fog up.

'Terrible about that murder,' Hackett said. 'Stabbed her through the eye and cut her diddles off. Like some sort of a ceremony. He'll do it again, I'd say. Wouldn't you?'

'Wouldn't I what?' I said.

'Say he'll do it again. They always do.'

'Not always.'

'Ah.'

After that brief skirmish something that had been standing rigidly between us sat down and folded its arms. I have nothing against the police, you know. I have always found them polite and attentive, with a couple of notable exceptions. One of the first things that struck me about them, at the time when I had to deal with them in the plural, so to speak, was their remarkable curiosity. They were like schoolgirls crowding round one of their number who has finally managed to lose her virginity. Details, they wanted all the dirty details. How they sweated, leaning over me and softly snorting, their nostrils flared, as I recklessly embroidered my squalid little tale for their delectation. *But hold on there*, they would say, laying a blunt paw softly but urgently on my arm, *the last time round you told it different*, and I would have to revise practically the entire plot in order to accommodate whatever new twist it was that my imagination, working in overdrive, had just dreamed up. And always at the end of the session there was that rustling and creaking as they sat back on their plastic chairs with a wistful, faraway look in their bruised and pouchy eyes; and then that release of breath, a soft, drawn-out *ahh* with a grace-note in it of what I can only think was envy. It is true, what has been said, that we get to know a man most intimately when he represents a threat to us. I believe I knew my interrogators better than their wives did. All the more strange, then, that I could not place Hackett. 'I was there the first time they brought you in,' he said. 'Do you not remember?' No, I did not remember, and to this day I do not know whether he was telling the truth or making it up for some shady and convoluted purpose of his own. I took him for a fool at first; it is one of my failings, that I judge people by appearance. He had, as I would discover, a way of playing with things that made me think of a big, slow, simple-looking cat toying with a captured mouse. He would approach a subject and then take a soft jump back and turn and pretend to fix his attention elsewhere, though one restraining paw remained always extended, with its claws out.

'Them paintings,' he said dreamily, frowning out at the rain. 'What do you think of them?'

The very tip of a thin blade of panic pricked my inflated consciousness and the last of the gas hissed out of the balloon of my euphoria and I came to earth with a bump.

'What paintings?' I said, too quickly, I'm sure, my voice quivering.

He laughed softly and shook his head and did not look at me. For a moment he said nothing, letting the silence tighten nicely.

'Tell me this,' he said, 'did you recognise them, at all?'

At that he turned his head and gave me a straight look. At least, it was as near to straight as he could manage, for his nose was pushed somewhat aside (early days on the beat, perhaps, scuffle outside a pub, a punch from nowhere, stars and blood), and that, along with his mismatched, pinhead eyes, made me think of those moon-headed stick figures with combined full-face and profile that Picasso in old age drew on the walls of that château of his at Cap d'Antibes or wherever it was. I almost laughed for fright.

'Recognise?' I said shrilly. 'What do you mean, recognise?'

His face took on a distant, unfocused expression, like that of a very old tortoise, and he sat for a long moment in silence tapping the rhythm of a tune with his fingertips on the steering-wheel. The light inside the fogged-up car was grainy and dense, as if the sky had descended on us. The rain ticked on the roof.

'They say,' Hackett said at last, pensively, 'that lightning never strikes the same place twice. But it does. And it has.' He chuckled. 'You were the first flash, so to speak.' I waited, baffled. Inside the silence small, tinny things seemed to tinkle. He glanced at me and grinned slyly and the tip of a purplish tongue appeared between his teeth. 'You wouldn't have heard,' he said softly. 'The insurance crowd asked us to keep it quiet for a while.' He paused, still grinning; he seemed to be enjoying himself hugely, in his quiet way. 'Whitewater House was robbed again,' he said.

I turned away from him as if I had been slapped. Breathe slowly. With my sleeve I wiped the window beside me. Three laughing girls with linked arms passed by in the rain. Above the street there was a tightening in the air and the great bell of the cathedral produced a single, reverberant dark stroke. I lowered my eyes in search of shadows and rest. The toes of Hackett's shoes gleamed like chestnuts. Twill; I had not seen a pair of twill trousers in thirty years. I went to school with the likes of Hackett, farmers' sons bent on bettering themselves, tough, shrewd, unloquacious fellows with an affecting streak of tentativeness, not my type at all. I treated them with indifference and scorn, but in secret I was made uneasy by them, daunted by their sense of themselves, the air of dogged authenticity they gave off. Real people: I am never at ease in the presence of real people.

'Half a dozen or more this time,' Hackett said, 'frames and all. They backed a van up to the side of the house and handed them out through the window. Knew what they were after, too.' He pondered the matter briefly and then glanced at me sideways and did his circus clown's smile. 'Must have had the help of an expert.' I was thinking of the Three Graces laughing in the rain. 'We know who they were, of course,' he said, thoughtful once more. 'They as good as left their calling card. It's a question now of . . . evidence.' He paused again, then chuckled. 'Oh, and you'll be interested in this,' he said. 'One of them gave the security guard a belt of a hammer and damn near killed him.'

A country road and a big old car weaving from side to side and veering to a halt in the ditch. The scene is in black and white, scratched and jerky, as in an old newsreel. All is still for a moment, then the car rocks suddenly, violently, on its springs and a voice cries out in agony and anguish. Welcome to my nightmares. I am always outside the car, never in it. Is that not strange? Hackett was watching me with quiet interest. I experienced then a flash of that old malaise that seizes on me now and then in moments of stress and extremity, bringing with it a dizzying sense of dislocation, of being torn in two; for a second I was someone else, passing by and glancing in through the window of my self and recognising nothing in this other's commonplace and yet impenetrably mysterious surroundings.

'Has he a wife?' Hackett said. I looked at him blankly. 'Morden,' he said gently and tapped me once smartly on the knee with his knuckle.

The rain stopped with a sort of swish.

'I don't know,' I said. It was the truth.

Suddenly then, and inexplicably, I experienced a sort of mild, mournful elation. Very strange. Hackett brightened too. In rapid succession he passed a finger under his shirtcollar, grinned, and plucked convulsively at the knees of his trousers. Three tics in a row: somehow I had hit the jackpot.

We parted then, as if we had settled something between us and for the moment there was nothing left to say. 'Toodle-oo now, Mr M.,' Hackett said, 'and good luck to you.' As I was getting out of the car he leaned across the seat and laid a hand on my arm. 'We'll have a talk again,' he said. 'I'm sure we will.'

I walked back slowly to the house through the shining streets. A molten rip had appeared in the clouds low above the roofs but the rain had started up again and fell about me in big awkward drops like flashing spatters of steel. There are times when I feel drunk though I have not touched a drop for days; or rather, I feel as if I have been drunk and now have begun to sober up, and that the fantasias and false perspectives due to inebriation are about to clear and leave me shocked and gulping in the face of a radically readjusted version of what I had taken the world to be. It never quite arrives, that state of pluperfect sobriety, and I stumble on baffled and deluded amidst a throng of teetotallers who turn from me coldly, tight-lipped, sweeping their skirts aside from my reeling path. As I walked through the rain now my mind raced throbbingly on a single thought. The thought was you. You had the power to push everything else aside, like an arm sweeping across a littered table-top. What did Morden and his pictures, or Hackett and his evidence, what did any of that matter, compared with the promise of all you represented? You see? – you see how I was lost already, careless even of the prospect of the dungeon once again?

As always, you had left your mark on the house, it resonated with your absence like a piano slammed shut. I climbed to the room, which already I thought of as *our* room, and sat on the chaise-longue in my wet mac with my knees apart and hands drooping between my thighs and gazed through the window for a long time at the rain spattering raggedly across the rooftops. Have I described the view from our eyrie? Spires and curlicues and beautiful rusted fire-escapes, and a big green copper dome that always reminded me of a cabbage; directly below, on the other side of the road, behind a hoarding and hidden from the street, was a vacant site with flourishing greenery where sometimes, at twilight, a fox appeared, stepping delicately over the rubble with brush down and snout up; beyond that there was a large, stately building, a church or meeting-house or something, foursquare and imposing, that I never could manage to locate when I was at street level. I was cold. Draggingly I turned myself about, a stone statue turning on its plinth, and walked with granite tread to where the pictures were stacked. Of course I had recognised them. I could close my eyes and see the walls of Whitewater House where they had hung, interestingly gapped now in my mind's eye, like a jigsaw puzzle with half a dozen pieces missing. I had recognised them and at the same time I had not. Extraordinary, this knack the mind has of holding things, however intimately connected, on entirely separate levels, like so many layers of molten silt. I turned and went to the couch and got between the sheets, wet coat and shoes and all, and lay on my side curled up with a hand under my cheek and felt my eyelids fall as if ghostly fingertips had closed them. Gradually the cold seeped out of my bones and I lay swaddled in my own fug, breathing my own smell, a mixture of wet wool, flesh, sweat and damp shoe-leather.

And here memory, that ingenious stage director, performs one of its impossible, magical scene-changes, splicing two different occasions with bland disregard for setting, props or costumes. It is still Saturday afternoon, it is still raining, there is still that rent in the clouds bright as a magnesium flare, and I am still lying between the smooth new crackly sheets on the chaise-longue, but now I have been divested of my clothes, and A. is in my arms, naked also, or nude, I should say, for she was never merely naked, my pearly, damp darling. That was the first time, as they say; very chaste it was, I can think of no better word, and almost absent-minded, as if we were outside ourselves, half looking away from this strange, laborious act in which our bodies were conjoined; looking away and listening in a kind of subdued astonishment to the far, small noises of a no longer quite recognisable world. The first time, yes, and in a way the last: never again that luxurious, doomed sense of something final, complete, done.

What do I remember? Tears at the outer corners of her eyes, her sticky lashes; the little hollow at the base of her spine, with its dusting of burnished, fair hairs; the hollow of her throat, too, a tiny cup full of her that I drank to the dregs; the sudden flash of her thigh, fish-belly white, with its thick, lapis-blue artery through which her very life was pulsing. She muttered things under her breath, words I could not catch, and I had the eerie sensation of there being a third with us for whose benefit she was keeping up a breathless running commentary. And once she said *No*, very loud, not to me but to herself, and went rigid, with her eyes screwed shut and teeth bared, and I waited in alarm, holding myself poised above her on arms quivering like bent bows, and slowly whatever it was went out of her and she gave a hoarse, falling sigh and clung to me, grinding her moist brow against mine. Then she fell asleep.

Once more I am lying on my side, facing as before towards the window and the dwindling rain, cradling her in my arm now as she snuffles and twitches, and my arm has gone numb but I will not shift it for fear of disturbing her, and besides, I feel heroic here, young Tristan watching sleepless over his *Irisch Kind*; heroic and foolish, unreal, anxious, exultant. And slowly there unfolded in me a memory from the far past, when as a child one summer afternoon on a holiday at the seaside I stepped out of a tin-roofed cinema expecting rain, fog, boiling clouds, and found myself instead standing in the midst of rinsed and glistening sunlight with a swollen cobalt sea before me upon which a boat with a red sail leaned, making for the hazed horizon, and I felt for once, for one, rare, mutely ecstatic moment, at home in this so tender, impassive and always preoccupied world.

The rain stopped altogether and the rent in the clouds turned into a broad sash of Marian-blue sky and A. woke with a start and frowned as if she did not know who I was. 'Look,' I said to her softly, 'look what we have done to the weather!' She peered at me closely to see if I was joking and, deciding I was not, laughed.

If ever I get round to writing that work of philosophy which I am convinced I have in me, curled up in the amnion of my imagination with its thumb in its mouth, it will be on the subject of happiness. Yes, happiness, believe it or not, that most mysterious because most evanescent of conditions. I know there are those – the mighty Prussians, for instance – who say it is not a condition at all, in any positive sense, holding it to be nothing more than the absence of pain. I do not fall in with this view. Don't ask me to compare the state of mind of two animals one of which is engaged in eating the other; the happiness I speak of has nothing to do with nature's fang and claw, but is exclusive to humankind, a by-product of evolution, a consolation prize for us poor winded runners in the human race. It is a force whose action is so delicate and so fleeting we hardly feel it operating in us before it has become a thing of the past. Yet a force it is. It burns in us, and we burn in it, unconsumed. I cannot be now as I was then – I may recall but not experience again the bliss of those days – yet I must not be led by embarrassment and sorrow and pain to deny what I felt then, no matter how shaming or deluded it may seem to me now. I held her to me, this suddenly familiar stranger, and felt her heart beating and listened to the rustle of her breathing and thought I had come at last to my true place, the place where, still and at the same time profoundly stirred, feverish yet preternaturally calm, I would at last be who I was.

Here she is, the moving mirror in which I surprised myself, poor goggle-eyed Actaeon, my traitorous hounds already sniffing suspiciously at my heels. Five foot two in her bare, her heartbreakingly bare, red little feet. Bust, thirty-four inches, waist . . . but no, no, this is no good. In the long-ago days when I took an interest in the physical sciences it was mensuration that gave me the most trouble – philosophically, that is – for how could anything in this fluctuant world be held still for long enough to have a measuring rod applied to it? (Have I said this before? I don't care.) And even if it were possible to impose the necessary stillness, would the resulting measurements have any meaning outside the laboratory, the dissecting room? Old What's-his-name was right, all is flux and fire wherein we whirl. Even the dead move, as they crumble and drift, dreaming eternity. When I think of A. I see something like one of those dancing, multi-limbed figures from an oriental religion, all legs and slender, S-shaped arms, her face alone always turned towards me, even as she spins and shimmers. She is the goddess of movement and transformations. And I, I am bowed down before her, abject and entranced, my forehead pressed to the cold stone of the temple floor.

I have a handful of images of her, fixed in my memory like photographs. When I summon one of them up a spasm of mingled pain and pleasure goes off in me like a flashbulb. The tones range from platinum-white through glass-grey and nickel to silky blacks, with in places a pale sepia wash. Here, look at this one, look: I turn from the window and you are lying on your front amid the tangled sheets, wearing only a short, satin vest, facing away from me propped on your elbows and smoking a cigarette – ash everywhere, of course – your knees apart and feet in the air, and with stopped breath I stand and gaze at the russet and pink crushed orchid between your thighs and, above it, the tight-furled little bud with its puckered aureole the colour of pale tea. You feel my eyes on you and turn your head and squint at me over your shoulder and smile the smile of a debauched child, wriggling your toes in a derisively jaunty salute. Or here, look, here is another one, do you remember it? This time you are at the window. You are barefoot and your skirt I mean your dress is unbuttoned. You stand with eyes closed and head leaning back against the frame and one leg flexed with a heel hooked on the low sill, your arms folded tightly, crushing your breasts outwards like pale, offered fruit. I say your name but you do not hear me, or hear me and pay no heed, I don't know which, and suddenly, as if summoned, a seagull, bigger than I would have thought possible, descends out of the sky on thrashing wings and hangs suspended for a second just beyond the glass in the bronze light of the October afternoon and seems to peer in at us, first with one agate eye and then the other, and sensing its annunciatory presence you turn to the window quickly just as the bird, screeching, with beak agape, goes on its way, downward into the shadowed chasm of the street.

At first in the weeks after she had gone I used to torture myself with the thought that I had not observed her closely or carefully enough, that when I still had the opportunity I had not fixed her sufficiently firmly in the frame of memory, but now that I am calmer (am I calmer?) I cannot believe that anyone ever can have been subjected to such unwavering, demented attention as I devoted to you. Every day when you arrived in the room (I was always the first one there, always) I turned on you a gaze so awed, so wide with ever-renewed astonishment, beseeching in its intensity, that I thought you must take fright and flee from me, from such need, such fear, such anguished happiness. Not that you so much as flinched, of course; my poor haggard glare was never fierce enough to dazzle you. All the same I insist that I looked harder at you and deeper into your depths than anyone ever did before or will again. I saw you. That was the point of it all. I saw you. (Or I saw someone.)

We had no night; it was always daylight when we met. Oh, the stillness of those pewter-coloured afternoons, with the muffled hum of the city below us and the sibilance of rain on the window and our breath white as thought in the motionless and somehow waiting air under that cranium-coloured ceiling. She did put up curtains, brown, hairy things that hung in lumpy folds like hides, but we never drew them. I wanted to look at her in the harshest light, to see the pores and blemishes and the little dark hairs that stood erect under my caresses; especially I treasured those times when, exhausted, or half asleep, she would lie sprawled across the couch, flaccid and agape, beached in forgetfulness of herself and of me; then I would sit by her side with my legs drawn up and arms clasped about my knees and study her inch by inch, from her gnawed fingernails to her splayed, unsettlingly long toes, devouring her slowly, minutely, in an enraptured cannibalism of the senses. How palely delicate she was. She glimmered. Her skin had a grainy, thick texture that at times, when she was out of sorts, or menstrual, I found excitingly unpleasant to the touch. Yes, it was always there, behind all the transports and the adoration, that faint, acrid, atavistic hint of disgust, waiting, like pain allayed, waiting, and reminding. This I am convinced is what sex is, the anaesthetic that makes bearable the flesh of another. And we erect cathedrals upon it.

I believe that she did not much like the thing itself, the act, as it is interestingly called, or not as we performed it, anyway; no, I believe it was the accompanying ceremonial that interested her, the eager play, the games of consequences, the drugged post-coital exchanges. Perhaps it is only in the bitterness of hindsight that I look back now and see a certain briskness always at the end. She would push me aside and sit up and reach for her cigarettes, as though she were folding up some item of everyday use, a deckchair, say, or an ironing board, and putting it away so that the real business could start. I remember once after the final paroxysm when I lay on her breast gasping like a jellyfish she squirmed out nimbly from under me and picked up a half-eaten apple from where she had set it down on the floor beside the couch and set to work on it again as carelessly as an interrupted Eve. I would not have been greatly surprised, or greatly displeased, for that matter, if I had looked up one day from my endless, vain attempt to burrow myself bodily inside her (I think of an actor trying to struggle into a marvellously wrought but too-small costume) and found her idly smoking a cigarette, or flipping through one of those glossy magazines in the pages of which she lived yet another of her flickering, phantom lives. I must not give the impression that she was indifferent or that she played her part with anything less than enthusiasm; it is just that she was, I believe, more interested in the stage directions than the text. But speeches, she was certainly interested in speeches. Talk was the thing; she loved to talk. Endless discussions. She would detach herself from my panting, pentapus embrace and sit up and wrap herself in the sheet, securing it under her curiously plump armpits with a deftness surely learned from the cinema, and demand that I tell her a story. 'Tell me things,' she would say, the tip of her sharp little nose turning pale with anticipation, 'tell me about your life.' I was evasive. It did not matter. She had enough fantasies for two.

She lied to me, of course, I know that, yet the things she told me (as distinct from the things that she did not) I think of not as lies but inventions, rather, improvisations, true fictions. The tales she spun had been breathed on and polished so often that the detailing had become blurred. There was the story of her family, and of her mother in particular. This mysterious woman – whom A. could not mention without narrowing her eyes and pursing up her lips as if to spit – though she was still malignly and, I suspected, exuberantly alive somewhere, was dead to her daughter. 'I don't want to talk about her!' she would declare, turning aside her head and holding up a hand with its turning cigarette canted at a trembling angle, and then proceed in a tight-throated drone to enumerate yet again the lengthy list of maternal enormities. The first time I heard of Mother she had been born in America, in Savannah, or Louisiana, or some other homonymous bayou of the Deep South, into a family of ancient lineage; in subsequent accounts, however, the birthplace shifted to Mississippi, then Missouri, and once even, if my ears did not deceive me, to Missoula, which, my atlas tells me, is a town in the Rocky Mountains in the northerly state of Montana, to where I, Melmoth the Bereft, shall journey on that circumferential pilgrimage I intend one of these days to undertake in search of my lost love. But Missoula! – where on earth did she get that from? Her father, she said, was Swiss. He had been – I heard it coming before she said it – a diplomat in the foreign service, and she had been brought up all over the place; and indeed, in her sleep she often spoke in what seemed to me foreign languages. (By the way, why is it, I wonder, that I always take up with restless sleepers?) About Daddy ominous hints were dropped; I pictured a dark, sleek-haired *gentilhomme*, sinisterly handsome – see his skier's tan, his chocolate-dark eyes, his multi-jewelled watch – idly fondling a pale little girl perched in his lap.

Did I believe her? Did it matter? Lolling there on our makeshift narrow bed in a daze of happiness I would listen to her for hours as she spun out her stories, and smoked her cigarettes, and picked at the callused skin along the side of her feet, now and then glancing at me sidelong, cat-eyed, gauging her effect, wondering how far she could go. In the early days, before I knew better, I would sometimes diffidently draw her attention to this or that discrepancy in whatever tale she was spinning and immediately she would retreat into a sullen silence outside which I would be left to stand, puzzled and repentant, with my nose pressed to the cold glass. I believed you, I believed you – how could you doubt it? Oh, my sweet cheat, I believed every bit of it.

Certain of her more outlandish claims retain for me even still a distinct tinge of authenticity at their core, even if the details were shaky. 'My trouble is,' she said one day, frowning as if into dark inner distances, 'there is only half of me here.' At first she would not explain, but sat with her arms clasped about herself, rocking back and forth and mutely shaking her head. At last, though, I got it out of her: she was the survivor of a pair of twins. Her double had come out dead, a tiny white corpse whose blood fierce little embryonic A. had leached from her to ensure her own survival.

A's mother let it be known that in her opinion the wrong twin had died. When as a child A. misbehaved, the Monster of Missoula, that Pasiphäe of the Plains, would chide her with the memory of little P. (a name had been chosen, a second christening gown had been bought). A. had grown up in a state of permanent, vague bereavement. She was a survivor, with the survivor's unshakeable sense of guilt and incompleteness. When she had finished her story she turned on me a strange, solemn stare. 'Maybe,' she said, 'maybe you too had a twin that died, and they didn't tell you.' We held hands and sat side by side in silence for a long time, clinging to each other like children who have frightened themselves with stories of hobgoblins.

There were other ghosts. I recall . . . dear Christ, sometimes I falter. I recall one stormy late afternoon, it must have been at the beginning of November, when the first real autumn gales were blowing. The buffeted house shuddered in its depths and there was a thrilling sense of things outside – top hats, toupees, wrecked umbrellas – flying and falling in the scoured, steel-grey air. It was such weather as makes me think always of the far past, as if my childhood had been one long, tempestuous twilight. We were in the draughty bathroom on the second-floor return, the only one in the house that had water and a lavatory that flushed. The pipes banged and the linoleum was buckled and often the flame in the coffin-shaped geyser above the bath would extinguish itself spontaneously with a frighteningly understated *whump*. The wind that day leaked sighing through the window-frame and the keyhole and under the door, and the air was gritty with steam that swirled in the waxy effulgence from the bare lightbulb that must have been there since electricity first came to Rue Street. I was washing

A.'s hair; we liked to play house like this (and, afterwards, mammies and daddies). She was in her slip, leaning over the big old chipped handbasin and clinging white-knuckled to the rim of it as if for dear life. I can see her there, the pink tips of her ears, the dark comma of wetted hair at the nape of her neck, the pale taut skin of her shoulders stretched on their intricately assembled ailettes of moulded bone, the slippery, silken slope of her back bisected along the dotted line of vertebrae. She liked to have her hair washed. It gave her the jitters, she said. She would squirm and shiver, and stamp from foot to foot, mewling in protest and cringing pleasure. As I crouched over her, with a crick in my back and my jaw clenched, I suddenly saw my son. It must have been the shape of her head in my hands that conjured him. I used to wash his hair, too, bending over him awkwardly like this on brumous evenings long ago when he was a child and I was still his father. My hands must have remembered the contours of his skull, brittle and delicate as a bird's egg, with those hollows at the temple as if a finger and thumb had pressed him there, and the bumpy little dome at the back where his hair was always tangled from the pillow. I shut my eyes and a wave of something, some awful burning bile, rose up in me and I tottered and had to sit down on the side of the bath.

A. must have felt that charge of grief pass through me, it must have crackled out of my fingertips into her scalp. She turned without a word, her hair in dripping rats'-tails, and took my head in her hands and pressed it to her breast. There was a scrawny, freckled place between her sternum and her collarbone that I found pitifully endearing, and there I nestled my ear and listened to the oceanic susurrus of her inner organs at work. I felt breathless and hiccuppy, as if I were at the end and not the beginning of a bout of tears. For I wept. Oh, yes, I am still a weeper, though I do not cry so often or so lavishly as of old. Was a time when hardly a day passed, or a night, that I did not shed my scalding quota. There is a barrier, a frontier of the emotions, where one must surrender – what is it: self-possession? dignity? grown-upness? – in exchange for the giddy and outlandish pleasure of abandoning oneself wholly to grief. It is not a crossing I often make. I weep, yes – but there are tears and tears. On the other side of that final boundary the ground drops clear away and one topples slowly, helplessly, into oneself, with nothing to break the fall and nothing to grasp except armfuls of empty air. She led me back upstairs (my God, if we had met Morden then, or his man!) and we sat on the couch and she held my hands in hers while I sobbed my heart out. Plump hot tears fell on our knuckles, each one printed with a tiny, curved image of the window in which the raucous grey day was rapidly dying. I recall the noise of the wind, a huge, hollow trumpeting high up in the air, and leaves and bits of twigs blowing against the panes, though that cannot be right, for there are no trees in the vicinity; perhaps they were fragments torn from the buddleia bush down in the waste site beside the house? We had a double-barred electric fire, an antique affair she had salvaged from somewhere, which burned now at our feet with what seemed to me a baleful, gloating redness that reminded me of the coke fires of my childhood. Often nowadays I toy with the notion of breaking into the house – I'm sure everything there is much as it was – and rescuing something for a keepsake, that fire, or a smeared wineglass, or a tuft of lint, even; from between the floorboards, perhaps with one of her hairs tangled in it; what I really want, of course, is the chaise-longue, but even in my worst throes I have to laugh at the image of myself, sweating and swearing like a cattle drover, bumping that recalcitrant big brute down endless flights of stairs. All the same, what would I not give to be able to throw myself down on my face upon it now and breathe deep its fusty, exhausted, heartbreaking smell.

My memory is up to its tricks again, conflating separate occasions, for now as I sit there weeping with A. beside me it is I who am undressed, under the cheap bathrobe that she had bought for me, while she is got up for outdoors in one of her expensive black suits and a pair of those needle-sharp high-heeled shoes the sound of which on bare wooden floors still tick-tocks in my dreams, always, always receding. I have the impression of a certain impatience, of exasperation, even, on her part; the tears of others, no matter how heartfelt, can be hard to tolerate. I was embarrassed myself, and even as I sobbed I had that hot, panicky feeling you get when the passenger beside you on a crowded bus begins to rave and curse. It was a long time since I had heard myself cry like this, so simply, so unaffectedly, with such heartfelt enthusiasm.

'I lost him,' I said, the words coming out in jerks and weepy plops. 'He just slipped out of my hands and was gone.'

A. sat with her gaze fixed on the floor beside my bare feet and said nothing. Disconcerted I suppose by her silence I peered at her anxiously through the mica-glitter of tears; she had the glumly patient air of someone dutifully waiting for a familiar and not very interesting story to end. I suppose I needed to impress her then, to do in words the equivalent of taking her by the shoulders and giving her a good shake. Besides, I had to live up to those extravagant tears. So I sat swaddled in my robe, swollen and blotched, with my hands bunched in my lap, like a big, bruised baby, and told her of my poor boy who was born damaged and died, and of my wife, that by now archaic, Minoan figure, with whom long ago I wandered the world until one day we found we had used up world and selves, and I left her, or she left me, and I went into free fall.

I wonder if she believed my tale, my tall tale?

But how good it felt, telling her. The crepuscular light, the silence all about, and her beside me with her face half turned away. I have made her wear her veil again; how like a grille it looks: the confessional, of course. Oh, absolve me!

Down in the street the newsboys were crying the evening editions.

'I know a man,' I said, 'who killed a woman once.'

She was silent for a moment, looking off from under lowered lashes.

'Oh yes?' she said. 'Who did he kill?'

'A maid in a rich man's house.' How quaint it sounded, like something out of the Brothers Grimm. The bad thief went to the rich man's mansion to steal a picture and when the maid got in his way he hit her on the head and killed her dead. 'Then they took him away,' I said, 'and locked him up and made him swallow the key.' And from that durance he is still waiting for release.

Such stillness.

But why am I in my bathrobe, when obviously she has just come in from outside? I could feel the little slivers of chill air that fell out of the folds of her jacket (three bright black buttons, cutaway pockets, a narrow velvet collar: see, I remember everything) as she stood up and walked tick-tock tick-tock to the window and stood looking out with her arms folded and her face turned away from me. Sometimes I seem to glimpse it through another's eyes, that simpler place, that Happy Valley of the heart where I long one day to wander, if only for an hour, hand in hand, perhaps, with my dead.

Day fails before the advancing dusk. I am there again, as if the moment cannot end. The wind bellows mutedly in the street and the window shudders, great indistinct dark clouds are churning like soiled sea-waves above the huddled roofs. My tears have dried, my face feels like glass. In the tin-coloured light at the window A. was turning to shadowed stone and when she spoke it was with a sibyl's unreal voice. She began to tell me the story of how when she was a schoolgirl in Paris she had run away from the convent and spent a night in a brothel, going with anyone who wanted her, twenty or thirty faceless men, she had lost count. She had never felt so real and at the same time detached, floating free of herself, of everything. She lifted her hand and made an undulant gesture in the dusk's dimming glow. 'Like that,' she said softly. 'Free.'

5. Capture of Ganymede 1620

L. E. van Ohlbijn (1573–1621)

Oil on copper, 7¾ × 7 in. (19.2 × 17.8 cm.)

Although he is not best known as a miniaturist, van Ohlbijn puts his skills, modest though they may be, to finest use when working on a small scale, as we can see from this charmingly executed little scene, a curiosity among this curious collection. What strikes us first is the artist's determination to avoid sentimentality – a determination the true result of which, some commentators believe, is a complete absence of *sentiment*, surely not the effect that was intended: a case, we may say, of throwing the bath-water out with the baby, or boy, in this instance. That doesn't sound right. Van Ohlbijn has combined in this work the homely skills of the Dutch genre painter that he was, with some scraps of learning brought back with him from a winter spent in Venice and Rome in the early 1600s. We detect influences as disparate as Tintoretto, in the dash and dramatic pace of the piece, and Pammigianino in the curious elongation of the figures, while the almost vertiginous sense of elevation and dreamlike buoyancy anticipates the skyborne works of Gaulli and Tiepolo. There is evidence also, in the softness of textures and the diaphanous quality of the paint surface, that van Ohlbijn on his Italian journey studied with application the work of Perugino and Raphael. The figure of Ganymede is admirably fashioned, being both an individual, wholly human boy (the painter is said to have used his son as a model), and an emblematic representation of ephebic beauty. How affecting is the conjunction of the creatural grace and delicacy of this young male, with his Phrygian cap and his mantel thrown back over his shoulder, and the ferocity and remorseless power of the feral bird that holds him fast in its terrible talons. In the eagle's muscled upward straining, its fierce eye and outstretched neck and flailing, bronzen wings, are manifested the power and pitiless majesty of the god. This is not our Father who is in Heaven, our guardian in the clouds; this is the *deus invidus* who kills our children, more Thanatos than Zeus Soter. Although the boy is bigger than the bird we are in no doubt as to which is the stronger: the talons clasped upon the narrow thighs are flexed with a peculiar delicacy yet we can feel their inescapable strength, while Ganymede's outflung arm communicates a deeply affecting sense of pain and loss and surrender. The gesture is at once a frantic appeal for help and a last, despairing farewell to the mortal world from which the boy has been plucked. In contrast, the attitude of the boy's father, King Tros, standing on the mossy pinnacle of Mount Ida, seems overstated and theatrical. His hands are lifted in impotent pleading and tears course down his cheeks. We do not quite credit his grief. He has the air of a man who knows he is being looked at and that much is expected of him. Why, we wonder, has the artist's judgment failed him here? Has he allowed an access of anxiety or personal sorrow to guide his hand into this overblown depiction of paternal distress? Those tears: he must have painted them with a brush made of a single sable hair. Remember how I showed them to you through the magnifying glass? Your breath forming on the picture, engreying the surface and then clearing, so that the scene kept fading and coming back as if appearing out of a mountain mist. There was a tiny mole on your cheek that I had not noticed before, with its own single hair. 'Why would he bother?' you said. So that one day, my love, you and I would lean with our heads together here like this in the quiet and calm of a rainy afternoon and be for a moment almost ourselves. Hebe in the clouds looks on as the boy is borne towards her in her father's claws. Does she see in him the usurper who will take her place as cupbearer to the deathless ones? She holds in her hands the golden bowl the god will take from her, his daughter, and give to the mortal boy. Everyone loses, in the end. Some little time after completing this painting van Ohlbijn, in grief at the loss of his beloved son and, so it is said, abandoned by a mistress, drank poison from a gilded cup and died on the eve of his forty-eighth birthday. The gods have a sense of humour but no mercy.

MORE IMMEDIATELY alarming to me than any of my own ghosts were the living phantoms who haunted the house. I was in constant fear that someone would click open the secret door some afternoon and discover us cavorting on the couch or sprawled steaming and exhausted on the floor with our limbs in a tangle. I am still amazed it never happened. Or maybe it did? Maybe Francie did get in one day when we were too absorbed to notice him – I believe that man could slip through a crack in a wall – and quietly withdrew again, pocketing our secret. He seemed to be always about, clambering up and down the house with that lopsided gait. He had an unnerving way of materialising silently out of doorways or on shadowed landings: a hand, an eye, that smile, and then that clicking noise that he produced out of the side of his mouth as if he were geeing up a horse. He had a little mocking salute that he would give me, lifting two fingers to his forehead and letting them fall lazily sideways. It amused him to feign large surprise when he came upon me, halting in his tracks with an exaggerated, wide-eyed stare and dropping open his mouth in a silent exclamation of mock amazement and delight. One day I met him with Gall the painter at the turn of the corridor outside our room. I had thought it was A. approaching and had been about to call out her name (ah, the eager gaiety of brand-new lovers!). He must have seen the alarm in my face. He stopped and grinned. Gall, slouching along in his wake, almost collided with him, and swore and gave me a bilious stare. Gall was a squat, bearded person with a big, unlikely-looking belly, as if a couple of cushions were stuffed inside his paint-stained pullover. He had very small, dark, sharp eyes and a clown's red nose. He carried himself stiffly, gasping a little and listing to one side, as though he were strapped too tightly into his clothes. This tense, leaning stance gave him an air of resentfulness and barely restrained hostility. (How I love them, these incidental grotesques!) I had the impression, even at a distance of yards, of unwashed flesh and undergarments badly in need of changing. 'Who's this?' he growled. Francie made elaborate and sardonic introductions. '. . . And this is Gall,' he said, 'artist and, like yourself, Mr Morrow, a scholar.' Gall gave a snort of phlegmy laughter and turned away, making an ill-aimed kick at Prince the dog, which stood at point on the landing with glistening snout delicately uplifted, seeming as always to be peering this way and that over the backs of a milling pack of its fellows. I was hot with anxiety, picturing A. hurrying up the stairs with her head down in that way she had and stopping dead at the sight of us. Francie was studying me with quiet enjoyment. 'You're looking a bit agitated,' he said. 'Are you expecting a visitor?' Gall had started down the stairs. 'Are we right, for Christ's sake?' he called back angrily. Francie touched my arm. 'Come on and have a drink with us,' he whispered. 'Gall is gas.'

We went down to the big empty room where I had first met Morden. The trestle or whatever it was still hung by its frayed ropes from the ceiling and the soiled white sheet was still draped from the high corner of a window. Frail sunlight of late autumn was arranged in trapezoids on the floor. We sat down on dusty bentwood chairs that cracked and groaned under us in geriatric complaint. Gall had a stone jug with a handle at the neck through which he hooked his thumb and hoisted the jug to his shoulder and drank a deep draught, his Adam's apple bobbing.

'Ach!' he said and grimaced, and wiped his mouth with the back of his hand.

'Good stuff, eh?' Francie said.

Gall offered me the jug. His eyes were watering. 'Poteen,' he said hoarsely. 'The missus makes it in the back shed.'

Francie laughed. 'Champagne is Mr Morrow's tipple,' he said.

They watched with interest as I took a tentative slug, trying not to think of Gall's wet little pursed-up mouth on the rim. No taste to speak of, just a flash of silvery fire on the tongue and then a spreading burn.

'Mind the backwash now,' Francie said gaily.

I passed the jug to him and he shouldered it expertly and drank. Now my eyes were watering.

'Spuds,' Gall said with satisfaction. 'You can't beat the spuds.'

As I think I began to say elsewhere, I have always had a distressing weakness for the low life. It is a taste that sits ill with what I consider otherwise to be a dignified, not to say patrician, temperament. In the old days, the days of my travels, I could sniff out the worst dives within an hour of arriving in this or that new place. The lower the haunt and more disreputable its denizens the better I liked it. Something to do with danger, I think, that thrilling, fluttery feeling under the diaphragm, and with transgression, the desire to smear myself with a little bit of the world's filth. For I never felt that I belonged in those squalid places – quite the opposite, in fact. I would sit on a high stool with an elbow leaning on the bar and a misted glass of something ice-blue and toothsomely noxious in my hand and watch for whole afternoons (daytime was always best) with admiration and a certain wistful enviousness the doings of people who in their small-scale wickednesses were more natural, more authentic, than I knew I could ever manage to be. They had, some of them, the men especially, a nervous elegance and an air of hair-trigger alertness that seemed to me the characteristics of the true grown-up, the real man of the world. Then there was the other type, of whom Gall was a fine example, all resentment and sullen self-absorption and bottled-up rage. Which kind would I be, I wonder? A mixture of the two, perhaps? Or something altogether other, and far worse. The jug came back to me and this time I took a good long fiery gulp and passed it on to Gall and grinned and with what was intended to be irony called out 'Cheers!'

They were discussing a painter of their acquaintance whose name was Packy Plunkett.

'He's only a piss-artist,' Gall said, 'that's all he is.'

Francie nodded thoughtfully.

'He can do the business, though,' he said, and winked at me.

Gall's pocked brow darkened.

'A piss-artist!' he said again, clawing violently and audibly at his straggly beard that looked like a species of lichen that had taken hold of his face.

The jug returned. How swiftly it was circulating. I recalled stories of wild men of the west driven mad by poteen, their brains turned to stirabout and their tongues rotted in their heads. It all seemed very funny.

I drank to their health again and said, 'Cheers!' more loudly this time, and laughed.

Gall gave me a sour look. '*Sláinte*,' he said with heavy emphasis, and turned to Francie and jerked a thumb in my direction. 'What is he,' he said, 'some sort of a West Brit, or what?'

Presently I noticed that the light was taking on a thickened, sluggish quality and somewhere at the heart of things a vast pulse was slowly thudding. I wanted to leave but somehow could not think exactly how to stand up; it was not a physical difficulty but rather a matter of mental organisation. This predicament was more interesting than distressing, and greatly amusing, of course. I felt like a rubber ball trapped out at the end of an elastic that stretched, fatly thrumming, all the way up the stairs to the secret room where I pictured A. waiting for me, squatting on the end of the couch, a cigarette smouldering in the corner of her mouth and one eye shut against the smoke, with her chin on her knees and clutching her cold feet in her hands, my monkey girl. I wonder if when you were with me you too experienced those swings between desire and tedium that I found so disconcerting. On occasion, even as I pressed you in my arms I would find myself longing to be somewhere else, alone and unhindered. (Why am I talking like this, why am I saying these things, when all I really mean to do is send up a howl of anguish so frightful and so piercing you would hear it no matter where you are and feel your blood turn to water.) There was a sort of trickling sensation in my sinuses and I realised with a faint start of surprise and, mysteriously, of satisfaction, that I was on the point of tears.

'The thing about my stuff is,' morose Gall was saying, 'the best of it is not appreciated.'

Francie chuckled. 'You can say that again,' he said, and the dog, lying at his feet, looked up at him with its head held at what seemed an admonitory tilt.

Gall's jackdaw eyes were filming over and his pitted nose had turned from cherry-red to angry purple.

I enquired, in a tone of grand accommodation, snuffling up those unshed tears, what kind of painting it was that he did (I think at that stage I still thought he could only be a house-painter). He threw me another soiled glance but disdained to answer.

'Figurative!' Francie cried, lifting his hands and moulding rounded shapes out of the air. 'Lovely things. Woodland scenes, girls in their shifts.' He clapped a hand on my knee. 'You should have a look at them, I'm telling you: right up your alley!'

Gall glared at him. 'Shut the fuck up, Francie,' he said in a slurred voice.

I began to tell them about my encounter with Inspector Hackett. It seemed to me a very droll tale, which I illustrated with large gestures and what struck me as a particularly witty turn of phrase. 'Is that so?' Francie kept saying; he was having trouble keeping his eyes in focus, and when he tried to light a cigarette he fumbled and let the whole package spill on to the floor, and Gall laughed loudly. When Francie had got his smoke going he sat nodding to himself and gazing blearily at my knees.

'Hobnobbing with the rozzers, eh?' he said, and we all laughed at that, as if he had cracked a fine joke.

The next moment, so it seemed, and to my large surprise, I found myself walking briskly if erratically up Rue Street, swinging my arms and breathing stertorously. The pavement was remark-ably uneven and the flagstones had a tricky way of rising up at the corners just as I was about to step on them. I had no idea where I was going but I was going there with great determination. The sunlight glared and had an acid cast to it. At the corner of Ormond Street, near the spot where A. had first spoken to me, there was parked a very large, old-fashioned American motor car of a pale mauve shade with tailfins and a stacked and complicated array of rear lights. As I approached, the driver's door swung open and with a swift, balletic, corkscrew movement a heavy-set young man leaped lightly out and placed himself in my path. I halted, snorting and heaving.

'The Da wants a word,' he said.

It took me a moment to recognise him as young Popeye, the one who had stood at the garden gate and glared at me the day Morden had taken me with him on that drive into the suburbs. There was something about him I seemed to know – I had seen it that other day, too – as if under the crustaceous accretion of rock-hard muscle there lurked a different, more delicate version of him, a ghostly Sweet Pea with whose form I was somehow familiar. Today he was dressed in an expensive, dark wool suit inside which despite his muscles he seemed lost, as if it were a hand-me-down from his big brother. Beads of sweat glittered in the nap of his close-cropped red hair. He bunched his fists and a nerve in his jaw danced.

'Your *father*?' I said with interest.

He opened the rear door of the car smartly and jerked his head at me. I leaned down. Sitting in the back seat like a stone idol was the pasty-faced fellow who had come in his kilt and shawl to join young Popeye at the garden gate and watch us that day as we drove away. He was enveloped this time in a vast overcoat with a broad fur collar on which his big, pale, pointed head with its lardy jowls sat as if it had been placed there carefully and might tumble off at the slightest movement. Very small eyes, soft-boiled in their puckered sockets, swivelled and took me in and a hand emerged from the folds of the coat and offered itself to me.

'How are you getting on?' he said; it was not a greeting but a question. I said I was getting on very well. His hand was soft and moist and cool; he shook mine slowly, solemnly, studying me the while. 'I'm the Da,' he said. 'Do you not know me? I know you. Get in and we'll have a chat.'

The springs in the seat twanged under me and I sank so low my knees were almost at the level of my shoulders. There was a strong smell of mothballs, from the greatcoat, I presumed. The sun in the windows was all spikes and sheer edges. Young Popeye slipped behind the wheel and started up the engine but we did not move; I was childishly disappointed; I would have liked a spin in this big crazy car. Popeye turned a knob and a fan came on and blew a blast of hot, metallic air in our faces. 'I suffer terrible from the cold,' the Da said. 'I have to have the heat and then I get the chilblains. It's fucking awful.'

So our conversation began. We discussed the climate and ways of coping with its vagaries, the provenance of his motor car, the incidence of spontaneous combustion among elderly ladies in the city in recent years, Morden's character ('Is he dependable, would you say?'), the stupidity of policemen (despite the fact that he was a notorious criminal, as he admitted with quiet pride, they had not managed to get him into jail since he had been a teenager, and then only for six months for shoplifting), the pastimes that make prison life bearable, the state of the picture market, the nature of art. I found all this perfectly agreeable and interesting. He was originally, he told me, a butcher by trade, although he had not practised for a long time, being in a different line of work nowadays. I nodded, saying of course, of course, one serious man of the world to another. I'm sure he explained many more things to me but if so I forgot them instantly. The hot breeze from the heater and the glitter of sunlight in the windscreen gave a sense of headlong movement, as if we were swishing smoothly down the boulevards of some great humming metropolis. After a time the Da ventured to unbutton his greatcoat and I noticed that he was dressed as a priest, with a full soutane and an authentically grubby collar.

He wanted me to tell him about art. He said he had just gone into the art business – Popeye in the front seat snickered at that – and he needed the advice of an expert.

'That one, now,' he said, 'that *Birth of What-do-you-call-her*, why would that be so special?'

I did not hesitate. 'Scarcity,' I told him, in a strong voice firm with conviction. My face, however, had a rubbery feel to it and I had some trouble getting my arms to fold.

'Scarcity, eh?' he said, and repeated the word a number of times, turning it this way and that, nodding to himself with his fat lower lip stuck out. 'So it's like everything else, then,' he said.

'Yes,' I answered stoutly, 'just like everything else, a matter of supply and demand, what the market will bear, horses for courses, and so on. There are not,' I said, 'very many Vaublins in existence.'

'Is that so?' the Da said.

'Yes, indeed. Scarcely more than twenty in the world, and few of them of such quality as the *Birth of What's-her-name*.'

In my mind I saw Morden's big surly face and through the murk suddenly I had a glimpse of the far-off state of sobriety and a shimmer of unease passed over me like a gust of wind passing over the surface of a still pool; dark, fishy forms were down there, nosing about. The Da pondered in silence for a while, his chin sunk on his breast and his hands playing together like piglets in his lap. Then he roused himself and put an arm around my shoulder and gave me a quick squeeze. 'Good man,' he said, as if I had done him some large service, 'good man.' He pushed me firmly but not ungently out of the door. When I was on the pavement he leaned sideways and with two fingers gaily blessed me with the sign of the cross and produced a cracked cackle of laughter. 'God go with you, my son,' he said.

I stood listing slightly and watched as the big pink car slewed into Ormond Street and roared off with a great fart of exhaust smoke. I think I may even have waved, though feebly.

I decided at once that what I needed was more drink, and set off for The Boatman. I found it eventually, after straying down a number of false trails. The pub was very dark and broody after the brightness of the afternoon streets. What month is it? October still? The barman was leaning on his elbows on the bar reading a newspaper and picking his teeth with a matchstick. I considered what would sit best with the remains of Gall's firewater and decided on vodka, a drink I do not like. I threw back three or four measures in quick succession and left.

There follows a period of confusion and distant tumult. I stumped along as if both my legs were made of wood from the thighs down, and there was a fizzing in my veins and my sight kept twitching distractingly with a regular, slow pulse. I remember stopping on a corner to speak to someone, a man in a cap – God knows who he was – but I could get no good out of him and lurched on, muttering crossly. A patch of sky, delicate, deep and ardent, fixed like a great sheet of limpid blue glass between the tops of two high, narrow buildings, seemed to signify some profound thing. I saw again from childhood a path through winter woods and was preparing to weep but got distracted. I bought an ice cream cone and when I had greedily sucked up the ice cream I lobbed the soggy cone into a litter bin five yards away from me with such accuracy and aplomb that I expected the street to stop and break into applause. I met Francie and Gall shuffling along like dotards with Prince stalking carefully at their heels. The dog's fur seemed to crackle with a sort of electric radiance. Francie pawed my lapels and kept repeating something incomprehensible, his jaw making spastic movements as if his mouth were filled with stones. I do not know what I said to him but it must have been affecting, for he began to blubber and pawed at me with renewed fervour, until Gall gave a high whoop and clapped him on the back, which sent him into a fit of horrible, stringy coughing. They passed on. Prince lingered a moment, looking at me speculatively as if it thought I might somehow be the explanation for all this amazing behaviour, then padded off after its master. That dog is going to bite someone, I'm convinced of it.

When I got home (shortly I shall say a word about home) the telephone in the hall was ringing. It had a tone of vehemence that seemed to suggest it had been ringing for a long time. I held it gingerly to my ear. There is something avid and faintly hysterical about the telephone that makes me always wary of it. The voice on the line was already in mid-flow. I thought it was Mrs Haddon. I leaned against the wall and laid my throbbing brow against its clammy coolness. *This place. Trying to murder me. I have to. You must, you must.* Not Mrs Haddon. Someone else. With a sudden surge of alarm I recognised Aunt Corky. Her voice boomed and rattled as if she were speaking from the bottom of an enormous metal tank. I bade her calm down but that only made her worse.

I managed somehow to find a taxi, a large, ancient, wallowing machine that seemed to progress in a series of sliding loops, as if it were spinning with locked wheels along the surface of a frozen river. I sat in the middle of the back seat with my arms outstretched and my hands braced on the plastic seat-cover. Buildings rose and toppled in the windows on either side and strange, staring people reared up and then dropped away behind us like ragdolls. The driver was a squat man with a flattened hat set squarely on a large, loaf-shaped head; he bore a remarkable resemblance to a stand-up comedian of my youth whose name I could not remember. He crouched over the steering wheel with his nose almost touching the windscreen. He seemed to be very cross and I wondered uneasily if when I had first got in I had said something to offend him that I had since forgotten. We slalomed on to the coast road. The sun was muffled in strands of insubstantial cloud and there was an unearthly, creamy luminance on the sea. The effects of the alcohol were fading and the acid of dread began to eat into my befuddled understanding. Hesitantly my mind reached out a feeler and touched this and that fizzing contact point – the pictures, Inspector Hackett, the Da and the Da's musclebound minder – and at each place I experienced a sharp little shock of fright.

We laboured up the hill road, gears groaning, and came to a slipping stop outside The Cypresses. I got out and spoke into the microphone and heard the lock disengage. How high up here we seemed, almost airborne. A seagull hanging overhead made a raucous, cackling noise disturbingly reminiscent of the Da's cracked laugh. When we arrived at the house the driver objected when I asked him to wait, but in the end he capitulated and sat hunched over the wheel in a sulk and peered after me suspiciously as I went into the porch and knocked at the glass door. My eyeballs burned in their sockets like cinders and there was a taste of hot rust in my mouth. The Haddons were waiting for me, standing side by side in the hall, him stooped and watchfully diffident and she staring off rabbit-eyed and grimly chafing her wrist. I could not help admiring again those nice legs of hers. 'Mr Morrow,' she said. There are times when I regret having chosen that name.

'Yes yes,' I said majestically, holding up a hand to silence her, 'I have come to take my aunt away.'

This was as much of a surprise to me as it was to them, and the force of it stopped me in my tracks and I stood swaying. The Haddons looked at each other and Mrs Haddon gave her head a toss.

'Well,' she said, 'I don't think there's any need to talk to us like that.'

Like what? I must have been shouting. We all hesitated for a moment, seeming to turn this way and that uncertainly, then wheeled about, all three, and marched in the direction of Aunt Corky's room. When we got to the foot of the stairs, however, Mr Haddon deftly sloped off. His wife did not register his going but marched on ahead of me, her sensible shoes pummelling the stair-carpet. Those legs.

I discovered Aunt Corky in consultation with her priest. Father Fanning was a weary-eyed young man, tall and thin and somewhat stooped, with a plume of prematurely white hair that gave him the look of a startled, ungainly bird. He wore a clerical collar and a green suit and sandals with mustard-coloured socks. He bent on me a keen regard and shook my hand warmly. 'Your aunt has been telling me about you,' he said with a curious emphasis that smacked to me of effrontery. Aunt Corky clasped her hands. 'Oh, he has been so good, Father,' she cried. 'So good!' Father Fanning made a steeple of his hands under his chin and smiled and nodded and let fall his eyelids briefly, like a stage cleric. My aunt was wrapped in a tea-gown with elaborate flame-coloured designs leaping up at back and front. She sat on the edge of the bed with the priest standing beside her; they might have been mother and son. Her feet were bare; the sight of an old woman's toenails is hardly to be borne. I found myself struggling with a rising tide of impatience, treading water and bobbing about annoyingly. I greeted my aunt in a level, accusing voice, and Mrs Haddon, as if she had been awaiting this cue, darted out from behind me and shouted at Aunt Corky, 'Mr Morrow has come to take you away!' There was an expectant silence as they waited on me. I understood, my mind grimly clicking its tongue at me, that there was no way out of what I had got myself into. A headache started up like a series of hammer-blows and made it seem as if I were being forced to bend towards the floor in definite but imperceptible stages. I asked Aunt Corky brusquely if she was ready. She glanced at me wildly and a shadow of panic, I thought, passed over her face. Mrs Haddon was suddenly brisk. 'She's all packed and ready,' she said to me, and went to the wardrobe by the window and like a magician's assistant threw it open with a flourish to reveal empty hangers and bare rails and a bulging carpet-bag on the bottom shelf. 'We have only to pop her into her dress and she's all yours!'

Sharon the nurse was summoned and Father Fanning and I were banished to the landing, where we loitered uneasily in an ecclesiastical fall of light from the coloured window there. I felt aggrieved and sorry for myself. I would have liked to hit someone very hard; Father Fanning must have mistaken for self-congratulation the speculative glint in the eye with which I was measuring him, for he nodded again with his eyelids gently closed and said, 'Yes, you're doing the right thing, the decent thing.' I looked at my feet. The priest lowered his voice to a holy hush. 'You are a good man,' he said. Really, this was too much. I demurred, giving a sort of leonine snarl and baring my side teeth at him. With gentle firmness he grasped my arm and shook it a little. 'Yes, it's true,' he said, smiling wisely; 'a good man.' He lifted a finger, with which I thought for a moment he was going to tap the side of his nose at me; instead he pointed aloft and his smile turned faintly maniacal. 'The man above is the one who'll judge,' he said. 'Oh yes?' I said. 'Then God help me.' His brow buckled in puzzlement but he continued gamely smiling.

The door opened and Aunt Corky issued forth at a shakily regal pace, tottering between the nurse and Mrs Haddon, who supported her on their arms. She wore a bulky fur coat with bald patches and a rakishly cocked hat with a veil of stiff black net (yes, a real veil, not one I have imagined for her). In that raggedy fur she bore a striking and obscurely distressing resemblance to an ill-used teddy bear I had been much attached to as a child. She looked at Father Fanning and me and her lip trembled, as if she feared that we might laugh. We descended the stairs with funereal slowness, the women going ahead and the priest and I behind them with our heads bowed and our hands clasped at our backs. A vague and restive band of old women waited in the hall to bid Aunt Corky farewell. I spotted the silked and sashed Miss Leitch among them but she showed no sign today of imagining that she knew me. They were murmurously excited, being unused, I suppose, to the sight of one of their company making an escape from that place not only in a conscious but also a vertical state. On the step of the porch Aunt Corky halted with a surprised and even distrustful air and looked about her at the lawn and the trees and the sea view as if she suspected the whole thing was a false front put up to deceive and lull her. The taxi driver was unexpectedly solicitous and even got out and helped me to lever the old woman into the passenger seat; perhaps she reminded him also of some worn-out, treasured thing from the past. She took off her hat and veil and eyed the *no smoking* sign pasted to the dashboard and sniffed. Mr Haddon appeared, lugging Aunt Corky's bag, and the driver had to get out again and stow it in the boot. We started up with a cannonade of shudders and exhaust smoke, and Mr Haddon stepped away backwards from us slowly, like a batman pulling away the chocks. From the porch the gathering of ancient maenads waved wiltingly, while Mrs Haddon stood to one side looking angry and ill-used. Sharon the nurse ran forward and tapped on the window, saying something, but Aunt Corky could not get the window open and the driver did not see the girl, and we drove off and left her standing alone and uncertain, biting her lip and smiling, with the big, spindly, gruesomely festive house hanging over her. 'Don't look back!' my aunt said angrily in a shaky voice, and pulled her neck down into her fur collar. *Oh dear God*, I was thinking, mentally wringing my hands, *what have I done?*

How odd it is, the way the familiar can turn strange in a moment. Home, what I call home, took one look at Aunt Corky and went into a sulk from which it has not yet fully emerged. I felt like an errant husband coming back from a night on the tiles with a doxy hanging on his arm. My flat is on the third floor of a big old crumbling narrow house on a tree-lined, birded street with a church at one end and a cream-painted, uncannily silent convent at the other. I inherited the place from another, real aunt, who died here, sitting alone at the window in the quiet of a summer Sunday evening. You will want to know these details, I hope. I have two big, gaunt rooms, one giving on to the street and the other overlooking an untended, narrow and somehow malignant-looking back garden. There is a partitioned-off kitchen, and a bathroom one flight down on the return. I should have brought you here, I should have brought you here once at least, so you could have left your prints on the place. The other tenants . . . no, never mind the other tenants. Brown light stands motionless on the stairs and everywhere there is the treacly smell of over-used air. We are a quiet house. By day despite the traffic noises we can hear faintly the tiny, dry staccato of typewriters in the offices on either side of us, though lately these lovely machines, which always make me think of the spoked car-wheels and cinema organs of my childhood, are being replaced increasingly by computers, whose keyboards produce a loose clatter like the sound of false teeth rattling. I like, or liked (your going took the savour from things), the vast, useless sideboard, the blue-black circular table with its breathed-on, plumbeous bloom, the dining chairs standing poised and wary like forest animals, the startled mirrors, the carpets that still smell of my dead aunt's dead cats. These rooms have a secret life of their own. There seems to be always something going on. When I walk into one or other of them unexpectedly – and who is there that would expect me? – I always have the impression of everything having halted in the midst of a stealthy and endless occupation that will quietly start up again as soon as I am out of earshot. It is like living in the innards of a vast, silent and slightly defective clock. Aunt Corky, when we had finally negotiated the three flights of stairs – it is evening by now – looked about her in the half-light with a last reserve of brightness and said, 'Oh: Berlin!' and like a surly child the place turned its back on her, and on me.

By now I was sunk utterly in despondency and so weary I seemed to be melting into the ground, like a snowman. I turned on the gas fire (it uttered a resentful *Huh!*) and sat Aunt Corky by it swaddled in her furs and went into the bedroom and changed the linen on my bed; the starched sheets when I shook them rattled like distant thunder. When I was done I leaned by the window to rest my fevered brain for a moment. In the wintry twilight the garden stood gaunt and greyly adroop. I did not know myself (do I ever know myself?). That is what home is for, to still the self's unanswerable questionings; now I had been invaded and the outer doubts were seeping in like fog through every fissure.

Aunt Corky settled in straight away, calling up old skills, I imagined, from her refugee days. She made a nest for herself in the corner where her bed was, draping her things over the back of a chair and on a towel rack that she had fished out of some cupboard or other. I kept my eyes averted as best I could from this display of geriatric rags, for I have always been squeamish in the underwear department. She, of course, was undaunted by our enforced intimacy. There was the matter of the lavatory, for instance. On that first evening I had to joggle her back down the stairs on my arm, a step at a time, and stand outside the bathroom door humming so as not to hear the sounds of her relieving herself. When she came out and looked up at the climb awaiting her she shook her head and made that soft, clicking noise with her lips that I took for one of the signs of her foreignness, and I thought with foreboding of chamber pots, and worse. Next day, without consulting me, she commandeered from the kitchen a handleless saucepan which she kept under her bed and first thing each morning emptied through the window into the yard three storeys below. I waited in fear for the tenants on the ground floor to complain, but they never did; what did they think was the explanation for it, this tawny matutinal deluge landing with a splat outside their kitchen window? She managed in other ways, too. She liked to cook for herself, having a particular relish for scrambled eggs. She even did some of her laundry at the kitchen sink; I would come home of an evening and find pairs of satin bloomers with elasticated legs – heirlooms, surely – and soggy and lugubriously attenuated stockings hanging above the gas stove on a clothes-horse I had not noticed was there, and all four burners of the stove going full blast. (Her way with gas was something I could not let myself begin to worry about; ditto her habit of smoking in bed.) As for her illness, whatever it was, she showed scant sign of it. She coughed a lot – I pictured her lungs hanging in rubbery tatters, like burst football bladders – and behind the fogbank of her perfume there was detectable an acrid smell, like the smell of tooth decay, only worse, that seemed to me the very stink of mortality. She had a look that lately I catch sometimes myself in my mirror of a morning: the pinched, moist gaze, the slackness, the surprise and sad alarm at time's slow damage. She seemed hardly to sleep at all. At night, lying on my makeshift bed on the sofa in the front room with my head skewed at one end and my toes braced against the moulded armrest at the other, I would hear her in the bedroom, her mousy scrapings and fumblings, as she moved about in there for hours, waiting for the dawn, I suppose, for those first pallid, hopeful fingerings along the edges of the curtains. She never complained of feeling bad, though there were days when she did not get up at all but lay in the jumbled bed with her face turned to the wall, her hands clenched on the turned-down blanket as if it were the lid of something closing on her that required all her strength to hold ajar. On those bad days I would come sometimes in the afternoons, still quivering from you, with your smell all over me, and sit with her for a while. Although she did not acknowledge me I knew that she knew I was there. It was like being in the presence of a creature of another species, whose silent suffering was happening in a different sphere from the one I inhabited. I held her hand, or should I say she held mine. They were unexpectedly peaceful, these occasions, for me. The light in the room, the colour of tarnished tin, was the light of childhood. I would see again afternoons like this in the far past and myself as a child at a window watching the day fail and the rooks settling in the high, bare trees and the rain like time itself drifting down. That rain: when it grew heavy the drops danced on the shining tar of the road and looked to me like so many momentarily pirouetting little ballerinas; that must have been the very first simile I formulated.

Father Fanning came to visit, in his green suit and sandals, with his startled crest of young man's white hair standing up like a question mark (Tintin! – of course, that's who he reminded me of). Aunt Corky was not pleased to see him; her enthusiasm for God and godly things had not lasted long. She listened in silence, impatiently, blowing streamers of smoke past his head, as he spoke in his earnest and friendly way of the weather and the Lord's goodness; he might have been a tiresome stranger she had met on holiday and been polite to and who now had tastelessly turned up expecting to renew a seaside intimacy. After a little while he became discouraged and departed sadly. At the front door he tried to tell me again how good I was and in the guise of giving him a friendly pat on the shoulder I propelled him firmly into the street and shut the door on him.

And so Aunt Corky became another strand in the thick, polished, frightening rope into which my life was being woven.

In the mornings I would wake with a knot of anxiety behind my breastbone, and for a minute or two I would lie stiff and staring as my mind strove laboriously to unpick this ganglion of hard-laid hemp. My days were a kind of breathless straining on tiptoe as I swung at the end of my fear between, on one side, Inspector Hackett and all he represented, and, on the other, Morden and the Da. Fear, yes, and something more than fear, a sense of there being another interpretation altogether of the things I thought I knew, of there being another world entirely, coterminous with this one, where another, wiser I grappled undaunted with terrible facts that this I could only guess at. And always there was the suspicion that for certain others I was a figure of fun, the one in the blindfold turning helplessly with outstretched arms in the midst of the capering crowd. Morden was at once evasive and scandalously blunt. 'I hear the cops are on to us,' he said to me one day with a shark's downturned grin. I stared at him, making a different kind of fishmouth. I had met him on Ormond Street sauntering through the morning crowds with the wings of his coat billowing and his crimson silk tie blowing back over his shoulder. I would often encounter him like this, going nowhere, relaxed and bored and faintly dangerous-looking, with a dead expression in his eyes. On such occasions he would drift to a stop and squint upwards at a corner of the roof of some distant building and begin to speak in a vague, distracted tone, as if we were already in the middle of a not very interesting conversation.

'Cops?' I said; it came out as a sort of frightened quack.

We walked down Rue Street. It was a blustery, brown day.

'Yes,' Morden said easily, 'Francie tells me you were accosted by a detective.' He glanced at me sideways with a bland expression. 'Fond of the boys in blue, are you?'

We came to the house and he looked on as I got out the key and opened the door. I had a sense of silent derision. Dealing with Morden was like trying to get a grip on a big, soft, greased, unmanageable weight that had been dropped unceremoniously into my arms. He stood with his head cocked to one side and waited, considering me. The door stood open, the hall held its breath. He grinned.

'I hear you met the Da, too,' he said. He grasped me by the arm and gave it an eager shake. 'Tell us,' he said, 'what was he dressed as?'

I told him glumly and he laughed, a brief, loud shout.

'A priest?' he cried. Behind him an eddy of wind lifted dust and bits of paper on the pavement and swirled them in a spiral. 'What a character!' he said, shaking his head. 'He skinned a man alive one time, you know, and tanned the skin and sent it to the fellow's wife. In a parcel, through the post. True as God, he did.' He stepped past me and crossed the hall and started up the stairs. He halted with a hand on the banister rail and turned to me again. 'Don't mind the Da,' he said good-humouredly. 'Don't mind him at all.' He went on up, humming, then stopped a second time and leaned over the rail and grinned down at me. 'Cops and robbers,' he said, 'that's all it is, the whole thing.' He liked that. He laughed again and trudged on and laughing disappeared around a bend of the stairs. '*Cops and robbers, I'm telling you!*'

So you see how it was. Oh yes, as I have said, I was afraid, of course, but my fear was of that hot, fluttery variety that half the time feels like nothing more than a keen sense of anticipation. Something in me, a snickering goblin crouched and expectant, always wants the worst to happen. I remember once seeing in a newsreel report of some catastrophic flood somewhere an emaciated chap clad in turban and loincloth bobbing along on the torrent in a tin bathtub with his arms folded and grinning serenely at the camera. That's me, with my knees in my chest, helplessly being borne downstream in a trance of happy terror as the shattered tree-trunks and bloated bodies go swirling past. If the paintings were genuine, they were stolen and I could go to jail for dealing with them. Simple as that. It was not prison, though, that I feared most, but the thought of losing you. (No, that's not true, why do I say such things – the prospect of prison filled me with boiling panic, at the very notion of it I had to sit down with a hand to my heart until I got my breath back.)

I have never been good at games, I mean the serious ones. I believe you really wanted to teach me how to play, I believe you did. There were times when I would catch you looking at me in a certain stilled, speculative way, with a smile that was hardly a smile, your head tilted and one eyebrow flexed, and I think now they were the moments when you might have taken pity on me and led me to the couch and sat me down and said, *All right now, listen, this is what is really going on* . . . But no, that is not how you would have done it. You would have blurted it out and laughed, wide-eyed, with a hand over your mouth, and only later, if at all, would I have realised the full significance of what it was you had told me. I never understood you. I walked around you, stroking my chin and frowning, as if you were a problem in perspective, a puzzle-picture such as the Dutch miniaturists used to do, which would only yield up its secret when viewed from a particular, unique angle. Was I very ridiculous? I say again, I don't care about any of the rest of it, having been cheated and made a fool of and put in danger of going back to jail; all that matters is what you thought of me, think of me. (Think of me!)

She it was who devised the games, she was mistress of the revels. I followed after her in my lumbering, anxious way, trailing my stick and pig's bladder, desperate to keep up. She was the initiator. She it was, for instance, who bought the fitting for the spyhole. It was the day that the third body was found, strung up by the heels on the park railings with throat cut so deeply the head was almost severed (the papers by now had found a name for the killer: the Vampire). When she came into the room, shaking rain-pearls from the hem of her black coat, I could feel her excitement – when she was like that the air around her seemed to crepitate as if an electric current were passing through it. She dropped her coat and handbag on the floor and plumped down on the couch and held out her upturned fist, smiling with her lips pressed shut, brimming and gleeful. My heart. 'Look,' she said, and slowly uncurled her fingers. I took the little brass barrel from her and peered at it in happy bafflement. 'Look through it,' she said impatiently, 'it's like a fish's eye.' I laughed. 'How will we fit it?' I said. She snatched the gadget from me and scanned the room through it, one eye screwed shut and a sharp little canine bared. 'With a drill,' she said. 'How do you think?'

I am not much of a handyman. She sat at my table smoking and watched me at work, offering facetious suggestions and snickering. After a long and bad-tempered search in the basement I had found a twist drill, an antique, spindly affair suggestive of the primitive days of surgery, and with this implement I bored a hole in the false wall, at knee level, as she directed. I asked no questions; that was the first rule in all our games. When I had screwed the brass lens into place she went outside and knelt to test it. (By the way, what of that gap in the plaster through which I am supposed to have had my first glimpse of her? Must have been fixed.) She came back scowling. 'You've put it in the wrong way round,' she said. 'It's for looking in, not out!' She sighed. 'You're useless,' she said. 'Listen.'

She had it all worked out. This is how it went. If we had an arrangement to meet at twelve o'clock, say, I was to come at eleven thirty and, without making a sound, kneel down at the spyhole and watch her for half an hour; then, at noon, I was to creep back out to the stairs and come tramping down the corridor as if I had just arrived. Sometimes, however, I was not to come early, and not to use the spyhole; nor was I to tell her which were the times I had been there unseen by her and which when I had not. In this way she would never know for certain if she was being spied on during the half hour before my arrival or if she was playing out her little charades for no one's benefit. I did as I was bidden, of course. What strange, shameful excitement there was in tiptoeing along the corridor – sometimes I went the entire distance on hands and knees – and putting my eye to that thrillingly cool glass stud and seeing the room beyond, radiant with silky light, resolve itself into a cup of swooping curves at the centre of which A. sat, a bulbous idol with pin-head and tiny feet and enormous hands folded in her swollen lap. This is how I always found her, sitting motionless and agaze, like tiny Alice waiting for the magic potion to take effect. Then slowly she would begin to stir, with odd, spasmic jerks and twitches. She would take a deep breath, drawing back her shoulders and lifting her head, carefully keeping her glance from straying in the direction of the spyhole; her movements were at once stiff and graceful, and touched with a strange, unhuman pathos, like those of a skilfully manipulated marionette. She would rise and take a step toward the window, extending one hand in a sweeping gesture, as if she were welcoming a grand guest; she would smile and nod, or hold her head to one side in an attitude of deep attention, and sometimes she would even move her lips in soundless speech, with exaggerated effect, like the heroine in a silent film. Then she would resume her seat on the couch with her invisible guest beside her and go through the motions of serving tea, handing him (there was no doubt as to this phantom's gender) his cup with a lingering smile and then demurely dropping her gaze and taking her lower lip delicately between her teeth and biting it until it turned white. Always the tableau began with these elaborate politenesses; gradually, however, as I shifted heavily from one knee to the other and blinked my watering eye, an atmosphere of menace would develop; she would frown, and shrink back and shake her head, pressing splayed fingers to her throat and lifting one knee. In the end, overwhelmed, her clothes undone, she would fall back slack-mouthed with breasts exposed and one arm outflung and a leg bared along its glimmering length to the vague dark hollow of her lap, and I would suddenly hear myself breathing. She would rest for a moment then, displayed there, her fingers idly playing with a strand of hair at the nape of her neck, and as the cathedral bell began to toll the noonday angelus I would get up stiffly and steal out to the landing and, composing myself as best I could (how the heart can hammer!), walk down the corridor again coughing and humming and breezily enter the room, by which time she would be sitting primly with knees pressed tightly together and her hands folded, looking up at me with a faint, shy, lascivious smile.

I wonder now if she devised all her scenarios beforehand or did she make them up as she went along? I was impressed always by how well she seemed to know what it was she wanted. Everything was at her direction, the words, the gestures, the positions, all the complex ceremonials of this liturgy of the flesh. *Tie my hands. Make me kneel. Blindfold me. Now walk me to the window.* How softly she stepped, like a sleepwalker, barefoot, with one of her own stockings bound tightly over her eyes, as I, half miserable and half excited, guided her across the room and stopped before the blank wall.

'Is this the window?'

'Yes.'

'Are there people in the street?'

'Yes.'

'Are they looking at me?'

'Not yet.'

The wall was pitted and scarred and there was the shadow of a dried-up water-stain shaped like a map of North America. Her hot little hand trembled in mine. Now, I told her, now they had seen her. And so powerful was the aura of her excitement that the scene began to materialise before me on the wall: the street and the stopped cars and the silent people staring up in the luminous grey light of the November day. She squeezed my hand; I knew what she wanted. Like a child being good she held up her arms and I bent and gathered her slip at the hem and lifted it slowly over her head, hearing the soft lisp of the silk as it grazed her skin. Now she was naked. The white wall reflected a faint effulgence on her breasts, her belly. She shivered.

'Have they really seen me?'

'Yes, they've seen you. They're looking at you.'

A sigh.

'What are they doing?'

'They're just pointing and looking. And some of them are laughing.'

A caught breath.

'Who? Who's laughing?'

'Two men. Two workmen, in their workclothes. They're pointing at you and laughing.'

She shivered again and gave a low gasp. I tried to take her in my arms but she stood rigid. Her greyed skin was cold.

'Why are you doing this to me?' she said softly. 'Why are you doing this?' And she sighed. And afterwards, when we were lying together slimed and sweating on the couch, she undid the stocking from her eyes and ran it thoughtfully through her fingers and said in the most matter-of-fact way, 'Next time, really take me to the window.'

She desired to be seen, she said, to be a spectacle, to have her most intimate secrets purloined and betrayed. Yet I ask myself now if they really were her secrets that she offered up on the altar of our passion or just variations invented for this or that occasion. One morning when I arrived at the house she was in the bathroom. I tapped on the door but she did not hear me, or did not choose to hear me. When I opened the door and slipped inside she was sitting on the side of the bath with a cracked mirror propped before her on the handbasin, cleaning her face with a pad of cotton wool. She did not look at me, only went still for a moment and drew in her lips to cut off the beginnings of a smile. She was wearing a loose shirt and her hair was wrapped in a towel. Her face without make-up was blurred, a clay-white, hieratic mask. I said not a word but stood with my hands behind me pressed to the door and held my breath and watched her. Steam swayed in the whitish light from the frosted window and there was the sharp tang of some unguent that made me think of my mother. A. finished with her face and stood up and unwrapped the towel and began vigorously to dry her hair, pausing now and then and shaking her head sideways as if to clear something from her ear. Our eyes met by accident in the mirror and immediately her gaze went blank and slid away from mine. Then, running her fingers through her still-damp hair, she hitched up her shirt and sat down on the lavatory and perched there for a minute, intent and still, her grey eyes fixed on emptiness, like an animal pausing on a forest track to drop its mark. A spasm of effort crossed her face and she was done. She wiped herself twice, briskly, and stood up. The cistern wheezed and gave its cataclysmic gasp. Her smell came to me, acrid and spicy and warm, and my stomach heaved languidly. She turned on the geyser then and glanced at me over her shoulder and said, 'Have you any matches?' I wanted to ask her if she always wiped herself with her left hand or was even that faked, too, but I did not have the heart.

But no, fake is not the right word. Unformed: that's it. She was not being but becoming. So I thought of her. Everything she did seemed a seeking after definition. I have said she was the one who devised our games and enforced the rules, but really this seeming strength was no more than a child's wilfulness. In the street she would dig her elbow into my ribs and stare slit-eyed at some woman passing by. 'Hair,' she would say out of the corner of her mouth. 'Exact same shade as mine, did you not notice?' Then she would shake my arm and scowl. 'Oh, you're hopeless!' Poking among the drifts of immemorial rubbish in the corridors, one of our favourite pastimes, we came upon a mildewed volume of eighteenth-century erotic illustrations (suddenly it occurs to me: had she planted it there?) which she would pore over for hours. 'Look,' she would say, in a hushed, wondering tone, pointing to this or that indecorously sprawled figure, 'doesn't she look like me?' And she would turn from the page and search my face with touching anxiousness, my poor Justine, yearning for some sort of final confirmation of . . . of what? Authenticity, perhaps. And yet it was precisely the inauthentic, the fragile theatre of illusions we had erected to house our increasingly exotic performances, that afforded us the fiercest and most precious transports of doomy pleasure. How keen the dark and tender thrill that shot through me when in the throes of passion she cried out my assumed – my false – name and for a second a phantom other, my jettisoned self, joined us and made a ghostly troilism of our panting labours.

Will you laugh if I say I still think of us as innocents? No matter how dirty and even dangerous the games we played, something childlike always survived in them. No, that's wrong, for childhood is not innocent, only ignorant; we knew what we were doing. Paradoxical as it may sound, I think it was that knowledge itself that lent to our doings a lightsome, prelapsarian air. Like all lovers, we, I (for how do I know what *you* felt?) lived in the conviction that there were certain things that in us came into being for the first time in the world. Not great things, of course – I was no Rilke, and you were no Gaspara Stampa – yet between us always there was that which seemed to overleap the selfish flesh, that seemed to overleap even each other and, quivering, endured, as the arrow endures the bowstring before being transformed into pure flight. And still endures.

She told me her dreams. She dreamed of adventures, impossible journeys. Of a great dane that turned into a unicorn and ran away. Of being someone else. How solemn she would be, lying on her front with her chin on her hands and the cigarette lolling at the corner of her mouth and the swift smoke running up in a shaky line like the rope in a rope trick. The lilac shadows under her eyes. Her bitten fingernails. That flossed dip at the base of her spine. In these sleepless nights I go over her inch by inch, mapping her contours, surveyor of all I no longer possess. I see her turning slowly in the depths of memory's screen, fixed and staring, too real to be real, like one of those three-dimensional models that computers make. It is then, when she is at her vividest, that I know I have lost her forever.

I could feel it coming, that loss; from the start I could feel it coming. Intimations abounded: a word, a sly glance, a smile too quickly suppressed. In my arms one day she suddenly went still and put a hand to my mouth and said 'Ssh!' and I heard with a qualm of terror the faint, remorseless sound of a telephone ringing somewhere down in the depths of the house. A telephone! If a burst of gunfire had started up it would not have seemed more outlandish. Yet she was not surprised. Without a word she slipped from my arms and wrapped herself in my bathrobe and was gone. I followed after her, nimble with apprehension. The phone was in the basement, an ancient, bakelite model lost among jumbles of stuff on the workbench. I stopped in the doorway. She stood half turned away from me with one foot pressed on the instep of the other and the receiver cradled against her shoulder. She spoke to it softly as if to a child. I could sense that she was smiling. After a moment she hung up and turned and walked towards me with her arms tightly folded and her head lowered. Suddenly, acutely, I became aware of my nakedness. She folded herself against me and laughed with a low, tigerish rattle at the back of her throat. 'Oh,' she said almost gaily, 'how cold it is!' I stood mute with unfathomable anguish, and for a second the mist lifted and I was afforded a heartstopping view of a far and altogether different country.

It was she who discovered No. 23. She had been watching the place for ages, she said. It was supposed to be a solicitor's office (someone had a sense of humour) but the people she saw going in and out did not look as if they were on legal business. Then one day she arrived in the room and knelt excitedly on the couch without taking off her coat and tugged me by the hands and said I must come with her, that she had somewhere she wanted to take me. We hurried through the streets. It was mid-afternoon, there were few people about. Under an iron sky the pavements had a scrubbed, raw look and whoops of icy wind waited around corners. No. 23 presented a grimy, disused aspect. It had a big shop-window with a brown curtain pulled across it and a high, narrow front door. A. rang the bell and grinned and pressed herself against me with the crown of her head under my jaw; her hair was cold but her scalp burned. I heard dragging steps approaching inside and Ma Murphy in her cardigan and slippers opened the door and drew back her head and looked at us sceptically. 'He's not in,' she said. She had a strong moustache and a bosom that reached to where her waist had once been. A. sweetly explained that it was not the solicitor we had come to see. Ma Murphy continued to regard us with suspicion. 'Two of yiz,' she said. If it was a question we had no answer. After another interval of dour consideration she stepped aside and motioned us in. I hesitated, as if it were the portals to the Chapel Perilous that I was breaching, but A. excitedly tugged my arm and I followed her, my Morgana.

Ma Murphy's broad backside swayed ahead of us up a narrow stairs. The place was dim and there was a smell of stew. A. squeezed my hand gleefully and mouthed something at me that I could not make out. On the first floor we were shown into a sort of parlour, low-ceilinged, ill-lit and chilly, with an over-stuffed sofa and net curtains and a table covered with oilcloth. Brownish shadows hung down the walls like strips of old wall-paper. Ma Murphy folded her hands under her bosom and resumed her sceptical regard. A. linked her arm more tightly in mine. I began to fidget.

'Yiz are not the Guards, are yiz?' Ma Murphy said with truculence.

A. shook her head vehemently. 'Oh no,' she said, 'no, we're not the Guards.' The woman fixed her eye on me. A. hurried on. 'We want a girl, you see,' she said.

I could feel myself blush. Ma Murphy remained impassive. Unable to sustain her colourless stare I turned with hands clasped behind me and paced to the low window and looked out; this was women's work, after all. Oh, I am a hound, and spineless, too. What was I feeling? Excitement, of course, the hot, horrible thrill of transgression; I might have been a sweaty little boy about to spy on his sister undressing. (Why do such moments always make me think of childhood? I suppose I am being reminded of first sins, those first, tentative steps into real life.) Outside, the grey was thickening; twilight already. A waft of melancholy rose in me softly, like a sigh. Below the window there was a narrow lane with dustbins and a jumble of lock-up sheds. A cat picked its way daintily along the top of a wall studded with broken glass. Why is it the detritus of the world seems to me always to signify some ungraspable thing? How could this scene mean anything, since it was only a scene because I was there to make it so? Behind me A. and the procuress were quietly discussing terms. I could have stayed there forever, glooming out of that mean little window as the winter day drew wearily to a close; not life, you see, but its frail semblance; that makes me happy.

Our girl's name was Rosie. She was a hard-edged twenty-year-old, slight but compactly made, with dyed yellow bangs and bad skin. She might have been the ghost of my daughter, if I had ever had a daughter. I addressed a pleasantry to her and in return was stared at coldly. She gave A. a cordial grin, however, and they struck up an immediate amity, and sat down side by side on the bed to take off their stockings, fags clamped identically in scarlet mouths and eyes identically averted from the smoke. The room was low and bare of everything except the bed and an office chair with a plastic seat. The bed had a disturbingly clinical look to it. Uneasily I took off my clothes and loitered by the chair in my drawers, feeling the small hairs rise on my skin, more from apprehensiveness than the cold. A.'s directions were simple: she and I were to make love while Rosie watched. That, Rosie said with a shrug, was all right by her; naked, she sauntered to the chair and, giving me an ironic glance, sat down and folded her arms and crossed her legs. Her shoulders were shapely, and her left earlobe was pierced by a tiny safety pin. A. lolled on the bed in her Duchess of Alba pose. The two of them considered me, quizzical and calm. I felt . . . perused. The consequences were inevitable. I muttered an apology, sprawled helplessly with my mouth crushed against A.'s neck. 'Don't worry,' she whispered breathily in my ear; 'just pretend.' She was pleased, I think. It was the way she would have wished it to be: not the act itself, but acting. And so for a quarter of an hour we toiled, miming passion, grinding and gasping and clawing the air. A. went at the task with especial energy, biting my shoulder and crying out foul words, things that she never did when we were alone and not pretending, or not pretending as much as we were now; I could hardly recognise her, and despite myself felt sad and faintly repelled. I avoided looking at Rosie – I could not have borne her disenchanted eye – but I was acutely conscious of her presence, and could hear the sound of her breathing and the tiny squeaks when she shifted her bare bum on the plastic seat. Halfway through our act she quietly lit up another cigarette. Afterwards, when she was putting on her clothes, I got up from the bed and tried to embrace her, in acknowledgement of something, I'm not sure what, and also, I suppose, as a rebuke to A. The girl went still and stood with her pants in her hands and one leg lifted, and sadly I released her. A. watched from the bed, and when Rosie was gone she stood up and laid her hand on my shoulder with a tenderness I had not known in her before that moment. 'We're just the same, aren't we, the two of us,' she said. 'Hardly here at all.' Or at least, might have said.

And that night I had the strangest dream, I remember it. You were in it. We were walking together through narrow, winding passageways open to the sky. It was our quarter, or an oneiric version of it – changed and yet the same – but also it was an open-air academy of some sort, a place of scholarship and arcane ritual: there was a hint of the Orient or of Arabia. No one was about save us. It was evening, overcast and darkly luminous, the sky low and smooth and flocculent above our heads. I was baffled but you knew our purpose there, I could feel you shivering with eagerness, your arm linked tightly in mine. We did not speak but you kept smiling into my face in that way you had, lips compressed and eyes shining with a kind of spiteful glee. We came to a pair of ornate doors, temple doors, they seemed, made of many intricately arranged interlocking blocks of polished wood through the interstices of which somehow a pallid daylight gleamed out from within. With a hieratic gesture and yet irreverently smiling and winking at me over your shoulder you reached up to the two wooden handles that were set very high, above our heads, and drew the doors open. Beyond was a narrow chamber, no more than another passageway, really, with a window at the end of it in which nothing was to be seen except a grey and glowing blankness that was a part of the sky or perhaps a clouded sea. Jumbled in this room and so numerous we hardly had space to make our way between them were what at first I took to be quarter-life-sized human figurines in contorted and fantastical shapes and poses, formed it seemed from a porous grey clay and stained with mildew or a very fine-textured lichen. As I walked here and there carefully amongst them, however, I discovered that they were alive, or animate, at least, in some not quite human way. They began to make small, sinuous stirrings, like things deep in the sea stirred by a once-in-a-century underwater current. One of them, a boy-shaped homunculus with a narrow, handsome head, perched on a high pedestal, smiled at me – I could see cracks forming in the mildew or lichen around his lips – smiled as if he knew me, or in some way recognised me, and, trying to speak but making only a mute mumbling, pointed eagerly past my shoulder. It was you he was showing me, standing with your strange smile in the midst of this magicked place. You. You.

6. Revenge of Diana 1642

J. van Hollbein (1595–1678)

Oil on canvas, 40 × 17½ in. (101.5 × 44.5 cm.)

The title, which is van Hollbein's own, will puzzle those unfamiliar with the story of Actaeon's ill-fortune in pausing to spy upon the goddess Diana at her bath, for which piece of mortal effrontery he was changed into a stag and torn to pieces by his own hounds. Van Hollbein himself was no scholar, despite the many classical references which appear in his work; like his great contemporary, Claude Lorrain, he came from a humble background, being the son of a corn-chandler from the town of Culemborg near Utrecht, and was largely ignorant of Latin and therefore had no direct access to the Virgilian world the poise and serene radiance of which he chose to ape in the work of his mature years. In this painting, the scene with which we are presented depicts the moment when Actaeon surprises the naked goddess (and, so it would seem from his expression, himself also), and therefore the action proper is yet to come; however, despite the limitations of his technique, the painter manages by a number of deft touches subtly to suggest the drama that will follow. Actaeon's stance, bent from the waist with arms lifted, has the tension and awkwardness of an animal rearing on its hind legs, while in the furrowing of his brow, where the drops of transfiguring water flung by the goddess still glisten, we seem to detect the incipient form of the antlers that presently will sprout there; and, of course, the dappled tunic that is draped about his thighs and chest and thrown over his left shoulder is obviously made of deerskin. Meanwhile the hounds milling at his heels are gazing up at their master in puzzlement and fierce interest, as if they have caught from him an unfamiliar, gamey scent. In the figure of Diana, too, turned half away and glaring askance at the gaping youth, we divine something of the violence that will ensue. How well the artist has caught the divine woman in her moment of confusion, at once strong and vulnerable, athletic and shapely, poised and uncertain. She looks a little like you: those odd-shaped breasts, that slender neck, the downturned mouth. But then, they all look like you; I paint you over them, like a boy scrawling his fantasies on the smirking model in an advertising hoarding. She is attended by a single nymph, who stands knee-deep in the shallows of the pool with the goddess's chiton and girdle folded over her arm and holding in her other hand, with curious negligence, Diana's unstrung bow. She maintains an odd, statuesque stillness, this figure, wide-eyed and impassive, her gaze fixed halfway between the goddess and the youth, as if she had been struck into immobility in the act of turning to look for the cause of Diana's startlement and dismay. Lowering over the entire scene and dwarfing the sylvan glade and the figures caught in their fateful moment are the wooded valley walls of Gargaphia, hazed and etherial in the golden light of afternoon and yet fraught with menace and foreboding. The temple built into the rocks on the right is unreal in its pale perfection and seems to gaze with stony sadness upon the scene that is being enacted under its walls. It is this stillness and silence, this standing aghast, as we might term it, before the horror that is to come, that informs the painting and makes it peculiarly and perhaps unpleasantly compelling. Just so the world must have looked at me and waited when

WHEN SHE URGED ME to beat her I should have known the game was up, or at least that it soon would be. After such knowledge, and so on. There are moments – yes, yes, despite anything I may have said in the past, there are moments when a note sounds such as never has been heard before, dark, serious, undeniable, a strand added to the great chord. That was the note I heard the day she clutched my wrist and whispered, '*Hit me, hit me like you hit her.*' I stopped at once what I was doing and hung above her, ears pricked and snout aquiver, like an animal caught on open ground. Her head was lifted from the pillow and her eyes were filmy and not quite focused. Sweat glistened in the hollow of her throat. A vast, steel-blue cloud was sneaking out of the frame of the window and the rooftops shone. At just that moment, with what seemed bathetic discontinuity, I realised what the smell was that I had caught in the basement that first day when she brought me there. My heart now seemed to have developed a limp. In a frightened rush I asked her what she meant and she gave her head a quick, impatient shake and closed her eyes and took a deep breath and pressed herself to me and sighed. I can still feel the exact texture of her skin against mine, taut and slightly clammy and somehow both chill and hot at the same time.

In the closing days of November a false spring blossomed. (That's it, talk about the weather.) Bulbs recklessly sprouted in the parks and birds tried out uncertain warblings and people wearing half-smiles walked about dazedly in the steady, thin sunshine. Even A. and I were enticed outdoors. I see us in those narrow streets, a pair of children out of a fairy-tale, wandering through the gingerbread village unaware of the ogres in their towers spying on us. (One of us, certainly, was unaware.) We sat in dank public houses and behind the steamed-up windows of greasy cafés. A. held on tightly to my arm, trembling with what seemed a sort of hazy happiness. I was happy, too. Yes, I will not equivocate or qualify. I was happy. How hard it is to say such a simple thing. Happiness for me now is synonymous with boredom, if that is the word for that languorous, floating sense of detachment that would come over me as I strolled with her through the streets or sat in some fake old-fashioned pub listening to her stories of herself and her invented lives.

It was she who first spotted Barbarossa. He was living in a cardboard box in the doorway of a cutler's shop in Fawn Street, a fat, ginger-bearded fellow in a knitted tricolour cap, that must have been left over from some football match, and an old brown coat tied about the middle with a bit of rope. We studied his habits. By day he would store his box down a lane beside the knife shop and pack up his stuff in plastic bags and set off on his rounds. Amongst the gear he carried with him was a mysterious contraption, a loose bundle of socketed metal pipes of varying thicknesses, like the dismantled parts of a racing bicycle or a chimney sweep's brushes, which he guarded with especial circumspection. Rack our brains though we might we could not think what use the thing could be to him, and though we came up with some ingenious possibilities we rejected them all. Obviously it was precious, though, and despite the considerable transportation problems it posed for him he lugged it everywhere, with the care and reverence of a court official bearing the faces in solemn procession. His belongings were too much for him to carry all together and so he had devised a remarkable method of conveyance. He would take the pipes and three of his six or seven bulging plastic bags and shuffle forward hurriedly for fifteen yards or so and set down the bags in a doorway or propped against a drainpipe; then, still carrying the precious pipes, he would retrace his steps and fetch the remaining bags and bring them forward and set them down along with the others. There would follow then a brief respite, during which he would check the plastic bags for wear and tear, or rearrange the bundle of pipes, or just stand gazing off, thinking who knows what thoughts, combing stubby fingers through his tangled beard, before setting off again. Of all our derelicts – by the end we had assembled a fine collection of them, wriggling on their pins – Barbarossa was A.'s favourite. She declared she would have liked to have had him for a dad. I make no comment.

One afternoon we found ourselves, I don't know how, in a little square or courtyard somewhere near the cathedral – we could see the bell-tower above us, massive, crazy and unreal – and when we stopped and looked about, something took hold in me, a feeling of unfocused dread, as if without knowing it we had crossed invisible barriers into a forbidden zone. The day was grey and still. A few last leaves tinkled on the soot-black boughs of a spindly, theatrical-looking tree standing in a wire cage. There was no one about but us. Windows in the backs of tall houses looked down on us blankly. I had the sense of some vast presence, vigilant and malign. I wanted to leave, to get away from that place, but A. absently detached her arm from mine and stepped away from me and stood in silence, almost smiling, with her face lifted, listening, somehow, and waiting. Thus the daughter of Minos must have stood at the mouth of the maze, feeling the presence of her terrible brother and smelling the stink of blood and dung. (But if I am Theseus, how is it that I am the one who is left weeping on this desolate shore?) Nothing happened, though, and no one came, and presently she let me take her hand and lead her away, like a sleepwalker. Someday I must see if I can pick up the thread and follow it into the heart of that labyrinth again.

Often in the middle of these outings we would turn without a word and hurry back to the room, swinging along together like a couple in a three-legged race, and there throw off our clothes and fall on the couch as if to devour each other. I hit her, of course; not hard, but hard enough, as we had known I would, eventually. At first she lay silent under these tender beatings, her face buried in the pillow, writhing slowly with her limbs flung out. Afterwards she would have me fetch her the hand-mirror from my work-table so that she could examine her shoulders and hips and the backs of her flanks, touching the bruises that in an hour would have turned from pink to muddy mauve, and running a fingertip along the flame-coloured weals that my belt had left on her. At those times I never knew what she was thinking. (Did I ever?) Perhaps she was not thinking anything at all.

And I, what did I think, what feel? At first bemusement, hesitancy and a sort of frightful exultation at being allowed such licence. I was like the volunteer blinking in the spotlight with the magician's gold watch and mallet in his hands; what if I broke something (*'Go ahead, hit it!'*) and the trick did not work and it stayed broken? From some things there is no going back – who should know that better than I? So I slapped at her gingerly, teeth bared wincingly and my heart in my mouth, until she became exasperated and thrust her rump at me impatiently like an urgent cat. I grew bolder; I remember the first time I drew a gasp from her. I saw myself towering over her like a maddened monster out of Goya, hirsute and bloody and irresistible, Morrow the Merciless. It was ridiculous, of course, and yet not ridiculous at all. I was monster and at the same time man. She would thrash under my blows with her face screwed up and fiercely biting her own arm and I would not stop, no, I would not stop. And all the time something was falling away from me, the accretion of years, flakes of it shaking free and falling with each stylised blow that I struck. Afterwards I kissed the marks the tethers had left on her wrists and ankles and wrapped her gently in the old grey rug and sat on the floor with my head close to hers and watched over her while she lay with her eyes closed, sleeping sometimes, her breath on my cheek, her hand twitching in mine like something dying. How wan and used and lost she looked after these bouts of passion and pain, with her matted eyelashes and her damp hair smeared on her forehead and her poor lips bruised and swollen, a pale, glistening new creature I hardly recognised, as if she had just broken open the chrysalis and were resting a moment before the ordeal of unfolding herself into this new life I had given her. I? Yes: I. Who else was there, to make her come alive?

The whip was our sin, our secret. We never spoke of it, never mentioned it at all, for that would have been to tamper with the magic. And it was magic, more wand than whip, working transfigurations of the flesh. She did not look at me when I was wielding it, but shut her eyes and rolled her head from side to side, slack-mouthed in ecstasy like Bernini's St Theresa, or stared off steadily into the plush torture chamber of her fantasies. She was a devotee of pain; nothing was as real to her as suffering. She had a photograph, torn from some book, that she kept in her purse and showed me one day, taken by a French anthropologist sometime at the turn of the century, of a criminal being put to death by the ordeal of a thousand cuts in a public square in Peking. The poor wretch, barefoot, in skullcap and black pyjama pants, was lashed to a stake in the midst of a mildly curious crowd who seemed merely to have paused for a moment in passing to have a look at this free treat before going on about their busy business. There were two executioners, wiry little fellows with pigtails, also in black, also wearing skullcaps. They must have been taking the job in turns, for one of them was having a stretch, with a hand pressed to the small of his back, while his fellow was leaning forward cutting a good-sized gouge into the flesh of the condemned man's left side just under the ribcage with a small, curved knife. The whole scene had a mundane if slightly festive, milling look to it, as if it were a minor holiday and the execution a familiar and not very interesting part of the day's entertainments. What was most striking was the victim's expression. His face was lifted and inclined a little to one side in an attitude at once thoughtful and passionate, the eyes cast upward so that a line of white was visible under the pupils; the tying of his hands had forced his shoulders back and his knobbled, scrawny chest stuck out. He might have been about to deliver himself of a stirring address or burst out in ecstatic song. Yes, ecstasy, that's it, that's what his stance suggested, the ecstasy of one lost in contemplation of a transcendent reality far more real than the one in which his sufferings were taking place. One leg of his loose trousers was hitched up where the executioner – the one with the crick in his back, no doubt – had been at work on the calf and the soft place at the back of the knee; a rivulet of black blood extended in a zigzag from his narrow, shapely foot and disappeared among the feet of the crowd.

I asked her why she kept such a terrible thing. She was sitting cross-legged on the couch with the photograph in her lap, running a blindman's fingertips over it. I took it from her. The once-glossy surface, cross-hatched with a fine craquelure, had the flaky, filmed-over texture of a dead fish's eye.

'Are you shocked?' she said, peering at me intently; when she looked at me like that I understood how it would feel to be a mirror. Her gaze shifted and settled on the space between us. What did she know? The penumbra of pain, the crimson colour of it, its quivering echo. She did not know the thing itself, the real thing, the flash and shudder and sudden heat, the body's speechless astonishment. I handed her back the photograph. It struck me that we were both naked. All that was needed was an apple and a serpent. Light from the window gave her skin a leaden lustre.

'Tell me about that man you knew,' she said. 'The one that killed the woman.'

She was so still she seemed not even to breathe.

'You know nothing,' I said.

She nodded; her breasts trembled. She found her cigarettes and lit one with a hand that shook. She resumed her cross-legged perch on the end of the couch and gave herself a sort of hug. A flake of ash tumbled softly into her lap.

'Then tell me,' she said, not looking at me.

I told her: midsummer sun, the birds in the trees, the silent house, that painted stare, then blood and stench and cries. When I had recounted everything we made love, immediately, without preliminaries, going at each other like – like I don't know what. '*Hit me*,' she cried, '*hit me!*' And afterwards in the silence of the startled room she cradled my head in the hollow of her shoulder and rocked me with absent-minded tenderness.

'I went to No. 23 the other day after you were gone,' she said. I knew that dreamily thoughtful tone. I waited, my heart starting up its club-footed limp. 'I went to see Rosie,' she said. 'Remember Rosie? There was this fellow there who wanted two women at the same time. He must have been a sailor or something, he said he hadn't had it for months. He was huge. Black hair, these very black eyes, and an earring.'

I moved away from her and lay with my back propped against the curved head of the couch and my hands resting limply on my bare thighs. A soft grey shadow was folded under the corner of the ceiling nearest the window. Dust or something fell on the element of the electric fire and there was a brief crackle and then a dry hot smell.

'Did you open your legs for him?' I said. I knew my lines.

'No,' she said, 'my bum. I lay with my face in Rosie's lap and held the cheeks of my bum apart for him and let him stick it into me as far as it would go. It was beautiful. I was coming until I thought I would go mad. While he was doing it to me he was kissing Rosie and licking her face and making her say filthy things about me. And then when he was ready again I sucked him off while Rosie was eating me. What do you think of that?'

I could feel her watching me, her little-girl's gloating, greedy eye. This was her version of the lash.

'Did you let him beat you?'

'I asked him to,' she said, 'I begged him to. While he was doing me and Rosie he was too busy but afterwards he got his belt and gave me a real walloping while Rosie held me down.'

I reached out gropingly and took one of her feet in my hand and held it tightly. It might have been one huge raw rotten stump of tooth.

'And did you scream?'

'I howled,' she said. 'And then I howled for more.'

'And there was more.'

'Yes.'

'Tell me.'

'No.'

We sat and listened to the faint, harsh sound of our breathing. I shivered, feeling a familiar blank of misery settle on my heart. It was an intimation of the future I was feeling, I suppose, the actual future with its actual anguish, lying in wait for me, like a black-eyed sailor with his belaying-pin. I am not good at this kind of suffering, this ashen ache in the heart, I am not brave enough or cold enough; I want something ordinary, the brute comfort of not thinking, of not being always, always . . . I don't know. I looked at the photograph of the execution where she had dropped it on the floor; amongst that drab crowd the condemned man was the most alive although he was already dying. A. squirmed along the couch, keeping her eyes averted, and lay against me with her knees drawn up and her fists clenched under her chin and her thin arms pressed to her chest.

'I'm sorry,' she said, a sort of sigh, her breath a little weight against my neck. 'I'm sorry.'

We parted hurriedly on those occasions, not looking at each other, like shamefaced strangers who had been forced for a time into unwilling intimacy and now were released. I would stop on the doorstep, dazed by light, or the look of people in the street, the world's shoddy thereness. Or perhaps it was just the sense of my suddenly recovered self that shocked me. As I set off through the streets I would skulk along, wrapped up in my misery and formless dismay, a faltering Mr Hyde in whom the effects of the potion have begun to wear off. Then all my terrors would start up in riotous cacophony.

Aunt Corky said there were people watching the flat. She had rallied in the unseasonably vernal weather. The brassy wig was combed and readjusted, the scarlet insect painted afresh but crooked as ever on her mouth. In the afternoons she would get herself out of bed, a slow and intricate operation, and sit in her rusty silk tea-gown at the big window in the front room watching the people passing by down in the street and the cars vying for parking spaces like badtempered seals. When she tired of the human spectacle she would turn her eyes to the sky and study the slow parade of clouds the colour of smoke and ice passing above the rooftops. Surprising how quickly I had got used to her presence. Her smell – her out-of-bed smell, compounded of face powder, musty clothes, and something slightly rancid – would meet me when I came in the door, like someone else's friendly old pet dog. I would loiter briefly in the porch, clearing my throat and stamping my feet, in order to alert her to my arrival. Often in the early days I was too precipitate and would come upon her lost in a reverie from which she would emerge with a start and a little mouse-cry, blinking rapidly and making shapeless mouths. Sometimes even after I had noisily announced my arrival I would enter the room and find her peering up at me wildly with her head cocked and one eyebrow lifted and a terrified surmise in her eye, not recognising me, this impudently confident intruder. I think half the time she imagined the flat was her home and that I was the temporary guest. She talked endlessly when I was there (and when I was not there, too, for all I know); now and then I would find myself halting in my tracks and shaking my head like a horse tormented by flies, ready to hit her if she said one word more. She would stop abruptly then and we would stare at each other in consternation and a sort of violent bafflement. 'I am telling you,' she would declare, her voice quivering with reproach, 'they are down there in the street, every day, watching.' With what a show of outraged frustration she would turn from me then, fierce as any film goddess, swivelling at the waist and tightening her mouth at the side and lifting one clenched and trembling fist a little way and letting it fall again impotently to the arm of her chair. I would have to apologise then, half angry and half rueful, and she would give her shoulders a shake and toss her gilt curls and fish about blindly for her cigarettes.

As it turned out, she was right; we were being watched. I do not know at what stage my incredulity changed to suspicion and suspicion to alarm. The year was darkening. The Vampire was still about his fell business and another mutilated corpse had been discovered, folded into a dustbin in a carpark behind a church.

The city was full of rumour and fearful speculation, clutching itself in happy terror. There was talk of satanism and ritual abuse. In this atmosphere the imagination was hardly to be trusted, yet the signs that I was being stalked were unmistakable: the car parked by the convent gates with its engine running that pulled out hurriedly and roared away when I approached; the eye suddenly fixed on me through a gap in a crowd of lunchtime office workers hurrying by on the other side of the street; the figure behind me in the hooded duffle-coat turning on his heel a second before I turned; and all the time that celebrated tingling sensation between the shoulder-blades. I was I think more interested than frightened. I assumed it must be Inspector Hackett's men keeping an eye on me. Then one morning I arrived home still shivery with the afterglow of an early tryst with A. and found the Da's big mauve motor car double-parked outside the front door. Young Popeye was at the wheel. I stopped, but he would not turn his eyes and went on staring frowningly before him through the windscreen, professional etiquette forbidding any sign of recognition, I suppose. He was growing a small and not very successful moustache of an unconvinced reddish tint, which he fingered now with angry self-consciousness as I leaned down and peered at him through the side window. I let myself into the house and mounted the stairs eagerly. I pictured Aunt Corky bound and gagged with a knife to her throat and one of the Da's heavies sitting with a haunch propped on the arm of the couch and swivelling a toothpick from one side of his mouth to the other. Cautiously I opened the door of the flat – how it can set the teeth on edge, the feel of a key crunching into a lock – and put in my head and listened, and heard voices, or a voice, at least: Aunt Corky, spilling invented beans, no doubt.

She was sitting by the fire in her best dress – you should have seen Aunt Corky's best dress – balancing a teacup and saucer on her knee. Facing her, in the other armchair, the Da sat, arrayed in a somewhat tatty, full-length mink coat and a dark-blue felt toque with a black veil (another one!) that looked like a spider-web stuck with tiny flies. He was wearing lumpy, cocoa-coloured stockings – who makes them any more? – and county shoes with a sensible heel. A large handbag of patent leather rested against the leg of his chair. Tea-things were set out on a low table between them. A half-hearted coal fire flickered palely in the grate. 'Ah!' said Aunt Corky brightly. 'Here he is now.'

I came forward hesitantly, feeling an ingratiating smile spreading across my face like treacle. What would be the rules of comportment here?

'I was just passing,' the Da said and did that cracked laugh of his, making a sound like that of something sharp and brittle being snapped, and his veil trembled. Dressed up like this he bore a disconcerting resemblance to my mother in her prime.

'I believe you're working together,' Aunt Corky said and gave me a smile of teasing admonishment, shaking her head, every inch the *grande dame*; she turned back to the Da. 'He never tells me anything, of course.'

The Da regarded me calmly.

'Is Cyril still out there?' he said. 'The son,' he told Aunt Corky; 'he's a good lad but inclined to be forgetful.'

'Oh, don't I know!' Aunt Corky said and cocked her head at me again. 'Will you take off your coat,' she said, 'and join us?'

I drew up a chair and sat down. I kept my coat on.

Cyril.

The Da took a draught of tea. He was having trouble with his veil.

'He was to blow the horn when you arrived,' he said. 'Did he not see you, or what?'

I shrugged, and said he must not have noticed me; I felt suddenly protective towards young Popeye, now that I knew his real name, and had seen that moustache.

There was a silence. A coal in the fire whistled briefly. The Da stared before him with a bilious expression, pondering the undependability of the young, no doubt. Really, it was uncanny how much he reminded me of my mother, God rest her fierce soul; something in the stolid way he sat, with feet apart and planted firmly on the rug, was her to the life.

Aunt Corky's attention had wandered; now she gave a little start and looked about her guiltily.

'We were discussing art,' she said. 'Those pictures.' She smiled dreamily with eyes turned upward and sighed. 'How I would love to see them!'

The Da winked at me and with mock gruffness said, 'Why don't you take your auntie down to that room and let her have a look?' He turned to Aunt Corky. 'They're all the same,' he said, 'no regard.' He put down his cup and heaved himself from the chair with a grunt and walked to the window, stately, imperious and cross. 'Look at him,' he said disgustedly, glaring down into the street. 'The pimply little git.'

While his back was turned I looked at Aunt Corky with an eyebrow arched but she only gazed at me out of those hazed-over eyes and smiled serenely. Her head, I noted, had developed a distinct tremor. I had a vision of her dying and the Da and me carrying her downstairs to the ambulance, I at the head and the Da, his hat raked at a comical angle and his veil awry, clutching her feet and walking backwards and shouting for Cyril.

The Da came back and resumed his seat, arranging his skirts deftly about his big, square knees. His fur coat fell open to reveal a black velvet dress with bald patches. He eyed me genially.

'Have you seen our friend at all?' he said. 'Mr Morden.' I shook my head. He nodded. 'They seek him here, they seek him there,' he said.

I considered for a moment and then asked him if he realised that the police were on to him. He only beamed, lifting his veil to get a better look at me.

'You don't say!' he said. 'Well now.'

I mentioned Hackett's name.

'I know him!' he cried happily, slapping his knee. 'I know him well. A decent man.'

'He asked me about the pictures,' I said.

His shoulders shook. 'Of course he did!' he said, as if this were the best of news.

Aunt Corky had been following these exchanges like a

spectator at a tennis match. Now she said, 'A headache for the police, I am sure, such valuable things.' We looked at her. 'Guarding them,' she said. 'And then there would be the question of insurance. I remember dear Baron Thyssen saying to me . . .'

The Da was watching her brightly, with keen attention, like Prince the dog.

'Oh, we don't need that,' he said, 'the Guards, or insurance, any of that. No, no. We can look after our own things by ourselves.' He turned to me again. 'That right, Mr M.?' M for Marsyas, slung upside-down between two bent laurels with his innards on show and blood and gleet dripping out of his hair. 'By the way,' he said, 'I had a dream about you last night.' He lifted a finger and circled it slowly in the air above his head. 'I see things in my dreams. You were in a little room with your books. You weren't happy. Then you were outside and this fellow came along and offered you a job. He knew you were a man he could trust.'

I think of fear as a sort of inner organ, something like a big pink and purple bladder, that suddenly swells up and squeezes everything else aside, heart, liver, lights. It is always a surprise, this sudden, choking efflorescence, I can't say why; God knows, I should be familiar with it by now. The Da's pale eye in its pachydermous folds was fixed on me, and now something in it flashed and it was as if his face were a disguise within a disguise and behind it someone else entirely had stepped up and put a different eye to the empty socket and looked out at me with casual and amused contempt, taking the measure of me, and I flinched and heard myself catch my breath sharply.

The doorbell rang, two short bursts and then a long, and Aunt Corky's teacup rattled. The Da, become his genial self again, grasped his handbag and stood up, grunting. 'There's my call,' he said. Aunt Corky smiled up at him sweetly, her faltering mind elsewhere by now. He took her hand and shook it solemnly. 'Goodbye now, missus,' he said. 'And remember what I say – water, that's the thing for you. Take five or six good big glasses of water a day and you'll be right as rain. I'm a great believer in it.' He nodded slowly, still shaking her hand, his head and arm moving in unison; then he turned and stumped to the door. On the way he paused and peered at himself in the mirror above the sideboard and adjusted his hat and veil. He winked at me over his shoulder and said, 'Are my seams straight?' I opened the door for him. It felt as massive as a bulkhead. My hand on the latch would not be steady. 'Well, ta ta for now,' he said, and wiggled his broad rump and went off cackling down the stairs.

When I came back into the room Aunt Corky gave me a roguish little grin and shook her head.

'The company you keep!' she said.

That was to be her last levee. She sat on for a while gazing vacantly before her and when she stood up she took a tottery step backwards and I was afraid she would fall into the fire. I held her arm and she looked through me with an expression of vast, vague amazement, as if everything inside her had been suddenly transformed and she could no longer recognise the features of this internal landscape. 'I think,' she said with a shake in her voice, 'I think I would like to lie down.' Her meagre forearm – a stick in a brown-paper bag – quaked where I held it. She leaned her weight on me and looked at the morning light in the window and gave a fluttery sigh. 'How bright the evenings are becoming,' she said.

I left her and fled back to the house in Rue Street, but you had left. I lay down in my coat again on the couch. Our stain on the sheet had gone cold but was still damp; I took some of the pearly slime on my fingertip and tasted it. Sometimes after we had made love and were walking through the streets she would give an involuntary shiver and make a face, turning her mouth down at the corners, and say accusingly, 'I'm leaking.' These small vicissitudes amidst the logistics of love were always my fault. 'Look at me!' she would cry, showing me this smear, that bruise, 'look what you've done to me!' And then a sullen flush would spread up from her throat and her face would go fat with resentment, and I would have to spend a quarter of an hour abasing myself at her feet before she would unbend and let me touch her. But afterwards how she would leap under me, lithe as a fish, her ankles locked behind my back and her poor bitten nails searching for a purchase in the quivering muscles of my shoulders. She smelled of brine and bread and something excitingly musty and mushroomy. Her spit tasted of violets, whatever violets taste of. She licked my hands, took my fingers one by one into her mouth and softly sucked them. In the street she would stop suddenly and draw me into a doorway and make me put my hand inside her dress; 'Feel me,' she would say, her breath booming in my ear, 'feel how wet I am.' But most affecting of all, I think, were the times when she forgot about me altogether, standing by the window in afternoon light with her arms folded, looking out vague-eyed over the roofs, or in a shop beadily scanning the magazine racks, or just walking along the leaf-strewn pavements, with her head down, thinking; what moved me, I suppose, was that at those moments she was most nearly herself, this stranger every inch of whose flesh I knew better than I knew my own. She could change from one second to the next, now child, now crone. She had a short-sighted way of peering into her purse, the tip of her grey-pink tongue stuck in the corner of her mouth, while she rummaged for her lipstick or a cigarette lighter, and crouched thus she would look like one of those ancient little bird-like women you see in off-licences buying their nightly noggin. I told her so once, thick-throated with emotion, thinking of her old and of me gone. She said nothing, only considered me for a beat or two in silence and then decided – I could see her doing it – that she had not heard me.

Despite the physical attentions that I lavished on her – the demented gynaecologist, speculum in hand – there were areas into which I did not venture. I never knew, for instance, what precautions she took, if she took any. I never thought about it; I could not conceive of her conceiving. She was already her own child, a frail, suffering creature to be nursed and fondled and cooed over. She would speak of herself – her health, her looks, her desires – with the transparently false off-handedness of a doting mother holding up her little girl for general admiration. There were things she must have, especially if they belonged to others, whose relinquishing of them was an added savour. My past was a place for her to plunder: my childhood, my family, my school friends (that one was quickly exhausted), first loves, the gradual disaster of adulthood, all was a playground for her imagination. She would have stories, she insisted on stories. She had a particular craving for the lore of life in prison (have I mentioned my prison days, I wonder?), and would sit rapt as I described – not without embellishing them for her sake – the sexual transactions, the rituals of punishment and reward, the fevered excitement and alarm of visiting-day, the strange torpor of afternoons, the nights restless with sighs and whisperings, the silence of those interminable, louse-grey dawns. It might have been the lost world of the Incas I was describing. How passionately, with what gentle abandon, she would give herself to me at the end of these narratives, sinking against me with her face lifted and pale throat exposed and her shadowed eyelids twitching.

These memories. Where is she in them? A word, a breath, a turning look. I have lost her. Sometimes I wish that I could lose all recollection of her, too. I suppose I shall, in time. I suppose memory will simply fall away from me, like hair, like teeth. I shall be glad of that diminishment.

We never spoke of the pictures, or Morden, or any of that, yet it was always there. It was as if at some immemorial time we had discussed everything and then put it aside, never to be mentioned again. Sometimes this feeling was so strong that I would wonder confusedly if there really had been such a conversation and that somehow I had forgotten it. On the rare occasions when I did let slip this or that reference to my predicament – for by now it had become a predicament – she would turn aside vaguely and her eyes would swim and her face become slack, as if she were suppressing a yawn. Yet I seemed to feel too an awareness in her, a sort of steady, perhaps resentful yet vigilant wakefulness, such as a fitful sleeper would sense in one sitting all night unmoving by his bedside. Did you betray me, my love? Well, I don't care if you did. If we had it all to do over again I would not hesitate, not for a second.

Now I fell asleep, huddled there on the couch in my coat with my knees drawn up and my arms clenched around myself. I had a dream of you. We were here together, but now there was a third with us, a great pale naked woman, majestic and matronly, with broad hips and narrow shoulders. Her white breasts were tipped with pink and her eyes, fixed dreamily on nothing, were of a washed-blue shade. She was sprawled between us where we sat on either side of the couch, unfettered and yet our prisoner. I touched her rosebud mouth and she made a vague, lost sound deep in her throat. You smiled at me with great sadness and I guided your hand and laid it on her breast; my own hand was buried in the thick fleece of her lap, which felt warm and dry and inexplicably familiar. She was us and yet not us, our conduit and ourselves. You leaned down and kissed that red, pursed mouth, and your blue-black hair fell over her face like a bird's wing.

When I woke the day was already failing. I was cold and there were pins-and-needles in my fingers. Something had followed me out of that dream, a dark, slow, dragging something. I lay blank and unmoving for a while with my eyes open, clutched in fear. I had thought, before Morden and the pictures and you, that I would never be afraid again, that I had been immunised against it. I got myself up and stood by the window lost in a kind of unfocused anguish. Around me the house squatted sullenly in silence. I wanted to put my face into my hands and howl. Something was moving under me, I felt it, the first, infinitesimal shift of the glacier.

I left the house. On the doorstep the cold air filled my mouth like water and made me gag. The false spring had ended and the air was bruised and darkened by the first of winter's winds. Why is it, I wonder, that certain brownish, raw, late days like this make me think of Paris? Is that where you are? I can see you in your black coat and needle heels clicking along one of those mysteriously deserted, teetering little streets – rue de Rue! – off the

Luxembourg Gardens. You stop on a corner and glance up at a window. Who is waiting for you in that shuttered room, with his smouldering Gauloise and smoky eyes and his air of moody insolence? Big hand-shaped leaves scrabble along the pavement. Children are at play in the Gardens under the shedding planes, their voices come to you like memories. You think you will live forever, that you will be young forever. I hope he abandons you. I hope he breaks your heart. I hope that one day without a word he will walk out of your life and destroy you.

Why do I goad myself like this? I am so tired, so tired.

In Hope Alley a man in a raincoat and a pixie's woollen cap with a bobble walked along sobbing harshly and wiping his raw and reddened eyes with the heel of his hand.

As I passed through those wind-haunted streets I had again that creepy sense of being followed, and felt again that tingling target-point between my shoulder-blades. I kept stopping to look in shop windows or tie my shoelaces and covertly scanned the streets. It is remarkable how strange people come to seem when you are searching anxiously amongst them for a particular face. They turn into walking waxworks, minutely detailed yet not quite convincing copies of themselves, their features blurred to anonymity, their movements stiff and curiously uncoordinated. Yet when at last Inspector Hackett's grinning, globular head and cubist countenance materialised out of the crowd I did not recognise him until he spoke. I had been expecting Popeye or the Da or someone even worse. He was standing under the archway in Fawn Street with his hands in the pockets of his buttoned and belted raincoat. He looked more than ever like a life-sized toy man, overstuffed, and tacky with too many coats of varnish. We shook hands; always that odd, impressive formality. 'How is it going?' he said, another of those ambiguous openers that he and the Da both favoured.

We went through the archway and turned on to the quays. The wind whistled in the spumy air above the river and the water heaved and tumbled like a jumble of big square brown boxes. 'Winter coming on,' Hackett said and stuck his hands deeper into the pockets of his rat-coloured mac and gave himself a shivery squeeze with his elbows. 'I suppose,' he said musingly, 'it takes a lot of work to become an expert? Lot of reading and so on?' He glanced at me sideways with his jester's grin. 'Of course, you had plenty of time for it, didn't you.'

We stopped. He leaned on the river wall and watched the jostling water for a while. Cold spits of rain were falling at a steep slant. I told him how the Da had come to the flat dressed in his fur coat and velvet dress. He laughed.

'That's the Da, all right,' he said, 'mad as a hatter. He writes to me, you know. All sorts of topics: how to cure cancer, the Pope is a Jew, that kind of thing. Stone mad. He knows I know he has those pictures. The question is, where are they?'

Sometimes I think all of the significant occasions of my life have been marked only by misery and fright and a sort of disbelieving slow sense of shock as I step outside myself and stare aghast at what I am doing. Your face appeared and hung in my head like a Halloween mask, gazing at me with lips pressed shut, warningly.

'Morden has them,' I said, in a voice so faint I hardly heard it myself, and immediately had a dismaying urge to weep. 'There is a room . . .' And in my head you slowly turned your face away from me and I remembered you lifting your hand and floating it on the air and saying, *Free*.

Hackett kept his gaze fixed on the river, frowning, as if he were idly doing calculations in his head.

'Is that so?' he said at last, mildly. 'And you'd say they're the real thing?'

'Yes,' I said, 'it's them; they're genuine.'

A wash of watered sunlight from somewhere briefly lit the emerald moss on the river wall and made it glisten. Hackett blew into his hands and rubbed them together vigorously.

'The only question, then,' he said, 'is how will he get them out of the country.'

We walked on. A bus bore down on us suddenly out of nowhere with a swish of huge tyres. In its wake a ball of air and rain churned violently. I was thinking, *What have I done, what have I done?* But I knew, I knew what I had done.

'By the way,' Hackett said, 'I told you he'd do it again, didn't I?' I looked blank and he gave me a playful nudge. 'The fellow with the knife,' he said. 'That's three now.' He squeezed himself again with his elbows. 'And more to come, I'd say.'

When I got home the house was silent. The bathroom door stood open, I saw the light from the bare bulb as I climbed the stairs, an expressionist wedge of sickly yellow falling across the landing and broken over the banister rail. What I took at first for a bundle of rags heaped on the floor in the open doorway turned out on closer inspection to be Aunt Corky. She lay with her head pressed at a sharp angle against the skirting board, and with one leg and an arm twisted under her. I thought of a nestling fallen from the nest, the frail bones and waxen flesh and the scrawny neck twisted. I assumed she was dead. I was remarkably calm. What I felt most strongly was a grim sense of exasperation. This was too much; really, this was too much. I stood with my hands on my hips and surveyed her, saying something under my breath, I did not know what. She groaned. That gave me a start. I became even more irritated: think of a stevedore, say, faced with an impossibly unhandy piece of cargo. I should not even have thought of touching her, of course, I had seen enough screen dramas to know better (*Don't try to move her, Ace, better wait for the doc!*). Impetuous as ever, though, I crouched down beside her and got her by an elbow and a knee and hoisted her across my shoulders in what I believe is called a fireman's lift. She seemed so light at first that for a second I thought that her limbs must have come clean out of their sockets and left the rest of her lying on the floor. The silk of her teagown felt like very fine, chill, slippery skin. She had soiled herself, but only a little, her old-woman's leavings being meagre; I was surprised not to mind the smell. I started up the stairs. It was a little like carrying an uprooted tent with the poles still tangled in it. I thought of Barbarossa and his precious contraption. I could feel Aunt Corky's bird-sized heart throwing itself against the cage of her ribs. 'Oh

Jesus, son!' she said, and I was so startled to hear her speak so clearly so close to my ear that I almost dropped her. At least, I think that is what she said. It may have been something entirely different.

It was a long way up the Via Dolorosa of that flight of stairs. What at first had seemed an easy burden grew heavier with each step and by the time I got to the top I was bent double and sweat was trickling into my eyes. I worried about getting the key to the flat out of my pocket – should I set her down or keep her balanced precariously on my back while I fished about for it? – but luckily she had left the door on the latch. Going through, I bumped her head on the door-frame and she groaned. Later on, Dr Mutter could not understand how she had survived the ordeal of that climb, with a broken hip and what must have been an incipient aneurysm. I meant well, Auntie, really I did. For those few minutes you were my life and all I had left undone in it, not to mention one or two things that I had done but should not have. I wanted to save you, to bring you back into the world, to knit up your poor shattered bones and make you whole. While all I managed to do was hasten your dying. I wish you had not left me your money.

I got her into the bedroom and unloaded her on to the bed as gently as I could; stevedore first, then fireman, and coal deliverer now. Aunt Corky and the bedsprings complained in unison. Her eyelids flickered open but her eyes were absent, trying to see into some impossible distance. I stood back, breathing; I knew what must come next. I got the teagown off easily enough (those stick arms!) but underneath she was bound in various strapped and tethered things which took a lot of tugging and swearing to remove. What a mysterious and compelling object the human body is. It struck me that this was the first time in my life, within remembering, at least, that I had looked at a naked woman without desire. I thought of you, and shivered, and hastily covered Aunt Corky's withered flesh with a blanket and went out to the kitchen to fetch a bowl of water and a rag. My movements were those of a frantic automaton. I knew that if I paused now to reflect for a second my nerve would fail me and I might slam shut the bedroom door and flee the house altogether and never come back. I returned to the bedroom and was faintly surprised to find my aunt still there, though how or where I might have expected her to have gone I don't know. I switched on the bedside lamp and then switched it off again; the glimmer from the window was ample illumination for the task awaiting me. I lifted the blanket and, holding my breath, removed the bundle of soiled rags from under her hips and cleaned her with soap and water as best I could. When I was lifting one of her legs aside I heard a gristly, cracking sound that must have been, I realised later, the broken ends of her hip-bone shifting against each other. When I was done I covered her up again – she felt frighteningly cold – and went down to the telephone in the hall on the ground floor to call for help. I had brought no coins for the phone and had to bound upstairs again. In my memory of that afternoon I am constantly on the move, covering the distances between bedroom and kitchen and stairs in great, mad leaps, like a demented ballet dancer.

I called The Cypresses. I was not aware it was that number I had dialled until Mrs Haddon came squawking on the line. I began shouting back at her at once, in agitation and furious hilarity. 'I need a doctor!' I cried, and kept repeating it, and she kept answering me with the same phrase over and over, which I could not make out; she seemed to be insisting that she had *told me so*; perhaps it was Dr Mutter's name she was yelling – Kehoe, Devereaux, something like that? – for in a lull in the uproar she informed me in a small, hard voice that the doctor in fact was there, was standing at her elbow, no less, and that he would call in on his way home, if he had time. This last addition started me off shouting again, until the retired hangman who lived in the ground-floor flat put out his bristly head and glared at me. I took a breath and looked into the black, breathed-on hole of the receiver and said quietly that my aunt was dying. More than the words, it was the sudden calm in my voice, I think, that had an effect. There was a pause, and Mrs Haddon put her hand over the mouthpiece, making a squashing sound that gave me the sensation of being pushed in the face, and then came back and said sulkily that the doctor would set out right away.

Trembling after this exchange, I hurried upstairs again. As I neared the open door of the flat I paused, hearing my aunt's voice, and a crawling sensation passed up my back and across my shoulder-blades. Who was she talking to? Quakingly I went inside and shut the door behind me and approached the bedroom on tiptoe. I decided that if it was the Da, who had somehow got in again without my seeing him, I would kill him. I even pictured myself coming up behind his broad back with a poker in my hand and . . . But there was no one, only Aunt Corky lying on her back talking to the ceiling. Her eyes were open but they still had that distant, preoccupied expression. The wind had slammed the door, she was saying, a dreadful wind had sprung up in the night and slammed the door shut. She spoke in awed tones, as if of some great and terrible event. Eerily the scene rose before me: the shadowed furniture crouched in stillness, a gleam of light on a polished wooden floor and a Biedermeier clock softly clicking its tongue, then a wary stirring as if something had been heard and then the great gust and the door swinging shut like a trap. Her big hand lay on the blanket, twitching; I took it in mine: it was chill and dry yet somehow slippery. I seemed to have been here for hours yet day still lingered in the window and the sky was a high dome of muddied radiance. I went and looked down into the tangled shadows in the garden and thought of the myriad secret lives teeming there. Rooks wheeled and tumbled in the wind-tossed sky like blown bits of black crape. I put my forehead to the coolness of a stippled pane and felt the soft throb of the world in the glass. Night was creeping up the garden. I did not know myself. Behind me the old woman whimpered. I began to pace the room and heard myself counting my steps. One two three four five six, turn. Time seemed to have faltered here; day surely was dead by now but still the sky clung to its tawny glimmer. Aunt Corky lay motionless with her eyes closed, like an effigy of herself, there and yet not there. I wanted to speak a word aloud and hear my own voice but I could not think what to say and anyway I was embarrassed; this was a special manner of being alone. One two three four five six, turn.

I recall that half hour with a strange and potent clarity. Nothing happened – precisely nothing happened: it was like time spent in a lift or waiting to hear news that will not come – yet I have the sense of an event so vast as to be imperceptible, like the world itself turning towards night. It was as if I were undergoing a ritual test or rite of purification: shadows, solitude, cawing rooks, the sleeping ancient, and I in the dimness pacing, pacing. When at last the doorbell rang, a sustained and somehow unfamiliar, harsh trilling, it sounded in my ears an urgently liturgical note.

When I opened the front door to him Dr Mutter stepped in quickly with a sideways motion, like a spy, or a man on the run. He was tall and awkward with a small, rather fine head set upon a long stalk of neck. He reminded me of those unfortunates who in the last year of school would suddenly turn into six-footers, all wrists and knees and raw-boned anguish. When he spoke he had a habit, picked up from Mrs Haddon, perhaps, of gazing off intently to one side, as if he had just been struck by a terrible thought to do with something else entirely. He shook my hand gravely, his eye fixed on a patch of wall beside my shoulder, and followed me up the stairs with weary tread, sighing and softly talking, whether to me or to himself I did not know. In the bedroom I switched on the light and he stood a moment contemplating Aunt Corky with his bag in his hand and his shoulders stooped. He hooked a finger under his shirt-collar and – shades of Hackett, this time – tugged it vigorously, throwing up his chin and sliding his mouth sideways, while his Adam's apple bounced on its elastic. 'Hmm,' he said uncertainly. Aunt Corky was an ashen colour and she seemed to have shrunk appreciably in the minutes that I was away answering the doctor's ring. Her wig of yellow curls was still incongruously in place. Dr Mutter laid a bony hand on her forehead. 'Hmm,' he said again, hitting the tone of gravity with more success this time, and frowned in what he must have thought was a professional way. I waited but nothing more came. I said I thought she must have broken something when she fell; I could not rid my voice of a note of impatience. He seemed not to have heard me. He turned to me but looked hard at the window. 'We'll have to have an ambulance, I think,' he said.

The telephone again, and another lip-gnawing wait. I paced while Dr Mutter muttered. Then the ambulance and the blue light in the street, and two jolly ambulance men with a stretcher, and at the door of each flat on the way downstairs a face peering out in eager sympathy. On the pavement I hung back while they stowed my aunt. The lighted interior of the ambulance reminded me of a nativity scene. The night roundabout this moving crib was wild and raw, with a black sky full of struggle and tumult. The blanket under which my aunt lay strapped was the colour of half-dried blood. One or two bundled passers-by slowed their steps and craned for a look. An ambulance man came to the open back door and held out a hand to me. 'There's a seat here,' he said. For a second I did not know what he meant. Dr Mutter was already seated beside Aunt Corky with his bag on his knees. In the neon glare both patient and doctor had an identical pallor. Reluctantly I climbed up to join them, queasily feeling the big machine tilt under my weight and then right itself.

The hospital . . . Must I do the hospital? A windy porch faintly illumined by the swaying light of what my memory insists was a gaslamp; within, a corridor the colour of phlegm where my aunt on her trolley was briefly abandoned like a railway wagon shunted into a siding. There was a warm, gruelly smell that brought me straight back to infancy. Somewhere unseen what sounded like a doctor and a nurse were listlessly flirting. Then a flurry of starched uniforms and rubber soles squealing on rubber floors and Aunt Corky was briskly wheeled away.

When I saw her again, in the aquatic hush and glow of a dark-green room somewhere underground, I hardly recognised her. They had taken off her wig; the few wisps of her own hair that remained were the same shade of rusty red as mine. How pale her scalp was, white and porous, as if it were the bone itself that I was seeing. They had removed her teeth, too; I wonder why? I touched her cheek; very firm, cool but not yet cold, and slightly clammy, like recently moulded putty. I stepped back and heard it again, more distinctly this time, that black wind sweeping through the stillness of the European night and the dark door slamming shut.

A hand touched my shoulder. I jumped in fright. First my heart was in my mouth and then I seemed to have swallowed it. Dr Mutter hung behind me at a pained angle. 'Have a word?' he said softly. I followed him to another subterranean room, a windowless cell with a metal table and two metal chairs and a bare lightbulb that shivered on its flex in time to the beat of some vast motor silently throbbing at the core of the building. We sat: The chairs gave out prosthetic creaks. Dr Mutter leaned down sideways suddenly as if to lay his cheek on the table, but he was only reaching into his black bag. He produced a dog-eared form and looked at it grimly in silence for a long, unhappy moment. Then he shifted his gaze to a far corner of the room and sighed.

'They're insisting she must have died before the ambulance came,' he said. His troubled eyes met mine briefly. 'I didn't think she was gone, did you?' I looked at my hands on the table; in the shivery glow from the bulb above my head they had a greenish cast. He sighed again, crossly this time, and stuck a finger under his collar and did that thing with his chin and sideways sliding mouth. 'I think they're just avoiding paperwork, myself,' he said crossly. 'Anyhow, it means I have to do the cert. Now . . .' He peered with misgiving at the paper before him and began to ask me questions about Aunt Corky that I could not answer. I told him I had hardly known her. He paused and nodded and sucked his pen. 'But she was living with you,' he said. I had no answer to that, either. It was an awkward moment. What could I do? Shamelessly I made it all up, dates and places, whatever he asked for; an invented life. I felt Aunt Corky would not mind. He wrote it all out happily; I would not have been surprised if he had started to whistle. Then we got to the tricky question of the cause of death and he became depressed again and sucked his pen and shifted in his chair, sighing and blinking, like a student sitting an examination for which he had not sufficiently prepared. He turned to me again hopefully. With diffidence I suggested heart-failure. He thought it over briefly and shook his head. 'Needs to be more specific,' he said. We brooded. He considered the ceiling while I stared at the floor. Next, I suggested stroke. He was doubtful but I persisted. 'All right,' he said, 'stroke it is.' Still he hesitated, then frowning he bent over the document and, having dithered for a final second, inscribed the word and sat back with an air of dissatisfaction and faint resentment, as if it were a crossword puzzle he had been doing and I had solved the final clue for him. He flourished the paper in my face, like something he was about to palm; I tried to read his signature but could not make it out. Then he stowed it in his bag and we stood up awkwardly, patting our pockets and looking about at nothing. I could sense him working up to something. Suddenly he took my hand in both of his and gave it a sort of anguished shake. 'I'm sorry,' he blurted, looking desperately past my shoulder, 'I'm sorry for your trouble,' as if . . . well, as if I had suffered a real bereavement; as if, indeed, I were in pain. How had he come by such an idea? I stared at him, shocked, and inexplicably dismayed, then turned away without a word. Amazing, as Morden would have said.

Outside, the night set upon me with a vengeance. Black rain fell across the shaking lamplight in the porch and the carpark was awash with wrinkled water. On the road the wind was smacking its huge hands on the streaming tarmac and passing cars dragged white-fringed tailfins in their wake. It took me a long time to find a taxi. The driver, humped and hatted, reminded me of the fellow who had taken me to fetch Aunt Corky from The Cypresses; maybe it was the same one, I would not be surprised. In the suddenly, definitively empty flat I threw myself on the couch – would I be able to get myself into that bed ever again? – and slept fitfully, hearing the nightwind keening for Aunt Corky. She came to me in a dream and sat beside me calmly with her labourer's big square hands folded in her lap and told me many things, none of which I can remember. I woke into an exhausted dawn. The world outside looked tousled and awry after the night's riotous gales. I was prey to an odd, fevered exhilaration; I felt buoyant and hollow, like a vessel that had been emptied out and scoured. The bedroom I avoided; the bathroom was not much better. I shaved with a shaky hand, and cut myself. I wanted to see you. That was all I could think, that I must see you.

7. Acis and Galatea 1677

Jan Vibell (1630–1690)

Oil on canvas, 18 × 27½ in. (45.8 × 69.9 cm.)

How calmly the lovers . . . I can't. How calmly the lovers lie. (As you lied to me.) How calmly the lovers lie embowered in bliss. In blissful unawareness of the watcher in the woods. Polyphemus the cyclops loves Galatea the nereid loves Acis the shepherd. The one-eyed giant plies the faithless nymph with gifts (see Ovid, *Metamorphoses*, Book XIII), to no avail. Acis, son and lover of a sea nymph, Acis must die, crushed by a rock the giant hurls, and then will be transformed into a river (presently Odysseus with his burning brand will settle in turn the cyclops' hash). Vibell's is a subtle and ambiguous art; is the subject here the pain of jealousy or the shamefaced pleasure of voyeurism or, again, the triumphant female's desire to be spied on by one lover while she lies in the arms of another? In this painter's dark and sickly world nothing is certain except suffering. The glorious, sunshot landscape against which the little triangular drama is played out, reminiscent of the landscapes of Watteau and Vaublin, is at once a stately pleasure park and a portrait of Nature rampant and cruelly supreme. The feral profusion of plants and animals seems a token of the world's indifference to human affairs. Polyphemus himself is dwarfed by the overarching surroundings amongst which he lurks: it is not he who is the giant here. See him crouching in the depths of the greenery (do you see?), his single eye staring, mad with grief and rage; is he merely hunched in pain or is he engaged in an act of anguished self-abuse? The artist's dirty little joke. I feel a strong and melancholy affinity with the lovelorn giant. The lions and bears, the bulls and elephants (it is apparent Vibell has never seen a real elephant), which are the cyclops' unavailing gifts to the uncaring nereid, roam the landscape as if lost in vague amaze, incongruous in this northerly clime, amidst these tender greens, soft umbers, limpid blues; soon, we feel, very soon they shall throw off puzzlement's restraint and then the slaughter will start. Under their great mossy rock the lovers lie entwined like twins in the womb. The pool of blue waters at the feet of Acis prefigures the transformation that awaits him, while the jagged point of rock above his head seems poised to shatter him. Galatea. Galatea. She is the daughter of Nereus. She will make a river of her slain lover. The rock will split and from the crevice will spring a sturdy reed, slender, wet, glistening. I am Acis and Polyphemus in one. This is my clumsy song, the song the cyclops sang.

I SHOULD NOT have gone to Rue Street in that raw and shaken, deludedly eager frame of mind. The morning had an air of aftermath, with fitful gusts of wind and torn clouds scudding and leaves and litter flying everywhere. I stepped along as if on springs, snuffing up the chill air through lifted nostrils and contemplating the mystery of death. This was a world without Aunt Corky in it. What had been her was gone, dispersed like smoke. Forgive me, Auntie, but there was something invigorating in the thought; not the thought that you were no more, you understand, but that so much that was not you remained. No, I do not understand it either but I cannot think how else to put it. I suspect it was a little of what the condemned man must feel when the last-minute reprieve comes through and he is led away rubber-kneed from the scaffold: a mingling of surprise and left-over dread and a sort of breathless urgency. *More, more* – it is the cry of the survivor – *give me more!* I stopped at the Ptomaine Café in Dog Lane and sat down amid the coughs and the fag-smoke and ate a monstrous breakfast, sausages and black pudding and a rasher sandwich and a fried egg singed brown around the edges and floating in a puddle of hot fat. *Che barbaro appetito, lalala la!* I even bought, from a dispenser the size of a coffin ('Give it a kick,' one of the regulars advised me with a sepulchral wheeze of laughter), a packet of cheap cigarettes, and though I have never been a smoker I sat there puffing away and smiling about me hazily. Sometimes I really think I must be mad.

In Rue Street three cars were parked crookedly outside the house, one with a plastic dog in the back window. The front door of the house was open wide, hanging by a hinge, though it gave an impression more of gaiety than violence, as if the damage were the result of a carnival crowd having forced its way through. A lumpy man in grubby but sharply pressed grey slacks and a blue blazer loitered in the hall with a cigarette ill-concealed in a cupped hand that was the size of a small ham. He gave me an uncertain look and said something that I did not catch as I swept past him and started up the stairs. On the first landing I came upon two more henchmen, standing about with the vacant, slightly peeved air of callers who had already been kept waiting an unconscionable time. They were wearing anoraks, and one of them had what at first I did not recognise as a snub-nosed submachine-gun resting negligently in the crook of his arm. They regarded me with interest. This pair also I disdained and went on up the stairs. At the door of the atelier yet another anorak stood guard; he too was armed. He was menacingly polite. He wanted to know who I was. I told him I lived here, which was almost true, after all. He frowned, and made an uncertain gesture with the snout of his machine-gun, waving me on. I swept past him haughtily with nostrils flared and head thrown back. I had an extraordinary feeling of invincibility. I could have walked through the wall if necessary.

I paused in the doorway, though, struck as always by the glare of white light falling from the tall, sky-filled windows. Morden was standing as he had been the first time I saw him, posed in profile against the backdrop of the draped sheet, his big flat face lifted to the light and his hands thrust deep in the pockets of his long overcoat. He did not turn. In the middle of the floor Inspector Hackett stood looking at his left hand, which was bleeding; he was subjecting it to a close and what seemed admiring scrutiny, turning it this way and that in front of his face. A little way off from him Prince the dog sat stiffly to attention, in an attitude at once defiant and abashed and licking its lips rapidly and noisily, its forelegs trembling. Francie squatted beside the dog with a hand on its scruff. He gave me an impassive glance.

'Ah, Mr M.' said Hackett. 'Come in, come in. You're just in time, as usual.' He seemed in high good humour, and was polished to a particularly bright shine today. He extended his hand proudly for my inspection; a drying trickle of blood led down his wrist and under his shirt-cuff. 'Will you look what the towser did to me?' he said. Together we contemplated the wound. 'More of a rip than a bite,' he said. 'See?'

There was a step behind me in the doorway and a tall, thin, skull-faced man in a three-piece suit of houndstooth tweed came in drying his hands on an enormous, snowy handkerchief. His small, bony head was broad at the brow and narrow at the chin, and he had a peculiarly prominent upper lip that made it seem as if he were wearing a set of stage teeth over his own. Blue eyes, very keen and watchful and spitefully amused. He had the manner, at once sleek and brisk, of a medical man – that handkerchief, those hands – and for a second I saw you sprawled on the chaise-longue in a tangle of blood-soaked sheets, one shoe off and one white hand dangling to the floor.

'Mr Sharpe!' Hackett said genially and pointed his wounded hand at me. 'Here's Mr . . . what is it again? . . . Mr Morrow. Mr Morrow – Mr Sharpe.'

Sharpe looked me up and down quizzically and sniffed. 'You are the art expert, are you?' he said. His blue glance glittered and I could see he was suppressing a snicker.

'Mr Sharpe is over from England,' Hackett said, his voice dropping a curtsey. 'I thought it would be a good thing to get another expert in.' Gently he smiled an apology. 'A second opinion, so to speak.'

Sharpe finished with the handkerchief and deftly tucked it into his breast pocket, then paced to the window with one hand in the pocket of his jacket and stood for a moment in thoughtful contemplation of the street. Still Morden had not turned. All waited. Inspector Hackett delicately cleared his throat.

'Yes,' Sharpe said, as if in answer to a question. He turned with a quick movement, suddenly brisk. He looked at Hackett, at Morden and at me. 'They are all copies,' he said. 'Every one of them.'

There was a beat of stillness, as if everything everywhere had halted suddenly and then slowly, painfully, started up again. Sharpe, gratified at the effect he had made, looked about at us with a faint, death's-head leer. Morden turned his face and gazed at me without expression. Hackett stood with his head tilted, faintly frowning, as if he were listening to something ticking inside his skull. He gestured vaguely at Sharpe with his bloodied hand. 'Here, give us a lend of that hankie,' he said. Sharpe drew back, startled. He hesitated, and reluctantly, with an expression of deep distaste, drew out the handkerchief and relinquished it. Hackett with thoughtful deliberation wrapped the cloth around his torn hand and then stood looking at the loose ends helplessly, until I stepped forward and tied them for him, and remembered as I did so a woman in a flower shop I used to frequent, in the days when I did that sort of thing, who could tie a ribbon into an elaborate bow with a deft twist of one hand. I could hear Hackett breathing; he exuded a hot, moist, constricted smell, the same smell a crippled uncle in my childhood used to leave behind him when he was lifted out of his wheelchair. Strange the things the mind remembers at a time like that.

'Yes,' Sharpe said again, pleasurably chafing together his pale, long-fingered hands, 'they are copies, no doubt of it. One or two are not bad, in their way. Done from photographs, I should think, probably those rather muddy ones in Popov's so-called *catalogue raisonné* of the Behrens collection.' A faint, sour smirk and Popov was dismissed. 'Two copyists were involved, I believe. Amateurs. The canvases and frames are Victorian, the pigments were supplied by the grand old firm of Messrs Winsor and Newton.' He frowned pleasantly and looked at his finger-nails. 'Such a quintessentially English name, I always think.' He allowed a sly, almost flirtatious glance to slide over me. 'I cannot imagine how anyone could have mistaken such daubs for the real thing.'

The dog detached itself from Francie and trotted forward silently and sat down beside me, folding itself into position with a deft, subsiding sweep of its haunches. I put my hand on its head. Its fur had the bristly, polished texture of plastic and smelled, not unpleasantly, of old carpets; the feel of it – how shapely that skull – imparted to my hand an incurious, companionable warmth. They say dogs can smell fear; perhaps this one could smell . . . what? Shock? But I was not shocked, not really. There had been an odd, unidentifiably familiar ring to Sharpe's announcement; it was like news so long awaited that when it came at last it was no longer news. My brain had slowed to an underwater pace. I wanted to sit down. I wanted to sit down in some dim, deserted corner and think slowly and carefully for a long time. There was much to be pondered.

Morden turned his head at last and spoke. 'I told you,' he said to Hackett, 'I told you they were copies.'

'Fakes,' Hackett said.

The dog growled softly and Francie slapped it on the snout.

'Copies,' Morden said again, with soft emphasis, and smiled.

Gall, I was thinking; Gall the painter and the piss-artist Packy Plunkett.

Hackett was examining his bandaged paw again. I admired his self-possession.

'They're signed,' he said mildly, in a faraway tone, as if he were thinking of something else altogether.

Morden gave a start of mock astonishment. *'Just what is it you're driving at, Inspector?'* he said in an Ealing-comedy accent, and Sharpe, who had been leaning against the window-frame with an expression of supercilious amusement, arms folded lightly on his prominent little chest, laughed. Morden came forward slowly, smiling at the floor and shaking his head. He stopped beside Hackett and contemplated him almost with compassion. Hackett frowned at the window.

'Have I tried to pass the pictures off as the genuine article?' Morden said. 'Have I tried to flog them to anyone? No. They're copies. I had them made. I'm an art-lover. I'm going to hang them in my house. In my house in France. My villa on the Riviera. Is that a crime?'

Hackett turned to him and—

Ah, I am tired of this. Shall I have Prince bite someone else, take a lump out of Morden's pinstriped calf or turn on Francie and tear out his throat? No, I suppose not. I stood stroking the dog's head and listened to them sparring, their voices coming to me buzzingly, as if from a long way off. I had sunk into a dulled, sleepwalking state, not unpleasant, really, and almost restful. The rug had been pulled from under my feet with such skill and swiftness that I had hardly noticed myself tumbling arse over tip and banging the back of my head on the floor.

Presently I found myself in the street with Hackett; we walked to his car in a shared, thoughtful silence. His men, silent also, had already packed up their guns and driven away. He got behind the wheel and started up the engine and let it idle. I stood beside him at the open door with my hands in the pockets of my mac. It had begun to rain, a faint, pin-like stuff that swayed and swirled in the gusting air. November. I told him that my aunt had died. He nodded seriously but said nothing and went on gazing through the windscreen. Could he have known about Aunt Corky? Was he so intimate with the details of my life? The thought was almost comforting. I have always wanted to be watched over. He heaved a sigh and put the car into gear. 'They'll have to do something about that dog,' he said absently. His hand was still bandaged with Sharpe's handkerchief, stiff now with drying blood. I shut the door on him and he crept the car away at the speed of a hearse.

I met Morden coming down the street with Francie and the dog behind him (Sharpe by now has been wrapped up in his tissue paper and safely stowed away). Morden had the look of a schoolboy who has pulled off a glorious prank. Full of himself, as my mother would have said. He was buried in his big coat with his hands in the pockets and the collar turned up against the rain. When they drew level he stopped and fixed me with his blankest look; yes, trying not to laugh, as always. 'Sorry about the pictures,' he said. 'Just a joke.' He nodded once brusquely and they passed on in file, the three of them, satrap and vizier and heraldic hound. Francie and the dog cast a backward look, both grinning. I shall miss old Prince.

Since I am no longer speaking to anyone except myself (and

maybe some dazed survivor of Armageddon, in footrags and squashed top-hat, idly turning over these scorched pages in his bomb-shelter of a night), I do not know why I should go on fussing over niceties of narrative structure, but I do. It troubles me, for instance, that at about this point I have a problem with time. After that Day of Revelation there is a hiatus. A day and night at least must have passed before Aunt Corky's interment but I have no recollection of that interval. Surely I would have tried to see you; surely, knowing all that I now knew, and with so much more still to know, my first thought would have been to confront you? But I stayed clear of Rue Street, where the gin-trap and the men with the guns were, and instead laid low in my hole, licking my wounds.

The sun shone for Aunt Corky's funeral, weak but steady, though the day was cold. The Da turned up. God knows how he knew the time and place. I was surprised at how glad I was of his presence. Aunt Corky too would have been pleased, I'm sure. The big mauve car came swarming up the cemetery drive, incongruously gay amid the sombre yews and gesticulating marble angels, and drew to an abrupt stop, its front parts nodding. Popeye in his outsized suit shot out from behind the wheel in his whirling way and snatched open the rear door, and with a heave and a shove the Da emerged and stood and looked about him with an air of satisfaction. Today he was wearing a plain dark suit and dark overcoat; the absence of a costume I took for a mark of respect for the deceased, unless this sober outfit were another, subtler form of disguise. Spotting me he advanced in stately fashion, breasting the air like an ocean liner through the waves, chest stuck out and the wings of his coat billowing, and gravely shook my hand. 'She was a grand woman,' he said, pursing his lips and nodding, 'grand.' Then he stood aside and gave slow-witted Popeye a glare and the young man awkwardly stepped forward and offered me a surprisingly delicate, fine-boned, fat-fingered little hand (where...? whose...?) and looked at my knees and muttered something that I did not catch. The three of us walked together to the graveside over the still-lush grass in a not uncomfortable silence; nothing like a funeral for promoting a sense of fellowship among the quick. The sky was very high and still and blue. The priest and the undertaker were there, and also, to my surprise, with his hands clasped before his flies and his head bowed, dark-suited Mr Haddon; in the open air his round, smooth face had a pinkish tinge and his fair hair seemed transparent. He gave me a studiedly mournful glance and lowered his gaze again. The ceremony was brief. The priest stumbled over Aunt Corky's consonantal surname. As soon as the prayers were done a canary-yellow mechanical digger trundled forward and set to work with strangely anthropomorphic, jerky movements, like an idiot child eating fistfuls of clay. I turned and made off at once, fearing to be spoken to by Haddon. The Da stuck with me, however.

We went to a pub close by the cemetery for what he called a funeral jar. I like pubs in the morningtime, with that stale, jaded, faintly shamefaced air they have, as if a night-long debauch has just stumbled exhaustedly to an end. This was one of those brand-new antique places with fake wood and polished brass and a great many very clean and curiously blind-looking mirrors. The sun coming in at the tops of the windows suggested strong spotlights banked up outside on the pavement. We sat in a pool of shadowed quiet at a table in the corner and Popeye was sent to order our drinks. The Da watched him with a gloomy eye and sighed. 'Have you any children yourself?' he said to me. 'I thought I heard you too had a son . . .'

Popeye returned, hunched in popeyed concentration with three glasses perilously clasped between his small hands, and the light caught his face and something leaped out at me for a second, something that was him and not him, and that I seemed to know from somewhere else (this is all with the benefit of shameless hindsight, of course). He set the drinks on the table. The Da lifted his glass in silent tribute to the dead. He drank deep of his pint and set it down and licked a moustache of froth from his upper lip. Then he leaned back at ease with his arms folded and began to tell me of the techniques he had developed for dealing with police interrogations, to which he had been subjected frequently over the years. 'The thing is not to say a word no matter what,' he said. 'Drives them mad. Do you know what the best trick is? Tell him, Cyril.' Popeye rolled an eye and chuckled and began to jerk a hand up and down in his lap with fingers and thumb joined in a ring. The Da nodded at me. 'That's it,' he said. 'Just take out the lad and sit there in front of them waggling away. Puts them off their bacon and cabbage, I can tell you.' He cackled. 'I'll try it on Hackett,' he said, 'when he has me in to help him with his enquiries.' He laughed again and slapped his knee, and then, bethinking himself and the occasion, he turned solemn again, and coughed and buried his nose in his pint glass. A restive silence settled on the table and Popeye began to fidget, looking about the bar in a bored fashion and whistling faintly through his teeth. The Da sat back and eyed me with an amused and speculative light.

'Where are they,' I said, 'the pictures? I mean the real ones.'

Popeye stopped whistling and sat very still, looking at nothing. The Da gazed at me for a moment, considering, then laughed and shook his head and held up a commanding hand. 'No: no shop,' he said. 'Respect for the dead. I'm in the export business now. Have another drink.' He went on watching me with a mischievous smile, playfully. 'Did Morden pay you for the work you did?' he said. 'Present him with a bill, that's the thing. List it all out: *to expert advice, such-and-such.* You earned it.' He paused, and leaned forward and set his face close to mine. 'Or did you get what you wanted?' he said. He watched me for a moment with a sort of stony smile. 'She's the genuine article, all right,' he said. 'A real beauty.' And he took up his glass and drained it and gave me a last, lewd wink.

The thinned-out sunlight seemed charged and sharpened as I ran through the streets to Rue Street: I have always lived in the midst of a pathetic fallacy. She was gone, of course. So were the pictures, my table, books, instruments, everything; the chaise-longue had been stripped, the sheets and pillows taken away. We might never have been there. I swarmed through the house, up

and down the stairs like a maddened spider, muttering to myself.
I must have been a comic sight. I had lost her, I knew, yet I
would not stop searching, as if by these frantic spirallings through
the empty house I might conjure some living vision of her out
of the very air. In the end, exhausted, I went back to our now
emptied room and sank down on the chaise-longue and sat for a
long time, I think it was a long time, with shaking hands on
shaking knees, staring at the roofs and the still sky beyond the
window. I know the mind cannot go blank but there are times
when a sort of merciful fog settles on it through which things
blunder in helpless unrecognition. Far off on a rooftop a workman
in a boiler suit had appeared and was clambering laboriously
among the chimney-pots; he seemed impossibly huge, with bowed
arms and a great blunt head and tubular legs. I watched him for
a while; what was he doing out there? Idly and with a grim sense
of exhilaration I considered what it would be to fling myself from
a high place: the receiving air, the surprise of such speed, and
everything whirling and swaying. Would I have time to hear the
slap and smash before oblivion came? Presently I rose to go, and
it was then that I found her note, scribbled in pencil on a piece
of grey pasteboard torn from a matchbox and attached to the arm
of the couch with a safety pin. It spoke in her voice. '*Must go.
Sorry. Write to me.*' There was no signature, and no address. I sat
down again suddenly, winded, as if I had been punched very hard
in the midriff. I have not got my breath back yet.

If only I could end it here.

I do not know for how long the noises had been going on
before I noticed them. They were not noises, exactly, but rather
modulations of the silence. I crept downstairs, pausing at every
other step to listen. The basement was dark. I stopped in the
doorway in the faint glow falling darkly from the high lunette at
the far end of the corridor. Linseed oil, turpentine, old-fashioned
wood glue. I remembered A. bringing me here that first day, my
arm pressed in hers, a shimmer of excited laughter running
through her. She had shown me what I could not see, what I
would not understand.

In the dark before me Francie laughed quietly and said, 'You too, eh? Where Jesus left the Jews.' His voice was blurred. I switched on the light and he put up a hand to shade his eyes from the weak glare of the bare bulb. He was lying on the floor beside the workbench on a makeshift pallet of rags and old coats. 'You wouldn't have a fag, I suppose?' he said. In fact, I had: the packet I had bought in the café that breakfast time an aeon ago was still in my pocket, battered but intact; the coincidence, or whatever it was, struck me as comical. He sat up and fished about in his pockets for a match. Had it not been for the ginger suit (lining lolling like a tongue from a torn lapel) and wispy red hair I might not have recognised him. His face was bruised and swollen, a meat-coloured puffball with rubber lips and purple and honeysuckle-yellow eye-sockets. One of his front teeth was gone, and each time before he spoke he had to organise his tongue to the new arrangement of his mouth. He held the cigarette in a shaking hand, the swollen index finger of which stuck out stiffly at an oblique angle. I sat down on the floor beside him with my arms around my knees. He smelled warmly of blood and pounded flesh. He squinted at me, and chuckled, and coughed. I asked him what had happened to him and he shrugged. 'Your friend Hackett,' he said. 'Brought me in for a chat. What could I tell him? Morden forgot to leave a forwarding address.'

I saw a long straight road with poplars and an ochre- and olive-green mountain in the distance. Paysage. My demoiselle.

There is an interval, I have discovered, a little period of grace the heart affords itself, between the acknowledgment of loss and the onset of mourning. It is effected by a simple, or impossibly complicated, piece of legerdemain by which a blocking something is inserted between the door-frame and the suddenly slamming door, so that a chink of light remains, however briefly. In my case curiosity was the wedge. Suddenly I was agog to know how they had done it, and why, to be told of the forger's art, the tricks of the trade, to be admitted to the grand arcanum. Not that I was interested, really. What I wanted, squatting with Francie there in the gloom of that Piranesian vault, was to have it all turned into a tale, made fabulous, unreal, harmless.

'Gall and Plunkett painted them,' Francie said with a shrug, 'and I did the framing.' He waved a hand, and winced. 'Down here. Day and night for a week. And what did I get for my trouble?' He contemplated his torn coat, his broken finger. 'We dried them under the lamps,' he said, 'they were still sticky when he showed them to you and you never noticed.'

Tarraa!

'What were they for?' I said.

He fixed me with a bloodied eye and seemed to grin.

'You'd like to know, now, wouldn't you,' he said.

Then he leaned his head back against the leg of the bench and smoked for a while in silence.

There really was a man called Marbot, by the way. Yes, he was real, even if everything else was fake. Amazing.

Francie sighed. 'And Hackett had poor Prince destroyed,' he said.

The world when I stepped back into it was immense, and hollowed out somehow. I saw myself for the rest of my days rattling about helplessly like a shrivelled pea in this vast shell. I walked homeward slowly, taking cautious little steps, as if I were carrying myself carefully in my own arms. The day was overcast, with a greasy drizzle billowing sideways into the streets like a crooked curtain. Things around me shimmered and shook, edged with a garish flaring like a migraine aura. In the flat I spent what seemed hours wandering abstractedly from room to room or sitting by the window watching the winter evening glimmer briefly and then slowly fade. I dragged Aunt Corky's bag from under the bed and went through her things. It was something to do. Lugubrious rain-light slithered down the window. I unrolled her yellowed papers; they crackled eagerly in my hands, like papyrus, they couldn't wait to betray her. She had been no more Dutch than I am. Before the war she had been married briefly to an engineer who had come from Holland to build a bridge and who abandoned her as soon as the last span was in place (the bridge later fell down, as I recall, with considerable loss of life). I sat on the floor and would have laughed if I could. What an actress! Such dedication! All those years keeping that fiction going, with foreign cigarettes and that hint of an accent. I wish I could have shed a tear for you, Auntie dear. Or perhaps I have?

In the days that followed I could not be still. I walked the streets of the quarter; peering into remembered corners. Everything was the same and yet changed. It was as if I had died and come back. This is how I imagine the dead, wandering lost in a state of vast, objectless bewilderment. I lurked in Rue Street watching the house. No one; there was no one.

When the story at last came out in the papers I was filled with indignation and proprietorial resentment; it was as if some painful episode of my private life had been dug up by these pig-faced delvers (*our reporter writes . . .*) and spread across eight columns for the diversion of a sniggering public. I did not care that my name appeared; it was my old name, and the mention was purely historical (*Previous Theft at Whitewater Recalled*), and I was grateful to Hackett for keeping me out of it; no, what galled me, I think, was the way the whole thing, that intricate dance of desire and deceit at the centre of which A. and I had whirled and twined, was turned into a clumping caper, bizarre, farcical almost, all leering snouts and horny hands and bare bums, like something by Bruegel. How could they have reduced such complexity to a few headlines? *Daring Robbery – Priceless Cache – Mystery of Pictures' Whereabouts – Security Man Dies.* It was all so impersonal, so . . . denatured. Morden was not named, though you could almost see *our reporter* squirming from buttock to buttock, like a boy in class with the right answer, dying to blurt it out. He was *a leading businessman with underworld connections*; far too dashing a description, I thought, for the distinctly loutish conman I had known. He and A. became *the mystery couple*. The Da was a *notorious criminal figure*. A Detective Inspector Hickett was quoted as saying that the police were following a definite line of inquiry. The butcher and the knave and the butcher's daughter linked hands and stumbled in a ring . . .

I saw A. everywhere, of course, just as I had done in the first days, after that first kiss. The streets were thronged with the ghost of her. The world of women had dwindled to a single image. There were certain places where I felt her presence so strongly I was convinced that if I stood for long enough, shivering in anguish, she would surely appear, conjured by the force of my longing. In Swan Alley there was a narrow archway beside a chip shop, it must at one time have been the entrance to something but was bricked off now, where buddleia grew and feral cats congregated, and where one dreamy November twilight we had made awkward, desperate, breath-taking love, standing in our coats and holding on to each other like climbers roped together falling through endless air locked in a last embrace. There I would loiter now, obscurely glad of the squalor, trying to make her appear; and one evening, huddled in the shadows under the archway, racked by sobs, I opened my coat and masturbated into the chip shop's grease-caked dustbin, gagging on her name.

This is all confused, I know, unfocused and confused and other near-anagrams indicating distress. But that is how I want it to be, all smeary with tears and lymph and squirming spawn and glass-green mucus: my snail-trail.

Barbarossa was still living in his box. I was surprised he had survived so far into the winter, huddled there in the cutler's doorway. I suppose he was pickled by now, preserved, like a homunculus in its jar of alcohol. How even the frailest things could endure, as if to mock me! It was surprising too that the owner of the shop had not had him shifted; it could not have been good for business, to have a character like that living on your doorstep, even if he was careful to absent himself discreetly during business hours. But the derelicts in general, I noticed, seemed to be getting more impudent every day, encroaching more and more upon the city, moving out of the back alleyways into the squares and thoroughfares, bold as brass, colonising the place.

At the cocktail hour they would gather with their bottles around an oily, dangerous-looking fire on that bit of waste ground by the bus depot and sing and fight and shout abuse at passers-by. Even when they approached me individually they could be surprisingly truculent. One of them accosted me in Fawn Street one evening, big strapping young fellow with a mouthful of crooked teeth, planted himself in my path with his hand stuck out and said nothing, just glared at me with one eye rolling like the eye of a maddened horse and would not let me pass. There was no one else about and for a minute I thought he might haul off and take a swing at me. Breath like a furnace blast and the skin of his face glazed and blackened as if a flaming torch had been thrust into it. Alarming, I can tell you. Why is it so hard to look a beggar in the eye? Afraid of seeing myself there? No; it's more a sort of general embarrassment, not just for him but for all of us, if that does not sound too grand. I gave him a coin and made a feeble joke about not squandering it on food and heard myself laugh and hurried on discomfited and obscurely shamed. Instead of which, of course, I should have taken him tenderly in my arms and breathed deep his noxious stink and cried, 'My friend, my fellow sufferer!' as the misanthropic sage of Dresden recommends.

Barbarossa had abandoned the tricolour cap A. had liked so much in favour of a much less picturesque, imitation-leather affair with ear-flaps. Also he sported now a rather natty pair of pinstriped trousers, the kind that hotel porters wear or ambassadors when they are presenting their credentials. I should very much like to know the history of that particular pair of bags. By the way, that beard of his: it did not seem to grow at all, I wonder why; or perhaps it did and I just did not notice it because I saw him every day? His girth was steadily increasing, I noticed that. On what was he growing so rotund? I never saw him eating anything, and the rotgut wine or sherry or whatever it was that he drank – always demurely jacketed in its brown-paper bag – surely could not be so nourishing that it would make him into this roly-poly, Falstaff figure? Perhaps, I thought, he was like those starving black babies one sees so many distressing pictures of these days, their little bellies swollen tight from hunger. He had a fixed course that he followed daily, squaring off the quarter in his burdened, back-tracking way: down Gabriel Street, across Swan Alley into Dog Lane, then along Fawn Street and under the archway there on to the quays, then into Black Street and Hope Alley and down the lane beside The Boatman and so back into Gabriel Street, as the day failed and the shops began to shut and lights came on in uncurtained upper windows, though never in ours, my love, never in ours.

I have a confession to make. One night when I was passing Barbarossa's doorway I stopped and gave him a terrible kick. I can't think why I did it; it's not as if he were doing me any harm. He was lying there, asleep, I suppose, if he did sleep, wrapped up in his rags, a big, awful bundle in the shadows, and I just drew back my foot and gave him one in the kidneys, or kidney, as hard as I dared. He had a dense, soggy feel to him; it was like kicking a sack of grain. He hardly stirred, did not even turn his head to see who it was that had thus senselessly assaulted him, and gave a short groan, more of gloomy annoyance, I thought, than pain or surprise, as if I had done no more than disturb him in the midst of a pleasant dream. I stood a moment irresolute and then walked on, not sure that the thing had happened at all or if I had imagined it. But it did happen, I did kick the poor brute, for no reason other than pure badness. So much violence in me still, unassuaged.

What *are* those damn pipes for? I cannot say. Not everything means something, even in this world.

One afternoon I witnessed a touching encounter. Iron-grey weather with wind and thin rain like umbrella-spokes. Barbarossa on his rounds turns a corner into Hope Alley and finds himself face to face with Quasimodo and rears back in obvious consternation and displeasure. They must know each other! I halt too, and skulk in a doorway, anxious not to miss a thing. The hunchback gives the burdened one an eager, sweet, complicitous smile, but Barbarossa, clutching to him his fistful of pipes, pushes past him with a scowl. Quasimodo, rebuked and near to tears, hurries on with his head down. *Compagnon de misère!*

In those terrible weeks I spent much of my time by the river, especially after nightfall. I liked to feel the heave and surge of water – for in the dark of course one senses rather than sees it – coiling past me like a vast, fat, undulant animal hurrying to somewhere, intent and silent, the slippery lights of the city rolling swiftly along its back. I'm sure I must have seemed a potential suicide, hunched there staring out haggard-eyed from the embankment wall with my misery wrapped around me like a cloak. I would not have been surprised if some night some busybody had grabbed me by the arm, convinced I was about to throw a leg over and go in. *Do not do it, my friend*, they would have cried, *I beseech you, think of all that you will be losing!* As if I had not lost all already.

But I knew I must not give in to self-pity. I had nothing to pity myself for. She had been mine for a time, and now she was gone. Gone, but alive, in whatever form life might have taken for her, and from the start that was supposed to be my task: to give her life. Come live in me, I had said, and be my love. Intending, of course, whether I knew it or not, that I in turn would live in her. What I had not bargained for was that this life I was so eager she should embark on would require me in the end to relinquish her. No, that was the wrinkle I had not thought of. Now there I stood, in the midst of winter, a forlorn Baron Frankenstein, holding in my hands the cast-off bandages and the cold electrodes and wondering what Alpine fastnesses she was wandering in, what icy wastes she might be traversing.

When I heard Aunt Corky had left me her money I bought champagne for the girls at No. 23 to celebrate my windfall. Yes, I had begun to go there again, but mostly for company, now. I saw myself as one of Lautrec's old roués, debouching from a barouche and doffing my stovepipe to the pinched faces watching with feigned eagerness at the windows. I liked to sit in the parlour chatting in the early evening while business was still unbrisk. I think the girls looked on me as their mascot, their safe man. In their company I glimpsed a simpler, more natural life: does that seem perverse? And of course there were the memories of you there, flickering in the dimness of those mean rooms like shadows thrown by a wavering candle-flame. That day after the reading of the will, when I arrived with my clanking bag of bottles, the place did its best to stir itself out of its afternoon lethargy and we had a little party. I got skittishly drunk and thus fortified had the courage at last to approach Rosie again, our Rosie. She is, I realise, beautiful, in her ravaged way; she has wonderful legs, very long and muscular, with shapely knees, a rare feature, in my admittedly limited experience. Also her skin has that curiously soiled, muddy sheen to it that I find mysteriously exciting (perhaps it reminds me of the feel of you?); this skin tone is the effect of cigarettes, I suspect, for she is a great smoker, unlike you a real addict, going at the fags like billy-o, almost angrily, as if it were an irksome task that had been imposed on her along with the rest of her burdens. At first she was guarded; she remembered me, and asked after you; I lied. She was still wearing that safety pin in her ear; I wondered idly if she took it out at night. Presently the bubbly began to take effect and she told me her story, in that offhand, grimly scoffing way they adopt when speaking about themselves. It was the usual tale: child bride, a drunken husband who ran off, kids to rear, job at the factory that folded, then her friend suggested she give the game a try and here she was. She laughed phlegmily. We were in what Mrs Murphy calls the parlour. Rosie looked about her at the cretonne curtains and lumpy armchairs and the oilcloth-covered table and expelled contemptuous twin steams of smoke through flared nostrils. 'Better here than on the streets at least,' she said. I put my hand on her thigh. She was a raw, hard, worn working girl, your opposite in every way, and just what I thought I needed at that moment. But it was not a success. When we went upstairs and lay down on the meagre bed – how quickly these professionals can get out of their clothes! – she ground her hips against mine in a perfunctory simulacrum of passion and afterwards yawned mightily, showing me a mouthful of fillings and breathing a warm, sallow fug of stale tobacco-fumes in my face. She had been better as a witness than a participant. Yet in the melancholy afterglow as I lay on my stomach with chin on hands and the length of her cool, goosefleshed flank pressed against mine – I think she had dropped off for a moment – and looked out through the gap under the curtain at the shivery lights along Black Street I felt a pang of the old, fearful happiness and gave her a hug of gratitude and fond fellowship, to which she responded with a sleepy groan. (None of this is quite right, of course, or quite honest; in truth, I remain in awe of this tough young woman, cowering before her breathless with excitement and fright, trembling in the conviction of enormous, inabsolvable transgression; it might be my mother I am consorting with, as Rosie wields me, her big baby, with a distracted tenderness that carries me back irresistibly to the hot, huddled world of infant-hood. Deep waters, these; murky and deep. She has a scar across her lower belly knobbled and hard like a length of knotted nylon string; caesarean section, I presume. What a lot of living she has done in her twenty years. I hope, by the way, I have made you jealous; I hope you are suffering.)

How powerfully affecting they are, though, these reflexive moments when you not only feel something but also feel yourself feeling it. As I lay on that frowsty bed in Ma Murphy's gazing down at that strip of windswept night street I had a kind of out-of-body experience, seeming to be both myself and the trembling image of myself, as if my own little ghost had materialised there, conjured out of equal measures of stark self-awareness on one side and on the other the fearful acknowledgment of all there was that I was not. Me and my ectoplasm. And yet at the same time at moments such as this I have the notion of myself as a singular figure, a man heroically alone, learned in the arts of solitude and making-do, one with those silent, tense characters you come across of a night standing motionless in the hard-edged, angled shadows of shop doorways or sitting alone in softly purring parked cars and who make you jump when you catch sight of them, their haunted eyes and glowing cigarette-tips flaring at you briefly out of the dark. *Esse est percipi.* And vice versa (that is, *to see is to cause to be*; how would I put that into bog Latin?) You see what you have done to me by your going? You have made me an habitué of this flickering, nocturnal demi-monde I was always afraid I would end up in at the last. Oh, I know, at heart I was ever a loner – who, at heart, is not? – but that was different to this. This is another kind of isolation, one I have not experienced before.

Yet I am not what you could properly call alone. There is a sort of awful, inescapable intimacy among us solitaries. I know all the signs by now, the furtive, involuntary signals by which the members of our brotherhood recognise each other: the glance in the street that is quickly averted, the foot tensely tapping amid the straggle of pedestrians waiting on the windy corner for the lights to change and the little green man to appear (the emblem of our kind, our very mascot!), the particular presence behind me in the supermarket queue: a pent, breathy silence at my shoulder that seems always about to break out into impossible babblings and never does. Children of the dark, we make diurnal night for ourselves in the bare back rooms of pubs, in the echoing gloom of public libraries and picture galleries, in churches, even – churches, I have noticed, are for some reason especially popular when it rains. Our favourite haunt, however, our happiest home, is the afternoon cinema. As we sit star-scattered there in that velvety dark, the lonely and the lovelorn, the quiet cranks and mild lunatics and serial killers-in-waiting, all with our pallid faces lifted to the lighted screen, we might be in the womb again, listening in amazement to news from the big world outside, hearing its cries and gaudy laughter, watching huge mouths move and speak and feed on other mouths, seeing the gun-barrels blaze and the bright blood flow, feeling the beat of life itself all around and yet beyond us. I love to loll dreamily there, lost to all sense, and let the images play over me like music, as you materialise enormously in these moving sculptures with their impossible hair and bee-stung lips and rippling, honeyed flanks.

Where are you. Tell me. Where are you. What we see up there are not these tawdry scenes made to divert and pacify just such as we: it is ourselves reflected that we behold, the mad dream of ourselves, of what we might have been as well as what we have become, the familiar story that has gone strange, the plot that at first seemed so promising and now has fascinatingly unravelled. Out of these images we manufacture selves wholly improbable that yet sustain us for an hour or two, then we stumble out blinking into the light and are again what we always were, and weep inwardly for all that we never had yet feel convinced we have lost.

What shall I do with myself? I could get a job, I suppose. Often I think it might be something as simple as that that would be the saving of me. Nothing serious, of course, nothing to do with science or art, none of that old pretence, that worn-out fustian. I could be a clerk, say, one of those grey, meek men you glimpse in the offices of large, established firms, padding about in the background furtive as mice, with dandruff on their collars and their suits worn shiny. I can see myself there, bleakly diligent, keeping myself to myself, suffering the banter of the younger clerks with a thin unfocused smile and going home in the evening to cold cuts and the telly. Dreams, idle dreams; I wouldn't last a wet week. The junior partner would be given the task of talking to me. *Ahem, yes, well* – frowning out of the window at the rain and jingling coins in his trouser pocket – *Oh, the work is fine, fine, very satisfactory. It's your manner, you see; that's the problem. A bit on the gloomy side. The girls complain, you know what they're like, and Miss McGinty says you're inclined to stare in a way she finds unnerving . . . Had a bereavement recently, have you?* Yes, sir; sort of.

I went to see Hackett. His office was in a big grey mock-Gothic fortress with wire mesh on the windows and a pillared porch where I waited meekly, trying to look innocent, while a bored young policeman in shirt-sleeves phoned the Inspector's office, leaning on his counter with the receiver tucked under his chin like a fiddle and looking me up and down with a gaze at once bored and speculative. Flyblown notices warned of rabies and ragweed. Two detectives in padded jerkins went out laughing, leaving behind them a mingled smell of cigarette smoke and sweat. Police stations always remind me of school, they have the same dishevelled, sullen, faintly desperate air. A billow of wind bustled in from the street, bringing dust and the smell of approaching rain. The young policeman's voice made me start. He slung down the phone. 'Third floor, first on the left.' Brief pause, a sour smirk. 'Sir.' They can always recognise an old gaolbird.

Hackett's office was a partitioned-off corner of a large, low-ceilinged, crowded room where angry-looking men walked here and there carrying documents, or sat with their feet on their desks or hunched over and glaring at big, old-fashioned typewriters. That schoolroom smell again: dust, stale paper, rotten apple-cores. Through the glass of his door Hackett motioned me to enter. He stood up awkwardly, smiling his shy smile. He wore a broad, greasy tie with a windsor knot, and his too-tight jacket was buttoned as always, the gaps between the buttons pulling agape like vertical, fat, exclaiming mouths. On the floor beside his incongruously grand mahogany desk an electric fire was tinily abuzz; the sight of it almost made me sob. In the corner, at a smaller, metal desk, an elderly policeman in uniform was poking with the smallest blade of a penknife at the innards of a half-dismantled pocket-watch; he was balding, and had the leathery look of a countryman; he gave me a friendly nod and winked. Crêpe paper decorations were strung across the ceiling, and there were sprigs of holly, and Christmas cards pinned to a notice board. One of the cards was inscribed *To Daddy* in tall, wobbly lettering. I would not have taken Hackett for a family man; I pictured two scale-models of him, globe-headed and chicken-eyed, one in britches and the other in a gym-slip, and had to think of death to keep from laughing. He saw me looking at the card and gave what I realised was a sympathetic cough. 'And you buried your poor auntie,' he said, and lowered his eyes and shook his great head slowly from side to side.

Despite everything I know, despite all the things I have seen, and done, I persist in thinking of the world as essentially benign. I have no grounds for this conviction – I mean, look at the place – yet I cannot shake it off. Even those – and I have encountered a few of them, I can tell you – who have perpetrated the most appalling wickednesses, can seem after the event as mild and tentative as any of . . . of you (*us*, I almost said). This is what is known, I believe, as the problem of evil. I doubt I shall ever solve it to my satisfaction. Hackett, now, with his shy smile and buttoned-up look of sorrow and sympathy, seemed the soul of harmlessness.

'I saw Francie,' I said.

Hackett beamed as if I had mentioned an old, fond friend of his.

'Yes,' he said. 'Had to give him a tap or two. The Sergeant there couldn't hear him and I had to keep asking him to speak up. That right, Sergeant?' The elderly policeman, without looking up from the intricacies of his watch, delivered himself of a rich, low chuckle. 'Brought the Da in too,' Hackett said. 'Couldn't get a thing out of him. Do you know what he does when—'

'I know,' I said. 'He told me.'

'Dirty bugger,' Hackett said, but laughed, rueful and admiring. He sat back on his swivel chair and laced his fingers together on his chest and contemplated me. 'I'd have had you in, too,' he said, 'but I knew you knew nothing.' He waited, smiling with fond contempt, but I did not speak. What was there for me to say? I was beginning to have an inkling of his sense of humour. 'Any word?' he said. 'Of your friends, I mean. Morden, and . . .' He raised his eyebrows. I shook my head. 'Oh, by the way,' he said as if he had just remembered, 'you were right about the pictures. Or about one of them, at least.' He leaned forward and searched among the papers on his desk and handed me a post-card. A crease ran aslant the coloured reproduction on the front like a vein drained of blood. The butcher's art. *Birth of Athena: Jean Vaublin (1684–1721)*. I turned it over. *Behrens Collection, Whitewater House*. It was addressed to Hackett. The message was scrawled in a deliberately clumsy hand: '*Who's the daddy of them all?*' 'He's fond of a joke,' Hackett said. He watched me with that gentle smile. He pointed to the postcard. 'They wanted to get that one out,' he said. 'They must have had a buyer for it. Some moneybags somewhere. The rest will be in store, for another day.' Brown light of the winter afternoon pressed itself against the meshed windows, the electric fire fizzed. In the office outside someone laughed loudly. Hackett gave himself a sort of doggy shake, and turned aside in his chair and set one shiny brown brogue on the corner of the desk and shut an eye and took a sighting along the toe. 'Seven fakes,' he said dreamily. 'Who would have thought the eighth would be the real thing? Not our friend Sharpe, anyway. Not when he had you to laugh at.' He looked at me again with that lopsided stare, that saddest smile. His eyes seemed crookeder than ever. A muscle in his jaw was jumping. 'We've been at this for years, the Da and me. It's like one of them long-distance chess games. He'll make a move, send it to me, I'll make a move, send it to him.' He swung his leg to the floor and leaned forward and shifted the invisible pieces before him on the desk. He smiled. 'He wins, I lose; I win, he loses. This time it was his turn. He stuck that real one in with the duds and gambled that we'd all miss it. And we did. But he wouldn't have cared if we had spotted it. He doesn't care about anything, only the game. I'm telling you, mad as a hatter.'

'What about the other seven?' I said.

He shrugged, and shifted bunched fingers this way and that over the desk-top again. 'He'll wait, then make another move. We'll see who'll win next time. It's a great match we have going.' He gazed towards the window with an almost happy sigh. 'Yes,' he said, 'yes: the daddy of them all.'

The Sergeant at the desk pressed something in the recesses of his timepiece and the mechanism resumed a tiny, silver chime.

Hackett and I walked down the echoing stairs. Below us men were talking loudly, their voices came to us in a blare. There had been another murder, the last, as it turned out. 'Bled her white,' Hackett said. 'It's a bad world.' On the last step a young detective sat staring at a splash of vomit on his shoes, grey-faced and breathing deeply, while two older men stood over him shouting at each other. They did not look at us as we sidled past. In the porch we paused, not knowing quite how to part. Outside, the grimed December dusk was flecked with rain.

'And the daughter,' Hackett said, 'you haven't heard from her?'

I looked at the rain drifting in the light at the doorway. Behind us the two detectives were still arguing.

'Daughter?' I said, and was not sure that I had spoken. 'What daughter?'

Hackett looked at me. I wonder what it was *he* thought of in order to keep himself from laughing?

'The girl,' he said. 'Morden's sister. The two of them; the Da is their . . .' He touched my arm with a sort of solicitude, awkwardly, like a mourner offering comfort to one bereaved. 'Did you not know?' he said.

What I thought of immediately was her telling me one day how in her bored childhood she used to spend hours alone hitting a tennis ball against the gable end of a house. At the time of course I pictured a tranquil suburb in the hills above some great city, dappled sunlight in the planes and a chauffeur in shirt-sleeves and leggings polishing the ambassador's limousine. Now what I saw was a mean terrace with defeated scraps of garden and a woman leaning out of an upstairs window raucously calling her name, while a toddler on a tricycle upends himself into the gutter and begins to whinge, and *pock*! goes the ball as the girl swings her racquet with redoubled fury. It was no dead twin that walked beside her always, but the ghost of that ineluctable past.

Birth of Athena. Behrens Collection.

Consider these creatures, these people who are not people, these inhabitants of heaven. The god has a headache, his son wields the axe, the girl springs forth with bow and shield. She is walking towards the world. Her owl flies before her. It is twilight. Look at these clouds, this limitless and impenetrable sky. This is what remains. A crease runs athwart it like a bloodless vein. Everything is changed and yet the same.

I saw her yesterday, I don't know how, but I did. It was the strangest thing. I have not got over it yet. I was in that pub on Gabriel Street that she liked so much. The place is fake, of course, with false wood panelling and plated brass and a wooden fan the size of an aeroplane propeller in the ceiling that does nothing except swirl the drifting cigarette smoke in lazy arabesques. I go there for the obvious reason. I was in the back bar, nursing a drink and my sore heart, sitting at that big window – I always think of windows like that as startled, somehow, like wide-open eyes – that looks down at the city along the broad sweep of Ormond Street. The street was crowded, as it always is. The sun was shining, in its half-hearted way – yes, spring has come, despite my best efforts. Suddenly I saw her – or no, not suddenly, there was no suddenness or surprise in it. She was just there, in her black coat and her black stilettos, hurrying along the crowded pavement in that watery light at that unmistakable, stiff-kneed half-run, a hand to her breast and her head down. Where was she going, with such haste, so eagerly? The city lay all before her, awash with April and evening. I say *her*, but of course I know it was not her, not really. And yet it was. How can I express it? There is the she who is gone, who is in some southern somewhere, lost to me forever, and then there is this other, who steps out of my head and goes hurrying off along the sunlit pavements to do I don't know what. To live. If I can call it living; and I shall.

Write to me, she said. Write to me. I have written.